STAR MAGE SAGA
BOOKS 7 - 9

J.J. GREEN

INFINITE BOOK

FATAL STAR

Prequel

Sign up to my reader group for a free copy of the *Star Mage Saga* prequel, *Daughter of Discord*, discounts on new releases, review crew invitations and other interesting stuff:

https://jjgreenauthor.com/free-books/

Books of the Star Mage Saga

ONE

Carina faced some tough decisions, but she'd already made one. She had decided to exclude Parthenia from the meeting to discuss the plans for the voyage to Earth. Her sister was pissed off, but it wasn't for the first time and it wouldn't be the last.

Plenty of other people were attending. Jackson had come as the representative of the Black Dogs, and Hsiao, the pilot, was there for obvious reasons. Carina had also invited Justus, the sole remaining Lotacryllan, due to his knowledge of the current sector's star systems. The ship's database held some information but it was centuries out of date.

There were two more attendees: Bryce and Jace. Bryce was essential. He knew her weaknesses as a leader and would counterbalance them. Jace's presence was important too. He was probably the wisest person on the ship.

Hsiao spoke first, giving her estimation of the length of the journey ahead.

"259 years?!" Carina exclaimed. "I don't understand. When you showed me Earth on the star map holo, it was in the same frame as the ship's position."

"Those maps cover vast areas. I thought you knew that. You've flown starships."

"Only a little. I basically managed not to crash them. You're sure it's going to take us that long to reach Earth?"

"I'm not making this up," the pilot said tetchily. "It'll take us a decade or so to slow down from maximum speed too, don't forget."

"I know, but..." Carina was at a loss for words. She looked to the others, wondering if they were as surprised as her at the pilot's revelation.

"We knew Earth had to be very far away for its position to be forgotten," said Bryce. "And the galaxy's tens of thousands of light years across. I suppose it shouldn't come as any surprise we have a long journey before us."

Jackson shifted in his seat, his prosthetic arm softly clunking on the tabletop. "I don't get what the big deal is. We'll be in Deep Sleep most of the time. Doesn't matter if it takes us two hundred or two thousand years to get to Earth, does it?"

"I don't want to leave the ship on automatic pilot," said Carina. "Remember the Regians? We need at least a skeleton crew up and around most of the time. And now we don't have the Lotacryllans..." she avoided looking at Justus "...there are even fewer of us. How are we going to manage it so we don't all die before we reach our destination?"

"Yeah, well," said Jackson, "we *did* have a skeleton crew when the Regians attacked, and we know how that turned out."

"You're seriously arguing we shouldn't bother leaving anyone awake because it won't make any difference?" Carina asked irritably. "That we're doomed whatever we do?"

Bryce touched her forearm. "Jackson has a point. The *Bathsheba* is a prize for any outlaw spacefarers who spot her, and as we leave the more densely populated areas there are going to be more of them. Maybe our real problem is how to defend the ship regardless of how many of us are awake or in Deep Sleep. We were boarded last time and we could be again."

Jace had been silent, stroking his beard, up until this point. But then he leaned both elbows on the table and said, "You're right, Bryce, and we must remember the detrimental effects of Deep Sleep too. If we do manage to rig up an automatic defense system, we still mustn't sleep the journey away. We need a timetable of waking and sleeping periods for everyone aboard."

"Great," muttered Carina. "Now we have two problems."

The older mage smiled. "We have two opportunities. One, to give the *Bathsheba* the best defenses we can, and, two, to figure out whose company we will have the pleasure of enjoying while we're awake. As I recall, Carina, going to Earth was your life's ambition. It looks like you may achieve it, and while you're relatively young. Not many can say the same."

"Or not so young," she said. "It sounds like I'll be an old woman by the time we arrive. What do we know about the safety parameters of Deep Sleep? Does anyone know how long it's safe to stay under?"

"I can check the database for information," said Jackson, "but we know that seventy-plus year stretch nearly did Calvaley in. Though he was an old guy to start off with. That probably didn't help."

A pang of sadness hit Carina. The old Sherrerr officer had been murdered by the Lotacryllans while she was away buying starship fuel. He'd given her sage advice on commanding the ship and its crew, and according to Bryce, he'd allied himself with the Black Dogs, warning them of the impending Lotacryllan attack. At one time, Calvaley had been a hated enemy, but he hadn't deserved such a brutal, ignoble death. She wished she had the benefit of his years of military experience now.

"Let us know what you find out," she said to Jackson. "I remember feeling like shit when I came out of suspension last time. I don't think anyone, young or old, should be under that long again. My guess is our bodies can only sustain maybe forty or fifty years of Deep Sleep, tops, before we suffer harmful effects."

"You should look up how long it takes to recover too," Hsiao commented. "We need to be awake at least that long before going under again."

"Got it," Jackson replied.

"How's the training with Bibik going?" Carina asked the pilot. Bibik was Hsiao's apprentice. She'd been teaching him the ropes for several weeks. Carina had taken some lessons as well, though she didn't feel confident to pilot the gigantic colony ship solo yet.

"Pretty well. He isn't a natural, but he's keen and he listens, which is more than can be said for most nineteen-year-olds. Er, present company excepted."

Carina chuckled. "As another nineteen-year-old, I don't see myself as an exception. But I hope I've been listening too."

"Absolutely," the pilot replied, also laughing.

"You sure about that?" asked Bryce.

Carina gave him a playful shove.

In truth, the need for competent people to check the *Bathsheba's* heading and progress regularly was vital. Hsiao, Bibik, and herself would be the bare minimum required to avoid a major disaster. The ship had sufficient fuel to take them the distance, but they couldn't risk traveling far off course. A mistake of a fraction of a degree meant a journey of millions of kilometers in the wrong direction.

"Could you check among the crew for another volunteer apprentice?" she asked Hsiao, who nodded.

"Good, we're making progress," said Jace. "If Jackson finds out the information we need, we can figure out the Deep Sleep schedule." Turning to the man, he added, "You might want to speak to Nahla about accessing the database. She's been digging around in there for a while."

The merc's eyebrows rose. "The kid?"

"Don't be fooled by the fact she's only as tall as your chest," said Bryce. "She's sharp as a tack."

"Noted," Jackson replied. "So, what about these defenses for the

Bathsheba? Seems to me that's the most important question here, not who's going to sleep and when."

It wasn't only the most important question, it was the hardest. If even the unintelligent Regians could overcome the colony ship's armaments, it meant the weapons were inadequate at fending off any determined attack.

"Can we improve our current stock?" asked Carina. "Do we have anyone among the Black Dogs who could assess them for potential improvements?"

"Doubt it," Jackson replied. "Our techs have struggled with most of the ship's systems. I don't think anyone's even taken a look at the weapons. I can ask."

"From what I've heard," said Hsiao tentatively, "our best weapon's your brother. The youngest one, I mean."

"Darius? A weapon?!" Carina exclaimed.

"Hey!" The pilot raised her hands in a gesture of placation. "It's just what I heard. He's the most powerful one out of all of you, isn't he?"

Carina's jaw muscles tightened as she tried to frame a reply. Bryce squeezed her forearm.

"But Darius will be in Deep Sleep for most of the journey," said Jace mildly, "like the rest of us."

"I know. I just thought he could—"

"What?" Carina asked tersely.

"He could...do one of those spells you do, like maybe..." Her words trailed off under Carina's hard stare.

"Maybe you should stop digging," Justus advised.

Hsiao clamped her lips together and looked away.

"What do you think we should do?" Jace asked the Lotacryllan. "You haven't said much yet."

"I've been too busy listening. I agree with all you've discussed so far. For my part, I'm grateful for the opportunity to accompany you all. After the behavior of my companions, it would have been understandable if you'd marooned me at the nearest habitable planet."

"You did nothing wrong," said Bryce.

"Even so. On my home world, I would have been executed for my association with the mutineers."

"You aren't on Lotacrylla," said Carina. "We aren't like that." She was calming down after Hsiao's suggestion that her little brother should be used as some kind of human shield.

"Fortunately for me," said Justus. "Regarding the ship's armaments, I recall my father talking about a place that specializes in them."

"An entire planet that specializes in producing space weapons?" asked Bryce.

"No, a space station. It orbits a star that lacks any naturally habitable satellites, and the star sits between three systems at war with each other. From what my dad said, the station plies a very good trade supplying each side with technology."

"Cool idea," said Jackson. "A market that never becomes exhausted. As soon as one side gets the latest weapons tech, the other two sides want it as well."

Carina sighed. "I'm not in love with the idea of a diversion from our route and more delay. We could pay for an armaments upgrade with ember gems, I guess, but I was hoping we could set out right away."

"On the other hand," Hsiao offered tentatively, "*I* don't like the idea of going into Deep Sleep not knowing if I'll wake up."

Carina frowned. What *was* it with the pilot? They'd gotten along pretty well up until now. Hsiao seemed to want to deliberately antagonize her.

"Can we trust the people at this station?" asked Jace. "What's to stop them seizing the *Bathsheba*?"

"It would be bad for their reputation," replied Justus. "Why would they do something unscrupulous when they're so successful?"

"Should we put it to a vote?" asked Jackson. "I like the idea of upgrading the ship's defenses. Like Hsiao says, it'll help us sleep better."

"I'm not sure it's necessary," said Carina, "but I'd rather do that than have a seven-year-old *child* as our first line of defense."

Hsiao rolled her eyes. "I only meant... Never mind."

"Let's vote," Carina said, though she was sure of the outcome.

Two

"When are we going to sleep?" Darius asked Carina as she entered her siblings' suite. He bounced into her arms, wrapping himself around her and nearly bowling her over.

"Hey," she admonished. "You're getting too big for this."

He certainly *had* grown. He was much bigger and stronger than the little boy she'd rescued from the Dirksens more than a year ago. More importantly, he seemed much happier too. Putting him down, she said, "We aren't going into Deep Sleep for a few weeks yet."

"Good!" Ferne exclaimed. "Oriana and I have lots of fashion design ideas we want to try out."

"Silly," said his twin sister. "It doesn't matter if we do that before or after we enter stasis, as long as we're awake together." She turned to Carina with a frown. "We *will* be together, right?"

"Don't worry. I know better than try to separate you two."

"We're *all* going to be together, aren't we?" asked Darius hopefully.

"The sleep schedule hasn't been finalized, but yes, we will."

"You don't have to include me," said Parthenia, a bitter edge to her tone. "I'd be fine with being awake while the rest of you are Sleeping."

Nahla looked up from the interface she'd been reading and put both hands to her face before rolling her eyes. Parthenia must have been sniping at her brothers and sisters while the meeting had been going on, taking out her anger on them.

She wasn't mad at her. If anything, she felt sorry for her. Feeling hurt by her exclusion from the meeting was natural, even if it had been necessary. More significantly, Parthenia's boyfriend Kamil had been killed while she was in the throes of her first love. She had to be still working through her grief.

"We'll be in Deep Sleep together," Carina said gently. "*All* of us. The voyage will be long. It's going to take centuries to reach Earth."

"Centuries?!" exclaimed Oriana.

"Of course," said Nahla matter-of-factly. "Didn't you know?"

"Not everyone has read the entire ship's database back to front and inside out," Oriana retorted.

Carina explained, "We don't have any choice except to leave the ship to run on automatic for years at a time. There aren't enough of us to always have even a few people awake for the entire journey. We would all age and die before we reached Earth. There's no point in trying to have a mage in every group not in Deep Sleep so we might as well stick together."

"The *Bathsheba* will fly without anyone awake?" asked Darius. His big brown eyes grew wide. "Like a ghost ship?!"

"Oooh, spooky!" said Nahla.

"But what if one of us wakes up and can't go back into Deep Sleep?" Darius continued. "He would be all alone, and he would get old while everyone else stays the same age. I could be an old man by the time you woke up, Carina!"

"That's not going to happen," she said, trying to sound reassuring, though her brother's words were painting a creepy picture in her head. She gave him a hug.

Nahla asked, "If we aren't going to sleep yet, what are we going to do? I thought we had all the fuel we needed to reach Earth."

"We're going to have the *Bathsheba* fitted with some equipment at a place called Lakshmi Station."

"Lack what?" asked Ferne.

"Lak-sh-mi," Carina repeated, more slowly.

"What a strange name," said Oriana. "Why is it called that?"

"I don't know. It's probably named after the founder. I'll explain more during din—"

"And *who* decided we're going to this station?" Parthenia interjected.

"The people at the meeting. We took a vote."

"But what if I don't want to go? What if other people on the ship don't want to go? Don't we get a choice?"

Carina sighed. "Jackson spoke for the Black Dogs, the biggest group among us by far, and he voted to go to the station, so if you're trying to make a point about democracy..."

"I'm trying to make a point about my free will!"

"We always do what Carina says," said Nahla. "She saved us from—"

"*I* haven't always wanted to do what she says," Parthenia spat. "And when I didn't, she made me."

She clearly hadn't forgotten the time Carina had been forced to Enthrall her to get her away from danger on Ostillon, and she would never forget.

"I was trying to save your life!" Carina protested.

"Don't be dumb, Parthenia," said Ferne mildly. "If you don't come with us, where will you go?"

"This isn't about alternatives," she replied. "This is about having a say."

"Well, you've had your say," said Ferne. "Now shut up and let's eat. I'm hungry."

Parthenia gave a huff of frustration, spun on her heel, and marched into her bedroom. Aboard a starship it was impossible to slam a door, but Carina guessed that was what her sister would have done if she'd had the chance.

"Phew!" said Ferne. "Now we can eat in peace."

"Don't be mean," Carina scolded. "She's upset."

Her sister was hurting, and her pain was apparently bringing all her past grievances to the front of her mind. Perhaps not allowing her to attend the meeting had been a mistake.

"Can we get some nice food at Lacks Me Station?" asked Ferne. "I'm getting tired of printed stuff. It doesn't taste the same as fresh."

"We can try, but they specialize in starship equipment, not general supplies."

After a disastrous visit to Magog, attempting to restock the ship, they'd been forced to go to Gog, a much sparser, more basic place where they could only buy fuel, not much else. She wasn't too concerned about fresh food, but they definitely needed the complex chemicals required for the nutrient solution in the Deep Sleep chambers. Ferne's question reminded her she needed to check how much they had in store, especially now she knew how long they would be Sleeping.

"What kind of equipment?" Darius asked.

"Uhhh, just stuff we need. Who's ready for dinner?"

―――――――

Later, as she was getting ready for bed, she said to Bryce, "I don't know what to do about Parthenia. She threw a fit today after I came back from the meeting. She was so angry I'd excluded her, she went into her room and wouldn't come out to eat. I think I made a bad call."

"Maybe. It wouldn't have hurt to have her there. I didn't know she felt so strongly about it."

"I knew, but I kept to my guns. I wanted to limit the numbers for efficiency's sake."

"Is that the only reason?"

"What do you mean?"

"Would one more person really have made a big difference?"

"I guess not." She frowned, confused. Why *had* she been so adamant Parthenia didn't attend?

"Do you think maybe you were trying to protect her?"

"Protect her from what?"

"I don't know. You tell me."

Carina sat on their bed. "Do you think I'm over-protective of the kids?"

"What?!" Bryce exclaimed, raising his hands in mock outrage. "No! Never."

She grinned sheepishly. "I suppose you have a point. But, to be fair, things have been dangerous and difficult for them for a long time, ever since their monster of a father took them out of their estate on Ithiya."

Bryce joined her on the bed and put an arm around her, pulling her close. "I'm only saying Parthenia has grown up over the last year or so. And even before that, from what you've said, she was older than her years. I know you love your family—our family—and you'd do anything to keep them from harm, but maybe it's time to start treating your oldest sister like an adult. It wouldn't have been a problem for her to come to the meeting, and it would have made her feel like she was being taken seriously. That means a lot when you're seventeen."

"Oh, Bryce..." she laid her head on his shoulder "...how can I be a good mother to those kids? I don't have a clue what I'm doing."

"No one is expecting you to be their mother, and you've already been an amazing older sister. But maybe it's time to loosen the reins a little."

"Yeah, I hear you. I'll apologize to Parthenia tomorrow."

"Good idea. I'm sure she'll come around."

He touched her chin and turned it toward his before kissing her.

Together, they fell backward onto the bed.

THREE

Carina was in the Twilight Dome when Hsiao arrived. Sitting in the shadows directly beneath an opaque section of overhead, repaired after the bomb blast, she was in a melancholy mood, thinking about the long journey ahead, and didn't feel like talking. When she saw the pilot come in, she shrank into her seat, hoping she couldn't be seen. She'd been avoiding Hsiao since the meeting. The pilot's comments about Darius still rankled.

But Hsiao's sharp gaze soon found her. "Carina! I thought you might be here."

"Yeah, just hanging out."

"Can I join you?"

No.

"I guess."

Hsiao came over and sat next to her before looking upward through one of the remaining transparent areas of hull, where a field of stars glittered in the black. "You've come to see Lakshmi Station?"

"Huh?"

"You can see it from here. Didn't you know?" The pilot pointed in the direction of a brilliant star outshining all the others.

"I figured that's where we're going," said Carina, "but that's the sun the station's orbiting, isn't it? It can't be the station itself."

"The brightest one is the sun, and at six o'clock there's the gas giant, the biggest planet in the system. Look between the planet and the sun. There's a tiny speck. Can you see it?"

Carina squinted. There *was* a pinprick of light at the spot Hsiao described. "Whoa," she breathed. "It must be *vast*."

"It's quite something, right? And the star it orbits is unusual too. It's spinning super slowly, and its spectrum is wild—neodymium, strontium, cesium. All kinds of heavy elements."

"Uhhh..."

"You wouldn't normally expect a star to emit anything like that."

"Okay," Carina replied. Hsiao was a bit of a nerd. Normally, she wouldn't mind listening to the pilot's monologues on obscure subjects, but today she wasn't in the mood.

Hsiao took the hint and was silent for a while. Then she said, "About your brother..."

"What about him?"

"I think you misunderstood what I was getting at in the meeting."

"You do, do you?"

"Yeah." The pilot squirmed uncomfortably. "I didn't mean he should be responsible for defending us if we're attacked. I only meant..." Her words faltered to a stop.

"What?" Carina turned to face her. "What *did* you mean? Look, Darius might be the most powerful mage in my family, and he might be able to do things the rest of us find impossible, but at the end of the day, he's just a little boy. And, more than that, what you have to understand is a lot of what he does hurts him. When we were on Magog and he guessed Kai Wei was a Dark Mage, it was because he felt the man's evilness and corruption. And when he knew the starwhale was in agony from the Regians' binding, it was because he *felt* her pain. Would *you* like to live like that?"

"No," Hsiao muttered.

"No, me neither, even if it meant I could do all the things Darius can. His abilities come at a price, and he doesn't have a choice about it. So when I hear people talking about him like he's a thing, something to be used for everyone's benefit, it pisses me off."

"All right! I get it."

Carina took a deep breath, and Bryce's gentle advice came back to her. Moderating her tone, she said, "I appreciate you coming to talk to me about it and trying to set things straight between us. I hope you understand now where I'm coming from."

"I do. I didn't know that about your brother, that he was sensitive in that way."

"I suppose, outside the family and Bryce, we don't really talk about what being a mage means. When I was growing up, I had it drummed into me that I had to keep my abilities secret, and my mother did the same with my siblings. None of us is comfortable with discussing this stuff with non-mages."

"I'd like to know more, if you're okay with talking about it. I think it's fascinating. I'd love to understand how it works."

"You and me both."

"You don't know?"

"The only explanation I've seen for mage powers is in the old documents we found on Ostillon. They were written by the mages who colonized the planet, though the stories were already ancient history at the time. They say the original mages believed they carried a genetic mutation, and the ability to Cast was unlocked when someone experimented with drinking mixtures of different substances. It does have to be something in our genes. That's how Kai Wei identified us on Magog, through the saliva samples."

"A genetic variation makes sense," said Hsiao, "but that doesn't explain *how* you do what you do. Transporting from one place to another, starting fires, healing people, locking doors so they can't be opened...none of it has any rational explanation according to the laws of physics."

"Beats me. It isn't something I think about. My grandma taught me how to Cast, the same as she taught me to read and write. Do you wonder about how you can read?"

"No, but..." The pilot's brow wrinkled. "I can explain *why* I can read. I can explain most things if I put my mind to it. I could tell you how the *Bathsheba's* engines work, for instance, and why it's odd Lakshmi Station's star emits heavy metal particles."

Carina shrugged.

Hsiao turned her gaze upward to the star field again and was silent.

Carina also concentrated on the speck that was the station, trying to guess how big it was. It had to be at least the size of a substantial moon.

After several minutes, the pilot said, "There has to be an explanation for everything, even if we don't know it yet. It took us hundreds of thousands of years to invent deep space engines, but we did it in the end. Maybe, one day, someone will figure out what makes mages different. Maybe one day splicers will be able to give anyone the same abilities."

"I certainly hope so. Life would be a lot easier."

Hsiao got to her feet. "For me too. I'd love to close my eyes and transport myself anywhere on the ship. The *Bathsheba's* way too big."

"I usually walk," said Carina, "though I can't deny it's nice to have the option of a shortcut. How long until we dock?"

"We've been slowing down for a while. A couple of days, assuming they allow us to dock right away."

"Why would we have to wait?"

"Lakshmi's a busy place. There's space traffic all around it. We've been picking up their advertising spiel for days too."

"We have? I didn't know."

"You should have a listen. It's illuminating."

FOUR

Lakshmi Station was shaped like two squares superimposed, creating an eight-pointed star. The *Bathsheba* approached the upper side, in the lane of space traffic.

Parthenia watched with Hsiao and a few of the Black Dogs as the station grew gradually larger on the bridge holo. The pilot would perform the maneuver to dock, but after that she would join the away party.

Parthenia wasn't going to the station. Carina had snubbed her again, but she had no interest in business meetings anyway. Father had forced her to attend too many meetings with clients on Ithiya. He'd made her Cast Enthrall on the unsuspecting men and women so they would agree to unfavorable terms. She felt sick and her skin prickled with anxiety just remembering. Participating in the process again would bring back many bad memories, though she didn't think Carina would pull the same underhanded trick to buy space weapons for the *Bathsheba*.

One of the Black Dogs, a woman called Van Hasty, quietly swore, expressing her wonder at the size of the station. "How far away are we?" she asked Hsiao.

"An hour."

"As long as that?"

"Uh huh. But we stop here. I'm reversing thrust to bring us to a standstill. When I've shut the engines down I'll fly the *Peregrine* the rest of the way. Bibik will be along soon to keep an eye on things while I'm gone."

The edges of Lakshmi disappeared and the station took up the entire view, the detail of its hull growing more defined as each second passed. Lines cut across the base of the points of the construction, channels of some kind, separating the triangles from the octagonal whole. More lines criss-crossed the main surface, creating an intricate pattern that Parthenia guessed was more decorative than practical. There would be conduits, service tunnels, air ducts, and much more running underneath the hull, but there was no reason for these to show on the outside as far as she knew. It looked quite pretty, if a space station could ever be called pretty, which was strange considering its trade.

"Shit," said Van Hasty, "I wish I was going with you, Hsiao. Must be all kinds of fun things to do there."

"You'll get your turn. As soon as we've figured out what we're doing about the armaments, everyone will get their R and R."

"I could do with it. How long has it been since we had a chance to let our hair down?"

"Stop complaining," said another Black Dog, Rees. "You went planetside with our friends the Regians. What more fun could you want?"

"Huh, *I* wouldn't call nearly being made a larva snack fun, but whatever floats your boat."

Rees's face creased as he grinned and he seemed about to fire back a quick reply, but his gaze slid to Parthenia and he hesitated before eventually saying, "You're welcome to float my boat anytime, and you know it."

"Yeah, you wish," said Van Hasty.

Parthenia inwardly sighed.

Rees was moderating what he said because she was present. The Black Dogs all treated her like a kid. Kamil had been the only one who didn't, and now he was dead. A sob welled up in her throat, but she swallowed it.

Carina treated her like a kid too, even though they were only three years apart. Her sister had apologized for not allowing her to attend the discussion about what to do next, but Parthenia knew she didn't really mean it. And she showed it when she left her out of the away party.

There had been a time when she'd thought Carina had begun to see her as more of an equal, but that was forgotten now. The next time something important had to be done, she would be excluded again.

She wished Magog hadn't been run by Dark Mages. She and Kamil could have stayed there, abandoning the journey to Earth. She could have had some kind of freedom. Now, her fate was tied up with her family's and the Black Dogs'. Whatever they did, she would be sucked into it. She had no choice and no say because everyone saw her as a child.

"Hey," said Hsiao, "listen to this."

She did something on her console and suddenly the bridge was filled with sound.

Welcome to Lakshmi Station, technology center of the sector!

What do you need? Space cannon? Mechs? The latest energy weapons? Whatever you want, you'll find it here, guaranteed! The most up-to-date, cutting-edge tech at your fingertips, all for a reasonable price.

Or maybe you're only looking for somewhere to get away from the stresses of interplanetary conflict? You've come to the right place. Bars, sim pads, leisure hotels, extra-friendly hosts and hostesses, anything and everything you need to relax and forget the war for a while.

The voice continued at a faster pace and in a more serious tone, *No personal arms allowed on site, and brawlers will be immediately and permanently expelled.*

The message began to repeat, and Hsiao turned it off.

"Extra-friendly hostesses?" Rees asked, grinning again. "I like the sound of that."

"*I* like the sound of the latest space cannon," said Van Hasty. "Waking up to a ship invasion was a nasty surprise I don't want to repeat. I hope Carina has the creds to get us the best."

"She's paying with the last of the ember gems," Parthenia commented. "I don't know how much they're worth."

"None of us does," said Hsiao. "They're a Geriel Sector thing. Never heard of them back home."

"She'd better watch out," Rees said, "or she'll get ripped off."

"Yeah," said Van Hasty ruefully, "it happens easily enough. You still up for a trip to the station after hearing that, Rees?"

"'Course. Why not?"

"Didn't you hear the bit about 'no personal arms' and 'brawlers expelled'?"

"Yeah, so?"

Hsiao laughed. "I'll explain it to him in simple terms. We're right in the middle of three warring systems, and they're all coming here to fill their weapon orders. *All* of them. What do you think the tension on the station's gonna be like?"

Rees's eyes widened and he whistled. "Holy shit. They'll be at each others' throats."

"He's got it!" Van Hasty exclaimed sarcastically.

Rees went on, "Cool. Can't wait to get down there."

"You're kidding, right?" asked Hsiao.

"Nah, who doesn't like a good bar fight?"

"Well," Van Hasty said, "you'd better not get caught or your R and R will be cut short, and you won't be getting any more."

"Yeah, I'll wait until I've spent some time with those extra-friendly hostesses before starting anything."

Van Hasty wrinkled her nose. "Ewww! Hostesses? Sex bots, you mean. What if they don't clean themselves properly between—"

Rees elbowed her, nodding at Parthenia.

Van Hasty gave her a glance and continued, "...turns?"

Parthenia clenched her jaw. "For goodness sake, I know what you were going to say. I know those words. You can say them around me without my ears falling off or my head exploding."

"Sorry," said Rees, "but you know what your sister's like. If she gets wind we've been treating you like another merc, our lives won't be worth living."

"Yes," Parthenia retorted bitterly. "I do know what my sister's like."

She stalked from the bridge.

FIVE

The umbilicus snaked out from the *Peregrine's* airlock. The ship's outer hatches were not compatible with the station's, so the away party was forced to enter it via the slightly more risky method, which meant EVA suits for everyone. At the farther end, Lakshmi Station waited.

"Okay," said Carina via her helmet's comm, "let's go."

She reached for the nearest handhold and pulled herself into the tube. As she moved out of the *Bathsheba's* a-grav field, she floated forward, her momentum carrying her almost too fast for her to grab the next bar.

The umbilicus was about twenty meters long. Glancing back to check the others weren't having any problems, she saw Hsiao, Jackson, and Justus in a line behind her. She wished Jace had agreed to come too, but he'd turned her down. He hadn't given much of an explanation, only saying he didn't know the first thing about space weapons or commercial negotiations.

The guy was a pacifist at heart and would never change.

She'd invited Bryce as well, though she had to admit the invitation had been half-hearted. He'd seemed to guess she would prefer him to stay on the ship and look after the kids.

Turning a bend in the umbilicus, she saw the station's hatch opening and the light of its airlock. She pulled herself onward to reach it. The station's a-grav quickly settled on her and she had to twist fast to get her feet under her before she hit the deck. Hsiao and the others arrived, the hatch closed, the airlock pressurized, and the inner portal opened.

On the other side, the passageway was empty. Carina removed her helmet and peered up and down it. "Huh?"

"What were you expecting?" Hsiao asked, tucking her helmet under her arm. "A welcoming committee?"

A muffled beeping was coming from inside Carina's suit. She unzipped it and opened the comm.

"Party from the *Peregrine* to proceed to Deck Five."

Justus said, "They want to check we aren't going to shoot the place up before they'll see us face-to-face."

"Makes sense," said Carina.

There was only one other exit from the passageway: a set of elevator doors. When they were inside, it didn't ask where they wanted to go. There was only one stop. The doors opened at Deck Five.

"Welcome to Lakshmi Station," said a man on the other side of a high desk. He and the desk stood behind a deck-to-overhead transparent shield. "You're from out-sector, right?"

"That's right. Uhhh, except one of us." She remembered Justus's planet, Lotacrylla, was in Geriel.

"I'm not from around these parts," said Justus. "So I'm probably not on your system either."

"Step forward one at a time for retinal scans," said the man, "and to receive your visitor ID code. From now on, if you don't show your code on request, you'll be immediately returned to your ship and your permission to enter the station will be permanently revoked."

Carina went first. After looking into the scanner, she had to present the inside of her wrist, where a laser etched a pattern. It stung a bit but didn't hurt too bad. When they'd all been scanned and received their codes, the man said, "Deposit your suits in the locker room to your left."

Carina asked, "Do you—"

"Locker room on your left."

She trudged to the room. She'd only been going to ask if there was somewhere to sell gems. Lakshmi was not Gog. It wasn't a backwater planet where people could barter for what they wanted. The traders here would only deal in creds. Heck, they probably had showrooms and catalogs.

Tall lockers lined the walls in the next room. Along with the others, Carina took off her EVA suit, hung it up in a locker, and closed the door. A square hole opened up.

"What's this?" she asked.

"You breathe into it," said Justus. "The locker records your breath signature. It'll only open if the same person breathes into it again."

Her stomach tightened. The last time her bio ID had been recorded, she, Darius, and Parthenia had been identified as mages. "Does it collect your DNA?"

"Only your breath chemicals, I think."

"You *think*?"

"I'm not a bio signature expert, Carina."

"It's only to be expected," Hsiao commented. "They need to use it for security."

"Yeah," said Carina, "but you know what happened on Magog."

"It's no big deal, is it?" asked Jackson.

"If they wanted your DNA," Hsiao said, "they would ask you for something different."

Carina sighed and leaned in to put her mouth to the square, hoping the station's security didn't want anything else. A soft snick emanated from the locker.

Next, they had to pass through a short, brightly lit tunnel. Carina went first, followed by Justus and Hsiao, with Jackson bringing up the rear. Carina stepped out the farther side.

"Scanning us," murmured Justus as he joined her.

"Yeah," said Hsiao. "They're probably looking at our insides too."

"They don't wanna see what I just ate," said Jackson. "That—"

An alarm sounded, and a metal plate slid across the tunnel, shutting Jackson inside.

"Shit!" Carina banged on the metal. "Jackson! Jackson, can you hear me?" She thought she heard some indistinct shouting, then silence.

"Uh oh," said Hsiao.

Carina turned around. When she'd exited the tunnel, there had been an open door in the chamber on the other side. Now the door was closed.

"Additional security check required," said a smooth female voice from an intercom. "Please wait."

"What the hell?" said Hsiao. "He wasn't trying to smuggle a weapon in, was he?"

"I hope not," said Justus. "We'll be screwed if he was. They don't *need* our business. If we're lucky, they'll only kick us off the station."

"What if we're not lucky?" Hsiao asked.

Justus didn't answer.

Tense seconds passed.

"Jackson isn't dumb," said Carina. "He can't be armed...can he?" As the words left her mouth, an idea about why the merc had been detained hit. But before she could state it, the metal plate slid back, revealing Jackson bare-chested. Two people in armored suits were walking away from him.

"It was your arm, right?" Carina asked.

The man's prosthetic was extensive, encompassing his entire right shoulder as well as the missing limb. Below the elbow downward it looked like a normal arm, but above that it was covered in a dull, flexi-metal skin. The cost-cutting of the cheaper coating on the upper arm and shoulder came as no surprise. The Black Dogs' former boss, Tarsalan, had been notoriously cheap.

Though Carina had always known about the prosthetic, she'd never seen the whole thing before. Jackson must have received quite an injury to lose so much of his body. He seemed embarrassed as he hastened to put on his shirt before answering her. Pulling the lower edge down over his hips, he said, "Yeah. They wanted to check I wasn't hiding a fancy gun."

The door at the opposite end of the chamber opened.

"Looks like we're good to go," said Hsiao.

"You know," said Justus as they walked out, "that might not be such a crazy idea. Fitting your arm with a gun, I mean. Once we're out of here, of course. Have you ever considered it?"

"Never thought about it," Jackson replied.

"Or you could get a natural arm regrown," Justus continued. "I don't know about where you're from, but it was a common procedure on my world. You're stuck in bed for a couple of weeks, but after that—"

"Never thought about it," the merc repeated in a harsher tone.

Justus shrugged.

Jackson's sensitivity was a little odd. Carina had heard him crack jokes about his arm many times. She guessed it was one of those cases where it was okay for *him* to joke about it, but not anyone else.

They seemed to have finally passed the security procedures. They stepped out into a busy thoroughfare humming with life, though not all of it was human.

In her short career as a merc, she'd encountered several alien species. Most had been humanoid. Evolution seemed to favor bipedal organisms for the development of intelligence. The similarity to humans made them not too hard to get used to. But the first alien she spotted at Lakshmi Station made her jump.

It scuttled like a spider, though the creature had more legs and skin rather than a carapace, and its head—what appeared to be its head—stuck up from the center of its body. It also wore clothes. Fabric draped over it and hung down between its legs. She wondered how long it took to get dressed, and if it was confusing trying to fit its legs through the many holes.

Ten or twelve black eyes ran around the alien's head like a crown and its face contained four orifices, the largest below the eyes and three more in a line below that. Fine, short, mottled gray fur coated its body.

The alien was making a beeline for them.

"Gross!" Hsiao exclaimed, backing up.

"Shit," said Carina. The creature seemed about to speak to them, but they didn't have a translator.

It drew to a halt in front of them, swaying slightly as it poised on its claws. "Welcome to Lakshmi Station. My name is Bongo. I'll be your guide for your free introductory tour."

"*Bongo*?" Carina asked.

SIX

A wave of sharp anger washed over Darius. Sadness, a sense of being alone, and something else he didn't know the word for—misery?—came with it.

Parthenia was back.

Though he hadn't seen her enter the living area because he was in his bedroom playing cards with Nahla, he felt her arrival clear as day, the same as always.

He recognized all his family by the patterns of their feelings. If someone had blindfolded him, he could have picked each of them out and even made a good guess about how far away they were. The farther they went, the fainter their broadcast became, until at four or five hundred meters they faded away.

He'd never let on how well he could feel his brothers and sisters. He thought Mother had guessed, but he'd never talked to her about it. When he was younger, he hadn't been able to keep his face straight or stop himself from crying when a wave of emotion bashed into him. She would cuddle him, surrounding him with her love, trying to help. It hadn't helped. She was too sad. Mother's sadness had been a deep, dark well no one could ever fill. Not even him. He'd tried, but he couldn't do it.

If his family knew the truth about how deeply they affected him, it might hurt them. They would be sad and guilty. He didn't want them to have those bad feelings. He wanted them to be happy. He didn't want them to fear or hate him.

"Hurry up," said Nahla. "It's your turn."

"Oh." He picked his next card and placed it on the pile.

Nahla was winning again. She always won, whatever game they played, but he didn't mind. He liked playing with her. Ferne and Oriana didn't spend much time with him anymore. They were busy designing and printing clothes. Nahla was often busy too, searching for information in the *Bathsheba's* database or translating the mage papers. But sometimes she agreed to play with him.

He liked Nahla best of all his brothers and sisters, except Carina, of course. He loved Carina so much it hurt. He would never forget the day she'd rescued him from the horrible Dirksen men who had cut him. Even then, before he knew she was his half-sister, he'd loved the way her care and concern wrapped around him like a big, soft blanket. Carina's pattern of emotions was strong and powerful. Every so often, it wavered into sadness, but mostly it was strong. He felt safe when she was nearby.

"I win," said Nahla, putting her final card on the top of the pile. "Better luck next time."

Darius gathered up the cards and began pushing them together to make a pack. "Do you want to play again?"

"No, I'm bored with this game. It's too easy."

"What about something else? We could play a different one."

"All the games are too easy."

"We could learn something new."

"Like what?"

"I don't know. Maybe we could find a new game on the database and learn the rules."

Nahla's face twisted as she considered his idea. Her feelings were mixed up. He guessed she didn't really want to play with him and she'd only agreed to be kind. She didn't want to say yes, and she was trying to think of a way to say no nicely.

"How about we do something else?" she asked.

"Like what?"

"Like..." She leaned closer.

He sensed a strange emotion in her—fear tinged with a little bit of excitement.

"Would you like to explore the ship with me?"

"Is that all?" Darius replied, disappointed. The odd feelings she was giving out had raised his hopes she had something interesting to suggest. "We've explored the ship lots of times. How about we volunteer to be models for Ferne and Oriana? They would like that."

Nahla wrinkled her nose. "I don't want to wear their silly clothes. And we haven't explored *all* the ship. I found a new place."

"You did?" He was surprised and excited. "Like the time you found the ember gems on the *Zenobia*?!"

She nodded. "Promise you won't tell anyone?"

"I promise."

Now he came to think of it, he had been sensing a secretiveness about her lately. "Why don't you want anyone to know? Maybe there are more jewels hidden on this ship. Carina could use them to buy us more stuff."

"You know what the grown-ups are like. If I tell them, they won't let us take a look. They'll say it's too dangerous."

"Well, it might be dangerous," said Darius, having second thoughts.

"It isn't." She frowned. "And even if it is, you could Transport us out of there, couldn't you?"

"Yeah, but..." He was still uneasy. If Carina knew they were planning on investigating a secret part of the *Bathsheba*, she wouldn't want them to do it.

"You promised not to tell anyone," Nahla reminded him. "If you don't want to come with me, that's okay. I'll go by myself. But you can't tell on me, okay?"

"I suppose so," he said grudgingly.

"Do you want to come or not?"

"Why didn't you go there by yourself already? Were you waiting until I agreed to go with you?"

"Kinda," Nahla replied sheepishly.

He didn't want to go. Starships weren't adventure playgrounds, as Carina had often said. There were garbage chutes and airlocks that you couldn't mess around with or you might end up in space. There were restricted areas near the engine that were deadly if you stayed there too long. There were boxes and machinery that could fall on you.

But if he didn't go with Nahla and something bad happened to her, she couldn't Cast to get herself out of trouble. All she could do was use the ship's comm, and the rescuers might not arrive in time. The *Bathsheba* was huge. If she needed an adult to help her, it could take too long for them to run there.

"I'll come," he said. "But if it looks dangerous, we have to leave right away."

"Okay," Nahla agreed, "but I keep telling you, it isn't dangerous."

"Let me get my elixir. Then we can go." He hopped down from his chair and grabbed his elixir bottle from the top of a cabinet.

They went into the living area, where Oriana and Ferne were drawing a design on an interface. Parthenia wasn't there. Darius could feel her in her bedroom, a bundle of heartache and unhappiness. He felt sorry for her, but whenever he tried to give her a hug she would push him away.

"Where are you two going?" asked Ferne as they headed for the door.

"Um, we're getting something to eat," Nahla replied.

"We only ate an hour ago," said Oriana. "You can't be hungry again."

"Darius is. He's a growing boy. He needs to eat all the time."

He elbowed her. Oriana and Ferne would think he was a greedy pig. Couldn't she think up a better lie?

"Bring us something too," said Ferne. "Some of those corn crackers. Carina will be back late from her trip to Lacks Me Station—"

"Lak*sh*mi," Oriana interrupted.

"That's what I said. Anyway, we won't be eating dinner until late and I need something to keep me going."

"All right," Nahla agreed. "Corn crackers. Do you want anything, Oriana?"

"Could you get me a brother who can speak properly?"

Darius and Nahla giggled.

Ferne rolled his eyes. "There's nothing wrong with how I speak."

"Should we get anything for Parthenia?" Darius asked.

"Ugh, no," said Oriana. "No point. She's given up on eating. I expect she'll miss dinner again too. She's still upset after *you know what.*"

Darius did know what. The young man Parthenia liked had died. When it happened, her feelings had hit him like a flash flood racing down a riverbed.

"Okay," said Nahla. "See you later. Come on, Darius."

SEVEN

"Where are you from?" Bongo asked.

He spoke through his upper orifice. The ones below were probably only for breathing, though why he needed three wasn't clear. The alien scuttled alongside Carina as they walked down the passageway. His head only came up to her waist, and when she looked at him she didn't know which of his many eyes to focus on. "You won't have heard of it. We're from outside Geriel Sector."

She didn't want to give him—or her—any more information than necessary. Justus might feel confident no one on Lakshmi would try to steal the *Bathsheba*, but she wasn't. She couldn't afford to be. The colony ship was all she had. That, and the little pouch of ember gems in her pocket.

"Outside the sector!" remarked the alien. "Fascinating. Well, you're all human, so it doesn't really matter. What brings you to the station?"

"We're interested in space armaments. Our ship is already heavily kitted out," she lied, "but we heard Lakshmi has some of the most advanced tech in the region."

"You heard right. You won't find better within the *sector*, let alone region."

"That's good to hear. I'm glad you can speak Universal. We don't have any translators. Do all the vendors speak Universal too?" She'd presumed they would be human, but Bongo's existence had made her realize they might not.

"You don't need to be concerned about translation. If an arms specialist can find a way to part you from your creds, he'll do it, even if it means he has to speak…" He concluded his sentence with a sound like someone gargling while at the same time trying to not throw up.

"Talking of creds," said Carina, "we don't have any."

Bongo stopped dead in his tracks and his head rotated as he scanned her with all his eyes. "Then how do you plan to—"

"We have valuable items we want to exchange. Is there a place we can do that?"

"What kind of valuable items?"

"I'd rather not say." And she certainly didn't want to pull out the gems to show him in the middle of the busy thoroughfare.

"I see. I can take you to some—"

A passerby stepped too close and caught his foot on one of Bongo's many outspread legs. The stranger stumbled, but at half his weight, the alien came off worse from the collision. He flipped right over onto his back, his head bending into his body.

"Damned spider creep!" the man yelled, getting to his feet.

"Hey, take it easy," said Carina. "It was an accident."

Bongo was struggling to right himself. The accident had drawn the attention of the crowd and a ring of bystanders was forming. Wriggling exactly like an arachnid, the alien was becoming a spectacle.

"Yuck," someone murmured. "Revolting."

Everyone watching was human, and they were having exactly the reaction most humans had when confronted with an insect or spider in distress— disgust. But Carina had always liked bugs. Nai Nai had discouraged her from making friends, fearing she would accidentally reveal her mage powers, and her planet hadn't evolved large life forms she could have as pets. So she'd taken to playing with invertebrates, constructing elaborate homes for them in her room, much to her grandmother's annoyance when they inevitably escaped.

She scooped Bongo up and set him on his feet.

Meanwhile, Jackson snapped to the crowd, "What are you gawping at? Move on. Nothing to see here."

"I can manage!" the alien exclaimed. He shook himself like a wet dog and reached up with a couple of claws to adjust the cloth hanging below his belly.

"Sorry," said Carina. "I was just trying to help."

"Are you all right?" asked Hsiao.

"I'm fine," Bongo retorted irritably. "Now, where were we? Currency exchange centers, right? I'll take you to some, and I'll show you the leisure and recreation facilities on the way."

"We aren't interested in leisure and recreation," said Carina, but he didn't respond. She guessed it was his job to take them on the standard tour.

What had been a bare, pedestrian transit tunnel opened out into a commercial zone. The congestion eased in the wider space, and the air was suddenly filled with scents of food, perfumes, and other, unrecognizable things. The noise increased, sounds of talking, footsteps, and a warbling singer echoing from the three-tier-high walls and walkways.

Justus continued on, unimpressed, but Carina, Hsiao, and Jackson halted to take it all in. Stores, restaurants, cafes, offices, and establishments she didn't even recognize ranged around them. She had always kind of known such places existed, but she'd never seen one. The course of her life had never given her the opportunity to visit a high-end market like this. From the way they stared, she guessed Hsiao and Jackson's backgrounds were similar.

Bongo was waiting patiently for them. Justus had turned around and walked back.

"You'll have plenty of time for shopping after the tour," said the alien.

They continued on. After a few minutes, Carina realized some of the people in the throng weren't actually alive. At first, she'd thought Lakshmi Station held more than the average share of attractive folk. Several of the men and women they passed were head-turners. But when the next one came along, she noticed there was something not quite right about the way she looked. Her skin, eyes, and hair were literally flawless, and her face and body was perfectly symmetrical. The other good-lookers were the same.

These had to be the 'hosts and hostesses' mentioned in the station's broadcasted advertising. Hsiao had explained they were androids and what they were for, and it was then she'd decided Parthenia and the other kids shouldn't come to the station, at least not until she'd checked it out. In fact, so far it was tamer than she'd imagined, but they'd hardly seen any of it yet. She didn't want to take the risk of exposing them to things beyond their years, especially considering everything they'd been through.

"Mind massage," Hsiao read aloud from a sign. "I wonder what that is?"

"Externally induced meditation," said Bongo. "It's pleasant, but nothing to write home about."

"Do you have sim modules here?" Jackson asked.

The alien emitted a long stream of air from its three lower orifices, causing them to flap and vibrate noisily. The effect was something like laughing.

Bongo had holes just for laughing?

"Do we have sim modules? Sir, we have the best sim modules in all Geriel Sector. Military, romance, sensual, adventure, historical, futuristic, theological, whatever you can imagine. We have sim modules that read your deepest fantasies and recreate them for you. And your worst nightmares too, though I wouldn't recommend that option."

"Cool," Jackson commented.

"After we figure out what we're doing about the armaments," said Hsiao, "we should get something to eat. I bet they have all kinds of weird, delicious stuff here."

"Probably," Carina replied, "but we aren't here to have fun, remember? We have a job to do."

"The Black Dogs are expecting some R and R," said Jackson.

"They're in a state of nearly constant rest and recuperation on the ship!" Carina protested. "Who started *that* rumor?"

"Uhhh," said Hsiao, "I just assumed..."

"Great," Carina muttered.

She was beginning to feel like a mother in charge of a bunch of demanding, whiny offspring. Didn't the mercs understand they were on a mission? It was a very long one, she had to admit, but the time for R and R would come later, after they'd reached Earth.

"I don't have any idea how many creds we'll get in exchange for the..." she coughed as Bongo's head swiveled her way. "Once we've bought the weapons and supplies, there might not be anything left over to spend on having fun."

She felt bad. The mercs had worked without pay for months. They'd joined her expedition to Earth mostly because they'd had no choice. It was either that or spend the rest of their lives hiding from vengeful Dirksens. She'd come to see them as extended family, but in reality they were work-for-hire soldiers who were working for no compensation.

An alien of the same species as Bongo approached through the crowd. As the two passed each other, they raised their legs and hit claws in a multiple high-five.

They entered a leisure and recreation area, which the alien insisted on showing them around, though Carina tried again to explain they weren't interested. Hsiao and Jackson made a liar of her anyway, expressing great interest in every place Bongo took them, from the 'hosted' lounges to the 'soaring rooms', where you could turn off the a-grav and fly, wearing wings. The latter seemed particularly silly. Aboard starships, losing a-grav generally meant imminent disaster.

Most of the entertainments were behind closed doors, which Carina was grateful for, though they did see one section open to the public: a hot spring 'lake', where bathers lounged and lazily swam. The creators had gone to a lot of trouble to make the place appear authentic, shipping in the rocks from a planet. The plants looked real, from the tall ferns that overhung the water to the moss on the pebble shore.

Finally, the obligatory tour of the recreation area was over and Bongo took them to a currency exchange booth. There was only room for three people on the customer side. Or, as it turned out, one human and a...whatever Bongo was. He crawled into the booth with Carina, and then no one else would fit. Hsiao, Jackson, and Justus waited outside, peering in.

Was it a set up? Was she about to be ripped off?

She decided to show the assistant only one of the gems and find out how much they were willing to offer before deciding whether to go ahead with the exchange.

Another of Bongo's species stepped out through a curtain into the back of the booth.

That explained why the counter was so low.

It *had* to be a set up. Bongo had brought her to a friend, relation, or associate to fleece her. Was he even an official guide? The sack-thing he was wearing didn't display any words or a logo.

He spoke with the sales assistant, using their mutual language. The sound reminded her of water running over rocks.

"Hey," she said, "could you use Universal? I'd prefer to know what you're saying."

"I was explaining to my cousin you'd like to conduct a non-standard exchange. She wants to know what you're offering."

Cousin, huh?

With a sense of unease, Carina drew out her pouch and removed one of the gems before returning it to her pocket. Squatting down, she put the gem on the counter but kept her finger on it.

A second round of bubbling dialogue ensued.

She picked up the stone and folded it inside her palm. "Universal!"

"I apologize," said Bongo. "If that's what I think it is, it's the first time I've ever seen one in real life. My cousin doubts it's genuine and wants to check for herself."

"Yeah, but..." She couldn't think of a nicer way to put it. "How do I know your cousin isn't going to run off with it and disappear, or take it out the back and swap it for a fake?"

"Wow," said Bongo's relative. "Rude much? If you don't trust me, you're welcome to take your business elsewhere."

"Don't be a stupid..." Bongo scolded, using a word from his language. "When are you gonna see another ember gem?" His head swiveled toward Carina. "It's clear you're from a rougher part of the galaxy. What you have to understand about Lakshmi Station is that it's tightly, I mean *tightly*, regulated. Just last week a cafe owner was found selling coffee from a printer as the genuine article. They spaced him."

"Spaced?!" Carina exclaimed, looking over her shoulder at her companions.

"Yeah, *spaced*. What do you think they'd do to my cousin if she tried to steal your gem?"

Carina still couldn't believe him. He could be spinning her a tale.

"The gem is real," she told the exchange owner. "Assuming I let you verify that, how much will you give me for it?"

Bongo's cousin named a sum that would have made Carina's eyes pop if she hadn't been carefully trying to keep a neutral expression. She'd made a similar exchange on Gog for starship fuel, and now she knew how badly she'd been screwed over. She wasn't going to make the same mistake again.

Bongo had begun babbling like a brook to his cousin, who replied at a louder volume. He upped the ante some more, rising onto the tips of his claws to lean over the counter. Were they arguing? It appeared so, but really Carina didn't have a clue.

He broke off abruptly and said, "We're going somewhere else."

"What?" asked Carina. "Why?"

"Because my cousin thinks she can retire early on a visitor's gullibility."

He crawled out of the booth, and she was compelled to leave too. A stream of liquid utterances from his relative followed them.

"Bongo," she said, trotting to catch up to the alien, "what's going on?"

He halted, rocking on his many legs. His head rotated, each of his eyes scrutinizing her before he replied, "Not many of you humans are nice to us. I get that we remind you of a creature you don't like, but we have feelings, you know? Before, when you helped me onto my feet, I was embarrassed, and I'm sorry I snapped. But I was touched by your gesture. It was a kind thing to do. To thank you, I want to get you the best deal I can, and my cousin wasn't going to give you it." He added, as he set off again, "She always was a greedy bitch."

Eight

Since the Lotacryllan men had gone away, the *Bathsheba* seemed bigger and more mysterious than ever. Darius was tempted to ask Nahla if he could hold her hand as they walked down the empty passageway, but he didn't want her to think he was a silly little kid. Instead, he held his elixir bottle more tightly. Like Nahla had said, if anything bad happened, he could easily Transport them back to their suite. "Where are we going?"

"Deck Zero."

"Deck Zero?" He hadn't known there *was* a deck zero. "What's down there?"

"You'll see." She gave him a quick, excited smile.

Nahla loved knowing things other people didn't. That was why she spent so long reading stuff in the ship's database and translating the mage papers. She'd kept the knowledge of the ember gems to herself for ages—actually took them and kept them until the others knew about them!

Ordinarily, that would have been bad. It was wrong to steal. But it had all turned out okay in the end and Nahla hadn't been punished. Maybe it was all right to steal from bad people like Lomang.

A shiver ran through him.

Lomang's feelings had been thick, dark treacle, strong and full of wants.

They arrived at the elevator. When they stepped inside, Nahla told it to take them to Deck One.

Darius protested, "But you said—"

"The elevators don't go all the way to the bottom."

"Why not?"

"I think they used to, then someone changed them."

"Why would they do that?"

"That's what I want to find out."

The elevator pinged and the doors opened.

"I'm not sure we should be doing this," Darius said uneasily as they stepped out. "There has to be a reason the elevators were fixed so they don't go to Deck Zero. What if something's living down there?"

"Nothing's living down there."

"How do you know?"

"Because it would need food and water."

"Maybe it has food and water. If it has the whole deck to itself, it could keep enough food and water to last a lifetime."

Nahla didn't like this answer. Her annoyance spread out from her in ripples. "There's nothing living there. That's dumb. Why would something choose to live there and never come out? We've been aboard the ship for months and no one's ever seen anything."

"It might only come out during the quiet shift, when hardly anyone's about. It might come out and take what it needs from our supplies."

Her sharp anger stabbed at him. "Do you want to come with me or not?"

"Ye-es," he replied. Now he'd had time to think about it, he wasn't sure he did. But if he didn't, Nahla would go there by herself. And if he told on her, he would be breaking his promise, and she probably wouldn't play with him for weeks. Then he wouldn't have *anyone* to play with. "But if we see that something's living there, we have to leave right away. We won't look to find out what it is. We'll tell a grown-up."

"Yeah, okay."

Her mood calmed, and he felt its cool draft.

Walking along the passageway on Deck One, he wanted to hold her hand more than ever. Hardly anyone came down here. Old, broken equipment that couldn't be fixed was stored here for spare parts, as well as things kept 'just-in-case' like out-of-date medications and supplies. The place had a creepy, neglected feeling, even though he knew it couldn't really feel anything and it was just his imagination.

Nahla stopped at a hatch. "We have to climb down the rest of the way."

It was a service tunnel for techs to use when the elevators didn't work or they had to reach something they couldn't get at any other way. A metal ladder led down into darkness.

"Lights will come on when they sense us in the tunnel," said Nahla.

"Okay," Darius replied nervously.

"I'll go first. Do you have somewhere to put your elixir?"

Darn it. He hadn't brought a bag with him. "I didn't know I'd have to use two hands."

"Can you tuck it in your waistband?"

"I guess so. I'll try."

"Whatever you do," said Nahla with a grin, "don't drop it on my head."

She climbed into the hatch and onto the ladder. He peered down at the top of her receding head. Lights lit up the tunnel, just like she'd said. He pushed his bottle into the top of his pants. He shouldn't be doing this. He wished Carina was here.

When he reached the bottom, he half-expected to find Nahla standing in the dark, but the lights worked the same as everywhere else.

"Hmph," she said. "Well, the sanobots certainly know about Deck Zero."

The place looked like as the rest of the ship. He wasn't sure what he'd been expecting—dust, cobwebs?—but it *was* kinda disappointing in a way. "Maybe there isn't anything special here. The people who owned the ship decided one day they didn't need this deck, so they closed it off."

"That has to be the most boring explanation I ever heard!" Nahla exclaimed. "There has to be a better reason than that. Let's explore."

She strode off, and he had to hurry to catch up to her while also taking his elixir bottle out of his pants. It looked like their expedition was going to be perfectly safe, but he still clutched the bottle tightly, just in case.

The first room they came to was stuffed with piles of clothes. The many-colored garments were stacked high, higher than he or Nahla could reach. She grabbed the edge of something and pulled.

"Don't do that!" Darius warned.

Too late.

The pile toppled over, right on top of her. She screamed, but in a giggling, happy way. She'd fallen down, and when she stood up, she was holding onto the piece of clothing she'd pulled out. It was a sparkly dress. Nahla held it up to her chest. The dress was much too long and wide to fit her. It was for an adult.

"Look at me!" she commanded. "I'm a beautiful *lady*." She pronounced the 'y' long and drawn out, *eeeee*. "Ferne and Oriana would love this. There are all kinds of clothes here. We should choose some to take back with us."

He looked around, wondering what they should take.

"Oh!" The dress had fallen from her fingers, or rather, most of it had. She was holding a straggly bit of it between her hands. She dropped it and, reaching down, she tried to pick up the fallen pieces, but they dissolved into tiny frag-ments. She pushed a hand into the mound on the floor. It collapsed into dust.

"These clothes must be really old," Darius remarked.

"Yeah, they must." Nahla frowned like she always did when she was thinking hard. "I hope that's all it is."

"What do you mean?"

She brushed the remnants of material off her hands and then brought them up to her face to look at them closely. Then she looked at him. "Do you feel okay?"

"Yeah. I-I think so." Now that she asked, he wasn't sure he did. Or was that only because she'd asked him? "Maybe we should go."

"Maybe, but..." She kicked the dusty pile. "Let's explore just a little bit more. Once we tell the others about this place, I bet they'll never let us come here alone again. We should take our chance while we can."

"All right, but just a few more rooms. Then we'll leave. If we don't go back soon, the others will wonder what's happened to us. And Ferne is waiting for his snacks."

"Okay. Just a few more rooms."

NINE

Holding her wrist under the scanner, Carina grimaced. Not that being scanned to enter the bar, the Mystic Supernova, was painful. It didn't hurt at all. Her pain was internal. She'd discovered that when she'd bought the starship fuel on Gog, she'd been royally swindled.

She was also deeply pissed off at Justus. He'd been with her when she'd made the transaction. How could he not have known the value of the ember gems? His dad had been a trader, for star's sake. Why hadn't he said something?

Hsiao must have seen her expression, as she whispered, "It's not a big deal, Carina. Get over it. We got a great price for the gems and we won't have to skimp on updates for the *Bathsheba*. Let's relax and have a good time."

Easy for her to say. *She* wasn't the one responsible for the only money they had and everyone's safety on the journey to Earth. "*Three* ember gems," she hissed back. "I paid three whole gems, just to fill up the tanks. I can't believe I was so stupid."

She imagined the Gogian fuel supplier laughing at her behind her back. She had only one consolation: the gem she'd given the Magogian ground dwellers would easily buy enough weapons and equipment to overthrow their Dark Mage masters.

"You weren't stupid," said Hsiao, maintaining her quiet tone as they were allowed through the security check. "How were you supposed to know?"

"But Justus should have known and told me. The gems are only found on his planet. Of all people, *he* should know."

"That isn't always the way, though, is it? The Lotacryllans are the wholesalers. They don't control the point-of-sale price, and they might not even know how much their export fetches in other parts of the sector. Justus said he wasn't from around here, didn't he? The station doesn't have him on its database."

It was a fair point.

"What does it matter, anyway?" Hsiao went on. "What's done is done. We have plenty left to get exactly what we need and everyone can have some fun too. I'd call that a win."

"Yeah," Carina grudgingly conceded, "I suppose so."

The volume of ambient noise increased as the doors opened and, Justus and Jackson joining them, they stepped into the bar. Wide stairs led down to an open space filled with people and dotted with bar islands.

"Just a couple of drinks," she announced, "then back to the *Bathsheba*. I want a good night's sleep before starting negotiations tomorrow."

The remaining four ember gems were exchanged and the creds deposited in an account, but she still had to decide how best to use them to fortify the colony ship against attack. The armament vendors had given a wide, varied range of options, and, as well as sleeping on it, she wanted to discuss the choices with the others.

A slide ran down to the lower level next to the stairs. She'd thought it was a gimmick, but as she began to walk down the steps, a long creature slid past her on its belly, slim, tentacle-like legs held high. When it reached the bottom, it slithered into the crowd.

"The kids are gonna have fun at Lakshmi," said Jackson.

"They aren't coming here," she replied. "Not the little ones at least."

"Aw, come on. You have to let them come to the station. When are they going to get another chance to see all the cool aliens? You could introduce them to Bongo."

Bongo had become somewhat of a friend while he'd been taking them to the currency exchanges and then on to the starship armament vendors. Carina was fairly certain his job only required him to show them the basics and then leave them to their own devices. Yet he'd gone above and beyond and offered to be their guide again when they returned.

"Bongo is one thing," she said. "What I'm not sure about is all the other things. Especially the sex bots."

"Hosts and hostesses," Jackson corrected.

"Right," she replied, rolling her eyes. "Hosts and hostesses."

"So we only have to show them our ID codes?" asked Justus, his eyes bright with excitement.

"Yeah," said Carina, "but—"

He disappeared into the crowd.

"Take it easy," she finished.

"Don't worry," said Hsiao. "He can't drink the budget. He won't even make a tiny dent in it."

"That's not what I'm worried about." She didn't want him getting himself into trouble. The story of the cafe owner who'd been spaced indicated there could be dire consequences for stepping out of line.

Just then, a man loomed up. Almost as big as Pappu, and he thrust his chest out aggressively.

"Wha' planet?" he demanded.

"Huh?" she asked.

"It's a simple question," he sneered drunkenly. "Wha' planet are you from?"

The long day, annoyance about being duped over the ember gems, guilt at being forced to exclude Parthenia again, and the stress of needing to make the best choices to defend the ship had all been getting to her *before* Justus had run off. Unprovoked hostility from this goon pushed her over the edge. "What planet are *you* from?" she spat back.

"The war, remember?" said Jackson softly. "He wants to know what side we're on."

"This section's only for Quintonese," slurred the man. "You're not from there, are you? Leave, now! 'Fore I help you on your way."

"No, we're not Quintonese," she declared, rearing up and glaring at him. "And we're not from Marchon, or the other side in your goddamned conflict, whatever the hell it's called. We're from out-sector and we're here to have a quiet drink, so get out of my face!"

"Selan," said another bar patron, pulling on the big guy's arm. "You'll get yourself thrown out. Leave them alone."

"Yeah, leave us alone, *Selan*!"

"Carina," said Hsiao, "cool it!"

The drunk grinned lopsidedly. "S'okay. Thought you were Marchonish. Your clothes are funny. But a Marchonish wouldn't have those balls."

His companion succeeded in pulling him away. Selan staggered off.

Jackson's heavy prosthetic hand landed on Carina's shoulders. "What were you saying to Justus? Something about taking it easy?"

"Carina has balls," joked Hsiao. "Who knew?"

"Bryce, probably," said Jackson.

"Let's get that drink," Hsiao said. "*Someone* needs to calm down."

Ten

When they returned to the *Bathsheba*, Bryce was waiting for them at the airlock. He was pale and sweaty, and he looked at Carina with dread in his eyes.

Before she could ask him what was wrong, he said, "I need to talk to you." He took her to one side while Hsiao, Jackson, and a somewhat unsteady Justus passed by them, walking into the ship.

"I'm not sure how to put this," said Bryce.

In all the time she had known him and through all the life-threatening situations they'd faced, she had never seen him looking so scared. "Stars, just say it! You're worrying the hell out of me."

He swallowed. "We can't find Darius or Nahla."

"*What*?!" A wave of icy fear hit. "What do you mean you can't find them?"

"They left their suite about an hour after lunch, saying they were just popping out to get snacks, but they didn't come back. Oriana and Ferne didn't notice until a couple of hours later. They were too engrossed in what they were doing. And Parthenia didn't leave her room until the alarm was raised. Everyone's been looking for them ever since, but there's no trace of them."

She felt numb. The mood in the *Peregrine* on the journey back had been so good. The visit to Lakshmi Station had been a great success. They had an account fat with creds and access to the best defensive tech the sector had to offer. They would be able to sleep peacefully the rest of the way to Earth, safe and secure. But none of it meant anything if something bad had happened to her brother or sister.

"But..." A realization broke through the tide of terror rising in her heart, creating an overwhelming sense of relief. "It's fine. I'll just Cast Locate." She reached for her elixir bottle. "I don't know why Parthenia and the twins didn't think of it. Darius and Nahla are probably hiding somewhere, enjoying the idea of us searching for them. You know what little kids are like."

"They tried that," said Bryce. "Oriana, Ferne, and Parthenia. They've all tried it over and over again. I told you, we can't find them."

"They can't find them with Locate?" she asked dazedly. "That's not possible. Even if they were..." she couldn't bring herself to say it "...Locate would always find them."

"Unless they were out of range. That's what Parthenia said."

"Yes, but..." Her mind was whirring. She couldn't think straight. How far did Locate operate? "The *Bathsheba* hasn't changed position since we left, has she?"

"No, or if she has, it's just a little from gravitational effects."

"Then the only way Darius and Nahla could move out of range would be—"

"Carina!"

It was Oriana. She ran down the passageway and hugged Carina tightly. Her eyes were red in her puffy face. "We can't find them!" she sobbed. "We tried everything. We looked and looked. I'm so glad you're back. Can you think of something else we can do? There has to be something else."

She was gazing up hopefully.

Carina tried to look calm. In truth, she was barely holding it together herself. It was up to her to be strong, to figure out a solution, to find the way out of a sticky situation, again. But she had nothing. She had no idea what could have happened to her little sister and brother or how to find out where they'd gone.

Ferne and Parthenia appeared. Ferne's expression was downcast, and Parthenia looked like Carina felt—utterly distraught.

"Let me think," Carina said. "I need to think." She began to walk, though she had no destination in mind.

"I'm sorry," said Parthenia. "I should have been watching them."

"No," said Bryce. "It's my fault. I should have stayed in the suite with you guys."

"It's nobody's fault," said Carina. "Neither of you could be expected to watch all the kids every second. They're old enough to look after themselves, and they should be smart enough to not put themselves in danger."

"They *should* be," muttered Parthenia.

"No other ship approached while I was gone?" It was a dumb question.

Bryce would have told her if that was the case, but she had to get the possibility of a kidnapping out of the way.

"Absolutely not," he replied. "Bibik and I searched all the scanner data three times. Nothing has come anywhere near the *Bathsheba* except the *Peregrine*. Even if a ship could avoid scanner detection somehow, the computer would have registered an airlock opening. There's been nothing. Not even a garbage evacuation."

"So they can't have left the ship. Which means they must be here somewhere, and that means they must be in range to Locate." She halted and swung toward Parthenia and the twins. "Is it possible your elixir is the problem?"

"I made it the other day," Parthenia replied defensively. "I've never got it wrong before."

"Okay, but let me try with mine. It's from an earlier batch. Does anyone have something of the kids' to use?"

"I have some of Nahla's hair from her brush and Darius's playing cards," said Oriana, taking them out of her pocket and handing them over.

Carina walked to the bulkhead and leaned her back on it. She unscrewed the lid on her bottle and, holding Nahla and Darius's personal items in one hand, took a swig. Closing her eyes, she concentrated. Casting under pressure was hard. It required focus, which was nearly impossible to achieve when you were worried something terrible had happened to people you loved.

She pushed away the black cloud of fear and went down into her mind. Locate was a seven-stroke character. Carefully, she wrote each glowing stroke in the darkness and sent it out.

She waited.

If the Cast worked, she should begin to sense her siblings, bright spots in the gray field of mental space.

Time stretched out, measured by each thump of her anxious heart.

She continued to wait, longer than she should have, past the moment she knew, deep down, she had failed.

Tears filled her eyes as she finally opened them. Unable to speak, she shook her head.

The four mages and Bryce stood silently in the passageway.

A flash of hope hit, though as she spoke she realized it was irrational. "What about Jace? Has he tried to Cast for them?"

"He tried many times," Parthenia replied. "He gave up and joined one of the search parties."

Despair descended again. If Jace could not Locate them, no one could. Only Darius was a better mage .

"Has Casting ever not worked for you before?" asked Bryce.

"Plenty of times," Carina replied, "when I was a kid and learning. But you can sort of feel if you did it wrong. Even if that wasn't so, it isn't possible that we're *all* doing it wrong. It can only mean they aren't here and searching for them is pointless."

Another idea occurred.

"Did the scanners pick up anything strange? Is it possible the *Bathsheba* was hit by something similar to what killed Lomang and Mezban?"

"We checked for that too. There was nothing out of the ordinary the whole time you were gone."

Dammit.

"They have to be here!" she exclaimed. "I can't explain why we can't Locate them, but they must be somewhere on the ship." She didn't add the final part of the sentence that sprang to her mind: *dead or alive.*

"If they're here," said Bryce, "we'll find them eventually. The *Bathsheba's* big but she isn't infinite. We won't stop looking until we've found them."

"Do you two remember exactly where they said they were going?" Carina asked Ferne and Oriana.

"All they said was they were going to get something to eat," Ferne replied. "Which to me meant the galley on our deck."

"If they wanted something that wasn't there," Oriana chipped in, "they would only have to go to the printer on the deck below. They should only have been gone half an hour at most, but it took us longer than that to notice they hadn't come back." As she spoke, her cheeks flushed.

"Look," said Carina, "I don't want any of you to blame yourselves." Yet she could empathize. What had happened wasn't her fault either but she couldn't help feeling somehow it was. "They must have gone to another place. How could they have gone missing between your suite and the galley or the printer? There's nothing dangerous in those areas, not even an airlock. They had to be going somewhere different and they didn't want to tell you because they knew you would try to stop them."

"That *does* sound like something Nahla would do," Oriana agreed. "I love her, but she can be sneaky."

"And Darius would go along with it because he wanted to please her," said Parthenia. "He wants to keep everyone happy."

"That's right," Carina agreed. There was no need to state the reason Darius needed the people around him to feel happy. "What were they doing before they left?"

"Playing cards," Ferne replied. "The cards were on the bed when we looked into their room to check they hadn't come back without us noticing."

His answer was no help. She couldn't see how playing cards could have led the two children to lie and go somewhere forbidden. "Has anyone checked Nahla's interface?"

"I did," Ferne said, "but there was no activity on it for the last couple of days."

"Doesn't sound like Nahla."

Bryce commented, "I checked it too. He's right."

"There's no way she didn't use her interface recently. She must have wiped the history to cover something up. What about the ship's database? Anyone check what she's been doing on that?"

ELEVEN

The old schematic of the ship Nahla had been looking at before she disappeared showed an extra deck that didn't exist on the more recent plan. Deck Zero.

Why had its existence been hidden? Carina couldn't think of any good reason why the ship's previous occupants would want to make a secret of an entire deck.

She peered down the service tunnel on Deck One. It disappeared into darkness, but that was innocuous. The lights were probably motion-activated the same as everywhere else.

"They're down there!" Oriana exclaimed, leaning over Carina's shoulder. "They have to be."

She launched herself at the opening, but Carina grabbed her and held her back. She understood the impulse. There was nothing more she wanted to do herself than to shoot down the ladder and find her siblings.

"Let me go!" yelled Oriana.

"She's right," said Bryce. "Hold on. We need to be careful. We don't know what's down there. If it's only another deck, why haven't Darius and Nahla come back yet?"

Fear and anxiety gnawed at Carina.

Stupid, stupid, kids.

If they were okay, she would ground them for a month.

If they were okay.

"What worries me most is that we can't Locate them," she said. "The only thing that can block a Cast is another mage, but usually you would feel it being blocked. I didn't feel a thing when I Cast earlier."

Bryce asked, "You're sure it would work even if they're…"

"Yes!" she snapped, then immediately regretted it. He loved those kids as much as she did.

"Yes," she repeated, more softly, touching his arm. "No matter what's happened to them, it would work."

Except…

She remembered cremating Ma's body in a shuttle's engine flare. You couldn't Locate someone if there was nothing left of them.

She comm'd Jackson. "Bring five Black Dogs and pulse rifles to Deck One ASAP."

"Pulse rifles?" asked Ferne. "What do you think is down there?!"

She turned to Bryce. "Could some of the Lotacryllans have re-entered after you spaced them?"

"It would be a miracle, but I have to admit I didn't check the logs. I don't know if any of the other airlocks were activated."

"Could we be carrying Lotacryllan stowaways?" asked Parthenia.

"If the Lotacryllans do have Darius and Nahla," asked Oriana, "why haven't they said anything? They would have asked for a ransom or…I don't know. It just seems weird they would keep quiet about it."

Carina could think of a dark reason why the men might have said nothing. They might be perfectly content with their situation, moving around the ship during the quiet shift, stealing enough food to survive, waiting for an opportunity to sneak away—waiting until everyone went into Deep Sleep. Then they could take over the ship and fly wherever they wanted. All they would have to do to ensure they never met any opposition was to turn off the stasis system.

If her guess was correct, the arrival of Darius and Nahla would have thrown a spanner in the works. It would be in the Lotacryllans' interest to silence the children, permanently.

The elevator doors opened and six Black Dogs emerged in full armor and armed.

"You suited up," said Carina. "Good idea."

One of them replied, his helmet comm switched to external, "No harm in being cautious."

It was Jackson. He peered into the service tunnel hatch and whistled. "You think the kids are down there?"

"Yeah, and I think they might not be alone."

"It'll be a tight fit in our suits, but I think we can do it."

"I'm coming too," said Carina.

"I didn't bring a spare rifle."

"I have my elixir. I'll be okay."

"Better to let…" ventured Bryce.

Carina gave him a hard stare, and he didn't finish his sentence.

"Let's go," she said. "We've wasted enough time."

Jackson managed to persuade her to allow himself and the other Black Dogs to climb down the service ladder first. After the last merc entered the hatch she followed. As she descended she listened for sounds of fighting, but there was nothing. At the bottom, she climbed out into a passageway the same as the others on the ship, empty except for the mercs.

"Carina," said Jackson, "you've gotta leave. My HUD's reporting low O2."

"Huh?"

"Get back up the ladder, or you'll be unconscious within a couple of minutes."

"But—"

"I don't wanna have to carry you *and* those kids. Leave. Now."

With great reluctance, she returned to Deck One. By the time she reached the top of the ladder, she'd begun to feel a little woozy. She climbed out and sat with her back to the bulkhead.

"Did you find them?" asked Oriana excitedly.

"No, I had to come back because the oxygen's low down there. It was lucky Jackson suited up. His HUD warned him."

"So that's why Darius and Nahla didn't come back," said Bryce.

She shared a look with him.

"What does it mean?" asked Ferne.

"It means there aren't any stowaway Lotacryllans," said Carina.

Oriana exhaled heavily. "Thank goodness for that!"

"But if you came back right away," said Parthenia, "that means the atmosphere must be really dangerous if you aren't wearing armor."

"Let's not speculate," said Bryce. "Let's wait and see what the mercs find."

Carina was holding it together the best she could. She didn't want to lose hope or upset her siblings by showing how she really felt, but a scene kept playing through her mind. She could see Jackson emerging from the hatch, carrying Darius in his arms, lifeless. Another merc appeared carrying Nahla, her body limp, her skin blue, her chest still.

She sank her head into her hands.

Bryce sat beside her and put his arm around her shoulders.

Seconds crawled past as they waited.

Her confusion about why the Locate Cast hadn't worked didn't matter anymore. All she could do was hope the inevitable wasn't true.

It couldn't be true.

"Someone's coming!" Ferne announced.

She leapt up and leaned in next to her brother at the open hatch. She saw the top of a helmet—a child's form rested over the merc's shoulder.

"He's got Darius!" Ferne yelled. "They found him!"

Carina backed out and pulled Ferne with her. "We have to make room." She took the lid off her elixir and put the bottle down, ready to Cast Heal.

When the merc reached the level of the hatch, she called out, "I'll take him!" and reached into the tunnel to lift Darius off the man's shoulder.

She laid the small figure down.

He was so tiny! So young.

"Is he breathing?" whispered Parthenia.

Darius was deathly pale. Carina put her ear against his chest.

The thump of his heart sounded. It was quiet and slow, but it was there.

A dam broke within her and tears flooded her eyes. "He's alive," she gasped. "He's alive."

Distantly, she heard Oriana announce, "They've got Nahla too!"

"Heal her, Parthenia." She was already sipping elixir. She placed a hand on Darius's chest and squeezed her eyes shut. With a great effort, she managed to control her ragged emotions and Cast Heal.

She opened her eyes, expecting her sweet brother's eyes to open soon too.

They did not.

Nothing had changed. He remained unconscious and just as pale. She thrust her ear against his chest again. His heart beat at the same slow rate.

Next to her, Parthenia had done the same.

"It isn't working!" her sister wailed over Nahla's motionless form. "Why isn't it working?"

TWELVE

Carina's understanding of the dreadful situation was confirmed by Jace later in the sick bay. Before he mentioned the problem, however, he asked how Darius and Nahla were doing.

"They're alive," she replied, her throat tight. "That's the main thing. The doc says it's going to be hard to tell how the oxygen deprivation has affected their brains until they wake up. She's put them under sedation to help them recover. We'll know more tomorrow when she begins to withdraw the treatment."

The children looked better than they had when they'd been found. As they lay in the sick bay beds with oxygen masks on their faces, their skin was pink and plump. But they'd been unconscious for hours, the oxygen-depleted atmosphere slowly sapping them of life. Black Dog medics had hooked them up to life-sign monitors, which displayed their steady heartbeats, respiration, blood pressure, and other figures. The screens provided the brightest light in the quiet room.

"I heard they were found on a deck no one knew existed?" Jace asked, sitting down.

"Deck Zero. It must have been abandoned decades ago. The *Bathsheba* is centuries old, and at some point the atmosphere management system began to struggle to maintain safe oxygen levels down there. Whoever was running the ship closed the deck off. I doubt even Lomang knew about it."

"But why isn't there a warning somewhere?"

"There is, on the computer, but the database is in the original colonists' script, remember? Some of it is converted to Universal now, but not all of it. Nahla must have found out about Deck Zero but she didn't fully understand what she was reading."

"No signs outside the service hatches?"

She shrugged. "There are no signs anywhere on the ship. Maybe the colonists didn't use them, or they were taken down. Who knows? It doesn't matter now."

Jace ran a hand through his hair. "Thank the stars they didn't die."

She nodded. "According to the doc, they wouldn't have lasted much longer if we hadn't found them."

Then Jace brought up the second awful event on both their minds. He said quietly, "You tried Casting Heal, didn't you." It was a statement, not a question.

She nodded again. The suffocating blanket of alarm and fear she'd been feeling tightened around her.

"It didn't work, right?"

She shook her head. There was nothing else to say.

"I've tried them all," he went on. "Every Cast I know. Rise, Fire, Break, Obscure, Transport, Lock, and the rest."

"None of them worked?"

He looked down. "Not one."

She'd tried some other Casts too. She tried to Lock the sick bay door and Cast Rise on the water in the beaker next to Darius's bed. These were simple Casts a mage child could do. Her experience mirrored Jace's.

A pause stretched out as the significance of their failures expanded.

"Have you ever heard of this happening before?" Carina asked.

"Never." He met her gaze. "You remember Magda?"

"Of course." How could she ever forget the old Spirit Mage?

"I listened to all her stories. I never heard a single one about mages losing their abilities."

She stroked the back of Darius's hand.

What did it mean?

She'd never imagined there might be a time she could no longer Cast. Mages retained their abilities until death, only losing the capacity in old age in the same way that old people's minds didn't work so well. Even with the evidence staring her in the face, she couldn't imagine no longer being able to Cast. She couldn't wrap her head around it. Her ability was a part of her, like talking, eating, and walking. Losing it felt like having a limb sawn off. "Do you have any idea what might have happened?"

"I'm as much in the dark as you. How have Parthenia and the others taken it?"

"We were all shocked when neither she nor I could get Heal to work. While we were waiting for the medics, we realized that might be why no one had been able to Locate Darius and Nahla, that it was because the Cast hadn't been working. Then the medics arrived, and after that...it's all a blur, honestly. I was so worried the kids were going to..."

Jace put a hand on her back.

"I comm'd Parthenia to tell her what the doc said but I haven't spoken to her or anyone else since. I don't know how they're doing. Bryce is with them."

"Would you like me to talk to them?"

"Please. Bryce loves them like his own, but he isn't a mage. He won't understand what this means or how they'll be feeling."

"I'm not sure I do myself yet. It's hard to take in."

"You can say that again."

He rose to his feet. "Darius and Nahla were found alive. That's something to be grateful for. Tomorrow will bring us more good news, hopefully. They're young and healthy, and that will help with their recovery."

"That's what the doc said. And today I discovered the ember gems are worth an absolute fortune. If I have to use it all to pay for medical treatment at Lakshmi Station I will."

"There are hospitals there?"

"They have *everything* there." She sighed. "I was so happy when I got back, looking forward to telling everyone about our good luck and deciding the best ways to protect the ship. And then *this* happens." She looked up at her towering friend. "Do you think it might be only temporary? That we'll get our abilities back?"

"Your guess is as good as mine. If it had happened after you'd returned from your trip, I would have wondered if you'd brought back a virus that had infected us. But the effect began earlier than that. My Locate Casts didn't work while you were gone. To find out whether the problem is temporary, we need to discover what's causing it, and at the moment I don't have any ideas. But I'll think about it. That's all we can do."

"That, and get used to being normal."

"You said it. I'll go and talk to the kids."

Normality. To be like 99.9 percent of the rest of humanity. It was a weird feeling.

There had been many times she'd considered her magehood to be more of a curse than a benefit. It had caused so much pain in her life. Ma had suffered years of torment due to it, and for Carina herself it had meant living with loneliness and constant fear of discovery.

Yet it was also a fundamental part of her identity, like the color of her eyes or her interest in bugs. It was *who she was*. If she could never Cast again, she would feel like a different person.

And what did it mean in terms of the journey to Earth? The reason she wanted to go there was to try to find a home where her family could live safely. She hoped things were different there now, thousands of years after mages had departed. But if none of them was a mage anymore, was there any point in making the long voyage? Might it not be better to find a quiet, backwater planet and live out their lives like regular people?

THIRTEEN

arina was in a long, dark tunnel. The air was humid and stuffy, and thick cobwebs stretched from wall to wall. She turned, trying to find a way out. At one end was impenetrable darkness, at the other, a pinprick of light shone. How had she come to be here? She couldn't remember.

All she knew was she had to get out.

She pushed through a sticky web, breaking it apart. Thick threads clung to her face and hair as she walked toward the light. She tried to pull them away, but they stuck to her skin and trailed behind her. Another web, and another effort to break it and pass through. At this one, something unseen scuttled away along the ceiling. The spot of light grew larger.

She was hot, sweating in the still, warm air. Her legs were already growing weary, though she didn't think she'd gone very far. Perhaps this was a high-g planet. She did feel heavier than usual. Or maybe there was something different about the air. It felt thick and syrupy.

Figures were moving in the light, silhouetted by its brightness. They were moving toward her slowly, shuffling. She could see three distinctly, but there might be even more behind, judging from the gray shadows in the brilliance.

She turned and looked back. Might it be better to retreat into the dark? But what lay that way was unknown. The least she could expect was more of the webs and the creatures who had made them.

She went on.

As the light increased, it grew softer. A cool wind blew from the same direction, drying her sweat. She could make out the first figure. It was a woman wearing a dress that fell to her feet, her long hair arranged carefully on her head.

Carina gasped.

Ma!

She ran into her arms and hugged the thin woman tightly. She felt so small, so frail, Carina was frightened she might hurt her. She let go and stared into her mother's deep brown eyes. "What are you doing here? Are you okay?"

Ma didn't answer, only smiled sweetly and pointed behind her.

Ba was here too!

He raised a hand in greeting, but before Carina could run to him she saw someone else she recognized farther down the tunnel. Hobbling forward, hunched over by age and long years of gathering semi-precious stones, was Nai Nai.

Tears sprang to Carina's eyes. She couldn't believe it. Here were three people who meant so much to her. Who to speak to first? She hadn't seen Ba since she was three years old, and Nai Nai had raised her, dedicating her life to protecting her and teaching her how to be a mage.

Then she saw the others.

Behind Nai Nai walked ranks of other people, all appearing familiar. She could see Nai Nai's, Ba's, and Ma's features in their faces. These were her ancestors, going back down the ages. Mages who had lived before her in different places and on other planets across the galaxy, all the way back for thousands of years to the people who had fled Earth.

"Carina," said a quiet, high-pitched voice.

She opened her eyes.

She was sitting down, bent forward, resting her upper body on a bed—Darius's sick bay bed.

She sat up.

He was awake and watching her. "Were you dreaming?"

"I think I was. How are you feeling, sweetheart?"

He looked healthy, and the fact he'd spoken to her was a good sign.

"I thought you were dreaming," he said. "You were talking. I think you said *Nai Nai*."

"I was dreaming about our family."

The family who had been mages for hundreds of generations. Was the line going to stop with her and her siblings? "How are you?" She stroked his hair. "I've been so worried about you."

He began to cry. "I'm sorry, Carina. I'm sorry I was bad."

"Hey," she said softly. "It's okay. We found you. That's the most important thing. What do you remember?"

"I was with Nahla on Deck Zero and—" he sat bolt upright. "Where is she? Is she—"

"She's still asleep."

Nahla's unconscious form hadn't moved while they'd been talking.

The sick bay door slid open and a medic appeared.

"How are my young patients?" he asked cheerfully, adding, "One's awake I see. Excellent."

"He seems to have fully recovered," said Carina.

"I certainly hope so. You are looking chipper, young man. If your sister would kindly step outside, I'll do some checks."

"No," Darius protested, "I want Carina to stay."

"It'll be fine," she said. "It's just for a few minutes, right?"

"That's all." The medic leaned down and fake-whispered in Darius's ear, "And I have candy Carina won't approve of."

Darius giggled.

"I'll see you soon," said Carina, stepping out.

While she waited, she rested her back on the bulkhead and folded her arms. Closing her eyes, she wished she could Send to Parthenia to tell her Darius was awake and was apparently okay. She could comm her, of course, but there was something special about Casting Send. It was a more emotional, meaningful act, in the same way an embrace felt different from hearing the words *I love you*. And Casting was something that drew them together.

All that appeared to be gone now, perhaps forever. If she couldn't Cast, she would need to learn a new way of being, like learning to walk again.

She comm'd Bryce.

"Fantastic," he said when she told him her brother seemed okay. "I haven't slept all night, worrying."

Guilt niggled at her. She'd left Bryce to look after her siblings again. She relied on him so much.

"How about Nahla?" he asked.

"She hasn't woken up yet. There's a medic in with both of them at the moment. I'll see what he says, but if Darius is all right I think Nahla must be too."

"Good. Let me know, okay?"

"Of course. What's been happening there?"

He paused before answering, "Jace came over to talk to the kids and..." he paused again "...they haven't taken the news they've lost their mage abilities very well."

Neither have I. "I guess it's only to be expected. It's a big shock for all of us. I never imagined this could happen."

"It's a bummer, but it isn't *that* big a disaster, is it? You're all still healthy."

"It's more than a bummer, Bryce. I don't think you really understand what this means to us."

"You're right. It *is* hard for me to understand. Oriana hasn't stopped crying since Jace told her and Ferne's acting like he just got hit by a truck. Parthenia hasn't left her room, though to be fair she hasn't left it much at all lately. Is it so bad to be an ordinary non-mage person like me?"

"No, but..."

"What?"

"I'm sorry. I can't explain right now."

The medic emerged from the sick bay room.

"I'll talk to you soon," she told Bryce before cutting the comm. "What did you find out?"

The man's expression stopped her heart.

"They're going to be okay, right?" she asked nervously.

"I performed cognitive function checks on Darius, and he doesn't seem to be suffering any major impairments." The medic looked down for a second before continuing, "Nahla woke up while I was working with her brother, so I ran the basic tests on her as well. The doc will be along soon to run more advanced checks, but it seems clear the hypoxia has caused some brain damage."

"What?" Carina breathed. "What kind of brain damage?"

"She's suffering memory loss and her gross motor skills have been affected. We'll be able to tell you more after the doctor's seen her."

"No! Poor Nahla."

"It's still early days. We'll begin treatment right away and do everything we can to help her regain her abilities."

"Will she ever be the same again?"

"It's hard for me to say," he replied, though his tone implied he was only trying to be kind. "The doctor will be able to give you a prognosis for her recovery."

"Thanks," said Carina quietly. "Can I see them now?"

"Go ahead."

FOURTEEN

"At last," said Parthenia sarcastically. "A gathering I'm invited to."

Carina bit back an equally acid reply. They were facing their greatest challenges yet, and her eldest sister had to make it about *her*.

"A very important gathering," said Jace. "Let's get started."

Carina had invited the older mage to the kids' suite to lead the discussion on what they would do to face the latest developments. Bryce was present as well as the mages and Nahla, who had curled into Jace's side on the sofa, sucking her thumb.

It was hard to look at her. Nahla had sucked her thumb sometimes in the earliest days Carina had known her. It wasn't hard to guess why the little girl had retained the baby habit. Her father had been a monster and their Dark Mage brother, Castiel, had mercilessly manipulated and later tortured her. What was harder to understand was the amazing resilience and adaptability she'd shown as soon as she was free of these two terrible influences. The thumb-sucking had stopped as the little girl bloomed.

Nahla had developed into a very smart, savvy child, despite all the trauma she'd endured, and her discovery of the ember gems had saved them all. Now her little escapade had resulted in brain damage that was probably irreversible, according to the doctor. She'd lost a lot of memories and cognitive ability, leaving her with the mental capacity of a child half her age. She also struggled with walking, using a knife and fork, and operating an interface. When the doc had shown her a screen, she hadn't even seemed to understand what it was. She could still speak, but with a limited vocabulary.

With treatment, the doc had said, she should make some progress, but it was most likely she would never return to the sparky, quick-witted youngster she'd once been.

The advanced tests on Darius had revealed he'd escaped his sister's fate, possibly due to his younger age or another factor they didn't understand. His brain seemed unaffected.

"Do you know why this has happened to us, Jace?" Oriana asked plaintively. "Why can't we Cast anymore?"

It was a pointless question. Everyone already knew what he would say, but Oriana appeared to hope if she asked again she might get a different answer.

"I'm sorry," he replied patiently. "I don't know."

"Which means," said Ferne, "we might get our ability back. If we've randomly lost the ability to Cast, we could randomly regain it."

"Being a mage isn't random," said Carina. "It's genetic. That's what I always guessed, and we found out for sure on Magog. They knew we were mages after they'd taken DNA samples."

"Then has something gone wrong with our genetic code?" asked Ferne. "Can that happen?"

"I talked to the doctor. He said space radiation damages DNA but the ship's hull and the EVA suits protect us from it. And if there had been a radiation breach, alarms would have sounded."

"True," said Bryce. "Anyway, Carina, you were away when whatever's happened to you all happened. If it was due to radiation on the *Bathsheba* you wouldn't have been affected."

"Are we sure it happened while Carina was visiting Lakshmi Station?" asked Jace. "We didn't notice the effect until we were searching for Darius and Nahla, but we could have lost our abilities prior to that. It will help to pinpoint the event if we all try to remember the last time we Cast successfully."

Carina thought back. It was hard to bring to mind the last Cast she'd made. She definitely hadn't done any Casting at Lakshmi for fear of being noticed. Before that... She frowned.

"It's so hard," said Oriana. "I can't remember. I don't do it very much anymore. There's no need to Cast on a starship where everything's close at hand and all we do is mess around all day."

"I remember," said Parthenia. "I Cast Locate five days ago for something I'd lost. It worked then."

"So," said Jace, "sometime in the last five days, we all lost our mage ability."

Silence settled over the room. Nahla snuggled closer to Jace, who wrapped a protective arm around her.

"I know it must be hard for you all," said Bryce, "but looking at it over the long term, does it really matter? Carina, you've told me so many times how hard it is to be a mage, always living in fear of discovery, facing the threat of slavery and torture. If this thing that's happened is permanent, you aren't at risk anymore. No one has a reason to capture or hurt you. Surely that's a good thing?"

"No, it isn't a good thing!" Oriana snapped. "How would you feel if I cut off your leg and told you how much fun you'll have hopping?"

"Cool it, sis," said Ferne. "Bryce is only trying to help us feel better."

"I'm sorry," Bryce said. "I'll shut up."

"Please don't," said Jace. "Your opinion is valued and welcome. We need to discuss this calmly and figure it out."

"Is there a lot to figure out?" Carina asked. "We don't know why this has happened so we don't know how to put it right."

"I've been wondering if it is related to our genes," said Parthenia, "but not in terms of damage, more like a genetic clock counting down. I don't know how it works exactly, but maybe mages' powers have been ticking down over millennia until now, and suddenly they're gone. No mages are able to Cast anymore. It's over."

"You mean it could have affected all the people we left behind too?" asked Ferne. "None of the mages back home can Cast now?"

"I'm just speculating."

"My most urgent concern," said Carina, "is what it means in terms of traveling to Earth. Is there any point now? Bryce was right when he said we have nothing to fear any longer—or at least no more to fear than regular people—so why should we continue our journey?"

As she spoke, the cream she'd been having when Darius awoke sprang to mind. Ma, Ba, Nai Nai, her great grandparents, great-great grandparents, and on and on, back in time, farther into the light. They all had one thing in common, but she didn't share it with them anymore.

Mentally dragging herself back to the present, she asked, "Why spend the money from the ember gems on fitting out the *Bathsheba* when we could use it to settle down somewhere?"

"You mean you want to give up everything you've worked for all this time?" asked Oriana.

"When you put it like that," replied Carina, "I want to say no. But going to Earth was my idea. I feel like I've hauled you and the Black Dogs along with me. I don't know if that was right. What's happened has made me rethink everything. It's all a mess in my head."

"Kamil and I might have settled down on Magog," Parthenia blurted. "*He* wanted to, anyway. I wasn't sure. He wanted me to give up being a mage, abandon the voyage, leave all of you behind, and live there with him." She finished with a croaky voice, and a fat tear ran down her cheek. She wiped it away with the back of her hand.

So that's what you two were arguing about, thought Carina. "I'm glad you didn't. I would have missed you."

"We all would have," said Ferne quietly.

Parthenia's confession subdued everyone to a second silence.

After a few minutes, Jace said quietly, "We have another item to discuss today. Nahla."

She'd fallen asleep, her thumb still in her mouth.

"What's wrong with her?" Darius asked timidly.

Carina realized she hadn't told him anything about his sister's medical status. The news had been a shock she hadn't quite recovered from herself, without the additional necessity of explaining it to her brother.

"She's...sick." What else could she say? How to explain to a seven-year-old that his sibling would probably never be the same.

"Her brain is hurt," said Jace gently. "That's why she's acting differently."

"Oh," said Darius. "Did it happen when we fell asleep on Deck Zero?"

"Yes, that's right,"

"When will she get better?"

"We don't know," replied Jace. "Maybe never."

"Oh no!"

"Nahla's going to need our help from now on," said Carina. "We'll have to be patient as she learns how to do things again."

"I can teach her," said Darius.

"I'm sure you'll be a great helper." Carina turned to the others. "I don't know how useful this discussion has been. We don't have any idea what to do to get our powers back, and I guess it's too soon to accept they're gone forever. Until we know that, we can't decide if we want to continue on our journey to Earth. But I do know one thing. We have to pour our resources into helping Nahla. At Lakshmi Station they have the most up-to-date medical facilities in the sector. I propose that I take Nahla there tomorrow and find out what they can do for her."

"I think we can all agree on that," said Bryce.

FIFTEEN

Parthenia hadn't spent much time aboard the late Mezban's ship, the *Peregrine*, and she wasn't in a mood to explore it now. Sitting on the bridge reminded her of the time Kamil had taken her to the *Duchess*, the Black Dog's crippled military ship that remained attached to the *Bathsheba*. He'd frightened her by not telling her where they were going, and she'd had to explain to him what being a mage really meant.

He'd seemed to try to understand how she had to be constantly vigilant to protect herself, though she wasn't sure he really had succeeded. It wasn't something easy for others to comprehend. Unless you grew up as a mage, unless you'd lived it, day in, day out, it wasn't possible to know how it felt.

Nor was it possible to understand how it felt when it was all taken away from you.

"Parthenia," said Carina, "I think you should know some things about Lakshmi Station. There are androids there called hosts and hostesses, and—"

"I know what you're talking about. You don't need to explain."

She'd been tempted to reply, *The sex bots? Oh, I know all about them,* just to embarrass and annoy her sister, but Darius and Nahla were here.

"You do?" Carina asked. "How come?" She was holding Nahla on her lap, though she barely fit, while Darius was next to Hsiao, who was showing him the flight controls.

"Some of the mercs were talking about them."

"Oh, okay."

Her sister looked worried and concerned.

"For goodness sake," Parthenia said irritably. "I'm not twelve. You don't have to protect me from that kind of thing. Do you really think that after growing up with Mother and Father I don't understand what happens between adults?" She was tempted to say more, about the times Father would stare at her with a certain look in his eye, or when he would stand too close and touch her too much and in the wrong places, but she didn't want to burden Carina. She didn't hate her *that* much.

Her sister looked deflated. She stroked Nahla's hair and replied, "I'm sorry. I was forgetting."

"Lucky for you. *I* can't forget so easily."

Carina sighed. "What I'm trying to say is, when we get to the station, be careful to stick with us. The place is huge and confusing and it's easy to get lost. It's also full of all kinds of people, mostly visitors from the three warring systems. There are strict penalties for breaking regulations, but I'm sure plenty goes on the station officials don't know about, or at least they don't find out about until it's too late."

"Yeah," said Hsiao, speaking over her shoulder as she sat at the controls, "Carina nearly got in a fight on our last trip. Jackson and I had to hold her back."

The pilot was clearly trying to lighten the atmosphere, but Parthenia wasn't in the mood for it. Carina seemed to feel the same.

After registering their looks, Hsiao gave a small cough and faced her console again. "So, Darius, do you want to take a turn?"

His jaw dropped. "Me? Fly the ship?"

"Sure, why not? I can trust you not to do anything stupid, right?"

"I won't, I promise!"

"Then scooch over and sit here." The pilot got up, and Darius just about leapt into her seat.

Hsiao opened a shipwide comm. "Belt up, everyone. Trainee pilot at the controls." Then she leaned over Darius to swipe the screen, stating, "Switching to manual."

As she fastened her safety harness, Parthenia smiled. She was touched by the pilot's kind gesture and sensitivity. Darius hadn't said much, but he'd been quiet and glum since finding out about his sister's problems. He probably felt guilty, and Hsiao was doing a great job of taking his mind off it.

Carina moved Nahla to her own seat and strapped her in. As Parthenia secured her own belt, the *Peregrine* suddenly dipped and her stomach seemed to rise above her head.

"Whoops!" said Darius, giggling.

Hsiao reached forward and gently moved his hands from the console.

"Take it easy, speedracer." A swipe of her finger brought the ship level again. "Did you think you were training to pilot a fairground ride?"

Nahla had squealed at the sudden movement, but then she started giggling too. "That was fun! Do it again!"

"No, thank you," said Hsiao. "Straight and steady, Darius, like I showed you."

He bent his head down as he concentrated on the controls. The ship continued on with small swerves and jumps for a few minutes. Then Darius's legs began to kick, which was a sure sign he was either bored or needed the bathroom. Hsiao appeared to recognize the signs too, as she said, "Is that enough for now?"

He nodded and closed his fingers, causing the *Peregrine* to swoop again. An alarmed yell came from the passageway. Someone had decided to ignore the pilot's order to strap in.

"Whoa," said Hsiao. "Switching to auto."

Darius unfastened his harness and jumped out of his seat before running to Nahla. "Did you see me flying the ship?"

"Yeah, that was really cool!"

"Did you see me Carina, Parthenia?"

"We did," Carina replied. "Do you want to be a pilot when you grow up?"

"Maybe. Nahla, do you want to..." The boy's voice faltered and his face fell.

"What's wrong?" Carina asked.

"I was going to ask Nahla if she wanted to look around the *Peregrine* with me, only..."

He didn't need to say any more. Everyone knew what had happened the last time he'd gone exploring with his sister.

"It's okay, sweetheart," said Carina. "As long as you stay out of restricted areas, there's nothing here that can hurt you."

His features brightened. "What about it, Nahla? Do you want to come with me?"

"Uh huh." Nahla tried to undo her belt but she couldn't manage it.

Darius leaned in and did it for her. She hopped down from her seat, and Darius took her hand. Together, they walked out.

Parthenia saw Carina's sad gaze following their youngest sister. Nahla now walked unsteadily with a pronounced limp. It was heartbreaking to watch. She knew exactly how Carina felt. "Maybe we'll find someone to help her at Lakshmi."

"I hope so." Carina looked drained and tired. She'd spent the entire night in the sick bay after they'd found the children, and she probably hadn't slept much since. "Maybe Bongo can help us."

"Bongo?"

"He was our guide the first time we went to the station. Nice guy. You'll like him."

———

Arriving at Lakshmi, Parthenia was initially under-impressed. The place seemed bare and boring. Yet the mercs who had accompanied them for their *R and R*, as they called it, weren't fazed by its appearance. As they completed the entry procedures they bantered with each other excitedly. The Black Dogs reminded her of big kids sometimes. Big, muscled, lethal children.

She had to have an ID code etched on her wrist, which was mildly painful, and then she passed through a scanner. When she stepped into the main area, her illusion about the station fell away. Sound and light crashed in on her. Lakshmi Station was humming with life and activity.

"It's quite something, isn't it?" asked Hsiao, raising her voice. "Have you ever been anywhere like it?"

"No, never." The closest comparison Parthenia could make was the spaceport at Ithiya. That had been thronged with hundreds of people too. It had been there Darius had spotted Carina and run up to her, thus revealing her existence to Father.

What would have happened to them if Darius hadn't seen their sister? Carina had rescued them from the Sherrerrs, escaping their flagship, the *Nightfall*. Would they ever have broken away without her help? Mother was already very sick by then, and Father had refused to have her transferred to a planet for treatment. After Mother died, they would have been stuck aboard the ship indefinitely.

With a heavy heart, she was forced to admit that without Carina, she and her siblings would still be enslaved to her father's clan, Casting to help Sherrerr businesses and military offensives, imprisoned forever in their gilded cages.

"Here he comes," said Carina.

"Are you sure that's him?" asked Hsiao.

"Yep, I'm sure."

"How can you tell?"

Carina shrugged.

Parthenia peered into the crowd of people and aliens, trying to see who they were talking about. From among the sea of bodies, an alien ran straight at them on many legs, its claws tapping the floor tiles. She took a backward step. Was it going to attack them? Where was the guide Carina had mentioned? Could he make the creature go away?

"Hey," said Carina as the creature reached them. "Thanks for meeting us."

"Hello again," it replied. "I got your comm. I have a few medical centers lined up. Wanna make a start?"

"Yeah. I brought Nahla's information from our ship's doctor."

She and Hsiao began to follow the alien, Carina holding Nahla's hand while Hsiao held Darius's.

This was Bongo?

Carina looked over her shoulder. "Are you coming, Parthenia?"

Sixteen

"Hey, Bryce," Jackson said, approaching him in the refectory. "Fancy a spacewalk?"

He put down his fork. "Now?"

"After you finish eating. Me and Justus were thinking we need to get visuals on the damage the Regians did when they boarded the ship. The diagnostics can only tell us so much. If we're going to upgrade her, we need to know what we're facing."

"Sure, but you should know I've never spacewalked before."

"That's what I thought. It won't hurt for you to get some practice. You can never tell when stepping into the black might come in handy. If it's an emergency, you don't want to be doing it for the first time."

"Okay. Sounds good."

"Meet you at Airlock D, this deck."

As Jackson left, Bryce shoveled the remains of his rice and beans into his mouth. His first spacewalk would be a good distraction from the current situation. He'd come to the refectory to get a break from Ferne and Oriana, who were taking the loss of their powers badly. They'd given up their usual activities and spent all their time lying around listlessly, occasionally attempting a Cast. When it didn't work Oriana would burst into tears and Ferne would stomp into their bedroom dramatically and throw himself on the bed.

Bryce was sympathetic, though he knew he couldn't properly empathize with the teenagers. But being around them brought him down too, and he was already upset about Nahla. He'd needed a breather.

Jackson and Justus were suiting up when he arrived at the airlock. The two men seemed in a good mood, laughing about something. Bryce edged past them to lift a suit out from the store. As he did so, he caught a whiff of alcohol.

He halted. "You two been drinking?"

Jackson replied, "I had a beer with lunch. Is that a problem?"

"I thought we aren't supposed to drink before going outside."

"Man, you sound like your girlfriend. Carina's no Cadwallader, but damn that woman's a hard ass. No offense."

"He's got a point," said Justus. "It *is* a little soon to go out after having a drink. Maybe we should wait a couple hours."

"Says the guy who could barely walk when we got back from Lakshmi."

"That was different. I wasn't planning on stepping into the black then."

"I had one beer!" Jackson exclaimed. "I've lost count of how many space-walks I've done. If I can't be trusted at the end of a tether after a single beer I might as well shoot myself."

Justus seemed to debate with himself for a moment before saying to Bryce, "Don't worry. It'll be okay. We're only taking a look around out there. If we were doing some work it would be different. But if you're not comfortable, you can join us another time."

The two older men continued to fasten up their suits.

They'd worked on starships most of their adult lives, whereas Bryce had only ended up on the *Bathsheba* by accident. He couldn't remember what his ambitions had been while growing up on Ithiya, but he knew they hadn't involved space travel. It was only after meeting Carina the idea of leaving his home planet had crossed his mind. But now this was to be his way of life for the next few years, he supposed he should learn all the ropes. "No, it's fine. I'll do it."

———

Starship a-grav didn't extend to the hull. You couldn't successfully walk on a ship's exterior if you were constantly pulled toward her 'base'. To compensate for the lack of gravity, EVA suit boots could be made magnetic so the wearers' feet clung to metal surfaces, and tethers attached the suit's wearer to the hull. Additionally, if spacewalkers became separated from their vessels, nozzles at their elbows and back could expel pressurized gas to control movement. A final safety measure was a constant positioning signal. Providing you didn't somehow end up very far from the ship, you could usually be picked up in time to save your life even if your suit sprang a leak.

In short, it was very hard to die on a spacewalk.

As he looked out into the cold, dark, airless expanse beyond the airlock's outer hatch, Bryce found these facts comforting. Yet it didn't change his impression of how vast, empty and *dead* it was out there. He'd become used to living aboard the *Bathsheba*, forgetting that only a few meters of hull separated him from—

"Comm check," came Jackson's voice inside his helmet.

"Check," said Justus.

"Check," said Bryce.

"You need to check your suit's levels too, Bryce," said Jackson. "Everything in normal range?"

He studied his HUD, mildly annoyed. He'd trained as a space soldier. He wasn't a complete greenhorn at wearing an EVA suit. "Yep."

"Okay, let's start aft and work our way forward. As well as the D airlocks we can reach airlocks C and E on Decks Three, Four, and Five. I'll take Five. Justus, you take Three, Bryce, you cover this deck."

"What am I looking for?"

"I expect we'll see acid damage from the Regian attack, but look for any kind of wear and tear too. Your helmet will pick up heat leaks. The computer is telling us the lasers are fully functional but this ship's damned old. Who knows when they were last checked?"

"Got it."

Jackson pulled the tether out from his waist, reached beyond the airlock and clipped it onto the hull. Then he grabbed the edge of the hatch, hauled himself through it, twisted sideways, and moved out of sight as the a-grav lost its grip on him. There were two clunks as his boots stuck to the metal.

"You're next," said Justus.

Bryce copied Jackson's movements and soon found himself looking at the outside of the *Bathsheba* for the first time. A metal plain stretched far and wide beneath his feet and 'above' it hung a void peppered with points of white diamond. The hull was also peppered, but with dents and scorch marks. Long scratches had been gouged from it too. The results of encounters with space debris over the centuries, he guessed. An aura hung around the edges of the ship, brightening the black—light from Lakshmi Station's star on the ship's far side.

"Give it a minute before you move around," said Justus as he emerged. "Helps to steady yourself and get your bearings."

He must have given the command to close the hatch, for it slid shut. Darkness closed over them like a blanket, alleviated only by the diffused light from the nearest star. Bryce's helmet switched to night vision and his view took on a steely tint.

Jackson was already several meters away, walking the high-stepping, long-striding gait imposed by magnetized boots. Justus also set off.

Bryce waited the advised minute, surveying the small laser weapons several meters distant from him, pointed toward the airlock. Their purpose was to defend against boarders. In the Regians' case that had been a bust.

He scanned for heat loss, but none showed. It was time to take a closer look.

He lifted a foot to break the magnetized contact. Weightlessness seized him and he wobbled. His sense of balance was all over the place until his foot met metal again.

Four lasers surrounded the airlock, mounted and angled to point at an edge of the square portal. The first laser Bryce checked didn't appear to have anything wrong with it though, despite Jackson's advice, he wasn't sure what he was supposed to be looking for. He connected with the ship's computer and searched for the device's schematics. When the image representing the laser's exterior came up it matched what he was seeing.

He moved toward the second laser.

"*Arghhh*!" Jackson cried out. "*Help! Help!*"

Then Justus's voice sounded in Bryce's helmet. "What's wrong? What's happened?"

Jackson yelled, "I accidentally activated one of the las—arghhh!"

He sprawled on his side, attached by one boot to the hull.

Bryce began to sprint in the direction of his injured shipmate...except he couldn't sprint. Each movement of his legs required breaking the magnetic hold, slowing him down to little more than a fast walk.

Should he use his pressurized gas pack to get him to Jackson's side faster? Justus was heading for their shipmate at a similarly restricted pace. He couldn't see exactly what was wrong with Jackson, but he must have been hit by a laser, which meant a suit leak. If they didn't get him inside quickly he would suffocate.

Bryce de-magnetized his boots and his feet lifted a fraction off the hull. The smallest push would send him floating away from the ship. He checked his tether and then fired a small spurt from the nozzles at his elbows and on his back. The effect was far greater than he'd anticipated. Within less than a second, he was tens of meters from the hull. The *Bathsheba* continued to recede from him at an alarming rate, the downed Jackson and run-walking Justus reduced to dolls on the expanse of pock-marked metal.

He adjusted the direction of the nozzles and angled his body forward before firing a second spurt of gas, even smaller than the first. He moved headlong this time, traversing a line parallel to the colony ship. That was better. His tether looped out below him, a reassuring link to safety.

Justus had almost reached Jackson.

Bryce cursed. He should have walked, not attempted this ridiculous effort.

Turning his head toward his companions, he fired a third burst of gas. By slow maneuvering and several corrections, he managed to bring himself back to the hull nearby Jackson. To Bryce's confusion, the man was standing by the time he reached him and acting normally. He didn't seem to be hurt.

Bryce realized he hadn't heard anything from either of his shipmates for a minute or so.

Then laughter exploded into his helmet. Jackson and Justus had cut their comms to him. They'd been laughing all the while he'd been making his way over.

When Bryce's boots finally snapped to magnetic contact with the hull, Jackson slapped him on the back. "It's good to know I can rely on you in a crisis."

"I haven't seen anything so funny in a long while," said Justus, gasping for air. "Thanks for that."

"Come on, fellas," Bryce remonstrated. But he knew there was no use in saying any more. The mercs loved to have fun at others' expense, even if it cut close to the knuckle sometimes. "Did you set me up right from the beginning or was this a last-minute joke?"

"Right from the start," Jackson replied. "Even gargled a mouthful of beer just so I could breathe it out on you." He leaned closer. "Word of advice. Don't *ever* go spacewalking with someone who's been drinking. Not even *just one beer*."

"Okay," Bryce said ruefully, "I get it." It was a hard lesson but well-taught. "Did you make up the part about checking the lasers too?"

"No, we do need to do that. Take a look at Deck Four C lock. I'll carry on checking this one."

Justus continued to chuckle as he high-stepped toward another set of lasers.

Bryce began the slow walk to Deck Four C.

He hadn't gone far, however, before Jackson exclaimed, "Holy shit!"

Half-expecting another prank, Bryce turned to see what he'd found.

Jackson was bent over a laser, pulling at something.

There was a blinding flash, momentarily wiping out Bryce's night vision. When he could see again, Jackson was collapsing and an object was floating away from him, spinning lazily in its own orbit.

It took Bryce a second to realize the object was an arm.

SEVENTEEN

Nahla looked glum, and Parthenia knew exactly how she felt. This was the fifth medical center they'd visited, accompanied by the strange alien-spider creature Bongo, and at each one her little sister had been questioned, prodded, poked, scanned, and tested. She didn't seem to understand what was going on, but she had to be exhausted. Parthenia only had to watch and wait as the medics did their work, and *she* was exhausted.

Nahla's prospects didn't look good. After an hour or longer of investigation, the conclusions of the doctors at the previous four establishments had been the same: there wasn't much they could do. While medical science had cracked the problems of regenerating every other human tissue and organ, triggering the brain into repairing itself remained elusive.

"You can expect to see *some* improvement," said the head of the latest center, "if you follow our treatment program. Nahla is young and her brain is still developing. Some of the functions that were lost in the hypoxia incident will be taken over by the remaining healthy areas. But will she ever return to her former state? I would say, according to what I've seen, it's unlikely."

"It would be hard for us to stay here for a long course of treatment," said Carina. "I was hoping something could be done for Nahla over the short term."

"Out of the question, I'm afraid. Your sister requires months of therapy to make any progress. I think perhaps you're underestimating just how much brain damage she sustained."

"But Darius was deprived of oxygen over the same period and he seems fine."

"With respect, you don't know that. I could run some tests..."

"No. No more testing." Addressing her siblings, Carina said, "Come on, let's go."

"Uh," the doctor murmured, "there's the small question of payment for—"

"Don't worry, I haven't forgotten. I'll pay on the way out."

"I'm sorry we can't help you."

Carina didn't reply as they left the office. At the receptionist's desk, she held her ID code to the scanner for the center to extract their fee. The figures on the screen were a drop in the ocean of the amount they had available, but creds weren't worth much when they couldn't help Nahla.

"If we could just Cast Heal," Carina muttered.

"What now?" Parthenia asked.

"Find Hsiao and Bongo. I want to talk to some weapons suppliers and get a feel for what we should buy for the *Bathsheba*."

"So we're still going to Earth?"

Carina sighed. "Honestly, I don't know. I don't know what the hell we should be doing anymore. But it won't hurt to explore our options."

Hsiao had balked at attending Nahla's fourth round of testing and had gone to find her merc buddies. Bongo had left them when they'd arrived at the fifth center, though he'd said he would be back soon. Carina had purchased the local comm and translation devices on her previous trip, and Parthenia waited, holding Nahla and Darius's hands on the busy thoroughfare, while her sister contacted the missing members of their party.

Bongo was the first to appear, dodging between the many pedestrians with ease. He was clearly accustomed to it, even avoiding the people who jumped in random directions, startled by his approach.

"Any luck?" he asked.

"Nope," Carina replied.

"Sorry to hear that. Do you want to try another place? There are a few—"

"There's no point. They're all going to say the same thing."

"You're probably right. The medical centers compete for custom so they're all pretty up to date on the latest treatments, though I would say they're best at combat injuries. Where to next?"

"Military equipment suppliers, I guess. Starship defense armaments."

"Um," Parthenia demurred.

"What?"

"The children are hungry and tired, and so am I. How about we find somewhere to rest and eat?"

"Yeah, you're right." Carina rubbed her forehead. "I was forgetting."

"If food and relaxation are next on the program," said Bongo. "I know just the place."

———

"Is Hsiao meeting us here?" Parthenia asked when they arrived at the restaurant, Etheric Edibles.

"I can't raise her," Carina replied. "She isn't answering her comm."

"What about the other mercs? She must be with them."

"Yeah, you're right. I'll try Van Hasty."

Bongo was speaking to the maître d'–another, different, alien. This creature was humanoid but extremely tall and thin and completely hairless. After a short conversation where Bongo explained all the humans were from out-sector, she—Parthenia had the impression the maître d' was female—beckoned them with a long-fingered hand and led them between the occupied tables to the rear of the restaurant. Her movements seemed full of effort, as if she was struggling with the local gravity.

"I can give you an hour and a half," she said. "I have a booking for this table."

"Thanks," Carina replied. "We won't be here that long."

"Did you manage to speak to Van Hasty?" asked Parthenia.

"No." Carina ushered Darius and Nahla onto the bench between her and Parthenia.

Bongo dragged over a low seat with a hole in the base and squatted on it, announcing, "I recommend the fungus and larvae. I've eaten it here before and it's delicious."

"The..." Parthenia swallowed. Table manners, especially when dining with guests, had been ingrained into her from a very young age. She smiled politely. "Is that a local specialty?"

"It's a Marchonish dish. Very tasty."

"Are you from Marchon?"

"Stars, no!" A bubbling sound came from the alien's orifices as he appeared to laugh. "My species' home system is a long way from here, and our culture is peaceful. We would never end up in a conflict like the Three System War."

"Fungus and larvae, hm?" Carina asked, scanning the menu.

You aren't serious? Parthenia mentally questioned her sister, but she didn't want to offend Bongo by speaking aloud.

She was about to ask their guide about the war when Carina continued, "The larvae *are* dead, right?"

"Well, they're frozen," Bongo replied. "So, technically—"

"Yeah," said Carina, "you're not exactly selling it. I think I'll pass." Her head down, she carried on reading.

Parthenia was also reading, trying to find something Darius and Nahla wouldn't reject out of hand. One of the noodle dishes seemed a fair bet. She made the suggestion.

"I want to choose for myself!" Darius exclaimed.

"I want what Darius wants," said Nahla.

"Fine," said Parthenia. "Let Carina know what you decide."

She wasn't particularly hungry. As she waited for the others to pick their dishes, she decided to try an experiment. She'd brought her elixir along. Carina hadn't wanted her to, but the small bottle of liquid hadn't triggered any alarms. She wanted to try a Cast. It could be something aboard the *Bathsheba* that was preventing them from working, or something in the ship's vicinity.

After checking no one was watching, she took the bottle from its bag at her waist and unscrewed the lid. Carina looked up at precisely the wrong time— from Parthenia's viewpoint—and saw what she was doing. Her sister gave her a severe frown and shook her head sharply.

"Is something the matter?" Bongo asked her, his many-eyed head swiveling from one sibling to the other.

"No, nothing at all," Parthenia replied, taking a sip of elixir while meeting Carina's hard stare. She closed her eyes. A small Cast would do for a test. Something simple. She wrote the Send character in her mind, followed by a message *You don't own me, Sis* and then released it.

From the lack of reaction on Carina's face it was clear the Cast had failed. Her heart settled like lead in her chest. Even at Lakshmi Station, she no longer had her special ability.

I'm no longer a mage.

The words in her head sounded unreal. It seemed impossible they were true.

Perhaps reading her expression, Carina's look became sorrowful and sympathetic.

Darius and Nahla called out their meal choice, which was something that sounded deep-fried and very unhealthy. Parthenia said she wouldn't be eating anything.

The food took only a few minutes to arrive. The center of the table retracted into a slot and the steaming dishes rose on the flat top of a column into the gap. Bongo reached over the tabletop with two limbs and picked up a bowl of something looking suspiciously like chopped up fungus peppered with frozen maggots. The maggots were rapidly thawing and beginning to wriggle. He placed the dish in front of him, scooped out a handful, or, rather, a clawful, of food and put it underneath his chair. When the claw reappeared it was empty.

That explained the hole in his seat.

Parthenia was deeply pleased she'd decided not to eat.

Thankfully, Darius and Nahla were too occupied by their own food to notice and make a rude comment. Carina, if she'd registered what the alien was doing, didn't react.

After waiting a few minutes, Parthenia asked, "Bongo, can you explain about the Three Systems War? How long has it been going on and what's it about?"

"Ah, do you want the official story or the truth?"

"What do *you* think?" Carina asked in return.

"I'll give you both, seeing as one kind of explains the other. But don't ever repeat what I tell you to a Marchonish, Quintonese, or Gugongian. You'll get yourself banned from the station, or worse."

Eighteen

Jackson had lost an arm but gained a Regian one. He was staring at the alien limb stupidly while his severed prosthetic dripped fluid.

"You need to get out of your suit," said Justus as the airlock's outer hatch closed and atmosphere hissed in.

Jackson raised his head. "What? Oh, yeah."

Bryce had expected the man to be in a worse condition, but his suit had only lost pressure to the top of the remainder of his arm. A seal had activated, preventing air from escaping and providing a tourniquet to slow blood loss.

"You know what this means?" asked Jackson.

The airlock's inner hatch opened.

Justus removed his helmet. "You fancied trying a different kind of arm?" He began to unfasten Jackson's suit for him.

The merc was clearly in shock, which wasn't surprising. Amputation via laser beam would shock the most hardened veteran, even when the limb in question wasn't made of flesh and blood.

Justus removed Jackson's helmet, and his voice switched from comm to natural as he said, "It explains how the Regians got around the laser defenses." As if suddenly hit by revulsion, he dropped the insectoid appendage. Black and shiny, it lay on the deck. The limb must have been stuck in the laser emitter ever since the Regian attack. It had traveled with the *Bathsheba* all the way to Magog and Gog and the millions of miles the ship had voyaged afterward.

"They swarmed them," Bryce said. "The Regians threw themselves at the lasers to give their buddies time to crack the airlocks."

"Yeah," agreed Jackson. "Their usual offensive tactic: overwhelm your opponent by sheer force of numbers, whether the enemy is another species or a weapon."

"Sick bastards," muttered Justus. "Step out," he ordered. He'd removed Jackson's suit down to his knees.

"Hey," the merc protested, apparently only just noticing what Justus had been doing, "I can do it." He pushed the legs of his suit down with his remaining arm and lifted his feet out of the boots. "I'm not a freaking kid."

"Does your arm hurt?" asked Bryce, wondering if the prosthetic had a biofeedback linked to Jackson's brain.

"Nah, it stung a little when the beam cut it, but the pain sensors shut down after that."

"Well, one thing's for sure," Justus commented, beginning to remove his own suit, "we've gotta replace all the lasers. They shouldn't misfire like that, even if someone's tugging at them like you did. But we would have to get rid of them anyway. I've never seen such antiques. They must be centuries old."

"Assuming we're still going to Earth," said Jackson, "and we need defenses."

"Why wouldn't we?" asked Justus.

Bryce explained, "Carina's reconsidering the options since she and her brothers and sisters lost their powers. She's not sure there's any point in continuing our journey anymore."

"That's news to me," said Justus. "Don't we get a say? If we don't go to Earth, I'm not sure where I'd go. Lotacrylla's closed to me now. I can't go back there after what happened to my old shipmates. I'd be executed for desertion."

"But you didn't desert," said Bryce.

"Doesn't matter. In my culture, it's all for one, not every man for himself. I'm expected to defend my company or die trying."

"No need to fret," said Jackson. "You're a de facto Black Dog now. Wherever we go, you come too."

"Says who?"

"Says me." Jackson patted his shoulder.

"Thanks. That means a lot. So, I guess you'll have to get that arm replaced now?"

"Yep. Another item on Lin's shopping list."

While the two men talked, Bryce had been taking off his suit and helmet and stowing them.

The remains of Jackson's prosthetic continued to drip on the deck. "Another antique to be replaced." His brow wrinkled and he lifted the short stump to peer at the end. "Feels weird. Never thought I'd lose it like this."

"How long did you have it?" asked Bryce.

"I don't know. Long time. So long it felt—"

Bryce's ship's comm bleeped an 'urgent' signal. He slapped it. "What?"

"You have to come to the bridge!" Oriana cried. "Right now! The ships are firing."

The three men sprinted down the passageway.

What a time for an attack! Hsiao, their only experienced pilot, was on Lakshmi with Carina. Would Bibik be able to perform evasive maneuvers? Could the mammoth *Bathsheba* even move evasively? Bryce assumed the other Black Dogs had been alerted and someone had taken charge of the ship's weapons, such as they were.

"Why the hell are they firing at us?" Jackson asked breathlessly. "We don't have anything to do with their stupid war."

"You'd think they would give us a warning at least," gasped Justus.

They reached the bridge and the doors slid aside, revealing Oriana, Ferne, Bibik, and a couple of mercs watching a holo playing in the center of the room.

"What's happening?" asked Jackson. "Have we taken any hits? Did you put up the force shield, Bibik?"

"Why would I do that?" the young merc replied mildly, raising his eyebrows at the newcomers' out-of-breath state.

Jackson said, "To defend the..." He paused and studied the holo closely. "Wait. They're not firing at *us*."

"Oriana," said Bibik, "I told you they would get the wrong idea from what you said. Sorry, guys. I think she got over-excited."

The scene playing out on the 3D image was of two fleets in battle—against each other. Pulse bolts streamed across space as the ships appeared to crawl slowly to new positions, though in reality they were moving fast.

"Sorry," said Oriana sheepishly. "I thought you would want to see it, Bryce."

"I do, but maybe explain what you mean a bit more clearly next time?"

"It's so cool!" Ferne exclaimed. "I think the one on the left is winning."

"Not so cool when you're in the middle of it," said Jackson. "Don't you know that? You must have been in some space battles in your time, youngster."

"Yeah, but this is different. It's like a vidgame."

"It's not a game when your life's at risk. You'd do well to remember that." Jackson's expression became serious and contemplative.

How many battles had he taken part in? It had to be a lot, considering the grizzled man's age, and the fact that he wasn't even sure how long he'd had his prosthetic arm.

Carina had told Bryce once that Jackson had taken part in the first attempt to rescue Darius from the Dirksens. How many of that team of Black Dogs were still alive? Not the captain, Speidel, certainly. Carina had spoken sadly of how he'd died in the second, successful attempt. Others had died since—Atoi, who had lost her life to the Regians, and Halliday, who had perished in a glider crash on Magog.

He guessed Jackson and Carina might be the only remaining survivors from the original rescue team. Mercenary life was generally brutal and short. If the old merc made it to their journey's end, where he could live out the rest of his life in peace and safety, that would be something.

Nineteen

"So," said Bongo, adjusting his position in his seat as if getting comfortable, "the official reason for the conflict between the governments of Marchon, Quinton, and Gugong is a territory dispute. There's a rogue planet roughly equidistant between the three systems, and each sovereignty claims it as its own."

"What makes the planet so valuable?" asked Parthenia.

"Nothing, as far as I'm aware, and I've done a fair bit of research into it. It's a small place, barely bigger than a moon."

"Nothing at all?!" exclaimed Carina.

"*Shhh!*" Bongo gestured downward with a claw. "This is a sensitive subject around here. You never know who you might offend. We..." he made a burbling sound "—that's the name of my people—we have to be careful to remain neutral about the war. Feelings run high, even after eighty Standard Years of fighting, maybe because of eighty years of fighting."

"They've been at war for eighty years?" Carina exclaimed again, equally loudly.

Bongo's head swiveled as each of his eyes glared at her in turn.

"Sorry," she said, continuing more quietly. "They've been at war for *eighty years*?"

"Eighty-three, to be exact."

"Over a worthless rogue planet?"

"He's already told us that," Parthenia reminded her.

"I'm just checking. It is a real war, right?" she asked Bongo, "with people dying and everything?"

"The estimated death toll passed into the hundreds of millions decades ago."

Parthenia asked, "How long have *you* been here?"

"This will be my fourteenth Standard Year at Lakshmi. I'll probably make it a round fifteen before heading home. I'll have saved enough by then to retire, providing I'm frugal. That's not to say I haven't enjoyed my work here, but you can only listen to the same biased, dogmatic opinions from each side for so long, you know? I can't tell you what a relief it was to hear you guys were from out-sector."

"I suppose it must be hard to stay out of the argument when you're right in the middle of it," Parthenia commented.

"You don't know the half of it. To keep the war going, the governments on the three planets feed their populations all kinds of propaganda, and the people believe it because, well, why wouldn't they? They never get to meet each other except here at Lakshmi, and then they segregate themselves. Most service jobs are carried out by non-humans. Prior to the recruitment drive for workers from other areas of the sector, the fighting on the station used to be a lot worse."

"What do their governments tell them?" Parthenia asked.

"Oh, all sorts of nonsense. That the other side beats their children, practices slavery, creates human/animal mutants, is planning to take over the sector, and so on. I forget who says what about the different sides. It's all bullshit, but there's no point in reasoning with them. They've been told this stuff all their lives. It's best to not get involved. They're in too deep."

"But they must interact with each other at least a little," Carina said. "We were accused of coming from the 'wrong planet' in a bar the other day, so it happens. It's kinda hard to believe they see and speak to the people from other planets and yet never question what they've been told."

"Some probably do question it," said Bongo, "but they don't dare to say anything. It must be hard to speak out when the war's gone on so long and everyone you know believes the propaganda."

"I think I understand," Parthenia commented. "They've been fighting for generations and the war has become a part of their identity. They're all invested in it. And every family must have people who died in the fight. Propaganda aside, that gives them a reason for hating their opponents and continuing the war. They want revenge."

"What an identity to have," said Carina. "I'm glad ours isn't like...wasn't..." She stopped speaking, firmly closing her lips.

Parthenia guessed exactly what her sister meant and what she'd nearly said.

The same thought had sprung to her own mind. From what she'd come to learn about mage culture, they were essentially pacifistic, like Bongo's species. It was a far better identity to have than to belong to a warlike society, but were they even mages any longer? Speaking softly to Bongo, she said, "You mentioned something about the real reason for the war."

"Ah yes," he replied before making his strange burbling sound again. "Now I'm wishing I hadn't." He tapped the two claws on the tabletop before continuing, "You must promise me you'll never mention this to another soul at the station, or to anyone among your crew who can't be trusted to not pass it on. You must *especially* promise me that, if you do mention it by accident, you never tell anyone it came from me."

"We promise," said Carina.

"Yes," Parthenia said, "we'll never speak of it." She checked Nahla and Darius, who definitely couldn't be expected to keep any such promise, but they were playing a game with the condiment bottles, oblivious to the conversation.

"Perhaps I don't actually need to tell you," said Bongo. "You seem like intelligent people. I'll give you some facts, and you can draw your own conclusions. I told you the war began eighty-three years ago, didn't I? Do you know how old Lakshmi Station is?"

"Eighty years?" Carina guessed.

"Wrong," said Bongo.

She tried again. "Seventy-five? Construction must have begun after the war started. Someone saw an opportunity to make money selling weapons to the three sides, and so they built the station."

"Wrong again," Bongo said.

"Oh!" Parthenia moved her hand to her mouth as the realization hit.

"Seventy?" asked Carina.

"No," Parthenia said. "Lakshmi isn't younger than the war, is it, Bongo? It's older, right?"

Her sister frowned. "But why...?" The frown disappeared and was replaced by open-mouthed horror. "Stars! You don't think—"

"The owners of Lakshmi Station are fabulously wealthy," Bongo interrupted, "and so are the arms dealers, medical professionals, and everyone else who services the war machine, including the governmental leaders."

Tears pricked Parthenia's eyes. "You said hundreds of millions have died?"

"The figures are probably into the billions by now, and that isn't counting all the injured, permanently disabled, orphaned, and bereaved."

Could it really be true? Could the war between the three planets only have come about in order to make a small group of people rich? She guessed some high-ranking individuals from Marchon, Quinton, and Gugong must have worked together to hatch the plan. They must have begun to build Lakshmi in preparation. Then when the time was ripe, they'd whipped up the planets' inhabitants into a frenzy of xenophobic hatred and staged an incident to trigger the war. She'd known some terrible people in her time—such as her own Father—but she'd thought his personality was rare. She'd been wrong. Lakshmi Station had to be making money for lots of people.

Carina echoed her thoughts. "Do you think everyone who profits from Lakshmi Station is aware of what's going on?"

"I can't say," Bongo replied. "I've never talked about it to anyone outside my own kind, and if you weren't from out-sector I wouldn't be talking about it with you, either. If the conspiracy was revealed and the populations turned against their governments, a lot of powerful people would lose everything. They would never risk it by allowing a blabbermouth to live." He bent his head forward conspiratorially. "That's the real reason I want to leave. *I* profit from Lakshmi Station along with everyone who works here. It makes me uncomfortable."

Parthenia murmured, "And by buying weapons here, we're complicit too."

"Don't be dumb," said Carina. "We didn't know about the reason for the war before we arrived, and we still don't for sure. Bongo could be wrong." She addressed him. "You don't know this for sure, right? You're only guessing."

Before he could answer Parthenia retorted, "It's a damned good guess. Think about it. What other reason could there be to go to war over a useless lump of rock floating in interstellar space?"

"Then the people are stupid for not figuring it out and doing something about it."

"Stupid, or brainwashed?"

"Same thing."

"How can you be so callous?" Parthenia asked her sister, nearly rising from her seat in anger.

Darius and Nahla, who had been happily chattering as they played their game, fell silent and looked from one sister to the other.

"I'm not callous," Carina said, "I'm just not interested in other people's wars. I have a family to take care of, and if it means striking deals with self-serving warmongers, that's what I'll do."

They were back to the old argument they'd had on Ostillon. Carina didn't feel responsibility toward her fellow human beings. Parthenia's anger eased. It was only to be expected. Carina had been alienated from non-mages for most of her life. She saw ordinary folk as different, with the possible exception of Bryce and Nahla. She didn't really care about other people and probably never would.

"Well, I think we should complete our business transactions and leave at the earliest opportunity," said Parthenia. "Now we're here, we don't have much choice about buying what we need, but I don't want to be a part of what's going on any longer than we have to."

"You won't hear any argument from me about that," said Carina, "but I wish we could do something for Nahla."

"Oh dear," said Bongo. "This is bad. This is very bad."

"Um, what?" Carina asked.

"Your companions are in deep shit."

Twenty

An hour earlier, Hsiao had found Rees, Van Hasty, and the other mercs enjoying their R and R in the Nebulaooze on the upper level of Deck Thirty-Two. Why they'd chosen this place was beyond her. Compared to the rest of Lakshmi, it was a real dive.

Most of the bartenders were Bongo's species, and they certainly needed their plentiful legs to serve the customers who crowded at every bar. The men and women looked like the lowest class of Lakshmi visitors—starship maintenance crews or space fleet grunts. Their clothes were the cheapest prints and were falling apart even so, their hair was shaggy and unkempt and some bore visible scars. Skin repair was cheap and widely available, so they were either too poor to afford it or were substance addicts, preferring to spend their limited funds on their kicks.

The décor matched the clientele. The furnishings were shabby and dirty, and the only decoration on the walls were stains and scuff marks. Underlying the smell of alcohol and the smoke of narcotic herbs were the odors of sweat and bad breath.

"What are you doing here, guys?" she asked when she reached the mercs' table, raising her voice over the hubbub.

"What's wrong?" Rees asked. "Don't like the atmosphere? Seems pretty cool to me."

His pupils were dilated, and Hsiao didn't think it was only due to the low lighting.

"It's a dump. Come on, let's go somewhere else."

"Relax," said Van Hasty. "Sit down and have a drink. I'll get you one. What do you want?"

"They don't have table service?"

It was another indication of the bar's poor quality. There were three standards of service in bars and restaurants: staffed by trained, professional servers (the highest standard), entirely automated, and staffed by low-skilled, badly paid migrant labor. This place clearly fell into the last category.

"It's not a problem," said Van Hasty. "I like seeing those spider-things pouring drinks. You know they can serve three people at once? It's like watching a show at the fair."

"I don't think we should stay here," said Hsiao. "There must be a million better bars than this. Why'd you pick it?"

Rees shrugged. "We just wandered in. If you don't like it, we can leave."

"Great. Let's go."

"Just have one drink while we finish ours."

Hsiao relented. One drink wouldn't hurt. "Okay. I'll have whatever you guys are having," she told Van Hasty.

The merc left the table and shouldered her way through the crowd. The patrons were tightly packed, but she was a tall, powerful woman and had no trouble in forcing a passage through the throng.

Hsiao pulled out a stool from under the table and sat down.

Rees turned to the merc sitting next to him and said something Hsiao didn't catch. He was smirking and his head wobbled as if he was under the influence of something.

Dammit.

The Black Dogs hadn't had a chance to unwind in months, and they'd come close to dying horrible deaths at the hands of the Regians. She knew from her years working with them what was coming next. They were going to really let loose and have a blast. Most likely they wouldn't be able to make their own way back to the *Peregrine*. They would have to be carried.

Though she wouldn't do the same herself, she didn't have a problem with it per se. The men and women risked death while they were on a job. It made sense that they lived their lives to the full while they still could.

But they were at Lakshmi Station.

Carina had lectured them on the severity of the laws here, but Hsiao had a feeling the mercs hadn't taken her as seriously as they should. Carina had a rep for being a hard ass, and the Black Dogs were used to bending the rules when out of sight of their commander. Cadwallader's iron-fisted leadership style had trained them to it. That, and the fact the average merc had the mentality of a teenager, spelled trouble in a situation like this.

Van Hasty returned with her drink. Steam or smoke curled from the bright violet liquid. Hsiao checked the glasses on the table. They were half full of the same cocktail.

Oh well, I got what I asked for.

She took a sip and winced as the sour, viscous fluid slipped down her throat.

Then it hit.

The room swam before her and took on a different hue.

She grabbed the edge of the table with her other hand. "What the hell is in this?"

"Who knows?" Van Hasty replied, lifting her own glass to her lips. "It's called Sudden Death."

"Sudden Death, huh?"

Hsiao carefully put her drink down.

A woman sidled up to Rees and placed an arm around his neck before bending low to whisper in his ear. Her large breasts performed a gravity-defying miracle as they remained inside her dress.

Hsiao took a double take. It wasn't a woman, it was a hostess, and not an expensive model. Even in the bar's dim lights her skin's sheen appeared artificial and her long, curly, chestnut hair looked fake. Rees reached up and cupped one weighty breast while his other hand disappeared behind her, or rather, it.

Van Hasty and Hsiao shared an *Ewww*! look.

In another moment, Rees was up on his feet and staggering off into the crowd, one arm around the hostess's waist.

"Seriously?" Hsiao asked Van Hasty.

"I know! I think he has a fetish."

A group of youngsters standing nearby had been edging closer to the table since Hsiao had arrived, pushed in by the sheer number of people jostling for space. The young people looked different from the rest of the patrons. They were well-dressed, their clothes intricately made, and the women wore jewelry that appeared authentic. They seemed oblivious to their encroachment on the mercs' space.

What were they doing here when they could obviously afford to patronize more upmarket bars? Perhaps, like Rees, they had a fetish for sleaze.

The crowd pressed closer, and a young man in the group stepped backward, bringing his behind right up to one of the mercs' heads.

Pamuk yelled, "Hey, I can smell ass!" Standing, she tapped the man on the shoulder. "I don't feel like sniffing your butt today. Find somewhere else to shove your backside, okay?"

In response, he grinned and grabbed her before grinding against her and saying, "If you don't like my backside, how about my front?"

Pamuk's elbow shot back and she landed a punch that had his eyes rolling up before he collapsed into his companions.

"Cut it out!" Hsiao hollered. "You'll get us all in trouble."

But she might as well have shouted into the void.

Another man in the group leapt at Pamuk, but Van Hasty was already on her feet and in his way with her fists up. The three remaining Black Dogs weren't far behind, and neither were their antagonists. Before Hsiao could say another word, a full-on brawl was taking place.

Rees reappeared from nowhere and dove into the combatants. The bar's patrons drew back, forming a circle of gawkers. The man who'd been punched unconscious lay at the fighters' feet, heedless of what he'd started.

Hsiao hesitated. Should she stay to help pick up the pieces when the mercs inevitably beat the rich kids to a pulp? Or should she leave and let them deal with their own problems? From what she understood of Lakshmi, there would be severe repercussions for the fight.

Loyalty made her stay.

TWENTY-ONE

Bongo's species was apparently telepathic. While Carina had been talking with Parthenia about the war, he'd received a tip off from a friend, warning him the mercs had been taken into custody and were in danger of being spaced.

Leaving Parthenia to look after Darius and Nahla, Carina raced with the alien to the security center where Hsiao, Van Hasty, Rees, and four others were being held.

"Why didn't I receive a comm about this?" she asked Bongo as they ran, dodging the ever-present crowds.

"You would have, eventually, but maybe not until it was too late. That's the way they do things around here. They inform the relatives and friends after the sentence has been carried out and pay compensation if the accused is found innocent on appeal. They call it retroactive justice."

"That's a hell of a system."

"It certainly keeps most everyone under control."

"Not the *Bathsheba's* crew, obviously. They don't know about the law around here."

"Well," said Bongo, "they just found out."

"I don't get it. Some meathead nearly started a fight with me the first time I visited. Why would he do that if the laws are so draconian?"

"It was probably all show. There's plenty of audacious talk goes on in those places, especially when people are buzzed, but hardly anything ever comes of it. Most visitors aren't that dim-witted."

The Fifth Point Justice Office where the Black Dogs were being held was kilometers away. Carina had to take the metro with Bongo for an hour and a half, changing trains twice, to reach it. Along the way, she'd asked him if there wasn't a faster way to travel.

There was.

A second network of tunnels for autocars connected all the areas of the station, but it was only available to a minority of Lakshmi residents, not visitors or migrant workers. By the time they arrived at the relevant district, she was a frazzled mess, out of her mind with worry she would be too late to save the mercs.

She still hadn't received a communication from the authorities that her companions were under arrest. To be on the safe side, she'd comm'd Parthenia, telling her to take the kids to the *Peregrine* and wait there. She couldn't risk them accidentally contravening the station's strict regulations. She wouldn't have time to fix a second problem.

This district was far quieter than the commercial zone. The metro car had been nearly empty as it pulled into the station at the end of the line, and the platform all but deserted. Overhead, the ceiling was so high it was lost in darkness, the lights on the walls too weak to penetrate it.

"It must cost a fortune to heat this place," she commented, partly to alleviate her anxiety as they entered the exit tunnel.

"It costs hardly anything at all," Bongo replied. "Lakshmi derives its power directly from its sun, with minute energy loss. The invention of the tech was one of the things that made the building of the station possible."

"Did the inventors share the knowledge with the local systems?"

"Guess."

"Of course not."

"It's one of the station's best-kept secrets."

When they left the metro, Carina had to hold out her wrist for her ID code to be scanned. Bongo seemed to have a free pass because his barrier opened automatically.

Outside, she stumbled and almost fell. A blue sky stretched wide above them, looking entirely authentic. It even had clouds. For a second, she'd felt as though she was suddenly walking on a planet surface. "Is that real?"

"It's an illusion, but a good one as I understand. Is that what the sky looks like on your home planet?"

She thought back. It had been a long time since she'd left the planet where she'd been born. "Yes, but it wasn't so blue."

"The Justice Office is this way,"

What color was the sky was on Bongo's world?

Only a few pedestrians walked the streets, which were lined with trees and shrubs, some in flower. The differences between here and the zone built for visitors continued to make its impression. Long-term Lakshmi residents had created a pleasant home.

She swallowed as she remembered it had been built with the blood of billions.

If only Bryce were here. She was afraid that when she met with the justice officers she might fly off the handle and ruin everything.

A tall, wide building of pale cream stone occupied center stage in the street. Pillars supported an overhang at the top of its steps, and beyond them stood a series of open double doors. Bongo led the way up the stairs, his many legs making short work of the climb. They walked through a set of doors into a huge lobby. Despite the size of the space, there was only one counter and one officer sitting behind it. A line six or seven people long had formed.

"Shit," Carina blurted as they joined the end of it. "This is fucking ridiculous."

"Calm down. Losing your temper will get you nowhere here. If we're lucky they'll only turf you out, but that'll be the end of your chance to help your friends."

She took his words to heart. While they waited, she closed her eyes and recalled the techniques Nai Nai had taught her to steady her mind and body. She took control of her breathing and mental focus as they moved closer to the front of the line. By the time they reached it, most of her tension had eased and she could address the person on the other side of the desk composedly. "Some of my companions were brought here, and I'd like to see what I can do to help them."

"Names?" the officer asked, not looking up from her interface.

Carina began to state them. Before she was halfway through, the officer interrupted, saying, "Yeah, they're here. They have some pretty serious charges. Causing a fracas, disturbing the peace, assaulting a justice officer. You're lucky you arrived in time to see them before their sentence is carried out. They're due to be spaced in fifteen minutes." She looked up. "You want to see them, right? Say a final goodbye and hear their last wishes?"

"No!" Carina yelled, her calm demeanor falling away in an instant.

The officer frowned and reached for a button on the counter.

"Sorry," said Bongo. "Please, there's no need to summon anyone. We aren't here to make any trouble. What my companion means is yes, we would like to see them very much. I understand there's a fee involved?"

"But can't we..." said Carina, the sound of her blood pulsing in her ears. "Isn't there anything...?"

Something hard and sharp touched her hand. She looked down. Bongo had put one of his claws on it. Was he trying to calm her, or console her?

"Yes, there is a fee," said the officer. "Let me see. It's per person, and there are seven in custody. Do you want to see all of them?"

"I, er, I don't..."

What a question. Of all the mercs who had gotten themselves into trouble, the only one she knew well was Hsiao. Did she want to see them only to say farewell before they faced an excruciating death?

"Yes," she replied, "all of them." Numbly, she held up her wrist to the scanner as the figure appeared on the screen.

"Through there," said the officer.

A door opened in the wall to the rear of her desk. Carina trudged toward it, every step leaden as she dreaded what lay beyond. Bongo scuttled beside her.

"Hey," called the officer, "she only paid for herself, not you too."

The alien hesitated.

"Ah, what the hell. Go ahead. I'm feeling generous."

TWENTY-TWO

The *Peregrine* felt silent and empty to Parthenia, despite the racket Darius and Nahla were making as they raced up and down the passageways. She'd never been the only adult aboard a starship before. It had been stressful enough finding the way to the right exit from Lakshmi and getting the children into their EVA suits and through the umbilicus by herself.

What if something went wrong?

Carina had seemed very anxious when she left the restaurant with Bongo. The mercs were in trouble and Hsiao was with them. What if Carina couldn't help them? Bongo had said they might be spaced. Lakshmi law was extremely strict, but she hadn't known it was *that* strict.

What if she had to take her siblings back to the *Bathsheba*? She didn't have a clue how to fly the ship. Darius probably knew more than her. If she had to resort to allowing him to take the controls, who knew what he might do?

The children had been playing for ages, and she'd been growing more and more irritated by their noise. She was tired, and she felt nauseated as well, as if she'd eaten something that didn't agree with her, though she hadn't had anything at the restaurant. Maybe that was the problem. Maybe she should have eaten something.

She strode to the open doorway to tell her brother and sister to be quiet, but what she saw changed her mind. She'd thought they were having a regular running race, though Nahla's limp would slow her down. But in fact Nahla had an arm over Darius's shoulder and he was helping her, not very successfully, which was causing them to giggle and shriek as they staggered along.

A lump rose in her throat.

"What's wrong, Parthenia?" Darius asked, picking up on her feelings right away.

There was no point in telling him she was fine. He knew she wasn't, and he would be hurt or confused by the lie.

"I'm wondering what's happening with Carina and the Black Dogs."

Darius and Nahla had drawn to a halt. Her brother said, "Why don't you ask her?"

"Lakshmi comms don't work outside the station."

"Oh. Then why don't you Send to her?"

"I can't."

Didn't he know?

"Why not? Did you forget your elixir?"

"No, I have some, but...Darius, we can't Cast anymore. Didn't anyone tell you?"

The little boy's eyes grew round. "No, no one told me. How come?"

"We don't know. It just happened. That's why it took us so long to find you when you were on Deck Zero. We were Casting Locate, but it wasn't working."

It seemed remarkable Darius wasn't aware the mages had lost their ability, but when she thought about it, it made sense. He'd been unconscious when they'd realized what had happened, and since then he'd been recovering with Nahla. He must have missed their discussions or he hadn't been listening properly.

"That's bad," he commented. "I like Casting."

"So do I."

"Will it come back?"

"No one knows. Maybe one day. I hope so."

"You're like me now," said Nahla.

"Yeah," Darius replied, crestfallen. "I don't feel like playing." He stepped out from under her arm.

"It's okay. Don't be sad. Let's run again."

But Darius walked away from her, heading for the bridge.

"Darius! I need you to help me run."

"I'll help you later. I want to rest." He passed Parthenia and sat in the copilot's seat.

"Will you help me run, Parthenia?" Nahla asked.

"Of course." She took her sister's hand. For a few minutes she trotted slowly alongside as Nahla hobbled up and down, but then Nahla said, "I want to stop. I'm tired."

Parthenia suspected she wasn't actually tired. She guessed she didn't find her older sister half as much fun to play with as Darius. "Why don't you go sit down for a while?"

"Is Carina coming back soon?"

"I think so."

When *would* Carina return? It had been hours since they'd parted ways. Surely she must have fixed the problem with the mercs by now. Not being able to Send to her was frustrating.

As she stepped into the bridge, Parthenia was confused to see Darius head down with his eyes closed and his lips moving silently. He appeared to be Sending to someone, though she knew that was impossible. She helped Nahla to sit down and opened an interface to give her something to do.

Darius continued to have a private conversation in his head.

Then she noticed her elixir bottle on the console in front of him. The cap was off and a few drops sat on the surface. He clearly hadn't believed her when she'd told him the mages could no longer Cast. He'd wanted to try for himself. Poor Darius. He was suffering the same shock and unhappiness she and their siblings had experienced. It would take time for him to get used to the fact.

He opened his eyes and looked up. "Carina says hi."

Parthenia froze. "What?"

"I *can* Cast. You were wrong."

"Darius, I..."

He *had* to be deluded.

"Darius, are you sure—"

"It's okay. Carina was surprised too."

Was it possible? He seemed very confident, and it wasn't like him to lie.

"Well, goodness!" Parthenia sat down.

No one had tested him. When they'd learned they'd lost their abilities, everyone had been so devastated, no one had thought to check if the same applied to their youngest brother. Even Jace hadn't suggested it. And Darius hadn't been aware of the news so he hadn't tested himself. But it was possible he was the odd one out. As a Spirit Mage, he was different.

"You really Sent to Carina?"

"Uh huh."

"That's wonderful. I'm so happy you can still Cast." What she said was true, but she couldn't help feeling somewhat jealous as well. What was worse, she knew Darius was aware.

"Me too! Now I'll be able to Cast for everyone, so it won't be so bad for you after all."

"Thanks, that's kind, Darius. What did Carina say when you spoke to her? Is she on her way back with the mercs?"

"No, she didn't talk about that. Parthenia, she was really sad, but she wouldn't tell me why."

TWENTY-THREE

The guard opened the cell door. As Carina went in Bongo said he would wait for her outside. The Black Dogs were a sorry sight. Rees had a black eye and a busted lip, Van Hasty's nose and knuckles were bleeding, and though Hsiao didn't have a scratch on her, Carina had never seen her look so down.

Did the mercs know they had about ten minutes left to live?

"Five minutes," the guard said. "That's all you get."

"But—"

"That's it. We need time to get them to the airlock. Gotta keep to the schedule, or there's hell to pay." He closed the door and the lock faintly hissed as it shut.

"What did he say?" Rees asked. "Something about an airlock?"

They didn't know.

"Thank the stars you're here," said Hsiao. "What took you so long? Can you get us out?"

"Or can you get us separate cells at least?" asked Van Hasty. "There isn't room to spit in here."

"What the hell were you all thinking?!" Carina yelled. "Didn't you hear the warning I gave you on the *Peregrine*? Hsiao, I can't believe you let this happen! You were with me on the first visit. You know how strict they are here."

"I know." The pilot winced. "I tried to stop the fight, but things got out of hand. When the guards arrived I kept my distance, but the bar patrons pointed me out and said I was with them."

"Great. Just great."

"Is it really bad? Do you know our sentence? Are we going to be here a long time?"

"No, you're..."

Carina choked up. Her chest heaved as she fought not to cry. She'd had her fallings out with Hsiao, but she counted the woman as a friend, one of very few. And though she wasn't close with Rees, Van Hasty, or the other mercs, they were like extended family.

Why oh why had she come to Lakshmi Station? The trip had turned into a disaster. The mages had lost their powers, and now seven mercs were about to die, including the only experienced pilot they had.

"We're *what*?" Hsiao asked. "Carina, what's wrong?"

"We could apologize to the guys we scrapped with if it would help," Rees offered.

"I'm not apologizing," said Van Hasty. "They started it."

Carina was tempted to ask what had happened. Where were the people the mercs had fought? Were they going to be spaced too? Or were the Lakshmi authorities picking on the outsiders?

But there was no time. They had only a few minutes left.

She took a deep breath. "Guys, there's no good way to say this, but your sentence for what you did is execution. You're going to be spaced very soon. If there's anything you want me to tell anyone, any message you want to pass on, you have to say it—"

Her words were lost in the mercs' cries of dismay and outrage. Rees got in her face and demanded she do something to save them. Van Hasty began wailing, while Hsiao only looked blank with disbelief.

"Shut up!" Carina shouted. "Shut up!" She pushed Rees's chest to get him away from her. "There's nothing I can do. I told you! I warned you. And then like a bunch of dumb morons you go ahead and get into a fight anyway. What did you think would—"

"*Carina?*"

The voice came from inside her head, and it was very familiar.

"*Darius?!*"

The mercs continued to holler and sob. A couple of them were banging on the cell door, demanding to be released.

"*Hey Carina,*" said Darius. "*What's up? Where are you?*"

"I'm...Darius, you can Send?"

"*Yeah, I can. Parthenia said we can't Cast anymore, but I thought I would try anyway, and I can! It's great, huh?*"

"*Yeah, it's great.*" She swallowed, grief and dread over the mercs' impending deaths at war with wonder and relief that Darius hadn't lost his mage ability.

"You don't seem very happy. Is something wrong?"

*"*Yes. No. I mean, I can't talk to you now. I'll see you later, when I get back, okay?*"*

"Okay. The Cast is fading now anyway. See you soon, Carina."

He was gone.

The mercs were quietening down, the reality of what was about to happen no doubt settling on them.

"How long do we have?" asked Hsiao, pale-faced.

"A couple of minutes at most."

"That's it?" The pilot's voice was a whisper.

"I'm sorry."

It was all too much. The tenuous grip she'd been holding on herself broke and tears overflowed her eyes. "I'm so sorry. If there was anything I could do…"

Silence descended except for Van Hasty's quiet sobs.

"No," said Pamuk, *"I'm* sorry. I should have kept my cool when that guy grabbed me."

"No point in going over it now," said Rees. "What's done is done. I never thought I'd go out like this. Thought I'd get killed in a battle, or my ship would get blown up, and that'd be it."

"I always knew the black would get me in the end," another merc muttered.

The cell door opened.

"Time's up," said the guard.

"Can't we have just another minute?" asked Carina, still weeping. None of the mercs had told her their last wishes yet.

"Time's *up*," repeated the guard. "Unless you want to step outside without a suit too?"

"Stars, I'm going."

She found herself suddenly enveloped in a tight hug. Hsiao had grabbed her. "I'm sorry for what I said about your brother."

"It's okay," Carina cried into her shoulder. "I forgave you days ago."

The guard coughed.

"I have to go."

"I know," said Hsiao, releasing her. "It's been good knowing you, Carina."

"And you."

"I hope you make it to Earth."

Carina took a final look at the seven men and women before leaving.

Bongo accompanied her as she plodded toward the exit. The other cells appeared empty, unsurprisingly. Most visitors to Lakshmi weren't so stupid as to get into a bar fight. But the mercs must have fought other people. Where were they? Why weren't they going to be spaced too? Or had they already been executed?

"What's happened to the others who took part in the fight, Bongo? Do you know?"

"No, but I guess they or someone they know paid the fine. Like I was saying at the restaurant, the people who profit from Lakshmi are fabulously rich, and it's usually only those types who get into—"

"*What*?!"

She had been so deep in despair, the sense of what the alien had said took time to filter through. "What fine?! No one told me there was a fine! Why didn't you tell me?"

"Oh, it's very expensive. You probably don't want to—"

"Where do I pay? Do I still have time?" She picked up her pace. "Where do I go? Tell me where to go!"

"The accounts section is...let me see...I'm not sure if I remember."

Swiveling to face the alien, she scooped him up and held him at eye level. His many legs uselessly windmilled in mid-air. "You'd better remember, fast. If my friends die, you're the next one who'll be spaced!"

TWENTY-FOUR

Though Bongo's culture was pacifist, his species didn't give a shit about each other, not if money was involved. He hadn't imagined for a second Carina would be willing to spend more than half the large sum she possessed to buy her companions' freedom. His omission had almost cost the mercs their lives, so it was with mixed feelings she said goodbye to him when she left Lakshmi Station for a second time.

As she pulled herself through the umbilicus to return to the *Peregrine* with the mercs, Hsiao spoke to her over the comm. "He really didn't tell you until after you left our cell?"

"Of course he didn't," replied Carina. "Do you think I would have let you all believe you were going to die as a joke?"

"It's just hard to understand. I mean—"

"He's a different species. You can't expect him to think like us."

"I know, but he seemed nice."

"He *is* nice, but remember how his cousin tried to fleece us? Money has an even higher value to them than to us."

"You'd think after living all that time at the station he would understand humans better. You said the other people in the fight had their fines paid too, so he's seen what we do."

"I asked him about that. He said that amount of money is nothing to rich Lakshmi-ites."

Hsiao whistled. "Holy smoke. I didn't realize the quantity of creds washing around that station even existed in the galaxy."

Carina reached the *Peregrine's* airlock and hauled herself inside. Van Hasty, Rees, and the other mercs were already waiting.

"You don't know the half of it," she said. "Wait until I tell you where the rich got their money." Her boots hit the deck.

When Hsiao arrived, Rees shut the outer hatch and activated pressurization.

"Where?" the pilot asked.

At the same time, Darius Sent to her. "*Carina? Are you back?*"

"Yes, sweetheart. See you in a minute." Her HUD showed normal atmosphere. She removed her helmet. "I have to see the kids. I'll talk to you later."

"Uhhh..." said Rees. He was holding his helmet awkwardly.

She paused. "Did you want to say something?"

"Yeah," said Van Hasty, her head down. "We're...uh..."

"We're sorry about the fight," said Rees.

"Yeah, we're sorry," Van Hasty echoed. "And we want to thank you for paying all that money to save us from..." She faltered.

"It's not a problem."

In fact, it was. With more than half their funds gone, they were now restricted on fitting out the *Bathsheba* with defensive weapons. The mercs' stunt could cost everyone their lives in the long run, but they knew that.

"Well, thanks anyway," Rees said.

The other Black Dogs nodded in agreement.

Carina quickly removed her EVA suit and set off to find Darius, Nahla, and Parthenia. Darius hadn't said where they were, but she guessed they would be on the bridge.

It turned out she was right. Darius greeted her with a hug and so did Nahla after she'd limped over. Carina's heart ached at the reminder that the visit to Lakshmi Station had been a disappointment on another level. It was hard to face the reality that her little sister would never be the same. In many ways she hadn't changed. She was still cheeky and adventurous, but she'd lost that spark of brilliance that set her apart.

"Isn't it wonderful that Darius can Cast?" Parthenia asked, apparently unable to keep the note of envy out of her voice.

Carina knew how she felt. She was happy for their brother yet she couldn't help feeling a little jealous too. "Yes, it is." Turning to Darius she said, "You always surprise us with what you can do. I'm glad we still have one mage in the family."

Another child his age would have taken her words at face value, but Darius felt the emotions underlying them. He smiled sadly. "I wish you could Cast too. Maybe you'll be able to again one day."

Parthenia put a hand to her head and squeezed her eyes shut.

"Are you okay?" Carina asked.

"Not completely. I've been feeling ill since we got back."

"Go and lie down. Hsiao will be here in a minute to fly us to the *Bathsheba*. One of the ship's doctors can take a look at you."

"Yes, all right."

It wasn't like Parthenia to agree so easily. Carina looked at her more closely. She *did* look pale. After the episode with the mercs, she didn't feel so great herself.

"What happened at the station?" Parthenia asked, halting in the open doorway. "What took you so long?"

"That's a long story, and not one for telling in front of the kids. I'll fill you in another time, but you should know we're not as rich as we were."

"Ugh, that's a shame. I hope we can still afford some treatment for Nahla."

———

When Carina arrived at the *Bathsheba*, she discovered another disaster had occurred in her absence. Jackson's prosthetic arm had been severed in an accident with the lasers on the hull.

"I don't believe it! I can't leave you guys alone for two minutes without something terrible happening. What'll it be next time I step out of the ship? Is she going to blow up? Is someone going to fly her into the star? Or invite the Regians to a party?"

"Calm down," said Bryce. "He only lost his prosthetic. It could have been a lot worse."

"It *is* a lot worse. I haven't told you what happened on Lakshmi yet."

"Yeah," said Jackson, "what went down over there? Van Hasty and Rees look like someone stole their puppy."

"Before you tell us," Bryce said, "you should know the second bit of bad news. It's probably better to get it all out the way now."

Carina pressed her palms to her face. "Are you sure I need to know?"

Bryce patted her shoulder. "Don't worry. No one's died."

"Thank the stars for that. Things were touch and go for a while on Lakshmi. I don't think I could stand another life and death crisis."

"Jace is in sick bay," said Bryce.

Her hands dropped to her sides. "What's wrong with him?"

"The docs don't know. They're still trying to figure it out. I went to see him and found him in bed. He didn't want to bother anyone. Kept saying he'd be okay after a good sleep. I called a medic to take a look at him and she recommended sick bay right away."

"Shit."

Parthenia was also feeling unwell. Was it related? She would have to tell her sister to get checked out.

"Is that it?" she asked. "No other catastrophes to report?"

"That's it. You can tell us what happened on Lakshmi now."

"Well..." said Carina, wondering where to start.

Then everything went black.

TWENTY-FIVE

Carina opened her eyes. She was on her back in a bed, and the air smelt faintly medicinal.

Sick bay?

She moved to sit up.

A thousand hammers beat on her skull and the room lurched. Her stomach began to force its way up into her throat. Swallowing hard, she lay down. She remained motionless, recovering, though her head didn't stop hurting.

The second time she tried to move, she only ventured to look to one side.

Parthenia was in the neighboring bed, her eyes closed.

This time, it was Carina's heart that lurched as she feared the worst. But her sister was only asleep, breathing regularly and gently. There was a pink flush to her skin.

She didn't attempt moving again. It only made the hammers beat harder. As she watched her sister, she went over what she remembered. She'd been talking with Bryce and Jackson. Jackson was missing his prosthetic, and Bryce had said something about...she frowned. Jace. He'd said Jace was in the sick bay.

Now she and Parthenia were here too.

Three mages all sick at once? It was too much of a coincidence. Something was going on. Was someone targeting the mages? It couldn't be anything to do with Lakshmi because Jace hadn't been there, and no one on the station knew about him. It had to be the work of someone aboard the *Bathsheba*.

Was that why they'd lost their ability to Cast? Had someone discovered a substance that would take away their abilities? It seemed unlikely. As far as she knew, no one understood how or why mages could Cast, so it should be impossible to know how to affect the process.

Plus, their sickness had begun days after they'd lost their abilities. The two things weren't related, or only tangentially. Everyone knew what had happened to them. It was possible their enemy had only decided to make their move because they felt safer now. Not that she or anyone else would have Cast to hurt them anyway, but they probably didn't know that.

Perhaps the person had spiked their food or drink. That might explain why Darius and the twins hadn't been affected. They tended to choose and print their own food.

She began to run through the people who had the opportunity to adulterate her meals or drinks. It was a short list. If the water dispenser in the galley nearest her suite had been contaminated, it would have affected far more people than just her. And she usually ate with Bryce. If their dishes had been poisoned, he should be in sick bay too.

An impossible idea began to form in her mind. Surely it couldn't have been—

Bryce walked in. "The doc comm'd to say you'd woken up. She said she'll be in soon. She's waiting for some test results. How are you feeling?" He drew up a chair and sat down.

"Like shit. What happened?"

"You fainted. Jackson caught you one-handed. It was pretty impressive."

"Fainted, huh?" Now she thought about it, she hadn't been feeling great for a while. The farce with the mercs at Lakshmi had distracted her. "And what were you doing while this was going on?"

"Watching in wonder." He was smiling, but then his expression turned serious. "You gave me a fright. The docs don't seem to know what's wrong with you."

"How long have I been out?"

"An hour or so."

"What about Parthenia? And Jace? Did the doc say anything about them?"

His expression grew more serious. "You can add Ferne and Oriana to the list. They're in another room."

"The twins as well?! Damn. Darius?"

"He's fine."

"Thank the stars."

"The docs think you all have the same problem, whatever it is."

"Makes sense." The throbbing in her head surged and she let out a groan.

Bryce gently touched the side of her face. "It's really bad, isn't it? Parthenia was saying she felt like buffaloes were stampeding through her brain before her sedative kicked in."

"She did? That's why they put her out?"

"Yeah, they said it would help her to get some rest. Carina, Darius told me he can still Cast. Is that right?"

"It is. He Sent to me when he was on the *Peregrine* and I was in Lakshmi. What a bunch of idiots we were to not check with him. I could have sworn I'd asked him to try a Cast, but apparently not."

"But if that's so, can't he Heal you all?"

"It doesn't work like that. Heal fixes injuries, like cuts, wounds, burns, and broken bones. It doesn't cure diseases. Don't you think I would have cured you when you had Ithiyan plague if I could? It would have been easy. And I would have Healed Ma in a heartbeat. You know that."

"Of course. I wasn't thinking."

She didn't go on to tell him Heal also couldn't save people near death. It wasn't strictly true. A Spirit Mage could do it, but only at the risk of killing themselves in the process. Darius had done it for her once, and she didn't want him to ever be put in the same position again. It was better to not remind Bryce of the fact.

She looked at her sleeping sister. They'd had their differences, but she didn't know what she would do if anything bad happened to her.

Watching her watching Parthenia, Bryce said quietly, "Have you ever considered the fact she might be your full sister?"

Carina almost sat up in surprise but managed to stop herself just in time, mindful of her aching head. "What makes you say that?"

"You look incredibly alike. Anyone who saw you would guess you were related. And though I only saw your mother a little, I'd say you both resemble her closely. I can't see anything of Stefan Sherrerr in Parthenia."

Carina had been three years old when Stefan had tricked Ma and Ba into revealing themselves as mages and taken them prisoner. She didn't know the exact dates it all happened, but it was possible Ma had already been pregnant Stefan raped her. She might not have known, or she might have kept the fact secret the rest of her life, fearing her tormentor would kill Parthenia if he found out.

"Stars," she said quietly, "you could be right."

"Something to think about. You share similar traits too."

"What kind of traits?"

"Oh, I'll let you figure that out."

Huh. They were both stubborn, argumentative, and sometimes difficult to get along with. It was definitely something to think about.

Though Bryce had spoken in a teasing tone, his face remained full of concern. "I'll ask the doc to give you a painkiller." He began to get to his feet, but at that moment Dr Asher arrived.

The Black Dogs had two military doctors: Asher and Baxter. Dr Asher was a woman in late middle age who had worked for the band ever since Carina could remember, and Baxter was a man in his twenties who had joined just before Carina reconnected with the band. He was young for a merc. Most had completed a few tours by the time dishonorable discharge, mental instability, or a traumatic event drove them to pursue professional soldiering.

To Carina's knowledge, Baxter had never explained why he'd chosen the more haphazard, riskier life among the Black Dogs over a space fleet career and guaranteed pension. And, as was usual, no one had asked him.

Carina preferred Dr Asher. She wasn't exactly what you would call motherly, unless motherhood entailed barking at people with any non-life-threatening ailment that they needed to get over themselves. But if she took your injury or ailment seriously, you could trust her to do her level best to help, and she never treated the kids with anything less than her utmost care and concern. Whereas Baxter was always distant and offhand, regardless of the severity of his patient's condition.

"I have to hand it to you, Carina," Asher said as she walked in, "you guys have us stumped."

"You don't know what's wrong with us?" she asked, grimacing.

"Not a clue. You're hurting, right?" Asher held up a pressure syringe.

Bryce helped Carina sit up.

"This won't knock me out, will it?" she asked as Asher lifted her sleeve. "I want to talk to you."

"No, it won't knock you out. It'll just take the edge off."

A cool blast from the syringe spread through her veins. The pain in her head eased. She could still feel it but the medication also made her care less. "You really have no idea at all what's wrong with us?"

"I know what you *don't* have. You don't have any of the hundreds of viruses our antivirals can tackle or a bacterial infection. You don't have cancer and you aren't suffering from radiation sickness. The tests didn't show any genetic abnormalities only manifesting now either."

Carina found her last comment interesting. Whatever was different about mage genes, it didn't show up as abnormal. "I was wondering if we'd been poisoned."

The doctor's eyebrows rose. "You too, huh? A tox screen was the first test I ran. Zilch."

"That doesn't mean we weren't poisoned though, does it? Only that the test didn't pick it up."

"Isn't that a little paranoid?" Bryce asked. "Who would want to poison you?"

"It was the first test she ran," Carina protested.

"It was, but I have a complete lack of faith in humanity," Asher countered. "It seems I'm not alone."

"So what happens now?" asked Carina.

"We continue to monitor you, and Baxter and I will rack our brains to try to figure out what's wrong. We haven't exhausted all the possibilities yet, only ruled out the most common ailments."

"How are the twins and Jace doing?"

"About the same as you, only Ferne and Oriana complain more."

"Does the order we fell ill in mean anything?"

"Not necessarily. You all exhibited symptoms within twenty-four hours. That's a standard range, given the variability of the human response to illness."

"Do you think it has something to do with losing our mage powers?"

"The correlation would certainly be worth investigating if we knew the first thing about what you do—or used to be able to do. But unfortunately we don't, so we'll be ignoring that for now. Unless, of course, you can shed some light...?"

Carina shook her head. "I'm as much in the dark as you."

"That's what I thought."

Twenty-Six

Carina had been in sick bay a week, and she was going out of her mind.

"Would you please stop huffing and puffing?" Parthenia snapped. "It's bad enough being stuck in here as it is without having to listen to you all day."

"I can't help it. Something's happening but I don't know what. Bryce hasn't been in to see us today and I heard a commotion outside this morning. Since then, it's been silent. Why hasn't anyone told me what's going on?"

"Because you're sick. They don't want to bother you."

"It's more of a bother *not* to know. Why the big secret? Why would knowing what's happening hurt me?"

"Because you would fret and worry and get annoyed when they won't let you stick your oar in for once."

"I wouldn't be sticking my oar in. I'd be giving them the benefit of my advice. Anyway, I'm the unofficial leader of the mission. If something important happens I should know about it, even if I am sick."

"Oh, it hurts to be left out?" Parthenia asked archly. "Who would have thought?"

Carina cast a glance at her sister. She wasn't looking at her as she spoke. She was watching something on an interface, propped up in bed.

They were both on high doses of painkillers, anti-nausea medication, and other medicinal treatments that counteracted their ever-worsening symptoms. If it hadn't been for the meds, neither of them would have been able to function at all. As it was, watching endless hours of mindless entertainment was about all they were capable of. That, and sniping at each other.

More than once, Carina had contemplated asking the docs to transfer her to another room. Spending time with Parthenia only added to her problems. She guessed they'd been put in the same room so they could keep each other company. What a great idea that had been.

She'd thought about Bryce's guess that they were full sisters. As the days had passed, she'd begun to believe he was right. From certain angles, Parthenia looked like a slightly younger version of herself. If they'd had the same hairstyle their similarities would have been even more apparent.

Personality-wise, their characters were not quite so alike, despite Bryce's hints, but their differences could be explained by their upbringing. Parthenia was far more fussy and particular, especially about things like manners and decorum. Carina couldn't have been more different. Spending your adolescence on the streets and then living among mercs didn't exactly teach you the refinements of polite society.

Their greatest difference was Parthenia seemed to feel responsible for the welfare of all humanity, while Carina—she freely admitted—only really cared about people she knew. That could be explained by their upbringing too. Parthenia had grown up the eldest child in a very dysfunctional family. She'd had the concept of duty to others drilled into her, whereas Carina had been trained by Nai Nai to look after herself and trust no one.

"Do you *have* to do that?" Parthenia asked, looking at her from the corners of her eyes.

"Sorry." Carina turned away. She hadn't mentioned Bryce's guess about their shared parentage and she wasn't sure she should. It might make her sister dislike her even more.

"What are you thinking?" asked Parthenia.

"I'm still wondering what's happening out there."

"For goodness sake! If that matters that much, why don't you go and find out?"

"You know, I think I will."

"No, I didn't mean it. We have to rest. That's what Dr Asher said."

"And it's doing us a lot of good, isn't it? We're getting sicker and sicker every day, and every day they up our doses. What's going to happen when they can't increase them any more? I can't stand lying here like an animal waiting to be slaughtered. I'm going to find out what's going on or die trying."

Even she had to admit her words were melodramatic. She didn't think they were close to death. She hoped they weren't, if not for her own sake then for Jace and her siblings'. But her current situation was beyond frustrating. She felt helpless and useless. She had to act. Pushing back her covers, she swung her legs over the side of the bed.

"Carina, cut it out. Stay where you are or I'll call the medic."

Carina had argued with the docs over their constant surveillance. Being watched all the time made her uncomfortable. She'd made them agree to turn off the monitoring when at least one of them was awake and able to sound the alarm. "Why do you have to be so damned prim and proper all the time? It's okay to break the rules now and then. That's what they're for."

"That isn't what rules are for and you know it. Look what happened on Lakshmi when the Black Dogs broke the rules."

"Parthenia, my dearest sister, would you please *shut up*?" Carina had eased herself down from her bed while they bickered and was now standing unsteadily next to it. Her prolonged inactivity had made her weak. Coupled with her illness, she could barely stand. She felt like getting back into bed and having a long nap, but it would seem like she was obeying Parthenia, and *that* would only happen over her dead body. She pulled on a robe and shuffled toward the door.

"Come back!" Parthenia called. "You're sick. Go back to bed." When Carina didn't respond, she continued, "You look pathetic. You're making a fool of yourself."

Carina winced. Not because the words stung, though they did a little, but because they weren't something Parthenia would ordinarily say. She was echoing her monstrous father. Stefan Sherrerr had probably said exactly that kind of thing to Parthenia and her siblings while they were growing up.

Not her monstrous *father*, Carina corrected herself. Her monstrous stepfather.

As she reached the door it slid open. She stepped out into the triage room, which was empty. In the center of the deck were a few spots of blood. Someone had been hurt!

Increasing her pace to a slow walk, she crossed the room to peer through the windows into the twins' and Jace's rooms. All were sleeping. Relieved that none of them seemed injured, she continued her journey, sneaking past the staff office and out into the passageway. Her legs were already aching. Her surroundings seemed to be underwater, moving to and fro as if in a choppy current. Propping herself with one hand on the bulkhead for support, she went on.

If only she could Cast Transport. The *Bathsheba* was so goddamned big and she wasn't sure where to go. She couldn't comm anyone. They would only alert the medics about her escape.

A little voice at the back of her head that sounded suspiciously like Nai Nai scolded her for being dumb, but something drove her on. She couldn't let others take over the running of the ship. What might happen to her siblings if she wasn't there to protect them? Ma had entrusted them to her care. She wasn't going to let her down.

She stumbled and fell.

The effort to get back to her feet threatened to take the last of her strength but she managed it. As she became upright once more, she heard distant voices. There seemed to be a lot of them. The Black Dogs must have got together for some reason. Were they fighting? That would explain the blood on the triage room deck.

It would be odd if the mercs were attacking each other. Though they weren't the most stable people, they'd generally gotten along pretty well since they'd escaped the Regians and dealt with the Lotacryllans' mutiny attempt. Adversity had bonded them more than ever, she'd thought. But maybe the trouble with Van Hasty, Rees, and the others at Lakshmi had divided them. The seven mercs were responsible for losing over half the ship's funds. That wouldn't sit well with the rest of the Black Dogs.

Weakness was overcoming her. If she tried to make it back to the sick bay and act like nothing had happened, she would never make it. Better to press on and hopefully find out what was being hidden from her. The voices were growing louder. She was heading in the right direction. She could even hear snatches of conversation.

"I've already explained," someone said, "this isn't a commercial venture."

Bryce.

"We understand," another voice replied. "We're here to appeal to your sense of human decency. Won't you at least consider our request? We have so much to offer you. Skills, creds, healthy females for breeding."

Healthy females for breeding?!

Carina let out a gasp. The deck seemed to rise up at her, and that was the last thing she remembered.

Twenty-Seven

"You have to stop making a habit of this," said Bryce as she came around for the second time.

She was back in sick bay. It was like she was living a waking nightmare: passing out, waking up in a sick bay bed; passing out, waking up in a sick bay bed. Yet it was better than not waking up.

"What's happening?" she asked groggily. "Am I going to be used for breeding?"

"*What*?!" Bryce put a hand to her forehead. "Are you getting another fever? You don't feel hot. Ohhh..." His features cleared. "You overheard the leader of the party from Marchon."

"Marchon?" Carina mumbled. Brain fog was clogging her thinking, but it still sounded wrong that people from Marchon were aboard the *Bathsheba*.

"I was going to tell you about it after we dealt with them. I didn't want to worry you unnecessarily."

She was about to say something similar to what she'd told Parthenia, that she worried more when she *didn't* know what was going on, but she couldn't utter so many words all at once. All she managed was, "What's happened?"

"We have visitors. Jackson and Justus are with them now. I wanted to check you were okay after the medics got you back into bed. You know, if I hadn't heard you fall in the passageway you could have been lying there a while before someone found you. Please don't do that again. I'm sorry, but I have to go now."

Her head was beginning to clear a little. She touched his arm. "Tell me what's going on."

He hesitated. "It would take too long to explain. Jackson and Justus need my input to sort this problem out. But you can see it all on the security vids. I'll find them for you."

Dr Asher burst into the room, her expression full of fury. "I'm reliably informed you were found unconscious in a passageway a hundred meters from here." As she spoke, she marched to Carina's side. "So you repay all my hard work in treating you by leaving your bed and wandering around the ship, hm?" She pushed up Carina's sleeve to her shoulder and pressed the cool steel head of a pressure syringe into her bicep.

The relief from confusion and aches and pains that spread from the injection was blissful.

"Listen to me, young lady," said Asher, leaning close. "As it apparently wasn't obvious to you that you need to stay put, I'm making it an express order. You've been warned. Defy me at your peril. I'll be back soon to see what damage you've done to yourself. One of my more deserving patients needs me right now."

She stomped out.

"Well, that's *you* told," Bryce remarked. "Seriously, Carina, that was a dumb stunt you pulled. You're not invincible, and you're not vital to the running of the ship. We can cope without your input and we want to. Everyone wants you to get better, not kill yourself." He reached for the interface next to the bed and gave commands for it to bring up the relevant vidfeeds. "Can you sit up?"

She nodded.

He helped her to a sitting position and swung the screen around on its arm so it faced her. "Take it easy. I'll come back and update you as soon as I can." He bent down to kiss the top of her head, and then he was gone.

While all this was going on, Carina hadn't been able to see Parthenia's reaction. Predictably, her sister was giving her a hard-eyed stare. As soon as their gazes met, Parthenia curled a lip in disgust and turned away.

A heavy weight settled on Carina's chest and her ribs felt constricted. She struggled to breathe, but it wasn't anything to do with her illness. Blinking away the blurriness in her vision, she told the interface to play the vids.

The first was a recording of the exterior of the ship. Another vessel was approaching—a battered, pockmarked craft far smaller than the *Bathsheba*. Most starships were. Her thrusters reversed and the ship slowed to a stop.

Frustratingly, there was no audio with the recording. The foreign starship must have hailed the *Bathsheba*. Carina would have liked to hear the conversation that took place, but her mind was too befuddled to find the recording made on the bridge.

The colony ship's weapons were too old and inadequate to protect her from a sustained attack, but no one aboard her would have gone down without a fight. No pulses had been fired, however, which meant the Black Dogs had agreed to meet the visitors.

A short, rigid umbilicus extended from the newcomers' ship and disappeared out of view as it attached to the *Bathsheba's* hull. The recording showed nothing more. The umbilicus wall was opaque, but the visitors must have crossed it and come aboard.

What had happened in the triage room? Who had dripped blood on the deck?

Bryce had found the vid for her.

She watched the sick bay doors draw apart and men pour in. A few were Black Dogs. Bryce was there too, but most of the rest were unfamiliar. Dressed in leathers, rough-shaven and shaggy haired, the men looked nothing like the people she'd seen on Lakshmi. She guessed only soldiers or wealthy citizens could visit the station. These men were different.

They were clustered around an individual who sagged, supported by his companions, his arms over the shoulders of two of them. Dr Baxter appeared from the staff room.

"Please help," said one of the men. "His bleeding won't stop and our blood generator's broken."

"All right. Put him over there."

But as the men moved the patient slipped from their grasp. There were too many people around him to see what happened, but Carina heard the thud of him hitting the deck. They gathered him up quickly and carried him to the bed. Conversations went on between the visitors and Bryce and the Black Dogs while Baxter did his work, but there were too many and the voices too indistinct to hear.

She watched intently. Where had the Marchonish man gone after Baxter treated him?

With surprise and alarm, she saw him carried into a room.

He was still in the sick bay?!

Ferne and Oriana were here, and Jace too. They were all ill and they could no longer Cast. What if the stranger tried to hurt them? She pushed the interface out of the way and moved to get out of bed.

"What are you *doing*?" Parthenia demanded. "Don't tell me you're going to get up again!"

"Someone's here, in the sick bay."

"What are you talking about? I think you're getting delirious. I'm calling Dr Asher."

But there was no need. An instant later, Asher walked in.

Her eyes took in Carina's position, half out of bed. Her lips pursed and her eyes narrowed. "Am I going to have to permanently sedate you, Carina Lin?"

"That man they brought in. The Marchonish man. Where is he? Is he still here? Is he under guard? Who's protecting the mages?"

"How did you...?" Asher's gaze drifted to the interface. "I see." Her expression lost some of its rigidity. "You don't have anything to worry about."

"I really wish," Carina said through her teeth, mustering the little energy she had, "people would stop telling me to not worry."

After giving an exasperated sigh, the doctor said, "The man from Marchon isn't currently in a position to do anyone any harm, considering he is under general anesthetic while having a damaged artery repaired. Does that answer your questions?"

Carina flopped backward onto her pillows and closed her eyes.

"Honestly," Asher went on, "your lack of confidence in others is alarming. Do you think you're the only person capable of doing anything around here? Or that we would put your siblings and friend at risk of harm?"

"No," Carina murmured, lifting a weary hand to rub her eyes. "I just feel so useless."

This seemed to soften Dr Asher's attitude somewhat. "Baxter and I are doing everything we can to get to the bottom of your illness, but you have to let us do our job and stop making things harder for everyone, okay?"

"Okay."

"Good. Now stop worr—" Asher paused and smiled, tight-lipped. "Remember, everything is under control on the ship. You should get some sleep. Would you like something to help you drift off?"

"No, I'm fine."

When Asher had left, Carina pulled the interface in front of her again.

Twenty-Eight

Darius peeked around the edge of the door into the mission room. The Marchonish men were lounging around, sitting on the tables resting a foot on a chair or leaning against the walls. A couple were lying stretched out on the floor.

They were waiting for something.

Bryce, Justus, and a few Black Dogs had gone into another room and closed the door. Darius guessed the visitors were waiting to be told something, and Bryce and the others had to decide what to tell them. Maybe it had something to do with the weapons Carina wanted to buy at Lakshmi Station. Maybe the men from Marchon wanted to offer them a better price.

He didn't like them.

They felt dark and dangerous, kind of like Castiel and that man on Magog, Kai Wei, but not quite the same. The darkness in the Marchonish men was cloudy and murky, while Castiel and Wei's had been hard and sharp, like a black diamond.

Nahla giggled behind him. "I want to see too," she whispered.

"Okay. Swap places." He let Nahla go in front of him to take a turn at watching the visitors.

He wasn't sure they were supposed to be here, but on the other hand, no one had told them to stay away. Everyone had been busy lately. First, they'd been talking about Carina and the others being sick, and now they were talking about the men who had turned up and asked to come aboard.

He hadn't been able to hear everything they said, but he thought they wanted to come with them to Earth. Their leader had said something about them being tired of the war, and wanting to start a new life somewhere else.

They'd spotted the *Bathsheba* near Lakshmi Station and so they'd come to find out who owned her.

He didn't think any one person owned her. Everybody owned a little bit of her, even him and Nahla.

Nahla looked over her shoulder and whispered, "They're so big and ugly."

That was a bit rude, and he didn't join in her giggles. But Nahla couldn't help it. She'd been different since the accident on Deck Zero. It wasn't only her body that was different—she couldn't walk properly anymore—*she* was different too. She wasn't interested in finding things out and she was always happy to play with him now. Before, she'd only played because she wanted to be kind. Now, he felt like *he* was the kind one.

At first, he'd been glad he didn't have to keep asking to get her attention. It was fun to have a full-time playmate. But then he'd felt bad. She was like that because she'd had an accident—an accident that was partly his fault. If he'd been thinking better, he would have Transported them out from Deck Zero before they fell asleep. Then Nahla wouldn't have been hurt. He still loved her, but he wanted the old Nahla back, even if it meant returning to being lonely sometimes.

"Hey," said a gruff voice, "we have a little spy."

"What? Where? Oh, yeah. I see her."

Oh no! Nahla had been spotted.

"Come here, little one. We won't hurt you."

Darius grabbed the back of her shirt. "Don't go in," he hissed. She didn't understand the men were bad.

"I want to!" she protested. She pulled her shirt out of his hand and limped into the room.

"That's it," said a voice. "What a cutie."

Darius didn't know what to do. Should he tell Bryce what Nahla was doing? They probably shouldn't be here. It was like Deck Zero all over again. Clutching his elixir bottle, he followed her. This time, he wouldn't let Nahla down.

She was smiling up at a tall man. This one looked older than the others, and though his friends' muscles showed on their stomachs and arms—they weren't wearing shirts, only vests, for some reason—the man Nahla was looking at was softer and flabbier. His gut overhung the top of his pants. If he'd been a Black Dog, the mercs would have teased him about it.

"What's your name?" the man asked Nahla.

"There's another one!" someone called out. "This place is a nursery. Kids everywhere."

"It'd be good if they'd let us fill it with our kids," someone else grumbled.

"I'm Nahla," Darius's sister replied, "and he's Darius."

He wanted to tell her to be quiet and to get out of here, but now he was in the room the men would hear him.

"Nahla and Darius," said the tall man. "Nice names. And you're a pretty little thing." He put a finger under Nahla's chin and tilted it up to look at her face more closely.

Darius didn't think anyone had ever told Nahla she was pretty. His family didn't talk much about how people looked, unless they were commenting on Ferne and Oriana's new clothes designs. Nahla seemed to like the compliment because she smiled wider.

"Take another turn about," said the man.

She frowned. She didn't understand, but Darius did. He clutched his elixir bottle tighter.

"Damn, I wish those mercs would hurry up and come to a decision," said a Marchonish man.

"I don't," someone replied. "They can take as long as they like, as long as they say yes."

"What do they have to talk about? We made them a great offer. Men, supplies, female companions. This is a colony ship but it's damn near empty from what I can tell. They need us. They need more bodies if they want to survive."

"You're right. How many have we seen? Ten, twenty? And all the time we've been waiting, we've seen no one else except these brats. Ship's damned near rattling like a pod with only three peas."

"You know, we might even outnumber them," a third man commented.

This drew a pause from the group.

Again, Darius knew exactly what was going through their minds. He would have to tell Bryce what he'd heard, but he wasn't going anywhere without Nahla. He wouldn't leave her alone with these men.

"Kid," the tall man said, appearing to remember her presence, "I said take a turn about."

"I don't understand."

"Walk around the room. Show us what you got."

Show us what you got?

Darius was confused too.

Frowning, Nahla stepped away from the man.

She'd walked badly ever since the accident. One of her feet dragged because her leg didn't lift it high enough and she had to rise up on the other leg. It made her go up and down when she walked. She looked a bit strange, but Darius had never said anything about it.

The tall man laughed. "This one's defective, guys. They should send her back to the shop." The other Marchonish men joined in his laughter.

Nahla halted and turned. She wasn't as smart as she used to be, but she wasn't so stupid she didn't know when she was being laughed at. Her hands clenched and she looked like she was going to cry.

"Be quiet," said Darius to the men. "Don't be mean."

"Aw, she your sister?" asked the pudgy one. "It's okay. We're just having fun."

"Come on, Nahla. Let's go."

She hesitated, but then set off toward him.

The men burst out laughing again.

Darius thought it would all be over when Nahla reached him and they would go, but one of the men walked in front of her, blocking her path. "Don't leave us, honey. We love to watch you. Walk over there." He pointed at the corner of the room.

Nahla tried to step around him, but he was too quick. Everywhere she tried to go he was there first.

His friends were laughing loudly now.

Nahla's face crumpled and she began to sob.

"Leave her alone!" Darius shouted. He ran over to grab her hand and drag her away, but the man thrust a hand into his chest and forced him back.

"Probably shouldn't do that," the tall man said. "They won't mind us messing with *her*, but it'll piss them off if we hurt one of their sons."

But the man blocking Nahla didn't take any notice. He pointed at the corner again. "Over there with your funny walk, little girl."

"No!" she yelled, her face red and wet.

Darius couldn't stand it any longer. He should probably go and find Bryce or someone else and tell them what was happening, but that would mean leaving Nahla alone, and who knew what the horrible visitors might do to her while he was gone?

He didn't have a choice. He had to protect his sister.

He unscrewed the lid from his elixir bottle and took a sip.

TWENTY-NINE

The Black Dogs had taken the men from the visiting ship into the mission room. That's where they'd been when she'd heard them talking. The security vid showed the mercs telling the men to sit down and explain why they were here. Thankfully, this vid had audio.

"Isn't it obvious?" a man who had introduced himself as Porcher asked. He was taller and older than the rest, though far less fit. He seemed to be their leader. "The same reason as you."

"Which is?" asked Van Hasty. She'd mostly healed up since the bar fight on Lakshmi, only the cut on her nose remaining.

Giving her a dismissive look, Porcher addressed his reply in the general direction of the male mercs. "We're colonists too. We want a better future for our sons. As it is, they'll have to choose between dying in battle or making a miserable living in a munitions plant or mine. We plan on leaving Marchon and settling somewhere else, preferably a virgin planet, but we're open to suggestions."

"What happened to the guy in sick bay?" asked Jackson.

"A disagreement that turned into a fight, that's all. Tensions are high on Marchon. Our government's been pushing for another assault on Gugong. Some of us want to stick it to them, others want peace, saying the war's gone on too long. People are going crazy. We're at each other's throats. The man responsible for the injury apologized when he'd cooled down, but we couldn't stop the bleeding. We're grateful for your help."

"You say you're colonists," said Van Hasty, "but you didn't come here in a colony ship."

Again, Porcher acted as though a male merc had spoken, focusing on them for his reply. "That's what we've come to discuss with you."

Van Hasty's eyebrows rose and she held a hand in front of her face, as if checking she existed.

Carina smiled.

Porcher's weird behavior hadn't gone unnoticed among the Black Dog men either. Jackson's gaze met Van Hasty's before he returned his attention to the Marchonish leader. "Let me guess. You want to be colonists but you're missing one essential requirement—a colony vessel. So you're here to hitch a ride."

With an abashed grin, Porcher nodded. "We spotted your ship ten days ago, but it took us a while to gather everyone and make our way to you. We've been planning this for years, though to be honest at times it seemed like an impossible dream. We've brought plenty of supplies as well as equipment for settling the new planet. Ground-breakers, seeds, water purifiers, generators, medicines, dwelling kits, the lot. And we're young and strong. We didn't bring anyone over fifty. I barely made the cut off myself." He smiled again and ran a hand over his hair.

"Over the years, as we talked about leaving Marchon, the biggest problem was we didn't know where to go. We're at war with the nearest habitable planets. We would never be accepted there. And, to be honest, we aren't exactly sure what the other options are. All we knew was we needed a bigger, more powerful ship than we had if we wanted to go anywhere else. And then you guys turned up. The galaxy's a big place, right? There has to be a better world, a better life for us somewhere."

Carina stopped the recording. She felt a smidgen of sympathy for the would-be colonists, despite their odd attitude to women. Decades of war must have taken its toll on their world. Rather than working to improve the general standard of living for all their citizens, their labor had been hijacked to increase the wealth of a small elite.

Stars, their *lives* had been hijacked, sacrificed in bloody, pointless military campaigns with enemies who were just as hoodwinked and ignorant.

But the Black Dogs didn't know that. She hadn't had a chance to tell anyone what Bongo had said. She'd fainted before she got the words out.

"Parthenia?"

"What?" her sister replied sullenly, not looking at her.

"After we got back from Lakshmi, did you tell Bryce or anyone else about the real reason for the Three-Systems War?"

"I was too busy vomiting. Should I have?"

"I was just wondering. You know about the Marchonish visitors?"

"I'm right next to you, Carina. How couldn't I overhear what Bryce said?"

A simple 'yes' would have been enough, but she let it go. "They want to join the ship. What do you think?"

"Join the ship to go where? We haven't decided if we're still going to Earth, remember? Personally, I'll be happy to survive another couple of weeks."

"You think you're going to die?!"

"I think *we're* going to die. You have the same disease, don't forget. We've been getting sicker and sicker, and no one knows why. Asher and Baxter are good doctors, but even they can't figure it out. What does that tell you?" Parthenia had been focused on her interface for most of this speech, but she turned to Carina as she asked her question with fear in her eyes.

"It tells me..." Carina bit her lip before continuing hastily, "We shouldn't worry about things we can't control."

"Nice cop out, Sis."

Carina rested her head on her pillows. *Were* they going to die? If they died, Oriana, Ferne, and Jace would die too. Bryce would have to raise Darius and Nahla by himself. Darius would be alone as a mage.

Strike that.

He was already alone as a mage. But with his brothers and sisters around, at least he would have people near him who knew what it meant.

The idea of Darius and Nahla losing their entire family was too painful to contemplate. She decided to concentrate on the problem of the visitors from Marchon. Two groups occupying the same ship for a long voyage had been a recipe for disaster in the past. The Lotacryllans had mutinied and murdered Calvaley, and they could have killed Jace too. But, thinking about it, the idea of living alongside the men from Lotacrylla had been doomed from the start. The mercs' introduction to them had been a hard-fought, bloody battle. How could anyone have imagined the two sides would ever get along?

The Marchonish colonists didn't have any history with the Black Dogs, and they would be coming along willingly, unlike the Lotacryllans, who'd had little choice in the matter.

As she saw it, the biggest sticking point was Marchon culture. Their dismissive behavior toward Van Hasty and the comment about 'females for breeding' were telling. If they did join the *Bathsheba*, she could foresee difficulties ahead as their poor attitude toward women came up against Van Hasty's fist.

A wistful pang hit her as she remembered Atoi. What would *she* have made of the Marchonish men? Something broken and bloody, probably.

But, maybe, if they were willing to accept a different way of thinking, it could work. It would certainly solve some of the problems she and the Black Dogs faced with manning the ship during her long journey. Greater numbers meant less time spent with the *Bathsheba* flying on automatic.

Was it worth the risk?

"What are you thinking about?" Parthenia asked.

"What we should do about the party from Marchon."

"You want to let them join us?"

"I haven't decided. What do you think?"

"Why should we help them? They're stupid, aren't they? They deserve everything they get."

Ugh. Parthenia was referring to their conversation at the restaurant on Lakshmi Station.

"I didn't say that exactly."

"Yes, you did. You said the people from the planets at war should just rise up and take over their governments, and they were stupid for not doing it."

Carina was silent.

"But things aren't so simple, are they?"

"Okay, I admit you have a point," Carina conceded. "Seeing them and hearing them speak throws a different light on things. So what do *you* think we should do with them, smartypants?"

"I think we should leave it to the Black Dogs to decide. They're the majority here, and since we lost our mage powers there's nothing special about us to give us any greater say in the decision-making." She sighed. "All I want to do is get better. Whether the Marchonish group stay or go, I only want to be well again."

Carina held out her hand across the gap that separated their beds. Parthenia looked at it for a moment before grasping it.

"Me too, Sis," Carina said. "Me too."

THIRTY

Darius opened his eyes. He was in the Twilight Dome, and Nahla was with him.

She hugged him tightly. "Thank you, Darius! Thank you for taking me with you."

"Of course I took you with me. You're my sister."

She released him and looked down. "I'm different from you, though. I can't Cast like you."

"You're not different anymore. I'm the only one who can Cast now. I'm the one who's different."

Nahla looked up and smiled brightly. "It doesn't matter. Those men were horrible, weren't they? I thought it would be fun to talk to them, but they were nasty."

"Yes, they were." Darius thought for a moment. "Let's stay here a while. I don't think it was a good idea to Cast in front of them, but I didn't know what else to do. If I'd left you there, they might have hurt you."

"I'm glad you didn't." She turned her gaze upward to the starscape shining through the transparent sections of overhead. "Look, it's so pretty."

Darius nodded. "Uh huh."

The old Nahla would have told him the names of the stars and planets, and probably what types and how far away they were too. All the new Nahla saw was their prettiness.

It hurt.

He sat down and tried hard to not cry.

"What shall we do?" asked Nahla.

"I don't know. Play hide-and-seek?"

The room seemed a good place for the game. It was full of tables and chairs of all different kinds, and there were bars in the corners and along the walls. The lighting was dim, too, which meant lots of shadows.

"Okay," Nahla agreed. "You hide first while I count."

"No, you hide and I'll count." He didn't feel completely safe here. He was worried the Marchonish men might be looking for them. Maybe they weren't done with teasing Nahla. The *Bathsheba* was so big the men would probably never find them, but it was better to be careful. He had to keep his sister safe.

He covered his eyes and began counting. As he counted, he heard Nahla moving around as she looked for a good place to hide. She wasn't being careful to be quiet. He could hear she'd gone to the left-hand side of the room.

"Thirty-four, thirty-five, thirty-six..." They hadn't agreed whether he should count to fifty or a hundred. As they were only playing in one room, fifty would be enough, but if he stopped there Nahla might say he was cheating.

He reached fifty and stoically continued, though he couldn't hear her anymore. She'd found her place to hide and was waiting for him.

"You can look for me now!" she called out.

He took his hands away from his face and rolled his eyes. She'd given her hiding place away, just about. She'd shouted from somewhere on his left, near the hull. Should he make a show of looking for her everywhere else first so she didn't feel bad about being found quickly? He set off.

But someone was comming him. "Hi, it's me."

"Hi," said Bryce, sounding relieved. "Where are you?"

When he told him, Bryce went on, "Darius, did you go to see the people from Marchon?" Before he could answer, Bryce added, "It's very important that you tell me the truth."

His guts seemed to squirm.

Nahla popped up from under a table. "Who are you talking to?"

"Bryce."

"What?" Bryce asked.

"I was speaking to Nahla."

"She's there with you? That was my next question."

"Yeah, she's here. Do you want to talk to her?"

"No, Darius. I can comm her too, remember? *Did* you go to see the Marchonish men?"

The tone Bryce was using, as well as his reminder to tell the truth, was making Darius uncomfortable. A hot feeling spread up from his neck over his face. "I, er..."

"If you did, it's okay. You didn't do anything wrong. No one told you to stay away from them. I thought you were both in your suite, but it doesn't matter. That's my fault, not yours. Only, I need to know if they've seen you."

"Yeah," Darius admitted. "We were spying on them, but they saw us. They..." he swallowed "...they were mean to Nahla, Bryce. Really mean!"

"I can believe it. What else happened?"

His distance from Bryce meant he couldn't feel his emotions, but he heard something in the man's tone. He was trying to make what he said sound unimportant, but in fact it was very important.

Bryce was asking if he'd Cast in front of the Marchonish men.

He wanted to deny it. Mother and Carina had told him many times he mustn't Cast around people who weren't mages. He wanted to explain to Bryce why he'd been forced to do it, how he hadn't any choice, but all that came out was a very soft, quiet, "I Cast Transport."

Bryce's heavy sigh rattled out of the comm button.

"Sorry," Darius added.

"You don't have to be sorry. You're just a kid. But it's made things tricky for us. Can you promise me something?"

"Yes, what?"

"That you'll stay right where you are. Some Black Dogs will be there in a couple of minutes."

"Okay, I promise."

"You *and* Nahla, right?"

"Me and Nahla."

"Great. And please don't Cast again, not unless your life depends on it."

"Or Nahla's!"

"All right. Or Nahla's." Bryce cut the comm.

"We have to stay here?" asked Nahla. She'd walked over while he'd been talking and must have heard the last part of the conversation.

"Yeah, but we can carry on playing, I guess."

"I don't feel like it." She slumped into a seat.

"What else do you want to do?"

"I don't feel like doing anything."

He sat down beside her.

"You know when you were showing me how to use my interface yesterday?" she asked.

"Uh huh." They'd watched a show together and she'd wanted to know how to find more things to watch.

"I found something I wrote on it before my accident."

"You did?" He feared what was coming next. Emotions were pouring out of Nahla like a waterfall tumbling over a cliff: sorrow, confusion, and worry.

"I didn't understand it," she said. "How come I wrote it, but now I can't understand it? How's that possible?"

He didn't know what to say. Even if he knew a doctor's explanation for what had happened to her—which he didn't—he felt she was asking something more. How could it be right that she'd gone from being so smart to someone who could barely read? He didn't know how to make her feel better.

Since they'd come to the Lakshmi Station system everything had gone wrong. Nahla and he had nearly died on Deck Zero and she would never be the same again; Carina and his other siblings had lost their special abilities, and they'd all gotten so sick he couldn't bear thinking about it. Then the people from Marchon had arrived, and now they knew he could Cast.

The doors opened and light from the passageway lit up the entrance, creating silhouettes of the four heavily muscled figures who stood there.

For a terrifying instant, Darius thought the Marchonish men had found them, but then he recalled his conversation with Bryce. He also noticed one of the figures had lost an arm.

"Hey, kids," said the one-armed man. "Uncle Jackson's here to look after you."

Thirty-One

Bryce closed the comm to Darius.

Shit. Shit. Shit.

Jackson had listened in to the conversation and immediately left with Rees and two more Black Dogs. Bryce didn't doubt the mercs would protect Darius and Nahla with their lives, but the situation was getting seriously out of hand. The group from Marchon had turned from an annoying problem into a real threat, and if he hadn't been paying attention to what a Marchonish man said, he might have missed it.

He'd sensed a change in the atmosphere when he'd returned with the mercs to the mission room. There was something different about the way the men looked at them, something hidden behind their friendly smiles and greetings. A menacing intent had entered their expressions. Jackson picked up on it too. He faked scratching his back to turn to Bryce and whisper, "Something's up."

"Do you think they've guessed our decision?"

"Nah, it isn't that." Jackson faced the group again, his eyes narrowing.

Porcher stepped forward. "We appreciate your consideration of our proposal and are anxious to hear your response."

Bryce had agreed to let the older man deliver the news. If Carina were well, she would probably have handled it, only she was so ill she had him seriously worried. Would she think they'd come to the wrong decision? Maybe not, though she would be pissed off no one had asked her opinion. But what help was her opinion when she clearly wasn't thinking straight?

"I'll get right to the point," said Jackson. "We've given your request serious thought, but the answer's no."

"I see," said Porcher, not losing his fatuous smile. "Are you going to grace us with your reasoning?"

"I guess you deserve that at least. Two groups on the same ship won't work. We tried it in the past, and the other group ended up taking a spacewalk with no suits. We're not prepared to take the same risk again. That's about the long and short of it, though several of us said they'd be happy to take your women."

"Our women!" Porcher echoed before bursting into guffaws. He turned, amazed and amused, to his companions, who shared his reaction. A short period followed where the Marchonish men laughed and Bryce and the mercs watched them in silence. When Porcher's laughter subsided, he wiped his eyes and said sarcastically, "A most generous offer. I can see why you would want our females, but they are not available."

Bryce had a strong suspicion he entirely misunderstood the mercs' motivation. He thought the Black Dogs wanted the women for sex and children, but it had been Van Hasty who had suggested accepting the Marchonish women onto the ship, in order to save them from men who treated them like cattle.

It didn't matter. Only the men were aboard the *Bathsheba*. The women were waiting on their ship and inaccessible. They would probably never learn they'd had a chance to escape their planet, but their men had refused on their behalf.

"So that's it?" asked Porcher. "We leave now and you continue on your journey without us?"

Jackson replied testily, "I'm not sure what else you expect. You came here uninvited and we were gracious enough to allow you aboard and listen to what you had to say. You asked and we answered. The discussion's over."

The tension in the room moved up a notch.

Jackson had anticipated trouble. Every merc was carrying a handgun. A condition of entry for the Marchonish party had been that they were unarmed.

That should have been the end of it. It would be suicide to go up against the mercs considering the imbalance of firepower. But the Marchonish men were surprisingly uncowed.

"What if we refuse to leave?" asked Porcher.

"I can't believe you would be so stupid," Jackson replied.

Still, the men didn't move.

"You're missing out on a great opportunity," said Porcher. "Maybe you should think it over some more."

"We'll escort you back to your ship now," said Jackson.

Porcher's arms jerked up, causing the mercs to reach for their weapons. He gave a fake yawn and stretched his arms out wide. "No need to get jumpy, boys. We won't outstay our welcome."

Someone muttered, "You already have."

Slowly and lazily, the men who had been sitting got to their feet. The others began to move slowly toward the exit, the Black Dogs stepping aside to give them room to pass. Some lacked Porcher's faux nonchalance and were grumbling and mumbling while they walked by.

"We didn't have to give up so easy," one of them said.

"Don't worry," his friend replied, "once we get the word out about that kid, they won't be going anywhere."

That was all Bryce heard before the men left. But he didn't need to hear any more. Dread rose up in him. There were only two kids on the ship the men from Marchon could have seen. He hadn't known they were in this section. The last time he'd seen Darius and Nahla they'd been playing happily in their room.

No one would have any reason to 'get the word out' about Nahla. She was only a little girl battling the effects of her accident. But Darius... There was a lot to be told about Darius, or rather one thing in particular. And if anyone outside the *Bathsheba* knew about it, a world of trouble could descend on their heads.

"Wait!" he blurted.

All movement in the room stalled.

"What's up?" Jackson asked. He was at the door, waiting for the last of the visitors to leave.

"I think we were too hasty," said Bryce. "We should talk it over some more."

Jackson frowned. "I don't think so. Everyone had their say and we voted so..."

"You're going to discuss it again?" asked a Marchonish man hopefully. "We don't have to leave?"

"No," said Bryce. "You don't have to go yet." He pushed through the throng to the doorway, where Jackson was eyeing him quizzically. He called down the passageway to the departing men, "Come back! Come back in here. We're going to have another discussion about your proposal."

Porcher had been leading his men back to the airlock. His head turned and he called back, "What did you say?"

Jackson said, "Bryce, what the fuck are you doing?"

Ignoring him, Bryce answered Porcher. "You and your men can stay here tonight. We need more time to—"

Jackson grabbed his arm.

"Trust me!" he hissed.

Jackson gave him a dark look, but he released his hold. "Yeah, you can all stay another few hours while we, er, hear some more opinions."

Thirty-Two

"We have to kill them," said Van Hasty. "What other choice do we have? After we've killed them, we board their ship, kill any other men we find, bring the women here and then blow the ship up. The women don't know about Darius, and if we leave the system with them right away, when they find out it won't matter."

Bryce couldn't help but think her opinion was colored by attitudes to gender in Marchonish culture, but she did make some good points. They couldn't risk knowledge of Darius's abilities to leak to Marchon or anywhere else. Even a non-aggressive society would be very interested in a kid with mage powers, let alone the three militaristic ones on the *Bathsheba's* doorstep.

Yet he still had nightmares over the time they'd spaced the Lotacryllans. He wasn't sure he could do the same thing again or be a party to it. He didn't like the Marchonish men and thought their attitudes were ridiculous, but they hadn't actually *done* anything threatening. All they'd done was put their case for inclusion in what they believed was a colonization expedition. It wouldn't be right to kill them for something they *might* do.

"I know what you're thinking," said Van Hasty, watching him, "but we aren't in court. We're not judges or a jury. We're talking about the life of a little kid and all the rest of our lives too. It's them or us. You know what the fuckers would do if they got a chance."

"We do," Hsiao agreed, "but how do you know their women won't do the same?"

"Why would they when we rescued them from those pricks?"

Bryce sighed and shook his head. "I wish Jace was well enough to be here."

Jackson snorted. "Jace would want us to invite every bastard in the three systems aboard."

He'd given over guard duty to other mercs, who were currently guarding Darius and Nahla in their suite while the Marchonish men had been taken to the Twilight Dome to sleep.

"He would try to find a non-violent solution to the problem," said Bryce. "That's what we're missing. There has to be an alternative to killing probably a hundred men and who knows how many women because some of them saw something they shouldn't have. It's so ruthless."

"The black's a harsh place," said Jackson in a tone that made Bryce grateful he didn't add a patronizing 'kid' at the end of his sentence. "You have to be ruthless to survive."

"If I might say something?" asked Justus.

He hadn't taken part in the first discussion, saying he was a guest himself so the decision should be up to the Black Dogs. But now the question had broadened out, he'd been invited to the meeting.

"Go ahead," said Hsiao.

"Whatever we do with the Marchonish, we have to factor in our business on Lakshmi. We aren't done there yet. We haven't upgraded the *Bathsheba's* defenses, and we were planning on re-stocking supplies before we left."

"Why does that matter?" Van Hasty asked.

"Because we're aboard the biggest ship in the sky. The Marchonish group saw us, and we can be sure plenty of others are watching and listening in our direction too. If one of our visitors manages to get word out during your proposed slaughter, Marchon military might turn its attention from its enemies to us."

"So you're saying we should complete our business before we kill anyone?" asked Van Hasty.

"Not exactly, but close."

Hsiao explained, "He's saying we need to finish dealing with Lakshmi before we deal with our problem here."

"That's it," said Justus.

"And what is our business with Lakshmi?" Bryce asked. "Carina hasn't been able to talk much since she got back, but as I understand it no one on the station could help Nahla."

"That's right," said Hsiao. "That's what she told me before she got sick."

"Damn," said Jackson.

"You need to talk to the doctors about replacing your arm," said Justus.

"That's not a priority right now. I'm left-handed, so it isn't a big deal."

Justus scoffed, "You're planning on going all the way to Earth one-armed when you have the best medical facilities in the sector right here?"

"He's right," said Van Hasty. "Stop playing the martyr and get it fixed. I don't want to fight beside you unless you have four functioning limbs. How are you going to suit up, moron?"

"All right! I'll get a new arm. But what are we gonna do about the assholes in the dome?"

"You know what I think," said Van Hasty. "Nothing anyone says will change that. I'm going to check on Carina while you guys make a decision."

Her departure brought a pause to the discussion.

Eventually, Bryce said, "There has to be another option than massacring a bunch of unarmed men."

"If there is," said Jackson, "I'm not seeing it. Not if we want to keep Darius out of the hands of the first space fleet that manages to board our ship."

"One child's life against a hundred others?" Bryce asked.

"One innocent life against a load of worthless shitheads," Jackson countered.

"What do you think, Justus?"

"I see both sides. I'm military too, and I've seen more soldiers die in a minute than we're talking about here. But I'm sick of fighting and bloodshed. If there's a way we can avoid murdering those men, I'm willing to hear it."

"I feel the same," said Hsiao. "I can see the necessity, and if we were measuring the worth of one life against another, I would say Darius deserves to live more than anyone we've seen from Marchon or anyone here. The kid has a special gift that could be used to do a lot of good and improve the lives of millions. We have a duty to protect him at all costs. Plus, as we know, if we allow a hair of his head to be harmed Carina will kill us all."

"True," Bryce agreed. "I'd rather face the Marchon, Quinton, and Gugong space fleets put together."

"But at the same time," Hsiao continued, "the idea of executing the men just because of something they know leaves a sour taste in my mouth."

"This is all fine and good," said Jackson, "but I'm not hearing an alternative."

"There has to be another solution," said Bryce. "What about taking them with us but marooning them somewhere along our way?"

"Too risky," Jackson replied. "Once they're all aboard, I'm pretty sure they will outnumber us. We would end up not waking up from Deep Sleep."

No one mentioned the idea of swearing the Marchonish men to secrecy. That was plainly ridiculous.

Jackson's comm chirruped.

"Porcher wants a chat," said a voice at the other end.

"Damn," said Jackson. "He must have guessed something's up."

"Maybe," said Bryce. "I'll come with you."

The Marchonish men had spread themselves out in the Twilight Dome, sprawling on the sofas and deck, making themselves at home in a way that left Bryce feeling uncomfortable. They were already acting as though they owned the place, and Porcher had an arrogant look in his eye.

"Over here," he said, beckoning.

Jackson calmly halted and tucked his remaining thumb into his belt, refusing to bend to Porcher's power play. The Marchonish man was forced to walk over to them. A smile and a scowl struggled for control of his face. "I was wondering how the talks are going."

"That's it?" Jackson asked. "That's why you made us come up here? You'll find out how the talks went when they're over." He turned to leave.

"That's not all."

"What else do you want?" Jackson growled, turning back.

"There's something else you should know."

"What?"

"Before we came here, we told a lot of people where we were going. Parents who were too old to come along, friends and relations who wanted to stay on Marchon. They'll be waiting for news. If they don't hear from us soon, they'll inform the Marchon Government, which will be interested in finding out what's happened to its citizens."

"That it?"

"That's it, for now."

After they left, Bryce said, "You were right. He's guessed this isn't any longer about whether they can join us. Do you believe what he said about the Marchon Government?"

"Why would it give a shit about a couple hundred opportunists leaving its system? But it shows they aren't going to patiently wait for days on end for us to make up our minds, and we can't forget about the men they left behind on their ship. I'm going to double the guards on the airlock and the dome door. We need to come to a decision fast."

THIRTY-THREE

A shadow fell over Carina, and she opened her eyes. A tall woman stood next to her bed, blocking the light.

"Van Hasty?"

"Hi." The merc dragged a chair over.

Carina winced at the noise of chair legs scraping on tile.

"How are you doing?" Van Hasty asked as she sat down.

"It's nice of you to come and see me." If this woman was paying her a visit she must be dying. Van Hasty wasn't renowned for her compassion toward her fellow mercs, or anyone else for that matter.

"No problem." She rested her hands on her spread knees, bent forward, and peered into Carina's face. "You look like shit."

"Thanks." Carina turned onto her back and tried to sit up.

After watching her for a couple of seconds in confused silence, Van Hasty helped her by grabbing her shoulders and hauling her upward. Then she bent her forward while adjusting her pillows and thrust her into them. "Is that better?"

"Uhhh..." Carina felt like she'd just finished Basic again with the Sherrerrs. "What's happening? No one's telling me anything."

"That's what I thought. We have a big problem to sort out. Hsiao and the guys are talking about it now, but you should know what's going on too. It concerns Darius."

"Huh?" She sat up straighter. "Is he okay?"

"He's fine, but... Let me tell you what's been going on." Van Hasty began to explain the events of the last few hours, during which Carina had been wondering why Bryce hadn't been to see her, and why Asher had looked so worried when she checked up on her.

As she listened, her heart beat faster. Before the merc had finished her tale, she guessed where it was headed and broke in, "They know about Darius's ability."

Van Hasty nodded grimly.

"*Dammit.*"

"Yeah."

"What are they going to do?"

"That's what they're talking about. I gave them my opinion and came to see you."

"Thanks, I appreciate it."

But Carina didn't know what to tell the merc. She could barely think, let alone get up and go to the defense of her brother, which was her first impulse. Since she'd collapsed in the passageway after trying to find out what was happening on the ship, she'd felt sicker and sicker. Moving her limbs was a Herculean task, an industrial compactor had set up in her head, and even thinking about food caused her to retch for minutes at a time.

Parthenia, meanwhile, seemed to have passed out entirely. She hadn't opened her eyes in hours. Carina wasn't sure if Asher or Baxter had given her a sedative or it was the effect of their illness. She couldn't remember if a doctor had given her something. Her memory was hazy as she'd drifted in and out of consciousness herself.

Seeming to sense she wasn't capable of forming coherent thoughts about the problem, Van Hasty got to her feet. "I shouldn't have bothered you. I didn't realize you were so sick."

"No, stay. Or...call Asher for me."

When the doctor arrived, Carina asked her for a stimulant.

"Why?" Asher looked from her to Van Hasty as if suspecting they were colluding to commit a crime.

"I have to think something through, but I can't. My brain won't work."

"Out of the question. You're already on the maximum doses of medications to control your symptoms, and you're far too weak. If I give you anything else it could stop your heart or give you a stroke. I don't think you understand how sick you are."

"Oh, I do. Believe me. But I have to be able to think. Darius is in danger. We all are."

"You mean the group from Marchon?" The doctor pursed her lips and frowned at Van Hasty. "It was very unwise to come here and bother her with this." To Carina, she said, "Other people are perfectly capable of dealing with the problem. Leave them to it and concentrate on getting better."

"Stop bullshitting me!" Carina spat, though her voice was pathetically weak. "I'm not going to get better. You said yourself you and Baxter don't have the first clue what's wrong with me. Only one outcome is possible now. I don't have much time left, but what time I do have I want to spend helping my brother. Give me something so I can think!"

The older woman stared at her, and for a second her stony expression broke, revealing anguish and guilt. She turned on her heel and marched out of the room without another word.

Van Hasty raised her eyebrows.

An uncomfortable pause followed.

Van Hasty said, "Do you think she's gonna—"

The door slid open and Asher returned, holding a syringe aloft like a weapon. She halted at Carina's bedside. "Do you take full responsibility?"

"Yes, I— *Ahhhh.*"

The doctor had forced the syringe against her upper arm and its contents exploded into her bloodstream. A cleansing wave washed over her. Suddenly she knew how it was to be completely well again. Her mind cleared, the ache left her muscles, and she no longer felt like a lead weight was holding her down on the bed. Then her pulse began to pound and her skin was instantly wet with sweat. Her hands began to tremble. But she could think. At last, she could finally think. "I might know a way. Just give me a minute."

"We have to kill them all, right?" said Van Hasty.

Carina glanced at her sister, pale, thin, and asleep on the neighboring bed. "Maybe not."

It took her longer than a few minutes to think up a plan, but when she had it, she felt confident it would work and she hadn't forgotten anything. She told Van Hasty. As she spoke, the stimulant started to wear off. The lead weight began to descend again, pinning her to the mattress. The hammering in her head resumed and the dreadful nausea returned.

Dr Asher had waited by her bed the entire time, watching the figures on the wall interface, tutting and shaking her head.

When Carina had finished her short explanation, Van Hasty said, "I'll tell them. They might not agree, but I'll tell them."

There wasn't anything else she could do. She was descending to the depths of her illness for what seemed the last time.

As Van Hasty was leaving, Carina asked Asher, "Am I dying?"

"I haven't given up hope yet, and neither should you."

Van Hasty halted at the door. "Everyone dies, Carina. The only win you get in life is outliving your enemies."

THIRTY-FOUR

Porcher reached out and grabbed Bryce's hand before shaking it forcefully. He did the same with Justus but, moving to shake Jackson's right hand, he hesitated, forgetting it was missing. He grinned and grasped his left hand instead.

He awkwardly nodded at Hsiao and Van Hasty, and then, redirecting his attention to the men, he said, "I can't thank you enough. You've come to the right decision. You won't regret it."

"We have some things to do before we leave the system," said Jackson. "You'll have time to get settled in. The *Bathsheba's* a big ship. There's plenty of room for everyone. I'd suggest spreading yourselves around rather than all of you settling in one spot. It'll help you integrate."

"Right." Porcher paused and smiled uncomfortably. "I think we would prefer our women to remain aboard our ship for now. Maybe when we begin our voyage we will bring them aboard. It will be necessary in order for them to go into Deep Sleep, naturally."

"You...what?" asked Van Hasty. "They can't come aboard?"

Bryce nudged her with his elbow. "We understand you might be worried about them mingling with the Black Dogs, but you don't have anything to fear on that account. I've lived with the mercs for over a year, and, contrary to their looks, they're very well behaved."

"Thanks for the glowing endorsement," Jackson muttered.

"Nevertheless," Porcher countered, "it would be better for all if our females stay apart from your company for the time being. Speaking as a Marchonish man, I can assure you that's what they want."

Van Hasty burst out, "Well, aren't they lucky to have you—"

"If that's what's best," said Bryce, "we'll take your word for it."

"It is," said Porcher. "Now, if you don't mind, I'll tell my men the good news. Then some of us will return to our ship to begin bringing our belongings aboard." Porcher left with a spring in his step.

"That's *that* done," said Jackson after waiting for him to pass out of earshot. "So we aren't as bad as we look?" he asked Bryce.

"Not quite."

Jackson cuffed his head, though not hard.

"I mean," Bryce went on, laughing, "you do have a few redeeming features."

Jackson cuffed him again.

"Quit it," said Hsiao. "He was only feeding into Marchonish prejudices. That's right, isn't it, Bryce?"

"Yeah, something like that." Bryce suddenly remembered Carina, whose idea they were following, and his chest grew tight. The way things were going she might not live to see the outcome of her plan. If the worst happened, how would he carry on without her? He would have to somehow for Darius and Nahla's sake.

Jackson's hand descended on his shoulder. "Coming with us to Lakshmi Station?"

"I don't know if I should. I think I should stay here to look after the kids."

"They're coming too."

"They are? But that wasn't part of the plan. Carina wouldn't approve. She would want us to keep them safe."

"That's why we have to take them with us," Hsiao explained. "The people from Marchon know there's something special about them. They saw Darius and Nahla disappear into thin air, so they're going to keep a very close eye on them from now on. It's much better for the kids to stick with us."

"Yeah," Bryce conceded, "you're right."

"Besides," Jackson said, "I'll be visiting medical centers to see if they can shed any light on what's wrong with the mages and talk to them about fixing my arm. I can ask about treatment for Nahla too. I might still find someone who can help her."

The proposal of bringing the children along on their next visit to Lakshmi was making more and more sense.

"It's a shame the mages are too weak to go to the station," said Bryce. "We should have taken them there earlier."

"They deteriorated faster than anyone expected," said Hsiao sadly. "It's taken everyone by surprise."

Only Jackson, Hsiao, Bryce, and now Darius and Nahla would be going to Lakshmi. Van Hasty would remain behind to keep an eye on the Marchonish men, and they couldn't risk taking any other mercs due to the events of the previous visit. A similar episode might bankrupt them, and they needed all the funds they had to purchase the space weapon Carina had suggested.

———

Bryce had heard so much about Lakshmi Station. Hsiao had described the hordes of people and aliens and the huge numbers of shops and facilities. Carina had told him about the friend she'd made, the guide Bongo. Even Darius had chimed in, talking about the range of weird foods on the menu at the restaurant where he'd eaten.

Yet none of it prepared Bryce for his first sight of the station from the *Peregrine's* bridge.

He'd never seen so many starships of so many kinds in one place. There were battleships being serviced, repaired, and fitted out, dwarfing the engineering vessels that flitted across and between them. Huge cargo haulers hung in space, too large to ever enter a planetary atmosphere. Commercial cruise liners floated along, sleek and luxurious, probably heading for exotic destinations. Or perhaps they were simply taking their passengers beyond any government's jurisdiction, where they could push the bounds of legal behavior without fear of repercussions. Private starships built for speed zipped along almost too fast to detect.

And the station itself was vast, easily the biggest man-made structure he'd ever heard of, let alone seen. It was hard to imagine how it sustained itself. How could there be sufficient people in the surrounding area to support it? But then, he reminded himself, three entire worlds contributed to its existence —billions of people, out of which probably only a fraction ever had the opportunity to visit. Though, from what he understood, hundreds of thousands lived on the station, either permanently or as part of an ever-changing contingent of migrant workers, shipped in from the three worlds and farther afield.

"Where do we dock?" he asked Hsiao, noting what looked like lines of ships vaguely spiraling out from several of the many points of the star.

"It wouldn't mean anything if I told you, but it's the same spot we've docked the previous two times. The station authorities seem to want to keep us in one area."

"Is visitor movement restricted inside?"

"Not officially. The last time I was here..." she looked abashed "...we were taken far from the commercial zone. Hours away. And I didn't see any signs prohibiting entry to anywhere. But my guess is most visitors never leave the district nearest their docking point. The place is too big, and you can find anything you might need in just one of the points of the star."

"What goes on in the middle?"

She shrugged. "I'm not sure, but maybe it's where the permanent residents live? The arms dealers, tycoons, business moguls, and so on. They probably don't want to mix with the shoppers and tourists."

"And they don't want to live on any of the planets."

"No, and we know why."

Van Hasty had returned from Carina's bedside with a horrific story. The war that maintained Lakshmi Station was artificially generated. Billions had given their lives so others could live in optimal luxury. It was no wonder the party from Marchon was desperate to escape.

Despite the magnificence of the station's appearance, it sickened Bryce to go there. Simply setting foot on it would feel like he was contributing to the injustice. And they weren't only going there, they were fueling the economy by purchasing a weapon.

He'd tried to speak to Carina about her plan before he left, but she'd been too out of it to have a proper conversation. He'd only been able to hold her, tell her he loved her and hoped she would get better soon. He'd said Darius and Nahla were okay and not to worry, but he wasn't sure she'd understood.

Silently, he watched the station grow larger until the point they were headed toward dominated the view.

THIRTY-FIVE

When Bongo heard Carina and Parthenia were ill, his legs lost some of their tension and his body sagged between them. "You should have brought them here. Lakshmi Station has the finest—"

"They're too sick," Hsiao interrupted. "It started after they got back from their last visit."

"You don't think they contracted their illness here, do you? The station managers are usually excellent at maintaining high levels of hygiene."

"Some of our crew members fell ill before they returned, people who have never been here."

"Then it's something aboard your ship?" He crawled backward a couple of steps.

"It's hard to explain why, but you don't have to be concerned about catching it. Carina and the others who are unwell are... Well, they're different from the rest of us. Everyone else on the *Bathsheba* is fine."

Bongo crawled closer. "I'm glad only a few of your crew members are affected. How can I help you today?"

Hsiao told him about the two purposes for their visit.

"Have you brought any samples for the staff at the treatment center to test?"

"We have." The pilot lifted the refrigerated box containing vials of bodily fluids and swabs from the patients.

"I hope you can find someone to help you. And I see you've brought the little girl back too. Maybe you'll be more successful this time. However, I can't be in two places at once. I can't take you to medical centers and to arms dealers. Let me ask my cousin if she's free to help out."

Whatever method of communicating the alien used, Bryce couldn't see. Bongo bounced gently two or three times, and then he seemed to be waiting.

Bryce occupied the time by watching the crowds and surveying the myriad of establishments lining the walkways around him. In reality, his mind was tens of thousands of kilometers away in the sick bay of a colony starship.

A figure two heads taller than the tallest person in the surrounding throng came striding toward them. Skin softly scaled, hairless, her pupils vertical slits, she was otherwise vaguely human, though there was no telling what lay under her shirt, pants, and boots.

"Ah, here she comes," said Bongo.

"That's your *cousin*?" Hsiao asked, her jaw going slack.

"On one of my mothers' side, far distant. And from a different planet, naturally."

Bryce and Hsiao exchanged a look.

"Scroocher," he hailed her as she neared them.

"Bongo." She leaned down to pat his head, which he didn't appear to mind.

"I'm about to show this young lady and her one-armed companion to several of our best hospitals. Would you accompany the remainder of the party to reputable starship weapons suppliers?"

"My pleasure."

Hsiao handed the medical samples box to Jackson.

"*Scroocher*," she muttered as they set off. "This place gets crazier by the minute."

———

By the time they reached the fifth arms dealer, Bryce had begun to despair. What they were looking for seemed impossible to find. When they explained to Scroocher the weapon they had in mind, hoping she could narrow down the field of prospective suppliers for them, she leaned her head back.

Was she thinking? Surprised? Comming Bongo?

Bryce had no idea.

Her head returned to vertical. "I've never heard of such a thing."

"Oh come on," said Hsiao. "A place like this? Best weapons technology in the sector? There has to be."

"Wait here," said Scroocher. "I'll see what I can find."

"Where's she going?" Bryce asked Hsiao as the alien disappeared into the crowd. "I can't believe she can't look up whatever she wants on the local net."

"It is strange," Hsiao agreed.

Turning to Darius, who had quietly accompanied them on every failed attempt to secure the specialized weapon, Bryce asked, "Scroocher is a good person, right? Can you tell?"

"Uh huh. She's okay. She's like a fizzy drink, sweet and bubbly."

"A fizzy drink?" asked Hsiao, squinting after the departing alien.

They had to wait half an hour for Scroocher to return, by which time they'd begun to wonder if she'd abandoned them. But then they spotted her scaly head weaving from side to side as she navigated the ever-present throng of visitors. When she arrived, she scrutinized them for a few seconds as if making up her mind about something. "Will this be your last visit to Lakshmi? If you can find the weapon you desire?"

"Yes," Bryce quickly replied before Hsiao said anything to the contrary.

If Jackson managed to find a medical center that could treat the mages, they might actually end up returning, but it appeared whatever Scroocher had to offer them was contingent on their never coming back.

Darius looked up at him, frowning.

Shit. The kid could tell when people were lying.

"Then follow me," said the alien.

Hsiao asked Bryce, "Are you sure—"

"Absolutely. If we get what we want, why would we return?"

Scroocher led the group to the other side of the concourse and for the rest of the way they stayed close to the wall, passing the entrances to the many and varied facilities. Noise blared from some, odors from others, and some were dark and silent, though people entered and left just the same.

When they arrived at the next stage of their journey, Bryce almost didn't see the exit point. Scroocher halted at an area of plain wall. Looking closer, however, it became clear a door stood there. Exactly the same color and texture as the wall, it was almost invisible.

Checking from side to side, the alien pushed it halfway open, creating a gap only just wide enough to slip through, and motioned everyone into it. Once they were all inside, she closed the door. It was only then the lights turned on in the passageway.

Bryce was reminded of the security area he'd passed through when they'd arrived at the station. No decoration marked the walls, and there were only two options for movement: forward or back the way you came.

Scroocher took them forward.

Hsiao gave Bryce a worried look.

He felt the same. They were clearly traveling into the less-orthodox regions of Lakshmi. If it had only been him and Hsiao he might only have felt more alert and wary, but he didn't like the idea of taking Darius with them. Ironically, this was even though the little mage was more capable than either of them of extracting himself from a dangerous situation, as he'd shown with the Marchonish men. Bryce had told him to bring his elixir as a precaution, hoping he wouldn't have to use it.

They left the noise and bustle of the regular areas of the station far behind as they traveled the nondescript corridor. Apart from themselves, it was nearly empty. They saw only one other person: a small, slight man with a long beard. He fast-walked past them. Neither he nor Scroocher acknowledged the other, as if pretending they hadn't seen them.

Bryce counted three plain doors the same as the one they'd entered by, lacking any sign or adornment, before the alien stopped at the fourth. Resting a hand on it, she said, "You never came here, you never met this person, and you didn't see anything, okay?"

"Okay," Bryce and Hsiao replied simultaneously.

"Okay," Darius solemnly echoed.

Scroocher smiled and ruffled his hair.

Then she opened the door.

THIRTY-SIX

A bald, fat man sat at a low table. His legs barely fit beneath it, and his gut hung over the surface like a dessert pudding waiting to be sliced up and served.

In each corner sat larger men with... Bryce did a double take.

For the first time since entering the station, he saw weapons.

The men were armed, pulse rifles held easily across their laps. As Bryce's gaze moved from the weapons to the men's eyes, one of them winked.

"Take a seat," said the fat man, sweeping a hand in the direction of low stools standing between them and the table. They were even lower than the man's chair, designed to put clients at a psychological disadvantage, no doubt.

"Cute kid," he added as they sat.

Hsiao shot Bryce a glance that expressed how he felt too—they were getting in far deeper than they'd intended. He wished Jackson were here. Even one-armed, the merc was better suited to this environment than he was or, he suspected, Hsiao. She was a good pilot, but she rarely saw combat or had dealings with lowlifes.

Scroocher hovered near the door, looking nervous.

"I hear you're in the market for a rather special space weapon," the man asked. "Am I right?"

"Yes," Bryce replied. "I'm—"

"No names!" The man held up a hand in warning.

Bryce continued, "I'm here on behalf of a friend who can't make it, but we'll do our best to describe the weapon she wants."

"Before we discuss it," said Hsiao, "I should check with another member of our party. He's seeking out medical treatment and if he's successful it'll affect our budget."

"No comm in here," the man said. "At least, not any you can access."

It was potentially a big problem. Unless they could speak to Jackson they wouldn't know if he'd agreed to pay some of their funds in return for a cure for the mages or Nahla. A new prosthetic arm wouldn't make a significant dent in their creds, but they had no idea how much they might have to pay for other treatments, which took priority over space armaments.

"Relax," said the man. "We're just talking, right? We can discuss payment later, if I have what you want." He poured a drink from a jug into two glasses and pushed them across the table before pouring another one for himself. The liquid was vivid purple and gave off a vapor.

"Sudden Death, right?" asked Hsiao.

The man smiled. "The lady knows her cocktails."

"Only take a sip," Hsiao murmured to Bryce.

He did as she suggested. Just a taste of the drink was enough to make him feel as though he was losing grip on reality. He guessed whatever was in it could be absorbed through the membranes inside his mouth and throat.

"What are you drinking?" Darius whispered, though in fact his voice must have been plain for everyone to hear. "Can I have some?"

The man and his two goons laughed.

"No, sonny," said the arms dealer. "This isn't for you. I see you've brought your own drink. Have some of that if you're thirsty."

Darius looked warily up at Bryce.

Bryce wasn't sure what exactly the look meant. Was Darius asking if he could drink some elixir to refresh himself? He didn't think so. He'd never seen any of the mages do that. Elixir didn't taste pleasant. You would have to be pretty dehydrated to consider drinking it not for its specific purpose.

Was Darius asking him if it was okay to Cast?

He couldn't imagine why the boy would want to. As a precaution, he gave a slight shake of his head.

The dealer focused on Bryce and Hsiao. "Now we've oiled the wheels, let's get down to business."

Bryce described what they wanted.

The dealer listened attentively. When Bryce reached the end of the description, he said, "Tell me about your ship."

"Is that really necessary?" asked Hsiao.

As they'd already discovered with the Marchonish men, the *Bathsheba* was a desirable prize. The last thing they should be doing was giving details about her to this shady character.

"It's necessary if you want me to supply a weapon to fit her," said the man. "Do you think space armaments are one-size-fits-all? This is complex equipment we're talking about. Are you serious? Do you want to do business or not?"

"We're serious," Bryce assured him. "Just cautious. I'm sure you understand."

He nodded. "A little caution is wise. But in this world you've entered there must also be trust. I'm trusting you just by allowing you to speak to me. If there's no reciprocation, our talk is over."

"We don't want the talk to be over," said Bryce.

Hsiao said, "I'll tell you about our ship." She gave the dealer the rough specifications. "I can send the details later via an encrypted comm."

He listened attentively, his gaze never leaving her face. "I can see where your reluctance comes from, but you have nothing to fear from me. I have no need for a colony ship. There's no better place to be than Lakshmi, and I have more wealth than I can ever spend. I only dabble in semi-legal armaments for the thrill. When you can buy anything and everything you want life loses its edge, if you know what I mean."

"Do you have the weapon we need?" Hsiao asked brusquely.

"I think I do, but indulge me a little further. What you're asking for is extremely expensive, as I'm sure you can guess. Why not use all those creds to purchase a range of armaments? Placing all your bets on only one is foolish, and you two don't strike me as idiots."

"We have our reasons," said Bryce. "Don't tell me you need to know those too."

The dealer held up his hands, palms outward. "That's your concern. Just offering a little friendly advice. So..." He turned to one of his men and nodded. The man got up and left the room by the rear door. "It will take me some time to arrange transportation and a team to fit the device. We're looking at 48 hours minimum to remove the equipment from storage and run checks, then another three or four days to ship and fit it, depending on what the team finds when they arrive at your vessel."

"A week?" asked Hsiao.

It seemed a long time to Bryce as well, but it was only to be expected considering the dimensions and complexity of the weapon.

"Roughly a week," the dealer confirmed, "give or take a day or two."

His man returned bearing a cred reader.

"We haven't talked about the price yet," said Bryce.

"I have a figure in mind."

"A firm figure?" asked Hsiao. "We don't have unlimited funds and, as I said, we aren't sure what else we might need to pay for."

"Reasonably firm. Naturally, I can't lose money on the deal. Your other expenses are not my concern. I require fifty percent down payment before you leave this room, the balance to be paid upon installation and successful testing."

"I'm guessing there's no written contract," said Bryce.

"If there were, you wouldn't be talking to me. You would be out on the concourse somewhere, listening to a one-hundred-percent-legit dealer telling you they can't help you."

Bryce shared an anxious look with Hsiao. If they agreed to the man's terms, they would be committing a large amount of the *Bathsheba's* crew's remaining money, possibly spending money already earmarked for medical treatment.

"What kind of figure are we talking about?" Bryce asked.

When the dealer answered, he and Hsiao drew in a breath. It was nearly all the creds remaining in the account.

"That's too much!" Hsiao blurted. "We can't afford—"

"Then you've wasted both our time," said the man, rising to his feet

"Wait a moment," Bryce said. "You said the amount isn't completely firm. Can you give us a discount? We have children aboard, who we're taking to find a new home." He rested a hand on Darius's head. The boy peered up at him.

"Trying to appeal to my humanity?" asked the dealer, sitting down. "I'm too cynical and jaded for that. But I would like this deal to go ahead. It isn't every day I get to sell such a specialized weapon. I'll knock off five percent."

"Five percent?" Bryce did the mental calculation.

Hsiao sadly shook her head at him. It was still far too much.

"It's too expensive!" exclaimed Darius, no doubt picking up on Bryce and Hsiao's anxiety.

Everyone except those two laughed, Scroocher included. She'd stayed by the door the entire time in silence.

"Is it, young man?" the dealer asked, smiling.

"I'm afraid it is," Hsiao said. "It does look like we've wasted your time."

Bryce was gutted. Carina's idea had been so good, but they didn't have a way of carrying it out, not if they also wanted to buy a cure for the mages' awful disease and pay other medical expenses.

The atmosphere in the room descended into mutual disappointment. The dealer stood up again and motioned to his men it was time to leave.

"I'm thirsty!" Darius announced as he unscrewed the lid of his elixir bottle.

Bryce's eyes widened. "Darius," he cautioned, instantly aware of what the boy intended to do.

"Very thirsty," he insisted and took a swallow of elixir. "That's better." He closed his eyes.

Darius's actions were so deliberate and odd, the arms dealer and his men stuck around to watch him.

A few seconds was all it took for the Cast to take effect.

The dealer's eyes lost their focus. "You know, maybe I was too hasty. Maybe I can give you a better deal. What do you say to a fifty percent discount?"

His men stared at each other, but neither intervened.

Bryce underwent an internal struggle. Darius had created a situation with many pitfalls, yet they would never be able to carry out Carina's plan without the weapon. "A fifty percent discount sounds great."

THIRTY-SEVEN

It wasn't until after Scroocher had taken them to meet up with Jackson and Bongo, and left them alone outside the treatment center, that Bryce could finally talk to Darius about his Cast. "What you did back there was kind but not very smart."

The boy looked glum. "Sorry."

"What are you talking about?" Hsiao objected. "He saved us a heck ton of money."

"For how long?" Bryce asked.

In response to the pilot's puzzled look, he went on, "Carina told me about the Cast Darius did. It has a time limit."

"Ohhh..." Understanding began to dawn in Hsiao's eyes. "How long does it last?"

"It depends on the mental sharpness of the victim. To me, that dealer seemed as sharp as they come. On the other hand, apparently Darius Casts like a hurricane. I suppose that means the effect will last a long time."

"As long as a week?" asked Hsiao.

"Maybe, but I doubt it."

"Holy crap."

Bryce knew how she felt. They'd tricked a dangerous, shady character into a deal that had most likely left him way out of pocket. At some point, he would cease being Enthralled and would wonder what the hell had happened to him. What he might do then was anyone's guess, but Bryce had a strong feeling no one aboard the *Bathsheba* was going to like it.

"Is there any way we can back out?" Hsiao mused.

"I don't see how. As I understand it, while he's under the effect of the Cast the dealer will feel compelled to help us, even if we refuse. Is that right, Darius?"

He nodded, looking glummer.

Bryce continued, "We could ask Scroocher to take us back and try to cancel the agreement, but he's going to put up a fight. He might even force us to accept his services without any payment. If he regains his normal mental state while his workers are attaching a pricey piece of equipment entirely free of charge, he's going to be even madder."

"I was only trying to help," Darius said sadly.

"I know. But next time, it would be better to ask before you Cast, okay?"

Darius's shoulders slumped and he didn't reply.

"Still," Hsiao said, "if we can swing it so we get the weapon without seriously pissing off the seller, that'd be a helluva bargain."

"*If*," said Bryce.

She was right, but he couldn't think of a way to do it. There was going to be a reckoning, sooner or later.

The doors to the treatment center opened and Bongo crawled out followed by Nahla and Jackson—Jackson with two arms!

"You got it done already?" Bryce asked.

"Yeah, but there's a small problem."

Two additional figures appeared one step behind him: armed guards.

"Did you order the weapon?" asked Jackson.

"Yes, but—"

"Then we have to leave right away."

"But—"

"It's either that, or we split up now. It's your call."

"We—"

"Are you with this man?" One of the guards approached menacingly, his pulse rifle angled across his chest.

"Why do you want to know?" asked Hsiao.

"Move," the guard said, aiming his rifle at her.

"What the...!"

"Do as they say," advised Jackson. "I'll explain when we get back to the *Peregrine*. Sorry, I had no idea this would happen. The doctors didn't tell me. They assumed I understood."

What followed could only be described as a forced march through Lakshmi Station. The visitors parted before them, gawping at the small party of humans and one spider-like alien being escorted like criminals through their midst.

"Did you find out what's wrong with the mages?" Bryce asked Jackson softly.

"No."

Dread gripped his heart.

"Not yet," Jackson hastily added. "The initial round of tests didn't bring up anything. I've left the samples with a center that offered to test for more obscure diseases."

Bryce didn't think Carina would want to leave the mages' DNA in the hands of strangers. She probably wouldn't have agreed to sending the medical samples to Lakshmi at all. But what was done was done. The Black Dogs' doctors were out of ideas, and if no one found a cure for whatever was ailing their patients, there was almost certainly only one outcome.

"How about Nahla?" Bryce asked. "Any luck there?"

The merc heaved a heavy sigh. "No." His voice quietened to a whisper as he went on, "I couldn't find anyone who could help her any better than our own medics, using therapeutic treatments. She'll have to live with the effects of hypoxia for the rest of her life."

Bryce looked at her. He loved the new Nahla just as much as always—she'd continued to be his non-mage ally in the family—but he missed the nimble-witted girl she'd once been.

The guards accompanied them all the way to the security zone, where Bongo said goodbye, and through the zone. They even waited at the station end of the umbilicus until they entered the *Peregrine's* airlock.

The outer hatch closed and sealed, and the airlock pressurized.

"What the hell was *that* about?" asked Hsiao, removing her helmet.

"Wait until we get inside," Jackson replied, "and I'll show you."

When everyone had stripped off their EVA suits and was waiting expectantly in the *Peregrine's* passageway, Jackson pushed up the sleeve covering his new prosthetic.

It looked extremely lifelike. Bryce hadn't studied the merc's arms in any detail, but he would have guessed the new device was virtually a mirror image of his flesh and bone one.

"It looks the same all the way up," Jackson said. "You can't tell where it joins my body." Relief and pride shone from his face.

Bryce hadn't realized how self-conscious the merc must have been about his old device. "Cool. But why the big fuss in the station?"

Jackson raised his arm and bent his elbow, so his fist pointed at the bulkhead. A rectangular section of his forearm split open, and a miniature gun rose up.

"*Shit*!" Hsiao exclaimed, taking a step backward. "You're permanently armed! Ha! Literally armed."

Jackson grinned. "My humerus is basically a power pack. If it begins to run low, I can charge it up overnight while I sleep."

"So that's why we had to leave immediately," said Bryce.

"Visitors aren't allowed weapons anywhere on Lakshmi," Jackson confirmed. "Not even weapons contained in prosthetics."

"*Especially* not contained in prosthetics, I bet," said Hsiao. "No one can tell you're carrying."

"But they didn't explain before you had it fitted?" asked Bryce.

"They only asked me if I'd completed all my other business," Jackson replied. "I'd ordered the supplies Carina had on her list. They'll be delivered soon. And Bongo said he didn't know of any hospitals better than the ones we'd already visited, so I reckoned I'd exhausted all the options regarding treatment for Nahla and finding a cure for the mages. I told the doctors I'd done everything else I'd come here to do, and they took me in for surgery right away. It only lasted an hour. They said it was a standard operation they perform all the time, on account of the number of wounded military they see."

Hsiao whistled. "You're a cyborg soldier."

The gun retracted into Jackson's arm and the fake skin closed over it.

"Stars," said Bryce. "The surgeons told you it was a standard operation? That means they're turning the soldiers in the Three-System War into cyborgs too."

"It figures," said Hsiao. "Every operation they perform is another stack of creds added to Lakshmi Station's profits."

"You can say that again," Jackson commented. "My arm was pricey, but I figured it was okay because we didn't have any other medical expenses."

"How much was it?" asked Bryce. "And how much did you pay for the supplies?"

When Jackson told him, it only took a little simple arithmetic to realize they'd been right when they'd told the arms dealer they couldn't afford what he was asking.

"How did you guys get on?" asked Jackson. "You said you managed to buy the weapon."

"We did," answered Bryce, "but there's a small snag."

THIRTY-EIGHT

Darius hated going to see Carina, but at the same time he couldn't help it. He needed to see her.

She looked so sick, so pale and thin and unmoving, it hurt him deep inside. Parthenia looked the same. So did Ferne, Oriana, and Jace in the other rooms. It had been days since any of them had spoken. They slept most of the time, and when they were awake they mumbled and moaned and didn't make any sense.

As if it wasn't enough to see them fading away from life, he could *feel* it too. In the past, before they were ill, he could have stood in complete darkness with any of them and known who he was with, just by the pattern of their emotions. He'd known Parthenia, Ferne, and Oriana's ever since he was little, and he'd learned Jace and Carina's soon after he'd met them.

But now their patterns were fading, like wallpaper exposed to sunlight for years.

As soon as he returned from his trip to Lakshmi Station, he wanted to see Carina again. He passed through the empty main sick bay area and pushed open the door to her room. At the same time, another door opened and Dr Asher appeared.

"Darius, what are you doing?"

"I want to see Carina." He couldn't look at the doctor. He had to look down and bite his lip to stop himself crying.

"I'm afraid you…" Dr Asher paused "…I don't suppose it will hurt. Go on in, but be careful not to disturb any of the tubes or wires, okay?"

"Okay."

His eldest sister looked even thinner than she had the last time he'd seen her, just before he went to Lakshmi. The bones of her face stuck out and her eyes seemed to have sunk in under her eyelids. She was attached to two machines by wires, and tubes ran out from under her bedclothes. The room was silent save for the quiet hum of the medical equipment and Carina and Parthenia's raspy breathing.

He sat down at Carina's side. One of her hands had a thin tube coming out of the back of it, but the other one was free. He held the free one. Though his sister was a fighter her hands were small, not a lot bigger than his own. "Hey, Carina."

She didn't answer. She was fast asleep.

"I came to tell you what happened at Lakshmi." No one else had been in to see her as far as he knew, and he thought she would want to hear how the trip went. "Jackson got a new arm and it's got a gun in it! It's awesome. I kinda wish I had one like it, but I like my real arms too, so maybe not."

He watched his sister, but she didn't react.

"Nahla... Nahla's the same. Jackson tried to find someone to help her go back to how she was but he couldn't." He swallowed. "She's different now. I think she knows it too. I'm not sure she's happy about it. I think she wants to be how she was before. But that's not gonna happen, right?" He paused. "I wish everything was how it was before."

He stared at Carina's limp fingers. "They got the space gun. Bryce and Hsiao, I mean. They met a man, a scary man. You know how Bongo looks like a spider? Well, this man—I don't know his name—he looked like a human on the outside, but he was a spider on the inside. Not a friendly spider like Bongo. He was the kind of spider that bites you in your sleep so when you wake up in the morning you don't know what that red mark is on your leg or why you feel sick. He was like that. But Bryce and Hsiao didn't know, and I couldn't tell them because the man was right there and he had two guards with guns and..." He took a breath and screwed up his face. "I did something bad, Carina! I Cast Enthrall to make the man agree to the deal for the gun. But I shouldn't have because when the Cast wears off the man will be really angry, and then what will he do? What will a man like that do to everyone?"

He swallowed again, hard. "And it's all my fault, just like with Nahla. I didn't Transport us out from Deck Zero when I should have, and now she'll never be better. The Marchonish men were bullying her and I took her away, but I had to Cast in front of them. That was wrong too. But maybe none of it will matter. Maybe the man selling us the space weapon will do something bad when the Enthrall Cast fades, and nothing I've done will matter anymore." He bent his head over her hand, and hot tears dropped onto it. "What should I do, Carina? What should I do?"

But his sister couldn't answer him. She'd slept all the time he was talking.

Would she ever wake up?

No one had told him what was going to happen to her and the other mages. All he knew was the doctors at Lakshmi couldn't figure out what was wrong with them. They were going to do more tests, but Bryce didn't seem to think they would find anything.

Bryce's pattern of feelings had changed, but it hadn't faded like the mages', it had grown darker and heavier. His face didn't match how he really felt. He looked normal most of the time, but his fear and sadness was an iron weight always dragging on him.

Darius rested his head on the bed next to Carina's hand.

If she and the other mages died he would be the only one left. He didn't want that. He didn't want to be the only mage. He didn't like being different from everyone else. They all treated him a little bit differently. He could feel a thread of wariness. They knew he could do things they couldn't; that if he really wanted to hurt them he could, very easily. Even Bryce treated him differently. He wasn't the same with him as he was with Nahla.

If he was the only mage, he would feel very alone.

He looked up at his sister's sleeping face. If only she could help him. She'd always helped him in the past. If she couldn't help him, he wanted to hear her voice at least, just a few words to give him comfort. But she was far away and she was journeying farther still.

———

A ship-wide alert had gone out. Darius was missing—again. Bryce couldn't rid himself of the gut-wrenching feeling that another disaster had occurred, only this time it was Darius who would be the victim. Nahla was safe here on the *Bathsheba's* bridge, but Darius had slipped away without anyone noticing.

"I'm sure he's fine," said Hsiao. "He's just wandered off and got distracted by something."

"Then why isn't he answering his comm?"

Hsiao didn't reply.

"The Marchonish men are on the ship," Bryce said. "We have to watch the kids. We have to know where they are at all times. How did he manage to get out of here without any of us noticing?"

Hsiao had come to relieve Bibik at the *Bathsheba's* flight controls. They had to maneuver to the rendezvous point with the arm dealer's vessel. Jackson and

Justus were on the bridge too. Justus had come to find out what had happened on Lakshmi. At some time during the general chatter, Darius had left. It could have been as long as twenty minutes ago.

Bryce's comm chirruped. As he checked who it was, he felt the blood drain from his face.

Dr Asher.

"What's wrong?" asked Hsiao. "Aren't you going to answer it?"

Ever since leaving to go to Lakshmi Station, Bryce had been dreading Asher contacting him. He'd visited Carina to say goodbye, even though she was permanently unconscious now. She'd looked sicker than ever. She was slipping away from him and there wasn't anything he could do about it. If Dr Asher had something to tell him it could only be bad news, possibly the worst news he would ever hear.

He accepted the comm. "Yes?"

"Darius is here in sick bay."

Relief hit him so hard he almost collapsed.

"He went into Carina and Parthenia's room ten minutes ago," Asher continued. "When I heard the alert, I checked and he's still there. He's asleep on Carina's bed."

"Thank the stars. You're sure he's all right?"

"It depends how you define it. Considering everything the poor child has been through, he's far from all right. But, physically, he's fine. Just very tired, I imagine. Do you want me to wake him up?"

"No, I'll come over there and carry him to his suite."

THIRTY-NINE

The men from Marchon had been making themselves at home—excessively so in Bryce's opinion. In the week since they'd come aboard, no one had caught sight of a single Marchonish woman, but the men ranged far and wide across the ship, showing their faces in all the areas the Black Dogs frequented and acting like the place was their own.

The mercs had kept their cool. No one had confronted the newcomers about their behavior yet, but tensions were simmering. It would only be a matter of time before they boiled over.

But today the focus of Bryce's attention had to be elsewhere. The arms dealer from Lakshmi Station had contacted them to say he was on his way with the weapon, accompanied by the technicians and engineers who would fit it to the ship and integrate it with her systems.

The work was already behind schedule. The dealer had implied the weapon would arrive earlier, and the delay had caused Bryce to assume the Enthrall Cast had worn off days ago. He'd thought the man had come to his senses, realized he'd been duped, and pocketed the deposit they'd handed over.

In the circumstances it wouldn't have been a bad outcome, though it would have meant that part of Carina's plan would be unfulfilled. Now it seemed the deal was going ahead, Bryce wasn't sure what to think. Was the arms dealer still Enthralled, or was he no longer experiencing the effects of the Cast and was coming to get his revenge?

They would soon find out.

In the days since departing Lakshmi they'd discussed how to fix the problem Darius's Cast had created, but they'd been unable to come up with a plan.

Bryce waited with Hsiao and Van Hasty at the airlock, ready to greet their visitors. Darius and Nahla were confined to quarters under express orders to not leave for the duration of the weapon fitting process. 'Uncle Jackson' and a rotating team of mercs were their protection from the Lakshmi Station-ites and Marchonish men.

The temptation to have Darius on hand to Cast them out of potential trouble from the arms dealer had been strong, but Bryce had decided against it. The boy's powers had worked against them recently. He couldn't risk more problems. Also, it was clear to anyone who knew Darius even a little bit that the boy was in a terrible mental state. It wouldn't be fair to place any more burdens on him. He needed nurturing, not responsibilities, though Bryce felt inadequate in that regard. There was only one person who could heal Darius, and not by a Cast but by her overwhelming love for him.

By some miracle, Carina and the other mages continued to cling to life, though how much longer they would last was unclear. The medical samples left at Lakshmi Station had yielded no results. The doctors there were just as confused by the mages' disease as were Asher and Baxter. When the seemingly inevitable happened, Bryce feared it would break the boy.

The arms dealer stepped from the airlock. His ship's hatches were compatible with the *Bathsheba's*, so he hadn't arrived via umbilicus wearing an EVA suit. Bryce guessed his vessel was an ancient model, like the Marchonish men's, only the dealer's would be refurbished and brought up to date, cherished in the way some people loved old autocar models. A cursory scan had told them the vessel was, nevertheless, bristling with armaments.

The dealer was better dressed than the last time Bryce had seen him. He wore a suit tailored to hide his belly and a wig of thick golden hair to cover his bald pate. Bryce thought he saw traces of make-up on his eyes and lips too. A man and a woman, similarly formally dressed, flanked him.

Bryce looked more closely at the dealer's eyes.

From the hazy, slightly unfocused look, he appeared to remain Enthralled! The length of time Darius's Cast had held was remarkable.

"Welcome aboard," said Bryce.

"Thank you. Members of my team are moving into place on the exterior of your ship. We will also need access to your existing weapons systems, engines, and bow infrastructure. My team leaders will organize the fitting from here." He didn't mention his companions' names.

"Hsiao and I can show you to the bridge. Does someone need to go to the bow section?"

"Me," said the woman, raising her hand.

Van Hasty departed with her.

"How long will the process take?" asked Bryce as he set off with the dealer and Hsiao.

"Barring any hiccups, about five hours. But there are always hiccups."

"As little as that?" Hsiao asked. "I thought you said it would take days."

"We made some adjustments before setting out. That was the cause of our delay. I thought it would be better to spend as little time out here and away from the station as possible."

"Why's that?" Hsiao probed. "If you don't mind me asking."

Bryce, too, wondered why the man was avoiding spending time at the *Bathsheba*.

"Haven't you heard? The Three-Systems War is heating up. Gugong has swapped sides and is now allying with Marchon. There are rumors a massive attack on the Quinton space fleet is planned. Interstellar space is big, but I'd rather be safe on Lakshmi if and when it kicks off. The speed and firepower of each side's battleships has increased exponentially over the decades, thanks to developers and suppliers like me. The risk is small, but I don't want to become collateral damage."

Bryce had to bite his tongue to avoid giving an angry response. The dealer didn't mind *other* folk being damaged by his business. Hsiao looked sour too.

"What are your plans after we finish our work here?" the dealer asked. "Are you leaving the system immediately?"

"We don't have any reason to stick around," Bryce lied.

"A wise move. Where's the young boy you had with you before?"

"He's playing in his cabin."

"Huh. Sweet kid. I never had any of my own. But there's still time."

How many tens of thousands of children had the man's business made orphans?

They walked onto the bridge. Bibik moved to rise from his seat, but Hsiao gestured at him to stay put. She took the male team leader to a weapons console and sat down with him.

While the pilot was guiding him through the *Bathsheba's* systems, it was up to Bryce to keep the dealer occupied—and to pray the effects of Darius's Cast would last until the work was completed and the people from Lakshmi were far, far away.

"How old is this ship?" asked the dealer. "I don't recognize the model."

Bryce wasn't sure how much it was safe to tell him. "We don't actually know. She seems to have had several owners before us. The database was originally in another language, not Universal."

"That old, huh? I thought so. She's held up pretty well, from what I can tell."

"We've had a few problems, but she hasn't killed anyone yet."

Not quite.

"They don't build them like they used to, not since the Colonization Period. Nowadays, battleships are where the money's at. People aren't interested in settling new worlds. Our ancestors found new homes and settled down. Even now, thousands of years later, most populations haven't exploited the full potential of their planets. There's no pressure to move on, you know? Not like there used to be in the old days."

Bryce thought of the group from Marchon, desperate to escape the home their ancestors had created. "Can I get you a drink?" he asked, dying to effect an escape of his own. "I can probably program the printer to create any cocktail you want."

"I appreciate the offer, but I never touch a drop of alcohol until a job is done and the equipment has passed all the tests. It's a little superstition of mine."

Shame.

If he could have got the man off his face, they wouldn't need to worry about—

It happened.

The dealer blinked and his pupils contracted, as if bringing everything around him into sharp focus.

Dammit!

Darius's Cast had finally run its course.

"What...what was I saying?" he asked uncertainly.

"You were telling me about your superstition," Bryce answered, clinging to a tenuous hope that if he carried on as normal, the dealer might follow his lead. He might not recall he'd sold his highly expensive space weapon at a huge discount for no reason whatsoever.

"Yeah, that was it. I never...I never..." He squinted at his team leader where he was hunched over the console.

Murmuring could be heard as the man liaised with workers outside the *Bathsheba*.

"How about I give you a tour of the ship?" Bryce asked brightly. "You said you don't know this model. You might find it interesting."

"I, er..." The dealer ran a hand through the golden mop on his head, which didn't budge a millimeter. The wig had to be cemented on. Or perhaps it was real hair, grown within days by a body modification clinic. "I think I would. She's old but a beauty, and unique as far as I know. You're lucky to have her."

The man really was a connoisseur of ancient spacecraft. No one else would have called the *Bathsheba* beautiful.

Hsiao looked over her shoulder as the dealer and Bryce got to their feet. Apparently noticing the panic on her friend's features, her mouth opened to an O. Then her jaw snapped shut. She pointed at the team leader's back and gave a thumbs up. She would keep the man distracted and cut off from the arms dealer for as long as necessary. Or, rather, for as long as she could.

Bryce escorted the dealer from the bridge.

FORTY

Thanking the galactic gods the *Bathsheba* was a vast ship that took hours to tour, Bryce guided the arms dealer to the top deck and Twilight Dome. Not only was it far from the bridge and the bow where his team leaders were working, it was usually fairly empty.

Except as he stepped inside, he remembered it was one of the areas the Marchonish men had taken for their own. They weren't blatant about their territory-claiming efforts—yet. They used more subtle methods, such as turning silent whenever someone not belonging to their group entered their midst, or pointedly commandeering all the available seats.

It was dumb of them to antagonize the very people who had agreed to help them out of a tough spot, especially before the journey had even begun. But the men had been made arrogant by their culture. They clearly saw anyone who was either female or not from Marchon as stupid and inferior.

Not that the Black Dogs took any notice. They knew exactly what the newcomers were attempting, and they would have none of it. All silences were ignored, and if there was nowhere to sit down, they would fetch more chairs from somewhere else.

In the Twilight Dome, no struggle for dominance was going on. The place was filled with the Marchonish. They'd discovered the stored drinks behind the bars, and a party was in full swing. Bryce hesitated at the door. Would this be a good or bad venue to draw someone's attention from the fact they were in the process of losing a huge amount of money?

The arms dealer liked to drink. Perhaps he could persuade him to break his superstition.

It was the ideal spot.

The dealer was gazing up at the partially filled-in transparent dome. "That must have looked great when it was whole. What happened?"

"Uhhh..." There was nothing to be gained in telling him about Mezban and her bomb, or the Regians. "A blowout. The structure must have weakened over the years."

"Yeah? Hm." The dealer peered upward, his apparently knowledgeable gaze traveling the struts between the overhead sections.

"Are you sure I can't interest you in a cocktail? What was it you said when we met? Something to oil the wheels?"

The Marchonish men were staring at them. Their tactical silence had fallen.

The dealer frowned. "Who are those guys? And what's their problem?"

"Just some passengers we'll be taking with us when we leave."

"I don't like the look of them. If you'll take my advice, you'll leave them behind, or drop them off at the first asteroid you see."

"Your advice is duly noted. Now how about that cocktail? It's going to be hours before your team is finished."

"My team... My team that's fitting your—"

"We found some ancient drink recipes in the ship's database. Unusual combinations you would never normally consider, but when you taste them they're rather special."

"No kidding? Well..."

"I'll mix you something. You don't have to drink it, only try a sip." Without waiting for a reply, Bryce strode to the nearest bar.

A surly man leaned on it. He lifted a lip before asking, "What do you want?"

"Get out of my way," Bryce hissed, shouldering the man aside.

"Hey!"

His companions grumbled and edged closer.

Bryce took no notice of them as he hastily splashed random liquors into a glass and finished the drink off with a squirt of soda. He'd never made a cocktail in his life. His concoction probably tasted disgusting, but he hoped to get the dealer drunk as quickly as possible.

If the man's stomach didn't immediately press eject when the drink hit it, this recipe should have the desired effect. When he took it over, the dealer accepted it graciously, saying, "Just a sip, mind. Otherwise it's bad luck." He lifted the glass to his lips and took somewhat more than a sip. Instantly, his eyes widened until the whites showed all around the irises. His face turned red. "That's..." he spluttered "...that's pretty good!"

"It is?!"

"I might indulge myself just a little further." He took a second drink and swilled the liquid around his mouth before swallowing it. He smacked his lips. After smiling like a child caught with his hand in the cookie jar, he slurped some more. "My! You must tell me what's in it."

"It's...er..." Bryce racked his brains. He didn't know the ingredients. He hadn't read the labels on the bottles. "It's a secret family recipe, I'm afraid. I really can't tell you."

The dealer waggled a finger at him. "There's no need to be mysterious. I won't tell anyone, and you're leaving the system soon, right?" He drained the dregs of the drink.

"I'm sorry, if I told you I would bring down the family curse on you, and who knows what might happen?"

The dealer considered this response for a second before shrugging. "Oh well, if this is going to be my only opportunity to enjoy your wonderful cocktail, you'd better make me another."

Shit.

"Sure." Bryce took the man's empty glass and set off toward the bar again. What had he used to make the drink? He definitely couldn't remember. He'd created the chance to render the dealer so drunk he would allow the deal to go ahead, only to fumble it.

"Remind me," said a voice directly behind him.

Bryce jumped in shock. He turned.

The dealer had followed him. "How much are you paying to complete your purchase today?" Despite the alcohol circulating in his system, the man's gaze was clear and hard.

"I'm not sure exactly. Let me get you that cocktail, then I'll look it up."

"No more drinks. Look up that figure right now."

"No problem. Come with me."

The Marchonish men watched with interest as he and the dealer walked to the door.

Bryce's mind was in turmoil. The dealer had clearly realized something was wrong. What would he do when he confirmed he'd been tricked? His battleship was easily a match for the *Bathsheba's* old, outdated weaponry, and he had a large team of workers, probably armed.

The doors to the Twilight Dome closed, shutting out the curious looks of the newcomers. The passageway stretched out left and right, empty.

What should he do? It would be hours before the dealer's team finished fitting the weapon. He couldn't possibly put off revealing the deal was a sham for that long. What would happen then? At the very least, they would lose the weapon they wanted and needed. At worse, they would lose the ship and their lives.

They were passing Jace's cabin.

On impulse, Bryce slapped the security panel and the door opened. He'd had access to Jace's suite ever since he'd fallen sick. Before he'd lost consciousness, he would occasionally ask Bryce to fetch him personal items.

"What are you doing?" asked the dealer. "What's in there?"

"We can access the computer via the interface here. It'll save us time."

The dealer blinked and leaned in. The lights came on, revealing a very ordinary cabin. Bryce's chest ached at the sight of small reminders of his friend, like the empty jug and the beakers from which Jace would drink cha.

"If you're sure..." The dealer stepped over the threshold.

Bryce was one step behind. As soon as they were both inside, he closed the door.

The dealer asked, "Where's the interf—"

Bryce's punch knocked him out cold. He snatched the comm button from the fallen man and searched him for weapons, relieving him of a gun in a shoulder holster before dragging him into the inner bedroom. He closed the door and locked it, and then returned to the passageway and locked the outer door too. Finally, he went into the suite's connections via the security panel and cut off its access to the ship's comm system.

With luck, no one would hear the dealer's hollers or banging. The Black Dogs wouldn't have a problem ignoring him, but the Marchonish party had no knowledge of the situation. The newcomers' involvement would only complicate everything.

The un-Enthralled dealer was safely out of the way for now. What to do with him next was a question for which Bryce had no answer. Carina hadn't included a duped, outraged, very dangerous man in her plan.

FORTY-ONE

When Bryce returned to the bridge, he found a holo on display and Hsiao and the team leader watching it.

"The battle's started!" Hsiao exclaimed

Streaks of light were speeding across space as the ships fired their pulse cannon. Long beams—particle lances—flashed out, carving into their targets. Tiny flecks representing fighter ships spewed from the bellies of larger craft, spread out, and turned in unison like a shoal of killer fish scenting prey.

The happenstance of the space battle was a welcome complication. It would serve as another distraction to the arms dealer's team, and hopefully it would encourage them to work fast so they could return to the safety of their station as soon as possible.

"How are you doing?" Bryce asked the team leader.

"Oh, uhhh..." The man returned his attention to the console. "I'm waiting for the engineers to give me the go ahead to begin synchronization. From what I've seen, it shouldn't be a problem." He added, "I'm Chi-tang, by the way. I don't hold with all that anonymity nonsense. It's not like you're going to implicate yourselves by giving us up to station security, is it?"

"So the weapon is actually illegal?"

"Oh yeah. About as illegal as they come, according to the current legislation on inter-system warfare. But my boss likes to stay ahead of the curve, developing new weapons ready for when they become legal."

"But what if they never become legal?" Hsiao asked.

"They always do. That's the way things have gone for the history of the war. The latest tech is one step ahead of the lawmakers, but the law catches up eventually. Whoa! Did you see that?"

Bryce checked the holo. A battleship had been cut clean in two. The halves were floating apart. Inside, rapid depressurization would be wreaking havoc, hurling crew into space, sucking them through hull breaches, slamming equipment into them. All personnel would be wearing EVA suits as a precaution against such an eventuality and section hatches would seal, but the loss of life would be massive.

Chi-tang stared, transfixed.

Bryce caught Hsiao's worried look. She had to be wondering what had happened to the dealer, but he had no way of telling her. Neither of them could mention the missing man without reminding Chi-tang of his existence. Then, right on cue, he turned from the horrific scene and asked, "Where's my boss gone?"

"I left him in a lounge...relaxing," Bryce answered lamely.

"Relaxing?" Hsiao echoed, her eyebrows lifting as if to say *You couldn't think of anything better than that?*

"No problem," said Chi-tang. "I need to check something with him." He tried to use his comm button to speak to the dealer but, predictably, received no response. "That's odd."

"A malfunction maybe?" Hsiao suggested.

"If it is, it's for the first time. We don't screw up stuff like that."

"Then he must have mislaid his button," said Hsiao.

"That's more likely. I'll have to go and speak to him face to face. Where is he?"

"In one of our lounges," Bryce replied, "really far from here. I'll go and get him for you."

"No, don't do that," said Chi-tang, alarmed. "He would hate the idea I was summoning him. *I* have to go to *him*."

"Well, I'm not sure where I left him."

"You're not sure...?"

Hsiao's eyebrows rose higher.

"I'll go find him." Bryce strode toward the door.

"No, I..." Chi-tang's focus switched to the console. "Great. An update."

Bryce slipped out quickly. He jogged down the passageway, trying to get out of sight before Chi-tang finished reading the message. Hsiao could make up an excuse about not being allowed to leave the bridge and tell the team leader he had to stay there too, for security reasons.

She would think of something.

Hours of the weapon installation process remained. They had to keep the workers from discovering the disappearance of their boss until then.

After that?

Bryce had no idea.

But one thing he did know was he had to apprise Van Hasty of the situation. She was in the bow with the other team leader, who they also had to prevent from trying to contact her boss. He didn't want to risk a comm conversation with Van Hasty the woman might overhear, and he had to do something while avoiding the bridge and awkward questions from Chi-tang. He took a turn and headed forward.

The first people he encountered as he arrived, panting, at the bow were Marchonish men.

Were these the same ones he'd seen in the Twilight Dome, drawn by the new activity on the ship? Or were these different? They seemed to get everywhere they weren't wanted, hanging about like a bad smell.

They drew aside as Bryce approached. He saw someone he hadn't seen for days: Porcher. The Marchonish leader had put on weight in his short time on the ship. A bulging stomach seemed to be a feature of leaders in the region.

"Just the man I want to see," said Porcher.

"Oh?" Bryce replied, slowing to a walk. "I'm busy right now." He carried on past Porcher, but the man followed him.

"Something's going on we weren't informed about. What is it? An adaptation to the ship?"

Bryce ignored him, scanning between the clustered bodies for Van Hasty.

"It's just, if you're doing something to the *Bathsheba* we should have been consulted, as per our agreement."

This comment drew Bryce to a halt. He faced the man. "What agreement?"

Entirely without shame, Porcher replied, "Our partnership in the running of the ship."

Bryce said darkly, "That isn't the agreement I remember. There *is* no partnership. We allowed you to join us. That's all."

"I don't recall the exact words, but it stands to reason we're an equal party in the venture, considering there are more of us than you."

"Your numbers don't mean anything, unless we're talking about the extra mouths to feed while you're out of Deep Sleep or the additional chemicals we'll need for the chambers. In fact, stacked up against the *colony ship* the Black Dogs own, your numbers mean a whole lot of nothing." Bryce fixed the man with a stare, his hands on his hips.

Porcher's men were reacting badly to the conversation, their grumbles growing louder. Porcher held Bryce's gaze for a minute, but eventually looked away, shrugged, and smiled. "There will be plenty of time for negotiations after we set out. As a goodwill gesture, we'll agree to whatever it is you guys are having done to the ship this time. In the future, we'd appreciate some consultation."

Not dignifying this bullshit with a response, Bryce forced his way through the men who had gathered around them.

Fifty meters farther on, he found Van Hasty. She was alone, standing next to an open maintenance access hatch, her pulse rifle slung across her back. "Are those assholes still hanging around back there?"

"Yeah."

There was no need for any explanation of which assholes she meant.

"Dammit. I can't get them to leave us alone. They don't take any notice of what I say. Half the time they pretend they can't hear me."

"Have they been interfering in the installation?"

"Not yet. The engineer's somewhere in there." She nodded at the open hatch. "I haven't seen her for half an hour."

"Good." Bryce brought her up to date on everything, finishing with, "So the longer that woman's in a tunnel and not asking where her boss has gone, the better."

"I'll keep her occupied as long as I can, but don't you think it's time we got things moving?"

"What, now? That isn't what we planned."

"I know, but we didn't plan on locking up a furious arms dealer either. We need to improvise."

Bryce considered for a moment. "You're right. I forgot to tell you the space battle our dealer was worried about has started."

"It has? That could work to our advantage. I'll comm Jackson and tell him to get the ball rolling."

"And I'll message Hsiao and tell her to start building power for the 'test'."

FORTY-TWO

Porcher wasn't difficult to find among his buddies. He was 'holding court'. A bunch of men surrounded him listening to him spouting off about changes needed aboard the ship.

Bryce asked the man standing between him and the Marchonish leader to step aside. When he sneered and refused, Bryce took out his gun and pressed the muzzle into his chest.

The man's eyes popped and he backed away, hands raised.

Porcher noticed the commotion. "Hey, what are you—"

Bryce advanced, aiming at him. "It's time you and your men returned to your ship."

"Huh? Why?" Porcher shot a narrow-eyed glance at his supporters, as if to say, *It's happening. You know what to do.*

"The deal's off," said Bryce. "Move."

"Now wait a minute. Let's talk this out like men."

"I don't see you moving. You have five seconds."

"This isn't fair! You said—"

"Four. Three."

"Okay, that's enough. You asked for this."

There was a flurry of movement. Two men grabbed Bryce from behind. His gun was wrested from his hand.

"I never liked you," sneered Porcher as one of the men handed him Bryce's weapon. "Jumped up teenager, barely out of short pants. It's going to give me great pleasure to—"

Jackson appeared behind him, suited up. Porcher jerked forward as something was thrust into his back.

"What?" Jackson asked. "I'm dying to hear what's going to give you great pleasure. Don't let me stop you."

Porcher grimaced. "Let's not be hasty. I wasn't really going to hurt the kid."

"Back off!" a Marchonish man yelled, pulling a gun from the back of his pants. "Let him go!"

They weren't supposed to carry arms on the ship. It was one of the conditions of the agreement. Not that the mercs had taken them at their word. They were frisked before being allowed aboard. But clearly someone had slipped up. Either that or they'd managed to break into one of the armories.

Another man darted forward to snatch Bryce's weapon from Porcher. "Yeah! Let him go!"

The men edged in, closing the space around Bryce, Porcher, and Jackson.

"Kill them both," someone urged. "Then we take over the ship."

"Nuh uh," said a voice from somewhere at the back. "That ain't happening."

Van Hasty had come up.

"It's the bitch!" a man called out.

A pulse round hissed. Van Hasty was taking the initiative.

The bunched-up men broke in a confused wave. Some were heading toward Van Hasty and some were running from her. Bryce was buffeted hard. Something heavy landed at his feet: the Marchonish leader, a smoking hole in his back.

"He killed Porcher!"

Jackson shot the man aiming at him next.

At the same time, Bryce ran at the other armed man and knocked him off his feet. He grabbed his gun. When the man wouldn't let go, he kicked him in the head. "Where's Van Hasty?" he gasped, rising with his weapon back in his hands.

Another tide was passing them. The Black Dogs accompanying Jackson had arrived. They crashed into the Marchonish men. The fight was brief. Any of the newcomers who didn't surrender immediately were executed on the spot. Most of them weren't dumb enough to put up a fight. As the struggle died down, only six or seven bodies lay on the deck.

The Black Dogs led the men from Marchon away, their heads hung low as reality caught up with them. Van Hasty brought up the rear, her rifle at her shoulder. When she reached Bryce and Jackson, she halted, gazing down at Porcher's corpse. "Damn. *I* wanted to kill him."

"You don't get everything you want," said Jackson.

"Ain't that the truth. Where to now?"

"A lot of them are in the Twilight Dome," Bryce replied, "but don't you have to wait here for the engineer?"

"Nah," she said. "I mean, yeah, probably, but the longer she wanders around trying to find someone to talk to the better, right?"

———

As they passed Jace's cabin, Bryce listened for sounds of the imprisoned arms dealer. No shouts or banging could be heard. Either he'd given up or Bryce's guess at the soundproofing afforded by two doors and a room in between was correct. Fifteen Black Dogs had already arrived at the dome as requested by Jackson and were waiting outside.

"This should be fairly easy," Jackson told them.

"Aw, don't say that!" Van Hasty protested. "You'll jinx it."

"We only want them back on their ship," Jackson went on. "But they don't get two chances to argue about it." He opened the doors.

A pulse round hit his breastplate, scorching it, though it must have been fired at some distance because it didn't seem to hurt him.

The Black Dogs had retreated to each side of the open doorway, out of the line of sight of anyone in the room.

"Dammit, Jackson," said Van Hasty. "What did I say about jinxing it?"

The Marchonish men had overturned the tables and chairs and used them to build a barricade. Word had reached them about their forced evacuation.

"Come out with your hands raised," Jackson called out. "You know there's only one way this can end."

"We're not going back to our ship! We're not going back to Marchon!"

"You're leaving the *Bathsheba*," said Jackson, "dead or alive. Whichever doesn't matter to us."

"Speak for yourself," Van Hasty muttered. "I don't want to scrape their bloody carcasses off the deck."

"We would rather die here like men!"

"Sure," Jackson replied. "Have it your way. You're pretty dumb men, if I'm honest, but if that's what you want." He nodded at the Black Dogs.

They piled into the room, rifles blazing.

Through the flash of rounds, some tentative hands rose beyond the barricade. A pulse hit one, turning it into a macabre torch. The hand disappeared, its owner screaming. Figures were moving in the shadowy room, running, darting into the corners.

Bryce had a feeling the man who had asserted the group's death wish hadn't been speaking for all of them. "They're giving up! They're surrendering."

The furniture was already ablaze. Fire-suppressing foam spurted from overhead. The mercs gradually ceased firing. Some men lay on the floor, groaning. Others peeked out from their hiding places.

"We'll go peacefully. Just don't shoot."

"Shit," Van Hasty muttered, surveying the smoking, charred scene. "What a mess."

———

While the two largest groups of Marchonish men were being rounded up, Black Dogs had been roaming the ship finding the rest of the individuals and giving them their marching orders. Despite their swagger, when it came down to it the men generally did exactly what they were told. Though perhaps that wasn't so surprising considering the proximity of rifle muzzles to their faces.

When the Black Dogs were confident all their unwelcome visitors had returned to their own vessel, they prepared to disable her engine. The group would be stranded in space but they would leave them with working comms. Someone would come to their rescue eventually. Then they could tell whoever they liked about the kid on the colony vessel who could disappear at will. The *Bathsheba* would be long gone.

Jackson, Van Hasty, and two merc engineers stood at the airlock, along with a plentiful guard in case the Marchonish men put up a fight.

"Right," said Van Hasty. "So after we kill their engine, that's when we get the women."

"We what?" asked Jackson.

"Are you deaf? We get the women. We can't leave them with those pricks."

"We never discussed this."

"We never discussed it because it's *obvious*."

"Not to me."

"What?!" Van Hasty's voice rose in outrage.

"How do you know they want to join us?" Jackson challenged. "No one's even seen one, let alone talked to any of them."

"Of *course* they want to join us. What's *wrong* with you? Haven't you lived alongside the evolutionary throwbacks controlling them for the past week?"

"And you're so much better, deciding for yourself what these women want?"

Van Hasty frowned at him. "After we kill their engine, we get the women."

Forty-Three

While the expulsion of the Marchonish men had been going on, Bryce had suited up. He decided to accompany the Black Dogs into the Marchonish ship, driven by curiosity as much as anything. No one from the *Bathsheba* had boarded her until now. He wanted to see the other half of Marchonish society the men kept so secluded.

The vanguard of mercs stepped from the airlock onto the foreign vessel.

"What do you want?" a voice called out. The man kept himself out of sight. "We did what you asked. We left your ship. Now leave us alone."

Jackson replied, "We have a couple more jobs to finish before we're done."

"What are you going to do? Porcher's dead and so are seven others. We've paid our dues. Let us go."

"When we've finished our business."

The mercs were advancing into the ship. Bryce was part of the rearguard, walking backward. In here, their enemy had access to weapons. The Black Dogs could meet some foolhardy resistance from men whose arrogance sometimes overrode their common sense.

The Black Dogs pushed forward.

Van Hasty was on point. "Bring out your women. We have a proposition for them."

"Ha!" the mystery man replied. "I bet you do. So that's why you're here. You want to steal them. We should have guessed. That's why you forced us off your ship. You never wanted us. You only ever wanted our females."

"This is the engine room," said Carter via helmet comm. "Blake, Rees, with me."

Three figures split off and disappeared. The rest of the mercs halted.

"We want to speak to the women," said Van Hasty.

"Like hell. You want them, you come and get them."

"Leave it, Van Hasty," Jackson said via comm. "It's not worth the risk."

"No, dammit. I'm not leaving until I've talked to them."

"Maybe they don't have any women," a merc joked. "Maybe they only exist in the men's imaginations."

"I had a girlfriend like that once," said someone else. "Best woman I ever had. Never complained about anything."

"Quit kidding around," Van Hasty snapped. "You're doing a goddamned public service here."

"Get out," said the invisible Marchonish man. "You're not having our women and that's the end of it."

A tense pause stretched out.

"Van Hasty," said Jackson, "unless you want to search every corner of this ship with hostiles at every turn—"

"Wait," she said before switching to external comm. "I get it. You know what their answer will be. You know they'll leave you in a heartbeat when they see the alternative. You know you don't stand a chance against real men."

"You said it, Van Hasty," someone commented.

"Shut up, idiot."

"That isn't true!" the voice yelled. "Bitch! You're just trying to manipulate us."

"If it isn't true, prove it."

Silence.

Then sounds of movement and muffled arguments.

Bryce had been watching the empty passageway that led back to the airlock. He risked a look over his shoulder, past the Black Dogs to the passageway ahead.

He was just in time to see the first woman appear.

He drew in a breath.

She was heavily pregnant, her swollen belly pressing against the thin fabric of her dress. Aside from her stomach, she was painfully thin. Her eyes were wide and frightened above her jutting cheekbones, and her long hair was an unkempt mess.

The mercs moved uneasily. Van Hasty's enforced rescue mission was no longer such a joke.

More women stepped into view. They differed in stature and coloring, but in their half-starved, fearful state they were alike.

Bryce quickly counted them before he had to look aft again. There were about twenty. Were there more who hadn't come forward? How many had been held back? They would probably never know.

"*Fuck*," Van Hasty whispered. Then over external comm, she said, "We're inviting you to come with us aboard the *Bathsheba*. We can't promise you anything much except food, your own space, and whatever else you might need. We're traveling out of this system, destination undecided. You're welcome to join us, but there will be no going back and you have to decide now, this minute."

Bryce's attention was inexorably drawn to the spectacle playing out behind him.

The pregnant woman's eyes shifted to the side, as if conscious of being watched.

"You don't have anything to fear," said Van Hasty softly. "We'll protect you."

The woman took a step forward.

"Ava!" someone yelled. "Don't you dare!"

She froze.

"It's okay." Van Hasty hoisted her rifle to her shoulder.

The woman took another step.

The mercs moved to aside so Ava could pass between them.

"Get back here!" a man shouted. "You're not taking my kid!"

He darted into sight.

Van Hasty fired and he fell.

The women screamed and ducked. Some ran toward the mercs, others sped away. More men appeared, firing. The mercs shot back. Bryce whirled to face the rear. Marchonish men were heading up the passageway. He began shooting.

"Fall back!" Jackson hollered. "Back to the ship! Carter, Rees, Blake, where are you?"

"Coming," Carter replied. "Their engine's dead."

Bryce was pouring round after round into the men blocking their escape. Their enemy was in armor, but the barrage began to take its toll. But Bryce's suit was heating up too. He marched steadily forward, forcing a passage to the airlock. Someone stepped right in front of him—one of the Marchonish women, panicking in terror. He thrust her behind.

The airlock appeared. The hatch remained open. Perhaps the Marchonish men had some brains after all.

Bryce ran for the airlock and laid down cover up one side of the passageway while his partner covered the other. The rest of the mercs and Marchonish women raced through the hatch. Bryce counted the women.

Five.

Only five out of the twenty or so he'd seen.

Five out of all the women on the ship had managed to get out.

Van Hasty was last to enter the airlock. The passageway was empty.

FORTY-FOUR

Bryce burst onto the bridge. He'd run here after taking off his armor, eager to tell Hsiao of the successful de-infestation of the *Bathsheba* and the handful of Marchonish women they'd saved.

Chi-tang turned to look at him curiously.

Shit.

The space weapon.

The dealer imprisoned in Jace's cabin.

The second part of the plan.

"Hey," Hsiao greeted him. She looked tired and anxious. Her efforts to keep Chi-tang distracted for the last several hours were telling on her.

Bryce gaped as he desperately tried to think of something to say.

"Our visitors left," was all he could come up with.

"Our visitors?"

"From Marchon."

"Oh." Hsiao's eyes widened. "Ohhh, *those* visitors. That's fantastic news."

"A few of them are staying though."

"They are?"

"I'll explain later." He faced Chi-tang. "How is the installation going?"

"It's complete. We're ready to move on to testing, but I still can't locate my boss. Did you find him? He needs to be here for the test."

"The test? The *test*? Excellent. Hsiao, could you...?"

"I'm on it." She moved to the pilot's console.

"Has everyone from your team returned to your ship?" Bryce asked Chi-tang.

"Definitely. It's far too dangerous for them to be out in the black when we fire the weapon. But my boss has to be here. Where the hell has he got to?"

Bryce shrugged. "Who knows? It's a big ship. He could be anywhere." He comm'd Jackson. "Phase two."

"Copy."

The comm went dead.

Chi-tang's brow wrinkled. "Look, I'm not an idiot. I know something's going on. What I can't figure out is, what? What are you guys up to?"

Without turning around, Hsiao replied, "It's better you don't know. You seem like a nice person. I don't want to get you into trouble." Into her mic, she said, "Strap in, everyone. We're going for a ride."

"I'm probably already in trouble," said Chi-tang sadly as he fastened his safety harness.

"Why's that?" Bryce slipped into the nearest seat.

"Because whatever it is you have planned, I'm sure my boss isn't going to like it. And when he realizes I've been here all this time while you did your thing, he's going to blame me for not stopping you."

"How could you stop us?" Hsiao asked. "You don't know what we're doing."

Chi-tang shook his head. "He isn't a reasonable man."

"Then why are you working for him?" The pilot was easing the *Bathsheba* into motion, trickling power into the engines from the large store the generators had built over the last few hours.

"I don't have a choice." Chi-tang scanned the bridge as if he expected the arms dealer to pop out. "He paid my school fees. It was the only way I could afford college. I agreed to work for him for ten years once I'd graduated. I was young and stupid and didn't understand what I was getting into. I thought when my ten years were up I would be free to do my own thing. But do you think a man like that will let me leave? I know too much now. I'll be working for him the rest of my life."

Hsiao and Bryce shared a look.

"Hang in there, Chi-tang," said Hsiao. "Things might not turn out how you expect."

She swept her screen, and the *Bathsheba's* thrusters burst into life, slamming Bryce into his seat.

It took a couple of minutes for the inertia compensators to fully kick in. During that time, it was all he could do to avoid passing out. Chi-tang *did* pass out. His mouth hung open and his head hung to one side. As the acceleration effects eased, his head flopped forward.

"Is the space battle over?" Bryce asked Hsiao.

"It only lasted a couple of hours, luckily for us. I would *not* have liked to fly into the middle of that. It was a slaughter. I don't know who won, if anyone."

"How long to our destination?"

Hsiao consulted her screen. "Twenty-one minutes eighteen seconds."

"We're that close?"

"We flew a lot closer when we came to the rendezvous point."

"We're going to need Chi-tang awake," said Bryce. "Unless he taught you how to fire the weapon."

"He didn't. We were supposed to receive the instructions after we paid the dealer the remainder of what we owe."

Bryce imagined the dealer, trapped, probably bounced and buffeted by the ship's movement. All comms to Jace's cabin cut, he wouldn't have heard Hsiao's warning. "Someone's going to be disappointed."

"Someone is already severely disappointed."

Chi-tang began to come around. He sat upright and blinked. "Where...? Oh, yeah." He looked worried.

"Now you're awake," said Bryce. "I want to talk to you about something."

"What?"

"This weapon we're in the process of buying, we need you to fire it."

Chi-tang looked from Bryce to Hsiao. "Why me?"

"Because we don't know how," Hsiao explained.

"But I could run you through—"

"There isn't time," said Bryce. "We'll only get one chance to make the shot. It has to be perfect. So it has to be you. You're the expert, right?"

"Yes, but..." Chi-tang swallowed.

"And in return," said Hsiao, "you can come with us."

"Leave Lakshmi Station?"

"Yes."

"Leave the system on a colony ship?"

"Yes."

He appeared to consider the offer. "I'm sorry. I can't deny it's tempting. I don't have anyone in particular I'd be sad to leave behind. My family were killed in a Quintonese attack and my best friend from school signed up as a space marine. He didn't even last a year. But my boss is smart and ruthless. You'll never get away with fooling him. Whatever your plan is, it won't succeed. I can't take the risk."

"Maybe if I tell you what you'll be firing at," said Bryce, "you'll change your mind."

"I'm listening."

After Bryce relayed the information, a smile broke out over Chi-tang's face. "I'll do it! That's a brilliant idea. I wish I'd thought of it myself. But you're right, it'll need perfect targeting to do the job correctly."

"Great," said Bryce.

"Less than fifteen minutes to arrival," Hsiao warned.

He unsnapped his harness and leapt from his seat.

Chi-tang was right. The arms dealer was a smart man. The easiest thing to do would be to kill him, but his workers might be more loyal than his team leader, and they were aboard a fully armed vessel. They would be deeply suspicious after not hearing from their boss for so long, and they might decide to inflict some damage on the *Bathsheba* to persuade the Black Dogs to hand him over.

As Bryce waited for the elevator to take him up to the top deck, the answer to his problem came.

Hsiao comm'd him. "Nine minutes."

"I know. I'm nearly there. I figured out what to do with the dealer. Chi-tang is still on board with the plan?"

"He's raring to go."

The elevator stopped and the doors opened.

———

As soon as Bryce had opened the door to Jace's bedroom, the dealer flew at him, red-faced, bruised, and furious. Bryce shot low to avoid killing the man. He needed him alive. The dealer screamed and collapsed, all his anger and energy gone in an instant. He rolled on the deck, clasping his right calf and yelling in agony.

Bryce cursed. He hadn't meant to hurt him so badly.

But when he looked more closely, the damage didn't seem serious. The pulse round had grazed him, burning his pants and skin, but not deeply wounded him. He threw the EVA suit at the dealer. "Stop yelling and put that on, or next time I'll aim higher."

"You'll regret this," the dealer seethed, but he did as Bryce had instructed, fumbling the zippers and clasps.

"Hurry up," Bryce urged, poking him with his rifle.

In a few minutes Chi-tang would fire the weapon. Then they would only have a short time to get out of range of the dealer's ship.

The man put on his helmet.

Bryce pushed the muzzle of his rifle into his back and forced him out of the cabin. The nearest airlock would do, he calculated. Once the dealer was outside, his men would be forced to decouple from the *Bathsheba* and pick him up, buying them precious moments. He checked the time. Fifty-three seconds remained until they reached their target. The ship would be decelerating quickly now.

The dealer was saying something and gesticulating as Bryce marched him along. He hadn't turned on his external comm, so Bryce had no idea what he was saying.

"I'll kill you for this!"

He'd found the external comm.

"I'll have you tortured until you beg for death!"

They were at the airlock.

Bryce opened the hatch and gave the man a hard shove, sending him through the opening and down, sprawling, onto the deck. He closed the inner hatch and immediately opened the outer one. It was against protocol, but it achieved the desired effect: the fast-escaping air expelled the dealer far away from the ship.

"Five," said Hsiao over the shipwide comm. "Four. Three. Two. One."

There was no need for any explanation. Everyone aboard knew what she was counting down to, with the exception of the rescued Marchonish women.

"We did it!" Hsiao announced. "We hit it perfectly."

No one was with him to celebrate, but Bryce didn't care. There would be time to celebrate later.

What mattered was the rogue planet, the excuse for decades of war, immeasurable pain and suffering and the loss of countless lives, and the source of the ill-gotten wealth of Lakshmi Station's elite, had received a hit from a weapon so powerful it would break it apart, leaving nothing but scattered rocks and a dusty haze.

It was over. There was nothing left for Marchon, Quinton, and Gugong to fight over. Their governments and corporations might scramble to find another excuse, but if the Marchonish would-be colonists were anything to go by, the populations were ripe for change. Hopefully, they had provided the catalyst.

He returned to the bridge.

Van Hasty was here and so was Jackson.

"Did you check on the kids?" Bryce asked him.

"They're doing fine, and they were very glad to hear the Marchonish men are gone."

Chi-tang was looking pleased with himself.

"What's happening with our business partner?" Bryce asked Hsiao.

"You mean our soon-to-be-ex business partner?" She looked up from the scanner. "His friends spotted him and are maneuvering to pick him up."

"Then it's time we left."

"That's exactly what I was thinking."

Van Hasty gasped. "Oh shit! What happened to the engineer?"

"She's still on the ship?" asked Bryce.

"She's still here somewhere. Where exactly is anyone's guess."

"She'll turn up sooner or later," said Hsiao, returning to the pilot's seat. Before she could issue the command to fasten safety harnesses, however, she received a comm. As she listened, her shoulders slumped. She gave a little *Oh!*

To Bryce's surprise, she collapsed onto her console and her shoulders began to shake.

"Hsiao?" He got up.

At the same time, Van Hasty noticed her. She reached the pilot first and leaned over her. "What's wrong?"

But Hsiao couldn't answer. She was sobbing her heart out. Deep, gut-wrenching sobs.

Her face a mask of bewilderment, Van Hasty removed Hsiao's comm button and spoke into it.

Bryce was close enough to hear Dr Asher answer. The doctor's words were crisp and formal, but her tremulous tone conveyed her struggle to maintain her composure as she said, "I'm sorry to inform you that Jace died a few minutes ago."

FORTY-FIVE

Bryce sat with his head bowed at Carina's bedside. He'd told her that her plan had succeeded. Everything she'd set out had worked, he'd said, with a few wrinkles along the way, though they hadn't managed to find a cure for Nahla. Still, she was healthy and seemed fairly happy.

The last part was a white lie. Nahla appeared down, in fact, and so was Darius. But Carina didn't need to know that. Should he tell her about Jace? Bryce doubted she could hear anything anyway. She was clearly near death herself.

He recalled collecting Darius from her bed. The boy had looked so sad even asleep. No one had told him Carina would pass away soon, but he knew. Of course he knew. Bryce wondered how he could even begin to offer the boy comfort when he was broken too.

He remembered the night he'd met Carina in the tavern on Ithiya. He'd watched her from a distance getting drunker and drunker, drowning a nameless sorrow like so many in that place. He'd followed her out into the street, drawn to her for some unknown reason. He recalled how he'd tried to steal from her to fund the meds he needed to keep himself alive, and how she'd woken and nearly killed him. The memories came flooding back: the journey over the snowy mountains to the Sherrerr fortress; persuading her to trust him on the Sherrerr ship, *Nightfall*, when they'd helped her family escape; her treacherous snake of a brother, Castiel; Sable Dirksen, malevolent and callous; Carina trapped in the battered mech on Ostillon; both of them riding horses when they left the Matching; sitting with her inside the eye of the space-traveling, sentient creature Darius had incongruously named Poppy.

They'd lived so much in such a short space of time, and now Carina's time was coming to an end.

What hurt him most was that he'd never had the chance to tell her how much he loved her. He'd gone to Lakshmi hoping he would be able to talk to her when he returned, but it was too late. She'd gone downhill so fast. After explaining the plan to Van Hasty, she'd never spoken again.

Dr Asher arrived. Her eyes were deeply shadowed and her face thin and pale. She'd suffered through the mages' illness too. Bryce couldn't imagine how hard it must be to lack the ability to help your patients, to be forced to watch young, healthy people wither away while you, the medical professional, stood by, helpless.

"I think you should call Darius and Nahla in here," she said.

A tight band fastened around his heart and chest. He swallowed and asked, "To say goodbye?"

Asher nodded. "It's advised. It will help them make sense of what's happening, and, eventually, it will help them come to terms with it."

Hardly able to get the words out, he said, "So she doesn't have long?"

"A few hours at most."

"And Parthenia?"

"She and the twins haven't entered the dying process yet, but they probably only have days left. Maybe a week or two."

His world was closing in around him, but somehow he had to find the strength to struggle through. "I'll go and get them." He forced himself to his feet and out of the sick bay. In a waking nightmare, he walked to the children's suite.

The door opened on familiar furniture. There was the table the family used to eat at together, and where Ferne and Oriana would create their unorthodox fashion designs. Across the living space was the door to Parthenia's room, where she would hide away refusing to speak to anyone. That was the sofa Darius and Nahla would sit on when they played cards.

Where were they?

He hadn't checked up on them since hearing the news of Jace's death and hurrying to Carina's side, fearing he might never see her alive again.

Did the children even know about Jace?

Heavy with guilt, he crossed the living area to their bedroom. Opening the door, he stuck his head around it.

Phew!

They were both here. Nahla was sitting on her bed reading her interface and Darius was asleep on top of his bedcovers.

Nahla looked up. "Hi Bryce! Something wonderful has happened."

"Has it? Tell me about it. I need to hear something wonderful."

"I can read what I wrote before."

"You can read what you wrote? What do you mean?"

"After I had my accident," she explained patiently, "I had to learn to read again. But it was hard and I was very slow. I used to ask Darius to read for me. One day I found something I'd written months ago, a translation of the mage documents. I couldn't understand it at all. But I tried to read it again just now, and I can! Listen."

She began to read aloud, fluently and confidently. Her intonation of complex sentences was perfect and her pronunciation of difficult words was correct. Bryce sank onto her bed. As he watched her, the truth dawned: the intelligent spark had returned to her eyes. He reached out to touch the interface, pushing it down.

She looked up, confused. "Did I read it wrong?"

"No, you read it perfectly. Could you do something for me? Could you walk to Darius's bed and back?"

She strode the ten steps swinging her arms.

Her limp had gone.

The old Nahla was back.

"This is a miracle!" he exclaimed. "You're the same as you were before. I wonder how it happened. What have you done since we returned from Lakshmi?"

"Nothing much. Just the usual. Except I had to play by myself because Darius wouldn't play with me. All he would do was lie on his bed and mope. How are Carina and the others? Are they getting better? It's boring staying in here with only Darius to talk to."

Bryce regarded the sleeping boy, and his elation over Nahla's miraculous recovery turned to despair as he remembered the awful news he had to convey.

Darius was lying on his back, his elixir bottle in his hand. The cap was off and from its position the bottle was empty. He must have drunk all the contents. That was strange. Why would he need to do a lot of Casting?

Horror bled into the edges of Bryce's mind. He looked at the sleeping boy more closely. For someone in a deep sleep, his chest was barely moving.

Was it even moving at all?

He thumbed his comm button. "Dr Asher? Please come to the children's suite immediately." He ran to Darius's side and listened to his chest. After two seconds of agonized waiting he heard one beat of the boy's heart.

Darius had saved Carina's life once, bringing her back from the edge of death. It was something only Spirit Mages could do, Carina had told him, but it was at the risk of losing their own lives. Had Darius Healed Nahla's brain, reinvigorating the dead cells, returning her to her original, highly intelligent state? And had he thereby put his life in the balance?

Just when Bryce thought his world could not become any darker, a new darkness descended. If Darius died, he couldn't see a way to go on.

Footsteps sounded in the outer room. Asher had arrived in record time.

But it wasn't the doctor who walked into the bedroom, it was Hsiao. Her grief over Jace's death still marked her features, but she managed a wan smile.

"I've left Bibik in control of the ship. I thought I would offer Darius some more flying lessons to help cheer him up."

"He's...He's..." Bryce struggled. The words wouldn't come out.

"Stars, Bryce, what's wrong?" She sat down beside him and put an arm over his shoulders.

"I think he might have done something really stupid."

"Huh?"

"I think he might have sacrificed himself for Nahla."

"What do you mean, sacrificed himself for me?" asked Nahla, looking up sharply.

He couldn't hide it from her. She was too smart. She would figure it out anyway.

"You know Darius is a Spirit Mage and the rest of your brothers and sisters are Star Mages?"

"Yes, of course. They don't talk about it much, but I do know that."

"Well, do you remember that time we went to the Matching, and Sable Dirksen had the place set alight?"

"It isn't likely I would forget something like that, is it?"

"Hold on," said Hsiao. "What did you say about Spirit Mages and Star Mages? What's the difference?"

"Spirit Mages are far more powerful," Nahla answered. Then her expression grew troubled. "Did Darius Cast for me? That's why I'm better?" She leapt up. "Is he going to be all right?

Asher ran in. "What's the— Stars, no!" She bent over Darius and lifted his eyelids. "He's out cold." She pulled a handheld scanner from a bag and placed it against his chest before running it over the rest of his body. As she read the display, a little of her tension visibly eased. "He has a steady heartbeat and respirations, but they're worryingly slow. Let's get him to sick bay. You can tell me what happened on the way."

Bryce lifted the boy into his arms.

Hsiao grabbed Nahla. "Why are Star Mages called that? Is it something to do with stars?"

"They aren't really sure, but it's believed they might derive their power from stars, while Spirit Mages derive theirs from the energy of the people around them."

"It was the star!" Hsiao yelled, so loud Bryce and Dr Asher paused in the doorway.

"The star at Lakshmi Station is abnormal," Hsiao continued. "It doesn't fit in any of the categories. It sends out all kinds of weird stuff. The star must have been affecting the Star Mages like a poison. First it killed their ability to Cast, and then it got to work on the rest of their bodies. Oh no! No! If I'd realized earlier, I could have saved Jace!"

She collapsed onto the bed, but Bryce could do nothing to help her. He had to get Darius to sick bay.

FORTY-SIX

They committed Jace's body to the universe the mage way, placing wood, water, iron, and earth with it. Unable to supply a real fire, they would cremate him in a blast from the *Bathsheba's* thrusters in the same way Carina had burned Ma's body all those months—years?—ago.

She clung to Bryce's arm as the ceremony took place, for physical as well as emotional support. By the time the short speeches were over, she was at the end of her strength.

Waking up had seemed like a miracle. After that last boost to her metabolism by the stimulant, her descent into her illness had been rapid. She could vaguely remember closing her eyes for what she thought would be the last time.

Then when she'd opened them again, it had been three weeks later. Jace had passed away, Nahla was better, and the Black Dogs had successfully carried out her plan, ridding the ship of the Marchonish would-be invaders, and probably also put an end to the Three-System War. What was more, the *Bathsheba* was now fitted with a weapon so large and powerful it should deter the most intrepid space pirates.

She wondered what Bongo had made of the news the rogue planet had been destroyed. Had he guessed she had something to do with it? Bryce had said his cousin had been there when they negotiated with the arms dealer. He had to know he'd been indirectly responsible for the destruction of the planet. She hoped the knowledge brought him some satisfaction.

She was certainly happy about it and she was grateful to Parthenia for her input. Her sister had changed her mind about other people's problems being none of her business.

They had gained seven new passengers while she'd been unconscious—eight if you counted the baby who was soon to be born. But they had lost one very important, very loved man, who Carina would never forget. She would miss his calm, gentle presence and wise advice.

The airlock opened. Six mercs carried Jace's wrapped body through the hatch carefully and respectfully. They gently placed him on the deck, saluted, turned, and marched out.

It wasn't quite the usual mage funeral, but Carina guessed Jace would have approved anyway. He and the Black Dogs had grown friendly over their time together, despite their opposing philosophies on life. But then again, Jace could make a friend of anyone, and who could have known him and not loved and respected him?

The hatch closed.

She closed her eyes and slumped against Bryce's side.

"Hey," he said softly. "Come on, let's find you a seat. I said you didn't need to stand. Everyone would have understood."

"I know, but I wanted to." She allowed him to lead her to the nearest room, where they found somewhere to sit down.

"I wanted to stay," she said weakly. "I should have stayed to the end."

"You're only missing the final part. It doesn't matter. Jace has gone. It's just his shell we were saying goodbye to."

"I know," she whispered, hunching over as tears spilled from her eyes.

Bryce pulled her close. "I don't know what to say to make you feel better. I'm going to miss him too, so much. But at the same time I'm glad there aren't five more bodies in that airlock."

"I'm glad the rest of us survived too. I really am, though it might not look like it. Especially Darius. He came so close."

"You *all* came so close. Asher told me you only had a few hours left and I had to go and get Darius and Nahla to..." He took a deep breath, paused, and pressed a finger and thumb to his eyes. When he'd mastered himself he went on, "Things could have turned out a whole lot worse. If we hadn't happened to leave the vicinity of that star in time, you wouldn't be here now."

"If only we'd left earlier," said Carina. "If only I'd figured out the star was having an influence on us. Hsiao told me there was something weird about it when we arrived. I didn't pay any attention. I was still angry at her over what she said about Darius at the meeting. I didn't think about the star at all after that. I still don't know how it affected us, but Hsiao must have been right."

"Right or wrong, I don't care. You're on the mend, thank the stars—though not the one powering Lakshmi Station."

Oriana peeked into the room. "There you are! We were wondering where you'd gone."

"I needed to rest a little," said Carina, "that's all."

"You'll feel better soon. Ferne and I are nearly back to normal. Dr Asher said it's because we're the youngest. Our bodies resisted the effects of the star longest. That's why Jace was the first to..." Her face twisted and she hung her head.

"It's okay," Carina said.

Parthenia also appeared and sat down next to Carina, resting her head on her shoulder. "I can't even remember the last time I spoke to Jace and now he's gone. I'll never get another chance to talk to him. Let's not ever fight again, okay?"

She appeared to be holding herself together, but the death of their friend had to be hitting her particularly hard. Jace had helped her and Darius when they were lost in the forest on Ostillon. He and Parthenia had always been close. In some ways he'd been the father she'd needed but never had, though who her true father was, Carina remained unsure. "I'll never fight with you again. I promise. You're right. You never know when it might be the last time you see someone you love."

"I'm going to hold you two to that," said Bryce.

Oriana lifted her head and wiped away her tears. "Is there any news on Darius?"

"He should be out of sick bay next week," Carina replied. "Dr Asher said he's making good progress."

"She also said he should never attempt to do the same thing again," Bryce said, "so it's up to us to keep an eye on him. I'm certainly never taking my eyes off any of you."

"That could get old fast," said Carina.

"You're just going to have to put up with me."

"Have you met any of the new people yet?" Parthenia asked.

"Maybe in a few days when I'm feeling better," Carina replied. "I noticed Jackson has a new arm."

Oriana said, "You should get him to show you what it does."

"Um, arm things?"

"More than that, but I won't spoil the surprise."

Nahla wandered in reading an interface. "Hey everyone. I looked something up and I thought you would be interested to know."

Seeing her little sister had returned to normal had been one of Carina's greatest joys on waking—until she found out the reason why. But it was good that she was better. "Okay, spill the beans."

"Lakshmi is the name of an ancient goddess who bestowed wealth and prosperity on her worshipers."

"No kidding?" said Bryce. "That makes a lot of sense."

"Are you talking about Lacks Me Station?" asked Ferne, also appearing at the door.

Oriana groaned. "I'm so glad we're leaving that place behind. I won't have to listen to you mispronounce the name all the time."

"We never even got to go there," Ferne complained.

"You didn't miss much, believe me," said Carina. "I'm very, very happy to be leaving it. And I guess now we have our ability to Cast back and we're mages again, we should continue with our plan to go to Earth."

"I think that decision requires a meeting," said Bryce.

"Yes," said Parthenia, "and don't leave me out this time."

Carina hugged her. "Don't worry, you're invited."

The ship suddenly dipped. The three children who were standing stumbled and Parthenia clutched her in surprise.

"What was that?" Ferne asked from the deck. "Is Bibik at the controls?"

The *Bathsheba* swerved upward and then jerked right.

"What's going on?" Oriana complained.

Hsiao's voice came over the shipwide comm. "Strap in, everyone, quick as you can. A strong gravitational field is pulling at us. The computer can't identify the source."

"Stars," said Carina, "can't we have a smooth, trouble-free passage for once? Is that too much to ask?"

CARINA'S STORY CONTINUES IN...

GALACTIC RIFT

(Amazon.com link. For your country's Amazon, scroll to the end of the book.)

Sign up to my reader group for a free copy of the *Star Mage Saga* prequel, *Daughter of Discord*, discounts on new releases, review crew invitations and other interesting stuff:

https://jjgreenauthor.com/free-books/

DOWNLOAD YOUR FREE READERS' GUIDE TO THE SCIENCE FICTION NOVELS OF J.J. GREEN

GALACTIC RIFT

ONE

The *Bathsheba* hung in darkness, the light of every star surrounding her blocked. The ancient colony ship sat in a cloud of all-enveloping pervasive dust stretching hundreds of light years. She had been shrouded for days, her fuel tanks slowly but steadily emptying as the Black Dogs' senior pilot, Hsiao, fought to free her from the inexorable pull of an unidentified gravity well.

Something had to be done, but Carina had no idea what. "Can't we catch a break for once?" she muttered to the void as scan data figures scrolled past on her interface.

"What was that?" asked Hsiao. "Do you have an idea?" Her features had grown more tired and drawn over the long hours she'd spent at the helm, trying every trick in the manual and a few more she'd come up with to try to break the ship free from the mysterious drag.

It was the quiet shift and they were the only two people on the bridge.

"Just talking to myself." Carina sat down and put her head in her hands. She'd barely begun to recover from her brush with death, courtesy of an anomalous star draining her life force, when the new problem had presented. She still felt weak but as de facto leader of the ship's company, the pressure was on her to find a solution.

"You know," said Hsiao, "if we don't do something soon, we won't have enough fuel to reach the nearest inhabited system, according to the chart."

"I know!" Carina exclaimed.

They'd dipped below the level of fuel needed to reach Earth three days ago.

Once the *Bathsheba* had reached her top cruising speed and everyone was in Deep Sleep, they could have—and would have—coasted for decades on minimal power. But fighting the pull of gravity required constant fuel expenditure. The dream of the final leg of their long journey had become just that. Their new reality entailed yet another stop at a civilized planet to refill the tanks. That was assuming they managed to escape whatever was dragging them in.

"Sorry," Carina murmured, her head slumping into her hands again.

"It's okay. I know I'm only stating the obvious."

"We're all repeating ourselves. We've run out of things to say."

The discussions and arguments had seemed endless. The situation made no sense. The gravitational effect on the ship should have also applied to the dust cloud. The particles should have been traveling toward the source too, yet they were not. The star charts showed no black hole, though they did mark the cloud. It was a vast area of cosmic dust of unknown origin. Nothing was known about what it contained either. Their course should have taken them past it, not through it.

"What is there to say?" Hsiao asked sadly. "We don't have any choices here. We're going wherever that damned drag wants to take us."

The bridge door opened and Bryce walked in. "Hey, ladies. Any change?"

"No," Carina answered, not moving her downcast posture. "No change."

"Well, I have some good news to cheer you up."

She lifted her head. "You've thought of something we can do?"

"No."

"Oh." She slumped again.

"You know our newest shipmate?"

"Uh huh."

Ava, one of the Marchonish women who had recently joined the ship, had given birth about a week ago.

"Her mother has decided what to call her. She's naming her after you, Carina."

"That's nice," she said without enthusiasm.

"It's a great honor," said Bryce. "You should be pleased."

"Should I?" All Carina could think was that another person was heading toward destruction and there wasn't anything she could do about it. And somehow it was her fault.

"Stars," Hsiao said. "That's terrible news!"

Bryce frowned. "Why?"

"It means we'll have two of them to deal with. Can you imagine *two* Carinas?"

"Very funny." She hauled herself to her feet. "I wish Jace was here. He was no starship navigator but he had the wisdom to help us face whatever was coming. I don't have a clue what to tell people."

Hsiao said, "The Black Dogs are all grown ups, with hairy bits, muscles, the lot. They don't need you to tell them anything."

"All right, but what do I tell the kids?" She turned to Bryce. "And the Marchonish women Van Hasty so kindly invited to join us? They would have been better off if they'd stayed with their slave-driving men."

"I'm not so sure about that," said Bryce. "At least here they get treated like human beings and they're free to do what they want, within reason."

"Fantastic," Carina said bitterly. "I hope they enjoy their final three days of freedom."

"Is that as long as we've got?" Bryce asked, eyes widening.

"We don't know! We don't know the mass of whatever it is that's pulling us in. The scanners aren't telling us a thing."

"Still nothing?"

She gave him a look.

"Okay, I'm the King of Stupid Questions. I just thought we should know something by now."

The bridge door opened again. Chi-tang had arrived. The former team leader of an underworld boss, he'd helped them destroy a planet that had been the excuse for an endless—and endlessly lucrative for some—war. In return, he'd earned passage on the ship. It was a decision he probably now regretted. He'd kept a low profile since Carina had recovered from her long sickness.

"I, er..." he began. But he didn't follow through. He looked at the three of them guiltily, as if something was weighing on his mind. "Things aren't looking too great for us, right?"

Carina replied, "You can say that again." She hadn't made an official announcement. The *Bathsheba* wasn't that kind of ship. Most news traveled among the company via osmosis. The fact of their perilous predicament had spread out the usual way.

"I thought so." He toed the floor pensively.

"If you've come to tell us something," Carina said, "it's best you get it off your chest. Because if things get any tenser around here I'm going to end up hitting someone."

"You got me," said Chi-tang. "I never could keep a straight face. Lost so much money at cards." He chuckled nervously. "I'm not sure it makes any difference, but I think I heard about this place."

"You knew about it?! Why didn't you say something?"

"I only just remembered."

Hsiao asked, "What do you know? Can you tell us how to escape it?"

"I can't, sorry. When I was a kid, I used to love studying history. Pre-war history, that is. Before the war started, the three systems around Lakshmi used to trade and travel extensively throughout the sector. Occasionally, ships would go missing. They were all in or near this region when it happened. Not all the time. Ships would pass near the cloud or even within its outskirts for years without incident, then suddenly one of them would vanish."

"Did any of them ever turn up again?" Hsiao asked.

"Not that I know of. Then the war started. The systems turned inward and focused their economic and technological power on defending themselves and defeating the other planets. The debate on whether to risk a journey in the vicinity of the cloud, or expend additional fuel to avoid it, became moot."

"And you're telling us this because...?" Carina asked icily.

"I just wanted to let you know."

She turned to Bryce and glared.

He held up his hands. "It was him who told you that. Not me. We're different people."

She returned her attention to Chi-tang. "So you remembered about this dangerous area of the galaxy after we entered it and now you're here to tell us it's dangerous but you don't know how to get out? Thank you so much. That's very helpful."

"I felt bad," said Chi-tang.

"We all feel bad. All of us." She looked down, clenching and unclenching her fists impotently. They'd come so far, through so many scrapes, surviving despite terrible odds. They'd lost friends and loved ones along the way, good people who hadn't deserved to die. It couldn't end here. She wouldn't let it. She looked up. "Cut the engines."

"What?" Hsiao asked.

"Fighting this thing is getting us nowhere. We're wasting fuel in a battle that's impossible to win. I said, cut the engines. Do it now."

The pilot blinked at her uncertainly but then lifted a hand to her console.

A shudder ran through the *Bathsheba* as the ship adjusted to the change in her motion. Now, she was moving with the current, hurtling headlong toward her fate. After a few seconds of acceleration force her inertia dampeners kicked in and it felt as though they were standing still. Nothing much had changed, except the faint vibration from the engine had ceased.

Comms began arriving at the absent communication officer's console.

Carina explained, "We might as well save the fuel we have left for whatever lies ahead."

Two

Odd scents emanated from the Marchonish woman's room. Sweet, milky, and sharp, they were not like anything Carina had smelled before, probably because she'd never been around a newborn babe and its mother. She'd gone to see the latest addition to the ship's company because it seemed polite considering the mother's choice of name, and because there was nothing else to be done except monitor the scanners for new data. Others could do that. The visit would also be a welcome distraction now the ship's fate was out of her hands.

The mother was called Ava, and she'd been the first to step forward when Van Hasty had invited the Marchonish women to switch sides. Her action had seemed to encourage the others to do the same, though sadly only five had made it under the Black Dogs' protection before they were forced to return to the *Bathsheba*.

One of Ava's companions had let her in. "She's through there," she whispered, nodding in the direction of the suite's bedroom.

"Is she asleep?"

"I don't think so, but Little Carina is. Never wake a sleeping baby."

Little Carina.

She smiled to herself, recalling Hsiao's joke. She wouldn't wish two Carinas on anyone either.

Ava did seem to be asleep, curled up on her side facing away from the door, the swaddled baby slumbering in a bassinet next to the bed. Someone must have found a printing pattern for the specialized furniture. Carina was confident they'd had no bassinets aboard.

She was stepping away, deciding to return later, when Ava turned over and smiled at her sleepily. "You must be Carina Lin. Come in."

"Hi," she replied, feeling awkward. "Is this a bad time?"

"No, I'm glad you're here. You're very welcome." Ava hauled herself to a sitting position, wincing.

Carina winced too, in sympathy.

"I wanted to thank you for helping me and my friends. There was no way we could have escaped without your help."

"I appreciate it, but what the Black Dogs did was nothing to do with me. You should thank Van Hasty from what I've heard, and the mercs who were with her."

"But you're the boss around here, aren't you? Your friends wouldn't have done what they did if they knew you wouldn't approve."

"That's debatable." It was true that she approved of the decision. When she'd heard about the rescue attempt, her only wish was that the Dogs had been able to save more of the women. "I'm glad you and your friends made it out, but I'm not really the boss. No one else wants the responsibility. If the Black Dogs don't like my orders they'll let me know soon enough."

While she'd been talking, her attention had drifted to her namesake. Only the baby's face showed, the rest of its body and head wrapped in a cloth. Red pimples stood out on the soft cheeks. "Is Little Carina sick?"

"You mean her rash? The medic said it's nothing to worry about, just her skin adjusting to being in air rather than water."

"Would you like me to fix it?"

"I didn't know you were a doctor too. Is there a cream you can give me?"

"I'm no doctor, but I can make the rash go away if you want."

"That would be great. I'm worried it makes her uncomfortable."

Carina took her elixir canister from her belt and sipped a mouthful of liquid. Laying a hand on the sleeping baby, she closed her eyes and Cast Heal. When she opened her eyes Little Carina's skin was free of blemish.

Ava's mouth had dropped open. "I heard you and your family could do magic but I didn't really believe it."

"It isn't magic, it's..." In the rare times she'd tried to explain Casting to non-mages, she'd never found the right words. That was because she didn't know herself how it worked and, she suspected, until scientists understood it, the words didn't exist. "It isn't magic," she repeated. "And it's a limited power, so don't get your hopes up expecting miracles."

Like dragging this ship away from whatever has her in its grip.

She had debated trying to keep her and her siblings' abilities secret from the Marchonish women and Chi-tang, but it would be difficult within the confines of the ship. Sooner or later, Darius or one of the twins would slip up and the cat would be out of the bag. It was easier this way and, well, they all might only have a short while to live anyway.

"I thought I might find you here," said Bryce, appearing in the doorway. "It didn't take long for your fame to go to your head."

Carina rolled her eyes and chose not to dignify his jibe with a reply.

"She's so cute," he went on, moving to the side of the bassinet. "Isn't she, Carina?"

"Uh, yeah." In truth, the baby looked like...a baby. "She's gorgeous," she added to the mother.

Ava beamed.

"Can I speak to you outside?" Bryce asked.

"Sure." As she left, she said to Ava, "Good luck, and let us know if there's anything we can do to help."

"You've already helped us more than you can imagine."

In the passageway, Bryce said, "What a beautiful baby. Ava picked the perfect name."

"You're a big suck up..." she kissed his cheek "...but I appreciate it."

"What do you think?"

"About what?"

"We might have a baby like that one day."

Her eyebrows shot up. "Are you insane? Have you forgotten we're most likely about to be crushed against a high-grav planet or annihilated in a black hole?"

"We've come this far. I have a feeling we're fated to survive."

"I wish I had your faith. What do you want to speak to me about?"

"Before that, I wanted to ask you, if we had kids, it would be a fifty-fifty chance they would be mages, right?"

"Bryce, I'm nineteen! Or twenty. I'm not sure. I've lost track. But I'm far too young to be thinking about kids."

"But maybe, one day."

"Something's messing with your head. Maybe the force that's pulling on the ship has affected your brain, like the star at Lakshmi Station destroying my mage powers."

He said wistfully, "I liked helping my parents with my brothers and sisters when they were little."

Shit.

She'd forgotten Bryce had abandoned his family forever when he'd decided to help her with her quest to reach Earth. "I'm not ruling it out. But—"

"You need to come back to the bridge. Something's come up. I don't think there's anything we can do about it, but you need to see it."

Hsiao had put the view outside the ship on holo. Van Hasty, Jackson, and Rees were on the bridge too.

Space had split.

The light-absorbing dust had disappeared and hanging in the void was a dark red, glowing chasm. It was a gash across the black, like someone had torn open the fabric of spacetime.

"How big is it?" Carina breathed.

"At its widest point," Hsiao replied, "about twenty-eight light years."

"*Light years*?!" She turned to Bryce. "Why didn't you tell me sooner? Why were you talking to me about having kids?"

Smiles passed between the mercs.

"What difference would it make?" Bryce replied. "What are you planning on doing about *that*?" He jabbed a finger at the holo.

"We could…"

"We don't have a hope of avoiding it," said Hsiao. "The pull on the ship is as strong as ever. We don't have the power to break free and if we try by the time we reach the rift our tanks will be empty."

Jackson said, "We're hoping we'll go through it and not get crushed in it. But it's just a hope. Hsiao's right. Whatever's gonna happen will happen, whether we like it or not."

"Do we have any idea what's on the other side?" asked Carina. "What do the scanners say?"

"They're telling us that's normal space," Van Hasty replied.

Whatever the tear in the galaxy was, normal it was not.

THREE

The rift seemed to occupy all space. To every side, above and below, the dark red expanse spread wide. Only a tiny sliver of regular vacuum and stars remained, far to the *Bathsheba's* rear as she slipped deeper and deeper into the anomaly. The attraction pulling her in was as strong as ever and they were no closer to figuring out what was causing it. In the weeks they'd spent trapped by the relentless pull, the scanners had failed to detect any high-mass bodies. But if gravity wasn't the cause of their predicament no one knew of any other explanation.

Carina was taking stock of their supplies. The majority consisted of chemical nutrients to keep them alive during long years of Deep Sleep. They also had mixes for the printers, edible and non-edible, and real food: powders and pastes for reconstituting, dry staples like flour, rice, and beans, dried meats, fish, fruits, vegetables, algae, and fungi, ready-made rations in packets and foil and whole, frozen foods to be thawed and cooked into tasty dishes on special occasions. The latter made up the smallest proportion. Lakshmi Station had also supplied them with water and—she peered at the figures and shook her head—Jackson had considerably upped the budget she'd allocated for alcoholic drinks.

She would have to remember to chide him about taking liberties while she lay dying in sick bay.

Their supplies weren't low yet but they couldn't continue eating them for months. If the ship was going to be traveling in the rift for an unknown amount of time, it might make sense to put everyone in Deep Sleep. They could schedule periodic awakenings for checking if they'd returned to normal space. They would survive longer that way, though not indefinitely. Eventually the chemical nutrients would run out and they would slowly, unconsciously starve to death. Perhaps that would be a better death than the current endless nightmare.

Their detour to Lakshmi Station had nearly been fatal, too, at least for her, Parthenia, Oriana, and Ferne. It *had* taken the life of their good friend, Jace. But in some ways the episode had been more fruitful than she'd expected. Lakshmi's specialism was starship weaponry, the source of its great wealth as it met the escalating needs of three warring systems, but it had also offered a range of ship's supplies. While she was out of action due to the deadly effect of the local star, her shipmates had taken full advantage.

The *Bathsheba* now sported one of Lakshmi's latest and most powerful weapons. Jutting from her bow was a device sufficiently powerful to blow apart a planetoid.

That had been another reason she wanted to conserve their remaining fuel. The Obliterator, as Bryce had taken to calling it, required a huge amount of power to operate. The arms dealer who had sold it to them, or, rather, who they'd stolen it from, had given it a fancier name based on tech jargon, but Obliterator seemed to fit better.

"What are you doing?"

Darius was poking his head into the little office.

"Hey, sweetheart. Just boring stuff. What have *you* been doing?"

He grinned at this tacit permission to disturb her and skipped into the room. He'd grown too big to sit on her lap, though it had taken a while for him to stop trying, so he contented himself with leaning against her. "I've been trying to invent new Casts."

"Oh you have, have you? I hope you haven't been doing anything dangerous."

"Not *really* dangerous," he replied after a moment's hesitation.

"Darius? What have you been doing? What does this new Cast do?"

Her Spirit Mage brother had invented two other Casts, Cloak and Guise. Cloak had proven very useful in the past, turning their ships and themselves undetectable and so helping them escape dangerous situations. He'd only used Guise for fun. The Cast enabled him to take on another's appearance and he'd played many tricks pretending to be someone else, in a typical seven-year-old's fashion.

"Well, I call it Heat. I guess it might be dangerous if I wasn't very, *very* careful. But I am so it's okay."

"Heat? Not Fire?"

"Fire makes things burn if they can burn, but Heat heats them up."

"So..." she looked around the room for something suitable 'you could make that hot?' She pointed at a metal-framed chair.

"Uh huh. That's easy." He unscrewed his elixir bottle.

"Just a little, okay?" she cautioned, worried the fabric seat might burst into flame.

Moments later, she gingerly touched one of the metal legs. It was pleasantly warm. "You're a smart boy. You know that?"

He smiled with pride.

"Strap in!" came Hsiao's warning over the intercom. "If you can't strap in, find something to hang onto."

"Darius," Carina blurted, "sit here." She leapt out of her seat, the only one in the room with a safety harness. After lifting him into the chair and fastening the straps, she comm'd Hsiao. "What's going on? And why wasn't I told about it?"

"I can't speak right now." The pilot cut the comm.

Cursing, Carina raced to the doorway and grabbed the bars on each side of it, handholds in case the ship lost gravity. The *Bathsheba* lurched violently, almost breaking her grip. Then the ship accelerated so fast she briefly became weightless. They came to an abrupt stop and a harsh shock juddered through everything, rattling her teeth.

"Carina," called Darius, "what's happening?"

"Don't worry, it's going to be okay." It was probably the biggest lie she'd ever told him. She had no idea if things would be okay. The *Bathsheba's* movements indicated they were far from it.

The extreme motions seemed to have stopped. "Hsiao, can you talk to me now?"

"Dammit. I tried my best. I'm sorry."

———

A starship had appeared, even larger than the *Bathsheba*. The scanners said it was roughly twice the size of the colony ship. According to Hsiao and the scan data, it had come from nowhere.

The ship's design was odd. Most of the structure consisted of a vast concave dish covered in spikes. That was all that was viewable from their present vantage point, but when it had appeared Hsiao had seen a pinnacle protruding from the opposite side. The new vessel's entire hull was the exact same color as a blue-green desert slime mold Carina had only ever seen on the planet where she grew up.

At the same time the ship had appeared, the source of the drag on the

Bathsheba had also become visible, Hsiao had said. Their ship had been caught in a beam all along. The pilot had seen a cylinder of pale light stretching from the prow into the rift. As the strange ship had approached, the light had vanished, and that had been the moment Hsiao had tried to make their escape.

She'd started the engine and slammed the ship into maximum acceleration, but almost immediately after the beam had disappeared, another had shot out from the new ship and fastened onto them. Now, the *Bathsheba* continued to be drawn deeper into the rift, this time pulled by another vessel. The new beam was undetectable but Carina guessed it was generated by the concave dish.

"All this time," she said, "something's been taking us somewhere. This isn't some weird astronomical event, it's personal. Someone wants us."

"Maybe not us in particular," the pilot replied, "but a starship. Chi-tang said vessels had randomly vanished over long periods of time. My guess is the dust cloud blocked comms. We don't have anyone to send a Mayday to, so we never tried, but the other vessels would have. The dust prevents messages from reaching anyone."

"Whatever. It's all by design. I don't know what happened to the people on those other ships, but I bet whoever took them has never encountered mages. I hope they find they've bitten off more than they can chew."

FOUR

"There's no point in trying to destroy it with the Obliterator," said Jackson. "The weapon probably *can* put that ship out of action if not blow it to pieces, but what then? The original attraction beam will fasten on us again or maybe they'll send another ship the same as the first, or a whole fleet to get their revenge. The point is, the civilization that constructed that thing can reach out across space and grab hold of a colony ship light years away. It's like nothing we've ever encountered. And that's speaking as a merc who's lived far longer than I should have in this business and seen more human and alien societies than I can count or remember."

He paused and flexed his prosthetic fist. "If this was a regular situation where some asshole was messing with us, I'd be the first to show them where they can shove their attitude. You know that. But it isn't. We can't come out guns blazing here or we might find ourselves in even worse trouble. We've gotta feel things out. Take it step by step if we're gonna get out alive and with our ship intact."

"Shit," said Rees. "He's channeling Cadwallader."

"You say that like it's a bad thing," Van Hasty commented. "I'm with Jackson. Say we do break free and put their ship out of commission. We'll be where we are now only with less fuel. Definitely not enough to get us out of this shithole we've been dragged into. Besides, a ship like that will have shields. Stands to reason. We might not take it out with the first or even fifth hit."

"So we just let them do whatever they want?" Carina asked. "Before the monster ship turned up I thought we were in the grip of some weird deviation from normal physics. Now we know it's personal, we can't let those people push us around. It gives them the wrong idea."

"I'm not saying we should let them push us around forever," Jackson replied, "but we can't go off half-cocked either. That would be dumb. We need to think this through."

"Jackson's right," Van Hasty reiterated. "We can't let our pride get in the way. We need to think long-term."

"I'm not talking about pride," Carina protested. "I'm talking about how they see us. So far, we've acted like prey, passively allowing ourselves to be towed. I wish I hadn't told Hsiao to turn off the engine and stop fighting. We've acted like victims so that's how we're treated."

"Seems like they're gonna do what they're gonna do," Rees said. "Doesn't matter how they see us."

"Yeah," Jackson agreed. "I get your point, Lin, but just because they think they've got us over a barrel, doesn't mean we can't hit back when the time's right. We have to think ahead and wait for our chance. They're not going to bring us all the way here just to kill us. They have something else in mind."

Exasperated, Carina turned to Hsiao. "What do you think?"

The pilot raised her hands. "I just fly starships. I let you guys figure out the hard stuff."

Bryce also didn't seem to want to contribute an opinion.

Carina gave up. "Looks like I'm outvoted."

"Hey," said Rees. "What about some mage stuff? Could your family do something?"

"I thought about it, but if we're planning on playing the long game like it seems we are, I think it's better if we keep our powers secret. Don't you?"

"Absolutely," said Jackson.

———

Carina tightened her grip on her pulse rifle, silently cursing the decision not to try to take out the vast vessel. It felt like giving up control, despite Jackson's assurance they were doing no such thing.

That was before the rest of the enemy ships arrived. Fifteen of them. *Fifteen*! They'd come at them all at once, their arrival masked by the giant ship, and spread out in all directions, making the question about firing the Obliterator moot. That was the disadvantage of the weapon. It was only effective against one target moving predictably. Against many targets moving along on differing trajectories, it was useless.

She waited. True to Jackson's theory, the enemy hadn't attacked, yet. But as with their mothership all attempts to hail them had fallen on deaf ears. They either wanted the *Bathsheba* or her crew or both. Four of their vessels had moved into position alongside, preparing for a face-to-face fight. What would the boarders be like? Would they even be human? She recalled the Regians and gave a shudder. They had barely escaped from the insectoid, time-shifting aliens. Some of them had not.

A dull thud hit the hull and reverberated through the deck. They were at the airlock. Another thud, rattling her teeth. She winced. She'd grown fond of the old ship and hated the thought of more damage being inflicted on her. The Regians had torn open the airlocks too.

A third thud.

"Weapons ready," she unnecessarily reminded the mercs in her team. Also with her were Viggo Justus, the Lotacryllan, and Chi-tang. The latter had been reluctant to join the defenders, saying his specialty was large weapons tech, not small arms. But Van Hasty had unceremoniously thrust a pulse rifle into his hands. The message was clear: as an adult, he had a duty to protect the ship.

Carina hadn't felt much sympathy for him. All the Marchonish women except for Ava had volunteered without being asked, lending a hand though they had never even held a gun.

The fourth thud did it. A terrible screech of wrenched metal parts came from the airlock. The attackers had breached the outer hatch. She activated the magnetic soles of her boots and reminded Chi-tang to do the same. He clutched his rifle nervously. She prayed he didn't kill someone on his own team. Then she ordered the ship's computer to close the emergency seals at each end of the passageway.

Movement could be seen through the tiny window in the inner hatch and, beyond the figures, the blackness of space. They had taken the outer door off completely. These guys were not messing around.

"What's happening where you are?" Rees comm'd. "Our uninvited visitors have nearly opened the door."

"Same here."

"Bryce's team too," said Rees. "In case you were wondering."

Something thunked against the inner hatch. The view of space disappeared, replaced by steel.

"See you on the other side," she said and cut the comm.

Wisps of smoke drifted from the bulkhead surrounding the inner hatch.

The hostiles were using a different method to break through the smaller portal. Some kind of machine was burning through the inner layer of hull. A red, glowing line in the shape of an oblong appeared. Smoke poured from it, sending the atmosphere filters whining with effort to clear it and Carina's

HUD readings haywire. The line turned white. Molten metal dripped onto the deck, melting holes in the tile.

"Back up," she commanded.

The team split into two, moving down the passageway.

They waited.

All nervous shuffling ceased. Attention was on the hatch.

After agonized seconds of anticipation, a tremor ran through it. Like a felled tree, the portal, carved from its support, toppled with a clang to the deck.

Her HUD flashed up an alarm as atmosphere flooded out. The escaping gases dragged her forward, ripping her off her feet. Others tumbled toward the ruined airlock with her. Some had managed to secure a hold and were only lifted up. Then all the air was gone.

She quickly scrambled upright, yelling, "Fire at will!" as figures poured through the breach.

Encased in matt black armor, their faces hidden behind deep black visors, they sprayed the mercs with pulse rounds.

She shot back. At the close range, her pulses should have had an effect, but the assailants' suits appeared unmarked. Her own was already growing hot from the hits she was receiving.

There was no cover in the open passageway. Unless she ordered the computer to open the emergency seals, depressurizing the ship and allowing the attackers more access, the fighting would end here, one way or another.

She gave the command to fall back.

The attackers moved forward with practiced ease, a tidal wave of firm intent. The passageway was alive with pulse fire as brilliant bolts of energy flashed. More attackers appeared behind the first, ready to replace fallen comrades, but none fell. The mercs were hopelessly outclassed by the superior tech.

A merc beside Carina collapsed, her suit smoldering.

Comms from Rees and Bryce sounded in her helmet. At their sites the experience was the same: the enemy's assault was powerful, relentless, and over-whelming.

It was time to surrender or die fighting.

The decision was made.

"This is it," she said over comm. "Drop your weapons."

FIVE

The journey down to the planet was bumpy and uncomfortable. They'd been herded directly onto steel containers inside the enemy ship and after many hours without food, water or toilet breaks, the containers were lifted onto space-to-surface transports. What followed was the worst flight Carina had ever experienced. The planet's atmosphere seemed highly turbulent as they were buffeted and jerked every which way, thrown into each other and the steel walls, before a heavy impact brought an end to the trip and their suffering.

Chi-tang and several mercs had upchucked on the way down, leaving Carina dangerously close to vomiting too. She hoped the kids, Ava, and the newborn babe's travel experience had been smoother.

Bolts rattled in their mountings, and the opening end of the container fell outward, slamming to the ground. A heavy cloud of dust swirled in, instantly choking her. Curses and coughing filled the space. The air holding the dust was frigid and dry. Lights penetrating it seemed artificial, coming from several sources rather than the sky. They had to be outdoors, so perhaps it was nighttime.

Men and women in fatigues, their faces enclosed in masks and breathing gear, lurched from the gloom, yelling. Their facial coverings made their words indistinct but the meaning behind the movement of their rifles was clear. Bruised, tired, thirsty, and hungry, Carina stumbled with the others toward the exit.

In her years as a merc visiting many worlds, she'd discovered each planet had its own subtle odor. Some smelled like malfunctioning sanitation systems, sulfuric compounds lacing the atmosphere. Others, heavily vegetated, held more pleasant scents that she could only describe as variations of 'green'. This world smelled acrid, as if its air was caustic. Was that the reason for the breathing apparatus? Did human lungs burn here?

Soldiers ran behind them to haul the worst-affected by the trip to their feet and force them out. More soldiers flanked her group on each side. They drove them down the shallow ramp created by the open side of the container. A gusting, moaning wind was lifting the dust. It swirled into her eyes and nostrils. She kept her mouth clamped shut and squinted. Barely able to breathe, let alone see, she gave up trying to survey her surroundings and focused on remaining upright.

As Jackson had said, they had a long game to play.

A patch of darkness loomed ahead. They were pushed toward it. After fifteen or so meters of rocky ground, her feet met concrete on a downward incline. The wind eased and the darkness increased. The dust seemed to diminish. Overhead lights flicked on. They were inside a tunnel.

Their guards closed in. The passage held five people walking abreast: two soldiers on the wings and three prisoners in the center. Three captors walked in front. When she turned to see how the rest of her companions were faring, the guard nearest her poked her with his rifle.

"Eyes forward."

She was startled. She'd heard two voices. The one she understood had come from somewhere below his mouth, but the words from behind his mask were incomprehensible. He was using a translator. These people didn't speak Universal.

They walked deeper, lights activating as they approached. The wind died away completely and along with it most of the dust, though the air remained hazy. A thick layer of fine particles covered the floor, piling up at the tunnel sides like snowdrifts. She was covered in the stuff, too, and her eyes smarted as the gritty grains fell from her lashes.

Another set of lights came on, revealing double steel doors ahead. As they approached, the doors rolled apart. They were forced into a large elevator, which descended for about fifteen seconds. At the bottom they stepped into a brilliantly lit, bare space covered in clean white tiles, floor, walls, and ceiling.

"Strip," a soldier ordered via translator. "Put everything in the chutes."

She cursed. She'd secreted elixir ingredients in her clothes and so had her mage siblings—wherever they were. She slowly undressed, hoping for a chance of retaining one or two items, but their captors were adamant the prisoners removed every last piece of clothing.

When everyone was naked, the soldiers filed out another door and the chutes snapped shut. Cold water erupted from nozzles in the ceiling and walls. She gasped and cursed again as the frigid liquid hit. There was no escaping it as it sluiced away the dust clinging to their skin. The dirty water disappeared down grilles in the floor.

Chi-tang said over the hiss of from the nozzles and the complaints of the mercs, "I'm starting to regret my decision to join up with you guys."

"I didn't think you were given much choice about it," Carina replied, her teeth chattering.

"Well, that's right, but I thought I was onto a good thing. Now, I'm not so sure."

"Are they disinfecting us?" Viggo asked. "Is that what this is about?"

"No idea," said Carina. "But one thing's clear. We're a helluva way off the beaten track. They don't even know Universal."

"They know it," said Viggo. "They just choose not to speak it."

The spraying stopped and the door the soldiers had vanished through opened. Beyond it was a second tiled room, but this looked dry and held clothes in piles on the floor. They filed through the opening, wet and cold.

The clothes were all the same color and style—plain yellow pants and shirts—but in different sizes. Along with the others, Carina sorted through the piles until she found garments that vaguely fit and then put them on. They'd also been given sandals.

"Haven't these people heard of underwear?" Chi-tang complained.

"If no boxers are the worst of our troubles," said Viggo, "we'll be damned lucky."

Carina squeezed the excess water from her hair and shivered as she fastened her shirt, wondering if Bryce and her family were being put through the same process. Their captors were treating them like cattle.

"Welcome to Sot Loza," said a voice.

A woman had entered the room. With her came warm air, wafting from the open doorway behind her. She wore a dark blue military uniform and her hair was tightly drawn up in a bun. As with the soldiers, she spoke through a translator.

"Some kind of welcome," Carina retorted. "What have you done with our clothes? Will we get them back?"

"I am Vice-General Queshm. Your induction is over and you're free to enter the city. You have freedom of movement within the city boundaries, but if you break any of our laws you will lose that privilege. The laws, along with more details regarding your lives here, are posted at your lodgings, where I will now escort you."

"What have you done with our stuff?!" Carina demanded. "Why have you brought us here? Where are the other people from our ship?"

"Come with me," said the Vice-General, turning.

"You'd better not push it," said Viggo.

Grumbling, Carina took his advice and followed Queshm with the others. She was growing deeply worried about her family. Darius and Nahla were too young to deal with this shit. Even Oriana and Ferne would be scared.

The Vice-General led them down a passageway and then out into a general thoroughfare. The atmosphere was warm and the caustic scent of the surface barely noticeable. People streamed past in each direction, though the emergence of the yellow-clothed newcomers onto the street soon provoked a stir. The pedestrians slowed down or halted to stare. A multi-person transport drew up and parked. Smaller vehicles drove around it, though the passengers rubbernecked as they maneuvered.

"Get aboard," Queshm barked. "Hurry up."

"Hey, beautiful," a man yelled. "When you get out, call me. My number's..." He reeled off the digits.

"Who's he talking to?" asked Chi-tang.

"Me, of course," Viggo replied.

Carina was studying the sky, or, rather, the ceiling of the underground city. It glowed a pale purple and wispy clouds moved across it. The effect was realistic. There was even a faint breeze, though she guessed from pumps that kept the air breathable more than an attempt to mimic an outdoor environment.

"You," Queshm snapped at her. "Move it."

The others were aboard the transport. She climbed the step into the vehicle and took an empty seat next to a window. First, she had to find her brothers and sisters and Bryce, and the rest of the *Bathsheba's* personnel. Then she had to work out the escape plan.

SIX

Outsiders are bound by all Sot Loza's laws. In addition:
    Outsiders must not leave their city's boundaries
    Outsiders must not wear any other clothing than their uniform
Outsiders must not fraternize with anyone below managerial caste
Outsiders must not take employment
Outsiders must not participate in activities that risk harm to their persons
Outsiders must eat and exercise regularly to maintain good health

The notice hung on the wall in the lobby of the single-story building where Queshm had offloaded them.

"We have to eat and exercise and not do anything risky?" said Viggo. "Weirdest rules for prisoners I've ever seen."

"We're not prisoners," Chi-tang corrected. "We're *outsiders.*"

Carina was trying to figure out the rules too. The most alarming was the edict to not leave *'their* city's boundaries'. Why not *this* city's boundaries? Did it mean some captives from the *Bathsheba* were being held elsewhere? Had they been taken to different locations all over the planet? It was a scenario they hadn't anticipated yet it made sense. Separating the new prisoners by thousands of kilometers made them easier to control. Her group only numbered twelve people, far too few to stage an escape attempt.

The requirement to always wear their uniforms also made sense. They would stand out like beacons among the general populace. What about the rules they mustn't get a job or fraternize with the lower classes? Was that because the poorer locals might help them?

Her biggest question was, why had they been brought here in the first place? The Sot Lozans had gone to an awful lot of trouble to get them to their planet. If seizing the *Bathsheba* had been their only motivation it would have been safer to kill her crew, not take them prisoner. There was always the chance they would try to get their ship back. The Black Dogs wouldn't disappoint the Sot Lozans in that regard.

Their new quarters consisted of a dormitory, communal washroom, refectory, gym, storage closet containing additional yellow uniforms and bedding, a laundry, and a room for leisure activities. The last held working interfaces but they couldn't use them. The spoken and written languages were not Universal nor any other language or dialect familiar to Carina or her companions.

The first facility she'd looked for was a kitchen, but there was none. It was the most important room if she was to create elixir. She could have used the heat source to set something alight. Naked flames and wood were going to be the hardest elixir elements to come by.

She left the lobby, returned to the dormitory, and flumped onto a bed.

"Hey, that's mine," Chi-tang protested, following her into the room.

Scowling, she replied, "Does it matter?"

"It does to me."

She found another bed, this time near a window looking out onto a paved yard a few meters square. The surrounding buildings were only two floors high. She guessed the fake sky wasn't far above them. The windows in the residence weren't barred and no guards stood outside. They were free to come and go as they pleased.

"Who wants to go and explore?" she asked the room generally.

"Not me," Chi-tang replied. "I'm exhausted. I'm going to get some sleep, so I'd appreciate a little quiet in here."

The Black Dogs had been doing their usual thing, bantering, slamming into things, and shoving each other around. At Chi-tang's complaint they quietened down somewhat but threw him dark looks. Trouble lay ahead if he didn't stop his whining. Carina couldn't find a shit to give. He was getting on her nerves too.

"I'll go with you," Viggo said.

They stepped out onto the thoroughfare. This place wasn't as busy as the spot where the transport had picked them up. They were on a long, straight road that stretched out of sight in both directions. The surrounding buildings seemed to be workplaces rather than habitations. Their blank, featureless facades dotted the roadway, where vehicles flew past at high speeds.

The same lilac sky as before hung overhead, and she could have sworn the same clouds floated across it, as if playing in a loop. The ceiling couldn't be far overhead but she wasn't sure how deep underground they were. The elevator that had brought them to this level hadn't traveled a long time.

"Wondering how to get up on top?" asked Viggo. "If you had your special liquid we could do it."

Was he being serious?

"Don't be dumb. We'd only find ourselves back where we were before, and we'd die there pretty quick."

"If it's all the same on the surface, maybe. But we don't know that. We only saw one area and they might have picked it intentionally to give us a certain impression."

"I didn't think of that."

"Something to think about. Which way are we going?"

She shrugged. "The direction we came from, I guess."

The ground was bedrock, gray and flat except for tiny grooves where the burrowing machine had cut into it. The same bedrock rose up beyond the buildings. The tunnel seemed to be about a hundred meters wide. Somewhere toward the top of its walls the rock's appearance turned hazy and faded into sky.

As they walked, Carina marveled at the feat of engineering the Sot Lozans had performed in creating their underground world. "Have you ever seen or heard of anything like this?"

"Never. Not in my sector or yours."

"The surface *has* to be uninhabitable all over, or else why would they go to all this trouble?"

Before Viggo could answer, a vehicle braked hard, pulled off the road, and parked. A woman got out. Wearing a fine-textured light blue pants suit and shiny black shoes, she walked up to them, smiling. Short, dark brown hair framed her face. She appeared older than Carina but not by much. Maybe mid-twenties.

She spoke but unintelligibly.

After taking in their expressions, she lifted a finger as if asking them to wait and then ran back to her vehicle. When she returned, she wore a small black cube on a choker. "Sorry, you're new, right?"

"If you mean have we been dragged across space," Carina replied, "light years off our route, taken prisoner, forced down to your planet, and are being held captive? That's right, we're *new*."

The woman gave an awkward cough and murmured, "I thought so. Can I give you a ride somewhere?"

"Where do you suggest we go?" Carina asked. "If you can take us back to our ship, that would be great."

"This area's only just been developed. There isn't a lot to do or see. I thought you might want to go into town."

"I appreciate the offer," Viggo said, "but it would be more helpful if you could explain to us exactly what's going on."

"Yeah," Carina echoed. "Why have we been brought here and when will we be released? When will we get our ship back?"

"You're kidding, right?" the woman retorted. "You're here to stay. You aren't going anywhere." She turned to Viggo. "Are you sure I can't show you around?"

Throughout the conversation, she'd focused mostly on him and now she looked expectantly at him for an answer. When he looked at Carina for her input, irritation flickered over the woman's face.

"It's up to you what you do," Carina said, "but from our experience so far I don't trust any of them. I'm not getting in her car."

"I wasn't asking *you*," the woman spat.

"I'm sticking with my friend," said Viggo.

"You're sure?"

"Certain."

She sighed and reached into her pocket. Pulling out a card, she gave it to Viggo, saying, "You can reach me here. Anytime, okay?"

Bemused, he took it.

Carina stared. *Damn. She really wanted to spend time with him, a complete stranger and newcomer to her world.*

The woman left, giving a final disappointed backward glance before climbing into her vehicle and speeding away.

Viggo held up the card to read it. The material was wrinkled and dog-eared, as if it had been in the woman's possession a long time.

"It's in Universal script," Carina remarked.

The information on it was scant. All it stated was a name—Hedran Mafmy—and a 9-digit number.

"One thing's for sure," she added. "You have a fan."

And by 'fan' she meant potential co-conspirator.

SEVEN

"This is it," said Carina over comm. "Drop your weapons."

Bryce slung his rifle over his back and raced from the airlock.

As well as a general command, her words were a signal to him in particular. He had to make his way to the suite where her family and the Marchonish woman, Ava, had sheltered while the battle for the ship raged.

The decision to separate Carina from her siblings when the *Bathsheba* inevitably fell into enemy hands had been a hard one to make. After hours of argument, the consensus had been if they were going to be captured they had to split up the mages. The children were too young to be parted from each other, but Carina working on her own would double the opportunities to use their powers. As well, if one mage's abilities were revealed, Carina or the children's might remain secret a while longer.

Now, the kids, Ava, and her baby were Bryce's responsibility. He had to stick with them at all costs and do his best to protect them from whatever their attackers had in mind.

The door to the suite was already open. Inside, Parthenia and the children bustled about, packing bags. In the midst of them Ava stood, clutching the swaddled babe, her eyes wide and frightened.

Parthenia halted and stared. "We've surrendered already?"

"Don't worry," he replied. "Everything's going as planned."

"I still think we should have fought," said Ferne, "to the bitter end if necessary. We mages could inflict a lot of damage before they took us out."

"And that's precisely why you aren't in charge of battle strategy," Oriana chided. "What's the point of fighting until everyone's killed? What good would that do?"

"Some things are worse than dying," he retorted. "Remember the Regian planet?"

"Shhh!" Parthenia put a finger to her lips and nodded at Darius. "We don't need reminding of unpleasant times."

Darius said, "I remember the Regians just as much as you do. And Poppy. Poppy was nice," he added wistfully.

Poppy was the name he'd given the creature who had helped them escape the time-shifters. If the animal was his main memory of their time with the Regians, who used humans as hosts for their eggs, he was lucky.

"The boarders will be here soon," Parthenia said. "Do we have everything?"

"I have everything I need," said Ferne, tapping the bottle of elixir on his hip.

"Don't make a show of it," Parthenia warned. "Remember what we agreed?"

Darius held up a holdall. "I have my bag."

"Me too," said Nahla.

"Then we're all set." She moved next to Ava and beckoned the others to do the same. She was pale and her expression grim.

The sound of pounding booted feet echoed down the passageway.

"They're coming," Bryce said. "Get ready."

He waited, peeking from the cover of the doorway, the muzzle of his rifle aimed in the direction of the approaching soldiers, silently praying that Jackson's hunch was right and their attackers didn't want to kill them all. If Jackson was wrong, Carina might already be dead. He swallowed. If the hostiles were planning on a massacre, he hoped he wouldn't live to see—

A figure rounded the corner.

Like the ones Bryce had fought at the airlock, the soldier was heavily armored and his visor allowed no glimpse of his face. Bryce aimed and fired. The pulse round hit but washed over the boarder's chest armor like a wave washing over a rock, except it left no trace. As he ducked back into the doorway, a round exploded on the frame.

"Be careful, Bryce!" Parthenia exclaimed.

"Stay back, and when they come don't put up any resistance." He dipped into the passageway again. Instantly, a round grazed his helmet. He moved his head behind the frame and fired blindly. He'd glimpsed three soldiers. The first was only meters away.

He tossed his rifle to the deck and raised his hands over his head. Taking a breath, he stepped out. But the attackers were primed to shoot. He took three or four rounds at nearly point blank range. His armor couldn't cope. Heat blazed onto his skin. In agony, he dropped to his knees and fell onto his front, redoubling the pain of his wounds. He writhed onto his back.

"Bryce!" Parthenia screamed.

Vaguely, he registered a kick. Someone took his rifle, then the soldiers stomped past him and into the suite. There were more of them now. Eight? Nine? They ignored him. By chance, he could see into the room and watched helplessly as the soldiers rounded up the kids. They grabbed their bags and threw them against the bulkhead, their contents spilling out. Ava was weeping. Darius's lower lip trembled but he was holding up. That poor kid had been through so much. Nahla glared at their captors defiantly as they forced the group toward the exit.

No sound came from the soldiers as they ushered the children and Ava away. Everything was done by gesture, but no doubt they spoke to each other via internal comm. From the way their heads moved and their gait, they seemed pleased to have discovered the kids. They were so pleased, in fact, they almost forgot him.

The group had reached the corner when one ran back to where Bryce sprawled in pain. He grasped Bryce's arm and tried to pull him to his feet.

He gasped in agony but the soldier had no mercy. He kicked his thigh and pulled harder on his arm. Somehow, Bryce managed to heave himself upright. He had to stay with the kids and Ava. He stumbled forward, hunched over, and followed the path the others had taken.

They headed for the airlock he'd been helping to defend and which the boarders had destroyed. The section had depressurized and the kids weren't wearing suits. How were the enemy planning on getting their captives through the airless space?

But when he reached the area his HUD told him it had breathable atmosphere. The airlock hatch, severed from its surround, lay on the deck, an oblong hole with melted edges where it had once stood. The children and Ava were not here. They'd been taken onto the enemy ship. He hobbled faster to try to catch up to them.

The far side of the airlock was a gaping hole and beyond it stretched a steel walkway. A rigid umbilicus led to the enemy vessel. At the end a huddled group was surrounded by soldiers. Ava and the kids.

He upped his pace, gritting his teeth against the pulsing agony of his chest and stomach. He wanted to call out to them and tell them he was coming but he couldn't. The group moved away to the right, guided by their captors. When he reached the same spot, his guard pushed him to the left.

"No," he grunted, trying to follow the children and Ava.

His guard blocked him and shoved him backward with two hands against his chest.

Bryce collapsed. The pain was too great. He pointed in the direction the children had gone. The soldier slapped his hand away and pointed left. His shoulders sagging, Bryce shook his head.

His captor snapped the neck seals on Bryce's armor open and wrenched off his helmet. He looked up and blinked as the cool air chilled his sweat. The black visor confronted him. The soldier barked a command and pointed again.

He couldn't understand the words but he knew the meaning. "I...have to... stay with—"

The guard jabbed his rifle into his chest.

He cried out.

"Okay," he muttered. "I get it."

With great effort, he staggered to his feet. He had to follow the order. He would be no use to the kids and Ava if he was dead.

His heart heavy, he shuffled off to the left, hoping he could find the others later.

EIGHT

The transport had returned. It pulled up outside the center and parked, visible from the refectory window. Carina and the others had gathered in the room hoping to be fed, but no evening meal had materialized. Instead, it looked like they were being taken somewhere.

"Should we just get aboard?" asked Chi-tang.

"No way," said one of the Black Dogs, a woman called Pamuk. "Who knows where it'll take us?"

Viggo suggested, "I don't think we're going to eat unless we get aboard that thing."

"That's the message I'm getting too," said Carina.

Chi-tang was already on his way out. His physique was on the chunky side and he loved his food.

"Man's stomach's gonna lead him to his grave," Pamuk remarked.

"You're right," Carina agreed, "but I'm hungry too." She followed Chi-tang. Another motivator was the hope she might see Bryce and her siblings.

In the end, everyone boarded. It was only then the transport departed.

Carina and Viggo had discovered on their excursion that their residence was a long way from anywhere useful. After walking for an hour they didn't come across any place where they could find out more about Sot Loza or how they might get off it. Their residence was in an area that effectively cut them off from most of the population. The only moments of interest after meeting Hedran Mafmy were the appearance of workers at the windows of buildings.

The Sot Lozans pressed their faces against the glass and watched as they walked by, but no one approached. Perhaps the people were not 'managerial class'.

The vehicle set off in the opposite direction from their arrival, zooming down the long, straight road. No side roads appeared. The new area was as bare and featureless as the section Carina and Viggo had walked.

Above, the pale purple sky faded to twilight and fake stars slowly shone out.

"They've gone to a lot of trouble," said Viggo, jerking his chin toward the display.

"To make it look realistic?" asked Carina. "Yeah. They want the illusion of living up top. But if they can't live on the surface, what do they do for food? Sot Loza is way off the trade routes. They can't import it."

"I guess we're about to find out."

The artificial twilight deepened as the vehicle took them to their mysterious destination. Lights winked on in the distance and shadowy constructions reared up in the drab landscape. The vehicle stopped at the edge of an unfamiliar metropolis. The wide tunnel opened out further, accommodating streets and houses, anonymous in the darkness.

More light shone from the windows of the habitation they'd parked outside. At the top of the steps stood a familiar figure: Queshm. Her hands were clasped behind her back and she gazed on them with a supercilious air as they climbed up to meet her.

"Go inside. You can eat and socialize."

Socialize?

"But I'm not dressed for a party," Carina muttered to Viggo.

"Me neither. My beard's a mess."

The room dedicated to the soiree sat directly beyond the open doors. Four long tables had been arranged in a quadrangle with gaps at the corners to allow passage for automated servers. Sparkling chandeliers hung from the high ceiling, and the chairs and table decorations were rich and sumptuous. Most seats were already filled by men and women in fine-textured, intricately patterned clothes. The yellow suits of the prisoners looked ridiculously out of place.

"Exactly one space for each of us," noted Pamuk.

Twelve chairs were empty, randomly scattered amongst the Sot Lozans.

"This must be what Queshm meant by socializing," Carina commented. "We have to pay for our supper with witty conversation."

"They'll be lucky," Pamuk said. "I never met a witty Black Dog."

Chi-tang set off for the nearest empty seat, saying, "I don't care what they want. I'm hungry." As he sat down, he was greeted in a friendly manner by his neighbors, as if he'd turned up to a regular dinner party.

Viggo asked, "What choice do we have except to go with it?" He left to find a seat too.

Carina pulled out a chair between a man and a woman. The woman wore a long, pale blue gown draped from her shoulders. Her jet-black hair hung loose down her back and a silver tiara held it away from her face. When Carina took the seat next to her she grimaced and looked away.

The man held out his hand. "Rano Shelta." He was black-haired too, strong-jawed and attractive in his pale gray, tailored suit.

She stared at the outstretched palm, her mind thrown back to Ostillon, where she'd discovered the true star map to Earth. In her earliest days on that planet, she'd been forced to attend a similar event held by Langley Dirksen, matriarch of her evil clan.

She smiled, recalling her outrageous behavior, stealing drinks and sweeping dishes from tables, furious at the coercion and her captivity. She'd tempered since then. Matured, maybe. She had no urge to disrupt the party regardless of how much she hated it, though the temptation to punch Rano Shelta in the face was strong. But that would get her nowhere.

She shook his hand. "Carina."

His startled smile of pleasure was interesting. What was he hoping from this encounter?

"Welcome to Sot Loza. What would you like to eat? I can recommend the—"

"You're speaking Universal. I didn't think anyone could around here."

His smile widened. "I took classes. I hope I'm easy to understand and my accent isn't too strong."

"It's fine. What were you saying about the food?"

"Ah, yes." He lifted a container and moved it next to her plate before removing the lid. "Try this. It's a fungus, rare even on Sot Loza. Fried in this way it's delicious."

Dubiously, Carina stuck a fork in a slice and transferred it to her plate. "Is that all you guys eat? Fungus?"

"We eat a wide range of food. You'll be surprised at what lives down here naturally and what we're able to grow. Take this, for example." He took the lid off another dish, revealing a lumpy yellow substance. "Can you guess what it is?"

She raised her eyebrows. "Eggs?"

"We call it seprex. It's made from bacteria."

"Uhhh...okay."

In response to her reaction, he added, "It's surprisingly tasty. Would you like to try some?"

"I think I'll stick with the fungus for now, thanks." She cut a piece and ate it. Her stomach was crying out for food, even though everything was unfamiliar. "Not bad." She swallowed her mouthful and cut another piece. "Do you all live underground?"

"That's correct."

"So the conditions on the surface are the same all over the planet?"

"With some variation. On this continent…"

The woman to Carina's right had turned to glare at him, causing his words to peter out.

"On this continent what?" Carina asked. "What were you about to say?"

He cleared his throat. "Conditions are particularly bad. The surface of Sot Loza is entirely uninhabitable. Tell me about your world. Where are you from?"

"Nowhere you would have heard of."

Other conversations were taking place around them. Low, murmured exchanges, as if the situation was completely normal and ordinary. The only remarkable thing about the scene was the yellow punctuation among the range of rich dinner party garments.

"Look," Carina said to Rano, "I know you aren't going to tell me, but I have to ask anyway. What the hell's going on?"

He shifted as if uncomfortable. "Let's just enjoy the evening. You must be hungry after your long journey. Are you sure you wouldn't like to try some seprex?"

"Maybe later."

As the dinner progressed she exhausted all the tactics that came to mind to get Rano to talk. She grew angry, she wheedled, she gave him the silent treatment. Nothing worked. He and the rest of the Sot Lozans appeared determined to maintain their masquerade.

It was only when she used the restroom she received the merest hint of a clue about what was happening and Sot Lozans' intentions. A human attendant staffed the room. The young woman in a dark gray uniform stepped forward to wash Carina's hands. In shock at the unusual treatment, she allowed the attendant to apply the soap and water.

As she dried her hands, the woman leaned closer and whispered, "It's better to go along with it and not ask too many questions. Life down here isn't too bad. You'll get used to it in the end." She took a step back and nodded, signaling her service was over.

Carina returned to her seat, trying to figure out what had just happened. What did the attendant's words mean? Had she been a prisoner, too, dragged to Sot Loza from a far distant sector? And was she now indoctrinated into the system, accepting her fate?

If washing people's hands was what her future held, Carina would have no part of it. She sat down, and Rano pushed a dessert dish toward her.

"Try this. It's a delicacy, usually only available at banquets."

She eyed the pink goop, no doubt another bacterial sludge. "I'm not eating your shitty slime. Tell me what's happening here. Why have you brought me and my companions to Sot Loza? Tell me what this is about!"

He had the decency to look abashed. Leaning in, he murmured, "In time, all will become clear. I cannot reveal any more. I'm sorry."

"Sorry doesn't cut it. You've diverted our ship, taken her from us, and now you plan on keeping us captive for the rest of our lives. You might as well have spaced us."

"Aw, come on. It isn't so b—" A gob of pink slime hit him in the face, splashed up by the serving spoon Carina had thrown in the dish.

A dull thud sounded, accompanied by a gasp of shock.

Pamuk, who sat opposite, had landed a punch on her neighbor's jaw. He crashed to the floor, still in his seat.

The blow triggered an eruption.

Someone screamed.

The Black Dogs were suddenly on their feet and attacking the Sot Lozans. They punched, choked, and grappled with the diners, lifting them from their seats and throwing them down before kicking and stomping on them. It was pandemonium, a riot of violence and pain.

Rano's head jerked to face Carina's, the whites of his eyes showing. He got to his feet and slowly backed away, hands raised. But she only stood up and separated herself from the action. Viggo and Chi-tang also elected to not join in the brawl.

The Sot Lozans didn't stand a chance. Though they outnumbered their 'guests' they weren't fighters. Crying out, groaning, and screeching, they suffered the onslaught as guards poured in and dragged the mercs off them.

The polished tiles were slick with blood. Bones had been broken. The diners' fine jewelry sparkled on the floor.

What had they expected would happen? You couldn't deprive a bunch of trained soldiers of their freedom and expect them to take it sitting down.

<h1 style="text-align: center">NINE</h1>

"**E**arth, metal, water, wood, and fire," Carina repeated. The list was only five items long yet two of her companions seemed to be struggling with it.

"Wood?" Chi-tang asked. "Like, from a tree?"

"Yes," she snapped. "Like from a tree."

"Come on, guys," said Viggo. "It isn't that hard."

They were outside, though near their residence, where they'd been dropped off after the dinner party. Most of the mercs had been hauled off somewhere. Only Pamuk had escaped the punishment, whatever it was, as she'd come to her senses after punching her neighbor and stopped her attack. Rather than going inside immediately the transport left, the four had walked a short distance down the road.

"But where the hell are we going to get wood around here?" asked Pamuk.

Carina sighed and slapped a hand to her face. "That's the problem. And it isn't only not having any wood that's an obstacle to making elixir. I don't know if I can make a fire."

"If we had some wood," Chi-tang speculated, "we could—"

"That's kinda my point!"

"Hear me out. Doesn't have to be wood. Any flammable material will do. If we short some wiring to make it spark, I can start a fire that way."

It was the first useful thing she had heard him say.

"Even with a fire, we still need wood," Pamuk muttered. "I bet it doesn't even grow on this planet. We'll never find any down here."

"I brought some with me," Carina said, "but it was in the clothes I was wearing when we were captured."

"That we had to throw away," Viggo said, "So if we find out where they put them..."

Carina shook her head. "Like they're going to tell us. They want us to wear these banana suits."

"Did your brothers and sisters have the elixir ingredients with them too?" Viggo asked.

"And bottles of elixir. But if they were treated the same as us they don't have them anymore." Anxiety and fear gnawed at her. Would she ever see her siblings or Bryce again? She forced the feelings down. She'd been separated from her family before but they'd found each other. They could do it again.

"One thing's for sure," said Viggo. "We aren't gonna find out where to get some wood by cutting ourselves off from the Sot Lozans. That event they made us go to tonight, it had a purpose even if they wouldn't explain it. If the Black Dogs hadn't started that brawl—"

"Ha!" Pamuk interjected. "More like a massacre."

"If they hadn't started that fight," he persisted, "we might have discovered something useful."

"No way," Carina said. "The guy I was with wouldn't drop a hint. Didn't matter what I said."

"Well, I thought I was getting somewhere with my neighbor," said Viggo, "until a Black Dog broke her arm. I'm pretty sure that's soured our relationship. Still, you catch more kultries with neinery than jadronic."

Carina stared. "You...what?"

"I understand," said Chi-tang. "You get what you want by being nice not nasty."

"Something like that," said Viggo.

Pamuk shook her head. "Being nice isn't a Black Dog's strong suit."

"Then they'll have to try," said Viggo.

———

One thing they hadn't realized at first was that they had a comm panel on the wall of the dormitory. It was a simple device, just a screen. Everyone had assumed it was an interface like the ones in the social area, and so useless unless you knew the local language. Then, out of idle curiosity, the morning after the dinner party fracas, Viggo read Hedran Mafmy's number into it. Carina was lying on her bunk, watching.

Seconds later, the blank screen was replaced by Hedran's face, wreathed in a smile. Viggo started with surprise. She reached for something offscreen and then hung her translator around her neck. "Great to hear from you. You decided to take me up on my offer to show you around?"

"I, er..." he glanced at Carina. "Can my friend come along?"

Hedran's face fell. "It would be cozier with just the two of us."

"I'm not looking for cozy. I'd prefer it if Carina came with us. If you're not up for that, then—"

"Sure," Hedran blurted. "Your friend is very welcome." Her expression said otherwise.

They arranged a time for her to meet them outside and Viggo cut the comm.

Carina raised herself up onto her elbows. "Of all the scenarios I imagined I might face after being taken prisoner, I never thought I would be third wheel on a date."

"Is that what it is?"

"What do you think? She has designs on you."

He gazed at his reflection in the screen and smoothed his beard. "That's understandable."

Carina chuckled. "Not saying you're ugly or anything, but the Sot Lozans seem to have designs on all of us. That's what last night was about. The guy I was with was trying to get me to like him. This whole situation is bizarre. We've been brought here to form romantic relationships with the locals. Why can't they get things going with each other?"

"Maybe their religion forbids it."

"Then it's the dumbest religion in existence and it would have died out before it even started."

"That's all I've got. My new girlfriend might shed some light. I'm guessing I'd better not tell her I prefer men."

Carina guffawed. "No, you'd better not."

The sound of a vehicle pulling up broke through the quiet hum of traffic.

Pamuk called from the refectory, where she and Chi-tang were still eating the breakfast that had mysteriously arrived overnight, "They're back!"

The Black Dogs who had been detained at the dinner party stepped into the building looking tired but unhurt. They'd been held in cells, they said, and forced to sleep on the floor, but no worse punishments had befallen them.

"Not much of a deterrent against doing it again," Viggo commented.

"No," Carina agreed, "but what would be the point? We can't punch our way out of this place. There are a helluva lot more Sot Lozans than us. We need firepower, but I haven't seen any civilians carrying weapons and the guards aren't going to give theirs up without a fight."

"If you and your siblings could use your talents that'll help."

"Yeah," she replied dubiously, "assuming we conquer the problem we talked about last night and we can find them. Even then it'll be tricky."

The mercs had spied the food packages in the refectory. In another second they'd piled into the room and begun to devour them.

"On the other hand," said Viggo, "we could out-eat our captors and starve them to death."

The vehicle that had brought the Black Dogs back pulled away and its place was taken by Hedran's conveyance. She climbed out, peered through the open doorway, and waved at Viggo.

"She's early," he said.

"She's keen," said Carina.

Hedran Mafmy wore a pink dress patterned with silver swirls. It wrapped around her waist and clung to her figure flatteringly. She'd gone to some effort with her hair, too, shaping the layers and bringing the front section to two points, accentuating her cheekbones. Her face was made up. Smudged dark gray lines defined her eyes and a darker shade of pink than her dress emphasized her lips.

Considering all her work was wasted on Viggo, Carina felt a little sorry for her.

He took the front passenger seat while she was assigned the lesser position in the rear. Expecting to be ignored for the duration of the trip, she focused on the exterior to see what else she could learn about Sot Loza. Hedran took them in the same direction they'd gone for the dinner party.

Now it was 'daytime' the 'sky' was replaying. Did the people responsible for it ever vary the display or the ambient temperature, giving the underground world the appearance of seasons? The same conditions all the time would get boring fast.

"This area seems empty," said Viggo. "Is it new?"

"You're a smart guy," Hedran replied. "That's right. This section was tunneled a couple of years ago, to join Laft, the town where you arrived, with Sarnach, the place I'm taking you. Before this section was opened traveling between Laft and Sarnach took two hours."

"Is Sarnach connected to the surface too?"

"No, just Laft." She paused. "I know what you're doing. You're trying to figure out ways to escape. I know it's hard for you right now but you have to forget about it. Even if you made it to an elevator, it wouldn't work for you, and if it did, you wouldn't last more than a few hours up top. It's unliveable up there. You can't see more than a few meters and the air fries your lungs. If you survived long enough to steal a shuttle to take you to your ship, you could never board it. We have hundreds of people on it and they would kill you. Escaping from Sot Loza is a suicide mission."

She might have been trying to put them off but in doing so she was giving useful information.

Viggo said, "It might make our fate easier to swallow if we knew why we're here."

"I can't tell you that. All I can say is, it'll become clear over time."

"In that case, what *can* you tell us? Do Sot Lozans have a list of permitted subjects to discuss with outsiders?"

"I can tell you our history, if you're interested."

"I'd love to hear it."

"Our ancestors arrived on a colony ship like yours, roughly fourteen hundred years ago, Standard. While most of the colonists were in Deep Sleep, there was an accident. According to the log the ship collided with an astronomical body of some kind—the data was incomplete. Whatever it was, it cut across and through the shielding on the fuel tanks, and as the pressurized fuel vented the force pushed us way off course. We sent out a Mayday but no one answered, unsurprisingly. We were far from any inhabited systems."

As Hedran had been speaking, a built-up area had come into view. The low buildings spread out as far as Carina could see. The Sot Lozans had been busy over the last fourteen hundred years.

"The skeleton crew awake at the time of the collision managed to seal the many leaks but only a little fuel remained, not enough to return the ship to her course or take her to inhabited regions. They had no choice but to remain on the new heading and hope to reach a habitable planet before the chemicals and power keeping everyone in Deep Sleep alive ran out. Their chances were slim but, as luck would have it, they came close enough to Sot Loza's system to use the remaining fuel to slow the ship down and achieve orbit."

Viggo said, "And I guess that, being a colony vessel, they were set up to survive a few years while they figured out a way to live here."

She nodded. "Despite the earlier misfortune, destiny seemed to have a hand to play in ensuring our presence on Sot Loza."

"Destiny?" Carina piped up. "Does your survival really mean anything? If your ancestors hadn't survived no one would be here to tell the tale, and in this galactic dead zone no one would ever find your planet or any evidence of a failed colonization."

Though Hedran had her back to her, Carina felt her scowl.

Without turning around, she said, "There are many of us who believe there's a deeper purpose to our existence on Sot Loza. I wouldn't go around voicing your opinion on the matter if I were you."

Viggo gave a small cough.

Carina sighed, silently cursing her own big mouth. So much for turning Hedran into a co-conspirator.

TEN

Bryce snapped his eyes open and sat bolt upright. He was on a bed in a small, bare room, and the door was closing. He leapt up to try to catch it, but blackness closed in and his head felt light. He crumpled to the floor, hitting his knees on the hard tile. The door slid shut.

Wincing, he shook his head to clear it. When his consciousness fully returned he got to his feet and stepped to the door. It was locked. As he'd suspected as soon as he'd come around, he was being held prisoner.

He touched his chest. His armored suit was gone and he was wearing a hospital gown. His burns seemed to have healed. The tile was icy cold under his bare feet. After trying the door a couple more times, he climbed back into bed.

What had happened?

As he recalled being separated from Carina's family, anxiety hit him. Were they okay? He hoped the people of this planet were treating the children kindly.

He remembered stumbling through the enemy ship, forced along by a soldier, until he reached a shuttle bay. He was pushed into a container holding the other mercs on his team. A seemingly endless journey full of pain followed. They must have landed but he had no memory of it or anything else.

The enemy had fixed him up. Jackson's guess that they didn't want to kill them had been correct. So what did they want? He padded across to the door once more and pressed an ear to it. Either the room was soundproofed or absolute silence reigned outside. He thumped it with a fist. "Hey! Let me out! What have you done with the children from my ship? I demand to see them! Hey, answer me!"

Nothing.

He marched to the opposite side of the room and slammed his hands on the wall. Jackson had said they had to take things step by step, but that had included him staying with the kids. Things had started to go wrong already. He had to get back to them.

From behind him came the sound of the door opening. He rushed over to it but halted in surprise when he saw who entered. It was the Marchonish woman, Ava, with her little one. As soon as she'd slipped in the door slid shut.

"Bryce," she said softly, "are you better?"

"Yeah, I'm fine. What are you doing here? What's happening?"

"The guard said I can only stay a few minutes. I just wanted to check up on you. I insisted on seeing you but they won't allow me to stay long. I'll tell the children you're okay. They're so worried about you."

"You're with the kids? Are they all right?"

"They're fine, just upset, but they'll calm down when I tell them your wounds have been treated."

"Can you tell them I'll get to them as soon as I can?" In his current situation there seemed little hope of that but he wanted them to know he was trying.

"Of course. But..." she looked up and around the room.

He was aware of people listening in on their conversation too.

"...be careful. They told us you won't be allowed to stay with us. You're going to go wherever they took the rest of the Black Dogs, and from what we saw, they didn't treat them too kindly. I don't want you to get hurt again."

"I hear you but don't worry, and tell the kids not to worry about me. I've been through some tough times and managed to survive this far. If I'm going to be with the Black Dogs I'll see Carina. Together we'll be able to figure something out." He didn't want to say more. It was important their captors didn't know Carina and the children were related.

The door opened and a guard stuck his head in. "Time's up."

Ava said sadly, "I have to go."

"Take care, and tell the kids not to worry."

She kissed his cheek. As she stepped through the open doorway, the guard moved out of her way.

He was alone again, but his solitude didn't last long. A couple of moments later the door opened again and a set of clothes was thrown in.

"Get dressed," the guard barked.

Bryce barely had time to don the gray garments and boots before the guard reappeared and ordered him out. He complied, the coarse material of his new clothes already making his skin itch. The boots were too large, causing him to shuffle.

A second guard waited outside. One in front and one following, they led him along the passageway and down some stairs. The rooms they passed weren't like his. There were windows in the doors and, from the interiors he glimpsed, they held medical equipment and interfaces. He even spied decorative pictures on the walls.

As they neared a door it opened and a medic walked out. She froze as she spotted him and his guards and ducked her head. Her expression was a mixture of embarrassment and fear. He didn't know what to make of it. Was she scared of the guards or him? And what was she embarrassed about?

They descended another set of stairs and then another. These steps circled a central open area. At the bottom stood a set of elevator doors. A guard pressed the button and they waited.

"You're taking me to the dungeons?" Bryce quipped.

Predictably, neither man answered.

The elevator certainly seemed to go down a long way. He guessed they must have descended to the basement. When the doors opened, the chillier, damper atmosphere suggested he was correct. The lighting was dimmer down here too.

Three doors along the passageway, the guards halted. One spoke into the security panel. The screen came alive, displaying the interior of a cell. The guard commanded the prisoner to move to the far wall. He or she must have complied because a moment later, Bryce was thrust in so hard he fell onto his bruised knees.

"Shit," said a voice. "I knew my living situation was too good to be true."

Bryce looked up. "Of all the cellmates I could have picked, you'd be the last."

"Likewise." Rees grinned and held out a hand. "Good to see you, kid."

Bryce took it and the heavily muscled merc jerked him to his feet.

He rotated his shoulder, checking it remained in its socket. "Thanks."

The small room held two cots and only one looked slept in. That's what the merc had meant about his living situation. He'd had the cell to himself up until now. Bryce eyed the toilet in the corner. He and Rees were about to become intimately acquainted.

Rees followed his gaze. "Yeah. I apologize in advance. I took a shot in the gut a few years back and my bowels have never been the same."

Great.

The merc was staring at his feet. "Wanna try swapping boots? Mine have been pinching my toes like a bitch."

He sighed in pleasure as he tried on Bryce's. Bryce discovered Rees's footwear was somewhat moist but did fit him better. He took the boots off and put them under his bunk to air out. "What's been happening? I don't remember much after being taken aboard the enemy ship. Have you seen Carina and the others?"

"You don't remember arriving here? That's no surprise. You were way out of it. There's not a lot to tell. We were taken underground and put in these cells, where we've been ever since—as far as I know. Our team was kept together but we didn't see anyone else from the *Bathsheba*. They seem to be keeping us separate. Until you turned up I was on my own." Rees stretched out on his cot and put his hands behind his head.

"We were taken underground?"

"Conditions on the surface are shit. High winds, thick dust."

"Prisoners move away from the door," a voice ordered from a speaker.

"Not again," Rees complained. "They do this every time they wanna come in here. Like I'm gonna jump two guards, put them both out of action, and break out of here all by myself."

"You want to try though, right? Admit it."

The voice repeated, "Prisoners move away from the door immediately."

The merc winked at him as he got to his feet. Bryce joined him at the far wall.

When the guard appeared, he pointed at Rees. "You. Come with me. You have to give a sample."

"A sample?" Bryce asked. "A sample of what?"

Rees shrugged.

ELEVEN

Carina poked her food with a fork. On her plate were some green beans, a grainy mash, and a square of an off-white, spongy substance she guessed was more of Sot Loza's ubiquitous fungi. Were the other items actually what they appeared to be? Or were they bacteria formed to give the right appearance?

"What's wrong?" Hedran asked angrily. "Isn't our food good enough for you? Would you prefer something from a ship's printer?"

"*Gee*," Carina muttered, digging her fork into the beans. "I was just wondering what it tasted like."

"Well now you'll find out."

Carina chewed, rolling her eyes.

Viggo had been doing a great job of making Hedran think he was interested in her, which was fantastic for the end purpose of squeezing out useful information, but at the same time her antipathy toward Carina had been honed. In ordinary circumstances she would have left the couple alone hours ago but, firstly, she had no way of getting back to the Outsiders residence, and secondly, she wanted to use the opportunity to find out as much as she could about Sot Loza.

Hedran had brought them to the restaurant after giving them a tour of Sarnach. The town reminded Carina of the place she'd grown up, though Sarnach was larger and less ramshackle. She guessed it was home to about fifteen thousand people. The low buildings appeared to squat under the overhanging sky. In the town of her childhood, poverty had prevented the constructions from being taller. Here, the reason was lack of space. It must have been cheaper to hollow out the subsurface on the horizontal rather than vertical plane.

Their host had shown them municipal centers built in a mildly interesting architectural style, food factories, entertainment venues with rudimentary sims, and a small park. Compared to Lakshmi Station, Sot Loza was laughably undeveloped if Sarnach was a typical example of life here. Hedran's pride as she took them on her tour was unfounded, but it was unlikely she'd ever been anywhere else.

Carina's heart had skipped a beat when she'd seen the trees in the park, but she'd quickly realized they couldn't be real. She'd confirmed her suspicion by running a hand down a trunk and feeling the leaves.

"They're artificial, of course," Hedran had said with a smirk. "How could plants grow down here?"

"With sufficient lighting they could," said Viggo. "Is energy in short supply?"

Hedran frowned as she replied, "We don't need plants."

The Sot Lozans couldn't be lacking a good source of energy. They needed plenty to create their underworld, and they'd built several starships as well as the behemoth that had dragged the *Bathsheba*. Plus, the attraction beam they sent across space would require vast amounts of power. Maybe it was only a case of prioritizing what was most important.

"Tell me," said Viggo. "Do you ever go up to the surface?"

"Why would I do that? Didn't you get a taste of what it's like before you were brought down?"

"I guess I'm not used to the idea of living my entire life underground. I can't imagine it."

"If you'd grown up here you wouldn't find it so strange."

Carina asked, "Do you have records of your ancestors' home planet? Do you know why they left?" She wondered if they'd come from Earth. The Sot Lozans' attraction beam had pulled the *Bathsheba* way off course, yet the rift was closer to Earth than her own sector and Ostillon, one of the first places mages had settled.

"Environmental degradation," Hedran replied. "At least, that's what the history vids say. Their world had frozen over. Though they could still survive conditions were tough and their lives were miserable. So they set out to find somewhere better."

"Fourteen hundred years ago?" Carina checked.

Hedran nodded. "Why?"

"It's not important."

Mages had left Earth, as far as she could estimate, much earlier. With the effects of time dilation it could have been eons ago. It was possible the planet had frozen over in the intervening time. If that was the case, going there could be pointless. "What was your origin planet called?"

"Lupa."

Lupa? It didn't ring any bells.

"You seem very interested in Sot Loza's past," said Hedran.

"We can talk about something else if you like. What other questions are you willing to answer? I mean, if you could let us know what this charade is about that would be great."

She grimaced. "You know the subject is out of bounds. Why can't you just be grateful I'm doing you this favor?"

"You aren't doing *me* any favors," Carina retorted. "It's Viggo you want. A complete stranger you wanted to pick up from the side of the road like a stray animal."

Viggo said, "Take it easy. I'd like to think my charms are easy to spot, even from a distance."

Carina pushed her plate away, folded her arms, and leaned back in her chair, biting her tongue. Her worries about her siblings and Bryce were gnawing at her, setting her on edge. It was hard to not get into an argument with Hedran. That was what Viggo's comment had been about. He was trying to defuse the situation.

"You're right," said Hedran. "It *is* Viggo I want." She turned to him. "You're an intelligent man. I'll give it to you straight: if you want to prosper here, you'll have to ditch your old associates and align yourself with a local. I can introduce you to influential people, give you somewhere nice to stay, and a good life. What do you say?"

"What do you expect in return?"

"Nothing at all for now, except perhaps..." she side-eyed Carina "...from now on we do things together, just you and me. I mean, it isn't like she's your girlfriend or anything, is she? She can't be. You must have better taste."

"I'm *right here*!" Carina exclaimed.

Viggo said, "Thank you for laying things out so plainly, Hedran. Now we all know where we stand. I'll give your proposal serious thought."

"Good. That's all I ask. I'm sure you'll come to the right—" Her hand flew to her ear and, as she listened, her expression changed from smug satisfaction to irritation. "I have to take you back to your residence immediately."

"What a pity," said Carina. "I was having so much fun."

Hedran was already on her feet. "Come with me."

"What if we don't want to?" Carina asked. "What if Viggo and I want to hang out around here a little while longer and smooch?"

Viggo chuckled. "We'd better go." He asked Hedran, "Is there a problem?"

"Something serious must be going down. The Security Chief is demanding your immediate return."

———

The pillar of smoke was visible from kilometers away. Except it wasn't exactly a pillar. The column only rose a short distance before billowing out sideways, drawn off by the air circulation system.

Vehicles Carina presumed belonged to the security services blocked one lane of the road and the traffic was backed up as it took turns to pass. By the time they reached the residence, flames flickered through the windows and fire was roaring.

A fire truck was spraying foam on the conflagration but to no apparent effect.

As they drew closer, Carina spotted figures struggling. The security forces were tussling with the mercs, trying to force them into vehicles. The Black Dogs were putting up an excellent fight. Several officers were incapacitated, lying on the pavement or leaning on their vehicles. They seemed to be unarmed, relying on brute force rather than firepower—a losing tactic when it came to men and women who were used to fighting for their lives and fighting dirty too.

They drew up and Hedran's car halted, her window opening. A man in uniform ran up.

It was Rano Shelta, from the dinner party! "Carina, you seem to be in a position of authority among your ship's personnel. Can you please come and speak to them? I need you to convince them to calm down and stop hurting my officers. I don't want to fire on them if I can avoid it."

"You're the Security Chief?"

"We didn't get around to it when we talked, but, yes, I am. If you could...?"

She climbed out of the vehicle.

Chi-tang was the only person from the *Bathsheba* not engaged in a fight. Many Black Dogs were trading blows with two or three security officers at once. The refugee from Lakshmi stood apathetically to one side, his arms hanging loosely. He had a guilty air about him, but she had more important work to do before she could get to the bottom of it.

"Hey, guys!" she yelled, raising her arms over her head. "The fight's over."

Either no one heard or they were all enjoying themselves too much to obey.

"Guys!" she yelled louder. "Knock it off!"

"Why?" Pamuk yelled back. "These assholes took our ship and won't let us go." A man barreled into her from behind and tried to get her in a bear hug. She reached back, grabbed him, and hauled him up and over, slamming him to the ground.

"Yeah," Carina agreed, "but this isn't going to get you anywhere."

"Doesn't have to," a merc commented, delivering a jab to an officer's face, causing his nose to spurt blood as the man staggered back. "Still feels good."

Carina turned to Rano. "I don't know what you want me to say."

"Whatever it takes to make them stop. I really don't want anyone to get shot."

It was an odd statement coming from someone responsible for security, and whose men and women were getting the shit kicked out of them. She shrugged and tried again. "If you don't stop they're gonna open fire. It's up to you."

This seemed to penetrate. Most of the Black Dogs had taken a hit at some point in their careers, and they weren't wearing armored suits. Firefights were a different matter from street brawls, and a merc who didn't understand that didn't live long.

"All right," Pamuk said, kicking an officer's knee in frustration, "we'd better call it a day."

Gradually, the mercs stopped resisting. The Sot Lozan security forces surrounded them but appeared reluctant to approach. The Black Dogs rubbed their knuckles and rolled their necks. They were bloody and bruised—though not as bloody or bruised as the Sot Lozans—but they seemed happy.

"How did the fight start?" Carina asked Rano.

"When we spotted their residence was burning, we came here to take them somewhere safe. That's all we wanted to do, I swear."

TWELVE

Their new accommodation was a three-story hotel in Laft. It was basic but better then the former place, which was now a charred, smoking skeleton. Here, they were to share rooms in pairs. Most importantly, the hotel had a kitchen, though it was off-limits to the Outsiders. Apart from a handful of staff, they had the place to themselves. If the hotel had held Sot Lozan guests, they'd been moved out before the prisoners arrived.

They were also closer to the elevator to the surface, though the prospect of their escape and re-taking of the *Bathsheba* seemed as remote as ever.

The mercs had gone to be treated for the minor injuries they'd received in the dust-up, leaving Carina, Viggo, and Chi-tang alone. Rano had left with the rest of the Sot Lozans after thanking Carina for her help.

"I did it for *my* people," she'd retorted, "not yours." It probably hadn't been the wisest thing to say considering that getting closer to the Security Chief could help their cause, but his friendliness made her skin crawl. She preferred Sable Dirksen's frank hatred over these two-faced shitbags.

As soon as he was gone, she took Chi-tang out into the crowded, noisy street.

"What happened?" she asked, though she already had a good idea.

"It was my fault," he readily admitted. "I was experimenting with the wiring, trying to see if I could start a fire for...you know."

"And you were successful."

"Too successful." His mouth turned down at the corners. "Things got a little out of hand."

"Just a little, but don't feel too bad. No one got hurt—"

"The Sot Lozan security officers did."

"Yes, but they don't count. None of *us* got hurt. And you figured out something important. Do you think you could do it again?"

He threw a glance at the hotel. "I don't see why not, assuming that place is set up the same. I won't let it get out of control next time."

"You don't need to do anything yet, not until we have the missing ingredient."

Viggo walked down the steps from the hotel and joined them. "I was wondering where you two had gone."

"Just talking business," Carina replied.

"I thought so. I've been checking out our new place of abode. Did you spot the kitchen?"

"I did, but even if we could get in there, it's irrelevant now. Chi-tang here was responsible for the fire at the other place."

Viggo's eyebrows rose. "I see. That throws a whole new light on everything."

"It makes sourcing the other material more important than ever." Carina felt she was on the cusp of a breakthrough. With elixir, she could do so much to put a permanent end to the Sot Lozans' control. "How did you leave things with your new girlfriend?"

"Easy there." He grinned. "I'm not the type of guy to rush anything. I like taking my time before making a commitment."

"You have a girlfriend?" Chi-tang asked. "Already?"

"You don't?" Carina asked. "What do you think that dinner party the other night was about?"

Light seemed to dawn in his eyes and his mouth fell open. Then he frowned. "Damn. I missed my chance."

Viggo laid a friendly hand on his shoulder. "Don't worry. I'm sure you'll have plenty more chances."

"Seriously," Carina said, "did you arrange another time to meet up?"

"In between all the mayhem of the fire and the brawl, yeah, we did. But she hinted very heavily that I should come alone so it could be *just us getting to know each other better.*"

"I'm hurt. I thought I'd made a new friend. When you see her, try to find out as much as you—"

"I get it. You don't need to spell it out. And you'll do the same with the security guy?"

"Rano?"

"If that's his name. Of all the people you could have sat next to at that party, you picked the Chief of Security. You hit gold."

"I suppose I did." The thought of cuddling up to the Sot Lozan wasn't appealing but he was as likely as any of them to know where she might find some genuine wooden material, and he was definitely interested in her. "One thing's for sure, they know where we are and who we're with at any time. As soon as the trouble with the Black Dogs kicked off, Hedran got a comm. Rano knew exactly where to find us. They probably know we're standing here in the street talking right now."

Pedestrians regularly looked at them as they passed though no one had stopped to address them directly. Perhaps none of them were managerial class and so Outsiders were off limits.

Viggo was running his gaze over the hotel facade. "You know, they might be able to pick up our voices even out here. We should be more careful."

Carina agreed, and they went inside. There was more to talk about, such as what might have happened to the rest of the *Bathsheba's* personnel, but it was all speculation. She could only hope that Bryce, her brothers and sisters, the Marchonish women, and the Black Dogs who had been taken captive were safe. She assumed they were having a similar experience to hers, though not the younger children. What would the Sot Lozans make of them? After her siblings' many trials she trusted them to keep their lips firmly shut about their abilities. They'd suffered far worse experiences than being kept in relative comfort, too. But how would their captors treat prisoners who were too young to 'get to know better'?

The Sot Lozans' behavior was bizarre. She could only begin to guess at their motivation. Was it something to do with their belief system, which seemed out-of-the ordinary according to Hedran's hints? Were Outsiders prized as romantic partners and that was why they were reserved for the higher classes?

She arrived at the room assigned to her and Pamuk. She lay down on the bed to think, but she found herself thinking about Bryce. Was he receiving the same attention from the Sot Lozans as everyone else? He had to be. Had he received offers he might find difficult to refuse? Almost certainly.

She turned onto her front and rested her chin on the knuckles of her folded hands. It didn't take her long to dismiss the idea. Bryce had made his feelings about her plain. He'd given up his entire family to follow her on her fool's quest. As long as he suspected she was still alive he would refuse temptation. *She* was certainly not tempted. Even in ordinary circumstances she would not have had feelings for Rano. He invaded her personal space, held eye contact too long, and for someone who had only just met her he was simply overly keen. It was obvious he wasn't interested in her as a person but what she had to offer. Which was…? What did she have that a Sot Lozan didn't?

There was only one way to find out.

She sat up and swung her legs off the bed. Scanning the walls, she discovered what she was looking for. The plain screen looked identical to the one at the former residence. That one was now melted and scorched somewhere in a pile of smoldering rubble, but this one might work in the same way.

Except…

She patted her pockets. Had Rano given her a card? She didn't think so. Despite the turbulent events surrounding their last two encounters, she doubted he lacked the presence of mind to give her his details. It was more likely that he hadn't seen any need to let her know how to contact him.

She walked up to the screen. "I want to speak to Rano Shelta."

One, two, three, fou—

His face appeared. "Carina! I'm so glad you got in contact. How can I help you?"

"I was wondering if you'd be interested in meeting up."

THIRTEEN

When Rees returned to the cell, he seemed physically unharmed. Bryce had been concerned about the 'sample' their captors had said they would take from him, but he didn't appear hurt.

"You okay?" Bryce sat up as the door shut and the lock engaged.

Rees waved dismissively. "Yeah." He lay on his bunk, putting his cupped hands under the back of his head.

"What happened?"

"Ah, wasn't a big deal."

"Did they just want a blood sample?"

"Yeah, well, something like that."

Something like a blood sample? What was *like* a blood sample? Bryce asked, confused, "Did it hurt?" He was a prisoner too. If the guards had taken Rees for a medical procedure the chances were the same thing would happen to him.

Rees gave him a look. "Let's not talk about it, all right?"

Of all the Black Dogs Bryce had grown to know and—mostly—like in the many months since Carina had recruited the band, Rees was the last one Bryce would have expected to be subdued and thoughtful, yet that was exactly how he would have described the man's demeanor. "Are you sure you're okay?"

Rees snapped, "I said I don't wanna talk about it."

The intercom crackled to life. "Prisoners move away from the door."

As soon as the two men complied the door opened and the same guard who had taken Rees appeared. He nodded at Bryce. "Your turn."

"It's best just to do what they say," Rees said. "Good luck, kid."

Bryce had been expecting to return to the upper levels and the medical center where he'd been treated. It seemed the obvious place for the enemy to take a 'sample' from him, but the guard led him deeper into the jail and down more stairs.

How deep below the surface were they? Was the medical center underground too? The location of their place of incarceration would make escaping the planet harder. No one had factored in that possibility.

A set of double doors blocked off the end of the corridor. The guard spoke into the security panel and the doors slid apart to reveal a clinically white, brightly lit room. Two steel work surfaces ran the length of it on each side, and people wearing blue medics' uniforms stood at them, working with equipment Bryce didn't recognize. He was relieved to see no operating tables.

"That way," said the guard, nodding at the end of the room, where a second set of doors stood.

The medics ignored him as he walked past them. Anxiety tightened his gut again. Perhaps the operating tables were in the next room. Rees had seemed unharmed but perhaps something different lay in store for him.

Beyond the second set of doors was a smaller room containing only three people: a man and two women wearing white uniforms. One of the women stood at an open freezer, mist from it dissipating into the air. As he entered, she closed it but he glimpsed rows of glass tubes. The man was working at an interface.

"Last one," the guard said.

"Great," said the other woman. "This is the one who was injured?"

"Yeah."

"So it's our first sample from him." She took a tube from a rack and held it out. "Spit in this."

They only wanted his spit? He relaxed. Why hadn't Rees told him? Carina had always been wary of giving others access to her genetic information but he didn't have anything to fear on that score. There was nothing special about his DNA.

"I'll create a new file," said the man.

Bryce spat into the tube and handed it back. The woman placed it into an open slot in a machine. She picked up a second container, also made of glass but wider and squatter, like a small cup. "We also need a semen sample. Go through there." She indicated a curtained alcove and pushed the container into his hands.

He almost dropped it. "You...?"

"You heard me. And don't take forever. It's been a long day and we're all ready to go home."

"Why?" he blurted. It was all he could think to say.

"I'm not here to answer your questions. Do as I ordered. I won't tell you again."

In one way it was a simple request yet he felt a huge reluctance to comply. Whatever the reason behind it, it had to be screwed-up. Were they genetically engineering military personnel? Or perhaps they were making human mutants, experimenting to see what special abilities they could give their creations. He'd heard of such attempts though they were outlawed on most civilized planets.

If either of his guesses was correct, he didn't see why they couldn't use their own genetic material. Why did it have to come from non-natives? Regardless, he didn't want any part of their experiments.

"No." He tried to return the container but the woman stepped out of his reach, so he put it on the table. "I'm not doing it."

"Don't be ridiculous. Get in there now and do as I say."

"No way."

"There's no need to be shy," said the other woman. "It's a natural act and we're all accustomed to working with these samples."

"I'm not shy. I'm just not doing it." He was feeling braver. What could they realistically do if he refused? Beating him up wouldn't help.

A terrible thought occurred. "What about our women? Are you using their genetic material too?" He had visions of the female Black Dogs undergoing operations or being impregnated against their will. He felt sick.

"That's no concern of yours," said the man.

"I don't agree. You're disgusting. Whatever it is you're doing, it's vile and you should be ashamed."

The guard cuffed him, hard, causing him to stumble.

"Watch out!" the woman next to the freezer admonished. "We have sensitive equipment in here. If you're going to rough him up, do it in the corridor."

The first woman said, "There's no point in roughing him up." She turned to Bryce. "I'm giving you one last chance."

"I told you, I'm not doing it."

Tutting, she stepped to the interface. The man moved aside and she swiped the screen, removing the data sets and said, "We have a non-compliant prisoner, male."

"Ugh, we were just about to pack up," a voice replied.

"I guessed so. We were nearly finished too. Can I send him up or do you want to leave it until tomorrow?"

"Send him. We'll get it over with."

Get what over with?

The woman nodded at the guard, who cursed and shoved him toward the door. "You have to make life harder for everyone, don't you?"

He forced him into the outer room, through it, and back into the corridor. Bryce wasn't sure what was going on. He clearly wasn't going to his cell. The guard was taking him someplace else. "What's happening? Am I going to be executed?"

"Ha!" The guard grabbed his upper arm and pushed him so fast they were nearly running. "If it were up to me you would, but luckily for you I don't make the decisions around here. Hurry up."

They mounted the steps that led to the cells but passed them by. The guard took him to the elevator and they ascended to the upper levels. He was back in the medical treatment area once more. As they approached a room, he spied something through the window that made his legs turn weak. It was what he'd been dreading: an operating table.

He halted.

The guard jerked him forward. "What did you think was going to happen? They're gonna get their sample whether you like it or not."

"No, I—"

"It's too late to change your mind now," the guard barked. "You've wasted enough of everyone's time."

Bryce had stopped walking but he was sliding toward the opening door, dragged by the guard. He swung his free hand around, forming a fist. The guard blocked the blow, grasped his arm, and kicked his legs out from under him. As his opponent bent down to grab him under his armpits, Bryce reared up, smashing his head into the guard's face.

There was a grunt of pain and Bryce felt the satisfying sensation of someone else's warm blood on his scalp. But then a blinding blow caught him on his ear, dazing him. Faintly, he heard the doors open and a sarcastic voice say, "My, this one *is* non-compliant."

FOURTEEN

"I have to say, this is more pleasant and natural than the banquet." Rano poured Carina a drink. "And I feel safer with only you as my companion." He winked.

She felt insulted. Did he think she was less able to inflict damage on him than one of the Black Dogs? She didn't voice her anger, however. She was supposed to be trying to get along with him. Instead, she imagined Transporting him up to the fake sky and letting him fall.

Picking up her glass, she asked, "What's this?"

"Wine, of course. We can get onto the hard stuff later." He winked again.

Carina cringed with second-hand embarrassment. "Made from grapes?"

"I don't know that word. It's made from—"

"Forget it. I don't want to know." She took a sip. It was alcoholic. She had to give it that. She took another swallow, fortifying herself for the task ahead. She hadn't paid a lot of attention to Rano Shelta the first time she'd met him. Her goal had been to find out as much intel as she could, not get to know him as a person. But if she was to gain his trust, she would have to be more attentive and friendlier. She gritted her teeth.

He'd brought her to a restaurant in Sarnach. It was an expensive place as far as she could tell. The servers were human and they treated Rano with extreme deference.

"This is nicer," she agreed. "The dinner party felt forced—until the fighting started anyway."

"Yes, the fights have been quite something. We were expecting some difficulties but not on that scale."

"You didn't expect us to object to what you've done?" She was incredulous.

"Treating people kindly usually makes them more amenable. Your group has been exceptionally combative."

"I wouldn't call..." she began hotly, but then she snapped her mouth shut while mentally continuing, *dragging a starship off course and taking her crew prisoner treating them kindly.* "If you find us unusual, that means you've done it before. There's a history of ships going missing in the area where your beam fastened on us. How long have you been doing this?"

He made a pained expression. "Carina, I would love to tell you more and I hope one day I will be free to do just that, but for now I simply can't. Let's talk about something else. I know hardly anything about you. Where are you from? What do you do?"

A server arrived with their dishes. Rano had ordered for her, due to the fact she'd recognized nothing on the menu. The server lifted a transparent tureen of green soup from their tray onto the table and added a dish of brown things swimming in a similarly colored liquid, and another dish of fried...

Her stomach did a flip. "Are those maggots?"

"You mean these?" He gestured at the crispy white grubs. "We call them krudrands. They have a delicate flavor, quite sweet. Though it depends on what they've been fed on. These are the best quality. You won't find better anywhere in Sot Loza. Try some." He scooped up a spoonful and, before she could protest, placed them on her plate.

They're dead. At least they're dead. "Is there any point in me telling you where I'm from? Do you even know the names of the systems nearest yours? I come from a place very far away, a poor planet no one's heard of."

"I guess that's a fair comment. About my unfamiliarity with the nearest star systems, I mean. We're far distant from everywhere. I could find out the names of the nearest systems if I looked in the archives but we Sot Lozans rarely bother with such stuff. We're very self-contained."

Insular, more like. "Why don't you tell me about yourself? You seem young to be Security Chief. Didn't anyone else want the job?"

He chuckled. "It *is* a hard job but, surprisingly, there's a lot of competition for it."

"So you have friends in high places?"

"Ha! I like your sense of humor. No, I didn't get a helping hand from an influential relative. I started young, worked hard, and I'm ambitious, that's all." He eyed her plate. "Not keen on the krudrands? How about some soup?"

The soup looked the least offensive dish. She ladled some into a bowl and peered at the contents. "This looks like algae. Am I right?"

"Well spotted."

She had some. It was okay. Algae was standard fare on many planets. Cheap and easy to grow, it could also take on a range of flavors. This was salty and aromatic. The warm liquid quelled her churning stomach somewhat but it didn't make the maggots look any more appetizing.

Questions ran through her mind. She had to find something made from wood. She wanted to find out why the Sot Lozans had brought them here. The answer might help them escape. She was desperate to know what had happened to her family, Bryce, Ava, and everyone else from the *Bathsheba*. But what could she ask that this man would answer? She put down her spoon. Rano had been eating the maggots, mixing them in with the lumpy brown stuff. When he saw her watching him he paused.

"Rano, it's clear you want a deeper relationship with me."

"I don't think that's any secret."

"It's also clear you're not going to tell me why."

"I can't. I'm sorry."

Do you even want to? "But how can I develop feelings for you when there are so many secrets between us?"

"What can I say? I hope you can take it on good faith that my intentions are honorable."

"I can't," she said dully, shaking her head. "It's asking too much."

"Perhaps, with time..." He appeared crestfallen, and she felt the absolutely tiniest smidgen of sympathy.

"The more time that passes, I'm only going to grow more resentful. I'm not as old as you but I've been through a lot and I know myself pretty well. Frankly, I hate Sot Loza and its people. You've deprived me of my liberty and self-determination. You try to dress it up, but that's essentially what you've done. Neither me nor my companions are the types to just accept our fate and make the best of things." She took a breath. Was she laying it on too thick? She didn't want to convince him the situation was entirely hopeless. She wanted him to believe it was salvageable—with a little give on his part.

He had slumped in his seat and a hint of defeat appeared in his eyes.

"But, maybe..." she went on.

He perked up.

"Maybe if you could make a gesture of that good faith you were talking about, I might begin to see things differently."

"Such as?" he asked cautiously.

"I haven't seen anyone else from my ship except the men and women I was with when I was captured. Are the rest of my companions alive?"

"Oh, yes. They're all alive. No one was killed during the capture, mostly because you saw the wisdom of surrendering quickly, and no one has died since being brought to Sot Loza."

The speed and clarity of his answer told her he was in close contact with the people holding her companions captive.

"Thank you. That's a relief."

With an undertone of guilt, he said, "I understand it must be hard for you to be separated from—"

"Please," she hissed, "spare me your pity." Instantly, she regretted her visceral reaction, but it didn't seem to anger him. If anything, he looked abashed. She pushed her advantage. "Can I see them?"

She knew what his answer would be, but her question had wider purpose.

"That isn't possible."

After refusing the big ask of her first request, he should find it harder to refuse a second, smaller one.

"Then can I at least know where they are? We had some children with us. I'm especially worried about them." She made sure to add a tremble to her voice. Lifting her napkin, she dabbed the corner of her eye and looked down. In truth, she was only partly faking her feelings.

After an awkward silence, Rano murmured, "I suppose it won't hurt to tell you the location of the children."

FIFTEEN

Sot Loza was divided into three zones, all dug out below the uninhabitable surface over centuries. According to historical records, the early years of colonization had been extremely tough. The colony teetered on the edge of oblivion several times, with hundreds of colonists dying of starvation or succumbing to the elements while waiting for the underground settlements to be built. But it had clung on despite all the adversities thrown at it.

Like most colonization attempts, the plan had been to create an agricultural economy first, ensuring food security before moving on to technological development after the colony had established itself. But the proposed methods of farming were all surface-based, relying on sunlight, rain, soil, clement weather, and moderate temperatures. Nothing had prepared the colonists for growing food underground. They'd been forced to use every ounce of ingenuity and invention to meet the challenge.

While Rano had been relating all this to Carina, he'd been drinking steadily. Was he working up his courage to divulge something he knew he shouldn't? She waited patiently as he wended his way toward telling her the location of her siblings. The more he drank, the more loquacious he'd become, lacing his words with many tangentially related facts and asides.

She'd let him talk. She'd barely eaten anything but had called for more wine and regularly topped up her dinner partner's glass. The restaurant slowly emptied of diners until it was just the two of them, alone at their table while the wait staff hovered in the shadows.

"So you see," he said, slightly slurring his words, "these dishes you don't seem to like very much, they're all the results of years of hard work and mental effort. A lot of them must be unique to our planet. They're a symbol of our survival."

"Sorry if I offended you. I didn't realize how important your food is to you."

"Yes, well..." He blinked and looked around the room as if noticing everyone else had left.

"You were going to tell me what happened to the children from my ship."

"I tell you what, why don't we continue this conversation at my place where I have some rather special liquor? It isn't far from here."

She assessed his state. He seemed too inebriated to be a physical threat, and more alcohol might loosen his lips even further. She agreed.

Rano Shelta's dwelling was within walking distance of the restaurant. They passed through mostly empty streets. Twilight hung over the town, just enough light to see by while still giving the impression of night.

He didn't attempt to hold her hand or put his arm around her as they walked along, for which she was grateful. She didn't want to sour the atmosphere by rebuffing him. After all the winking going on when she'd first arrived at the restaurant she'd been apprehensive he would overstep, but if anything tipsiness seemed to have made him less confident and more subdued.

They arrived at a house that fronted directly onto the street, detached from the others. Like all the buildings it was two storys tall. Single windows bordered the door on each side, and three windows sat in a row on the second floor. The place was small for the Chief of Security, but then perhaps it was old, built in a time when space underground was more scarce.

Rano pressed the security panel and the door opened. He led her to a living room on the right, telling her to take a seat while he got their drinks.

The living room window was opaque and played a vid of a waterfall in a lush forest accompanied by the gentle sounds of falling water and birdsong. Taken aback at experiencing something so un-Sot-Lozan, Carina stared.

Rano broke her trance by handing her a drink. "It's beautiful, isn't it? Nice to come home to after a long day at work. I never tire of it."

"Is it a recording of your origin planet?"

"It's supposed to be, though I don't know for sure. It could be entirely artificial, a sim. I like to tell myself it isn't."

She ruminated on the trees bordering the water. "Doesn't it make you wish you could live somewhere like that or at least visit?"

"That would be like wishing I could time travel into the past."

She sniffed the drink and took a cautious sip. It was strongly alcohclic with a flavor she couldn't identify. "Don't tell me what this is made from."

He smiled. "Okay."

She sat down. He joined her but didn't sit too closely as she'd expected him to. It was odd. The drunker he got the less annoying he became. It was the opposite of what she'd expected based on life experience. He sipped his drink, an arm over the back of the seat, his chin slumping toward his chest.

Was he about to nod off?

"You were telling me Sot Loza has three zones," she said. "I take it the children from my ship aren't in this one."

"Huh?" His head snapped up. "Oh, yeah. The three zones. There was a civil war four hundred years back. It was a political thing. Up until then Sot Loza had been governed by a single ruler. A hangover from the early days of colonization. A series of strong-minded figures had carried the population through the hard times. Some people thought it was time to elect the governing body. Before that, the Leader had chosen the members and retained right of veto on their decisions. Democratic elections had been the political system on our home planet and this new faction said we should return to it. Others disagreed, saying the Sot Lozan system had worked for us so far, and there was no reason it couldn't continue to work."

Carina clenched her jaw, aching to snap at him, telling him she didn't give a shit about his planet's history, but she had to be patient. He would either tell her where her family was or he wouldn't, and pressuring him wouldn't work. Besides, if he passed out while he was droning on about his world she would be free to search his house undisturbed. The sight of the trees in the vid had made her wonder if he owned wooden artifacts from his origin planet. Perhaps such things were prized.

"This zone stayed out of the fight," he went on. "We said we would go along with whichever system the winners chose. The war was short and bloody. The zone that fought for elections won. Sot Loza's Leader was executed." He sighed. "It was harsh, but if they hadn't killed her she could have tried to rally support and start another war."

"Uh huh," Carina remarked in a monotone.

"It's interesting..."

Is it?

"...Prior to the war, the three zones were separated by kilometers of rock. They'd been settled at different stages of the colonization. This one's the oldest. Twice in the past a group had split off, deciding they wanted to open up a mining site to create a new zone, though under the overall authority of the

Leader. Over the centuries, new dialects developed and then entirely different languages. Here, we don't speak Universal anymore—"

"I *had* noticed."

"But one of the other zones still does, as a second language. That's the youngest zone."

"Is that where the children from my ship are?"

"Yes," he replied, as naturally as if he were telling her something insignificant, "that's where they were taken. The zones were joined up by tunnels forty years ago, and linguists expect the languages to merge again eventually."

She closed her eyes and rested her head on the seat back. Her siblings were far away but at least she had an idea of where they were. How were they getting on? She was in a constant state of anticipation, hoping to receive a Send from one of them, probably Darius, whose Sends were powerful enough to cross the planet.

"You're tired," said Rano. "I should take you back to your hotel."

"I'm not tired. Just thinking."

"What about?"

"Life's hard here."

He appeared about to protest, so she held up a hand to stop him. "Hear me out. I understand that you're proud of what you've achieved, and you should be. In the history of galactic colonization I don't think a colony has ever been established under such terrible conditions. But things are different now. You have starships that could take you away from all this, to underpopulated planets where life is much easier. Maybe you don't have the capacity to transport everyone all at once, but over time you could do it. All of you could walk in sunlight and wind, swim in oceans and rivers, stand under waterfalls like the one playing on your window screen, instead of burrowing underground like rats and eating maggots. You must know it's possible, yet you choose to stay here. I don't get it."

He reached out a hand to cover hers. "Don't worry. In time, you'll understand."

Sixteen

Though Rano had been pretty drunk by the time Carina left, she hadn't managed to squeeze any more intel out of him. It was only to be expected, she'd reflected as she'd walked back to the hotel. He was the zone's security chief, after all. You didn't get into positions like that by being an idiot. He must have only divulged the location of her siblings because he thought she wouldn't or couldn't act on the information.

Pamuk was out of it and snoring when she entered their room. She went to bed feeling a little more hopeful about the situation. The kids were alive at least. She was confident Rano hadn't lied to her. On the other hand, she knew for certain that they and the rest of the Black Dogs were far away. Most likely, the *Bathsheba's* personnel had been split into three groups, each group allocated to one of Sot Loza's zones. Keeping them apart made sense. There was strength in numbers, and if any one group managed to escape they would face the difficult choice of abandoning their companions or risking re-capture by trying to get the others out too.

For her, there was no dilemma. She would free her brothers and sisters, Bryce, the Marchonish women, and the Black Dogs or die trying. The mercs were less important to her than her family but she felt responsible for their predicament. If it weren't for her they would still be working their old sector, not on this hare-brained escapade.

As nebulous ideas on how to resume their journey swirled around her mind, she fell asleep.

———

Someone was shaking her.

"Wake up. Chi-tang's found some wood. Wake up!"

"Ugnnnhhh." She turned onto her back and squinted, her eyes gritty.

Pale lilac light glowed through the window. Someone had pressed the 'Dawn' button.

Pamuk stood over her. "Chi-tang reckons he knows where we can get some wood."

"'kay." Her tongue seemed to have swollen to twice its usual size and it moved in her mouth like a slug that had lost its slime. The meaning of Pamuk's words began to filter through. "Wood?"

"Yeah, wood," the merc snapped. "You remember that stuff—"

"Hey!" She rose onto her elbows and hissed, "What are you thinking?!"

Pamuk appeared to suddenly remember where she was. "I mean, I just thought it was interesting..."

Carina rolled her eyes. "I'm gonna get up, then we'll go for a walk, okay?"

"Yeah, sure."

Ten minutes later, she was out in the street with Chi-tang, Pamuk, and Viggo. Chi-tang was buoyant, full of energy as he almost skipped along. Carina's steps were leaden. She'd only had three hours' sleep. They walked toward the town center, where the elevator to the surface was located. Few people were about at this early hour. When no one was within hearing distance, she said, "So what exactly did you find, Chi-tang, and where is it?"

"Uhhh..." He hung his head. "I'm kinda regretting saying anything now."

"Why?" Carina asked, deflating. "Aren't you sure this thing is made from genuine wood?"

"Yeah, that's one problem. I spent most of my life on Lakshmi. There's not a lot of natural products there. I'm not sure if I'm right. I'm no expert."

"That's okay," said Viggo. "If you're wrong, you're wrong. You tried, right?"

"Yeah, but..." Chi-tang continued to hesitate.

"What's the other problem?" Carina asked irritably. Her head was pounding. "Spit it out."

"You guys are gonna try and get this thing, aren't you?"

"Well, duh," said Pamuk.

Chi-tang went on, "I was thinking, you might get hurt for something that I'm not even sure is what I think it is. And, anyway, is it even worth it? I kinda like it here. Maybe sticking around wouldn't be so bad, especially when trying to leave could be a big disaster."

Carina said, "I didn't know there were *small* disasters. You're forgetting several facts and, no, I'm not going to spell them out to you. Think about it. The point is, we want that wood and we're going to try to get it. So, where is it?"

He huffed a sigh. "That's the third problem."

Carina suppressed an urge to punch him.

"I made a friend. A Sot Lozan. And I like her. I'm beginning to think I like her a lot. I don't want anything bad to happen to her while you guys do your stuff."

"How long have you known this person?" Viggo asked.

"I only met her yesterday but we really connected. Deep down, you know?"

Viggo met Carina's gaze. "I can cautiously say your relationship may not be as meaningful as you imagine it to be."

"You don't know her!" Chi-tang protested. "She's wonderful. Really nice."

Carina muttered, "Give me strength."

Viggo placed a friendly hand on Chi-tang's shoulder. "Have you considered that this woman may have an ulterior motive for being nice to you?"

"I knew you would say that. You've been saying the Sot Lozans have brought us here for a purpose, that there's something weird going on. But can any of you tell me what that purpose is? Do you know why we're here?"

"Just because we don't know the answer," said Carina, "that doesn't mean there isn't one or that it isn't bad. Is this person your first girlfriend?"

Chi-tang looked down. "I never had time for relationships before. The boss I was working for kept me too busy. And, to be honest, no one seemed interested anyway."

"My man," said Viggo, extending his reach over Chi-tang's shoulders and grabbing him in a sideways hug. "You have plenty of time to get a girlfriend. Take it from me, you don't want to get too involved too early on in the game. Play the field."

Carina rolled her eyes, scarcely believing that getting off the planet would involve giving relationship advice to their accidental pick-up from Lakshmi Station. "We don't have time for this bullshit. We're prisoners. The Sot Lozans took our ship. They're holding people I love captive and I might never see them again if you don't get your head out of your ass and tell us where the hell you—"

"Keep your voice down," Viggo urged.

"Yeah, cool it, Carina," said Pamuk. "Everyone's on edge, not just you." She leaned closer to Chi-tang and said in a hushed tone, "You've seen the Black

Dogs in action. If you don't want to get their attention, cough up where this thing is you claimed you saw."

He paled. "I wish I hadn't said anything now."

"Well, you did," said the merc, "so you better follow through."

"All right, all right." He raised his hands in exasperation. "Last night, I went out with the hotel manager. She took me back to her place and...you know."

"We know," said Carina. "And?"

"And she had a beautiful house. Her family own a string of hotels all over Sot Loza. There was this display case in one of the rooms upstairs and something in it caught my eye. It was a bowl, very simple and plain. Not like the rest of the ornaments, which were all shiny and fancy. So I asked her what it was, wondering why it was in there with all the expensive stuff. She said I had great taste, that I'd noticed the most valuable item. She said it was one of the few surviving objects from the colonization era, and it must have been brought on the colony ship from their origin planet because it was made from a plant that died a long time ago. It has to be wood, right?"

"What color was it?" Carina asked.

"Dark brown, almost black."

"Could be what we're looking for," said Viggo. "Did you handle it?"

"I didn't dare ask. The case was locked."

"What was the security like at the house?" asked Carina.

"Tight. A fence, guards, house security system, the works."

"Figures. Do you think you can disarm the security?"

"I can try but I'm not promising anything."

Leaving Sot Loza was not going to be easy.

SEVENTEEN

When Bryce came to he was back in his cell. The dimly lit, drab ceiling that swam into focus, the sensation of lying on a hard, lumpy mattress, and the noise of Rees's snoring told him so. He ached everywhere. The guard had roughed him over before handing him to the medics. After that he vaguely remembered a mask descending over his face, then blackness.

An ache in a particular part of his body told him the operation he'd undergone had been what he'd suspected. What the Sot Lozans couldn't get him to give up freely they'd taken by force. He adjusted his position, sparking fresh pain, and a groan escaped.

The sound of snoring ceased.

"You're back in the land of the living?" Rees asked.

"Looks like it," Bryce muttered through swollen, bruised lips.

"They did you over pretty good."

"I can tell."

"Was it because you wouldn't give them a sample?"

"Uh huh."

"Shouldn't get hung up about it. It's no big deal."

"Right. I'll bear that in mind. How often have you had to do it?"

"Every couple of days. If that's the worst we can expect, we should count ourselves lucky."

"I'm not doing it."

There was a rustling sound as Rees moved on his bunk. "Look at me, kid."

With some difficulty, Bryce turned onto his side to face the older man.

"Don't get a stick up your ass about nothing. They could be doing a whole lot worse things to us. All we need to do is sit tight, do as they say, and try not to—"

"Have you thought about what they're using our samples for?" Bryce asked.

"Not for a second. Why would I care?"

"You don't care if they're using your genetic material for human experimentation?"

"I don't give a shit what they're using it for. Whatever it is, that's on them, not me. It's their responsibility, and if they didn't get it from me they would get it somewhere else. That stuff's not exactly hard to come by."

"All right," Bryce seethed, "if it doesn't faze you that you might be fathering babies born to live in pain, or actual monsters, have you considered what they must be doing to Carina and maybe Parthenia too, and the Marchonish women? The female Black Dogs?"

"What do you mean?" Rees asked uneasily.

"What they're asking from us is easy to deliver. It's different for women." He didn't want to go into more detail because the idea made him feel sick.

"Okay, point taken. But what difference would it make if I refuse? They'll just take it, the same as they did to you."

"It'll show them what they're doing isn't okay."

"Yeah," Rees scoffed, "like they care what we think."

"Even if it makes no difference, you'll keep your integrity."

"Ha! That's a damned fancy word. Talk to me again when you can grow a beard, kid."

"I might be younger than you but that doesn't mean I haven't lived, or that I haven't learned right from wrong. That's something you seem to have forgotten."

"Kill enough men and you'll soon learn there isn't any right or wrong. There's only living another day or getting smoked."

Bryce was silent. He didn't know how to reach this hardened merc and make him understand. He also wasn't sure he should, or could, or that it was worth it. Men like Rees had endured adversities he couldn't even imagine and seen inconceivable horrors. Who was he to lecture him on morality?

Another idea occurred. "We've been here days. Don't you think something should have happened by now?"

"Yeah," Rees replied quietly. "The thought had crossed my mind."

"Something must have gone wrong. And if it has, that means we aren't getting out of here anytime soon. If we don't want to spend the rest of our lives as lab rats we can't just sit here twiddling our thumbs."

"Maybe, but what can we do? It's just the two of us. Have you seen any other Black Dogs?"

"No, I can't even figure out if they're in nearby cells."

"Me neither. The guards are being careful to keep us all separated."

The light flicked from dim to full.

Prisoners, move away from the door.

Bryce and Rees locked eyes. Had their conversation been overheard? Were they about to be punished?

Blinking in the brighter light, Bryce got slowly and painfully to his feet and joined Rees, who stood with his back to the far wall.

When the door slid open, the guard jabbed a finger at him. "You're to come with me." As well as being armed, this one carried a thick baton. His partner waited behind him.

"Already?" Bryce asked. "I only just got back."

"Move!"

"They must have loved your sample," Rees joked.

"Yeah, top quality stuff." Bryce shuffled across the cell. As he left, he caught a glimpse of Rees's look of concern. Then he was alone with the guard.

"Where are you taking me?"

The guards didn't answer.

They passed locked cells, enigmatically silent.

"Hey!" he yelled. "Any Black Dogs here?"

The baton hit him in his midriff. An *Ooof!* exploded from his mouth and he doubled over.

"Try that again and next time it'll be your kidneys," the guard hissed. "Now move."

Bryce staggered forward. No reply had come from the cells, but they could be soundproofed. He'd never detected any noise from outside his own.

They were moving toward the elevator again. Was he about to undergo another operation? What would the medics take from him this time? Or was he about to take part in their experiments in another way? He fought the urge to vomit, not only triggered by the blow to his stomach.

When they reached the elevator, the guards took him right past it.

So he wasn't returning to the medical center after all.

The passageway turned a corner and widened out. Here, the walls were more brightly colored and cleaner and more lights shone overhead. The atmosphere seemed better too. The air smelled sweeter and less dank.

They stepped into a new section, where a dark tunnel replaced one wall. It was a transport line. The platform was empty. They waited only a few minutes before a single carriage swept in and drew to a stop. The passengers who alighted were all in medic uniforms. They cast glances at Bryce but ducked their heads, avoiding eye contact.

"Where are you taking me?" he asked again as the guards pushed him into the car.

A surreal feeling settled over him. It was like he was going on vacation with two stern, strict uncles who weren't about to take any shit from their nephew. A few passengers remained in the carriage, and they turned their heads as if to pretend he didn't exist. He and the guards didn't sit. At the next stop, they forced him off.

Ignoring his aches and pains as well as he could, he took careful note of his surroundings. It was interesting, and perhaps useful, to know that there was a public transportation system so close to the prison. The map he'd seen on the train had shown it was a closed loop of ten or twelve stations. Their names hadn't meant anything. They hadn't indicated what was at each stop, such as an elevator to the surface or a spaceport.

The guards walked him down a narrow, circular tunnel. At the end, they climbed a long flight of steps. Near the top, Bryce halted in amazement. He could see the sky. It was pale lilac and clouds scudded across it.

A guard grabbed his elbow. "Get up there. We haven't got all day."

They stepped out into a street. It looked ordinary, like you might see on any planet, though not many people were about. A longer look at the sky told Bryce it was early morning or dusk. He couldn't see a sun.

A vehicle was waiting. They boarded it and ten minutes later it drew up outside a single-story building set back from the street. Bryce was completely confused. No scenario he could imagine explained what was happening. Was he being transferred to this new place due to the conversation he'd had with Rees? If so, why hadn't the guards simply put him in another cell?

The double-doored entrance opened at their approach. Beyond it stood five familiar figures.

Parthenia ran forward to hug him but drew up short. "Oh, Bryce!" she breathed. "What have they done to you?"

EIGHTEEN

The feeling he was in a weird dream hadn't abated. Bryce sat in the living room drinking tea with Carina's siblings as if it was just another rest day aboard the *Bathsheba*. Meanwhile, two armed guards stood at the door, one looking inward the other out into the rest of the house, and they were trapped on an alien planet with currently no prospect of leaving.

Ava was here, too, somewhere. She'd come, babe in arms, to briefly say hello before disappearing, presumably to give him time alone with the kids.

He was having trouble keeping it together. Parthenia was the problem. She couldn't help it, but she looked so like her older sister his mind was crowded with Carina. What was happening to her? Had their captors—the Sot Lozans, the children had told him—been experimenting on her? When he'd seen the kids his hopes had briefly lifted that Carina was here too but she was not. None of her brothers or sisters had seen or heard of her since leaving the ship.

"I wish I could make you better," Oriana whispered, lines of concern creasing her forehead as she peered at him.

She meant she would have Cast Heal if she could, which meant she could not. The kids didn't have elixir and hadn't managed to make any. He didn't know which ingredient they were lacking and they couldn't tell him, not with a guard listening to every word they spoke.

"I look worse than I feel," he replied. "Don't worry about me."

"What about everyone else?" Parthenia asked. "Have you seen them? Are they all right?"

Again, there was a subtext. She wanted to know about Carina but couldn't reveal their relationship.

"I'm cellmates with Rees. He's fine, or as well as you might expect considering we're being held prisoner. I don't know anything about anyone else, sorry."

"Oh." Parthenia's shoulders slumped. She'd undoubtedly been hoping for a hint that her resourceful sister was in the process of arranging everyone's escape, or at the very least that she was okay.

He wished he could have reassured her, if not about their imminent release from captivity then Carina's well being. If only. There was one subject they could discuss without fear, however. "What I don't understand is, why am I here? Do any of you know?"

"That's easy," Ferne replied. "We begged them to let us see you. We told them you're our friend and if they wouldn't show us you're alive and well then we would stop eating. It was yesterday we made the threat, though we've been asking to see you ever since we were taken from the ship."

"I see. So that explains why Darius is stuffing his mouth with cake."

The little boy gave him a crumb-speckled grin.

"Are you all okay?" Bryce asked. "Have you been treated well?"

Parthenia replied, "Apart from keeping us prisoner, everyone has been very kind. We don't like the food very much but they've given us plenty and a wide range of it too. We're allowed out under supervision so we've been exploring as much as we can."

This was bad news. If the kids had free rein to find what they needed for elixir and they'd been unsuccessful, it meant one or more of the items was scarce or entirely absent. "What have you discovered about this place?"

Parthenia told him the Sot Lozans lived entirely underground and had done so ever since they'd discovered the planet centuries ago. The colonists had intended to go somewhere else but an accident on their ship had driven them many light years off course.

"It isn't horrible here," Oriana added, "but it isn't very nice either. I don't want to spend the rest of my life on this planet. They keep telling us we'll get used to it eventually."

"We won't," Nahla said vehemently. "*I* won't. I hate it. It's so boring. And it's outrageous that they stole our ship."

Bryce couldn't help smiling at the little girl's anger, not in a patronizing way but because she was so forthright in front of the guards. Nahla was fearless, despite having no mage powers.

"Try not to give up hope," he said. "Maybe the Sot Lozans will see sense soon and let us go. How are they treating Ava?"

"Like a queen," said Ferne. "They seem to like her best of all of us. No one knows why. Even she can't figure it out."

"It's because she has a baby," Darius commented.

"Huh?" Ferne's lip curled in skeptical puzzlement. "That's a stupid reason. What makes you say that?"

"They get all warm and fuzzy inside when they see it."

Parthenia frowned at him, warning him not to mention anything else pertaining to his mage abilities.

He looked down, abashed.

"Hmm, come to think of it," she said, "you could be right."

"I *am* right!"

She turned to Bryce. "They're very patient and gentle around Ava. It would make sense they're being especially careful because the baby is so young and vulnerable."

He tried to reconcile this side of the Sot Lozans with the treatment he'd personally received from them. He couldn't.

"They're more patient than me," said Oriana. "The little thing never seems to stop crying. I'm never having children. They would send me crazy."

"Good," said Ferne, "because if you did I would be the worst uncle in the galaxy. Now I've experienced living with one I agree with you. All they ever do is cry, eat, and poop."

Parthenia reached out and touched Bryce's hand. "I'm going to speak to the guards and ask them if you can come and live here with us. You're part of our family. We should be together."

A rush of emotion hit him. Again, her resemblance to Carina, coupled with his fears, were overwhelming.

NINETEEN

Carina rubbed her sweaty palms on her pants. She didn't think she'd ever been so nervous on a raid, not even when she'd gone with Captain Speidel to rescue Darius from his Dirksen kidnappers. Was it because she didn't have any elixir? Even if she'd never intended to use it, she'd always taken some with her when she'd been a Black Dog. Just having a flask on her hip gave her a sense of security. If she was in a bad spot she could Transport out, or if she was wounded she could Heal herself. Elixir was a great backup plan. Now she was as vulnerable as a non-mage and she didn't like it. She felt naked.

Being unarmed didn't help either. But, strangely enough, that didn't bother her as much. As well as the Lotacryllan, Viggo, her merc companions were Pamuk, Mads, and Berkcan, seasoned warriors, well-trained and veterans of many battles. Military conflict had weeded out the worst fighters in the Black Dogs—though they had lost some of the best, too, through sheer bad luck. She recalled Cadwallader, Atoi, and Halliday. All good people. Good friends. All gone.

She swallowed and blinked as she peered out from her hiding place, hoping they would not lose anyone tonight. It wasn't likely. The Sot Lozans seemed intent on handling their prisoners with kid gloves. But it wasn't impossible.

The residence Chi-tang had brought them to was out of town. A wide, two-story house stood behind tall railings and a large gate. Lights from the windows shone brightly in the darkness, illuminating the open ground in front of the house and the guards standing each side of the gate. Were more guards patrolling the site? None had been spotted yet.

"How much longer before they go to bed?" Pamuk whispered. "It's already late."

"How would I know?" Carina replied. "We'll have to wait as long as it takes. Be patient."

They were in the construction site opposite Chi-tang's girlfriend's house. Someone seemed to be building a mansion to rival her family's, in the usual habit of the rich trying to out-do each other. Their cover was the portable office of the site. The place was empty now all the workers had gone home.

Viggo said, "Have you noticed how quiet it is here at night? At home, even out in the desert there would be noises. The wind in the dunes, the calls of nocturnal animals, the scrape of creatures moving through the sand. Here, there's nothing."

"That isn't right," said Pamuk. "You can hear something. Listen hard."

Mads and Berkcan were still, and the little group listened. One of the guards outside the house they were staking out shifted position and Carina heard the faint rustle of his uniform. Then there was nothing. Except, it was not quite nothing.

"I can hear it," said Viggo. "What *is* that?"

"Fans," Carina replied, the moment recognition hit her. "I remember feeling a faint breeze when we stepped out of the elevator. The Sot Lozans must run fans to keep the atmosphere breathable."

"You can barely hear the hum," said Pamuk. "Only at night when there's no traffic around. It took me a while to figure out what it was. I bet the locals aren't even aware of it."

"Yeah," Carina agreed. "Probably not. They grew up with it."

The downstairs lights in the residence went out. Only two upstairs lights remained on.

"Ha," said Viggo. "Not long now."

Carina wasn't so sure. Chi-tang had gone into the house with his date a couple of hours ago. She guessed it would still be another hour or so before he could sneak down and open the front door.

It was the only signal he could give them and—not being a fighter—the only help he could offer. The man lacked the skills and guile to steal the bowl from its display case, so they were forced to do it themselves.

She chewed her lip. Was five too many for the raid? Or were they too few? But they couldn't have brought any more mercs along. The Sot Lozans seemed to know where every Outsider was at all times. The five of them simply slipping out of the hotel and walking out here under the cover of darkness had been risky.

First one and then the other upstairs light went out.

"This is it," Viggo said, his tone tense.

"No, it isn't," said Carina. "Take it easy."

"Yeah," said Pamuk. "Relax." She leaned her back on the wall of the flimsy office. "Shit, I can't wait to get out of this place and back to the ship. Sot Loza is more boring than Deep Sleep."

"But you aren't aware of anything in Deep Sleep," Carina replied, puzzled.

"Exactly."

"So they don't compare."

"That's what I mean."

Pamuk's answer wasn't enlightening but Carina left it. There was no understanding mercs sometimes. She wondered how Jackson and Van Hasty were doing, and Hsiao. Of all the Black Dogs she got on with the pilot the best, probably because Hsiao usually thought things through before she acted.

"C'mon," Viggo muttered. "How long's Chi-tang going to take?"

"Longer than a minute, I hope," said Pamuk, "or his new girlfriend's gonna be disappointed."

Her fellow mercs sniggered.

Carina peered up and down the road, though she couldn't see far. Night enveloped the gray strip now the house lights had gone out. Only the faux stars and the glow of street lights in Laft lit the darkness.

"Can anyone actually *see* the front doors?" Pamuk asked.

In truth, it was practically impossible. Carina wasn't sure she could differentiate between any aspects of shadowy facade. An open door would only look like a slightly darker patch.

Pamuk cursed. "We didn't think of this, and we can't comm him to tell him to give us a clearer signal."

"We could try to get closer to the gate," said Viggo. "We might see the doors better then."

"And we might not," Pamuk replied, "while the guards will certainly see *us*."

Dammit. Carina tried to think of a way around the problem but she couldn't. How could they tell if the doors opened in near pitch blackness? "We'll just have to do our best. We need that bowl. It might be the only piece of wood in all Sot Loza."

"We could forget about it and come back another night," Viggo suggested. "We'll see Chi-tang tomorrow. We can agree on a different signal. One that will actually work in these conditions."

"I don't know," said Carina. "I'd rather take our chances now. There's no guarantee the bowl will even be there after tonight, or that we'll be able to come out here again without being noticed. The Sot Lozans are probably looking for us already, wondering where we've gone. After tonight they'll watch us more closely."

"Lin's right," said Pamuk. "We won't get this chance again. We've been treated pretty nicely but we're still prisoners. We can't forget that."

"Then maybe we can think of another—"

"*Shh*!" hissed Pamuk. "Did you hear that?"

Carina strained her ears, but the only sound she could detect was the faint hum of the ventilation fans. "What do you think you heard?"

"A door opening."

She squinted at the front of the house. Was the site of the doors darker than the rest of it? "It's too soon. He can't have snuck downstairs yet."

"I swear that's what I heard," said Pamuk. "We need to move, now. Before someone notices the open door and closes it."

"Okay," said Carina. "Let's do it."

The group ran out from their cover and about thirty meters down the street, moving softly and quietly. When they reached the spot opposite the corner of the fence they darted across the road. If the estate guards saw them they didn't raise an alarm. Pamuk in the lead, they jogged along the fence line, not stopping until they were out of sight of the guards.

Mads made a stirrup from his hands. Pamuk put a foot in it and he boosted her up. She grabbed the top of the railings and pulled herself over. There was a soft thunk as her dark figure landed on the other side.

It was Carina's turn next. A moment later she hit the ground next to Pamuk. In another few seconds, Viggo joined them. Mads and Berkcan would wait to help them climb back over the fence, assuming they didn't get caught.

Three cars were parked on this side of the house. They ran behind them to the wall and then up to the corner. Peeking out, Carina saw the guards. They faced outward, toward the road. It was only then it struck her how odd their presence was. The owners of the house were rich—there was no doubt about that—but armed guards seemed overkill. Sot Lozan society didn't appear particularly lawless or violent.

She had no more time to think about it. Pamuk was on her way to the front door. Viggo quickly followed her and Carina brought up the rear.

The merc had been right. The front door was wide open. They walked unimpeded into the hallway.

"Chi-tang?" Pamuk whispered, almost inaudibly.

No answer came.

TWENTY

Minutes had passed, and there was no sign of their companion. They were alone in the large, dark hallway. The house was silent. A pale glow spilled down from the second floor. Open doorways led to the downstairs rooms, all seemingly empty. The household had gone to bed, and so had Chi-tang, apparently.

The plan had been that he would disarm the security, open the door, and wait for them inside before taking them to the bowl. Was he hoping that if he wasn't present for the robbery he wouldn't be suspected of helping, and he could continue his romantic relationship with the rich daughter?

"Where the *fuck* is that idiot?" Pamuk hissed. "I should have known he would half-ass it."

"What do we do now?" murmured Viggo.

"Anyone remember which room the display case is in?" Carina asked. "Did he say it was upstairs?"

Pamuk replied, "Yeah, but I'm pretty sure he didn't mention where."

"We can't search everywhere," said Viggo. "The house is full of sleeping people. We're bound to wake someone up."

"We would wake them up when we smashed that case open anyway," Pamuk countered.

"Yeah," Viggo replied with forced patience, "but then we would leave, fast. If we wake everyone up before we find the bowl—"

"*Okay.* I get it."

"We have to try," said Carina. "Come on." She tiptoed up the wide, central staircase. The deep carpet helped to mask the sound of their footsteps.

At the top, the reason for Chi-tang's omission in not describing the location of the display room became clear. Four corridors led from the staircase, lit at intervals by tiny wall lights not much brighter than candles. At the end of each corridor another crossed it. The upstairs space was like a warren.

They picked one corridor at random.

A closed door confronted them.

They halted.

Could this be the right place? Carina asked the others with her eyes.

Viggo shrugged.

It might make sense for the display room to be close to the central area. She pressed an ear against the door. From inside the room came the distinct sound of someone snoring.

She shook her head and they moved on.

The next door stood ajar. Carina stuck her head in the opening. Screens bedecked the walls and a holo projector stood in the center. It seemed to be a room for entertainment or education.

At the next room no sound could be heard but the door wouldn't open, and so on they went.

They'd reached the end of the corridor. Pamuk took the left turn and Carina and Viggo followed.

The farther they got into the Sot Lozan mansion, the faster Carina's heart raced. They were moving away from their escape route and increasing the distance they would have to run when they smashed open the case to get the wooden bowl. She guessed they were already so far from the front door that the guards would easily reach it before them, and then what?

She didn't think their punishment would be unbearably severe but the object of their crime—the bowl—would be taken from them, and they would face very awkward questions about why they wanted it.

Pamuk had stopped at a door and was listening. She grinned at them and made an obscene gesture to indicate the activity she could hear going on within. Viggo leaned in to listen too. Carina rolled her eyes and stepped past them. A short way along the corridor they caught up to her.

"I think that was Chi-tang," Pamuk whispered in her ear.

"You're disgusting," Carina muttered.

Three more doors yielded no results. When she listened at the fourth, she heard an odd sound she couldn't identify. It was a quiet rhythmic hiss, a mechanical noise, not human. She beckoned Viggo closer to get his opinion. He listened and then gave a baffled look.

Whatever was going on in the room, she doubted it had anything to do with displaying ancient artifacts, so she walked past it. Pamuk was already at the next door, which stood open. She entered the room and immediately emerged from it again, wildly gesticulating.

She'd found it.

They went inside and closed the door.

Tall, glass cabinets occupied much of the space. It was easy to see why the owners had picked this room to display their most precious items. The floor-to-ceiling windows would allow in plenty of light during the daytime. Even at night, the starlight glinted beautifully on the cabinets and gilded their contents.

There were tiaras, necklaces, brooches, rings, and hairpins. Some lined, open boxes held only single gems. Another cabinet displayed ceramic art, highly decorated. The next she looked into contained portraits carved into flat pebbles—the colony's founders?

She felt a tap on her shoulder. Viggo tugged her arm, bringing her to a corner display. On the third transparent shelf sat a small, plain bowl. Perhaps it was dark brown as Chi-tang had said but in the dim light it looked black, and it was so small it must have been for a baby.

She nodded. This had to be it. She tried the cabinet door but it didn't open.

Pamuk waved them back and took a fist-sized rock from her pocket.

Carina held her breath. They were far from the only exit. Too far. But if they didn't want to spend the rest of their lives on this backward planet, they had no other options.

Pamuk slammed the rock into the glass.

It bounced back. The glass was not glass but a transparent material, fortified against breaking.

"*Shit!*" Pamuk grimaced and rubbed her shoulder.

"Be quiet," Carina urged softly. Pointlessly, she tried the lock again. The wooden bowl tantalized her, sitting innocently on the shelf, the answer to so many of their problems. They'd come all the way here, searched for it, and found it, but it remained beyond their grasp.

"Let me try again," Pamuk whispered.

"That's never going to work," said Viggo, "but I thought of something that might. Help me lay this thing down." He reached for the top of the cabinet while Pamuk took the bottom.

The items inside shifted, sliding from their shelves as the angle altered. Viggo and Pamuk moved slowly but some noise was inevitable. Carina winced and looked furtively at the door. They were bound to wake someone up. A sense of hopelessness hit her. Maybe they should leave now.

Viggo was scanning the other cabinets. He strode to one that looked emptier than the others, squatted down, and wrapped his arms around it.

"Oh, I get the idea," said Pamuk quietly. "We'd better get out of the way."

Carina got the idea too. The cabinet's legs tapered to a narrow point.

Viggo heaved the display case up and carried it over to the prone one.

Carina put her hands to her face as she watched in trepidation.

He smashed it down, driving the point of one leg into the transparent surface.

It cracked.

But he'd made a racket. The objects in the cabinet he was holding clattered against the sides. The crack had been loud.

"Do it again," Pamuk prompted.

The second blow split the crack into shards, which collapsed into the cabinet.

"Get it!"

Carina reached inside. She'd kept her eye on the bowl the entire time. She flicked aside the splinters and grabbed it before shoving it into her shirt. "Let's go!"

They sped through the room. Viggo tore the door open and they piled through the doorway. Carina ran only a few steps before she crashed into Viggo's back. He'd jerked to a halt. In another second, she saw why.

Guards were already at the end of the corridor.

It was too soon for them to have heard the disturbance and run inside, or to have been alerted by someone in the house. They must have noticed the open front door.

Her heart sank to the pit of her stomach.

Why hadn't they closed the door?

Still, their idea had been stupid and pointless as soon as they'd found out the display room was so far from the exit.

The guards advanced, weapons drawn.

"Don't move," one called out, "or we'll shoot."

"In here," said Pamuk, opening the nearest door. "Maybe we can climb out of a window."

It was the room where Carina had heard the strange, mechanical noise. She darted inside, Viggo close behind her. It was a small anteroom with bare white walls and shelves containing what looked like medical equipment. There was also a tall metal cupboard, which Viggo dragged across the door.

There was no time to ponder these anomalous items. Pamuk was on her way through a second, heavier door. The mechanical noise burst out as she opened it.

She screamed.

Carina had never heard a merc scream.

Pamuk stood in the open doorway as if frozen.

Carina peered around her and had trouble stifling her own scream.

Viggo, looking over Pamuk's shoulder, only breathed, "Holy shit."

In one corner of the room was a hospital bed. The machine they'd heard stood next to it, and tubes ran from the machine to the figure lying on the bed.

Carina couldn't tell if it was a man or a woman, but not because the room was dark. There was sufficient light from the machines to see that the person was one giant, weeping, open sore. The machine was breathing for him or her, and liquid and nutrients seemed to be running through lines to the remains of the person's face and chest.

"Th-the window," Pamuk stammered.

Carina tore her gaze from the figure. The window was indeed open a few centimeters.

Had the patient even registered their arrival? It was impossible to know.

Viggo pushed past and marched to the window. He opened it to its fullest extent. "You two go first. You're lighter than me and less likely to break something."

A scraping sound could be heard from the anteroom.

"Hurry!"

There was no time to argue. Carina took a glance at the ground one floor below, barely able to make it out in the darkness, and leapt. As she landed, she rolled to absorb the impact. Getting to her feet, she was amazed to discover she seemed unhurt.

Pamuk hit and grunted. She also rolled, but when she got up, she hobbled as she walked to Carina.

Viggo's form was a silhouette against the dim light shining through the window above.

He seemed to hesitate.

A flash lit him up. He groaned and fell, impacting the ground with a sickening thump.

The odor that emanated from him was nauseatingly familiar. He'd taken a hit from a pulse round. The guards must have broken through into the room.

"Viggo!" Carina cried out.

He'd taken a hit at nearly point blank range, unarmored. He'd had it.

"Leave me." The words were a sigh on his exhaled breath.

Pamuk pulled on her arm. "We have to go."

Light flashed.

They were being fired at.

I could Heal you. I could save you.

But she could not.

Her merc training kicked in and, tears filling her eyes, she stepped away from his body.

Pamuk was limping heavily. She put the woman's arm over her shoulder and grabbed her around her waist. They stumbled toward the fence.

A pulse round exploded next to her foot, burning through her shoe. Stifling her cry of pain she pushed on. Raised voices came from above. The guards were arguing.

No more fire came.

They were at the fence. Though they were far from the spot where they'd scaled it, Berkcan was ready, hanging down. He and Mads must have seen or heard the commotion and run to meet them. Carina helped Pamuk up reach the outstretched hands. As soon as the merc was over she took a short run and leapt, forcing herself to ignore the pain from her foot.

She was on the other side of the fence.

They disappeared into the night.

They'd done it.

They had the bowl, but it had cost Viggo his life.

TWENTY-ONE

It was three in the morning and Carina's foot was aflame by the time she reached the hotel with Pamuk and her other partners in crime. The walk back to Laft had been brutal. As well as the pulse round burn she'd suffered, Pamuk had badly twisted her ankle jumping from the window. With two of them injured their journey had been slow, and the need to avoid detection meant they'd stayed far from the highway. Stray rocks and spoil from tunneling littered the open ground. Each time Carina had tripped on something the agony that lanced from her burnt foot was indescribable.

The streets of Laft were just about empty at the late hour. They'd walked from the edge of town to the hotel without encountering another soul. As Carina mounted the steps to the lobby, she nursed a hope that they might have gotten away with their escapade. In the back of her mind she knew she was being delusional, but the pain and the long trek had addled her mind.

Vice-General Queshm was waiting for them. The sadistic glitter in her eyes told Carina she'd seen them approach. She'd probably had tabs on them since they stepped within Laft's boundaries, but she'd let them walk the remaining kilometers exhausted and injured, prolonging their suffering out of spite.

Soldiers waited inside the door. The Black Dogs who had remained behind stood on the staircase, watching.

"Seize them," Queshm ordered. "Search them, and then bring them to me, along with anything you find."

Firm hands grasped Carina's arms and she was force-marched away from the entrance. She didn't have the strength or willpower to put up a fight.

Viggo's body in the dust below the mansion's window was an image she couldn't banish from her mind. Limply, she allowed herself to be manhandled. The soldiers slapped and jabbed her as they searched. When they came up empty-handed, she was the first to be taken to Queshm.

The Vice-General was seated at the hotel manager's desk. After running her gaze from Carina's toes to her head, she nodded at the soldier who had brought her in. The man left.

"Your companion is dead," said Queshm.

"I thought so."

"The guards at the Varvara Estate didn't notice he was an Outsider before they shot him. They thought you were there for a purpose other than stealing the family's valuables. It was nighttime and the room you were in was dark, so they didn't notice the color of your friend's clothes. It was an easy mistake to make. They will be punished nevertheless."

"Because they shot one of us?" She was confused. If the guards' employers didn't want them to use deadly force on intruders, why did they give them guns?

"Because they killed an Outsider."

"I didn't realize we were so important."

Queshm slammed her hands on the desk and rose stiffly to her feet. She walked around the desk and up to Carina before leaning in until their noses nearly touched. "You didn't realize you were important?! What the hell do you think has been happening here?"

"I don't know. You tell me. You've all been screwing around with us ever since you took us prisoner."

Queshm moved away. "But you've been treated well. You can't deny it. Believe me, things could be a lot worse for you."

"Doesn't matter how well you treat us. We're still prisoners. If you're so nice and kind, let us go. Give us our ship back." Carina paused as a fresh wave of pain from her foot washed over her. "What do you mean, things could be a lot worse? Are you talking about the rest of us, the ones you took to the other zones? What have you been doing to them?" It hadn't occurred to her, after Rano told her that her siblings were in another zone, that their experience of Sot Loza might be different from hers. Sudden fear seized her, masking the discomfort from her injury. "If you want to treat us well, let us see the rest of our ship's personnel. How do we know you haven't killed them?"

Amusement flickered over the vice-general's face. "No one's been killed."

"I don't believe you. I want to see them."

"If you had been compliant that might have been arranged, but now it's out of the question. You've demonstrated that you can't be trusted. We can't take the risk."

"Compliant with what?!" Carina spat. "*What* are we supposed to be complying with?"

"You could start by not breaking into highly respected families' homes and stealing from them. What was it you took, by the way? Is another member of your gang carrying the item?"

Carina didn't answer.

After a moment's silence, Queshm returned to her seat. "Oh well, I'll find out soon enough. The Varvara family will take an inventory and figure it out. What I don't understand is, why do it in the first place? What use would you have for a valuable item? You lack the connections to make a profit from it."

Carina only regarded her steadily.

Queshm sighed and shook her head. "Naturally, your actions mean freedom of movement is now restricted for all Outsiders. No one can leave this hotel unless accompanied by a Sot Lozan with the necessary clearance. I will send a medic to your room to attend to your injury."

This seemed to be a dismissal, so Carina limped out into the lobby. Pamuk was waiting with two soldiers. They exchanged a look as Carina passed by.

———

"I'm going to kill Chi-tang when I see him," Pamuk seethed. "Slowly."

She was lying in the bed across the room from Carina, her ankle wrapped up. A medic had attended to Carina's foot, too, and she was in less physical pain.

She was lying on her side, facing the merc. She was angry with Chi-tang too, but even if he had met them in the hall as planned, things would probably have gone the same way. "We should have closed the front door," she replied dully.

"Huh?"

"If we'd closed the front door the guards wouldn't have come into the house until later, after they heard the noise of the cabinet breaking. Maybe they wouldn't have heard it at all and we could have snuck away."

"There's no point in speculating. But Chi-tang might have thought to close the door. He deviated from the plan, like a moron."

"He isn't a merc, just an engineer, and a young one."

"He's older than you."

Carina had no answer to this. Their pick-up from Lakshmi was older, in his early twenties. Yet in many ways he was younger than her. Young and naive.

"We might not see him again anyway. He could have already shacked up with his new girlfriend."

"It'll be lucky for him if he does."

Carina understood how Pamuk felt. To be betrayed by a teammate was devastating and infuriating, especially when someone had died. If Chi-tang had been a Black Dog and had no good excuse for his behavior, at the very best he could have expected a severe beating. But she couldn't share Pamuk's anger. She was too heartsick for Bryce, her brothers and sisters, and Viggo. Over their time on Lakshmi Station, the Lotacryllan had become a friend. She had lost too many friends.

"What do you think was wrong with that person in the bed?" Pamuk asked.

"No idea." Carina turned onto her back. "Whatever it was, it was bad. They looked barely alive."

"Yeah, and they weren't gonna get better. No one comes back from that. If I'm ever like that, I hope someone does me a favor and pulls the plug."

"Me too. I don't get it, though. Why wasn't that person in hospital? Why were they being kept in that room?"

"They'd been brought home to die, of course. The same thing happened to my uncle. He lived on Ithiya and caught the plague. When he got too sick and the splicers couldn't help him anymore, my cousins took him home so he could die in peace, surrounded by the people he loved."

Carina turned onto her side again to stare at Pamuk. "Your uncle had Ithiyan Plague?"

"You've heard of it?"

"Yeah, I..." It was the disease Ma had died of and that Bryce had suffered from until his parents found him and paid for his treatment. But she didn't want to go into her personal history. "I've heard of it. I'm sorry."

"Don't worry about it. We weren't close."

A fellow merc stuck his head in. "Chi-tang's back."

Pamuk leapt from her bed and then gave a yelp as her twisted ankle hit the floor. "I'm gonna kill him. I'm gonna throttle his goddamned scrawny neck." She hobbled out.

"Pamuk, slow down," Carina called after her. "At least wait to hear what he has to say."

She hopped across the room, grabbing the door frame for support, leaned into the corridor. Pamuk had reached the end of it and was face to face with Chi-tang, hands on hips, though not—yet—hurting him. He appeared terrified, justifiably. Carina was a bit scared of Pamuk too, and *she* hadn't done anything to piss her off.

"Where were you?" Pamuk demanded. "We had to find that goddamned room all by ourselves."

Chi-tang stammered, "Ch-Ch-Cheepy woke up and came downstairs. I had to go back up with her. She wouldn't wait for me."

"You could have put her off! Told her a lie or something."

"She wouldn't take no for an answer. I can't help it if I'm irresistible."

Pamuk's fury dissolved and let out a great guffaw. Roaring with laughter she collapsed to the floor and slapped it, wheezing out, "Someone help me. I'm gonna piss myself."

Boots hammered on the stairs. Someone was running up. Someone in a hurry. Pamuk and Chi-tang turned toward the interruption. A merc ran from the stairwell and down the corridor, carrying something in his hands. Wordlessly, he handed it to Carina.

It was the bowl.

They'd stashed it among some rubble as they made their way back.

She took it into her room and held it up to the window. It was risky. She suspected their every move was being watched, but she had to know. Pamuk appeared at her side, along with Chi-tang and the merc who had brought the bowl.

She ran her fingertips over the dark brown surface, judged the weight of the thing, and peered closely at it.

The bowl was utterly smooth with no blemish. There was also no sign of the grain she expected in a wooden object. She turned the bowl over. A maker's mark had been stamped into the underside. The stamp was clearly melted into the material.

Her legs lost their strength and she slumped to her bed. The bowl toppled from her hands.

"It isn't made from wood."

Twenty-Two

Unless she was with a Sot Lozan Carina couldn't leave the hotel. After a restless night, she'd spent the next day in the lounge. It was dusk, yet she hadn't eaten since returning from the raid and even now she didn't feel hungry. They had gone to all that effort, suffered injuries, and lost Viggo, for nothing. It had all been a waste of time.

A couple of Black Dogs were here too, puzzling over the content on an interface. To her disgust, she realized they were trying to figure out the meaning of words in the Sot Lozan language. She turned from them to stare morosely out the window. Pedestrians passed on the street, some giving the hotel glances. The prisoners' new location was famous. Was the burglary popular news as well?

She didn't care. She felt like she was standing at the bottom of a pit. Up above was a circle of daylight, real daylight, not the Sot Lozan fake sky. And somewhere out there were all the people she loved. Yet the pit was deep and the sides were smooth. There was no way of getting out.

"Someone wants to see you."

The hotel receptionist stood in the doorway, disdain written on her features.

Carina got to her feet. Who could it be? The only person she could think of was Rano Shelta. Was the Security Chief still interested in a relationship with her after her escapade? A spark of hope lighting up, she walked out into the lobby.

Hedran Mafmy awaited her.

She halted in her tracks.

"It's Carina, isn't it?"

"Y-yes?"

"I've come to take you for an excursion if you're interested."

There was something in Hedran's tone Carina couldn't define. And her expression was odd. Her face looked pinched, as if she was holding something in.

Still, the only way Carina was going to get out of the hotel was in her company. "Okay." She accompanied the Sot Lozan down the hotel steps. Her car was parked next to the curb.

"Get in," Hedran said. It sounded like an order.

Carina began to have second thoughts.

"Are you coming with me or not?"

Carina climbed into a front seat.

Hedran input the destination. The car waited for the traffic to clear and then U-turned. They headed to the outskirts of Laft and then onto the highway to Sarnach. The drive would take them past the house she'd broken into, where Viggo had died. She didn't doubt this trip had something to do with him. Hedran hadn't spoken a word since leaving the hotel.

The house appeared on the side of the road, enigmatic behind its fence. It was hard to imagine the previous night's events had taken place. She recalled the skinless figure with melted flesh, kept alive by machines.

Hedran checked the road behind, reached out, and pressed a button on the dashboard. The car slowed to a stop, its engine running. She pressed a second button, the dash opened, and a steering wheel emerged. Pedals rose from the floor. Taking the wheel, Hedran guided the car off the road and into the bare, undeveloped wasteland.

A bad feeling crept over Carina. "What are you doing? Where are you taking me?"

There was barely enough light to steer by, but Hedran must have done something to stop the vehicle turning on its headlights. She clearly didn't want it to be seen from the road.

"Stop," said Carina. "Let me out." She tried the door. It was locked.

"Calm down. We're nearly there."

Nearly where? There was nothing out here. Behind them, cars passed by, their occupants oblivious to the rogue vehicle.

Hedran pressed a pedal, drawing the car to a halt. "Have you ever been to the edge, Carina?"

"The edge of what?"

"Get out and I'll show you."

The door locks clicked open. Outside, the air was the same ambient temperature as always. It was dark and the stars hadn't achieved their full brightness.

"Walk that way," Hedran said.

Carina could only just make out her arm and hand as she pointed. Keeping a wary eye on her, she stepped in the indicated direction. A few paces later she walked right into a solid surface. She'd reached the edge of the tunnel.

"That's the limit of this section," Hedran whispered in her ear.

Carina jumped. The minute she'd stopped watching the Sot Lozan, she'd approached her closely. She turned. "Get away from me."

"Feel it. Feel the rock."

"Why? It's just rock. What are you doing?"

"It isn't only rock. It's the substance that encloses my world. It's all around us, above, below and on every side. Wherever we live, there it is. If we want to go somewhere new, we must bore it out, meter by arduous meter."

"I don't give a shit about your world. You're the ones choosing to live here. It's not my problem. Or at least it wasn't until you made it my problem. If you've finished with the geology lesson you can take me back to the hotel."

"I brought you here so you can see what it means to be Sot Lozan, to always be hemmed in, confined."

"Like I said, I don't give a sh—"

Hedran had made a quick movement. The glint of a blade flashed.

Carina took a step back. She hit the wall. The car was on one side, the wall to her rear, and Hedran in front. The only way out lay to her left.

Hedran moved up close. Her voice soft, she said, "You took it away from me. My only chance for life, the only way I would ever be able to create something beautiful. And now it's gone. Because of you."

Her arm jerked upward. Carina knocked it to one side and grabbed Hedran's wrist. Her other hand came up to grasp Carina's neck. She head-butted her. Hedran gasped and warm blood from her nose spattered Carina. Her free hand went to her face while she tried to wrench the knife-wielding arm from Carina's grip.

Carina punched her jaw. She staggered backward. There was distance between them now but they remained joined by Carina's hold on her right arm. Carina twisted her wrist. "Let go!" she said through clenched teeth. "Let go of it!"

Hedran squealed with pain but the knife remained in her hand. Carina kicked her. Another squeal. "If you don't let go I'll break your fucking arm."

The knife dropped.

Carina released Hedran's wrist to pick up the knife. Instantly, the woman ran. She leapt after her, launched herself at Hedran's back, and together they hit the ground. The whoosh of breath that escaped the Sot Lozan's lungs said Hedran wouldn't be moving for a while.

Carina felt for the knife in the dark. She found the blade first, slicing open her thumb. Cursing, she grabbed the handle.

Hedran's silhouette had changed. She'd turned onto her back and was lying still, gasping. Carina crawled over to her and knelt on her, a knee on each arm. She placed the tip of the knife at her throat.

"Don't," Hedran panted. "Please, don't."

"Tell me why your people brought us here. I want the truth. Everything, do you understand?"

"I can't. I'm not allowed."

"You brought me to this place to kill me, which means no one's watching. There are no cameras, no microphones. I can do what I like. No one will come to help you. I can slit your throat and make it fast. Or we can take it slow, one cut at a time until, a few hours from now, you bleed out." It was like another person's words were coming from her mouth. Carina heard herself as if from a distance, or as if a stranger was talking, not her. It wasn't only the meaning of the words that shocked her inner self, it was the cruelty, the enjoyment in her voice. Her fears for her siblings and Bryce and grief for Viggo were sending her mad.

"Please," Hedran whimpered.

"Tell me." She pushed the knife tip in.

Hedran screamed and writhed. "I'll tell you! I'll tell you."

Carina moved the blade away a fraction until it only rested on her skin. "Speak."

"It's, it's the radiation that does it. That's why we have to live underground. It isn't only because conditions on the surface are bad, it's just much safer down here anyway. But it doesn't give us complete protection. The radiation is too strong, and it seeps in too, in a gas from the rock. We have to keep the fans running all the time to extract it."

Radiation? The idea had never occurred to her, but it explained one thing. "I saw something—some*one*—at that house we broke into. There was something very wrong with them. It was like their flesh was melting away. Was that radiation poisoning?"

Hedran nodded. "You mean Nur Varvara. He spent too long on the surface, testing out a new idea for a habitation. It didn't work. He was stubborn, ignored all the warnings, and now he's dying. His family are keeping him alive as long as they can but a lot of people think it's time he was put out of his misery. The guards thought you were fanatics there to do what the family won't."

"That's why they have guards?"

"They've received death threats, and not only for Nur."

As Carina pondered this revelation, Hedran twisted under her. "I've told you what you wanted to know. I want to go now."

"You haven't told me anything that explains why you brought us here, and why your people have done the same thing for centuries."

"I told you, it's the radiation."

"So what about the radiation?"

"It kills us, young. Have you seen any really old people?"

Now Carina thought about it, she hadn't.

"I've only ever seen them in ancient vids and sims from the old planet. No one on Sot Loza lives past fifty. Only a few people make it that far. There are euthanasia clinics all over the place."

Hedran still wasn't giving the full story. She was holding something back.

But Carina had figured it out anyway. "You can't have kids."

She felt the other woman's body go limp.

"It's hard," said Hedran softly. "Most of us freeze eggs or sperm soon after we start producing them and they're stored in lead-lined vaults. Getting pregnant and growing a baby to full term are fraught with problems. So many fetuses die of medical complications or abnormalities before they're even born. If we can get fresh genetic material from people who haven't grown up saturated by radiation, it multiplies the chances of success. And the influx of new genes from offworld helps prevent us from becoming inbred."

It was the real answer Carina had wanted ever since the attraction beam had fastened on the *Bathsheba*. Finally, things made sense.

Except for one thing.

"Why don't you leave? This planet is a terrible place. The children you're so desperate to have will lead horrendous lives. Who would wish that on their child?"

"It's all we have!" Hedran exclaimed. "It's everything our ancestors fought for, the reason they suffered and endured, to give us life, a future." Her voice quiet again, she continued, "Besides, if you grow up here, you're doomed before you reach adulthood. If I were to leave tomorrow it wouldn't help me. Wherever I go, tumors will kill me before I grow old." She began to weep.

Carina got to her feet. Keeping hold of the knife she walked toward the road, the sound of Hedran's sobs growing fainter.

Twenty-Three

Parthenia's request that Bryce could live with the siblings and Ava had been denied, but he was allowed to visit and he wasn't required to give any more 'samples'. Only Rees had to attend the regular medical appointments. The merc predictably joked that it was because Bryce's donations weren't worth having. Bryce suspected it was rather that their captors didn't want him bruised and battered when Parthenia and the others saw him.

For this latest visit, the children had managed to persuade the guards to allow him to accompany them on an excursion. Darius had done an excellent job of hanging onto the head guard's hand, looking up at him with puppy eyes, and asking him plaintively if Uncle Bryce could come too.

It was his first proper experience of the world outside the prison. As they walked down the street where the children lived, accompanied by armed escorts, it took a while for him to shake the impression he was on the surface. The Sot Lozans had done a good job with the sky. It appeared to stretch for kilometers but it had to be only a short distance overhead. It wouldn't make any sense for it to be as high as it appeared. Tunneling out the underground area would be time-consuming and expensive.

The kids had been here long enough to have found favorite places to go. Their most favored place was within walking distance. Parthenia stepped sedately beside him, Darius held his hand, and Oriana and Ferne walked ahead. Nahla had elected to stay at home. She was learning Sot Loza's native language. It was typical of the smart little girl to seize the opportunity to learn something new, and her knowledge might come in useful.

Passersby took longer-than-necessary looks at the children. It wasn't so odd, considering four bodyguards surrounded them, yet there seemed to be more than idle curiosity in the glances. In another context Bryce might have said the onlookers appeared wistful or even hungry, as if Parthenia and the others were precious yet unattainable.

They rounded a corner, and the place the children had picked for the outing came into view. It was the first sight of green Bryce had experienced in all his time on Sot Loza. Lush grass grew next to a wire fence and pushed through it. Beyond the fence the sward spread wide, wildflowers dotted among the tall stalks.

Another novelty hit his senses: the sound of children playing.

"It isn't very nice being kept prisoner," Parthenia remarked, "but we love coming here."

Oriana added, "It reminds us of the grounds of our estate on Ithiya."

"Where you lived with your father?" Bryce asked, surprised that she seemed to be making a happy association with her former home.

"And Mother," Oriana replied as if in explanation. "Mother was with us too."

"I can see how it's hard for you to understand," Parthenia said, "but we do have happy memories of our childhood. It wasn't all bad. I think Mother shielded us from the worst of it. I know she did with the younger children. I remember more than they do, but even I recall some peaceful, pleasant times. Father wasn't always home, and when he was away we were quite content."

"I miss Mother," Darius murmured. "And C—"

"We all do," Parthenia interrupted. "We all miss her."

Another new sight opened up for Bryce. The park had the usual trees and flower beds, but it also contained low hillocks. Everything he'd seen on Sot Loza so far had been flat. In one section a climbing wall rose about fifteen meters, and children in safety harnesses were climbing it. There were adventure playgrounds with slides, rope bridges, tunnels, dens, swings, zip lines, and all the usual equipment. More children swarmed over it.

"Have you noticed it?" Parthenia asked, spreading her arms wide.

"Noticed what?"

"The breeze!"

She was right. A soft wind blew, rustling the grass, flowers, and leaves of the trees.

"There isn't a breath of movement in the air anywhere else," she went on.

"Because we're underground," Bryce commented, musing. "There must be fans somewhere."

"Yes," said Ferne, "but we've never been able to discover them. Though the guards bring us here, they don't let us out of their sight for a minute and they restrict where we can go. I would love to try the climbing wall but they won't let me."

"They say it's too dangerous," said Oriana, "but the other children are allowed on it."

Indeed, only children were climbing, their parents watching anxiously from below. In fact, parents were everywhere, gazes fixed on their offspring.

"I only wish it were real," Parthenia remarked.

"What do you mean?" The park seemed real enough to Bryce. Aside from the doting mothers and fathers, the place seemed very similar to parks on Ithiya and, he presumed, most other planets humans had colonized.

She stooped, grabbed a handful of grass, and tugged it. Nothing came up.

"Hey," said one of the guards, "cut that out."

She scowled at him. "It's fake. All of it. The meadow grass, flowers, everything. Nothing's real."

The children couldn't make elixir because they couldn't find any wood. He recalled how the guards had torn their bags from them and tossed them away on the *Bathsheba*. Their other belongings had been taken from them too, including elixir ingredients.

"What are you going to do?" the guard who had spoken before demanded. "Make your minds up or we'll take you back."

"That one," said Ferne, pointing at the central, largest play center. "I want to go on that one."

It was also the busiest center. Thirty or forty children were playing on it, running up and tumbling down the two hillocks, lining up to take a turn on the zip line that ran between them, throwing plastic chippings at each other in the play pit, and playing on the other equipment, screaming and yelling.

"Would you push me?" Darius asked Bryce. The swing was a wide dish of netting, currently empty.

"Sure."

Darius climbed onto the dish and lay down, spreadeagled.

"Hold on tight!" Bryce gave the dish a hard push and stepped back.

The dish swung high and Darius giggled wildly. It was a bittersweet moment. In another life, another place, accompanying Carina's siblings to the park would have been an ordinary event. Over the time he'd spent with them he'd grown to love them like family, yet here they all were, trapped in this godforsaken place, held against their will by people whose designs were as yet opaque.

Parthenia chatted with one of the guards as the children played. It was the one who looked at her too long and in a way that made Bryce's ire rise. In an earlier, whispered conversation she'd told him this guard had made a habit of walking into her room without knocking and hovering over her whenever he was on duty.

Bryce gave the swing another push.

"I want to practice climbing," Ferne announced loudly.

"You're not allowed," a guard barked.

Yet Ferne marched determinedly toward the wall.

"Hey, come back here," shouted the guard, going after him.

Ferne ran.

At the same time, Oriana pushed another girl down a slope, making her scream with alarm. The girl's parents rushed over, got in Oriana's face and yelled at her. A guard stepped forward to intervene.

Bryce gave the swing the hardest push yet. As it reached its zenith, Darius launched himself off it. As he landed, he collapsed dramatically and began hollering as if in agony. "I broke my leg! I think I broke my leg!"

As the third guard sped toward them, the one Parthenia was speaking to moved away from her, but she grabbed his jacket and rose onto her tiptoes to kiss him.

While the guard checking on Darius knelt down beside him, Bryce slipped away. He dipped into a tunnel running under a hillock and crawled to the opposite end. Looking out, he spotted a father focused on the altercation going on between a guard and the parents Oriana had offended.

"Hey!" he called out.

The man turned toward him.

"My kid's hurt herself in here. Could you help me get her out?"

The man hesitated, clearly reluctant to leave his own child unwatched.

"Please."

He bent down to look inside the tunnel. He squinted, trying to see the imaginary child in the darkness. Bryce seized him and hauled him all the way inside.

"Sorry," he said as he punched the man's jaw. The father was dazed but not out.

"Sorry," Bryce repeated as he knocked his victim's head against the concrete tunnel wall.

That did the trick.

Bryce ripped off his prison uniform and, in an agony of fumbling and breathless tension, removed the man's clothes and put them on. Now he could blend in with the locals.

The alarm had already been raised. The guards were shouting, telling the parents to look for an escaped prisoner. Bryce emerged from the tunnel, pulled his new garments straight, and walked quickly to the exit.

Twenty-Four

"Rano Shelta," Carina said into the interface. "I want to speak to Rano Shelta."

"You're wasting your time," Pamuk said, twisting her pinky in her ear. She withdrew her finger, inspected the treasure she'd excavated, and flicked it onto the floor. "He isn't going to answer." The merc was lying on her bed in the room they shared. They'd been roommates for twelve days, which was twelve days too long.

"He will eventually. He has to. The allure of my healthy reproductive status will be too seductive for him to resist." Her tone was light and ironic as she slipped into the customary merc banter, but in reality the notion sickened her. Ever since she'd discovered the truth behind the Sot Lozans' weird behavior, she'd struggled to wrap her head around what they were doing.

Kidnapping innocent spacefarers? Using their non-irradiated status to provide fresh, healthy gametes and inject new life into the gene pool? And all just so Sot Lozans could prolong their screwed-up existence on their poisonous planet.

Naturally, she'd told all the Black Dogs everything she'd learned from Hedran Mafmy. If their rooms were bugged and the security forces heard her, she didn't care. There was nothing to be lost by pretending they didn't know their captors' dirty little secret. The mercs' movements were already restricted and they had something the Sot Lozans' desperately wanted: the ability to bear healthy children. So what could they seriously do to hurt them?

The small comfort the nauseating revelation had given her was that her siblings and Ava's baby were probably receiving good treatment, wherever they were. She'd been worrying about them ever since the taking of the *Bathsheba*. But she still didn't know what had happened to Bryce.

"Rano Shelta," she repeated.

The screen remained silent and blank.

She flopped onto her bed.

"You're giving up?" Pamuk asked.

"No."

Silence.

"Okay," said Pamuk. "I'm gonna get something to eat. You coming?"

"I'm not hungry."

The merc walked to the door but then she turned and said, "You know, maybe we should stop fighting the inevitable."

"What do you mean?"

"Maybe Jackson was wrong. Playing the long game doesn't seem to be getting us anywhere. It might have been better to go out in a blaze of glory fighting the bastards. Better than defeat and a slow death on a dead end world."

"Is that how you really feel?"

"I'm just saying, for the first time ever, I'm starting to think there might not be a way out."

Coming from someone like Pamuk this wasn't idle speculation.

Carina sat up. "Are you guys planning on doing something dumb?"

The merc looked evasive. "Noooo..."

"Yes, you are."

It would be typical of the Black Dogs if, faced with being trapped in domestic tedium forever, they would rather seek a quick end, taking as many hostiles with them as they could.

"Don't do it," Carina said. "Whatever it is, don't do it. There's still hope we can get out of here."

"I never said we were going to do anything, but you have to admit, we're truly screwed. You can't get what you need for you-know-what and neither can your sibs. We have no way of getting back to the ship, and even if we did, we would never leave the system without their giant vacuum cleaner pulling us right back in again. When we first got here I thought we had a sweet deal. Spend a little time with the weirdos who wanted to wine and dine us while we figured out how to get them to leave us alone, then flash, bang and we're back on the *Bathsheba*, grabbing some decades-long shuteye on the way to Earth."

The bulky merc sighed before continuing, "But here we are weeks later, one good man down, and no farther on with getting away from this place. I don't have the patience for this shit and I'm sure as hell not going to be some guy's brood mare. So, while I'm not saying anyone's planning on doing anything rash and bloody, if something like that were to happen, could you blame us?"

"Yeah, I could," Carina replied vehemently. "Absolutely. We've hardly been here five minutes. There's lots of things to try yet."

"Like what?"

"Like I'm not going to tell you, am I? Someone could be listening in."

Pamuk narrowed her eyes. "I'm gonna get something to eat."

As she left, Carina lay down again.

Shit.

If she didn't come up with something soon the Black Dogs would take matters into their own hands, and then who knew what might happen, except that it would be violent and perilous for everyone involved. Though she had to agree that things looked bad she was far from giving up. She had her family to think about, and Bryce. She would fight to her dying breath to at least see them again.

But the Black Dogs were not like her. They lived in order to...*live.* And the life the Sot Lozans proposed was no life at all to them.

Maybe she should have killed Hedran Mafmy out in the dead lands between towns. She would have been the primary suspect and so perhaps in great danger, but it would have made the Sot Lozans realize who they were dealing with. Perhaps they would have understood it was safer to allow this latest set of victims to go on their way.

Maybe I should have killed Hedran just for the pleasure of it.

Pain shot up from her palms. She realized she was gripping her hands into fists so tightly her fingernails were biting into her flesh. She relaxed her hands. She mustn't lose it. The Black Dogs might not be able to keep their heads but she must. She had to.

"Carina?" said a tired, melancholic voice.

It was Rano, speaking to her from the interface. She leapt up and ran to the device. "I'm here."

The man's face was wan and downcast. "I'm not sure if I should be doing this. Why do you want to speak to me?"

"I-I was wondering if you had any more of that horrible liquor you gave me the other night."

A sad smile. "There's plenty more but why do you want it if it tastes so bad?"

"I'm a masochist. Didn't I tell you?"

"You must have forgotten to mention it."

"I did. So, what do you say? Want to have another go at getting me drunk and taking advantage of me?"

"I wouldn't ever..." he replied, shocked. Then, "You're kidding, right?"

"What do you think?"

"Hm. I think I'll take a chance."

"Great. Will you pick me up? Only some idiot made a stupid rule about us not being allowed to leave our hotel without a Sot Lozan accompanying us."

"That idiot would be me. I'll be there in five minutes."

———

"As I understand it," he said while she climbed into his vehicle, "you know all about my world now, and why you're here."

"I wouldn't say I know *all* about your planet. I mean, you must have forgotten some fascinating snippets of local history in the lesson you gave me the other night, but I know the main parts, yeah."

"And I think I'm also right in saying you're not going to reveal who told you."

So he didn't know what had happened in the barren wastes with Hedran. It wasn't so strange. Like the rest of the prisoners, she'd come into contact with many Sot Lozans. The only person he could know for sure hadn't given the game away was him.

"Why would I betray someone who did me a big favor?" she asked. "Why subject another person to punishment?"

"Is that how you see your lives here? As a punishment?"

Her jaw dropped. "Not exactly a punishment because we didn't do anything wrong. But what do you think this is to us? A ride at a funfair? You stole our ship! You've trapped us here on your deadly world. Did you think you were helping us out?"

"Does it really matter where you live out the rest of your lives? You were on a colony vessel, planning to settle somewhere. Why not Sot Loza?"

"You *have* to be joking."

His jaw clenched and he looked away from her, out into the darkness. He seemed to be wrestling with something. His conscience?

"Why don't we talk some more over that nasty drink of yours," she suggested.

"Let's do that."

At his home, he not only had the noxious brew he'd offered her before but also crispy snacks in a bowl. When he offered her the bowl as they sat down, she took one and ate it without asking its origin. It was better not to know. The snack was quite nice.

"Now the beans have mostly been spilled," she said, "will you spill the rest of them? If I have to stay here what can I expect? It's been clear from the start that you guys are trying to partner up with us. We get the idea is so you can become parents. That's right, isn't it?"

He leaned back and spread an arm over the back of the sofa. "There's no point in denying it so I won't. But I do like you, Carina. I like you as a person, not just because of the opportunity you offer."

"That's easy to say, but if I wasn't from offplanet would you even be interested?"

"I admit it's hard to know for sure. I like to think so."

"How old are you?"

"Thirty-six."

"How old do you think I am?"

"Mid to late twenties?"

She shook her head. "Try again. I'm about twenty. I'm not sure exactly. Things get muddled when you do a lot of traveling in space."

His eyebrows popped up. "I didn't realize. You look..." He faltered to silence.

"It's okay. You can say it. I know I look older than my age. I've had a hard life, with one thing and another. What do you think about being my partner now?"

His brow furrowed, but his internal conflict only lasted a brief moment. "The age difference doesn't have to be a barrier. You don't only look older than you are, you act older. Your hard life has made you grow up fast."

"Thanks, but..." She'd been about to tell him he'd just proven to her that his desire to be a father superseded everything, all notions of decorum, integrity, and morality. But insulting him wasn't going to get her anywhere.

"What?"

"Never mind." She took a sip of liquor. "Can you clear up some questions I have about life here?"

"I can try," he replied guardedly.

"As I understand it, everyone dies from tumors while still relatively young. How does that work out? I haven't seen anyone who seemed to be sick or lots of hospitals. How can your society function if it has to care for huge numbers of people suffering slow, lingering deaths?"

He grimaced. "It's rarely slow and lingering. Most Sot Lozans choose to take the quick way out when their illness begins to interfere with their everyday lives. Everyone knows a tale of someone who didn't self-euthanize and it isn't a pretty one. There are retirement clinics all over the place. You just haven't spotted them because you don't know what you're looking at."

"Still," she said, "I would have thought it would be hard to know when it's time to go. It must take years from diagnosis until—"

"You don't get it. We've been living and dying like this for centuries. The progress of the disease is well known and it's the same in virtually all of us. From the appearance of the first tumor we have about six months, tops."

"That fast?"

He took a breath and let it out slowly. "There's a drug we take that suppresses the effects of radiation. It's in all the food in trace amounts. If you eat a normal diet you get enough of it for your body weight. Once the drug stops being effective the disease takes over quickly. Coming from offplanet you and your companions will live much longer than me. You have a head start, and the drug is working in you now, fortifying you."

"That's a relief to hear. Another thing—is it only the managerial class who can reproduce? I don't understand how you maintain your population."

"Only higher-ranking Sot Lozans can pick a partner and have children directly with him or her. Once the match has been made, you would be expected to also donate your eggs for sale to the general public."

Carina coughed up the drink she'd been swallowing, spraying it over her front.

Donate her eggs?

If the need to escape hadn't already been great, it had suddenly become imperative. Any child of hers conceived with a Sot Lozan had a fifty percent chance of being a mage. And not only her children, but Parthenia's and the rest of her siblings once they matured. Rano had thrown another ingredient into the disastrous mix.

He was patting her back. "Are you okay? Would you like some water? That drink is pretty strong."

"I'm fine," she croaked. "It just went down the wrong way."

When she'd recovered, she said, "I appreciate your honesty. I have to confess when we first met I thought you were a bit of an asshole. But I can see now there's more to you than meets the eye."

He smiled. "I'm glad I'm making a better impression."

She reached out and squeezed his hand.

His smile widened.

Viggo had been right. You really did catch more kultries with neinery than jadronic.

Twenty-Five

The goods in the store were unfamiliar. When food had arrived in the prison cell or at the home where the Sot Lozans were keeping Carina's family and Ava, it had been prepared. They were strange meals to be sure, but cooked and presented on bowls and plates in the usual fashion. Here, the packages, boxes, and packets displayed pictures Bryce didn't recognize and the names were in the Sot Lozan's native language.

One piece of information he was able to glean from looking at the diagrams and numbers was that nearly everything needed to be cooked or at least prepared in some way. To do that would require access to a kitchen and the only place he had access to was the street.

A shopper approached down the aisle, and he silently cursed. He'd deliberately come here in the early hours of the morning to avoid other people. He waited for her to pass, but when she reached him she stopped. He put the product he was looking at back on the shelf and moved away but not before she let out an *Ough*! of disgust and lifted the back of her hand to her nose.

Yes, he smelled.

It had been three days since he'd escaped. He'd been sleeping rough and the only water he had access to was in public restrooms, where washing his face, neck, and pits was the best he could do. Even that was risky. The authorities must have put out the alert that a prisoner had escaped and anyone washing themselves in a restroom basin would look suspicious.

More worrying than his odor, however, was the growling ache in his belly. He was faint with hunger, and being weak and unable to think straight wasn't going to help get anyone off this planet. He had to eat. Dining at a restaurant or cafe was out of the question. He had no qualms about running off without paying for his meal but, again, he couldn't afford the danger of being seized or attracting attention.

He picked up another packet. It showed a child eating green gloop with a manic smile on his face, as if the gloop were the tastiest thing ever. That was a similarity between all the food items—they all portrayed children or babies, and the youngsters were all ecstatic to be consuming the product. Apparently, no adult Sot Lozans ever ate. Their culture seemed obsessed with youth. It explained Darius's observation that the guards felt 'warm and fuzzy' around Ava's baby and why their treatment of the kids was kinder than that of the rest of the prisoners.

He put the packet back and moved on. There had to be something here he could eat. It was the first grocery store he'd found that had a manual checkout. The others had been run in the usual style of automatically registering the customers' credit as they entered and subtracting the cost of their purchases when they left. Here, you had to scan the codes on the packets and your credchip.

Or not.

The woman who had been disgusted by his smell left the aisle. He checked in the other direction. The area was empty. He picked up three packets of green gloop and slipped them inside his shirt. Swiftly, he headed toward the front of the shop. The scene beyond the doors was dark, the road deserted.

The doors pulled apart at his approach. He stepped into the widening gap.

An alarm blared out.

The doors snapped closed, catching his leg.

He gave a gasp, twisted and wrenched it free.

He was out.

He ran, favoring his unhurt leg. Next to the store was an alleyway. He raced down it. At the end he turned right, darted across the street, and then sped down a second alley.

And so on, and so on, until he'd been running for twenty minutes and he was out of breath. He'd put around a kilometer between himself and the scene of the crime before he stopped. Would the Sot Lozan authorities study recordings of the shoplifter? He had no idea if petty crime was common or rare here. Regardless, he'd had to take the chance his stealing would reveal his rough location. He had to eat.

In the nook between a wall and a fence, he sat on the ground. One thing to be said for Sot Loza was that the temperature was always mild and it never rained. He took out the three packets from his shirt and placed two of them beside him. He had to feel rather than see how to open the third, tearing apart the box in the darkness. Four thick sachets were wedged inside. He pulled one out and used his teeth to rip a corner open. Something wet oozed out.

He sucked at the hole.

The paste that hit his tongue was salty and gritty. Though it was almost flavorless, there was something about the texture that made his stomach rebel as he swallowed, forcing the substance back up his throat. He grimaced and swallowed again. Then he squeezed more from the sachet into his mouth.

Adjusting his position, his hand brushed the two packets on the ground. Could he manage to eat all three tonight? The thought of it made him retch, but he would have to try. He had an important job to do.

———

The following morning brought an aching stomach, cramped back, and sore head. He sat up. He'd gone to sleep resting his head on his arm, but at some point in the remainder of the night it had slipped onto the hard ground. After three nights in the open with little to eat and no shelter, exhaustion was creeping up on him. The time he had to act effectively was running out.

The problem was, he had no map of the town. When Nahla had explained in whispers how to get from the park to the place, her instructions had been complicated. Though he'd thought he'd committed them to memory, when it came down to actually making the journey he'd become lost. It was only now, after days of searching, that he knew exactly where he was and how to get to where he needed to be.

The familiar lilac sky occupied the gap between the walls and pedestrians passed by along the road at the alley's exit. He'd slept late after his long night, thankfully unnoticed in the shadowy corner.

After twisting his torso from side to side to ease the knots in his back muscles, he got to his feet, catching sight of the empty packets from last night's meal. His stomach lurched and he sweated as he fought down nausea. His mouth felt like a sand pit.

He smoothed down his wrinkled, dirty clothes and walked to the alley's end. When the road was fairly empty, he stepped out nonchalantly, as if on a shopping expedition or on his way to work. His first stop was a public restroom he'd made a mental note of yesterday. As well as being thirsty, he needed to smarten up if he was to avoid attracting attention.

The restroom was empty. He bent down and took a long drink from the faucet before splashing water on his face. As he stood up he saw his reflection in the mirror. What a sight. His eyes stared out from dark hollows, his skin was cadaverous, and he'd grown a bedraggled beard. He hadn't looked so bad since the time he'd been slowly dying of Ithiyan Plague.

He wet his hands and dragged them through his hair, flattening it. There wasn't a lot else he could do to improve his appearance.

Outside, the street was growing busier. Lunchtime had to be approaching. The timing was fortunate. It was easier to remain anonymous in a crowd. The museum was only ten minutes' walk away. When he arrived, a short line had formed at the entrance. He joined the end. He had no idea how he would get inside without money to buy a ticket. Maybe he could sneak in.

He reached the ticket machine and realized his plan was hopeless. A barrier and turnstile stood between him and the museum's interior. He couldn't walk past the machine and jump the barrier without being seen. Then, no doubt, an official would be along soon to throw him out.

Someone behind him spoke. He turned. The speaker was a young woman and she looked mildly annoyed. She'd spoken in the local language and he hadn't understood a word but he guessed she'd told him to hurry up.

He made the universal open-handed gesture that meant he had no money. It was a desperate measure but then his situation was desperate. She frowned at him as if he were stupid, reached past him and pressed some keys. Then she gestured for him to go through the turnstile.

No money was required. The visitors were only inputting information— what information he had no idea. Elation washing over him, he pushed through the barrier. Now all he had to do was to find the object Nahla had discovered in her long searches of the Sot Lozan net.

That, and steal it.

The latter was definitely going to be the harder task.

Twenty-Six

Growing up in a small town on Ithiya, Bryce hadn't visited many museums, but he got the general idea. They usually had a theme, like science, technology, the natural world, or a period of history. This one was devoted to Sot Loza's colonization. *From the Fateful Accident to Winning Against All Odds* Nahla had translated from the website.

Her conversation with him had taken place directly in front of the guards, none of them understanding its significance.

"Look what I found, Uncle Bryce. There's a museum all about Sot Loza and it's right here in this town."

"Is there?" He'd sat down beside her to take a look at the screen.

"Uh huh. It's *so* interesting."

"Museums are boring," Oriana said.

"Unless they're about textiles," Ferne added.

"This one isn't boring," Nahla protested. "It has objects that are hundreds of years old." She scrolled through the pictures, showing relics from the colony ship, a replica of one of the first dwellings, the text of a colonist's diary, an early example of locally made clothing, and the stages of developments in food production. There were also titles to special exhibits.

"That's cool," said Bryce. "Can you read what those words say?"

"This one..." she pointed "...says *Sounds of the New Planet* and the next one is *Going Underground.*"

"Maybe you can go there one day, if the guards allow it."

"Hmm." She surveyed the two men keeping watch over them. "Maybe. But they don't usually let us go where there are lots of people crowded together. They say it's too easy for us to get separated and lost."

Neither of the guards commented but they didn't deny what she was saying either. Of course, by 'get separated and lost' they'd meant, 'slip away and escape.'

Angling the interface subtly away from their scrutiny, Nahla said in a quieter tone, "There's something *really* cool I want to show you." She brushed the screen with her fingertips, bringing up an image of a box on a pair of odd legs.

"What's that?" asked Bryce.

"Don't you know?" She chuckled as if he were a little stupid. "We had one at our estate. Mother used it for all of us. It's for babies."

"What is it?" Darius peeked over the edge of the screen. "Oh, a cradle. Yes," he went on authoritatively, "when the baby cries you put it in and then you push the cradle to make it rock. That's what these are for." He pointed at the legs. "That's why they're curved. Babies like rocking. Ava rocks hers all the time."

"It's because it reminds them of being inside their mothers when they were walking about," Nahla explained.

"Oh yes," said Darius. "That makes sense."

Bryce was silent. The reason Nahla was showing him the cradle had just hit him.

It was made of wood.

"Do you like it?" Nahla asked pointedly.

"Uh, yeah," he'd replied. "Looks great."

A cradle.

Where was the cradle among all these exhibits?

The place was dimly lit and filled with shuffling visitors, slowly making their way past the displays. He followed in their wake. Unable to read the signs, he had no idea where the cradle might be. He would just have to search everywhere until he found it.

He passed artifact after artifact: tech items from the home planet, artworks, ancient medical equipment, an original Deep Sleep cell from the colony ship, reports from the first media station, so many things. The visitors seemed deeply impressed by the exhibits as if they were extremely valuable, though they were only old and mundane. He saw no cradle.

He grew tired. The gnawing hunger that had forced him to steal yesterday had returned, and last night's slumber had not been restful. Sleeping outside on hard asphalt, the prospect of discovery constantly at the back of his mind, he'd barely snoozed. Pins seemed to be stabbing at his eyes and he stifled a yawn.

A doorway opened into darkness lit by moving light. Recorded audio leaked out. A vid or holo was playing in the side room. He stepped inside, grateful for the opportunity to sit down.

The show was ending and the audience was filing out. He took a seat at the back and rested on the wall. More attendees dribbled in. The few that came close to him altered course, his unwashed odor perhaps deterring them. The screen faded to black, replaced by figures counting down to the next showing. His eyelids grew heavy and he began to drift off.

A blast of sound signaled the beginning of the vid, jerking him awake. More visitors had arrived during his brief nap.

A starship floated in space. He recognized it instantly—it was the ship that had dragged the *Bathsheba* the final part of her unwilling voyage to the planet. So the locals had converted their original colony vessel to a hauler. The camera zoomed in and the ship's hull melted away, revealing an operating engine. The image was not realistic as far as he understood, only a representation. Lights moved through channels inside the machine, which was not the way space-going engines generated power.

A second burst of sound, this time accompanied by a flash of light. The scene cut to an asteroid speeding through the void on a collision course with the ship. Another cut, and the view was inside the colony vessel once more, only it showed the crew running about in a crazed panic.

Bryce smiled. In his experience, starship crews didn't react like that when faced with disaster. There was a lot more standing around open-mouthed and staring while a few people made stupid suggestions about what they should do.

The asteroid hit, tearing a rent meters wide in the hull. Fuel sprayed spectacularly into space. The audience gave a collective sigh of awe.

So this was the Fateful Accident?

After the inevitably melodramatic reactions from the crew, the story grew more boring. The vessel was clearly off-course, a fact unknown to the apparently hundreds of thousands of colonists in Deep Sleep, if the scene involving the vast rows and columns of cells was historically accurate. Meanwhile, the crew ran through a series of attempts to return to the original heading.

Bryce's eyelids began to close again. Warm and comfortable, his hunger pangs abating, and the danger of imminent re-capture far away, he fell deeply asleep.

He jolted awake so violently the people in front of him turned and stared.

How long had he slept?

Through at least one entire showing of the vid. It was showing the asteroid strike again. And the place was packed. The chairs each side of him were occupied, despite his unpleasant scent. He should get up and look for the cradle, but he didn't want to attract additional attention by forcing his way out. He decided to stay to the end.

The crew repeated their ineffective attempts to recover from the disaster that had befallen their ship, then the vid moved to a new phase in the planet's history. The colonists began to settle the planet. The vid showed several hundred awakened from Deep Sleep, presumably those with the necessary skills to begin construction of the settlements. But conditions on the surface were atrocious. It was exactly as Rees had said—a nightmare of howling winds and scouring dust.

But something else was also wrong. The settlers were falling ill.

The audience, which had been shuffling, murmuring, coughing, and rustling snack packets as they surreptitiously ate, became still and silent.

It was a grisly scene. The earliest colonists took to their beds or collapsed as they worked, sores erupting on their skin, teeth and hair falling out, eyeballs bleeding. The vid displayed an expanse of gravestones buffeted by swirling dust clouds.

Bryce wrinkled his nose. So the surface harbored diseases too? It was no wonder the colonists had delved underground.

More and more of them died. The graveyard stretched wider. Then the accompanying music changed from slow, sad tones to upbeat, soaring rhythms. Work hollowing out the underground sped up. New buildings were constructed, roads, hospitals to treat the people exposed to the disease above ground.

Time seemed to march forward at a rapid pace. The colony ship appeared again, this time emitting an attraction beam that held another vessel at its farther end. When the two ships reached the planet a shuttle flew from the newcomer to the surface, now miraculously calmer. After landing the ramp descended and smiling, waving figures walked down it. Sot Lozans greeted them joyously, shaking hands and slapping backs.

What a propaganda piece it was. Did the general public know what really happened to people their authorities seized from space?

The show was over and the audience was leaving. Bryce got to his feet and filed out with the rest, even more determined to find the wood the kids needed to make their elixir. He guessed Carina must be facing the same problem. All they needed was a little of the precious natural material.

There it is!

Directly opposite him as he exited the viewing room stood the cradle. It was smaller than he'd imagined. Maybe that, along with his fatigue, was why he hadn't noticed it before. Its soft luster and grain and the wearing on the side from the touching of many mothers' hands told him it was authentic. It must have come all the way from the origin planet, perhaps a precious family heirloom.

The museum remained full of people. It would be a while before it closed. He had plenty of time to find somewhere to hide.

TWENTY-SEVEN

"I hope it isn't too soon to say I told you so," said Rano.

"That depends on what you're talking about," Carina replied, though she knew exactly what he meant.

They were driving to Una, the main city of the zone and the first settlement on Sot Loza. Carina had expressed a desire to get to know more about the planet and Rano had jumped at the opportunity. From his comment it was clear he had the impression that she was coming around to the idea of remaining here.

"Isn't it obvious?" he asked. "Look at us. I'm showing you the sights. We're getting along pretty well. This is very different from the Newcomers' Banquet, wouldn't you say?"

"You mean that night when my friends kicked off? I didn't even know it was called that. No one told us a thing. All we could figure out was that we wouldn't eat unless we boarded the transport that took us there."

He winced. "It might have been better to give you all more of an explanation. I'll bear that in mind in future."

So the Sot Lozans were planning on bringing *more* victims to their planet? Carina felt sick. If she managed to help everyone from the *Bathsheba* escape, she wanted to do it in a way that would make their captors think twice about pulling the same stunt again.

"You know," said Rano, "I don't think I ever told you my ancestors were Outsiders."

"I don't think you did. Where were they from originally?"

"I don't know. It was one of my great-grandparents."

"How often do you pull people in from space?"

"Roughly once per generation. The geneticists calculated that was how often we needed the injection of undamaged genes to maintain the planet's population and health. We try to do it as rarely as we can."

"Every thirty or forty years?"

"About that. So you can see how special you are to us and why we might come across as heavy-handed. I won't have another opportunity to be with someone like you."

She seemed to recall Chi-tang saying that ships disappeared less frequently. So the Sot Lozans were taking them from other galactic routes too.

"Carina?"

"What?"

He was looking at her as if he'd expected a different reaction to his weak attempt at an apology.

She forced a smile and patted his hand. "I forgive you. Now I know the whole story I can see why you're desperate for new blood. If you didn't do what you do, you would die out."

He nodded. "We nearly did. Hundreds of thousands died in the first century. That's another reason we need new genes added to the pool. The bottleneck reduced our genetic diversity considerably. When you think about it, our survival has been a miracle."

"It certainly has." Carina tried to sound genuinely enthusiastic. Inside, she was wondering what else the Sot Lozans might consider doing to ensure their colony's success. Torture? Genocide? Was nothing off limits?

"You aren't convinced," Rano said flatly.

She sighed. She was a terrible actor. "As a victim of your people's methods it's hard for me to wrap my head around your reasoning."

"It *is* too soon for me to say I told you so. Give it time. I'm sure you'll change your mind. As you said, you're the victim here so it isn't going to be easy for you to see my side of things. But plenty of societies have been forced to commit unsavory acts in order to survive. We aren't any different."

The road from Sarnach to Una was lined with buildings. It was clear that Sarnach was a satellite town, probably originally a mining site. Then, as the colony became established the town had developed and businesses and homes had been built along the adjoining route.

Una was something new. Three- and four-story buildings had appeared in the distance. Carina leaned toward the car's window and looked up. The sky was higher, the 'clouds' weirdly elongated as they moved across the slope.

"The ceiling engineers never ironed out the kinks in that effect," Rano explained. "Everyone is used to it now."

"The chamber is taller here? Closer to the surface?"

"For the first underground settlement the colonists tried to build something that mimicked where they'd come from. It took a while for them to figure out that wasn't optimal for protecting against radiation, so the level is slightly higher here. It's better in places like Sarnach and Laft and the other zones, which were dug later. But it's still within safe parameters. Plenty of people live in Una and their life expectancy is about the same as in the rest of the planet."

"Thanks, that's reassuring." She was unable to extract the note of sarcasm from her voice.

Rano gave her a sidelong look.

You catch more kultries with neinery than jadronic. "Where are you taking me?"

"The tallest place in town. There's a restaurant with a great view of the city."

She grimaced.

"Is something wrong? I thought it would be nice to eat and chat. I want to get to know you better. All we've talked about so far is Sot Loza and a little bit about me."

"Nothing's wrong." Perhaps a great view of the city would be useful. "Sounds good."

He'd reserved a table next to a window. As he read out the menu and explained what each dish was, Carina looked out over the expanse of buildings and streets. She spotted several factories.

"You pick for me," she interrupted. "What's that place over there?"

He followed the line of her pointing finger. "Textiles plant. It supplies all Sot Loza, just about."

"What about that?" She pointed to another set of buildings.

"A bacterial food factory."

"Hmm."

"Are you looking for something in particular?" he joked. "What's your specialty?" He went on, more seriously, "Not that you would need to get a job. I make more than enough to support us both plus any little ones that come along."

She suppressed a shudder. There was something in what Rano had said that reminded her of Stefan Sherrerr. The little that she'd softened toward the security chief turned to stone. There were layers to this man. Deep underneath everything, he was psychopathic. He didn't see her as a real person, only a thing that could offer him something he wanted.

They were all psychopathic. All the Sot Lozans had to know what their authorities did to ensure their survival, and they all went along with it. Perhaps it was a result of the weeding out of the colonists that went on in the early years. Only those who truly didn't give a shit about anyone else had lived long enough to reproduce. Environmental pressures had selected the very worst of them.

"I'm rushing ahead again," said Rano apologetically.

"Just a bit. I heard that there are giant fans circulating the air and removing radioactivity. Where are they?"

"On the surface. A network of ducts runs through the crust, opening out at intervals in the ceiling. You can't see them. The sky effect disguises them."

"But I thought no one could live on the surface. Who runs the fans?"

"Ah, er..." He paused before continuing as if reluctantly, "They're mostly automated, but technicians go up there on a rota for service and maintenance."

"Isn't that dangerous?" She recalled the skinless figure in the mansion she'd burgled.

"It is, somewhat. Measures are taken to protect the workers."

She waited for him to explain more.

"Let's talk about something else."

"I'd rather look at the view for a little while. Why don't you put in our order?"

While Rano selected the dishes, her mind ticked over. She doubted she would ever be able to create elixir, and it appeared her siblings were facing the same problem. She had to think of another way to escape Sot Loza, and fast, before the Black Dogs gave up hope.

Twenty-Eight

ryce's greatest fear was motion sensors. If they were part of the museum's security system, as soon as he stepped from his hiding place he would set them off. Then he would have minutes or even only seconds to grab the cradle and get out—somehow. He hadn't figured that part out yet.

In fact, he hadn't figured hardly anything out. All he knew was that he had to get that wooden item to the kids at all costs, even if he ended up dead. If he didn't manage it they could never do it by themselves. The guards would be keeping a tighter rein on them than ever. They probably wouldn't be allowed out on any more excursions. He only hoped they weren't being punished for helping him.

He peeked out. Beyond the replica hut from the early days of colonization, all was still and silent. He hadn't heard movement or voices for at least a couple of hours. The place had closed ages ago. Then cleaning bots had done their work, thankfully identifying him not in need of sanitation. Perhaps their sensors had told them he was organic. Since then the place had been silent.

Tiny floor lights lit the walkways, fortunately. Otherwise he would have been forced to blunder around in the dark.

He peeked out again.

Motion sensors?

Not a thing moved.

How much longer should he wait? Another few hours. After stealing the cradle he would have to get it to the kids. It wasn't the kind of thing you could easily hide, and their house was a couple of kilometers away. Carrying a priceless artifact through the streets would have to wait until the early hours when no one was about. He adjusted his position to ease his cramped muscles and tried to forget that he was famished before settling down to wait.

Footsteps.

He tensed, listening.

The steps were purposeful, heavy, and accompanied by faint creaks. It sounded like a man, fairly heavy, and approaching.

Bryce leaned out a fraction so half his head and one eye moved into the hut's open doorway. This section of the exhibit was in darkness so he wasn't concerned he would be seen. Coming down the walkway was a figure turned almost entirely black by the minimal lighting. The floor lights gilded the buttons of his uniform and made the mustached face spectral with shadows.

The lights glinted from something else: the handgun at his hip.

In one sense, the appearance of the museum guard was a relief. If someone was patrolling the place it meant there were no motion sensors. In another sense it was an added worry. How could he get away with his prize without attracting the armed man's attention? The outer door had to be locked. He'd been planning to bust his way out but the guard would put a pulse round in his back before he'd made it ten meters.

Okay, okay.

He had plenty of time to come up with a foolproof plan.

———

Hours later, he had nothing.

No plausible explanation for being here if discovered and challenged.

No smart trick to disarm the guard.

No masterful scheme to get through the locked outer door.

That wasn't quite right. He now knew the guard performed his walkabout roughly every half hour. He had counted out the seconds and minutes three times in a row to make sure.

What he didn't know was where the man went after he'd passed by.

Did he return to an office a minute away or did he complete a full circuit of the museum? A circuit would make sense, which meant that if Bryce waited fifteen minutes after the guard passed by before making his move, he would get a good head start.

The guard was coming.

He sauntered past, the same as he had the last eleven times.

The man was regular. He had to give him that.

One, one thousand. Two, one thousand. Three, one thousand.

Fifteen minutes later, Bryce quietly slipped out from his hiding place. Slowly and cautiously, he rose to his full height and scanned around. The artifacts took on a new appearance in the quiet darkness. Surrounded by babbling visitors they'd looked smaller as well as boring and drab. They seemed to have grown larger and more ancient. They were performing their intended purpose in this place, creating echoes of the lives of the people who had made them and used them but were now long dead.

Chilled not only by the cooled atmosphere, he quickly stepped over to the cradle. Heart racing, he stooped to pick it up but then snatched his hands away just in time.

He was so nervous he'd forgotten to check if it was attached to an alarm.

A careful visual inspection told him it didn't appear so.

He reached out again, heart in his mouth, and lifted it.

It was surprisingly heavy for such a small object.

He had the wood. All he needed to do was get it to the kids.

There was still no sign of the guard. He walked softly toward the exit. Prickles ran down his spine as he imagined the guard stepping out in front of him or yelling at him to stop or he would fire. He saw himself stumble and fall, his back destroyed and smoking from a pulse round.

He'd made it to the turnstile!

It was locked, of course. No problem. He leaned over it, lowered the cradle to the floor, and then jumped the barrier. The road beyond the glass wall and doors was empty, lit palely by street lamps.

The doors were locked too.

He checked the lobby walls for a release mechanism but found nothing. There was nothing on the doors themselves. They had to be locked remotely, and so they could only be opened the same way.

Only two or three minutes had passed since the guard had made his recent round of the museum. Would it be better to attempt to break out or go back and try to find another exit? Perhaps there was an emergency door that opened from the inside in case of fire. But that would mean risking meeting up with the guard.

Bryce hesitated, indecision gnawing at him.

Something sounded softly behind him.

Footsteps?

He hefted the cradle to shoulder level and flung it at a window.

With a *boing* it bounced back and hit him, smacking into his forehead.

At the same time, a siren blared.

He found himself on his knees, dazed, the cradle rocking on the floor, blood running into his eye.

Fuck, fuck, fuck.

His head pounding a protest, he grabbed the cradle. Its impact with the window had shaken its joints loose and it shifted as he grasped it close. He leapt up. He had to find another way out.

He threw the cradle over the barrier, loosening it some more, and then joined it. Without breaking his stride, he snatched it up and darted back into the display area.

There was the guard, heading straight for him.

"Stop, or I'll shoot!"

Everything was playing out as he'd feared.

He kept on running, heading directly for the guard.

"I said, stop, or I'll…"

Bryce lifted the cradle in front of him as a shield.

It was wood. If a round hit it, it would scorch and burn, maybe even catch fire, but the energy wouldn't pass through it to his hands.

For some reason the guard didn't fire. Was he reluctant to damage the ancient artifact? He continued to shout warnings until, at the last minute, he tried to step out of Bryce's way.

He'd left it too late.

The cradle hit him full force in the face, and Bryce knew how bad that felt. It knocked the guard out cold.

Yes!

Now all he had to do was get out, and quickly. The alarm would have alerted more people than just the guard. He raced toward the back of the museum, through a plain door with a sign, and down some stairs. He came to another door, unmarked. Was it the back exit?

He tried it and cursed when it didn't open. He put the cradle down and kicked the door, punched it, and kicked it some more. He'd got so far. Only a single stupid door stood between him and—

He ran back up the stairs, two at a time, through the door, and back to the guard. The man was coming around.

"Hey," he mumbled. "You…"

Bryce had his gun.

"You…that's fine," said the guard, lifting his hands. "You take it."

Bryce sped back to the cradle and aimed the gun at the door's lock. He held down the trigger until the lock was a mess of seared, smoking, melting metal. Then he gave the door a mighty kick. It burst open. Warm night air flooded in and he was looking into a narrow lane.

As he seized the cradle, it broke apart. The rockers, base, and sides clattered to the floor. He was holding two spindles, one in each hand.

It didn't matter. All the kids needed was a single piece of wood. It was good that the cradle had broken. Now he had less to carry. He tucked a spindle into his shirt and stepped into the lane.

Vehicles with flashing lights stood at each end, blocking it.

TWENTY-NINE

The interface on Carina's hotel room wall bleeped. Though it remained blank, Rano's voice said, "Carina? Can I speak to you?"

"Urghnnn," said Pamuk, turning over in bed. "Wha's th' time?"

The Black Dogs had been awarded a delivery of Sot Lozan liquor, perhaps as a gesture of goodwill. While Carina had been visiting Una with the Chief of Security, they'd drunk it all at once and smashed the place up. Pamuk had been sleeping off the after-effects.

Carina told her to go back to sleep and padded over to the screen. "You can turn on the visual. There's nothing here you shouldn't see."

His face appeared.

"Are you planning another trip for us?" she asked. The last one had been enlightening.

"This is a professional call, sorry, though I enjoyed yesterday a lot."

"Me too," she replied, clenching her jaw. "Is there something I can help you with?"

"There is. I...uhh..." His expression turned pained. "I was in two minds about asking you this. Would you accompany me to Grantha?"

"Sure, but I don't know what it is."

"My mistake. Grantha is one of the other zones."

Her heart leapt. She struggled to keep her features neutral. "I'm fine with that. It'll be interesting to see another part of Sot Loza."

"Good. I'll be there soon."

"Rano?"

"Yes?"

"You haven't told me why you want me to do this."

"Um, they've been having problems with a member of your ship's personnel. I thought, as you do a good job of keeping your group calm and reasonable—aside from that little incident at the Varvara Estate—it might help if you talked to him."

She'd become her group's de facto leader, probably due to her image of being the non-violent one. If only Rano knew. She glanced at Pamuk, on her back and snoring, a line of drool running from her mouth, one eye blackened and a cut on her forehead crusty with dried blood. At some point in the previous night's party, she must have gotten into a fight.

Calm and reasonable?

He obviously didn't know about last night's events yet, or perhaps it was all just another excuse to spend time with her.

"See you soon," she said.

The only way to reach the other zone was via an underground rail line. They drove to the station and boarded the train's front carriage, reserved for high-ranking officials. Only two other passengers occupied the space: a couple in expensive clothes who seemed to recognize the security chief, for they nodded at him deferentially. Carina spotted a lump on the man's throat. Before he could notice her staring, she averted her gaze.

They took seats in the opposite corner.

"Does that man have a tumor?" she asked quietly as the train started.

"They're probably taking a final tour of all the zones before he goes to a euthanasia center. A lot of people do it."

The train quickly accelerated. Lights flashed past.

"Do you know the name of this person we're going to see?" She'd been telling herself it had to be one of the Black Dogs. Of everyone from the *Bathsheba*, they would be least able to tolerate their captivity. Yet she also feared it might be one of the kids. Ferne and Nahla could be very strong-willed.

"I don't, sorry, only that it's a male."

The journey took hours. They alighted at the first station in Grantha, and Rano took her into an elevator. "We're going to a medical center."

"The man's hurt?"

He winced. "I'm sorry. I wanted to tell you but I've been putting it off. Grantha treats Outsiders differently from Una. We prefer a gentler approach, encouraging rather than forcing you to join our society. It usually works, given time. Grantha is more heavy-handed."

"You didn't tell me that! Why didn't you tell me? I assumed everyone's experience was the same. Are the children in this zone?"

"Don't worry. The heavy-handed approach doesn't extend to minors. The children are perfectly safe and unharmed."

"How can I believe you when you already lied to me?" She hesitated to ask to see them. No one seeing Parthenia and her side by side would fail to notice they were sisters.

"I haven't lied to you, Carina. Not once."

"Not telling me something I should know is also a lie," she spat. "Just a different kind."

"There's no need for you to get upset."

"I'll decide that."

The elevator stopped and the doors opened. In strained silence, she accompanied Rano to a nurse's station, where he introduced himself and asked where the patient was.

Dread dogged Carina's footsteps as they walked toward the room. She'd guessed she was going to see a merc but perhaps she wasn't. Seeing a Black Dog in a bad way wouldn't be pleasant but there was a worse possibility.

Rano halted. "This Outsider escaped and spent several days on the run. He was hurt during his recapture so he was brought here for treatment. That was when the Grantha authorities reached out to me, asking my advice, and I offered to bring you over to speak to him. Outsiders are valuable to us for all the reasons you now know. At the end of the day, we don't want them hurt any more than they want to be hurt. It would be in everyone's interests if you could persuade your shipmate to be more accepting of his situation."

"Escaped? What do you mean? Are my friends being held prisoner?"

"Your own movements are restricted. You know that."

She frowned. "You're lying to me again. I want to see this man." She stepped up to the door but it remained shut.

"You don't have the clearance to enter."

"Open it!"

"Perhaps you should calm d—"

"*Open it.*"

Sighing, he placed his hand on the wall panel and the door slid open.

Carina didn't recognize the patient at first, he was in such a bad way. Swathed in dressings, connected by wires and tubes to two machines, exposed skin swollen and purple, all she could tell was that the figure was male. She stepped closer. The man's eyes were closed but opened at her approach.

Then she recognized him.

"*Bryce!*"

Her legs turned weak and she dropped to her knees.

"You know him well," Rano said, tension edging his tone.

"What have you done to him?" she blurted. "What have you done?"

"Not me, Carina. As I said, the Grantha authorities…"

But she didn't hear any more. It was like Viggo all over again. If she only had elixir she could Heal him. She could take away his suffering and make him healthy. But she couldn't. She was crippled and weak.

"Bryce," she sobbed, burying her face into the pillow next to his head and taking his hand. A voice inside told her she shouldn't give away her feelings but she couldn't help it. He was so badly injured it was clear he could have been killed. They'd nearly murdered him.

"It's okay," he murmured through thick lips. "I'm okay. 'S good to see you."

Why had the Sot Lozans done this to him? It must have been the same as had happened with Viggo. Somehow, they couldn't have known he was an Outsider.

"I'm beginning to think this wasn't such a good idea," said Rano tensely. "I confess I didn't know the extent of this man's injuries. They're as much of a surprise to me as they are to you."

She rose to her feet and whirled to face him. "You bastard! You're all bastards, and you're insane. A bunch of psychopaths, trapping innocent people, bringing them to this hellhole, forcing them to-to-to…" She didn't have words to express how she felt. She returned to Bryce's side. Kneeling down once more, she leaned close and whispered softly in his ear, "I'll get you out. If it kills me, I'm going to get you and everyone else out, and I'll leave this planet a smoking ash heap."

"We should go." Rano touched her arm. "I can see this was a mistake."

She slapped him away. "Get your slimy Sot Lozan hands off me."

"That's enough! I've been patient with you, but you don't get to speak to me like that. I'm not just anyone, you know."

"What are you going to do? Beat me up? Send in goons to work me over? Are you going to put me in a hospital bed too?!"

Rano was speechless, his cheeks flushed.

She got up and bent down to gently kiss Bryce. "Hold on," she muttered. "Just hold on."

He blinked a silent acknowledgment.

THIRTY

Clawing her way back in Rano's affections after displaying her feelings for Bryce wasn't going to be easy, but she had to do it. On the train ride back to Una the security chief was mostly silent. When he did speak he was stiffly polite. She hoped his problem wasn't only that he'd seen how she felt about another man. She hoped he was at war with himself after witnessing the brutality inflicted on Outsiders in another zone. He'd done a great job of convincing himself that the habit of Sot Lozans in snatching people from space wasn't so bad. Bryce was evidence to the contrary—evidence that was hard to ignore or explain away.

When the train stopped at the station, she said, hating herself, "I'm sorry for losing it at the medical center. When I saw my friend I was very shocked. I wasn't expecting that."

He seemed to soften a little. "Neither was I. If I'd known he was that bad I wouldn't have taken you there. Outsiders would never be treated like that here in Una."

She was reminded of Calvaley, the former Sherrerr officer killed by the Lotacryllans. He'd maintained that the Sherrerr cause was for the greater good, overall, and that was why he supported it. Though he'd died nobly in the end, he'd been a liar like Rano, lying to himself as much as to everyone else. "I'm glad to hear it. For what it's worth, I didn't get the impression you could be so savage and merciless."

He smiled tightly. "Thank you. That means a lot."

As they'd been speaking, they'd exited the station.

"I'll arrange an autocar to take you back to your hotel," he said. "I have to go straight to work. Lots to do. I'm going to speak to my counterpart in Grantha."

"About the Outsider?"

"I'm not happy about what I saw today."

"Will I see you later?"

"Do you want to?"

"I do."

His smile relaxed. "I'll pick you up at the usual time."

When she arrived at the hotel the mercs were up and sitting around the lounge they'd just about demolished, listless and morose. Their state clearly wasn't only about their hangovers. They'd reached the end of their tethers about the situation.

"Where's Chi-tang?" she asked.

"Screwing his girlfriend," Pamuk replied.

"As usual," someone added.

"I'm surprised he hasn't worn it off," said someone else, eliciting a half-hearted chuckle from the room.

"It isn't like you didn't get your chance," Pamuk said.

The speaker shrugged. "What's the point? The women here only want one thing. I don't want to be used. I'm more than a piece of meat, you know."

This brought louder laughter.

"Where have *you* been?" Pamuk asked her. "Buddying up with the enemy again?" She seemed to be only partly joking.

"Hey, come on," Carina retorted. "You don't really think I'm going over to their side, do you?"

"I don't know. You aren't here most of the time. Where were you last night when we were partying? And where did you go today? You haven't told us yet."

"I was with Rano last night and we went to the other zone today." How much should she tell them? The mercs were in a precarious state, on the edge of doing something rash and likely to get them killed. The news that the Sot Lozans had severely hurt Bryce might set them off. "He asked me to speak to a merc who was having a hard time."

"Who did you see?" asked Pamuk, sitting up.

Carina picked a missing merc at random. "Karl, but he didn't want to talk to me. Not with Rano hanging around."

"I don't blame him," Pamuk said. "How did he look?"

"Fine. I think everyone over there is just getting impatient, the same as here. But we need to wait a little while longer. We're working on things. I can't say more." The fact that the Sot Lozans might be listening in was a handy cover for her lack of ideas or updates.

"As soon as you need us, let us know."

"I will."

As she climbed the stairs to her room, Chi-tang returned. A roar of jeering and laughter went up in the lounge. She left the mercs to their fun.

———

Rano took her to a holo show. The scene was a setting from the origin planet, and it was pretty realistic. They seemed to be in a forest. Trees and undergrowth surrounded the path they followed. The air was fragrant and moist and filled with the sound of running water from an invisible waterfall.

"This is one of my favorites," he said. "I paid to get the place to ourselves. I hope you like it."

"It's nice." She caught his disappointed look. "I mean, beautiful. It's really beautiful."

His features brightened. "If we follow this path it takes us to a lookout."

They ascended the trail.

"Are you feeling better now?" he asked. "After our visit to Grantha, I mean."

"Did you speak to their security chief?"

"I did, and she apologized. She said the officers responsible will be disciplined."

Carina wasn't sure she believed him. Then again, she was a liar too. She had lied to the Black Dogs for expediency's sake. "So my friend will be treated better now?"

"Absolutely. And he's predicted to make a full recovery."

"That does make me feel better."

He reached for her hand and she didn't resist, though his touch made her skin crawl. The trail turned left and ended at a ledge with a guard rail. The view was spectacular and not at all representative of their short climb. They appeared to be hundreds of meters high. A lush green canopy spread out in front of them, undulating on the uneven ground and also as a gentle breeze swept through it. Steam rose from the treetops and brightly colored birds flitted from branch to branch.

"It's quite something, isn't it?" Rano asked.

"It is." She recalled seeing something similar on a planet she'd visited in her merc days, but she hadn't been able to stick around for long.

"Carina." He took her shoulders and turned her to face him. "I think *you're* quite something too."

"Do you?" She steeled herself for what was to come.

As he kissed her she willed her body not to stiffen, forced her hands not to shove him into the abyss. She was nauseated to her core but she couldn't show it.

Finally, it was over. He put an arm around her shoulders and they stood together, taking in the view.

"I can't tell you how much tonight means to me," he said. "You'll never regret it. I promise."

"I know I won't."

As they drove back to the hotel, she said, "Can I ask you about something that's been bothering me for a while? I don't mind if you can't tell me."

"We'll only find out if you ask."

"I've been wondering about the attraction beam that brought my ship here. It must be immensely powerful. How does Sot Loza generate so much energy?"

"Uhh…" He glanced at her and appeared to mentally debate with himself. "It isn't a big secret. All our energy comes from a solar array, deep in space. The power runs the planet and can be used to create and sustain the beam. Does that answer your question?"

"It does, thanks. It's pretty simple. I've heard of other planets using similar systems though not to such a great extent."

"Here on Sot Loza we've had to be very inventive and adaptable to survive. If only the rest of the galaxy knew about us. We'd be famous."

If the rest of the galaxy knew what you were doing you'd be wiped from the star map.

He dropped her off with a promise to arrange another activity tomorrow night. Carina mustered as much enthusiasm as she could as she agreed, secretly hoping she wouldn't have to continue faking it much longer. At some point, probably fairly soon, Rano would expect her to take a step she wasn't prepared to take.

Chi-tang was alone in the lounge.

"Where is everyone?"

"They were all invited to another dinner party."

"You didn't get an invitation?"

"Nope. Like you, I'm already taken." He smirked.

"How are things going?"

"Good. Really good."

If they ever got the chance, would he even want to leave the planet? She wasn't sure.

"Come here." He patted the seat beside him.

Cautiously, she sat down.

He leaned close.

She leaned away. "What are you doing?"

"Stop kidding around. I want to tell you something."

"Uh, okay."

He put his lips close to her ear. "I found out something important. The planet and the attraction beam that dragged the *Bathsheba* in are powered by a massive solar array."

"I know."

"You do? Damn. I thought I'd discovered something important."

"It is important. I only found that out myself today. Chi-tang, did your girlfriend tell you about the array?"

"Of course. Why else do you think I'm seeing her?"

"I didn't get the impression you were mining her for secrets."

"Not at first, maybe. But then I realized what a perfect position I was in. Her family are right up there."

"They don't mind that you let a bunch of burglars into their house?"

"Meh, I got Cheepy to cover for me. She told them she left the door open by mistake."

He was certainly full of surprises.

"Cool. Let me know what else you find out."

Thirty-One

Three days had dragged by and Carina was no closer to getting her family and companions off Sot Loza or re-taking the *Bathsheba*. She had learned so much intel through one means or another, but all her knowledge was useless. What was needed was a shift in the power balance or an 'in' she could exploit. At the moment their captors held all the cards, and she was fast losing hope that things might change.

Everyone seemed to sense it. The usual banter between the Black Dogs had dried to a trickle. They took out their frustration on the things around them and each other, getting in each others' faces and starting fights just for the hell of it. Chi-tang was rarely at the hotel and seemed to have moved in full-time with his girlfriend, and Rano was becoming insistently physical. It was hard to keep him on a string, reeling him in when he began to give up on her yet dangling him loosely when his attentions grew too much to bear. She'd seen others play that game over the years but she was no expert in it herself.

Things could not continue as they were. Something had to give. She had a horrible feeling it would be the mercs.

Then, on the morning of the fourth day after her visit to Grantha, everything kicked off.

She woke to unusual sounds of activity. She was often the first to wake, the Black Dogs often lounging in their beds until midday or later. But this morning Pamuk was already up and gone from the room. Noises were coming from the corridor—determined footsteps, banging, shouts, and laughter.

What was going on?

She got up, rubbing her eyes, and padded to the door. As she opened it a merc marched purposefully by. He looked oddly bulkier than she remembered, as if his muscles had expanded overnight.

"Hey, what's happening?"

He turned and slowed his pace but didn't stop. "Uh, Carina. You, uh, better ask Pamuk." He ran down the stairs. As she watched she realized why he looked odd. He was wearing many layers of the yellow Outsider Suits.

What the...?

She trotted to the head of the stairs and peered down. Mercs were moving around on the first floor. "Pamuk? Is Pamuk there?" When no reply came she descended, barefoot and cursing.

All the Black Dogs were dressed in the bizarre many-layered costumes. Several were already sweating heavily. In the underground world's mild temperatures one set of clothing was plenty for staying warm. It was only when she spotted someone carrying a kitchen knife the penny dropped.

Shit!

"Stop! Everyone stop what you're doing right now! Put everything down and come into the lounge so we can talk about this."

The mercs had piled on all the clothes they could wear as a poor form of body armor, and now they were gathering objects they could use as weapons.

"The time for talking's over," said Pamuk, emerging from the bustling men and women. "Now it's time to act."

"Whatever it is you plan on doing, it isn't going to work. You're all going to get yourselves killed."

"If we stay here we're already dead. What difference does it make?"

"Yeah," someone remarked, "I'd rather go out now than in twenty years when the tumors get me, and after I've fathered a thousand bastards who'll die the same way. This is better by a long shot."

"We can still get out of here safely," Carina protested. "Don't throw everything away when we're so close."

Pamuk thrust her face into Carina's. "Tell us the plan and we'll stop, here and now. Right, guys?"

The movement around her ceased. Carina swallowed. "You know I can't do that."

"Bullshit. Look, it's nothing personal. I like you, even though you're a shitty roommate. But you've been stringing us along for weeks with your promises of a way out of here. We've been screwed ever since we arrived, we just didn't know it. We should have called it quits after we broke into the mansion. It's time to do what needs to be done."

"This is so senseless. There's always hope. Always."

"You don't get it, do you? It's different for you. You have people you want to see again, people you want to stay alive for. We don't."

Carina scanned the faces surrounding her. "That isn't true. You have all the other Black Dogs, and you have me. I don't want to lose any of you. We've been through so much together. Too much to give up so easily."

"We're not giving up," said Pamuk. "We're taking back control."

"No, you're not! This is dumb. Look at you all. How long do you think you're gonna last wearing five banana suits and wielding chair legs? C'mon, see sense."

They ignored her and continued to gather their supplies.

"I won't let you do it," Carina announced, running to the exit. She stood in front of it defiantly, a hand on each side of the frame. "I won't let you leave."

"Aww," said Pamuk, with only a touch of sarcasm. "She's so cute."

In another few minutes, the mercs had finished their preparations. Carina hadn't changed position. She wasn't going to let them out.

"You still here?" Pamuk asked as they came face to face again.

"I'll fight you," Carina said. "Every one of you."

The mercs chuckled.

"You know you don't mean that," said Pamuk. Reaching out, she picked Carina up under her armpits, moved her to one side, and gently set her down. "Let's go," she said over her shoulder, and the party of Black Dogs jogged down the outer steps.

Carina ran after them. "Where are you going? At least tell me that. Maybe I can help you."

Pamuk frowned. "You're not gonna tell that security chief?"

"Of course not."

"All right, well, we're going to take the elevator to the surface, steal a shuttle, fly to the *Bathsheba*, and take back the ship. You're welcome to come along."

"That's insane. You'll never make it."

Pamuk shrugged and joined the rest of the mercs, who were moving away.

Carina caught up to her. "What about the rest of the Black Dogs? Aren't you going to try to rescue them?"

"They had their chance, same as us. If we could help them we would. They'll understand."

Cursing, Carina halted. There was nothing she could say or do to change their minds. She became aware she was barefoot and in pajamas, attracting as much attention as the group of mercs. She raced back to the hotel, bounded up to her room and threw on clothes and boots before running downstairs again.

When she reached the street the Black Dogs were out of sight. She sped after them.

———

She hadn't been back to the spot where she'd entered underground Sot Loza since she'd arrived. She recalled the doors that led out to the street, where the transport had been waiting. No signs marked the portal, the place where Outsiders were brought to begin their journey of assimilation.

How many captives had arrived here and at similar places in the two other zones? How many lives had the Sot Lozans destroyed in their quest to ensure their world's survival? One was too many, yet it had to have been thousands if not tens of thousands over the centuries.

Were the Black Dogs the only ones who had made a stand? She would never know. But what did seem certain, as she gazed at the mercs forcing their way in the doors, was these were determined to succeed or die trying.

They must have reached them before anyone realized what they were attempting. A wedged chair leg was preventing the doors from closing, and a pitched battle was going on inside and outside between the mercs and guards. One Black Dog was already down, hit by pulse fire. The suits of others were blackened and smoldering from rounds that had grazed them. Pedestrians were fleeing the scene though some hung around in horrified fascination. Flashes of fire cut across the gap between the doors from the firefight going on within.

Pamuk emerged, armed. Swinging from left to right, she took out the Sot Lozan guards. The mercs seized their rifles and someone grabbed the downed merc, hauling him inside the building. The fighting going on within seemed to be over. Could the Black Dogs really make it to the surface?

A rumble distracted Carina.

A military transport had appeared at the end of the street.

Another approached from the other side. Each vehicle held at least twenty personnel. Forty soldiers?

She darted across the road and ran between the wedged doors. A round passed close by her head, momentarily blinding her.

"Shit, Lin," Pamuk admonished. "Next time, holler before you run in. You decided to join us after all?"

"Forty hostiles will be crawling up your asses in about half a minute. Can you get into the elevator?"

"Not yet. We can't get through this goddamned door."

All the Black Dogs were jammed into the lobby, dead and dying guards at their feet. The defenders had managed to seal the inner door during the initial attack. Someone had a pulse rifle trained on it, filling the air with choking smoke as the energy melted the surface, but the chances of burning through the door in the next thirty seconds were slim.

"You've had a good run, guys," Carina said. "If you surrender now, you'll live to fight another day."

Pamuk cuffed her and leaned in close. "Don't *ever* let me hear you say that again." She turned to her comrades. "We make our stand here."

The Black Dogs knelt or stood as they saw fit, rifles at the ready.

Carina couldn't leave them. Though it would save her life, though she might see Bryce and her brothers and sisters again, everything in her rebelled against walking away from these men and women who had fought on her behalf so bravely and for so long.

She picked up a rifle and waited.

Thirty-Two

They'd put the least badly wounded in a group cell. Carina lay on the bare floor, resting on her back to keep a distance between her wound and the hard surface. She was better off than many. She'd only taken a hit to her shoulder, forcing her hands to open and her rifle to fall from her paralyzed fingers. Mads, Berkcan, and Ola, who occupied the cell with her also had non-life-threatening wounds, though no doubt they were painful.

No one spoke.

The others could be asleep, but she doubted it. Sleep didn't come easily when your body was burned and blistered. But it wasn't only discomfort keeping her awake. It was the realization it was over.

In response to the latest outrage, the Sot Lozans had taken off the gloves. The soldiers who had attacked the mercs at the elevator site hadn't used their customary restraint. They'd sprayed the lobby with fire, putting an end to the escape attempt in less than a minute. She didn't know who had survived, if there were any more still living than her and her cellmates. The soldiers had roughly dragged them out without checking them over. She'd been one of the few who had tried to crawl away before being seized and brought here.

Then, nothing.

They'd been left without medical treatment, food, or water for hours. No one even passed by the cell. The message was clear. This latest set of Outsiders was now no more than farm animals. They would be allowed to live but only because their bodies contained cells that were rare and valuable in this doomed, toxic world. She had lost all credibility with Rano Shelta. He would know she'd been messing with him all along. He would never contact her again. That was no great loss. In fact, the knowledge she would never see his face again or feel his disgusting hands on her was a relief.

She shouldn't have listened to Jackson. All his talk of playing the long game had come to nothing. They should have fought back with everything they had from the moment the Sot Lozans had latched onto them, and taken out as many of the bastards as they could.

They would have been beaten, for sure. The enemy had developed unusual, powerful technologies during their years of separation from the rest of the galaxy. The *Bathsheba* didn't have the power to break away from their attraction beam, nor could she fight off several ships at once. Jackson had been right that resistance would have ended in disaster, but they would have all been together at the end. They would not have wound up as slaves, used for breeding like beasts. The Sot Lozans were no better than the Regians. They were worse, in fact. At least the Regians sedated their victims.

The lights went out.

Still, their captors hadn't acknowledged their presence. So they were expected to sleep now, in pain, hungry, and thirsty? To her left, someone groaned. If only she could help him, but she was impotent, useless.

She would never see Bryce again, never know if he'd recovered from his injuries, never know if he was safe. She would never see her siblings either. There would be no more bickering with Parthenia, no more of Ferne and Oriana's fashion shows, no brilliant revelations from Nahla, and she would never feel sweet Darius's arms around her neck.

She put a hand to her face, ashamed even in the darkness as silent tears slipped from her eyes and ran into her hair. Heaving a wretched sigh, she tried to will herself asleep, seeking oblivion. After a while she managed to slip into a light doze.

Something had changed.

Her eyes opened.

The cell remained dark, the breathing of her companions loud in the silence. Not all were asleep. One inhaled and exhaled with effort as if in pain. Was that what had disturbed her?

She sat up. Perhaps if she screamed and hollered enough she could force the guards to get the merc treatment.

"Mads," she whispered, "is that you? Are you okay?"

"Carina?" a voice hissed. "Are you here? Where are you?"

It was not Mads who had answered. The voice she'd heard made her wonder if she was still asleep. Had she dreamt it? It couldn't be true.

"Parthenia?" she asked in a squeak.

"You *are* here," her sister answered.

There was the sound of movement. Carina got to her feet and reached out, hardly believing this was real. Her hand brushed clothing. Parthenia touched her elbow. In another second they hugged. Carina winced and gasped.

"You're hurt," Parthenia whispered. "I'm so sorry."

"No, it's fine." Adjusting her position she hugged her sister again, fresh tears spilling out. "Are you really here? I'm not imagining it?"

"I'm here." Parthenia softly chuckled. "I'm really here. I can't believe it either. I've missed you so much."

"What's going on?" asked Mads. "Who's that? Who are you talking to, Lin?"

"Shhh," she told him. "Be quiet. We might be able to get you out."

"Take this," Parthenia said, feeling down her arm and then pushing a bottle into her hand.

It felt comfortingly, reassuringly full. "You don't need it?"

"We have more. Lots more."

"Thank the stars." Maybe their ordeal would soon be over. Carina unfastened her shirt and put the bottle inside before buttoning it up again.

"And take these," Parthenia said. She gave her an assortment of small objects. There was no need for her to explain. They were all things their siblings had handled, items that would allow Carina to Locate them. She'd carried similar things with her when she'd been taken from the *Bathsheba*, but she'd been forced to throw them all away, severing her from her family.

"Is there something of Bryce's here?" she asked, not sure she wanted to hear the answer.

"The piece of gauze is his. We cut it from one of his dressings."

Carina breathed in sharply.

"He's okay," Parthenia said. "Oriana Healed him and we have him hidden at our house."

Thirty-Three

As Bryce had stared at the law enforcement vehicles waiting near the rear entrance of the museum, ages seemed to pass, though it was probably only seconds, before he finally figured out what to do.

He'd picked a vehicle and run toward it. "Help! There's been a break in. Someone's attacked the guard! Please, help!"

Two officers climbed out. "We got an alert a few minutes ago. Do you know what happened?"

"I saw the window at the front was broken and I thought thieves must have broken in. When I looked inside I saw two men beating up the guard. I don't have my comm with me so I ran in to help him, but the men took off. I followed them to this exit. Did you see them?"

"No, but we only just got here."

"Maybe the other officers did," Bryce said, edging away. "Anyway, you seem to have the situation under control."

"What did the men look like?"

"Uhh, it was hard to see. It's really dark in there. You'd better check on the guard. He looked in bad shape." He began to walk off.

"Wait, we need you to give a statement about what you saw. What's your name?"

The other officer was murmuring into his comm button.

"Connor...Cradle," Bryce replied. "Look, can I drop by tomorrow to give a statement? Only I'm already late and my—"

"Connor Cradle? Why kind of stupid name is that?" The man moved closer and peered at him, then wrinkled his nose.

"You should probably focus on catching those thieves. I promise I'll—"

"Hey, where do you think you're going?"

Bryce had stepped backward and turned. "Sorry, I really have to go."

"Get back here!"

He ran.

Connor Cradle? What the hell had he been thinking?

He had no ID and a quick check of their database would tell the officers no one with that dumb name existed.

"It's him, dammit!" one of the officers exclaimed. "It was him all along."

Bryce flew down the road. Due to his long wanderings on his quest to locate the museum he knew the area well. A busy shopping district, it was a maze of small streets and alleys. He darted down the first opening he saw. A flash of light and hiss burst behind him. Yells and running footsteps followed. He dashed past an alley and took the next, hoping to confuse his pursuers.

But the night was quiet and it was impossible to disguise the noise of his movements. Before he reached the end he heard someone enter the alley behind him.

"He's here! This way!"

Bryce sped up. He ran like his life depended on it, and perhaps it did. If he was caught he would never be allowed out again, and the kids would never get what they needed to set everyone free.

He'd barely eaten for four days, he'd slept rough for four nights, and he'd spent hours crouched in darkness, waiting. He was already cramped, sore and exhausted, but he had to squeeze out the remainder of his strength. It was the last chance they had.

He swerved into a lane, sped to the end, turned left into the rear entrances of a set of shops, vaulted a low fence, hesitated and then went right. He was moving so fast he was becoming disoriented.

And all the while, his pursuer was on his tail.

Which way was it to the kids' house?

He couldn't remember. This place looked unfamiliar.

He was lost.

A major road appeared ahead. Even at this late hour vehicles passed up and down it.

Ah! He knew where he was. But running up the road would lead to him getting caught. He would be too easy to spot.

He dashed around the corner and instantly halted, his chest heaving. Pressing his back against the wall, he tried to quieten his panting, without much success. His lungs were aflame. Aside from the vehicles, the road was empty.

The officer ran out.

Bryce grabbed him, shoved him down, and kneed him in the face. Then he threw the man against the wall. As he hit the ground, he kicked him in the head. After quickly checking he was out, Bryce shot up the road. The vehicle occupants would wonder who was the strange man in such a hurry but he couldn't help it.

If he could just evade capture a few more minutes.

Where was the turnoff?

That street?

No.

That one?

No.

There!

A vehicle slammed to a halt next to him.

Bryce tried to force more speed from his legs but they had nothing left to give.

The vehicle doors opened and slammed.

Pulse fire exploded on the wall.

They hadn't even given him a warning. They had to know he'd hurt one of their own.

He rounded the turning into the kids' street.

Just let him get another fifty meters.

Four houses. Just four houses.

He felt for the spindle in his shirt. As he'd been running it had rubbed against his chest. His hand encountered warm wetness and mangled skin. In his flight he hadn't even noticed. He took the spindle out.

Three houses.

Heated light splashed against a fence, sending out furious hisses.

Two houses.

Pain roared from the back of his thigh.

He stumbled.

One.

As he fell, he launched the spindle in a high arc. It sailed through the night, barely visible, and disappeared.

At the same time another pulse round hit him in the back.

His howl of agony was cut short as his face smacked into the ground. His nose broke and his gums split open on his teeth. Boots pounded the pavement and stopped next to him.

"You're under arrest," a voice barked.
There was a grunt and someone kicked him in the ribs.
"Stop resisting," the voice commanded.
Another kick.
He jerked into a ball, his arms over his head.
"I said, stop resisting!"
Another kick.
The kicks kept coming until he slipped into a deep, black void.

THIRTY-FOUR

As she waited through the night, Carina's hand kept creeping to the elixir bottle in her shirt, seeking out its comforting reality. She still couldn't quite believe Parthenia had been here in the cell with her. The bottle was the only firm evidence she had, that and Mads' memory of their whispered conversation in the dark.

But, no, she was forgetting something. She was also healthy again and free of pain. Her first Casts since leaving the *Bathsheba* weeks ago had been to Heal herself, Mads, and the sleeping mercs. They would have a pleasant surprise when they awoke—two pleasant surprises. Not only would they find themselves miraculously better, they would discover they were about to take part in an escape plan.

The temptation to return with Parthenia to Grantha had been great. She would have given a lot, risked a lot, to see the rest of her siblings and to reassure herself with her own eyes that Bryce had been Healed too, even if she could only see them for a few minutes. But her sister had explained that the house she was living at was heavily guarded and their numbers had increased since the children helped Bryce to escape. Parthenia had been pretending to take a bath while on her visit to Carina, and to Transport her to the house, even for a few moments, was too dangerous.

After hearing the commotion of the law enforcement officers beating Bryce up outside, and finding the piece of wood he'd stolen for them in the yard, it had taken them days and a great deal of ingenuity to create elixir under the guards' noses. Ava had helped with the subterfuge by telling them that, in her culture, her baby had reached a milestone that had to be celebrated by bathing it in a special, holy, liquid.

"Apart from setting her free," Parthenia had said, "the guards will do anything for Ava. *Anything.* They used to have a soft spot for Darius as well, because he's the youngest I suppose. But they don't trust him now, not since he faked breaking his leg."

"Faked breaking his leg?!"

"I can explain later. We need to figure out how we're going to do this."

There was a lot. The Black Dogs and Ava's companions, the other women from Marchon, were spread out across Sot Loza. They had to locate and free them all. Then they had to get the *Bathsheba* back under their control. Finally, they had to leave the system, free from the threat of the attraction team. A bonus action would be preventing the Sot Lozans from continuing their barbaric custom.

So much to do, and each step brought risks. The kids had a plentiful supply of elixir but sooner or later the enemy would cotton on to what was happening. Though they wouldn't understand Casting completely they would spot its weaknesses, such as the time it took and the need for the special beverage. The mages had to keep them guessing as long as possible.

Carina adjusted her position. Mads had gone to sleep, true to his pragmatic merc nature, but she could not. As the night passed, she mentally went over the details she'd agreed with Parthenia, trying to anticipate problems before they arose. By the time she heard distant sounds of movement hinting it was early morning and the prison was waking up, tension and fatigue riddled her.

Mads turned onto his back and stretched his arms out.

"About time," she murmured. "How can you sleep in a situation like this?"

"I sleep the sleep of the innocent."

"Ha, funny. Wake up Berkcan and Ola."

The cell remained pitch dark. She heard him crawl to their companions, who had slumbered heavily since being Healed.

"Rise and shine," Mads said, no doubt roughly shaking them. "It's time to go."

The mercs responded with grumbles and grunts.

Ola said sleepily, "Go where?"

"Grantha," Carina replied. "Only we have a few things to do first."

When everyone was fully awake, she outlined the plan. Then she took out the elixir bottle and removed the lid.

"Hold on," said Berkcan. "I'm not sure about this. Can you explain again how we get outside the cell?"

"I Transport you. I would Unlock it but that could trigger the alarm. Don't worry. It doesn't hurt. You won't feel a thing."

"But I'm not a mage."

"You don't have to be a mage, stupid. I can Transport objects too."

"But I'm not an object either."

"C'mon," said Mads. "Quit being a crybaby. You've been around Lin and the kids long enough to realize they know what they're doing."

"Well, you know," Carina said. "There *is* another option."

"What's that?" asked Berkcan eagerly.

"I leave you here. You pick. Ola and Mads, you're going first." She swallowed elixir, closed her eyes, and Cast. When she opened her eyes she tapped the cell door. An answering knock came. "Made up your mind?" she asked Berkcan.

"Shit. Just do it. But I swear, Lin..."

She ignored him, already Casting.

She was in the passageway outside the cell with the three mercs. This area was lit.

"I just realized," said Ola, "I don't hurt anymore. Did you do that?"

"Yeah, but save your thanks. We have work to do."

It was impossible to tell if there were more Black Dogs in the surrounding cells without Transporting inside them to check. The doors had no windows and they couldn't access the data using the security panels on the wall. She guessed the surviving mercs were elsewhere receiving medical treatment. Everyone at the elevator lobby except her group had been in bad shape, possibly dead. She didn't want to waste elixir looking in every cell just in case she was wrong.

They had a different target.

The door at the end of the passageway was locked, but this one had a window. On the other side was a stairwell going up and down. It appeared empty. Whatever early-morning noises that had filtered through to Carina a few minutes earlier had now ceased.

"They'll be upstairs," said Mads. "The guards always take the best spots."

Another two swallows of elixir and all four of them were on the other side of the door.

"What happens if you use all that stuff up?" whispered Berkcan.

"If we don't make it, my sister will find me and bring me more."

"How?"

Carina frowned at him.

"Shut up," Mads hissed. "This way." He crept up the stairs.

Carina followed with Ola. Berkcan brought up the rear.

They had to climb three flights before they reached something other than passageways and cells. Mads crouched beside the door and pointed at it, then held up four fingers.

Four guards? It was a lot for them to take on unarmed, but they had a fantastic advantage. Carina was confident that the Sot Lozans had never experienced a vengeful Black Dog appearing out of nowhere before.

"Can you do all four of us at once?" Mads asked softly.

"I can try." The trick was being able to join them in her mind and Transport *Things of this kind* rather than individuals. Everyone was wearing their dumb banana suits—torn, scorched, and bloody, but essentially the same. That would help.

"What happens if it doesn't work?" Berkcan asked.

"You stay here forever."

"Just me?"

Shaking her head, she unscrewed the elixir bottle lid. Then she paused. If she could see the guards through the window...

There weren't many Casts that could hurt people. Most of the banal ones like Lock or Clear would have no effect on them. The one that could kill, Split, was excruciating and horrible to witness. On the other hand, there was Enthrall.

She gestured for Mads to move out of the way. Peeking through the window, she noted each guard. One sat at a desk. Another lounged against a wall. The other two were consulting a wall interface.

She could divide Enthrall into four at a pinch but it would weaken the Cast, perhaps so much it would be ineffective, especially if one of them was particularly strong-willed.

Instead, she targeted desk man.

His eyes took on the characteristic glazed look. She pressed her face against the window and waved to attract his attention.

"What are you doing?!" Berkcan demanded.

The guard had seen her but his face betrayed no reaction.

She beckoned.

Automaton-like, he got to his feet and tottered toward the door.

The lounging guard noticed. His voice muffled by the barrier, he said, "Farver, what are you doing?"

Farver had reached the door and was already obeying Carina's gesture to unlock it.

"Farver!"

The mercs burst into the room. Mads rushed the noisy one, slamming a fist into the man's jaw and felling him. Berkcan and Ola went for the two at the interface, barreling into them before they could raise the alarm. Blows from their own rifle butts sent them to the same nirvana as Mads' target. Farver had watched the proceedings slack-jawed. Carina took his handgun.

"How long will he stay like that?" Ola asked.

"It's hard to tell. Depends on his personality."

"Let's get them all into a cell, fast," said Mads.

"Yeah," Carina agreed. "Then it's on to our next stop."

THIRTY-FIVE

It would still be nighttime in Grantha though it was morning here. Now they had two rifles and two beamers it was time to go to her family. Carina took out the bracelet Nahla had fashioned for Parthenia from packaging. After wearing it for several days her oldest sister would have imbued it with her 'signature'. Carina Located her in the vast gray expanse in the Casting mind. For safety's sake, she sent Mads and Ola first rather than attempting to Transport all of them that distance at once. Now it was her and Berkcan's turn.

As she took his arm he opened his mouth to speak.

"I swear," she said. "One more word…"

His lips snapped shut.

Another mouthful of elixir, and she was back in darkness, except this darkness was warm and comforting. She could sense her sibling's presence and see her shadowy form.

Parthenia's arms wrapped around her and she whispered, "You made it!"

"You're here! You're here!" squeaked a voice.

"Darius?"

The little boy grabbed her around the waist and he buried his head in her stomach. "I thought I might never see you again."

"Me too, but I'm here now. Everything's going to be okay, I think. Are Mads and Ola here?" She could already see Berkcan's bulky form next to her.

"They're over there, near my bed," Parthenia replied. "I thought I'd better move away before you Cast again so everyone didn't bump into each other. We can't make too much noise or someone will come in to check on me."

"Where are the others?" Carina asked. "And where's Bryce?"

"The twins and Nahla are in the bedroom next door. They know what's happening but not when exactly because we couldn't set a time. They might be asleep. Bryce is still in his hiding place in the roof. I couldn't speak to him at all yesterday after we hid him so he doesn't know what's going on."

"Can I go up there?" asked Carina.

"You could Transport into it, though the space is very cramped. We can't risk anyone going out into the main part of the house yet. Guards are on watch all day and night."

"We should take them out now," Mads growled softly. "Get the ball rolling."

Carina said, "We do everything in order, and that means waiting for dawn. Except I really want to see Bryce, and he should be in on this too. I'm going up there. Wait for me."

She had never known the Transport Cast to land anyone within a solid structure and she vaguely remembered Nai Nai telling her it wouldn't, that if the Transported wouldn't fit in the available space then it simply wouldn't work. Nevertheless, a little anxiety nagged at her. It was not enough to overcome her need to see Bryce, however.

Something was digging into her back and her legs were tightly wedged. She breathed a quiet groan of discomfort. Again, she was in darkness, but this time she was surrounded by boxes.

Something else, soft and warm, lay against her body, breathing gently. She touched him. "Bryce? Bryce, wake up."

"Who's...?" he murmured. "Carina? Is that really you?"

"It's me. I can't move, though. Can you help me?"

"We're right under the eaves. Wait a sec." He felt down her legs and grabbed her calf, helping her to wiggle one leg and then the other free.

"This is insane," she said as they cuddled. "How long have you been here?"

"Only a day. Parthenia arrived in my hospital room last night."

"Are you really okay?" She felt his face, gently running her fingertips over his features. The swelling seemed to have gone down.

"I'm a hundred percent better. Oriana did a great job Healing me."

"But it must have hurt so much before the kids helped you. How did it happen?"

"It was revenge for something I did. It doesn't matter now. It was worth it to get the kids the wood they needed. Stars, I've missed you." He pulled her close and kissed her. "Are *you* okay? I've been so worried about you. Has anyone hurt you or operated on you?"

"*Operated* on me? No, nothing like that. The Sot Lozans went easy on us, or they did until the Black Dogs got tired of waiting and tried to get to the surface. I thought you were being treated the same."

"It sounds like our experiences were different. The only Black Dog I've seen since the attack on the ship is Rees. As far as I know he's still imprisoned and so are the other mercs, while the Sot Lozans experiment on them."

"What the hell?" She tried to square Bryce's report with Ranc Shelta wining and dining her. She couldn't. He'd said that the zones didn't treat Outsiders the same, but it sounded like the rest of the *Bathsheba's* personnel had been subjected to some very dark shit.

"It's bad, Carina, especially for the women. We have to help them."

"We will, as soon as we can. But we can't rush anything or we'll screw up."

"I know. Step by step. As soon as you need me I'll be ready."

She held him close, aware that if things didn't go according to plan this might be her last opportunity.

He murmured in her ear, "That was smart thinking of you to push some strands of your hair into my hand in the hospital."

"You were so badly hurt I didn't know if you would even notice. I only thought of it when I recognized you. I didn't know who I was coming to see. All I'd been told was I was supposed to speak to a merc who had been acting out. If it hadn't been you, I doubt anyone else would have understood what I was doing. And, of course, I didn't know if you would see the kids or be able to give them my hair so they could Locate me." She added quietly, "Bryce... Viggo's dead."

"No! How? I thought you said you were treated well."

"It was a stupid accident. We were trying to steal something, something we thought was made of wood. It turned out we were wrong. Viggo got shot because they didn't see his Outsider clothes in the darkness."

"Outsider clothes?"

"Gee, our time here really has been different."

"Not for much longer."

"From now on we stick together, whatever happens."

He kissed her again. "Whatever happens."

Carina?

Parthenia was Sending to her.

What is it?

We can hear the new guards arriving. They'll be taking over from the others soon and someone will look into my room to check on me. I've hidden the mercs in the closet but there's no more room in there. Don't come down until I tell you it's safe.

Got it.

"Who are you talking to?" Bryce asked. He'd learned how to tell when she was mentally conversing with her siblings.

"Parthenia. We have to stay here a little while longer. Then we act."

Thirty-Six

What Carina really wanted to do to the Sot Lozan guards was to hurt them. She wanted to punish someone for Viggo's death, Bryce's beating, the injuries and possible killings of the mercs who had tried to escape, and for whatever other terrible things the people of this vile planet had done. Someone should suffer and pay the price of their evil acts.

But she knew it was her pain and anger talking. Sot Loza had brought out a side of her she didn't like and wanted to forget. Besides, hurting the guards would upset the kids, and any shouts or cries of pain might alert passersby. Ava was also against violence. Gentle, sweet Ava, a steady, calm presence in the children's lives ever since they'd been taken from the ship, had objected. Carina found she couldn't look into the woman's soulful, pleading eyes and argue for a vengeful payback.

As soon as the usual rounds of checks by the incoming guards was over, Carina had Transported back to Parthenia's room, this time with Bryce in tow. He'd stretched luxuriously after his long incarceration in the cramped space. Then it had been a matter of waking the other children and Ava—though everyone was careful to not wake the baby—and holding a brief conference in Parthenia and Darius's room to decide their next steps.

When they'd agreed exactly what to do, Darius walked out into the living area, rubbing his eyes.

Nahla, peeking out with Carina, quietly giggled. "He's a good actor."

"Morning, kid," said a guard lounging on the sofa. "How'd you sleep?"

"Uh, okay." Darius walked past the man into the kitchen, where he poured himself a drink from the jug on the counter.

The guard stood up. "What's that you're drinking? Is it something good?"

"Uh uh," Darius replied, shaking his head.

"Then why are you drinking it? Don't you want... What's wrong?"

Darius had closed his eyes and was clearly concentrating hard.

"Hey, I said..." The guard had been walking toward the kitchen but his footsteps slowed to a stop, his arms fell limply to his sides, and his jaw dropped.

Darius opened his eyes and grinned. "Got them!"

Carina cautiously stepped out of the bedroom. From her new vantage point two more guards were visible, one at each exit, with similarly vacant expressions as the first.

"Did you get the ones outside too?"

"I think so."

He probably had. Darius tended to underestimate the strength of his mind-blowing Casts. He'd most likely not only Enthralled all the guards for the next 24 hours, possibly inflicting mild though permanent brain damage, but also caught any nearby pedestrians in his blast. She'd been a little apprehensive about asking him to make the Cast, worrying she or the others might fall victim to friendly fire.

Ferne and Oriana went into the yard and, taking the Enthralled guards by the hand, led them into the house. Then the mercs relieved the guards of their weapons and pushed them into Parthenia's room, where they tied and gagged them all securely.

Now it was time for part three: to find and gather all the remaining captured personnel from the *Bathsheba*. This part was bound to be way more difficult.

Bryce knew where Rees and presumably other Black Dogs were locked up, but the big question was where were the rest of the Marchonish women? After hearing Bryce's explanation of what had happened to him and Rees, Carina was deeply concerned for their safety. Nahla had been plumbing the Sot Lozan net for information, with success. It was obvious that some of the people from the ship must have been taken to the third zone on Sot Loza, Bago, and she'd discovered an area where she suspected they were being kept.

"Now what?" asked Mads.

Bryce replied, "Now we go break your buddies out of prison."

"What buddies?"

"Rees, Harlow, and the rest. You know who I mean."

"They're no buddies of mine," Mads replied, grinning. "Maybe we should leave them there."

"I'll tell them you said that."

"Are we going to the prison now?" Darius asked.

Carina replied, "Yes, but you're staying here, remember?" It had been a hard decision to leave him and Nahla in the house with only Berkcan as protection, but they were unlikely to free the mercs without a firefight and she didn't want to put the younger kids in danger. If Sot Lozans discovered what had happened at the house and burst in, Darius could Transport himself, Nahla, Ava, her baby, and Berkcan to safety.

"I want to come!"

"It's out of the question, so don't bug me, okay?" She turned to the others. "Are you ready? Do we have the prison coordinates?"

"I can help," Darius said.

Carina sighed. "I know you can, but we can do this ourselves."

"I can Cast Heat."

She paused. "I didn't think of that."

"What's Heat?" Ferne asked. "Have you invented another Cast?"

His question went unanswered as Carina considered the possibilities. Darius waited for her answer.

"I can stay with Ava," Oriana offered.

"All right," Carina relented.

"Yay!"

"But you stick behind me at all times, okay? Now let's do this before the Sot Lozans catch on to us." She suspected the out-of-action guards and mysteriously empty cell she'd left behind had been discovered. The Una authorities would be checking recordings to find out what had happened.

"You didn't explain what Darius is talking about," said Bryce.

"You'll see."

———

It was impossible to be precise about where they appeared at the prison. The ideal spot would have been within its depths near the cells. They could have released the captured mercs and Transported them out of there without too much fuss. As it was, they materialized next to a set of elevators.

"This is the outer section," said Bryce. "We need to go that way."

Though the area was deserted, the sudden appearance of armed mercs and assorted children must have been immediately picked up by the prison staff. By the time they reached the lower depths, a defense of armed guards had been assembled. Carina spotted them first as she rounded a corner. A pulse round flashed past as she hastily stepped back.

"We know who you are," a voice shouted out. "You're the Outsiders who disappeared on Una. If you think you're going to rescue your friends, think again. Give yourselves up or those kids with you might get hurt."

"The only ones who'll get hurt are you guys," Carina replied. "We're in a hurry. Bring the prisoners out and we'll leave quietly."

"Not going to happen. You'll be taken and interrogated and, believe me, you won't like it."

They had to be wondering how she and the mercs had managed to move to the zone unnoticed, and how they'd appeared in the prison from nowhere. The speaker was also stalling for time. Guards would be on the way to attack them from the rear, sandwiching them in.

"Do your stuff, Darius," Carina said. "They're about ten meters away."

The great thing about her little brother was that, despite his incredible abilities, he was never cocky. He only seemed happy to please her as he drank elixir from his flask. She hated to think what such amazing mage powers would have done to someone like their Dark Mage brother, Castiel. The boost to *his* already hugely inflated ego would have been vast, and he wouldn't have hesitated to inflict even more horrors on the people under his control.

"Arghhh!" came a guard's cry.

"Shit!"

"Damn!"

The space resounded with the metallic clatter of many scorching-hot pulse rifles hitting the floor.

When Carina peeked again, the guards were disarmed and nursing burnt hands.

"What do we do with them?" asked Mads as he followed her around the corner.

She softly replied, "Wait until the kids are out of sight and then shoot them." It wasn't revenge, she told herself, just pragmatism. "We don't want them coming after us. You don't have to kill them, just incapacitate them."

Ola had heard her. "Feels bad to shoot someone who can't fire back."

"They've been keeping innocent mercs captive," Carina argued. "And you should have seen what Sot Lozans did to Bryce."

The guards put up a fight despite their burns, but the mercs quickly forged a safe passage for everyone with brute force and stayed behind while Carina, Bryce, and the kids went ahead. Soon, there was the hiss of pulse fire, shouts, and cries. Then the mercs caught up.

Bryce found his former cell and Carina Cast Unlock, revealing a surprised Rees. The mercs thumped and slapped him in their usual celebratory style, and then it was time to find more members of the band. The kids raced up and down the passages Unlocking all the doors in the vicinity, sometimes three or four at once. It was a risky tactic, considering they might be releasing dangerous Sot Lozan criminals too, but now that their captors knew they were facing something out of the ordinary, time was of the essence.

When they'd gathered all the mercs they could find, Rees asked, "Now what? We fight our way out?"

"No," replied Carina, "first you're coming with us on a little trip. Then you're going to help rescue Pamuk and the others trapped in Una."

THIRTY-SEVEN

Back at the kids' house, the guards remained Enthralled and no one from the Grantha authorities had turned up. But how much longer did they have before someone saw the children on the security recordings at the prison? They couldn't stay here any longer.

The place was full of rescued mercs. Carina began to wonder how she would deal with them all plus—hopefully—the ones still in Una and Bago. Her plans about what to do when everyone was rescued were hazy.

"On to Una next?" Bryce asked.

"Yeah, but..." She bit her lip.

"You're wondering if you can Transport all of us?"

"Exactly. I mean, we can do it, but it'll take time, and that's not exactly helpful for a surprise attack. Also, how will we get everyone to the ship?"

"I was hoping you had that part figured out."

"I barely had *this* part figured out. Stars, this is hard." Even if they got everyone to the surface the conditions up there were so bad they wouldn't last long. If they didn't find and fight their way aboard a shuttle fast, they would be weakened and recaptured. They would be back at square one *and* the Sot Lozans would know what they were dealing with regarding the mages, who would never be allowed near the ingredients to make elixir again.

They'd played their trump card. Now they had to win.

"We've topped up," Parthenia announced. "We have as much elixir as we can carry."

"I'm ready," said Oriana. "I don't want to miss out on the action again."

"Where's Pamuk and the rest of them?" asked Rees. "In another prison?"

Carina shook her head. "They jumped the gun and tried to make their own escape. The ones who survived must be in a medical center."

"*Fuck*," Rees breathed.

"We can Heal them but we have to get to them first."

"You know where they are?"

"Not exactly, but I know someone who does."

———

They arrived at Rano's house in batches. Carina Transported in first with Bryce and Rees. She appeared in Rano's living room, site of his drunken revelations about the history of his world. The waterfall played in the window space. There was the sofa where they'd sat. There were his ornaments. It was all horribly familiar.

"Whose house is this?" asked Bryce.

"Una's Chief of Security."

"You've been here before?"

He knew she could only Transport to somewhere she'd previously visited if she didn't have specific coordinates.

"I'll tell you all about it later."

Parthenia arrived, two mercs in tow. All Carina's siblings had become better mages since leaving the Sherrerrs, the regular meditation she'd taught them honing their powers.

Carina walked to the doorway and listened. Had Rano left for work? She wasn't sure what the time was in this zone. If he had, it would make everything more difficult.

Parthenia disappeared, leaving to bring more mercs over. At the same time, Ferne blinked into existence with two of the fighters. It was as if they were alighting from an invisible train.

Still, there was no sign of Rano.

She stepped to the stairs and looked up.

A figure moved quickly out of sight.

He must have heard them speaking.

She bounded upstairs. "Bryce! Rees!"

A door shut before she reached the landing. She turned on the spot. Which one had it been?

Bryce and Rees came running up.

"We have to find him fast before he can comm anyone." She ran for one door while the men headed for the other two. Her door slid open and there

Rano was, back to the window, his finger on his ear. His lips stopped moving and his eyes widened as she burst in.

Without breaking pace she hurled herself at him and drove her shoulder into his stomach. He crashed into the window, bounced off it, and they both slid to the floor. The heel of her hand thrust against his cheek, she held his head down as she dug into his ear with her other hand and popped out the comm.

"Who were you talking to?" she demanded. "What did you tell them?"

"Carina," he said, his speech distorted by the pressure on his jaw, "who are those people?"

Bryce had walked up and stood over them, hands on hips.

"You know who they are," she replied. "Tell us where you put the rest of my companions, here and on Bago."

"I don't kn— Arghh!"

Bryce had kicked his back. A chuckle came from Rees, who stood in the doorway.

"I think he might have got a comm out," said Carina.

"I know," said Bryce. He knelt on one knee and leaned close to Rano's ear. "We can inflict a lot of damage on you before your friends arrive, and, believe me, I'm in the mood for it. I'm the guy you came to see in hospital."

Rano's gaze roamed Bryce's face, shock permeating his features. "How...?"

"Where are the others?!" Carina yelled.

He closed his eyes and screwed up his face as if bracing himself for what was to come.

"You've seen something of what we can do. Arriving out of nowhere is only a part of it. Think about what else we're capable of. Think about what we'll do to those circulation fans on the surface, keeping the air moving and removing the radioactive gas, if you don't let us go. Think about what we'll do to the solar array. How do you fancy living with no power, slowly roasting in radiation? Do you really want to return your civilization to its beginnings, each day a struggle for survival? That's how it's gonna be if—"

"You can't do all that."

"Do you wanna find out?"

Resolve seemed to ooze from his body. Perhaps he'd concluded it wasn't worth the risk, that there were more people Sot Lozans could drag from space if these ones got away. He murmured a couple of names, adding, "The first is an Unan medical center, the second place is in Bago."

She released her hold. "Tie him up," she told Rees.

"My pleasure."

From downstairs came the noise of people moving about. The mercs and mages had continued to arrive. Picking up Rano's comm, she left Rees to deal with him and went with Bryce to talk to the mercs. The bulky men and women filled the living room and spilled out into the hallway.

She outlined the situation to them, continuing, "We have a limited number of mages to help free our shipmates, and then we need to get everyone up to the *Bathsheba*."

"We'll steal a shuttle," said Mads.

"No need," said Parthenia. "We can use Transport."

"For so many?" Carina questioned.

"If we do it in batches, like we did just now, we can manage it." Parthenia turned to her siblings. "Right?"

Ferne, Oriana, and Darius nodded enthusiastically.

"You did it before, Carina," said Oriana, "after we escaped the *Nightfall*. You moved us all to Ostillon. I couldn't have managed a Cast like that then but I can now."

"That was different. We were passing over the planet surface and I had to set you down randomly, not knowing where you would appear. We don't even know exactly where the *Bathsheba* is. If we miss our mark, whoever we're Transporting will die."

"I know where she is," said Nahla. "Her position was the first thing I looked up when I figured out how to read the Sot Lozan language."

"You're amazing," Darius said, admiration shining in his eyes.

She shrugged. "Honestly, it isn't very different from Universal. The ship's in geostationary orbit, or she was the last time I looked. I can check."

"You're my *best* girl," exclaimed Carina.

"Hey!" Oriana objected.

"You're all my best girls."

Ferne chuckled. "Me and Darius aren't."

Carina said, "Now we just have to figure out how to comm Van Hasty, Jackson, and Hsiao. I have to let them know we'll be there soon to help them take back the ship."

THIRTY-EIGHT

I
t was decided.

Bryce would take Darius and Oriana with him to Bago, while Carina would rescue the mercs at the medical center with Parthenia, Ferne, and Nahla. The Black Dogs split into two teams to go with each party. Then everyone would rendezvous on the *Bathsheba* as soon as their work was done.

As the most powerful mage, it seemed glaringly obvious that Darius should go to Bago, where the nature of the situation was opaque, yet Bryce was uncomfortable with taking the little boy away from Carina. She knew him best, especially his strengths and vulnerabilities. But the medical center job was likely to be straightforward and it made sense that Carina would be in the first group to return to the *Bathsheba*, when the fighting was likely to be heaviest. Though she was a mage she had also been a Black Dog and she worked well with the mercs.

"They're coming!" someone shouted.

Something heavy and solid hit the front door. The security chief's comm must have got through, and now his officers weren't wasting any time in coming to his rescue.

Carina grabbed Bryce and kissed him. "Good luck. See you back at the ship."

She took a drink of elixir then she was gone.

Another blow resounded from the door. It cracked at its hinges.

"Who should I Transport first?" Darius asked.

"Mercs," Rees answered. "We'll be ready with cover when you guys arrive."

Bryce nodded agreement.

Darius drank from his bottle and most of the remaining Black Dogs disappeared.

"Wow," said Oriana. "That was a *lot*. Now do the rest of us."

"Okay."

The door shattered and jagged splinters exploded. Armed men in uniform ran in—

Bryce was on a wide, dusty plain under a twilit sky. The atmosphere was cold and clammy. The mercs who had arrived before him were standing around looking confused.

As soon as Rees saw Darius he said, "You sure you got the right place, kid?"

"Uh huh. I Transported everyone exactly where Nahla said."

"She must have got it wrong," said another merc. "Or that security chief lied."

"Shit," said Rees. "What're we gonna do? Carina and the others will be at the medical center by now. Should we join them or go straight to the ship?"

"We can't leave," Bryce said. "We can't just abandon all those women."

It had been clear after the prison rescue that the Sot Lozans had sent half the Black Dogs to Una and the other half to Grantha. The Marchonish women apart from Ava had been sent to the third zone.

"I don't wanna leave without them," said Rees, "but we don't have a choice. No one's here to give us directions."

Oriana grabbed Bryce's arm and gazed up at him tearfully. "Those poor women. There has to be *something* we can do."

"I could Send to Carina and ask her," Darius offered.

"She'll be busy," Bryce replied. They had to figure this one out themselves.

He strode away from the group. One thing he'd noticed during the time he'd spent sleeping rough was that every surface not paved or decorated with artificial plants was covered in grooves, presumably marks left by the excavating machines. In this place, he couldn't see any grooves. The ground appeared natural. Flat, irregular rock covered by fine dust stretched as far as he could see.

"Oh!" Oriana, who had also wandered away from the group, had tripped and fallen. As she got onto her hands and knees, she said, "There's something here."

When Bryce joined her she was examining a round metal plate lightly covered in dust. He squatted down for a closer look. The plate was slightly raised from the surrounding rock. "Shit. We're at the right coordinates but the wrong depth." He stood up. "This must be some kind of natural cavern."

"Then where's the light coming from?" Rees asked.

Mads looked up. "The sky shining in through cracks, maybe? If it is, we need to leave, fast. This planet's hot with radiation."

"*That's* why everyone lives underground?" asked Bryce.

"It was Carina who found out. Darius, get us out of here."

"Wait." Bryce pushed the edge of the plate. It moved. He pushed harder and it slid to one side, revealing a hole with rungs leading down. "We can get in this way."

"I don't like it," said Rees.

But Oriana swung herself into the hole and began descending.

Rees spat on the ground. "What's up with the mage girl? Does she think she's invincible?"

Darius followed his sister.

"I'm going after them," said Bryce. "You can do what you like, but if you want to get to the ship you'd better stick with me and the kids."

"All right," Rees grumbled. "I was only worried about the radiation."

"Then come down here."

The shaft descended in utter darkness. They climbed downward for about five minutes before reaching the bottom, where the rungs disappeared and the tunnel turned at a right angle. They began to crawl, the line of mercs shuffling and complaining in the dark.

"What's this for, do you reckon?" Rees asked.

Bryce pondered. "Escape route to the surface?"

"Maybe an escape route *from* the surface," said Oriana. "It's very dusty, as if it hasn't been used in years."

"I'm sorry I got it wrong," said Darius. "I wish I knew how deep to go. Then I could Transport everyone there."

"Don't worry," said Bryce. "These goons could use some exercise."

There was a small thunk and another *Oh*! from Oriana. "I bumped my head. I think I reached the end."

"That's it?" Rees asked. "What do we do now? Go back? I can't turn around."

Oriana said, "I can feel a...a..."

A crack sounded, like a seal snapping open, and light from a widening chink flooded the tunnel.

"Careful," Bryce quietly warned.

Oriana's features were illuminated as she peered through the chink. "It's a facility of some kind," she whispered.

"Is there anyone around?"

"I can't *see* anyone. Should I climb down? There are indents in the wall."

"Let me look." Bryce squeezed past Darius until he was alongside her and took a peek.

They'd arrived at the edge of a large, circular room, surrounding an inner, round chamber. Everything—walls, floor, and ceiling—was clinically white and brilliantly lit by bright overhead lamps. The indents in the wall Oriana had spotted were the only dusty spots in the place.

The Marchonish women had to be in here, somewhere. Bryce's guess was they were inside the inner chamber. Why they were there and how they could be rescued, he wasn't sure.

"I want to go down," Oriana murmured plaintively.

"We should go in there and search," said Darius.

Bryce had misgivings but he had to agree. Something strange was going on and the realization only increased the imperative to put a stop to it. "I'll go first. Then Rees and Mads. Oriana and Darius, you come down after them. If we need any more mercs I'll holler."

He lifted the hatch and leaned it against the wall, then holding onto the edges of the opening he lowered himself through it, feeling for an indent with his toes. When he had purchase he climbed down, lightly jumping the last meter.

Rees and Mads were soon beside him. Oriana came next. Darius's head and shoulders appeared in the space.

"You have to go feet first," Bryce explained.

Darius frowned. He turned around and dangled his legs out of the hole, swinging them around randomly.

Bryce sighed. "Jump and I'll catch you."

The little boy dropped and he caught him under his armpits before setting him down and calling up quietly to tell the mercs above to close the hatch.

A second later a soft swish sounded. A door had opened somewhere out of sight.

There was no way of telling where the new arrival would go. Mads ran one way and everyone followed him. They huddled against the inner chamber wall as footsteps echoed nearby. Darius sipped elixir.

The footsteps paused. Had the newcomer heard them?

They started up again, coming closer.

Mads and Rees lifted their rifles.

Darius shook his head, mouthing *I Cloaked us.*

Bryce pushed the muzzles down.

A man appeared, his gaze sweeping the room. He looked directly at them but didn't react. Then he walked away. There was another swish and silence returned.

"Word must have arrived from Una," said Mads. "The security chief has told them to expect us."

"That man was definitely checking the area," Oriana agreed.

"So let's find those women and get out of here before he comes back." Bryce was already walking around the inner wall. On the outer wall on the opposite side of the room was the door the searcher had entered through, and facing it was the entrance to the chamber. It slid open at his approach. What he saw made him take a step back. The door slid closed.

He'd glimpsed a sight that set his heart racing in horror. As Oriana and Darius neared him he pushed them away. "Don't go in there."

"Why?" asked Darius.

Ignoring him, Bryce asked Rees to wait with the kids and took Mads in with him. Beds ringed the room and on them lay the women from Marchon, unconscious under bedsheets, drips running from their arms.

His fears about human experimentation seemed to have been realized. Had the women been impregnated? Or were the Sot Lozans only feeding them with artificial hormones in order to harvest their eggs? "We have to detach the lines and wake them up." He ran to the first woman.

"They're out cold," said Mads, approaching another victim. The strong man's voice trembled as he went on, "We'll have to take them as they are."

"Then let's make it look like they're sleeping at least."

Over the next minute the two men removed the medical equipment attached to the women. Bloody trails formed on the sheets but they covered up the stains as well as they could. When they'd done their best to improve the scene, Bryce let Darius in. The little boy's big brown eyes widened until the whites showed all around.

"It's time to Transport everyone to the ship," Bryce said. "Can you send the women first with some Black Dogs for protection?"

Who knew what was going on up there, but whatever it was it had to be better than life on Sot Loza.

THIRTY-NINE

"What the hell took you so long?" Jackson demanded. "You've been gone ages."

"Now isn't the time for explanations," Carina replied.

"Yeah," Van Hasty said, echoing Jackson's complaint. "Do you have any idea what it's like hiding for weeks on Deck Zero, living and sleeping in an EVA suit? Every time I needed to take a dump I had to—"

"Quit whining," said Hsiao, handing out ear comms to the new arrivals. "Carina's right. Save your bellyaching for later. We have a job to do."

Carina nodded her thanks. "Bryce and the rest of the Black Dogs should be here soon. What's the situation?"

They were in the storage area, where Jackson had taken them after she'd alerted him that she was back.

"Not too bad," he replied. "There are about fifty hostiles, but that's down from a couple hundred when they took her over. They spend most of their time on the bridge, though. That's where they are right now."

"The bridge? All of them?"

"I don't know for sure. It's hard sneaking around, you know." It wasn't like Jackson to be so tetchy. His irritation had probably originated in his fears about his shipmates.

The bridge was the worst place for an assault. The Sot Lozan crew would have ready access to all the ship's controls and the bridge had the best security, along with the engine room.

Yet she had Parthenia and Ferne with her as well as Pamuk—now Healed—

and many more mercs. Plus, they knew the *Bathsheba* inside out, unlike the thieves who had stolen her.

"We can do it," she said. "It'll have to be fast and smooth, but we can do it. Afterward we'll comb the ship for stowaways before we set off."

Van Hasty asked, "But what's to stop the other ships from firing on us when they know what's happening?"

"That's why we have to be super fast. The Sot Lozans now know we can Transport but it might take them a while to imagine we could travel all the way up here. If we had Darius with us he could have Enthralled them all at once before they got a comm out, but he's with Bryce. I don't want to wait for him to arrive. So speed is the word."

"Fair enough," said Jackson. "Let's hit the bridge."

Carina told Nahla and Ava to stay in the storage area until someone told them it was safe to come out.

Maneuvering on home turf was far easier than Transporting around an unfamiliar planet. The mercs quickly and quietly spread out and approached the bridge from different areas of the ship. If anyone encountered a Sot Lozan en route Carina didn't hear about it. The order was shoot to kill on sight. They were taking no hostages and showing no mercy.

A few minutes later, she was in the passageway leading to the bridge, repeating the plan to her siblings. Jackson, Van Hasty, and Pamuk would be going in with them. She opened her elixir bottle. "Ready?"

Parthenia and Ferne nodded. The mercs gripped their rifles.

She Cast.

As she opened her eyes, pulse rounds were already hissing out. The Sot Lozans hadn't been slow to fire as she and the others had appeared. Perhaps they had guessed they might have unwanted visitors. Parthenia and Ferne sheltered behind Van Hasty and Pamuk as instructed. She ducked behind a console.

Jackson took a hit and collapsed, but there was nothing she could do. She had to Cast again. She pinpointed the Sot Lozans nearest her, drank elixir, wrote the Enthrall character in her mind, and sent it out.

The hissing quietened but not entirely. As she looked out again, a round flashed past, hitting Jackson where he sprawled on the deck. His rifle lay by his side. His attacker, the remaining non-Enthralled Sot Lozan, ran for the exit. Jackson weakly lifted his prosthetic arm. The forearm opened and a barrel rose up. He aimed and fired, hitting the man in the back. He fell flat on his face between the opening doors.

Parthenia raced to the downed merc, gulping elixir. She might save him if she Healed him before he slipped away.

"Is that all of them?" Pamuk asked Van Hasty, shooting the man at the exit in the back again and finishing him off.

Van Hasty appeared to be taking a mental tally of the hostiles, dead, injured and still living. "Nearly, I'd say." She comm'd the other Black Dogs and told them to sweep the ship.

Hsiao peeked in. "Is it all over?"

"Bar the shouting," said Pamuk. She strode to a wounded woman trying to rise, put a boot on her back and pushed her down.

The pilot gingerly stepped over the corpse between the doors. "What are we going to do with those?" She nodded in the vague direction of the Enthralled Sot Lozans.

"Transport them to the surface, I suppose," said Carina. "Let them take their chances."

Pamuk said, "I vote we space them."

"I'm not a hundred percent against it, but as we haven't been attacked I'm guessing they didn't manage to send a comm. Another of their ships might notice little freezing figures floating in space."

"I don't think so," Pamuk countered. "Space is like really, really big."

"I'd noticed." Carina was wondering what had happened to Bryce. It had been some time since he'd gone to Bago with Darius and Oriana.

Jackson groaned and stretched.

"He's going to be okay," Parthenia said brightly.

Van Hasty grimaced. "Now he's gonna make us listen to his stories about what a big hero he is."

"I heard that," said Jackson.

"You were meant to."

Carina sent out a shipwide comm, asking if anyone had seen Bryce or anyone else they were expecting to arrive from the planet. In answer, she received a Send from Oriana. *We're back. Where are you?*

When she told her, Oriana said, *I'll Transport him to you. He wants to talk to you urgently.*

When Bryce appeared, his features were pale and riven with distress. "We have to use the Obliterator on that place, wipe it from the galaxy."

"What's wrong? What happened down there? Did you get the women?"

"We got them. They were... *shit*. I don't even know what they were doing to them, but we can't let them get away with it. We have to stop the Sot Lozans from hurting anyone else."

A pulse round hissed. Pamuk had shot the woman under her foot. "What?" she replied to their questioning looks. "I believe him."

Carina believed him too.

Parthenia must have seen her expression change to grim resolve. "You can't just kill these people in cold blood."

"If the roles were reversed," Carina replied, "what do you think they would do to you?"

Her sister clutched her hands into fists. "The roles *aren't* reversed. We don't have to be as bad as them. We can be better."

Bryce was shaking his head. "You didn't see what I did. If you had, you wouldn't say that. Those people have to be stopped. I don't care how."

Carina gave Van Hasty and Pamuk a look. They understood immediately and began to herd the ambulatory Sot Lozans from the bridge. Jackson got up to help them.

"Where are you taking them?" Parthenia asked.

Out of your sight. The mercs would be back soon to deal with the wounded. "Ferne, Parthenia, go and find Darius and Oriana. From the sound of it they'll need your help tending to the Marchonish women."

"But..." Parthenia objected.

"They do need you," said Bryce.

Setting her lips, she marched out with her brother.

Hsiao was at her console. "Luckily, those assholes haven't messed things up too much and they filled the tanks. I've reset the coordinates to Earth."

"Better get over to the Obliterator," said Carina. "We have a few things to do before we leave."

The pilot's eyebrows rose. "You're going ahead?"

"I don't think we have any choice if we want to leave with a clear conscience." She leaned on the back of Hsiao's chair. "They have a solar array feeding energy to the planet. Can you find it?"

"Hmm... Yeah, got it."

"Don't fire yet. They also have structures on the surface housing fans that keep the air underground sweet."

Hsiao searched. "Quite a lot of structures on the surface. Hard to tell what they are."

"The fan housings are probably made from lead to protect the service engineers from radiation."

"Ah, yeah. That kind of information helps. Got them."

"And then there's that big bitch that towed us here."

"How could I miss her?"

"She goes first, so she can't send out her beam, then the array, and then the fans. That'll put the Sot Lozans out of action for a long while and make them think twice about what they did."

"The rest of their ships could still come after us."

"If they're dumb, they might. If they're smart they'll concentrate on protecting their remaining resources."

"Whatever you say. Hey, shouldn't Chi-tang do the honors? He knows this machine better than—"

Carina slapped her forehead. "Chi-tang! I forgot all about him."

FORTY

T he noises in the dark bedroom were unmistakable. Cringing, Carina gave a small cough.

The noises didn't stop.

She gave a louder cough and pre-emptively covered her eyes with one hand.

A woman gasped. "Did you hear that? I think someone's in here."

"Someone *is* in here," Carina said.

There was a small scream.

"Chi-tang, I need to talk to you." She'd considered simply Transporting the man out of there, but the concept of free will bothered her. There was always the possibility that, despite what he'd said, Chi-tang might think he'd found True Love.

The light came on. There was another scream and the sound of rustling bedding.

Carina lifted her rifle and pointed it in the direction of the rustling, peeking between her fingers. "If you try to leave, if you try to comm, I'll shoot."

"Not me, I hope," said Chi-tang.

"Even you."

The pair had pulled the covers up to their chests, so Carina removed her hand from her eyes. "Chi-tang, we're leaving. You have now, this moment, to decide if you're staying or coming with us."

"Huh," said the young woman haughtily. "I don't know who you are or how you got in here, but he's *my* Outsider and you can't have him."

"I don't particularly want him."

Chi-tang looked hurt.

"Not like that anyway." She locked eyes with the pick-up from Lakshmi. "We're about to mess this place up, badly. I'm giving you fair warning."

"In that case…" He leapt out of bed and began hastily pulling on his pants.

"Where are you going?" asked the woman. "Don't believe her. She doesn't know what she's talking about. No one can hurt Sot Loza. No one."

"I'm sorry, my love, but they really can."

"But how?" Her gaze traveled from her lover to Carina. Something seemed to register. She announced, urgently, "I want to come with you."

Chi-tang picked up his shirt. "Err…"

Carina said, "You aren't invited."

"I'm sorry," Chi-tang repeated. "It's been wonderful, but I have to—"

The woman had grabbed him around the waist. "Don't leave without me. I want to come too."

"Not happening," said Carina, leveling her rifle and aiming at her head. "Back off."

But the woman gripped tighter and moved behind his back.

Carina.

She winced. Darius was Sending. Or, rather, he was blasting her mind apart with his megaphone Cast.

You have to come back immediately. Hsiao says the Sot Lozans are hailing us. If we're going to fire on them we have to do it now or they'll get their shots in first.

Okay, I understand. I'll be right there. "Dammit," she muttered, slinging her rifle over her back and opening her elixir bottle.

"Wait," said the woman. "I changed my mind. I want to st—"

Carina appeared on the bridge. Chi-tang and the woman were in the same position. His shirt was open and she was entirely naked as she clung to him. The bedclothes hadn't been included in the Transport. She squeaked and tried to cover herself with her hands.

Hsiao stared. "Who's *that*?"

"Don't ask."

"*Another* pickup?" Van Hasty's tone was scornful.

The woman was flushing furiously. "How did I get here? Take me back immediately!"

"Chi-tang," said Hsiao, "glad you could make it. You might want to guide me through this."

———

The Sot Lozans did the smart thing, for once. Their energy source destroyed, their population at risk of slow suffocation and radiation poisoning, they conserved their resources and didn't send their remaining vessels after the *Bathsheba*.

The ship's personnel spent the following weeks recuperating. Medics nursed the Marchonish women back to full health. The children returned to their usual games and antics. The mercs' banter reached new heights of obscenity, when no youngsters were around, as they recounted their experiences on the strange planet. Carina grieved Viggo Justus, a good friend gone too soon.

The time was approaching when the *Bathsheba* would be set on automatic and everyone would enter Deep Sleep.

One day, fears overwhelming her, Carina went to the Twilight Dome to be alone for a while. Their journey so far had been dogged by bad luck. Would they even make it? And if they did reach Earth, what would the planet be like? Yet they'd come so far and at the cost of so many lives, they had to go on. They had to try, and not only for their own sakes.

Ever since Nai Nai had taught her about the Star Map and explained that it showed the origin planet of all mages, Carina had hankered to go there. As she'd grown and learned about the persecution of her kind, her resolve had strengthened. Then, at the Matching on Pirine she'd met Magda, the Spirit Mage, and finally confirmed that Darius was a Spirit Mage too. Born once a generation, only these mages could bring the others together. Magda had died and Carina had taken Darius away. Without a Spirit Mage her people were lost. She had to try to find a safe home for them.

"I thought you might be hiding in here," said Bryce.

His arrival dissolved the anxious meanderings of her mind. She smiled, "Busted."

"You're escaping Chi-tang and Cheepy, right?"

"Not particularly. Are they fighting again?"

"Do they ever stop? I'm thinking maybe one or both of them should go into Deep Sleep earlier than the rest of us."

Carina chuckled. "I'm sure Jackson can arrange it."

"He might need to or Van Hasty will provide a more permanent solution." He sat down and put his arm around her.

She recalled the time he'd given her the mage love band he'd made for her. She'd never taken it off. "Bryce, I hope you aren't still thinking about us having kids, because that's a long way away, if it's ever going to happen."

"Kids? Don't worry. I like the ones we already have. Sot Loza kinda put me off the idea."

CARINA'S STORY CONCLUDES IN...

NEVER WAR

(Amazon.com link. For a link to your country's Amazon, scroll to the end of the book.)

Sign up to my reader group for a free copy of the *Star Mage Saga* prequel, *Daughter of Discord*, discounts on new releases, review crew invitations and other interesting stuff:

https://jjgreenauthor.com/free-books/

(If you don't receive an email, check your spam folder.)

DOWNLOAD YOUR FREE READERS' GUIDE TO THE SCIENCE FICTION NOVELS OF J.J. GREEN

Untitled

NEVER WAR

ONE

Wet. Groggy. Cold.

Carina opened her eyes and immediately started shivering. She'd been through this same scenario countless times over the years, but the repeated experiences didn't make it any easier. She couldn't see a thing. A blurry veil shrouded her vision. Yet she knew what she was looking at: the inner wall of the Deep Sleep chamber she had stepped into three years previously—she hoped it was three years, and that nothing had gone wrong to shorten or prolong her time in stasis.

"How do you feel?"

Bryce.

She remembered he'd been scheduled to wake up a week before her. "I can't see a thing."

"I'll wipe your eyes."

She felt a soft cloth move over her eyelids. When she opened her eyes again she could make out his dark figure leaning over her.

He took her arm. "This way, ma'am. Your carriage awaits."

She chuckled as she climbed out of the chamber, his grip steadying her. He wrapped a blanket around her and she sat in the a-grav medic chair. Bryce would take her to sick bay for a checkup and then she would spend the next few days recovering. Her digestive system would start functioning again and her heart would become accustomed to beating at its normal rate, not the beat-per-hour of Deep Sleep. Stasis Dreams—wild, colorful escapades of her imagination, impossible scenarios, fantastical creatures, visions of people long dead

—would fade from her memory. They were already slipping away. Providing she suffered no permanent after-effects, in less than a week she would be entirely back to normal, as if she hadn't spent years unconscious, leaping forward in time.

How different this was than her first experience of Deep Sleep, when the Regians had taken over the ship and put Lomang and Mezban in charge. Then, she'd been hauled from her chamber, freezing and slippery, by the giant, Pappu. And the Lotacryllans had killed Cadwallader in cold blood, before the man even had the chance to wake up.

She bowed her head.

Bryce put a hand on her shoulder. "Thinking about Cadwallader?"

She nodded.

He squeezed her shoulder.

It was the same every time. Whenever she woke from Deep Sleep she was reminded of the lieutenant-colonel's death, though it had happened decades ago and light years across the galaxy.

So many had died. Atoi, her long-time merc comrade, Jace, the wise, patient, kind mage who had helped her so much, Stevenson, the *Duchess*'s pilot and her port in the stormy sea of her youth, Viggo Justus, the honorable Lotacryllan, Calvaley, the former Sherrerr officer, Halliday, who had protected Darius with his own body during the glider crash on Magog, and Captain Speidel, who had been like a second father to her. There had been more deaths. More than she wanted to recall.

Had it been worth it?

Bryce hadn't said anything. He was probably waiting for her to come around fully before he gave her the news. The mind took time to adjust during the first days after Deep Sleep and facts would slip in and out of memory.

She would find out the news soon enough. Yet even if they'd succeeded, on a deeper level her question had no answer. Cadwallader, Atoi, Stevenson, and Halliday had been Black Dogs who knew the risks of the lives they'd chosen. Viggo and Calvaley had been military men too. Jace had been a civilian, but he'd also been a mage, and the mage creed was that they helped each other, always.

Was her goal worth the sacrifice of those who had helped to achieve it? She didn't know the answer and never would, no matter what happened.

Fogginess invaded her thoughts and she slipped into a doze.

When she woke again she was in sick bay and people near her were talking.

"*Shhh!* Oh, look, you went and woke her up, just like I said you would."

"Sorry, Carina."

She smiled. Her brothers and sisters were standing around her bed. "It's all right, Ferne. No need to tell Darius off. It's good to see you all again. Is everyone okay?"

How time had changed them. During the periods they'd spent out of Deep Sleep on the long journey, everyone had aged. Tracking the passing birthdays during long-distance space travel was impossible, but Darius had grown to a young man, dashingly handsome and as sweet-tempered as ever, while Nahla was about twenty and very serious. Ferne and Oriana were in their mid-twenties. As they'd gone through puberty Ferne had shot up but Oriana had stayed the same height—a fact Ferne enjoyed reminding her about frequently. Parthenia had moved into her thirties and had grown to resemble their mother so much that sometimes the sight of her gave Carina pangs of grief.

"We're all fine," Parthenia said. "I was allowed out of bed this morning. How do you feel?"

"Good." Carina pushed herself upright. "I could almost say I'm getting used to Deep Sleep."

"Don't say that," Darius warned. "You'll jinx it and we'll have to do it again."

"No way," Oriana whined. "I'm never getting into one of those chambers again. It's like dying, and you never really know if you'll wake up."

Though the risk of dying was small it was one of the dangers of Deep Sleep. Sadly, one time they had lost a Black Dog. It was a big relief to know Bryce and her siblings had been successfully revived.

"So," she said, "is anyone going to tell me what's happening? Did we make it?"

Darius was about to say something but Parthenia interrupted him. "Before we answer that, we have something to show you. I'll just check with Clarkson that we can take you out."

The doctor grudgingly gave her permission. However, she stipulated that Carina was not to walk anywhere due to the danger of falling and hurting herself. The a-grav seat was employed once again to take her out of the bay and into an elevator.

"Where's Bryce?" she asked as they ascended.

Nahla replied, "He's with Hsiao, Jackson, and Van Hasty on the bridge. They're going over the scan data. It's *very* interesting."

Naturally, Nahla must have been examining the data too. She might have changed physically over the years but she had remained as inquisitive as ever, to the point of positively snooping.

"In what way is it interesting?"

"We can talk about that when you're back to normal," Parthenia replied. "What we're about to show you will be enough for today."

They were going to the uppermost deck of the *Bathsheba*, and Carina knew exactly what that meant. Excitement began to build in her stomach.

The elevator doors opened and, surrounded by her siblings, she maneuvered her chair down the passageway. They halted outside the doors to the Twilight Dome. How often had she been here, looking out at the starscape? So many events had taken place in the space beyond those doors.

They went inside.

The lights were out. The only illumination was the starlight shining in through the transparent roof.

Except stars were not the only things shining out in the velvety blackness of space. She moved to the center of the room and looked up.

"It's beautiful, isn't it?" Darius whispered.

Hsiao had positioned the ship so the object occupied the middle of the wide view.

A sapphire and emerald orb swathed in pearl-white clouds sat among the stars.

"Yes, it is," she breathed.

It was the most beautiful planet she'd ever seen.

Earth.

Two

"Hey, Lin. You look like shit." Van Hasty's greeting as Carina stepped onto the bridge made her smile. "You look worse. Did you spend the past five years awake?"

"Nah, I only feel like I did."

How old was the merc now? She had to be in her early forties. The long voyage had weighed heavily on the Black Dogs. The military men and women hadn't dealt well with years of inactivity. They thrived on action and risk, yet there had been little else to do since leaving their last port of call, Sot Loza, except spend time with other people—not their greatest strength.

Carina's family had fared better. They'd grown up, developed their self-identities, and honed their skills. They were ready for whatever new adventure awaited them on Earth.

"Don't pay any attention to her," said Hsiao. "You look great."

Carina slid into a seat at a console and opened the screen. "Where are Bryce and Jackson?"

"Checking for signs of damage."

"Did something happen while we were in Deep Sleep?" The chances of an asteroid strike were tiny but not non-existent.

"There aren't any reports but it doesn't hurt to get a visual."

She brought up the files of data pertaining to Earth. "So, what do we know?"

"A lot," the pilot replied. "Too much, almost. Have a look and you'll see what I mean."

The scan data *was* interesting, as Nahla had said. The most interesting thing about it was that it went back thousands of years. The *Bathsheba*'s scanners had been detecting attenuated, garbled comm signals light years before the ship arrived in Earth's system. Earth was *old*. She recalled a meeting with Jace and Cadwallader after the taking of the *Bathsheba*, where, with Jace's help, the lieutenant-colonel had calculated seven thousand years had passed since mages left Earth. The data completely fit in with his guess.

Seven thousand years since her ancestors had left? It was an impossibly long time to imagine. Hundreds of generations of mages had lived and died, and she and her family were the first to return. What would they find?

The stories of the mages leaving told of pitched battles as the non-mages tried to force them to stay and fix the problems humanity had created for itself: a volatile climate, constant war, poverty and suffering for the vast majority of the population. But all the people could offer in return for the mages' help was persecution and servitude. They'd had no choice except to take advantage of the newly developed interstellar starship engines and depart, seeking worlds where they could live in freedom without fear.

And look how well that turned out.

"What do you think?" asked Hsiao. "What's the plan?"

"Stars, give me a minute."

There was no plan. Their actions depended upon what they found upon arrival, and what they'd found was almost too much information to digest.

As the *Bathsheba* had neared her ultimate destination, the data had become clearer and more recent, naturally. Over the long years, the ship's computer had done an excellent job of analyzing the language and translating it to Universal. Carina searched the media broadcasts, personal conversations, entertainment shows, company communications, and educational programs for mentions of mages. There weren't many, but there were some. However, everything she read or heard pertained to the fabled image of her kind—mages were imaginary beings from fairy tales, something akin to witches and wizards. There was no mention of Casting except in relation to casting a spell. She saw nothing about the Characters, and the only references to elixir related to something called the Elixir of Youth.

It was all nonsense. Had humanity entirely forgotten about the real mages they'd driven away millennia ago? It seemed impossible. She felt she was missing a clue.

"Are you going to sit there all day?" Hsiao asked. "Decisions need to be made, Carina."

She straightened her back and stretched out her arms, noting with surprise she'd been going over the data for a couple of hours. Before she could answer, the bridge door opened and Bryce and Jackson walked in.

"Glad to see you're finally paying us a visit," said Jackson. "Your bed got uncomfortable?"

She rolled her eyes as Bryce leaned down for a kiss. "Everything shipshape?"

"The old girl's holding up well," he replied. "Just a few scratches still self-repairing on the hull."

"Did you run an armaments check?"

"Does Pamuk fart like a horse? All checked and ready for action."

"Let's hope it doesn't come to that." Her brief dive into the wealth of data about Earth indicated it wasn't steeped in military conflict. Aside from some minor, civil wars, the planet seemed relatively peaceful. Of course, information about defense capabilities wouldn't be available for cursory inspection.

"Come on, Carina," said Hsiao. "How are we going to do this? You've had the entire voyage to think about it."

"Introduce mages to Earth? That's going to take some thinking about."

"No, I mean where am I to park this ship? She isn't exactly petite or hard to notice. Anyone watching the skies will pick us up soon, if they haven't already."

"Ahh, I see what you mean. I'll ask Darius to Cloak us."

"Will that work?" Bryce asked.

"We'll try it. He can't Cloak the *Bathsheba* indefinitely anyway. Someone's going to notice us eventually. We'll just have to deal with it when the time comes. Hsiao, I can see that Earth has a large, tidally locked moon. After Darius has Cast, take us to the far side. We can hide there while we figure things out."

"Got it."

Carina Sent to her youngest brother to make the request.

Now they'd finally arrived at their destination taking the next step felt hard. She'd been focused on getting here, fighting to overcome all the obstacles that had stood in their way. Their actual arrival in Earth's system seemed anti-climactic and the days ahead foggy and obscure. She'd wanted to find a place where mages could live in the open without fear. Then they might finally be able to use their powers for good, to improve the state of humanity. But how to get to that point was a mystery.

As if sensing her anxiety, Bryce said, "One step at a time."

She breathed deeply and exhaled. "Yeah, one step at a time."

———

Over the thousands of years that had passed following the mages' departure from their collapsing home planet, Earth's climate had stabilized, the cities had regrown, and technological development seemed to have resumed. The human population stood at three and a quarter billion—the largest of any world Carina had ever known. No single power or organization governed the planet as far as she could tell from the data. Even if there were a single entity to approach, she wasn't sure if that was wise.

As the *Bathsheba* hung in geostationary orbit on the far side of Earth's moon, she pondered the facts over and over, the weight of her predicament growing heavier and heavier day by day, until one day at the start of an active shift Darius came to see her in her cabin. Bryce had gone to breakfast and she was listening to the computer's translation of the latest broadcasts from Earth, trying to make sense of what she was hearing.

He leaned in at the open doorway and immediately her heart lifted. Though she loved all her brothers and sisters equally she shared a special bond with Darius, first forged when she'd rescued him as a frightened child, tortured by Dirksen thugs. He was tall now, taller than Bryce and Ferne, but to her he would always be that little boy who had entrusted an anonymous young merc with his life.

"Hey, Carina. I saw you weren't at breakfast."

"Not hungry. How are you doing? Come in and talk to me. I'm sick of listening to this nonsense from Earth."

He smiled at her invitation and sat next to her on the bed. "What nonsense is that?"

"Ugh, I don't know. It's a news channel, but I can't make head nor tail of who they're talking about or why. What have you been doing?"

"Well..." he paused and looked at her from under thick, dark brown bangs "...I've been waiting."

"Waiting for what? Oh, you mean..."

"Yeah. We're all waiting for you to—"

"Decide what happens next." She grimaced. It was embarrassing. In all the years it had taken them to journey to Earth, she'd had plenty of time to think through the possibilities of what they might find and come up with strategies to meet her goals, but now she was here she had nothing to suggest.

Darius said, "Maybe we should just go down there and see what happens. We could do that re...re... That thing the military does."

"Recon. Yeah." Reconnaissance would definitely be a good idea. There was only so much you could learn listening to broadcasts. In fact, lately she'd found the practice left her more confused than enlightened. Getting boots on the ground would reveal a whole lot more about human society on Earth and what mages might reasonably expect in terms of treatment.

Sending a team to the surface was the obvious move, but something held her back.

Darius asked softly, "Are you worried about what might happen?"

"Uhh..."

When her youngest brother asked questions like this, they were rhetorical. Though he couldn't read her thoughts—or at least he'd never admitted to being able to do it—it was no secret that he knew how she felt. He knew how everyone in his immediate proximity felt. As a Spirit Mage he couldn't help it. No one liked to mention his ability because it made everyone uncomfortable, including Darius, but they all knew it.

"I guess I am a little worried," she confessed. "So many people died to get us here," she continued, her voice catching in her throat. "What if it wasn't worth it? What if there's nothing for us on Earth? We've come so far, lived out so many years just flying through space. Most of your childhood has been spent on a starship..." Her words petered out.

Darius wrapped an arm around her shoulders. "And I couldn't wish for a better one. I've grown up among the people I love. What could be better than that? Do you think I would have had a better time living with my father?"

She sniffed. "Good point. I'll let you have that one."

"You know, I think Mother would be so proud of you. Look at everything you've done. You saved her children from the Sherrerrs, and you've done everything in your power to protect us, even to the extent of stealing a colony ship."

"It wasn't *exactly* stealing," she demurred, in an effort to lighten the mood. Their mother was never far from her thoughts.

He went on, "And you've brought us halfway across the galaxy to find us somewhere safe to live, somewhere we can be ourselves. Mother couldn't have asked any more from you, and neither do we. Neither does anyone on this ship. We all know the dangers, Carina, and if we didn't accept them we wouldn't be here. We're with you, come what may."

She was silent.

"So you're sending down an away team today?"

She swallowed. "Do I have a choice?"

"Maybe you can choose who's going to be in it."

"Thanks."

"To an extent."

THREE

The argument had been going on too long.

"Ferne and Oriana," Carina snapped, "you're staying here, and that's the end of it. There will be plenty more opportunities to visit Earth. Heck, hopefully one day you'll live there and you will have all the time in the world to explore, but for now we need mages aboard the ship."

"So let Parthenia and Darius stay," Oriana whined, pouting.

Carina had seen that pout many times over the years but familiarity didn't make it any less irritating. "Parthenia is the oldest and most experienced of all of you, and Darius is the best at Casting. That's why I've picked them and whether you agree with it or not, that's my decision."

"Leave it, sis," Ferne said irritably. "You won't change her mind. You know what she's like."

What I'm like?

Darius said, "I don't mind sitting this one out if it'll make things easier."

"It won't make anything easier," Carina replied. "You're coming."

"And I suppose Bryce is going too?" Oriana asked.

"Bryce is in the away team, yes. I suppose you don't like that either."

"Figures."

"Leave it, Oriana!" Ferne repeated.

"Nahla isn't coming either," Carina said. "She isn't complaining."

"Nahla's more interested in analyzing all the data from Earth," Oriana retorted.

Ferne tugged her sleeve. "Let's go and find something else to do."

"We've done everything there is to do around here," Oriana objected, "a thousand times over. I want to walk on grass again, feel the wind, and look up into a blue sky."

"And you will," Carina said, softening. Everyone on the *Bathsheba* felt the same. Though the ship was vast, living aboard it didn't compare to being planetside, and no one had been planetside in a very long time. "The next time the shuttle goes to Earth, you'll be on it. I promise."

Oriana turned and left the bay without saying another word. Ferne said, "She'll be all right soon enough. She's just bored. That's all."

"I know. I understand."

"Good luck, everyone." Ferne also left, passing Bryce as he entered.

"What's up with Oriana?" Bryce asked. "She gave me her death glare in the passageway a minute ago."

Parthenia replied, "She's just being herself. Who else are we waiting for, Carina?"

"Hsiao's flying us down. Jackson and Pamuk are on their way too. Van Hasty's going to keep an eye on things here while we're gone. I thought it was best to keep the team small. The more people we have the greater the risk of someone getting into trouble. When we have a better idea of what to expect we can increase the numbers."

"Do we have translators?" asked Parthenia.

"Oh, yeah. I was forgetting." Carina handed out the devices, which hung around the neck.

Bryce asked, "Do *they* have translators? Or are they going to think these are weird?"

"They do, but the ones I've seen in vids clip to the ear. I couldn't get the printers to fabricate them. These will do."

Bryce fingered his doubtfully. "What about clothes? Aren't we going to stick out?"

"We're going to stick out regardless. It will look more suspicious if we try to blend in and fail spectacularly. People will wonder what we're trying to hide."

"Right, so what's our story? You weren't planning on announcing we've just arrived from outer space, surely."

"I'll go over it on the way there."

Hsiao walked into the bay accompanied by Pamuk. The two looked comical next to each other. Pamuk dwarfed the petite pilot by half a meter and was brawny while Hsiao was slight. Carina was not a small woman herself, but the female mercs made her feel that way sometimes. She vividly recalled the burly merc simply lifting her out of the way when she tried to prevent her from leaving their residence on Sot Loza.

Pamuk was picking her teeth. "Jackson not here yet?"

"He's on his way," Carina replied, recalling Bryce's remark about the merc farting like a horse. She hadn't met many horses in her time but his observation was spot on. And she was about to share a cabin with her. Perhaps Van Hasty would have been a better choice. But there were few people she felt comfortable entrusting the *Bathsheba* to while they were gone.

Jackson arrived.

"We're all here," Carina said. "Let's go and take a peek at Earth."

"Hold on," said Jackson. "I've been checking the manifest. Thought you could use an update on supplies and so on."

"Good idea, but I'll take a look later. I've put off this trip long enough."

He continued, "I also wanted to make sure everyone was accounted for before we left. We're two people down."

She blinked. "That isn't possible. How could we have lost two people over the last leg of the voyage? I mean, even if the computer hadn't recorded something happening to them, they would have been missed by now."

"I've passed on the information to the medics. I guessed they must still be in Deep Sleep, and I've a good idea who they are."

"Who? Ohhh..." She cringed. She'd entirely forgotten the people in question too.

Bryce chuckled. "It's Chi-tang and Cheepy, right?"

"Bingo," Jackson said.

Their two 'pickups'—one from Lakshmi Station and the other from Sot Loza—had been nothing but trouble. Separately, they were bearable, Chi-tang more so than Cheepy. Chi-tang was their resident expert on the *Bathsheba's* primary weapon, fondly nicknamed the Obliterator. In some ways he was quite smart, though not in the area of human relationships. Cheepy was a spoiled rich girl. As Chi-tang's first girlfriend, she'd made a split-second decision to accompany him to the ship before Carina had rained hell on her planet.

Despite the fact that her decision had probably been wise she'd regretted it, loudly and at great length, ever since being Transported to the *Bathsheba's* bridge. She mostly blamed Chi-tang for her predicament and, after immediately breaking up with him, had hounded him with her complaints ever since.

The Black Dogs were seriously lacking in the compassion department. Although Cheepy's presence on the ship wasn't exactly Chi-tang's fault, the mercs blamed him for having an annoying ex-girlfriend. Consequently, the two had been sentenced to far longer periods of Deep Sleep than everyone else had to endure, and, it seemed, now the *Bathsheba* had reached her destination, no one had wanted to wake them.

Carina said, "The medics will get on it while we're gone. Chi-tang and Cheepy will be up and around soon."

"Awesome," Pamuk commented. "Something to look forward to when we get back."

FOUR

Darius Cloaked the shuttle all the way down, making them invisible to detection. Carina had picked a small town on one of the larger continents as their first experience of human society on Earth. The town's population was around 20,000. She hoped this meant it wouldn't possess the high-tech monitoring that city authorities used for security, yet it also wasn't a tiny, backwater place where newcomers would attract immediate attention.

Hsiao set down in a clearing in the forest that bordered the town. They had arrived in the early morning. The sun was just rising, and the shuttle's scanners told them no human-sized life forms were about for kilometers around, though the vessel's descent spooked some large specimens of local wildlife grazing in the open space. Perhaps the animals sensed by instinct that an object was approaching from above. Once the vessel was down they covered it in a camouflage blanket Carina had printed.

After they had hammered in the spikes that held the blanket in place, she took a few steps back to assess the results.

The blanket wasn't entirely effective viewed from the side. It worked by deflecting the light hitting it, guiding the waves around the object it covered. So at first glance the clearing looked empty but it was also faintly blurry or smudged. An aerial view was probably more convincing, and that was what really mattered. Satellites and passing aircraft would soon spot a starship shuttle that had appeared from nowhere, but the chances of hikers or hunters stumbling upon the shuttle were low.

"It's not too bad," Bryce commented.

"It'll have to do."

"Let's go meet some Earthlings," said Jackson.

They shouldered their packs, containing water and food supplies, and set off, leaving Hsiao to wait for them at the shuttle. They were unarmed. Earth seemed generally peaceful and civilized, and the last thing they wanted to do was to get into a firefight. In the event of a conflict they would walk away. The mages could Cast them out of trouble if things got dicey. The object was to not attract attention.

The forest was cool, humid, and quiet. Large ferns and small, thorny shrubs covered the ground between the trees. Carina had mentally debated the possibility of Transporting everyone closer to the town, but she didn't dare risk someone spotting them materializing out of thin air. Without a good knowledge of exactly where they would be Transporting to it was a real possibility.

There was no trail nearby. Forced to push through the undergrowth, they were soon dirty, sweaty, and scratched by thorns. If their unusual clothes didn't attract attention when they reached the town, their appearance surely would. It couldn't be helped.

They headed downhill, trying to seek out a water course. They didn't find one, but they did hit upon a path of sorts, leading through the trees and roughly in the right direction. They were nearing areas frequented by humans at last.

Darius kept lagging behind, and after calling a halt for the fifth or sixth time to allow him to catch up, Carina grew irritated. She told the others to wait for her and stomped back up the path to find her brother.

He was standing still, a hand resting on a tree trunk as he gazed upward at the canopy.

"Darius," she snapped. "What are you doing? You're slowing us down. We don't want to be walking back through these woods in the dead of night."

"We can Transport back to the shuttle," he said simply, his attention remaining on the tree.

"Well, yes, but..." she spluttered. "What *are* you doing?"

"It has feelings, you know."

"The tree?"

He gave her a 'what do you think I meant?' look, but only said, "They're faint, but I can feel them."

"Right." She regarded the tree. "How does it feel?"

"Calm, and..." he frowned "...content."

"I guess that's how a tree *would* feel. If you're done communing with the vegetation, it would be great if you could join us."

"Sure."

"That was a little mean. Sorry

."

"It's okay, sis."

They walked down the trail, Carina going in front. It occurred to her that Darius had spent more than half his life aboard a starship. This was his first experience of a natural environment in a very long time. She said over her shoulder, "If you want to do that kind of thing—talking to the trees, I mean—I don't mind, but we're in a hurry today."

"I wasn't talking to it."

"Whatever you want to call it, it's fine, but—"

"I get it, Carina."

They caught up to the others and continued the trek. The woodland began to thin out. A place for eating picnics appeared ahead of them, ten or twelve wooden tables with benches dotted about and a children's climbing frame in the center. No one was here, however.

Then, beyond the trees, Carina spotted her first Earth dwelling. She pointed. "Look."

The habitation seemed to be *made* of earth too. Thick bricks of what looked like dried mud formed the walls of the single-story home. The roof overhung the walls, and it was alive. Living plants grew all over it. In some areas vines dangled all the way to the ground.

"Should we knock at the door?" asked Jackson. "Introduce ourselves as visitors from outer space?"

"Quit kidding around," Carina said.

It was mid-morning. The sun had risen above the trees and was shining through the open window shutters of the house. She couldn't spot anyone, which implied they also hadn't been spotted.

"I don't understand," Parthenia said. "I thought Earth was quite techno-logically developed. That house looks very simply constructed, and there are no power lines running to it."

Jackson replied, "You'll get many different levels of living standards on a planet. That place only represents one of them."

Bryce, who had walked away from the group to take a look from a different angle, asked, "Is that a well?"

"No electricity *or* running water," Parthenia commented.

"Let's head farther into town," Carina said.

They took a route that led them around the house and mostly out of sight of it. A wide dirt track ran down a slope from the forest and through low scrub. Beyond it was the town proper, though it was difficult to spot at first. The reason for this was the fact that the roofs of all the town's habitations were similarly covered in green plants, causing them to blend into the landscape. What gave it away was the regularity of the houses and roads laid out in a grid.

They saw their first people of Earth, riding bicycles or walking.

"Where are the cars?" asked Parthenia.

There were none.

"Well, one thing's for sure," said Jackson, "we aren't going to look weird for walking into town."

"Someone's coming," Bryce said.

Six people were approaching up the track. It was not a family group. They were all adults, and their clothes were similar. All wore dark blue slacks and a white top. Carina was confused. Were they wearing a uniform? There was sufficient variation in their clothing to imply it was not, but the similarities were too great to be random chance.

"What do we do?" Bryce asked. "Run? Fight?"

"Speak," Carina said. "We speak to them. This is a fact-finding mission, remember? We aren't doing anything wrong so whoever those people are they shouldn't be a threat. We stick to the story. We're from a remote island they probably never heard of, on vacation, just walking through the woods. I'll do the talking."

When the leading woman in the party arrived within speaking distance, she called out to them.

Carina's translator repeated the words in Universal: "Hello. Welcome to Earth. You're under arrest."

FIVE

Carina ran.

Among the many conversations they'd had during the flight down, one thing they'd agreed was that if they were attacked, they were to split up and meet back at the shuttle. Hoping the others remembered the plan, she raced for the trees.

The police—or whoever those people were—didn't have weapons out, so she might reach cover before any of them got a shot off.

She thudded through the long grass, shouts of *Stop! Wait!* echoing in her ears. There was also the sound of a scuffle, as if someone had been caught. Guiltily, she hoped it was Jackson or Pamuk, who were used to being manhandled. Hell, after the interminable, boring voyage, they might even enjoy it.

The trees were only meters away.

She might make it.

"You!!" a voice directly behind her called. "I order you to halt."

Oh, sure. Anything you say.

She reached the shade of the canopy. She'd nearly made it. Once she was in the forest she would be much harder to hit.

There was an explosive sound—not a detonation, but more like a discharge with force—something flashed across her vision, and suddenly her arms were pinned to her sides and her legs forced together. She fell, face forward, onto the dirt.

Pounding footsteps came to a stop next to her head. "You should have listened and done what you were told," the voice complained. "This is completely unnecessary."

Carina's cheek pressed into the prickly woodland floor and her hair had flopped over her eyes. All she could see was empty nut shells from the tree and the boots of her captor. Her limbs were tightly pinioned. She guessed her assailant had fired some kind of entrapping device. Her arms and legs felt as though they were tightly wrapped. Perhaps what she'd seen had been the cords or ribbons flying around her body.

"Wait here," the voice said. "I'll be back for you in a minute."

Like I have a choice about it.

Over the years, as Bryce and she had grown into the familiarity of a long-married couple, though, technically, they weren't married, he'd grown sufficiently comfortable to tease her about her magehood. Whenever she screwed up, such as by programming the printer incorrectly and creating a disgusting dinner, he would say something like *Being magic didn't make you a great cook, did it*? Or if they were doing target practice and he beat her, he would patronizingly comment, *Never mind. One day you'll learn how to Cast a great shot.*

That was the thing with non-mages. They imagined being able to Cast was some kind of cure-all, a fix for each and every situation. But there were so many limitations they didn't take into account. Here on Earth, she couldn't risk Casting in front of the natives. The whole point of being here was to find somewhere safe for her and her family. They couldn't reveal their secret without risking the beginning of the whole slavery-and-torture cycle that mages in distant parts of the galaxy devoted their lives to avoiding.

But even if she could openly Cast here, how could she possibly drink elixir, create the Transport character in her mind, send it out, and wait for it to take effect, in the time available before she was captured? Running away was the faster, more effective, and pragmatic solution.

Not that it had worked this time around.

The boots returned. "Right. Let's get you on your feet." A hand grasped the back of her shirt and helped her stand upright.

She was staring into the face of a sandy-haired, hazel-eyed young man, roughly mid-twenties. Like the other Earth men, his hair reached his shoulders and he was clean-shaven. Most of the men on the *Bathsheba* had given up on shaving regularly. Even Bryce had a short beard.

"Where are my companions?" she asked, peering over his shoulder. She caught a glimpse of a group being led away, but only heads and shoulders were visible as they descended the slope.

She looked down. Her body from her chest to her knees was encased in thin, transparent threads.

"Is that a translator around your neck?" The man leaned closer. "If I free your legs, do you promise not to run? There's no point. I'll just catch you again with this." He gestured at a box on his belt. "It won't be fun to plant your face in the dirt again, will it? You might get hurt."

He reached toward her face. She flinched and pulled back.

"Take it easy." He brushed her cheek and nut shells that had embedded in her skin dropped to the ground.

For a law enforcement operative, he was being excessively polite.

"I'm not promising anything," she retorted. "Let me go. You've got no right to hold me captive. I haven't done anything wrong."

His eyebrows lifted. "That translator is so cool. I've never seen one like that before. I'd love to take a closer look at it but we really need to go now. I'm going to free your legs. Please don't run. I'd rather not hurt you."

He took a short knife from a sheath in his belt and slit the threads enveloping her thighs. "It's only a short walk to the station. You go in front, where I can keep an eye on you."

She might have been able to get away from him. She could have kneed him in the balls and fled into the forest. But there was no way she would be able to cut the threads around her torso by herself, and it was a long trek back to Hsiao at the shuttle. She also had no idea where the captured members of her party were being taken, and she clearly stuck out as a stranger. Somehow, the man knew she wasn't even from Earth. Rescuing her companions could be impossible in the circumstances.

She stepped in the direction of the trail.

"Glad you're finally seeing sense," the man said as he followed her. After a few more steps, he added, "So, where are you from?"

"What makes you think I'm not from Earth?"

"Huh? Oh, you mean what the sergeant said." He chuckled. "You don't speak English, so I guess she must be right."

The situation was becoming more and more bizarre. English had to be the name of their language.

"So what if I don't speak English?" she said.

He chuckled again. "Most people speak English. Except you and your friends, that is. I mean, I'm not saying there's anything wrong with it, but you can't deny it. You must be from offplanet."

They had walked down the slope, giving her a better view of the group ahead. Darius, Parthenia, and Bryce had been caught. Pamuk and Jackson must have got away and would be heading back to the shuttle.

"I know what you're thinking," the man said. "You're thinking we didn't catch all of you. But we will. It's only a matter of time."

"Where are you taking us?"

"You'll wait in the lockup until the magistrate arrives. He has the final decision on what to do with you, but you'll probably go to the central court in Bridgeford. After that, who knows? The capital, I suppose."

"But we haven't done anything wrong," Carina protested.

"You're illegal aliens, from outer space of all places! I'm sorry, ma'am. I didn't write the laws, but it's my job to enforce them."

"How did you know we were here?"

"Sensors in the woods, of course."

"They detect people? Aren't people allowed to wander around in there?"

"Absolutely. I go up there all the time with my friends. But you triggered them."

"How?"

"Like I said, you're illegal. Set off the alarms."

"But how?"

"You'll have to ask a technician. I don't know how they work. How did you end up in the forest?"

She didn't answer. As they drew near the group in front, Parthenia looked back and her face fell. She must have been thinking her eldest sister had escaped and might help her, Darius, and Bryce out of their predicament. Carina gave her an apologetic smile.

They caught up to the group and Darius also noticed her. "Oh, no. Not you too."

"Don't worry. Everything's going to be fine."

Bryce smirked.

They were escorted into town. It was an odd place. For a human habitation it was remarkably alive. The roadways—or perhaps it was better to describe them as pathways as no motorized vehicles ran on them—were paved, but everywhere else was green and growing. Grass surrounded each building, but it couldn't be described as lawn. The blades grew fifteen centimeters tall and other low-growing plants dotted the sward, some in flower. Shorter plants covered the roofs. Even the walls were growing surfaces, holding pockets of trailing vines.

Carina asked her affable law enforcement officer, "Why is everything so green?"

"What do you mean?"

"There's vegetation everywhere."

He frowned. "Why wouldn't there be?"

They passed through the open doorway of an official-looking building. A sign in English hung over the portal, but naturally she couldn't read it.

A woman in blue and white sitting behind a desk rose to her feet as they entered. "The aliens! Well, isn't this something? What are those things?" she asked, pointing. "Wait, I understand." She marched over and lifted Carina's translator to her lips. "What's your name?" The device converted her words to Universal. Without waiting for a reply, she laughed. "I love it." She stared Carina in the face. "Say something."

"Uhhh..."

The translator didn't repeat the utterance, and the woman's features expressed her disappointment. "Does it only work one way?" she asked Carina's captor.

"No, it works both ways. We had a little conversation, right?" He turned to Carina for confirmation. "Go on, say something for the sergeant."

In a tone of amazement, she asked, "This is your *superior*?"

When her translator conveyed her words in English, the sergeant's eyes grew hard, and she gave a cough before straightening her jacket. "Put them in the cells. I've notified the magistrate and he'll be here shortly."

As Carina and her companions were led away, the sergeant said, mockingly, "Take me to your leader." Then she burst into fits of laughter.

Six

There were only two cells, and one was already occupied. A man in ragged clothing lay on his back on the bunk, snoring loudly.

"You don't mind all squeezing in together?" the officer asked, "only I don't want to wake Brian up. You'll be cozy."

Carina stared at him while he ushered them into the cell. He cut the threads binding their upper halves, stepped out, and closed the door. She tried it, wondering if the kindness of their captors extended to not actually locking them in. It didn't open—probably magnetically sealed.

"You have to admit," Bryce commented, "for local law enforcement, they're pretty nice."

"Nice enough to imprison us," she muttered.

Darius sat down on the bunk, which was suspended from the wall on chains. "So...do we Transport?"

"Shhh!" She scanned the ceiling, walls, and floor, and bent down to look under the bunk. Though she didn't find any security devices, she remained unconvinced they weren't being monitored. Pretending to take a sip of water because she was thirsty, she swigged elixir, and then Sent to Darius and Parthenia: *No Casting. We don't know who's watching or listening, and we definitely don't want anyone to guess we need our elixir. They'll know all they have to do to control us is to take it away. We use Transport to escape only as a last resort.*

Her brother and sister signaled their understanding with their eyes, and Bryce clearly knew what had passed between them. He'd been a member of the family so long, little needed to be explained to him.

Their incarceration almost immediately after setting foot on the planet was definitely a setback, but it wasn't necessarily a disaster. For one thing, the authorities didn't seem to know where the shuttle was. If things got dangerous, they could get back to it. Pamuk and Jackson were probably already on their way there. In the meantime, the fact-finding mission could continue, though somewhat more restricted than she would have liked. She had already learned a lot. Earth natives seemed to be obsessed with natural environments, to the extent they grew plants everywhere they could squeeze them in. And their police service was remarkably friendly and casual. Nothing made much sense but maybe things would become clearer later.

She said, "Let's wait for the magistrate the sergeant mentioned. Maybe we can find out from him or her exactly what we're supposed to have done wrong."

The cells were down the corridor from the station entrance. She pressed her face against the transparent wall, angling for a look at what was going on. The wall that separated the cells area from the rest of the station was transparent too, but she didn't see much except a couple of police officers passing to and fro.

"Sit down," Bryce said. "We've been walking all morning. You must be tired."

"I'm fine."

Parthenia snapped, "You don't have to be on guard all the time, Carina."

She ignored her. The years they'd spent on the *Bathsheba* might have dulled her siblings' sensitivity to the dangers mages faced, but they hadn't dulled hers. She also had a sense of desperation that wouldn't allow her to relax her vigilance. If her family was to ever find a safe place to live, this was their last shot. She couldn't screw up.

Activity in the reception area increased. Several officers ran to the door, and there was a struggle as someone was brought in. Shouts and exclamations resounded dully through the barrier.

Darius got up and joined her. "What's that? Is something going on?"

"They've caught someone else, I think."

"Who?"

"I can't see. I only got a glimpse."

"Is it one of the mercs?"

"Maybe. Whoever it is, they're putting up a hell of a fight."

As they'd been talking, the sound of furniture banging about joined the noises of the altercation. Frustrated by her inadequate view, Carina pushed her face harder into the wall. Naturally, it didn't make any difference.

Three figures approached, the central person being held and dragged by the other two.

"It's Jackson."

Judging by the blood trickling from his scalp, the merc had been subdued by a blow to the head. He seemed barely conscious as he was forced to walk the distance to their cell.

"Stand back," one of the officers ordered. It was the man who had captured Carina. His affable demeanor had disappeared. He was pale and looked shocked. She guessed most of his prisoners were more compliant than a Black Dog who hadn't been in a fight for too long.

As they crowded into the far side of the cell, Jackson was brought in.

"He is one of your companions, right?" the officer asked. "Only, he's very dangerous." With the help of his colleague, he laid Jackson down on the bunk.

"Yes," Carina replied. "He's our friend."

"A friend? You should know, he killed someone. But he won't hurt you, I suppose?"

"No, he definitely won't."

The officer seemed relieved. He nodded to his fellow and they left the cell. With the door closed, he continued, "The doctor is on her way to take a look at him. If he comes around and turns violent, give a shout. The cells are monitored. Someone will definitely hear you."

So there *were* hidden surveillance devices.

As soon as the officers had left, Jackson swung his legs over the edge of the bunk and sat up, ruefully rubbing the back of his head.

"You shot one of them?" Bryce asked.

"Had to." He surreptitiously touched his prosthetic forearm, which concealed a weapon. "Didn't help in the end, obviously. That stuff that wraps around you is really effective."

The officers who had finally caught him must have thought he'd thrown his gun away. Someone was probably searching for it in the woods even now.

"They seemed astonished," Parthenia said.

"More like appalled," said Carina. "I get the impression this is a very peaceful society." It boded well for her aims, but if she was right Jackson was in a lot of trouble. They'd all become used to violence and death, moving on from one battle or conflict to the next. What were the repercussions somewhere these things weren't commonplace?

Parthenia dabbed at his wound with the hem of her shirt. "I would help, but..." She glanced at Carina.

"Don't worry," the merc growled. "I get it."

"Where's...?"

Jackson shrugged. So Pamuk, at least, had escaped. The monitors the officer had mentioned couldn't be placed throughout the whole forest or she would have been picked up. It was a shame neither she nor Hsiao were mages and couldn't receive Sent messages.

The man in the cell opposite stirred, moving his legs weakly. He turned onto his side and promptly fell off his bunk, hitting the hard floor with a thud that made it through two walls. While he was staggering upright, the officer returned.

"Now then, Brian. Take it easy. Get back into bed." He leaned nonchalantly on the wall, peering at the inmate without particular concern.

"Wanna go home," Brian slurred.

"You're not ready yet. Get some more sleep."

"I wanna go home." He thrust his hands into his pants pockets and rested his chest on the barrier. "The missus will be wondering where I am. Give me the shot and I'll be on my way."

To be fair, Brian did appear to be sobering up by the second.

"You know the law. Drunk and disorderly gets you twelve hours' jail time, for your own safety as much as everyone else's. You've only been here seven hours. You've got five hours to go."

"Come on, Matt. Give me the shot and no one will be any the wiser. I need to get home to the missus."

"You can comm her."

"If I comm her she'll know where I am."

It seemed an odd comment. Maybe comms were easily traceable here.

"Have a word with Betty," Brian went on. "Go on. Do a man a favor."

"Oh, all right."

"That's what I like to hear."

As the officer left to 'have a word with Betty', Brian noticed his fellow inmates. He stared, his bleary eyes sharpening their focus while his jaw slowly dropped.

Darius gave him a small wave.

He pulled a hand out of his pocket and waved back, his mouth continuing to hang open.

The sergeant—Betty?—appeared. She cast a dark look at Jackson before turning to the opposite cell. "Matt tells me you're agitating to leave, Brian. You know that's against the rules. What'll happen if it gets out that I let you go before your time was up?"

"But it won't get out. I won't tell a soul, I promise."

"Hmm... You'll give me your word?"

"Cross my heart and hope to die."

"And you'll attend the recovery course we booked you onto?"

"I'm looking forward to it. I've been wanting to turn over a new leaf for a long time."

"Okay, you can have your shot, but if I see you back here again you'll have to serve twenty-four hours. Do you understand?"

"Clear as crystal, Betty."

But before the sergeant could follow through with their agreement, she was called back into the reception area.

Her expression was grave when she returned. A man in late middle age walked behind her. Ignoring Brian, who watched with interest, Sergeant Betty said, "Here they are. They're all yours. Good luck with them." Gesturing at Jackson, she added, "That one's the murderer."

SEVEN

The handcuffs were made from a similar material to the cords the officers used to bring down suspects who were running away, except they locked. Officer Matt snapped the transparent bracelets around Carina's wrists.

"You're armed now," she commented.

He was carrying a handgun in a shoulder holster. "Uh-huh." He didn't look at her as he moved to Parthenia to put on her handcuffs.

Another officer—a beefy guy they hadn't seen before—had apparently been assigned to Jackson, who was hobbled as well as handcuffed. His wrists were behind his back too, while the other prisoners' hands were secured in front of their bodies.

"Why are you armed?" Carina persisted. "You weren't before."

Matt nodded at Jackson. "Courtesy of your friend here. The *murderer*," he added, shaking his head.

"I take it you don't see a lot of dangerous criminals."

He didn't answer her. His attitude toward her and her companions had changed. The friendliness was entirely gone and he wouldn't even make eye contact. The magistrate waited outside the cell with Betty, watching the prisoners being prepared for transfer. They were to go somewhere for a preliminary hearing. No one had explained any more than that.

"What did they do?" a voice called out.

Brian's release had been delayed by the magistrate's arrival, and he remained in his cell. He was craning his neck, trying to see around Betty. "Who are they? Did one of them kill someone?"

"Be quiet," said Betty over her shoulder, "or I'll make you wait for that shot."

"I was only asking!" Brian protested.

Two more officers waited with the magistrate and Sergeant Betty. With Jackson's minder and Matt, that made four. Despite the fact they were transporting a *murderer* the authorities still hadn't thought it necessary for their officers to outnumber the criminals.

They were led from the cell in single file, Matt in front. The man assigned to Jackson walked beside him, and the remaining officers brought up the rear. They took them out of the station. A crowd had gathered. Word appeared to have gotten out that some unusual criminals had been taken into custody. The people seemed to be local townsfolk, and they gawped in the usual way, obviously enjoying the fact they had something new and interesting to gossip about.

Bryce commented, "We're famous."

"But not in a good way," said Carina.

Parthenia muttered. "So much for remaining inconspicuous while we investigate Earth society."

Carina had expected to see a vehicle awaiting them, but there was only the crowd, which had spilled onto the road. Bicyclists were being forced to dismount to navigate a passage.

"Break it up," Matt ordered. "Nothing to see here. Move along, please!"

The people ignored him.

He tutted, elbowing a particularly nosy man aside as he forced his way through the throng.

"Stand back!" Jackson's guard commanded. He had greater success. The onlookers shuffled backward a few steps, murmuring and pulling faces.

"Where are we going?" Carina asked Officer Matt's back.

"Where do you think?" he snapped, without turning.

"How would I know? I'm new around here, remember?"

"Bridgeford."

The crowd followed them down the street, attracting new members.

"Why don't we go by car?"

He threw her an annoyed look. "We *are* going by car."

A cry like that of a warrior going into battle came from somewhere beyond the crowd. The people surged, pushed forward by those behind them. Some stumbled into the prisoners. Jackson's minder yelled and shoved at them, warning them to move back.

"What's going on?" Bryce asked.

Jackson said, "I think I recognized that—"

A burly figure pelted through a gap and crashed into Matt, shoulder to shoulder, felling him like a bowling pin.

Pamuk.

"I got you!" she hollered. "Carina! Bryce! Everyone, this way!"

Carina was frozen with shock. They were surrounded on every side, and the officers escorting them were armed, and Jackson was hobbled. Where did Pamuk think they were going?

The prisoners looked at each other uncomfortably.

"Come on!" Pamuk rammed the nearest people. "Get out of the way. Come on, guys!"

Carina half-heartedly followed her into the passage she was forcing, more out of sympathy and solidarity than any hope of escaping. Bryce came with her, his face a picture of secondhand embarrassment.

Jackson's guard pushed past them and laid a heavy hand on Pamuk, spinning her around. She threw a fist, smacking into his jaw. He staggered and drew his weapon. The crowd tried to move out of the way, tripping and falling into each other.

Carina jumped on his back, lifting her handcuffed wrists over his head and wrapping her legs around his waist. "Pamuk! Run!"

Hands clutched her, trying to rip her off the guard.

Pamuk grabbed at the gun, tugging hard. The guard fell forward, and everyone went down. Whoever had been holding onto Carina landed on top of her. She could feel the burly guard underneath her, arching his back as he tried to get up. Where was Pamuk? She had to be on the bottom of the pile.

What if the guard fired? Pamuk could be killed. And if she wasn't killed right away she would be injured and the mages would have to Heal her in front of everyone or let her die.

"We surrender!" Carina yelled, her face pressed into the guard. "Don't shoot!"

"I don't surrender!" Pamuk's voice was muffled but her words were clear.

"Yes, you do!"

"No way. Get off me you great lummox!"

"She doesn't mean it."

"Yes, I do."

The pressure on Carina's back lifted and she could breathe again. Hands fastened around her waist and hauled her to her feet. The guard managed to climb to his feet. As he did so, Pamuk appeared to finally realize the hopelessness of the situation. She leapt up and turned to run. But Officer Matt—the person who had picked Carina up—was already reaching for his belt, though not his gun she was relieved to see.

The crowd had scattered. Matt had a clear shot, and Carina had her first clear view of the device that had been used to bring her down out in the forest. Long, liquid lines spurted from the black box, gaining solidity in the air as they went. The ends touched the fleeing Pamuk and then the rest of the lines whirled around her, wrapping her up like a spider wrapping a fly.

She toppled to the ground. But even that didn't stop her from trying to get away. She wriggled on her stomach, inching forward.

The other officers had corralled Parthenia, Darius, Bryce, and Jackson together and were holding them under threat of being shot. Matt rubbed a bruise on his head that must have been sustained when he fell.

Jackson's guard dealt with Pamuk. He walked over to her and put one boot on her back. "Where do you think *you're* going?"

The merc cursed. She was so loud and vile Carina was silently thankful Darius was just about a grown man. The guard fiddled at his belt and brought out a pair of handcuffs and a small knife. Slitting the threads nearest Pamuk's hands, he freed them sufficiently to draw her wrists together behind her and fasten the cuffs around them. Then he cut through the remaining threads, grasped her shirt at the neck, and jerked her to her feet.

"Thanks a lot," she said sarcastically. The remark was addressed at Carina.

"Hey, I was the one trying to save you from being shot."

"I was the one saving *you* guys! Why didn't you run when I told you?"

"Because how in all the hells would we ever have got away?!"

The guard barked, "Shut it. Both of you. Matt, you watch this one and her, right?" He meant Pamuk and Carina. "I'll take the murder suspect. Let's go while we have space to move."

The bystanders were regaining their confidence and approaching again.

The situation was bizarre. Why were they walking along a street, out in the open? In her time as a merc and even afterward, on all the worlds she'd visited, she'd never encountered such lax security. Perhaps Pamuk's idea that she might be able to free them wasn't so insane. If she'd been armed and had a vehicle, she might have done it.

"So where is this car you're taking us to?" Carina asked Matt as they continued.

He didn't answer her only snapped at the people in his way. Considering he was an armed police officer, they seemed surprisingly unafraid.

They approached a wide, open entrance. Tape had been strung across it at waist level, and the other side was empty. Matt halted and lifted the tape, telling Carina to go under it. When everyone in their group was on the other side, he warned the crowd that anyone who attempted to follow would be placed under arrest. Some of them seemed tempted, nonetheless.

They stepped onto an escalator that descended to a lower level.

"Hey," Carina said.

Matt, who stood on the step below her, didn't turn around.

"Hey." She poked him with a finger.

"Carina," Bryce warned.

"Don't worry. He's a nice guy. I can tell."

Bryce rolled his eyes.

"Officer Matt, I thought you said we were going by car."

"We are. That's enough questions."

The escalator ended at an open, tiled space. Carina got the impression it was a public space, but that the public were being excluded for the moment. They followed Matt under one of several archways and halted. They were standing on a station platform.

"We're going by *train*?"

"How else would we go?" Matt asked in return. "Here comes our car now."

A railway car sped toward them, borne along on the single rail track.

EIGHT

"Let me get something clear," Carina said, "you don't have vehicles that run on roads on the surface?"

They had the carriage to themselves. Long lines of seating ran down each side. It seemed to be a regular model for public use that the police had commandeered for transporting the prisoners. Matt sat between Carina and Pamuk, Jackson's minder sat next to him at the far end of the car, and the two remaining officers flanked Darius, Bryce, and Parthenia.

"I said," Matt replied testily, "that's enough questions."

"But we're from offplanet, remember? How do you expect us to learn about Earth if you won't tell us anything?"

"Not that again. Be quiet."

Pamuk's nose was bloody from where she'd hit it on the ground. As she wiped it on her sleeve, Matt glanced at her, and then fished in the top pocket of his jacket. He pulled out a tissue and dabbed at the blood.

Pamuk's eyes grew wide and her mouth fell open.

Matt folded the tissue in half and dabbed some more with the clean section.

"Wh-what the stars are you doing?" the merc stuttered.

Carina chuckled. There was nothing that could alarm a Black Dog faster than someone being nice to them.

"Seeing to the welfare of my prisoners," Matt muttered. "What do you think?"

Pamuk stared at Carina as if to check she wasn't imagining things.

Across the carriage, Jackson guffawed.

"Quieten down!" snapped his guard.

Jackson stifled his mirth. Matt put the tissue away, and Pamuk relaxed. Lights in the tunnel sped past. There was little sound, only the rush of air as they sped along the tunnel.

"How far is it to Bridgeford?" Carina asked.

Matt replied, "We'll be there in a few minutes."

"So, not far. Does everyone get around like this?"

He heaved a sigh. "Yes, everyone gets around like this. You're trying to tell me it's different where you're from?"

"What about freight transports?" said Jackson's guard. "Maybe that's what she means."

"Oh, the overground system. You mean going by freeway?"

"I don't know," Carina replied. "Do I?"

Matt said, "Heavy loads of freight are sometimes transported on freeways. The network is a little more extensive than rail."

"But what about people? Don't people travel by road?"

"I suppose people could go that way too, hitching a ride. But I don't know why anyone would."

"Can't they travel by themselves?"

"How would they do that?"

"In cars."

"But we're in a—"

"Not this kind of car. One that goes on roads."

"I don't know what you're talking about. I think we must do things differently on *Earth*. Where are you from, by the way?"

In some ways, it was a hard question to answer. "You wouldn't have heard of it."

"Maybe not, but it must have a name."

She told him the name of the impoverished, backwater planet where she'd grown up, two galactic sectors and a lifetime away.

"You're right," said Matt. "Never heard of it."

———

At the Bridgeford stop—the train ran straight through several intervening stations—the immediate area had been made off-limits to the public. The news of their arrival must have traveled ahead. A crowd pushed against a temporary barrier erected around the station exit.

"Do criminal suspects usually receive this kind of attention?" Carina asked Matt.

"The interest is all on account of your friend there." He jerked his chin at Jackson.

"So there aren't many murder cases?"

"First local one I've heard of. I don't think there were any in my parents' time either."

Pamuk whistled. "You guys live in a fairy tale."

"Is it like that all over?" asked Carina.

"People generally don't go around killing each other. Is that what it's like where you're from? What a horrible place."

Carina began to worry about what might happen to Jackson, given that his crime was so rare. Judging from the expression on the man's face, he was worrying about it too. Killing a pursuer was a reflex action for a merc. She'd lost count of how many people she'd killed in her days with the Black Dogs. She'd killed a fair few subsequently too.

Did the crime carry a death sentence? If the worse came to the worst she would Transport Jackson to safety, regardless of whether that entailed revealing her powers.

At the edge of the cordoned-off section stood four armed men and women, wearing uniforms the same as Matt's. He made the prisoners wait at the station exit while he talked to them. When he returned his expression was glum.

"Sad to say goodbye?" Carina asked.

"I've been seconded to the NPS—National Police Service—apparently, for an open-ended period, due to my 'familiarity' with the prisoners." He huffed disconsolately. When his colleague, Jackson's guard, laughed, he added, "So have you."

The man's face fell.

"You two can go back," Matt said to the officers guarding Bryce, Darius, and Parthenia. "This way." He gestured for everyone to follow him.

The Bridgeford Police Force appeared to be more respected than the one in Matt's town. The crowd stayed back as they walked to the detention center. However, the town itself didn't seem very much different from the place they'd just left. Carina guessed they had to be in the central district, but none of the buildings were taller than two stories, and they were all verdant, with green roofs and trailing plants dangling down the walls. Some vehicles passed by that were larger than the bicycles they'd seen in the other place—covered three- and four-seaters and some pulling trailers—but all were pedal-powered.

"I like it here," Darius commented to Carina. "Don't you?"

"To be honest, I'm still trying to wrap my head around the place."

Parthenia said, "Darius, only you could be literally wearing handcuffs and on your way to a place of incarceration to await an unknown fate, yet still see the positive side."

"I quite like it too," said Bryce, glancing around. "The air's clean and I like seeing plants everywhere. It feels like we're in the countryside even downtown."

"I suppose it *is* nice," said Carina, "but it's also weird. You're forgetting the sensors in the woods. What kind of government monitors their citizens to *that* extent? You can't even go for a picnic without the authorities knowing about it? I wouldn't like to live like that, with zero privacy."

Matt had overheard her. He said over his shoulder, "Those sensors are there to track kids who wander away from the picnic site. The government doesn't keep tabs on everyone's movements. Why would they?"

"Then how come you picked us up?"

"You're not chipped and clearly not from around here."

"Is it so obvious we're offworlders?" Carina repeated.

Matt's open, honest features creased into a confused expression. "I-I'm not sure."

Jackson's guard leaned close and whispered in his ear. Matt nodded and said firmly, "No more questions."

They arrived at the detention center. After climbing the steps into the building, they passed through two sets of double doors, each requiring a security check from two of the local police officers. Two guards stood on the inside of the inner doors. They scanned the right hands of all the officers before allowing them and the prisoners to pass.

The Bridgeford Police led them downstairs to a lower section, where a woman in uniform sat at a desk. "Murder suspect first."

His guard brought him forward and removed his handcuffs and hobble, she told Jackson to empty his pockets and place everything on the table.

Carina threw Parthenia and Darius a look.

Their backpacks with their supplies remained at the first police station and Jackson said he wasn't carrying anything. His guard confirmed this.

"Search him again," said the woman.

The guard patted him down thoroughly. "He's clean."

Except for the gun in his forearm.

"All right. Put him in cell five." As the guard led him away the woman looked at Carina. "Her next."

Matt brought her over and took off her handcuffs.

"All personal items on the table."

Uh oh. "Can I keep my water? I'm thirsty."

The woman glared at her. "All personal items on the table."

Carina hesitated, taking stock. She could possibly Cast in time to Transport everyone out of here, all the way back to the shuttle. Or she could create a diversion that would allow Parthenia or Darius to do it. But that would give the game away. No doubt their images had been recorded. Casting in front of all these people would give them a rep that would follow them all over the planet.

"If you refuse to comply," the woman said, "this officer will remove the items for you."

With a heavy heart, Carina unfastened the belt that held her elixir canister, folded it, and put it down. Then she pulled from her pockets the sundry bits and pieces she carried to help her Locate her siblings and also placed them on the table.

"That's it?"

She nodded.

The woman scooped everything into a bag then got up and walked around the table. After giving Carina a cursory search, she said to Matt, "Cell nine."

He led her away, taking her to the last cell in the row.

"Are they splitting us up?" she asked.

"They don't mess around in Bridgeford."

Shit.

She and her companions wouldn't even be able to communicate. Being captured on their first day on Earth was bad enough. Now things were getting worse. "We'll see you again, though, right?" The friendly officer might be their only chance of escape.

He grimaced. "I'm sure I'll be around."

The cell door opened. The interior was tiny, just a bunk and a small cupboard. How long would she have to spend here awaiting her fate? Matt's comment about the authorities being on the lookout for offworlders had deeply unsettled her, though she couldn't put her finger on the reason.

"In you go," said Matt, lightly touching her back.

She resisted and glanced up the corridor to where Pamuk's handcuffs were being removed prior to her being processed by the woman at the desk.

"Where's Jackson?" she asked.

"The murderer? Cell five. But you won't be able to talk to him. You have to go inside now." His voice had a slightly pleading tone to it, as if he was reluctant to force her.

"But where exactly is he? I just want to know."

Matt pointed at the blank door diagonally opposite. She spotted the tiny 5 above it.

Memories of Sot Loza were flooding back. Her confinement on that planet hadn't been as bad as it had been for others from the *Bathsheba* but it had been bad enough. Before that the Dark Mage on Magog had tried to trap the mages in his palace. Earlier, the Regians had captured them to turn them into living meals for their offspring. And, in the very beginning of this crazy adventure she'd been living ever since rescuing Darius, the Dirksens and the Sherrerrs had wanted to enslave her and her siblings. There was always someone trying to deprive her and the people she loved of their freedom.

No more.

Matt said, more firmly, "Into the cell, n—"

She slammed her elbow into his stomach. Air exploded from his mouth and he doubled over. She sped down the corridor, hoping he wouldn't be able to shout for a few seconds. Racing into the admissions room, she dove for the bag of her belongings behind the desk, yelling to Darius and Parthenia, "You know what to do!"

She caught a glimpse of Pamuk throwing herself on one of the officers and Bryce attacking the other. Jackson's guard seemed to have left. She got hold of the bag, but the Bridgeford officer snatched it at the same time. They wrestled, the woman yelling at her to let go. Carina managed to open it. She shoved a hand in. Her fingers closed on the smooth, hard elixir canister. She pulled it out, relinquishing the bag. The woman flew backward and landed on her backside. Instantly, she leapt up and ran at Carina, who performed a high kick, connecting with her jaw. The woman's eyes rolled up and she keeled over.

Despite being handcuffed, Darius and Parthenia had managed to drink elixir and were Casting.

"Get away from those people you're fighting!" Carina yelled at Bryce and Parthenia. She unscrewed the lid of the canister and took a swig.

"Hands up!" Matt must have got his breath back and followed her.

She was writing the Character in her mind. Unsure of who Parthenia and Darius were Transporting, she included Bryce and Pamuk. You couldn't over-Transport someone, so it didn't matter.

"Everyone, put your hands up," Matt repeated, "or I'll shoot."

The Character was written. She sent it out.

The last thing she recalled before the Cast took effect was someone grabbing her arm.

NINE

"Not again!"

Carina opened her eyes. She was back in the forest, next to the clearing where they'd concealed the shuttle. The Cast had worked and she'd escaped imprisonment.

"First Cheepy, and now him," Pamuk complained. "Can't you be a bit more careful?"

She turned around and came face to face with Matt, who had the look of someone suffering a large and unwelcome surprise. *Damn.* Her Transport had carried him along with her. "Sorry about this."

"What the...?" Pale and sweaty, he turned a circle, gaping. "Where am I?"

She checked everyone else had made it before reassuring him. "Don't worry, I didn't bring you far. You can probably walk home from here."

"No, he can't," said Bryce. "Parthenia, could you Unlock me?" He was still wearing handcuffs.

Parthenia replied, "In a minute. I have to do my own."

"I'll do all of us," said Darius.

"Why not?" Carina asked Bryce. "We're back in the—"

"Think."

Matt knew exactly what they'd done, or if not exactly, he knew they'd done *something* to move themselves and him kilometers across the landscape. The other officers back at Bridgeford Detention Center had only seen them disappear. That was bad, though a better alternative than being locked up. But Officer Matt knew more—too much, in fact. "Oh, yeah."

He seemed to be coming to the same understanding, for he was beginning to slowly edge away from the group.

"You should hang around here for a while," Carina said.

Three sets of handcuffs opened and fell to the ground.

He seemed to suddenly recall he had a gun. He lifted it and pointed it at her, then pointed it at each of them in turn, all the while backing up toward the trees.

"Stay here with us," Carina said. "I promise no one's going to h—"

He ran.

Pamuk raced after him only a few steps behind, her boots thumping into the soft leaf litter, and Bryce followed. All three disappeared under the overhanging branches. Loud rustling and the sound of twigs breaking came from under the canopy, and flashes lit up the shadows as Matt fired.

"He won't get away," Parthenia remarked.

"No," Carina agreed.

A corner of the camouflage sheeting over the shuttle lifted and Hsiao emerged. "I thought I heard talking. I wasn't expecting you back so soon. How did it go?"

"Terribly," Parthenia replied.

Darius said, "It only took us a couple of hours to reveal our abilities."

"I think that must be a record," said Hsiao. "Where are the others?"

"Long story," Carina said. "Pamuk and Bryce will be back soon with a visitor. Meanwhile, I have to retrieve Jackson." She swigged elixir.

"Where from?"

"Jail." She closed her eyes.

"Not his first time, I bet."

"Probably."

"Good luck," said Parthenia.

Darius added, "Be careful."

She was within the confined space of Jackson's cell. The merc lay on his bunk, hands behind his head. "What took you so long?"

"I've only been gone five minutes! Stars."

"Where did you go?"

"Back to the…" Her lips snapped shut and she cast a glance around the cell. "Get ready."

Jackson swung his legs over the edge of the bunk and got to his feet.

The cell door opened. The woman who had checked Jackson and her into detention, plus another Bridgeford police officer stood in the entrance.

Damn.

As she'd suspected, the cell was being monitored. She lifted her canister to her lips. "Cover me," she told Jackson from the corner of her mouth.

He pushed up his shirt sleeve.

The female officer gasped, "What are you doing? Put that down! How do you do that? Shoot! Shoot th—"

Carina was in the forest again, her merc friend by her side.

"Hey, Jackson," said Darius.

"Hey, kid." He rolled his shoulders and surveyed his surroundings. "What happened to Pamuk and Bryce? Didn't they make it back?"

"They're fine," Carina replied. "They're around here somewhere."

The undergrowth parted, and Pamuk and Bryce appeared from amongst the foliage, Matt suspended between them. In the scuffle to apprehend him, he'd sustained a cut lip and the skin around one of his eyes was swelling and turning purple. Carina winced. The man hadn't done anything to hurt anyone. He'd just been in the wrong place at the wrong time, or rather, grabbing the wrong person at the wrong time.

"Couldn't you two be more gentle?" she chided.

"Did you want us to capture him or not?" Bryce retorted.

Jackson squinted at the police officer. "Why did you bring *him* along?"

"I didn't do it on purpose. It was an accident."

"You mean like Cheepy?" Jackson shared a look with Pamuk.

"Yes," Carina replied between her teeth. "Like Cheepy."

"Cuff him, Jackson," said Pamuk. She held Matt's gun in her other hand. As she passed the man over, she tucked it into the back of her pants. "What now?"

"Well," said Parthenia, "as our first foray into Earth society was pretty much a disaster, maybe we should return to the *Bathsheba* and rethink our strategy."

Carina sighed. "First of all, let's not discuss our business in front of the prisoner."

"I didn't hear anything," said Matt. "Nothing at all. And I promise, if you let me go, I won't remember anything about any of this."

"So how are you going to explain disappearing along with the rest of us? When you're asked how you managed to arrive in this forest from nowhere, what are you going to say?"

"I-I'll tell them I don't remember. I could say I hit my head." He gestured at his swollen eye.

"And your lip happened to walk into a fist too? No one's going to believe you. I'm sorry, but you're sticking with us, at least until we figure out what to do with you."

He hung his head.

"Don't worry," said Darius. "You won't come to any harm. We're nice people."

"Pamuk isn't," Jackson said.

She shoved his shoulder.

He continued, "And neither are Rees or Van Hasty, come to think of it. And Carter and Blake are absolute ass—"

"That's enough of a rundown on the Black Dogs," Carina interrupted. "Jackson, you stay with the prisoner. Everyone else, over here." After they'd walked some distance away, she went on, "I'm inclined to agree with Parthenia. We need to leave for a while and debrief before thinking up a new way forward. Clearly, just walking into town isn't going to work. We stick out too much."

"And we don't have any idea what we're doing," said Darius.

"There is that too."

"But we can't take the prisoner with us," said Pamuk. "He's seen what you guys do. He's already a liability, and if we take him back to the ship he'll see everything. We'll never be able to let him go. It might be better and kinder to get rid of him now. It's either that or keep him in the brig forever."

Carina sucked in a breath. "I'm fairly confident Officer Matt won't think it's better and kinder to kill him now."

"We can't kill him!" Darius exclaimed. "That would be terrible."

"It's only a suggestion," said Pamuk.

Parthenia said, "We've come a long way over many years and we aren't leaving anytime soon. Who knows what the future holds? It's still early days. We can't leave the prisoner behind so we have to take him with us. After that, we'll have to see how things pan out. But I agree, we can't kill him. There's been enough death on our journey. Let's not sully our endeavor with more of it."

"You're right," said Carina, admiration for her sister swelling in her chest. "You're absolutely right. Okay, the prisoner comes with us."

"If his mind was blown by our Casting," Darius said, "I wonder what he'll make of the *Bathsheba*?"

TEN

Carina wasn't sure exactly what Officer Matt made of the colony ship as he stepped down from the shuttle, but it wasn't good. She was behind him. All she could see was his back, but it was clear from the way his chest expanded and contracted rapidly he was going through something.

She called out to Bryce, who was walking in front, "Check the prisoner."

He turned just in time to catch Matt as he collapsed. Bryce supported him, holding him under the arms as his head lolled against his shoulder, and then gently eased him down to the deck. Matt was out cold. She guessed traveling to a starship must have been too much of a shock.

The mission members crowded around the prone figure.

"I'll Heal him," said Darius.

"No, get a medic, just in case it's serious. He might have something wrong with him. If he has we need to know what it is."

"It's not my fault," said Pamuk defensively. "I didn't hit him that hard."

Jackson tutted. "Always the guilty conscience."

"I'll comm sick bay," said Hsiao.

By the time the medics arrived Matt was already coming around. After a quick assessment they decided he'd probably only fainted but they would take him in for 24 hours for observation. Pamuk and Jackson went with them to arrange security.

Ferne and Oriana appeared.

"We heard you were back," Ferne said. "How did it go?"

Oriana added, "We thought you would be gone for days. I take it there was a huge disaster due to the fact we weren't with you."

"There was somewhat of a disaster," Parthenia replied, "but it would have been the same whether you were with us or not."

"Still," Ferne said, "it's our turn next, right, Carina?"

"Nothing's been decided yet. We've only just got off the shuttle, for star's sake. We need to think things through." Though it had been years since his death, she missed Cadwallader more than ever. He would have had a plan B, or at the very least they could have bounced ideas off each other. She also missed Jace and his gentle, steady good sense and kindness.

Oriana whined, "Are you going to tell us what happened or not? You can't leave us hanging."

"I'm exhausted," Parthenia said. "If you want my side of the story you'll have to wait for it. I'm going to lie down for a while."

"I'll tell you," said Darius, "but first I want something to eat."

"You can talk and eat," Ferne said. "Come on."

Carina watched the four siblings walk out of the bay. Bryce wrapped an arm around her and she sighed as she rested her head on his shoulder. "Parthenia's right. That was a huge disaster. What made me think we could just appear on Earth and everything would be fine? That they would accept mages, leave us alone, and we could all live happily ever after?"

"I don't think you ever thought that, did you? We all knew it wouldn't be plain sailing. What we didn't know was what the problems might be."

"I guess you're right. Let's go and eat, preferably somewhere far away from Ferne and Oriana and their interrogation."

They took an elevator to Deck Seven, printed some simple food in a small galley, and went into the Twilight Dome. Luckily, it was empty, possibly because all that could be seen through the transparent overhead was the dusty, rocky, gray, barren surface of Earth's moon. Scan data showed there had once been research stations beneath the surface but all had been abandoned. No humans lived there now who could spot the vast starship in geostationary orbit on its far side.

They sat and began to eat. Carina picked at her noodles and vegetables.

After a few moments Bryce said, "Spit it out."

"Huh?" She paused, her fork poised halfway to her mouth.

"Whatever it is that's bothering you."

She put the fork down. "Isn't it obvious? How are we ever going to make a success of this? The people on Earth are a bunch of weirdos. They grow plants in every available crevice, their police aren't usually armed, and they get around in underground tunnels. I noticed something else, too.

There were no fields for crops or for farm animals. How the heck do they eat?"

"We only saw a small area. Maybe there weren't any farms around there. And we only saw a couple of towns in one country. Earth won't be the same all over. No planet is like that. You should know. You've seen enough of them."

"Do you think we should try another country?"

"It wouldn't hurt."

"But the news of what we did in that detention center will be all around the globe by now. They must have vids of us. There were cameras everywhere. Jackson even had one in his cell. So our faces will be known as well as our ability to disappear and reappear at will. Wherever we set foot, we'll be noticed, and then someone will be along to arrest us."

"Maybe we could go somewhere very remote, where there isn't much technology."

"Hmm..." The place where she'd grown up had been similar to what Bryce had described. It had been very poor. No one could afford expensive tech, and few people could afford any tech at all. Nai Nai hadn't had anything to connect her with the outside world. She'd relied on the customers for news about what was going on in the outer world, though Carina suspected her grandmother might have also Sent with other mages. She wouldn't have told Carina about it while she was too young to keep a secret. In fact, that might have been how she knew Ba had died, not because she had a 'feeling'.

"Your food's getting cold," said Bryce.

"I'm not hungry." She put the plate down. "Maybe you're right. Maybe we could go somewhere far from civilization, but what would be the point? The reason we're here is to find a place where mages can live in the open, where we're accepted for who we are, and no one tries to exploit us. If we have to hide away out in the wilds, I'm back to square one. That's how I grew up. It was a better experience than my siblings', at least until Nai Nai died, but it wasn't much of a life. I don't want to live in fear anymore. Is that too much to ask?"

"No, it isn't. But I think you're being too pessimistic. So our first try didn't work out. So what? We can try again. We have a whole planet with billions of people, and we've only just arrived. If you thought everything would be easy, you were expecting a lot. It might take years for humans on Earth to understand your family and learn how to deal with them fairly."

"Ugh, it's already taken us years to get here."

Yet he was right. She *was* being impatient.

"Have you thought about other mages?" he asked.

"Others? On Earth?"

"The documents you found on Ostillon confirmed the old stories that mages came from Earth. Even if they all left the mutation might have reappeared. There might be mages down there, only they don't know what they are."

"They didn't all leave. The documents say some chose to remain but go into hiding." With Nahla's help, over the long years of the voyage, she had translated everything in the ancient papers. Naturally, there was no way to check whether the translation was accurate, but their version made sense.

"There you go," said Bryce. "If the ones who stayed behind passed down their lore the same as the colonizers, there are mages on Earth now who can help you."

"That's a big if. It would have been safer to give up practicing their abilities."

"The mages who left didn't."

"But they had new worlds all to themselves for decades, perhaps centuries, before the ordinary humans caught up to them. They..."

He was giving her a steady stare.

"All right," she conceded. "I guess I am being too negative. Maybe it's because I hate to think of those poor people living there for millennia, frightened of their powers being revealed and suffering the same hatred and persecution as their ancestors. And it would mean that my quest is hopeless, that Earth isn't a safe haven and never will be."

"We've barely arrived, Carina. Stop over-thinking things. We can try again somewhere else. Only we'd better take Ferne and Oriana this time or we'll never hear the end of it."

He continued to eat and she watched him, thankful for his presence in her life. Then something about him distracted her.

After a few moments he noticed. "What's wrong? What are you looking at?" He lifted a hand to the spot above his left ear that was her focus.

"Oh, nothing. Have you finished?" She offered to take his plate.

"Have I got a cut there?" He pressed his fingers against his scalp. "I can't feel anything."

"I forgot to ask you, how did you take down Matt?"

"Pamuk threw a stone to make the undergrowth rustle, and when he fired at it I tackled him from behind. Then Pamuk took over. You know what she's like. But you're changing the subject. What's so interesting about my hair?"

"You...er...you're going gray. Did you know?"

"No, I didn't." A brief look of concern flitted over his features, but then he shrugged. "It's only to be expected, I suppose, after living with you all these years."

She chuckled and playfully punched his arm. "I'm to blame, huh?" Then she grew somber and she continued in a softer tone, "Do you have any regrets? Answer honestly."

He'd left his family behind to be with her, abandoning them with a note to say he was safe but he had something he had to do. That would have been the last his parents and siblings had heard from him, and with the time dilation effects all of them would be long dead.

"No, I made my choice, and you can't live with a choice like that while holding onto regrets. I would have driven myself crazy. And it was the right choice."

"Thanks. I needed to hear that."

"No problem. It's the truth. Hey, we're forgetting something. We don't need to rely on all those quadrillions of bits of data about Earth anymore. We have our own shipboard source of intel now."

"Of course. Officer Matt."

ELEVEN

Matt was looking better when Carina went to see him a few hours later. He was sitting up in bed, and Ava was fussing over him, adjusting his pillow and pouring water into a cup. The Marchonish woman hadn't spent much time out of Deep Sleep on the long voyage. She'd said she didn't want her little girl to spend most of her childhood living on a starship. But the time she had spent awake she'd asked to be trained as a medic, to give her a source of income when they reached Earth. On Marchon, women had been expected to stay at home and not undertake paid employment, which would bring great shame on their families.

Carina had a soft spot for Ava, who had lived with her siblings on Sot Loza and, to an extent, been a mother figure while Carina could not. Now, her daughter was four years old and Ava had her hands full with working and looking after her. Consequently—and partly also due to the mages spending more time out of stasis—the two families had drifted apart, though Carina still felt warmly toward her, though she remained embarrassed that she'd named her daughter Carina.

"How's our patient?" she asked.

"He's doing very well. All his vitals are normal. It's most likely he suffered a bout of low blood pressure as he disembarked the shuttle. It isn't uncommon in people not used to space travel."

The color had come back to Matt's cheeks and he definitely looked perkier. One of his wrists was handcuffed to the bed frame.

Carina asked, "Is he well enough for a chat?"

"Absolutely. I wouldn't have a problem him being discharged today, but Dr Asher is being cautious as usual. She's given him one of your translators."

Matt's attention was focused on Ava until she'd left the room. When he turned to Carina and Bryce, caution overshadowed his features. "What do you want?"

Carina perched on the side of his bed. "We aren't any happier about this situation than you. I didn't intend to take you with me when I Transported to the forest. It was an accident. But now you're here we're all going to have to make the best of it."

"And what does 'making the best of it' mean exactly?"

"We're not sure yet. As my brother was telling you, we aren't bad people. No one here will hurt you, or at least not unless you force them. You should know most of the people on this ship are trained mercenaries and they haven't had a fight in a very long time."

"You're keeping me here against my will. If that isn't hurting me I don't know what is."

"Believe me, you don't want to find out. Like I said, we haven't come to a decision about what to do with you, but in the meantime perhaps you can help us."

"Why would I do that?"

"Call it doing us a favor."

"I don't owe you anything."

"No, but..." She appealed to Bryce with her eyes.

He sat on the other side of the bed. "Look, friend, you're at a big disadvantage. Carina is trying to be nice because she feels guilty about dragging you into this—"

"I wouldn't call threatening me with mercenaries being nice."

"...but the facts are you're all alone with no way of even contacting anyone, let alone leaving. All anyone knows is that you mysteriously disappeared along with a bunch of prisoners. For all they know, you're in on it with us. Otherwise, why would you disappear too? If you never go back, no one will ever be any the wiser about what happened to you. So it's in your interest to do whatever we say, isn't it? That way, we might be inclined to feel kindly toward you."

Matt shifted uncomfortably, his gaze traveling between them. "What do you want me to help you with?"

"We need to know about Earth," Carina said.

"Earth?" He laughed. "Odd question. It's a big place. Could you whittle that down a bit?" As she tried to decide what would be most useful to know, he went on, "Maybe if you told me who you are and what you're trying to do it would help."

"Ugh, where to start?" She wasn't sure it was safe to tell him *anything*.

"How did you move me from Bridgeford to the forest? I thought you must have drugged me somehow, but you said it happened like I experienced it, disappearing in one place and a second later appearing in another. I've seen it plenty of times on shows, but that's just a trick. You're saying it really happened?"

She didn't answer. Mage powers were the last thing she wanted him to know about.

"Can all aliens do that?" he asked hesitantly.

"Aliens? We're not aliens. We're human, like you."

"But we're on a starship, right? A very big one, from what I can tell. That smaller ship we were on brought us here. Only aliens travel on starships."

"That's not true," said Bryce. "Humans invented space travel millennia ago. We travel on starships all the time."

His eyes lit up. "I get it now! You're members of that cult. What's it called? The Exodus Testifiers. You did drug me. All of this is made up."

"We're...what?"

"Exodus Testifiers. Don't try to deny it. I'll give you credit, though. You had me fooled for a while there."

Bryce said, "What the hell are you talking about?"

"If you let me go now, I'll say you treated me well. You'll get off with a light sentence, maybe just a few months in a psychiatric hospital."

"Matt," Carina said, "what's an Exodus Testifier?"

He laughed again. "Nice. Keep it up. This is hilarious. Where did you get the money for all this? All those props and special effects must have cost a fortune. And are the people members of the cult too, or did you pay actors?"

"We haven't paid anyone anything. This is all real."

"No, it isn't," he said patiently. "I understand you enjoy pretending, but it's time for the games to stop. Kidnapping a police officer is a serious crime, and you can add assault to that charge." He prodded his swollen eye. "You need to release me and you need to do it now, before you get into even more trouble."

He was so earnest, for a brief moment Carina had the weirdest sense that perhaps he was right. Could she be living in an illusion? Could her life up until now be the imaginings of a sick mind? Then she snapped back to reality. "Everything that's happened to you is exactly as it seemed. You were Transported to the forest. You traveled on a space shuttle, and you are aboard a starship. Her name is the *Bathsheba* and she used to be a colony ship. We acquired her in deep space two galactic sectors from here, and we've traveled for decades in stasis to come to Earth."

Matt shook his head in wonder. "It's marvelous how deeply you believe that bullshit, despite all the evidence to the contrary. Tell me, where are you from? And what did you used to do, before you got sucked in I mean?"

Carina locked gazes with Bryce. How could they convince Officer Matt of the truth?

"Maybe we should call Clarkson," Bryce said.

"Yeah, good idea."

The doctor could assess Matt's mental state. He could be experiencing a psychotic break. The shock of all that had happened to him might have placed too much stress on his mind, and this was his way of explaining everything.

"Dr Clarkson will check you over again," she said. "She won't be long."

"No more checks. You must let me go. Now." He rattled his handcuff on the metal bed frame. "People will be looking for me and it won't be long before they trace my chip. You don't stand a chance. Save yourselves and give yourselves up."

Carina rose to her feet. There was no point arguing with him. He was completely convinced he was right.

As she and Bryce walked to the door, Matt shouted after them, "You won't get away with this! Things are going to go very badly for you if you don't release me immediately!"

When they were outside, Bryce went into Clarkson's office while Carina comm'd Nahla.

"Hi, Carina," she replied. "I heard you were back. How did it go?"

"Not great, but I have another problem I'd like your help with. You've been looking at the information we have on Earth, right? Did you notice anything about Exodus Testifiers?"

"What a strange name. No, I don't think so. I'm sure I would remember if I did."

"Could you look it up? Find out everything you can about them."

"Happy to, but why? Is it something to do with mages?"

"No, nothing like that. I accidentally kidnapped a police officer, and he thinks that's what we are. Exodus Testifiers. And unless we can convince him otherwise, I don't think he's going to tell us anything useful about Earth."

"Hold on. Rewind. You accidentally kidnapped a police officer?"

"Don't start. Pamuk gave me enough grief already, all the way back on the shuttle."

TWELVE

Though the translations of the mage documents were all on the ship's database and readily accessible via any interface, Carina sometimes liked to handle the ancient papers themselves. There was a sensation of connectedness and deep nostalgia to be had from touching the sheets created by her ancestors thousands of years ago. And she had worked so hard and so much had been sacrificed to attain them. Some people had sacrificed their lives. The documents were precious—priceless, in fact. What value could be placed on something so unique?

She had taken them from the safe and brought them to the cabin she shared with Bryce. In the early days of the journey, a techie had encased the brittle, aged papers in a transparent substance to preserve them, and now they slid easily between her fingers. One by one, she placed them on the bed, spreading them out. The same handwriting had been used on all of them, but the author hadn't signed their name. Similarly, no signature gave away the identity of the artist who had created the sketches of the mages' mountain home, their first attempt at a sanctuary for their kind. Perhaps the writer and artist had been the same person. Had he or she ever imagined that their creations would still exist thousands of years later and be the remaining source of written lore of mages?

The door chimed.

Nahla had come to see her. Carina invited her sister in.

"You got those old papers out again?" Nahla asked, eyeing the unconventional bedspread. "Didn't we squeeze every last drop of knowledge out of them?"

"Yeah, I reckon we did, but I still like to look at them. Can I get you a drink?"

Nahla shook her head. "Don't let me stop you though." She sat at the table. "I like coming here. Ferne and Oriana did a wonderful job with your room."

The twins had excelled as interior decorators during the voyage, expanding on their first vocation as fashion designers. They had printed wall hangings and paintings and created matching textiles for the cabin. Carina had allowed them free rein as an indulgence, which had resulted in a daring mix of colors and patterns, but the effect had grown on her over time.

"You should let them do yours." Carina sat opposite her sister.

Nahla shuddered. "Too risky. It worked with you, but who knows what they might come up with for me? And then I would have to pretend I liked it or they would be offended. Besides, there's no point now. We won't be living here much longer."

"I'm not too sure about that. From what happened on our first try, I think it's going to be hard to do what we want."

"Hmm. I bumped into Parthenia on my way over. She told me a little of what happened. At least no one was hurt."

"That's about the best that can be said. It's nice to see you, but I take it this is more than a social visit." Nahla's preference for research over company was well-known. "Are you here to tell me what you found out about the Exodus Testifiers?"

"You know me too well." She opened the table's interface and navigated to a personal file. After opening it, she turned the display to face Carina. "That was quite the rabbit hole you sent me down. Fascinating stuff. And it throws a whole new light on human civilization on Earth. Read the top entry."

EXODUS TESTIFIERS – Conspiracy theorists or mentally ill?

John Markham (name changed for anonymity) is an unprepossessing man. Pass him in the street and you wouldn't look twice. Grey-haired, mid-fifties and well into middle-aged spread, he's even wearing the trademark cardigan and slacks typical of his generation when he allows me into his home. I ask him if he's married, but Markham is single—perhaps unsurprisingly. It would take a special kind of person to tolerate living with someone so deep into their obsession.

Most of us have a hobby or pastime. Many of us have several. We all need something fun and interesting to do for leisure, whether it be sports, outdoor pursuits, crafts, or more esoteric activities. But few take things to the level John has, and he isn't alone. It's estimated there are more than ten thousand Exodus Testifiers spread across the globe and, what's more, their numbers are growing.

I first came across John's writings on an ancient history forum. That's one of my interests. I'd heard of Exodus Testifiers but I'd never encountered one in the flesh, so to speak. Knowing it wouldn't be long before his words were gone, I copied everything he wrote. Inevitably, the mods banned him about an hour later, but by then I had a treasure trove of his thoughts, beliefs, and, some might say, ravings. I read them avidly, and my eyes were opened to this bizarre cult.

I had to know more. Perhaps I was developing an obsession of my own?

John must have known his opportunity to voice his views to the general public would be brief because he'd given his contact details in one of his posts. No sooner had I found him than a meeting was set up. He seemed eager to introduce a new potential disciple to the fellowship.

His home is testimony to his beliefs. Images of starships adorn every centimeter of the living room wall. Models of the vessels sit on every available surface. He invites me to take a seat, moving aside a pile of odd packages. When I ask what they are, his answer surprises me, even though I thought I knew what I was getting into.

"Rations," he says with a grin. He picks one up. "Freeze-dried curry. Add water and heat it up—after steaming your rice, of course—and, bingo, a healthy meal." He picks up another package. "Ice-cream." He pulled a face. "That one isn't so nice. But if you were in a survival situation it would be very welcome, I'm sure."

"Survival situation?" I ask. "Is that what this is about?"

"That's only a small part of it. Survival just happens to be my particular interest."

"I see. I'm new to this. Would you be able to sum up the core Exodus Testifiers' beliefs in a sentence or two?" I reach into my pocket for my interface. "Do you mind if I record our meeting—for me to listen to later in case I forget anything?"

His expression turns sharp and suspicious. "You aren't a journalist, are you?"

"No, no. Just an interested citizen."

"Only the media has a tendency to make fun of us. Testifying is a serious pursuit. We have plenty of evidence to back up our claims, but academics are too frightened of upsetting the status quo to pay any attention to it. The minute anyone knows you're a Testifier, everything you say is ignored and dismissed."

"I won't make a recording if you don't want me to." I slip the interface back into my pocket.

He relaxes. "One or two sentences? That's hard, but if I had to summarize, I'd say we basically believe that, for a period of two or three thousand years, humans regularly left Earth in order to colonize other worlds."

"Let's be clear. You aren't talking about Mars, Venus, or other planets in the Solar System. You mean planets light years away."

"Exactly."

I decide to humor him. I get the impression that the slightest questioning of his beliefs will make him shut up tighter than a clam. I gesture at the many pictures and models of space-going vessels surrounding us. "In ships like these?"

Carina's jaw dropped. She lifted her gaze to Nahla, who was watching her with amusement. "What did I just read?"

Nahla chuckled. "There's more, if you're interested. Lots more."

"He...doesn't think people ever left Earth?"

"Not just the writer. Most of the population. Exodus Testifiers are the exceptions."

"But how is that possible? It doesn't make any sense. Even if the people on Earth gave up on space exploration, they can't have forgotten about it. There has to be plenty of evidence to show what happened in the past."

"Apparently not. And, thinking about it from a data storage perspective, it isn't so strange. Computer systems change over time. What was accessible a few centuries ago could be completely corrupted or irretrievable now. Data doesn't persist in the same way as those mage documents on your bed. And reporting styles change too. Present-day archaeologists might misinterpret an ancient media report about a colony ship's departure as fiction rather than fact."

"But what about shipyards? They're huge. There has to be something left of them."

"Most starships are built in space, remember. They would have fallen to Earth, probably crashing into an ocean. There might be something left of component manufacturing plants, but an excavation wouldn't necessarily reveal the exact purpose of the discovered artifacts. That would be open to interpretation, and people tend to explain evidence in the context of their culture and perspective."

The enormity of the misunderstanding was hard to swallow, but one thing was clear: Officer Matt genuinely thought they were crazy cultists, living out a fantasy. She didn't know how to persuade him to accept that he and most of the rest of humanity was wrong. Whatever they showed him, he would believe it was an illusion. If they took him on a tour of the ship, he would think it was an impressive set. If they showed him the view from the Twilight Dome, he would say it was a vid.

"So," said Carina, "if we were to go to Earth and announce that we were space travelers from another galactic sector, the descendants of colonizers who left millennia ago, no one would believe us?"

"Not only that, there's a good chance you would be locked up—for your own good. As the article implies, Exodus Testifiers are often believed to be mentally unwell."

"But what if we showed them the *Bathsheba*? No one could deny we were telling the truth then."

"Right, but if you did that, how long do you think you could hold onto her? The arrival of an actual starship from outer space would blow apart the current understanding of humankind's history. My impression so far of Earth societies is that they're generally friendly, non-violent, and free. But that doesn't mean someone won't decide the shockwave of the revelation would be dangerously destabilizing, and seek to remove the evidence from scrutiny. And let's not forget about all of the *Bathsheba*'s tech and weaponry. Less well-meaning individuals would be very keen on getting their hands on them."

Carina rubbed her temples. "We could hold them off, but not forever." And announcing their presence in such a loud fashion was the last thing she wanted. "Thanks for doing the research. The results have been illuminating to say the least."

"It wasn't difficult, and it was fun. I'm sorry if I've created more problems for you." Nahla rose to her feet.

"It's better I'm aware of them now than find out the hard way."

"Let me know if there's anything else I can help you with."

As Nahla left, Carina had a brief vision of a small, frightened girl, recently released from her Dark Mage elder brother's control and traumatized from being trapped in a shuttle cabin with Stevenson's body. She'd come a long way. She was now a confident young woman and the smartest person on the ship. She deserved a good, happy, fulfilling life. They all did. But the chances of achieving it were looking increasingly remote.

Carina returned to the mage documents spread over her bed. How to turn what she knew into a successful outcome? How could they integrate into Earth society safely and live openly, without hiding fundamental aspects of themselves?

Her gaze alighted on the drawings depicting the mages' mountain hide-away. It had to be ruins by now, if any of it remained at all. It was doubtful she would learn anything useful there, yet she had a hankering to visit anyway, if only to walk in the places her ancestors had trodden, imbibing their spirit. But no location was given—understandably, considering the dangers they'd faced.

She tilted her head. Surrounding the stone-walled edifice was the mountain landscape. The lines of the ridges stood out clearly against the sky. Buildings, towns, and cities rose and fell, constructed by humans and destroyed by nature. But mountains didn't change for tens of thousands of years, or at least not significantly.

She comm'd Nahla. "There's something else I'd like you to do."

THIRTEEN

Carina pulled the copy of the mage document from her bag, studied it, and then scanned the view. Thick gray cloud cloaked the sky, obscuring the mountain peaks. Snow glinted on the highest peaks.

Oriana peered over her shoulder. "This is it. It has to be. Look, Ferne. What do you think?"

Her twin, without asking, took the sheet from Carina's hands and frowned over it before handing it back. His eyes narrowed as his gaze swept the view. "Maybe. But I wouldn't get your hopes up. After all this time, there won't be anything left."

"That isn't the point," Oriana countered. "That's right, isn't it, Carina?"

She shivered, turned up the collar of her coat, and pulled her hat lower. She was already regretting bringing her brother and sister along, but without a good excuse she hadn't been able to say no. The twins were intense and had only grown more so during the voyage. Just being around them was tiring.

In truth, she didn't know how to answer the question. She had no good reason for being here except that she had to do *something*. Parthenia, in the interests of having a mage aboard the ship, had stayed behind this time. So had Pamuk, Jackson, and Bryce. They were known to Earth authorities—as was she, but this whole thing was her idea. It was her responsibility to make it work.

Though the rest of the Black Dogs and the Marchonish women were gagging to visit Earth, she'd decided to limit the new away team to Darius, herself, the twins, and Hsiao. They needed Darius to Cloak the shuttle but he was staying with it, along with Hsiao. Until they knew more about the local systems it wasn't safe for anyone from the *Bathsheba* to be here. Matt had said they were 'not chipped'. Any one of them could quickly be spotted as an 'alien' and picked up. On the other hand, they were on an entirely different continent, so who knew what might happen?

"Carina," Oriana repeated, "did you hear me?"

"I heard you. You're right. I don't expect to find the hideaway." However, the mountains in the place Nahla had suggested did match the sketches made by a mage thousands of years ago. The habitation the mages built had sat in a high pass, which was indicated on the drawings but obscured from view when looking from below. "I think there's a path over there."

Hsiao had landed the shuttle as close to the site as possible, but in the rocky landscape they still had many kilometers to travel. It was exactly as the mages had intended. They'd deliberately made their home difficult to reach in order to discourage unwanted visitors. Any non-mages who made it there were turned away, and sometimes they died in the wilderness. That had been the start of the enmity toward mages, the beginning of the motivation behind their exodus.

Exodus Testifiers.

Did they believe in mages too? Or did they only know about ordinary humans' galactic colonization attempts? Would it be worth talking to a Testifier?

"We should Transport up there," said Ferne.

They were nearing the narrow gap in the undergrowth Carina had spotted.

"Is that wise?" Oriana asked.

If you didn't know exactly where you were going, Transport was a little risky. One time, Carina had ended up waist-deep in a swamp.

"There's nothing between us and our destination except trees," Ferne replied. "What could possibly go wrong?"

"Don't say that," Oriana warned. "That's inviting trouble."

"We could leapfrog from here to that slope over there. That'll halve the distance we have to travel."

"I don't suppose it'll hurt," said Carina. The less time spent trekking the better, for several reasons. She pointed out a particularly tall pine. "I'll take us all there." She sipped elixir, Cast, and then opened her eyes, instantly tumbling over and landing on her side in thick leaf litter.

Oriana had done the same.

Ferne laughed. "You two are hilarious. Didn't you realize the ground would be at an angle?"

Carina got to her feet, brushing dead pine needles from her clothes. "Next time, you're Transporting us." She helped her sister up.

It was darker among the tall, overshadowing trees, and the air was colder. Her ears had popped as she'd arrived.

"Smart move," Oriana grumbled. "Now we can't see where to go. Which way is the pass?"

"It would have been the same if we'd walked here," Ferne retorted, "only we would be a lot more tired."

With the sun obscured by a blanket of cloud, it was hard to tell directions, but one thing Carina did know, and that was they had to go up. "This way."

She headed up the slope, weaving through the trees. They didn't grow thickly at this altitude, and if her guess was correct, they would soon thin out before disappearing altogether. Her years aboard a starship were taking their toll. She toiled upward, puffing and panting, hearing the gasping breaths of Ferne and Oriana behind her. Soon, she was sweating despite the cold.

"Maybe…" Oriana said "we should…take a…chance…and—"

"Forget it," Carina said. "We could Transport to an edge of a precipice and fall off."

"And perform the fastest Transport ever before we hit the bottom," added Ferne.

As Carina had predicted, the trees soon disappeared. They scrambled over rocks and slipped on shale as they drove themselves steadily upward.

"We could do lots of small jumps," Oriana called out.

Her voice sounded distant.

Carina halted and turned. Her sister stood about thirty meters down the slope, leaning on a boulder.

Ferne yelled, "We would use up all our elixir, silly. Come on, it can't be far now."

"I don't suppose someone could carry me?"

They ignored her in the way only siblings well-used to—and tired of—their brother's or sister's shenanigans could. In a few moments the sound of Oriana's dogged footsteps came from behind as she crunched her way over the stones. Somehow, she managed to convey her annoyance in every step.

When they reached the pass it appeared suddenly. One minute they were working their way up yet another steep rise, one of seemingly countless others, and the next flat ground stretched out before them. The area separated two steep mountainsides and was strewn with loose rock. In the gap a sliver of blue sky peeked from the lowest stretch of the pass. Everywhere else was gray, misty, and chill.

"We've found it," Oriana breathed. "It has to be it."

Carina pulled the document from her backpack. Next to the image showing the view of the mages' hideaway from afar was a close-up version. "No, it's wrong. We've come the wrong way. *Damn.*"

"Let me look."

She handed the sheet to Ferne and then sat on the cold ground, exhausted.

They were clearly in the wrong place. The document showed a bigger area and an outer section of the building, where the mages would receive visitors and test their abilities before either welcoming them or sending them away, depending on the results. Though it might be too much to expect that anything would be left of the mages' construction, the mountainside shouldn't have changed very much. This place was markedly narrower. She guessed there was another pass between another pair of mountains in the range, or perhaps Nahla's suggestion was incorrect.

"You silly goose," said Ferne. "This *is* it." He squatted down beside her and pointed at the spot in the picture where the mountain slopes met. "The angles of the slopes are identical to how they are now."

"Maybe, but there's nowhere near the same amount of space. How could the mages have fitted *that* here?" She prodded the curved protuberance with its wide double doors and window slits. The image showed two figures at the door, giving a clue to the building's size. "There's no way there's room."

He straightened up and gazed from one slope to the other. "But it was so long ago..." he mused. He thrust the toe of his boot into the ground, sending up a spray of rock shards and dust.

"Hey," Carina protested, "watch out!"

"This has all fallen from the slopes, weathered away by the elements. Do we know how long ago mages left Earth?"

"Cadwallader estimated it once. He said it was about seven thousand years ago, based on Jace's knowledge of the number of generations who had lived in our sector."

"Cadwallader? So that must have been before we were kidnapped by the Regians, and since then we've been forced even more light years off course. With time dilation, we can add at least another thousand years to the figure. Eight thousand years." His chin tilted up as his attention focused on the surrounding mountains again. "A lot of rock could have fallen in that time, enough to narrow the pass considerably."

Carina got up, brushing rough pebbles from her backside. Could he be right? The angles of the slopes *were* the same.

"You two!" Oriana called, stepping out from behind a rock.

Carina hadn't noticed she'd disappeared.

"While you've been slacking off," Oriana said, "*I've* been working. I've found a cave entrance. Come and take a look. It seems to go back really far."

FOURTEEN

The cleft in the mountainside was barely wide enough to pass through. They all had to take off their backpacks and edge sideways. Once they were inside, however, the gap quickly opened up. Carina found herself standing in a space the size of a small room. The ground was flat and sandy, and the walls... She stepped closer. The walls resembled others she'd seen before, on a planet far distant half a lifetime ago. "This is it," she whispered. "They were here."

The walls were smooth and polished, like the pebbles Nai Nai used to make, and like the walls in the mountain castle on Ostillon where she'd found the mage documents. Whatever Cast had been used to create the surfaces, hollowing out the mountains' interiors, had been lost as far as she knew. Certainly, Nai Nai hadn't taught it to her and neither had Ma taught it to her siblings. But the similarity was unmistakable.

"Yay!" Oriana exclaimed. "We found it!" She hugged her brother and then Carina, but Carina couldn't return the gesture.

All energy had drained from her limbs and she felt numb.

"It's like the place the Dirksens took over, isn't it?" Ferne asked.

She nodded.

"That's right," said Oriana, running her fingertips over a wall. "I remember now."

He and Oriana had been around thirteen years old when they'd gone with Carina to find the documents. They'd fought alongside the Black Dogs, and they'd been present when Sable Dirksen had shot Darius. It was no wonder the place had left an indelible mark on their memories.

"I need to sit down," Carina said. She walked to the edge of the chamber and slumped to the floor. Burying her face in her hands, she wept.

"What's wrong?" Ferne asked. "I would have thought you would be happy."

"Oh, shut up," Oriana admonished. "She is happy. She's just having a moment." She sat beside Carina and put an arm over her shoulders. "Take as long as you like. We have all day to explore, and now we know where it is, we can come back whenever we like."

Carina sniffed and mumbled, "Thanks."

In fact, she wasn't sure she was crying with happiness. She wasn't sure what she felt. Images of Nai Nai and Ma had flooded her mind, along with the faces of all the people who had died during their journey. She wished she could pull herself together and do what she'd come to Earth to do, but the ghosts of the past seemed to always drag at her, holding her back.

"Have you noticed something?" Ferne asked. "It's light. It should be much darker in here. There's hardly any light coming from the way in, but we can see perfectly well. The walls and ceiling must be faintly glowing." As he'd been speaking he'd wandered around the chamber. "There's a way out," he said as he reached a protuberance. "I'm going to see what else is here."

"Wait," said Oriana. "We shouldn't split up."

"Don't worry. If you can't find me, shout, and if I don't hear you, Locate me."

"Ugh, he's so inconsiderate."

"He's just excited," said Carina. "I'm feeling better now. Let's see what he's found."

On the other side of the protuberance was an arched doorway carved into the rock. There was no question now that *someone* had lived here, if not the mages. And if it was the mages, had they left anything behind?

The opening led to a tunnel with similar doorways at regular intervals. Ferne was peering into one. "Nothing here, just empty rooms. I wonder what they used to be for?"

"What's that noise?" Oriana asked.

"What noise?" Ferne wrinkled his brow. "I can't hear a thing."

"Shhh! Listen."

Carina heard it too: a faint soughing like the wind in a forest, rustling the leaves and branches.

"Oh, yes," said Ferne. "It's coming from that way." He strode down the tunnel, leaving Carina and Oriana hurrying to catch up.

"Slow down," Oriana complained. "We're already exhausted from all the climbing."

Typically, Ferne took no notice. If anything, he seemed to speed up. "It's getting louder," he called over his shoulder. "We're on the right track."

The tunnel sloped downward, diving deep into the mountain. In her hurried glimpses of the rooms they passed, Carina saw only empty, bare spaces. Whatever had once been inside had either been taken by the mages or decayed to dust.

Meanwhile, the noise was growing louder and becoming more distinct. It didn't sound like the wind anymore. It sounded like—

"Whoa!" Ferne had halted at a portal larger than the others, seemingly transfixed by what lay beyond.

A gust of cool, moist air hit Carina, and she knew her guess at what the noise was had been correct. She joined Ferne at the opening. In a high cavern, the sides lit by the same glowing material that illuminated the place, a waterfall cascaded into a deep, dark pool.

"This must have been why they chose it," Oriana said excitedly, clapping her hands. "An endless supply of water to make elixir."

It had occurred to Carina on the way up that the mountain was a dry place, devoid of the brooks and rills she would have expected to see. It seemed clear that the majority of the snow melt and rainfall in the higher regions was funneled inside the mountain, emerging in this cavern.

"Marvelous," said Ferne, stepping over to the pool. "I'm going to try some."

"Are you sure it's safe?" Oriana asked.

He stooped and scooped a handful of water into his mouth. After swallowing, he gasped. "It's freezing. I felt it all the way down to my stomach." He smacked his lips. "Tastes nice, though."

"You're probably going to catch a horrible disease," said Oriana, "or a parasite."

"Why? The mages must have drunk this all the time."

"They would have boiled it to make elixir, and to drink too."

He pulled a face. "Oh well, if I get sick I'll Heal myself."

Carina?

Darius was Sending to her.

Hey, sweetie. What's up?

Did you find the hideaway?

We're pretty sure we did. We're here now, inside the mountain. It took us a while, but—

I think you should leave.

Huh? Why? We only just got here.

I have a bad feeling. I don't know what it is, but it's coming from near where you are.

"Who are you talking to?" Oriana asked.

"It's Darius. He's saying we have to get out right away. He has a bad feeling."

Ferne scoffed, "He's always having a bad feeling about one thing or another. It's probably indigestion."

"It might be something serious," Oriana replied doubtfully.

"We should listen to him," said Carina. The twins might have forgotten Darius as a little boy saving all their lives more than once, but she hadn't. "Get ready to Transport back to the shuttle."

"What could possibly be dangerous in here?" Ferne asked, opening his arms wide. "We've only just arrived. There must be lots more to see."

"I'm not going to argue," Carina said. "If you won't Transport yourself I'll do it for you."

It went against mage code to Cast on others without their permission, but when it came to protecting her siblings she was prepared to make an exception.

"*Fine.*" Ferne snatched his elixir flask from its holder.

"We can always come back later," Oriana placated.

There was movement on the far side of the cavern. Three figures had appeared at the entrance.

"Who's that?!" Oriana had seen them too.

"Hurry up." Carina swallowed elixir, her gaze fixed on the figures. In her peripheral vision she saw her brother and sister Casting.

One of the newcomers raised his hand and pointed. They'd been seen. Nothing of what was said on the other side of the cavern could be heard over the rushing of the waterfall. One of the other men was doing something else.

Closing her eyes, she wrote the Character in her mind and sent it out. At the same time, she retained what she'd just seen.

The figures were all male. They'd been standing in the shadow of an overhang, which obscured them almost to silhouettes. She hadn't been able to tell their ages or even what they were wearing. All she'd been able to see was the man pointing, and the other one... He'd been drinking from a container! Had he been Casting?

Had his Cast activated before their own, Transporting them to another destination?

She opened her eyes.

There was grass beneath her feet. The air was warm and dry. There were voices.

"Carina," Oriana said, "you made it, thank goodness. Who were those people?"

"Where's Ferne?" she asked, turning. "Is he here?"

"Yes, I'm here. No need to tell me off," he added ruefully. "Darius was right and I was wrong."

Darius was here too, and so was Hsiao. Beneath the camouflage sheet, a tiny piece of the shuttle peeked out. Everyone was safe.

"I don't know who those people were," she said, "but one thing's for sure —they weren't there to welcome us with open arms. It's time we went back to the ship."

Fifteen

"You said we were from offplanet," Carina leaned closer to Matt, causing him to edge backward. "What did you mean? You don't believe humans have ever left Earth. Why would you say we're offworlders?"

His comment had come back to her as she'd traveled from Earth to the *Bathsheba*.

"I-I was being sarcastic."

"Sarcastic about what? That we were offworlders?"

"Y-yes!"

"Carina," Darius said, "give him some room, then maybe he'll be able to answer you properly."

They were in the brig, where Matt had been taken after his discharge from sick bay.

Carina moved away from his bunk and folded her arms. "Is this better?"

Matt swallowed. "A little."

Darius asked gently, "Can you explain why you made that comment?"

"I didn't really think you were from outer space..." The Earth man shifted in his seat and plucked at the cuff of his shirt "...though what I've seen here has made me question that."

Was he trying to mollify them, thinking that if he played into their Exodus Testifier fantasy they would treat him well?

"I was referring to the General Alert. You must know it." He added hastily, "Though of course if you really are aliens you wouldn't have heard of it."

"Just tell us what it is," said Carina.

"The General Alert is the warning everyone learns at school, to be on the alert for aliens masquerading as regular people. When the sensors in the wood picked up the presence of humans who weren't chipped, we joked about it at the station."

"Not chipped?" Before he could explain, Carina went on, "Oh, I get it. You have ID chips embedded in your hands." She'd recalled the police officers having their hands scanned. "Everyone on Earth has them?"

"Nearly everyone. Every so often someone turns up who had theirs removed. People who want to disappear for whatever reason. Sometimes they can't get a fake one or it doesn't work. It's against the law, so we arrest them. Before we could process you, your friend killed one of my colleagues. Then things got serious."

"We're sorry about that," Carina said. "You see, where we come from violence is normal. Jackson was only trying to protect himself."

Matt didn't answer. He probably thought she was indulging in her delusion.

"I'm interested in the General Alert," said Darius. "How long has it been in place?"

"I don't know. Since before I was born."

"And it involves being aware that aliens might be walking among you disguised as ordinary humans?"

"Basically."

"How would you be able to tell who these aliens were?"

"Well, for one thing they wouldn't be chipped, hence the joking at the station."

"What else?" asked Carina.

"They would be able to do things humans can't."

"Like?" Darius prompted.

"Like start fires spontaneously, open locked doors, disappear from one place and reappear in an—" He gave a small gasp. His wide-eyed gaze traveled from Darius to Carina and back again. He looked down. "No," he said softly, as if speaking to himself. "No, it can't be." He looked up and grinned nervously. "Neat trick."

"Where does the warning come from?" Carina asked.

"I don't know."

"You said you learned it at school. Does that mean it isn't serious? Is it a boogeyman thing?"

"No, it's serious. I guess it must come from the government. I never really thought about it, but I've seen the warning on websites, notices, that kind of thing."

"If we give you access to Earth information channels, could you find an example?"

Hope bloomed in his features.

"You'll only be able to browse."

Hope faded. "Okay, I'll try."

They left the brig and walked in silence. There was no need to state the obvious. The situation was the last Carina had expected. If she'd discovered that mages were known about and feared on Earth she would have been disappointed but not surprised. But a society prepped to hate and fear them? How had it come about and why? And why weren't they given their real name, rather than portrayed as aliens?

She comm'd Nahla.

"You're back? Good trip?"

"No."

"Oh dear. Maybe next t—"

"While you were looking at the Earth data, did you come across something called the General Alert?"

"Doesn't ring a bell. I can do a search."

"What about warnings to watch out for aliens?"

"No...wait. Yes, I did see one. I thought it was a joke."

Great. "Could you check for the General Alert? And anything to do with aliens with special powers."

"On it."

Darius said, "We need to do something with Matt. We can't keep him here forever. He hasn't done anything wrong or tried to hurt us."

"He locked us up!"

"He was only doing his job."

"Well, what do *you* think we should do with him?"

"The next time we go to Earth, we should take him with us and leave him somewhere safe. He'll be able to make his way home."

"But then what? He'll tell everyone about the *Bathsheba* and all the people on it—the 'aliens'. Then everyone will be on the lookout for us wherever we go."

"Will he tell them we're aliens? Or will he say we're a bunch of crazy Exodus Testifiers who pulled a stunt on him? That's what he seems to believe."

"He might believe that, but there's the evidence of us disappearing from the detention center and Jackson disappearing from his cell a few minutes later. Matt might not believe what really happened, but he'll find it hard to explain those disappearances, and his superiors will expect him to explain. You can be sure about that. In fact, things might be even worse for him than we thought.

We—I—brought him with us. The police might think he was colluding with us."

"Hmm," Darius mused. "Didn't think of that. I guess he'll have to stay here a while, until we can think of a way of getting him home without creating problems for him."

Van Hasty appeared in the passageway. "I want to talk to you, Lin, face to face."

Darius said, "Uhh, I'll see you later."

He often escaped when an emotionally charged moment was imminent, and from the merc's expression, it seemed this moment was about to be especially so.

"What do you want?" Carina asked cautiously.

"I want to know exactly when the Black Dogs are gonna set foot on the first freaking planet we've arrived at in ten years."

"It's too soon for you all to go down there. You know that."

"Is it? It might be too soon for you guys, but we don't have your agenda. There's no reason we can't have some R&R."

"There are plenty of reasons. For one thing, you don't have embedded ID chips like everyone else on Earth. The minute you try to go anywhere, get a job or whatever, people are going to start asking you some very hard questions."

"So what? We'll just say we're from offplanet. There's no law against it."

"You don't underst—"

"We're going stir crazy. We've *been* stir crazy for years. Now the waiting's over and we're at our destination. We expect to get off the ship. Soon. If you keep stalling, something bad's gonna happen."

"Like what?" Carina asked, putting her hands on her hips. "Are you threatening to mutiny?"

Van Hasty's eyes narrowed. "No one ever made you captain. You took that on all by yourself. It's hard to mutiny when you don't have anyone to mutiny against."

Carina took a breath and exhaled. Van Hasty, like many of the mercs, could flip into anger on a trigger switch. It was time to de-escalate. "If the Black Dogs go planetside they could jeopardize everything we've worked for. As it is, our presence is a secret. I want to keep it that way for now. I need to figure some things out. As soon as I have, you all get your R&R. Permanently."

It was a long way back to inhabited regions of the galaxy.

"When? How long is it gonna take you to figure things out?"

"I don't know. I can't give you a date."

"You've got a week. No longer. After that, we take things into our own hands." Van Hasty walked away.

"Hey, wait! You can't hand out an ultimatum. You don't even know the situation down there."

"One week, Lin." She was nearing the bend in the passageway.

"I'll tell Hsiao to refuse to fly you down!"

"We've got Bibik, and, anyway, Hsiao isn't as much on your side as you might think." Van Hasty was gone.

Carina's hands fell to her sides.

Sixteen

Ferne and Oriana lounged on cushions on the floor, Parthenia and Darius were on Carina and Bryce's bed, and Nahla and Bryce sat at the small table.

Darius shifted sideways to make room. "Do you want to sit here?" he asked Carina.

"No, thanks. I'll stand." She knitted her fingers. "Are you all sure no one knows where you are?"

"Bibik doesn't know," Parthenia said, "but I'm not happy about it."

She'd been in a relationship with Hsiao's co-pilot for over three years. Nahla and Ferne also had serious partners, and Carina felt bad asking them to keep the meeting a secret from them. "I appreciate whatever little white lies you've had to tell, and I promise this won't be forever, but I don't feel like we have a choice. The Dogs are turning against us. If they knew we were holding a mages-only meeting they might take it the wrong way."

"Bryce and I aren't mages," Nahla said brightly.

"You're honorary mages," said Ferne.

Carina said, "You're family. Maybe that's what I meant."

"And Bibik isn't my family?" Parthenia asked archly.

"You know what I mean. Please don't make this any harder. I'm doing my best to find a home for us, a *real* home. But it isn't working out. I need your help."

"We'll do everything we can to help you," said Darius. "Just tell us what you need."

"That's the problem. I don't know what I need. I don't know what to do. Those three men turning up at the hideaway, and Matt's revelation about the General Alert has thrown everything into question."

Ferne eyed her. "You're *positive* you saw one of those men Casting?"

"A hundred percent."

"*I* didn't. Did you, Oriana?"

She shook her head. "Sorry, Carina, but all I saw was some shadowy figures. They could have been anyone and they could have been doing anything. It was too dark to see."

"When you say you saw one of them Casting," said Bryce, "what do you mean? Only, to someone who doesn't know what you're doing, it just looks like you're taking a drink and closing your eyes."

"That's right," Nahla said. "If I hadn't grown up with mages, I might not even make the connection between what you do and the effect of the Cast. How do you know he wasn't simply drinking something?"

"Don't you think it's a weird thing to do?" Carina asked. "You find some strangers in a cavern and the first thing you do is quench your thirst?"

Parthenia shrugged. "It isn't *that* strange."

"All right." Carina gritted her teeth. "What about Darius's bad feeling about them? When has he ever been wrong?"

"Can you tell us any more about that, Darius?" Parthenia asked. "Did you get any indication of what the men intended, or anything else?"

"Very little, sorry. The feeling was faint—due to the distance, I guess."

Carina said, "The fact that he felt anything at all at that distance tells me at least one of those men is extremely malevolent. Perhaps they all are. And they wished us harm."

"How do you know?" Parthenia asked.

"I just do."

"So you're a Spirit Mage now?"

Darius raised his hands placatingly. "Let's not argue. We need to help Carina, and each other, if we're ever going to live on Earth."

"I'm just concerned that we act based on reality and don't allow ourselves to be spooked by meaningless shadows. We have enough problems facing us without inventing more. There are these ID chips the police officer mentioned, and the fact that the population is on the watch for evidence of Casting."

"Exactly," said Carina. "Doesn't that strike you as oddly specific? Who has been priming them and why?"

"It *is* odd," Parthenia conceded, "but for now all it tells me is that we need to be careful. We can't give anyone cause to even suspect our abilities."

"But we've been forced to be careful all our lives," protested Carina. "Earth is supposed to be our chance for something new."

"Perhaps, with time, we can introduce the idea that mages aren't anything to be feared, and that there's a lot we can do to help people, providing we're allowed to live our lives as we please."

"Stars," Carina muttered. Parthenia sounded so naive. Had she forgotten all the trials and difficulties they'd faced as mages in the past? Had she forgotten everything Ma had gone through? "Before that incident in the mountain, I might have agreed with you that was a possible way forward. Now, it sounds futile and dangerous. It's clear that someone's been waiting for mages to turn up, someone who wants ordinary people to view us as enemies. Think about it. Those men arrived soon after us at the hideaway. Somehow, they knew we were there and they came to challenge us. At least one of them is a mage too. If his Cast had worked before ours, who knows what might have happened?"

"His alleged Cast," Ferne commented.

"Whatever. I'll take that seat." She flopped down on the bed between Darius and Parthenia.

"I found out some information about the General Alert," Nahla said.

"Shoot."

"The earliest instance I can trace occurred fifty-one years ago. It started in one country and gradually spread across the globe over fifteen years or so. Now, it's given out to most schoolchildren up to the age of fourteen. Then, the public information notices take over. They appear where most adults would see them fairly regularly. It seems to be an effort at subliminal programming to be on the lookout for activity that defies known physical laws, as mages do."

She added, ruefully, "Transporting out of the detention center as you did is exactly the kind of thing that would attract a great deal of attention, even more than it would somewhere the General Alert didn't exist. Actually, it already has. I thought I would check for repercussions, and they're all over the place. The recording of the incident has gone viral. Your faces must have been seen by everyone on the planet."

"Fantastic," Carina said. "So much for keeping a low profile."

"I'm glad we *didn't* go with you now," said Oriana.

"We would have been famous—for all the wrong reasons," Ferne quipped.

Carina straightened up. "I suppose there are warrants out for our arrest, Nahla?"

"What do *you* think?"

Ferne said, "It was lucky no one saw you or Darius when we went to the mage hideaway."

"*Some* people saw me," said Carina.

The room fell silent. No one appeared to have anything else to offer the discussion.

If they went planetside they would be apprehended, if not on sight then when it became clear they weren't chipped. It was a disaster. Everything was working against them. And it felt personal. It was as if someone had deliberately arranged things to make Earth the last place mages could live safely.

She announced, "Whoever organized the General Alert has to be connected to the people we saw inside the mountain. This is all too much of a coincidence."

"How do you figure *that*?" Oriana asked. "Nahla said the alert started decades ago. We've only just arrived."

"I can't explain it. It just makes sense. Someone is out to get us, and they nearly did. If it weren't for Darius's warning they would have succeeded. There's only one thing to do. I have to go back to the mountain. I want to find out who those men are and get to the bottom of what they have against us."

"That's insane!" Bryce exclaimed. "If you're correct you'll be walking right into their hands. And Darius has told us they're evil. It's a suicide mission."

"What alternative is there? Until I fix this problem Earth is off-limits. Our voyage will be a waste of time, and all those people who died to get us here will have died for nothing. I can't turn around and go back. I would be making those sacrifices meaningless." She swallowed hard and blinked away tears.

Darius put a hand on her arm. "They're gone, Carina. Nothing you do will affect them."

"It affects *me*."

A second silence fell.

"I'll go with you," said Parthenia.

"What?"

"I'm coming with you. As you said, we won't solve this mystery any other way. And if it comes to a mage battle you'll need another mage on your side. I can repel his Casts with Repulse while you defeat him."

"I thought you said we shouldn't be spooked by meaningless shadows."

"And I meant it. How else am I supposed to discover whether I'm right if I'm not there to see with my own eyes?"

Carina got to her feet and crossed the room to her sister, leaning down to hug her. "It'll be like old times. Do you remember when we blew up the Twilight Dome with Mezban's bomb?"

"How could I forget? It was the first time you didn't treat me like I was a silly little girl who needed protecting from herself."

Ouch.

If there was one thing Parthenia could be relied upon for it was speaking her mind.

"Those days are long gone," Carina said. "It'll be dangerous, but I would love it if you'd come."

SEVENTEEN

Everything was the same as before. The mountainside was quiet except for the wind passing over the rocky slopes, and there was no sign of the men. Carina paused at the gap that led into the ancient mage hideaway. The atmosphere had taken on a different feeling. Previously, she'd begun to accept this really was the home of her ancestors. She's started to enjoy a sense of awe and wonder from being here. Then the strange men had arrived and forced her to flee. Now, the dimness beyond the cleft seemed ominous and threatening.

"This is it?" Parthenia asked, peering in.

"We thought so. The shape of the slopes matches the sketch, only the pass is smaller. Ferne thinks it's due to erosion. The outer keep is entirely gone, but Oriana found this entrance. What's inside is like the mountain castle on Ostillon where we found the documents."

"That doesn't sound conclusive."

"No, but... It feels right. It feels as though they were here."

"Hmpf." Parthenia didn't say more, letting the skeptical vocalization stand.

"And the walls glow in a way I can't explain."

"That doesn't mean someone else can't explain it, someone who knows about these things. There could be a perfectly rational explanation. And I've never heard of a Glow Cast. Have you? How would it last all these years?"

Ignoring the unanswerable question, Carina said, "We saw the men fairly deep inside, in a large chamber with a waterfall. I don't know how they knew we were there. I'm worried that entering the cave set off an alarm, and that if we go in we'll do the same, only this time they'll arrive faster. There could even be someone waiting for us. It's only been a few days."

"How do you know the men don't simply live in the caves and your arrival spooked them?"

"I don't know for sure, but everything from here to the waterfall was uninhabited. I'm sure of it. There was dust over everything. No one had been there in a very long time. And look around you. There's nothing here. How could anyone survive here unless they were mages?"

"Well, we *want* the men to arrive. We need to find out who they are."

"We do, but we have to be in control of the situation this time. No more surprises." They'd brought sidearms along this time. The holster on Carina's hip felt awkward. It had been a long time since she'd been involved in a firefight, and though everyone on the *Bathsheba* had kept up with their training, she didn't relish the thought of engaging in armed combat.

"Then why don't we Transport in?" asked Parthenia. "If walking into the cave triggers an alarm we can avoid it. You can take us both to the waterfall."

"All right. Let's do that." Carina swigged elixir and sent out the Cast.

As she opened her eyes, the cool, humid air of the cavern hit her and the thunder of falling water filled her ears. She'd Transported them to the place she'd been standing when she'd spotted the men. She checked the opening on the far side of the waterfall, but it was empty. So far, so good.

Parthenia was already stepping away from her, heading for the pool. "It's quite something, isn't it?" She'd raised her voice to be heard over the waterfall's noise.

"Shhh!" Carina urged, joining her and adding, more quietly, "It's possible someone heard us talking the last time we came here, and that's what alerted the men."

"I very much doubt anyone can hear us over that thing." Parthenia nodded at the towering cascade. "Shall we explore further? I'd love to know what's through there." She indicated the opening where the men had been standing.

"Me too, but we have to be careful." Parthenia's breeziness was making Carina uneasy.

They skirted the perimeter of the wide pool. Translucent crustaceans crawled in the clear water of the shallows. The central area was obscured by mist.

"I have to admit," Parthenia commented, "this does remind me strongly of the mountain castle on Ostillon."

"Feeling more persuaded I'm right?"

"I never said you were wrong, but I know how much this means to you. It's easy to see evidence for something when you want it to be true."

They'd reached the exit. Her pulse quickening, Carina signaled Parthenia to stay back. She drew her gun and peered out. A passageway crossed the exit traveling in two directions. It was empty.

"Left or right?" Parthenia asked.

The right-hand path sloped upward. On Ostillon, the mages had placed their documents in the highest part of the castle, in an open-air chamber that commanded a view of the surrounding lands. Had the mages who had fled Earth left something behind to tell their story?

"This way," said Carina, turning right. She walked a little ahead of her sister, one hand on her elixir canister, the other carrying her sidearm. Parthenia had drawn hers too.

As before, openings led from the passage. Some revealed dusty, bare rooms, others were the beginnings of more passages. If there had ever been doors to the entrances they'd long since rotted away. A deep silence pressed in on Carina's ears, broken only by their soft footfalls. She almost began to believe the men had been figments of her imagination, but Oriana and Ferne had seen them too.

Why hadn't they arrived this time? Had Transporting into the cave and avoiding the outer entrance really foiled them?

"What's that?" Parthenia asked.

"What?"

"That, on the floor. Be careful!"

Carina looked down just in time to see an irregularity in the dust-covered ground as she trod on it. She barely registered the faint striations in the uniform surface before a click sounded and the rattle of heavy chains burst out. A metal cage slammed down.

Parthenia screamed.

The edge of the cage had hit her feet. She collapsed, gasping, outside the cage, but the weight of the heavy metal pinned her. Blood oozed from her shoes.

Carina was trapped inside. Her first instinct was to seize the bars and attempt to lift it. She couldn't move it a centimeter. She began to come to her senses. She took out her elixir canister to Transport them both out of here, back to the shuttle. Then she could Heal Parthenia.

"Ha!" a voice said. "We knew you would be back. Can't resist the place, huh?"

Carina turned. A tall figure was striding toward her—a female figure, but her stature was more like a man's. Had this been one of the people Carina had seen before, mistaking her as male? She was the size of Van Hasty and Pamuk.

Now wasn't the time to find out. Carina lifted her canister to her lips. But before she could drink, she froze. As the woman had walked closer, her face had been revealed in the half light. Carina's grip tightened on her container.

"No need for that," the woman said. "Why don't you stay here a while?" She closed her eyes. She was about to Cast. She must have drunk elixir before announcing her presence.

Parthenia's whimpers were another distraction. Fighting her shock, Carina forced a mouthful of elixir down. It was a matter of who could Cast faster. The woman had a head start on her. Should she Cast Repulse and block whatever the stranger planned to do with them? Or should she go straight to Transport to take them away from danger?

She had a better idea.

She took out her gun and fired.

———

She was standing in grass in sunshine. Parthenia lay on the ground, rolling in agony, her feet crushed and bloody. Carina fell to her knees. "I'm here, sweetheart. Just a moment." She placed a hand on her poor sister's ankles and Cast Heal, praying the elixir she'd swallowed a few seconds ago remained effective.

Gradually, Parthenia's moans faded. She relaxed onto her back and lifted a hand to her forehead. "That was *awful*."

"Are you sure you're better? Can I take off your shoes and check?" Irrational though it was, she wanted to reassure herself the Cast had worked.

"Be my guest." Parthenia sat up and inspected the damage. "Ugh, they're ruined. I only printed them yesterday."

The shoes were soaked in blood. Carina carefully slipped them off. "You Transported us out? I don't know how you managed it."

"It was hard to concentrate but I thought you would have your hands full. It never occurred to me the place might be booby-trapped."

"Me neither." She removed Parthenia's blood-encrusted socks. Her feet were whole and unmarked. Carina took a deep breath and exhaled. "You're fine."

"I know." Parthenia patted her arm. "You can relax. It was a good idea to shoot that woman. A pulse round is always faster than a Cast. Did you get a chance to see if you hit her before you were Transported?"

"No, but if it wasn't a kill shot she'll just Heal herself—or get someone else to do it for her. Did you notice anyone else?"

"It was as much as I could do to Cast, dear. I wasn't making detailed observations."

Carina chuckled. "Sorry." She took in their surroundings. Parthenia had

Transported them to within a short distance of the shuttle, where Hsiao and Darius waited. Though she didn't like the idea, they'd been forced to bring their youngest brother along to Cloak the shuttle on their journey to Earth. "We should get back to the shuttle." She began to put her sister's socks on but Parthenia told her she would wear the shoes with bare feet.

They began the short walk, Parthenia padding gingerly in her wet shoes.

"There was no warning from Darius this time," Carina said. "The woman must have arrived after I triggered the trap. Did you..." she hesitated "...did you get a good look at her?"

"From my position on the floor, looking past you while enduring unbearable pain? Not a *very* good look, no."

"So you didn't see her face?"

"Carina, what are you trying to say?"

"She...uhh...you're going to find this hard to believe. Do you at least believe me now about the men I saw, and that one of them was Casting?"

"I do. I admit you must have been correct. What new revelation do you have for me?"

"The woman—she might have been as burly as a female Black Dog, but she...she looked like Ma."

Parthenia halted. "Are you sure?"

"It isn't the kind of mistake that's easy to make."

"But you were freaked out, and you must have been thinking about mages and our history and so on. Maybe—"

"She had Ma's face. She looked even more like her than you or me. I'm not wrong, and," she added with some heat "I'd appreciate it if you would stop dissing everything I say."

"I'm sorry, but I don't understand how that's possible."

"It isn't. Not any way I can think of. But it's true."

EIGHTEEN

They were nearly at the shuttle—Carina thought she could see its faint outlines under the camouflage sheet—but there was no sign of Darius or Hsiao. Parthenia was peering around in a confused way too, and she opened her mouth as if to call out, but Carina put a hand on her arm, silencing her.

Something wasn't right.

She stepped off the track, taking her sister with her, and crouched in the undergrowth.

Parthenia did the same, whispering. "What's wrong?"

"I don't know."

If the pilot and their brother were in trouble, Darius would have Sent a message.

"They might have gone for a walk," said Parthenia softly. "It must be boring waiting for us with nothing to do."

Carina couldn't explain her feeling, so she just gave a shake of her head. She took out her elixir and swigged a little. *Darius, where are you? Is everything okay?*

Carina. Thank the stars. They took my elixir. They knew exactly what they were—

The sudden cut off in his reply sent a shockwave of alarm through her body.

Darius! Darius!

Parthenia grabbed her arm. "What's wrong? Has something happened to them?"

Sorry, Darius Sent, *They're hurting Hsiao, trying to make her tell them where the shuttle is. Please help, Carina. I can't do anything without my elixir.*

Where are you?

His description wasn't helpful. He and Hsiao had gone for a walk, as Parthenia guessed. All he could say was they'd walked roughly south for about fifteen minutes, and they were surrounded by trees—exactly like everywhere in this place.

If it were only a matter of Transporting Darius out of danger, she could have done it. She had a fix on him. But not Hsiao. She couldn't Transport the pilot unless she could see her, and it sounded as though hostiles were in close contact. She definitely didn't want to take any of them along by accident.

Hold on, she Sent. *We'll be there as fast as we can.*

"What's happening?!" Parthenia demanded as Carina opened her eyes.

"Someone's got them." She peered out, checking for movement, but the forest was still. She slowly rose to her feet.

Parthenia also stood up. "Who?"

"No idea. But whoever it is, they know all about mages. They took Darius's elixir off him. And they know about the shuttle, but they don't know where it is." She left out the part about the attackers torturing Hsiao. "I only know roughly where they are. We can Transport some of the way, but we'll have to be very careful. The woods must be crawling with people looking for us."

"You think the woman we saw in the caves is connected to this?"

"She has to be. It's all connected. Are you ready?"

Parthenia nodded and grasped her arm again.

"Take your gun out."

"What?"

"We have to be ready for anything."

With a look of distaste, her sister drew out her sidearm.

Before Transporting them, Carina checked the level of elixir in her canister. There was plenty but, as always, her supply was finite.

They appeared in a patch of open ground, a glade, surrounded by trees. Instantly, they sank down. The sunlight was warm on their backs and insects buzzed and crawled in the grass.

"I can't hear anything," Parthenia whispered. "Can you?"

Aside from birdsong and insect noise, their surroundings were quiet... except... Carina strained her ears. "I can hear them."

Easing through the undergrowth softly, she led Parthenia toward the faint sounds of voices. One was deep, demanding, and insistent. The other was shrill with pain and fear. She couldn't make out what they were saying, but she was in no doubt that the higher voice was Hsiao's and the other was her interrogator's. She hoped the pilot would resist a little longer. If the enemy found the shuttle it would make escape trickier.

Parthenia hissed, "I can see them."

An arching, thorny stem had snagged Carina's pants. She put away her gun to carefully detach the stem before looking in the direction her sister had indicated. In between the tree trunks in the distance was a group of figures. She made out ten or eleven gathered into a circle, facing inward.

Shit.

Hsiao and Darius would be in the center, the objects of attention. If she could only see Hsiao she could extract her, but the men and women blocked her view. "We have to get closer." She took out her weapon and they crept on. Then she halted. "Wait a minute." She sank to her haunches, pulling Parthenia down with her, then swigged elixir and Cast. *Darius, we know where you are but I need a line of sight to Hsiao. Can you do something?*

I'll try.

Thanks. Be careful.

"Carina," whispered Parthenia, her tone strained. "I think we've been spotted."

As she spoke, the cracking of twigs and rustle of bodies forcing a path through vegetation burst from the rear. Only fifty or so meters distant, men were heading their way.

Carina leapt up. "Run!"

They sped toward Hsiao and Darius. Keeping her focus on the group, she zigzagged through the forest, hoping to reduce her chances of being hit. Sure enough, pulse rounds hit the trees to each side, searing and scorching the bark. The scent of burning wood filled the air along with the snap and crackle of flames.

The people holding Darius and Hsiao seemed to have noticed what was happening. Pulses began to fly from that direction too. She was running from danger into danger. Where was Parthenia?

Shouting erupted from the captors. There was a scuffle going on. Darius had to be creating a distraction. The group was breaking apart. She caught a glimpse of Hsiao, and her heart lurched. The pilot was on her knees. Her hair glinted with wetness. Blood?

She could get her out. She had to get her out. But she needed a few seconds to make the Cast—a few seconds she didn't have. The minute she stopped running and dodging she would be shot or captured.

Suddenly, from nowhere, Parthenia was at her side. "Do it! I'll cover you."

They stopped near a bunch of ferns. Carina crouched down. Through the leafy stalks she could just make out Hsiao. Darius seemed to be struggling with two men. The other hostiles had spread out and were heading their way. A pulse grazed the ferns, setting them alight.

Parthenia was firing, sweeping her weapon to the front and back. "Hurry!"

Checking Hsiao's position again, she drank elixir and closed her eyes. Her sister's panting breaths sounded in her ears. Heat glowed on her cheek. The fire in the fern was spreading. A shriek came from somewhere close by. *Hsiao*.

She Cast.

Hard deck was under her knees. The noise and heat were gone. "Hsiao?!"

The pilot was curled on her side, holding her head, moaning. Her face was a mask of blood, dripping from cuts on her scalp, but she was alive.

Darius was also here in the shuttle passenger cabin but so were the men holding him. They stared wildly, their mouths gaping. Carina strode the two short steps required to reach them and shot two in the head. The third had time to raise his hands and mutter a plea before she shot him too. The awful scent of burned human flesh oozed from the bodies.

"You probably didn't have to kill them," Parthenia protested.

Always the pacifist, she'd turned soft over their long voyage.

"I think I *probably* did," Carina retorted. "Have you seen what they did to Hsiao?"

Darius dropped to the pilot's side. "Someone give me elixir, please!"

"Thank the stars it's all over," said Parthenia, handing him her canister.

"I told them," groaned Hsiao. "I told them. I'm sorry."

"You told them where the shuttle is?" Carina asked.

The pilot couldn't answer, only grimace and nod.

"I'll Heal her," Darius said, "and we can fly out."

Carina darted into the pilot's cabin and checked the sensors. People were moving toward the vessel. A few minutes ago the woods in this area had been empty. Had the people been Transported here? She started up the engine.

"What are you doing?" Parthenia asked from the doorway.

"What does it look like?"

"But we haven't removed the camouflage sheet."

"No time." She jabbed a finger at the approaching figures.

"Can you fly it?"

"It's been a while but I'll have to try. Tell Darius to Cloak us as soon as he's finished Healing Hsiao. And you all need to strap in."

Parthenia disappeared.

Carina gave a command and her seat harness snaked over her, closing with a click. After setting the coordinates, she grabbed the controls and guided the shuttle upward. Resistance from the sheet registered on the display. She ignored it. Outside, the vessel would be rearing up from among the trees, ripping the cover from the ground, and the whine of her engine would reverberate through the forest.

An alarm sounded and the pilot's interface blinked. They were being fired upon, but she doubted the enemy carried more than small arms. As soon as Darius Cast Cloak, they would be invisible to their attackers anyway.

While she flew them away, more pressing problems bothered her. Who was the woman in the caves and why did she look like Ma? And how had someone guessed there would be a starship shuttle waiting for them in the woods?

<h1 style="text-align:center">Nineteen</h1>

Bryce was in the shuttle bay. Reading her expression as she descended from the shuttle, he said, "Another bad trip?"

"You know that saying about the third try being the lucky one?"

"Er...third time lucky?"

"That's it. It isn't true."

"At least you all got back in one piece. That's the main thing."

Darius, Parthenia, and Hsiao were heading for the exit.

"Hey," Carina called after them, "see you in the mission room in fifteen minutes for debriefing."

No one replied as they left.

"That's a bit harsh," said Bryce. "Maybe you should give them more time to rest."

"Time is exactly what we're running out of. The Dogs gave me a week to figure this out before they take matters into their own hands, and we're one day down already. If they're let loose on Earth with no prep can you imagine the carnage? Honestly, I don't care if they screw things up for themselves. That's on them. They're big enough and ugly enough to run their own lives. But I don't want them to ruin our chances of living peacefully and openly."

"What happened down there? You sound desperate."

"Ugh..." She put a hand to her forehead. Where to begin? Before she could explain, a woman dashed into the bay—the last person she wanted to talk to right now, or ever.

"There you are!" Cheepy announced in a triumphant tone. "How come I haven't seen you since I came out of Deep Sleep? You've been avoiding me, right? I suspected you were hogging Earth all to yourself, and it's true. How many times have you been planetside now?" She got up close to Carina's face. "How many?!"

Hogging Earth to myself? "I'm glad to see you're over the effects of stasis. Things on the surface are tricky at the mo—"

"Don't give me that bullshit. You want to be the only person who gets to go down there and have all the fun. You, your family, and your cronies." She gave Bryce a look of disgust. "I won't stand for it. I never wanted to come on this stupid voyage in the first place. You tricked me into it, taking me away from everything I knew and everyone I loved."

"We've discussed this a million times," Carina said between her teeth. "You were the one who wanted to leave Sot Loza. It isn't my fault you changed your mind at the last second. And if you'd stayed, there's a good chance you would be dead by now. So you should really be thanking me."

"*Thanking you!* That's rich. You consigned me to living with thugs and weirdos, and I should thank you?!"

It had been a long, harrowing day. Something snapped. "Do you think I *want* you here, you nasty, whiny, stuck-up b—"

"Let's go," Bryce interrupted. "Gotta do that debriefing, remember?"

Cheepy's glare followed them out of the bay. If she'd been even remotely intelligent, Carina would have been worried about leaving her alone with the shuttle. She was sufficiently stupid to try to fly herself to Earth in it. However, she didn't possess anywhere near the smarts to even start the engines. The worst she could do was injure herself trying, and Carina secretly hoped she did.

"Am I a thug, a weirdo, or a crony?" Bryce asked as they walked down the passageway.

"All three, and an adorable thug, weirdo, and crony too."

On the way to the mission room they encountered Chi-tang, who was creeping about surreptitiously, peering over his shoulder.

"She's in the bay," Carina told him.

"Uhh, thanks." Chi-tang headed in the opposite direction.

———

Van Hasty and Jackson had invited themselves to the debriefing. Carina eyed them as they came in and sat down. She didn't say anything. She had to concede they had a right to attend. "I want Officer Matt here too. Is he still in the brig? And what about Nahla?"

"She's on her way," Parthenia replied, "along with Ferne and Oriana."

Another attendee had appeared: Ava. "I heard you're going to talk about Earth. Is it okay if I listen?"

"Of course," replied Carina, mentally chastising herself for forgetting about the Marchonish women. They were so meek and mild, so self-effacing, forgetting them was easy. Ava was the most outspoken of the bunch, but that wasn't saying a lot.

Jackson comm'd the brig guard to bring Matt, and everyone waited. Nahla came in with the twins. Lastly, the man from Earth arrived, wearing handcuffs.

"I don't think those are necessary," Carina said to his guard, nodding at the cuffs. What exactly would Matt do in a room full of mercenaries and mages, and if he escaped, where would he run to?

The guard unlocked the restraints. Jackson told him he would comm when it was time for the prisoner to return to the brig.

"Do you really need to keep him confined?" Ava asked. "I'm sure he won't do any harm."

"That's just your opinion," Jackson growled.

"And I'm entitled to it," Ava retorted, her eyes narrowing, "as his medic."

"I won't do anything," said Matt. "I promise. Anyway, I haven't done anything wrong. You don't have any right to lock me up."

Carina huffed in exasperation. "Oh, give him a cabin, for star's sake. We have more important problems than a deluded Earthman wandering around the ship."

"*I'm* the deluded one?" Matt gave a slight shake of his head. "I don't think so, though I have to admit, the effort you guys have put into this is impressive. You've learned a whole new language, built this fake ship, printed strange clothes... You've invented an entire history for yourselves too. You know, if you worked as hard at something else—a career, for instance, or a business—you could go far."

"What's he blathering on about, Lin?" Jackson snapped.

Putting her face in her hands, Carina wondered if they should take Matt's translator and only return it when they were ready to speak to him.

Bryce patted her back. "Shall we start?"

Darius spoke first, explaining what had happened to him and Hsiao. His report was simple and didn't contain much more information than Carina already knew. He and the pilot had gone for a walk, imagining the woods were empty. They'd *seemed* empty, until the men had pounced on them and, before Darius had a chance to Cast, they'd snatched his elixir canister. Then Hsiao's torture had commenced. Why no one had hurt Darius, who also knew the shuttle's location, hadn't been revealed.

Parthenia then told the story of what had happened in the caves. The time line of events showed that Darius and Hsiao had been attacked only minutes after the cage had slammed down over Carina. The connection was clear.

"So after I sprung the trap," Carina said, "someone sent—probably Transported—a team to the forest to find a starship shuttle. They knew that was how we arrived. Darius, did you get a bad feeling about a presence in the mountain like you did before?"

"I didn't, but I was distracted by the attack on Hsiao and me."

"They wanted to prevent us from returning to the ship," said Parthenia. "They wanted to cut off our avenue of escape and keep us on Earth."

Carina took in a breath. "There's something else to tell you. Parthenia can't confirm it because she didn't have a clear view, so you only have my word, but..." she focused on her siblings "...I'm absolutely certain the woman in the caves looked like Ma."

"She looked like Mother?" Oriana repeated. "How?"

"She just did. I can't explain it any better than you."

Jackson said, "You all look kinda alike, and you said the woman was a mage. It isn't that strange, is it?"

"There are thousands of mages," Parthenia snapped. "Probably tens of thousands, who look nothing like each other. Jace didn't look like us, did he?"

"Fair point," Jackson conceded.

"What does it mean?" Oriana asked, with a troubled expression.

"I don't know," Carina replied. In truth, on the shuttle ride back to the ship she'd formed a suspicion, but she didn't want to air it, not without more proof. Her idea was outlandish and she would sound unhinged, yet it was the only possible explanation.

She turned to Matt. "Have you followed everything so far?"

"I understand what you've said. Whether I believe it..."

"Whether you believe it or not doesn't really matter. Just imagine that what we've been saying is true. Have you ever heard of anyone who can do the things me and my family can—Transporting to locations and Healing injuries, for instance?"

"Never. Or, at least, not outside children's stories and vid dramas."

"Is it possible you just don't know about it?"

"No way. Something like that would be big news."

Parthenia said, "So mages on Earth are living in secret, the same as everywhere else. Disappointing, but perhaps to be expected."

Carina couldn't deny it.

"The situation is worse than that," said Nahla. "Not only do mages live in fear of persecution on Earth, a set of them are waiting for others to arrive from space, and whatever they intend, it isn't good. You don't trap people in cages or torture them to be friendly."

"They knew we would go there," Carina said. "They know the mountain hideaway is the only place returning mages could go if they wanted to connect with the past."

"I discovered something that might be relevant," Nahla announced. "Fifty-three years ago, the media reported that a starship had arrived from outer space and was in orbit around the planet. The reports were quickly discredited and, from what I can tell, most were deleted. I only found a few, hidden deep in the archives."

"So some other mages made it back before us," said Ferne. "The group in the caves must have attacked them too."

"And had all news of them removed from public view," Oriana added.

"There's no reason to think they were mages," Parthenia countered. "They could have been any returning colonists. Perhaps there's a conspiracy to keep Earth natives ignorant of the possibility of human life existing on other planets. Perhaps the information about the departure of colony ships wasn't lost, but is a deliberate attempt to erase history."

Carina said, "But why would the authorities not want anyone to know about people leaving the planet in the past? Matt, what's the general opinion about the possibility of colonizing other worlds? Is it something people talk about?"

"Not seriously. If there are other habitable planets out there, they're so far away it would take several lifetimes to reach them. A space journey that long isn't practical."

"You've never heard of Deep Sleep?" Carina asked. "I mean, putting people into a state of stasis for years at a time, where they're only just alive?"

"Sounds like science fiction."

"The tech has been forgotten," said Nahla, "along with starship engine drives. No one on Earth could build a colony ship even if they wanted to. But the impression I get is that there isn't much interest. Earth people are content with their living conditions, and it isn't hard to see why. It's a peaceful place with little hardship. Most of the population lives a long, happy life."

"Sounds idyllic," said Oriana.

"It isn't idyllic if you have to hide an important part of yourself," said Carina.

Van Hasty spoke for the first time. "I've listened enough. Me and Jackson came here to find out if there's a reason the Dogs can't go planetside, and all we've heard is mages this, mages that. You've got no reason to keep us here except that our arrival might upset your little plan to live happily ever after doing your magic tricks whenever you feel like it."

"I have to say," Ava interjected softly, "I agree. My friends and I have waited years to reach a place we can finally call home. Many of us are in relationships. All we want to do is to settle down and raise children, and Earth sounds ideal."

Though Van Hasty and Ava spoke separately they voiced the sentiment from the non-mage contingent aboard ship. Lines between the mercenaries and the Marchonish women had become blurred over the years as they'd fallen in love and formed partnerships. Carina's heart was heavy as she responded, "That isn't unreasonable. I want the same for my family. I'm just asking for a little time."

Van Hasty stood up. "What you want could take an eternity. You've got six days, Lin. Come on, Jackson."

The mercs departed.

"I'll go too," Ava said. "Unless there's something else I should know?"

Carina shook her head.

"Matt, come with me. I'll find a cabin for you."

Only Carina, her siblings, and Bryce remained in the mission room. No one spoke. What was there to say? They faced a problem that could take years to solve, and they had mages actively working against them.

The only thing she knew for sure was that however they tackled their anonymous enemies it had to be done in secret. Any whisper of a violent conflict related to their kind would tarnish their reputation forever among the ordinary, peaceful people of Earth, destroying the chance of mages ever living openly.

Twenty

Regardless of the urgency of the situation, Carina had to sleep. After a quick dinner she went with Bryce to their cabin and got ready for bed. As soon as they were under the covers Bryce wrapped his arms around her. "Try not to worry too much. We'll figure things out. We've got through worse things than this."

"I know, but—"

"And we've made it this far. If it wasn't for your determination we could never have done it. You should be proud."

"Yeah, but—"

"Go to sleep."

He knew her well.

He added, "Unless you want to…?"

"Too tired, sorry."

"Sure." He snuggled closer.

Warm and secure, her weariness overcame her anxiety and she drifted off.

Hours later, something woke her. She wasn't sure what. Bryce was lying on his back, quietly snoring. It couldn't have been that. She was well-used to his sleeping habits, as no doubt he was to hers.

A tiny light overhead gave the cabin minimal illumination, just enough to avoid utter darkness. Bryce's bare chest rose and fell. She laid a hand on it, appreciating the familiar sensation. At the meeting, Ava had mentioned the wish of the couples aboard to settle on Earth and raise families. Bryce had voiced the possibility for them, too, a long time ago. Though their experiences on Sot Loza had dissuaded him of the urgency, she hadn't forgotten the suggestion.

She had no practical objection. The only problem was, the odds of their offspring being mages was fifty-fifty, and she didn't want to bring a child into the world where they might be feared and hated, perhaps exploited. She would never forget the life Ma had endured. Creating a new person, knowing that a similar life for them was a risk—no matter how remote—was something she could never do.

But that didn't mean she and Bryce couldn't be happy. Over the course of the voyage her feelings for him had deepened and she was in no doubt that at the Matching on Pirine, when mages had the opportunity to find their life partners, she'd made the right choice.

Raising herself up on one elbow, she leaned over to kiss his lips. It took him a moment to wake up and when he did he was a little startled until he realized what was going on. Then he returned her kiss.

She said, "I'm not so tired now."

He smiled and turned onto his side, taking her into his arms. They kissed again.

Her ear comm chirruped.

"Shit." She reached for the side table, where it lay, and popped it into her ear. "Yeah?"

"Get to the bridge, Lin," Jackson said. "You want to see this."

"It's Jackson," she told Bryce. "Something's up. You should come too."

After hastily pulling on some clothes, they jogged through the passageways. Jackson didn't provide any updates along the way, so she guessed whatever the issue was it couldn't be that urgent. What she saw as she walked onto the bridge contradicted her assumption. "What the hell?!"

In the center of the bridge hung a holo, representing what she assumed was readings from the short-range scanners. Somewhere near the *Bathsheba* was a space-faring vessel. She didn't recognize the type but it wasn't much bigger than a regular shuttle.

"How long has *that* been here?"

"Only a few minutes," Jackson replied. "Comms has been trying to hail her, but no luck so far."

The comms officer was speaking into her mic. She looked over and gave a slight shake of her head.

"Keep trying," Carina ordered.

"It has to be from Earth," said Bryce.

"Well, duh," said Van Hasty. "Unless you know of another inhabited planet in this system."

"No need to guess how they found us either," Carina said. "*Dammit.* I was so busy worrying about our problems I didn't think about the repercussions of what happened today. If the hostile mages know we arrived from space, they know there's a colony ship somewhere close by."

Van Hasty added, "And the obvious place to hide around here is behind this big ol' satellite."

"Now they found us," Jackson said, "what do we do about it? If they didn't mean nasty business they would answer our hail. Is it time to turn on the Obliterator?"

"That old thing?" Van Hasty scoffed. "We haven't used it in years. Someone will have to dust off the cobwebs or it might blow *us* up instead."

"Sounds like a job for Chi-tang."

"Uh-uh." Van Hasty shook her head emphatically. "That's a negative. If we get him in here his goddamned loud-mouthed girlfriend's gonna follow him in."

The irony of the burly female merc calling Cheepy loud-mouthed wasn't lost on Carina, but she kept her opinion to herself. "Do we know if it's carrying weapons?" She studied the holo but it was hard to tell what might be armaments.

Jackson replied, "If she is, she hasn't used them." He checked his console. "Scanners aren't detecting anything powering up."

"It would take balls to fire on a ship a hundred times the size of your own," Bryce commented.

"If their mission isn't offensive," said Carina, "and they don't want to talk, they're here for surveillance. They want to know what they're up against. While we've been chatting they've been taking readings, finding out as much as they can about us. Let's not give them the luxury."

"I'll comm Chi-tang," Jackson said.

"No, wait." She chewed the side of her thumb. The *Bathsheba* could easily destroy the little vessel, providing her captain was stupid enough to stick around while the Obliterator built energy. But there was the need for secrecy to consider. Astronomy might no longer be of much interest to people on Earth, but there had to be a few die-hards with telescopes who wouldn't fail to notice a sudden massive burst of power on the far side of the moon. Keeping a violent conflict hidden from Earth eyes was paramount.

Besides, there was another good reason to not destroy the enemy vessel.

"I don't want to annihilate the ship," she said, "just scare it off."

"We can do that easily," said Jackson. "We can fire this bird's pulse cannon across her bows. That should give them the willies."

"Yeah," Carina agreed. "Do it." She sat down, keeping her gaze focused on the holo image.

"If the pulse cannon don't do the trick firing up the Obliterator will," Bryce said reassuringly, taking the adjacent seat.

The cannon fired. Streaks of light streamed above and below the enemy vessel. There was no need for a repeat of the warning. Her thrusters spurted and she slipped from sight, disappearing over the moon's rocky horizon.

"I dunno," Van Hasty said ruefully. "Maybe we should have destroyed that ship while we could. They can't have many space-worthy craft, and we don't want them to think we're pussies."

"They don't need spacecraft," Carina replied. "They must know the reason we came all this way is because we want to settle on Earth, so winning a space battle isn't important. The battle for what we want is going to take place on the surface. Blowing their ship up wouldn't have made any difference. They wouldn't risk putting anyone important in danger. But this way..." she got to her feet and opened a screen "...we can read her trace."

Jackson laughed. "And find out where she goes. You always were a smarty-pants, Carina Lin."

"Too smart for her own good," said Van Hasty. "Six days."

Twenty-One

The shuttle swept low over a vast tree canopy, stretching to the horizon on every side. Blazing sunlight glinted from every leaf under an azure sky.

"*This* is where the vessel landed?" asked Bryce.

He was crowded into the pilot's cabin with Carina and Parthenia, who had insisted on returning to the surface despite Carina's protests.

"Somewhere hereabouts," Bibik replied, nodding toward an undefined spot a few hundred meters below.

Carina decided to voice the obvious question. "But how?"

Bibik shrugged. "That's for you guys to figure out. Just let me know where to set this bird down."

That was another unanswerable question.

"Do another circuit," Carina replied. "We need some time to think about it."

They returned to the passenger cabin.

"Maybe the scan data is wrong," said Parthenia. "We should comm the ship and get someone to check it."

"I checked it twice already." Carina slumped into a seat. "I wouldn't bring us all this way without confirming it. This is where the spy ship landed."

"Maybe they have a special Cast that allows them to dissolve trees," Bryce said.

"And regrow them in a day?" asked Carina. "That isn't what's happened, believe me. I have an idea what it is, but I don't know what we can do about it."

"It's Semblance, right?" asked Darius.

"Yes!" Parthenia exclaimed. "That's it! It has to be."

"Semblance?" Bryce frowned. "That's a new one, to me at least."

"No, it isn't," said Carina. "You remember the Dirksen headquarters on Ostillon, in the mountains?"

"Oh, yeah. The entrance was fake."

"We encountered the same Cast on Magog. The boundary of the Dark Mage's estate was false. You could step through it and see the real boundary, the same as we stepped through the rock into the mountain castle. Semblance creates an illusion mirroring something nearby."

"I get it now. The trees aren't real. They're obscuring a shuttle landing site."

"It doesn't really help, though, does it?" Parthenia asked.

Carina replied, "At least we've confirmed this is mage work—ancient mage work. I didn't know about Semblance until we encountered the mountain castle, and I didn't have a name for it until we met the Dark Mage, Wei, on Magog. My grandmother never taught me the Cast, and Ma didn't teach it to her kids. So I guess it must have been forgotten by the mages in our sector."

Darius said, "I wonder what other Casts Earth Mages can do that we can't?"

"Who knows?" asked Parthenia. "Not too many, I hope. But, to return to my point, knowing that the shuttle landing site is there even though we can't see it isn't helpful. Even if we could figure out exactly where it is, we can't land there ourselves. Assuming Bibik could set us down in an open spot, Darius can't keep our shuttle Cloaked forever."

Bryce groaned. "You mean we have to trek in? How far? Conditions down there must be shit."

"And there will be snakes and spiders," Parthenia added. "But I don't see a way around it."

"It isn't as bad as it looks," said Carina. "We can Transport part of the way. If we can't see the landing site we have the rough coordinates from the trace data. I'll ask Bibik to find the closest place to land, then we'll take it from there."

She returned to the pilot's cabin to speak to him, but deeper problems were bothering her, problems she wanted to understand better before she mentioned them to the others. Why had the people who had spied on them constructed a secret base deep within a jungle and obscured it with Semblance?

Nahla had scoured Earth's news media reports and found no mention of a spacecraft visiting the Moon and returning, yet surely it must have been noticed, if only by people who watched the skies as a hobby. Somehow, these people were being silenced. So the base was hidden from regular view and whoever was running it had influence within the highest level of Earth governments.

Why go to all this trouble to keep their activities secret, and how were they managing it?

Something nefarious was going on, and it didn't only involve mages.

———

Parthenia and Bibik were taking a while to say goodbye before the party set off to find the shuttle landing site. Carina waited patiently. The two had been serious for a couple of years, and after what had happened to Hsiao it was natural that Parthenia would be concerned about leaving her partner alone, tens of kilometers from help on Earth and hundreds of klicks from his merc buddies on the *Bathsheba*. He wasn't a mage so he couldn't Send if he needed them, and they couldn't be sure their comm would work over the distance.

"It was nice of Bibik to volunteer to bring us down," Bryce commented as they waited.

"I think he felt obliged," Carina replied. "Hsiao would have done it but it wouldn't be right for her to take all the risks."

Darius said, "I could stay with him if that would be best. I don't mind."

Carina shook her head. "We need you too." *More than you know.*

The area nearest to their anonymous enemy's base sufficiently open to land the shuttle was a sandy beach at the edge of the jungle. The place was utterly deserted. No signs of human habitations or activity were visible. Though it was conceivable people lived within the jungle bordering the ocean, they couldn't be technologically advanced and so it was unlikely they posed a threat.

They waited in silence as the waves rose and fell and the steady sea breeze ruffled the palm tree leaves. From somewhere in the forest came the shrill cry of a bird.

Parthenia emerged from beneath the shuttle's new camouflage sheet, which mimicked the edge of the shoreline. She looked as though she'd been crying, but her expression became neutral as she walked over, trudging through the loose sand.

Darius put a hand on her shoulder. "I'm sure he'll be fine. We're in the middle of nowhere, and no one will have spotted where we landed. I was Cloaking the ship. They didn't know where it was on our last trip."

She stiffened. Brushing her hair from her eyes and ignoring her brother's reassurances, she asked, "Are we Transporting directly there? No stops?"

"I don't see any point," Carina replied. "It's a long way, but I'm sure Darius can manage it." Looking at her brother, she added, "Right?"

"I can do it, but how close do we want to be? They might be expecting us."

"Hmm. You're right. They might have guessed we would track their ship's trace. In case they've posted lookouts, shall we say one K out? We can check things out as we get closer and reassess." She scanned the others' faces for approval.

Bryce grimaced but said nothing.

Darius made his Cast, and they appeared on a raised portion of ground, thick tree trunks surrounding them. They seemed to be alone. Unfortunately, the high elevation didn't give them a good vantage point. All that could be seen was ranks of trees hung with vines and moss descending down the slope. The line where reality ended and the Semblance began was impossible to spot.

The humidity was stifling. Carina was instantly coated in sweat, and the local insect life had discovered them almost as quickly. A flying creature alighted on the back of her hand and began to probe with its proboscis. She killed it with a slap.

"Anyone know a Protect Against Bloodsuckers Cast?" Bryce asked hopefully.

"Sorry, but no," Darius replied. "I could try to invent one but it would take me a while."

"Another time." Bryce took out an interface from his backpack, consulted it, and pointed. "The shuttle landing site is that way."

"Should I Cloak us?" asked Darius.

"Save it for when we really need it," Carina replied. "I think we're okay for now."

"We waited too long on our first mission to Earth," Parthenia countered. "Maybe it would be a good idea to use it pre-emptively."

"We have quite a walk ahead of us over rough terrain. If Darius Cloaks us the entire way he'll use up his elixir supply."

Parthenia shrugged. "I'm just saying, we might not have been captured on our first mission if—"

"I hear you. We'll Cloak when we're two hundred meters out or if we spot anyone."

They set off down the slope.

After five minutes of battling invertebrates literally after their blood while also slithering down the leaf mold and loose soil, clinging to plant stems and draping vines for support, Carina cursed. "Why the hell did they build a freaking shuttle landing site out here?"

Bryce asked, "You mean why not somewhere more convenient, like an air-conditioned shopping mall?"

"That's exactly what I mean."

"We could browse the latest fashions while fighting our enemies," said Darius. "Ferne and Oriana would be totally on board with that."

Parthenia murmured, "I hope Bibik is all right."

As they reached the lower ground the insect life increased. A black cloud descended, and soon every square centimeter of open skin was under attack. Carina pulled her shirt sleeves over her hands and the hood of her jacket over her head, but her efforts barely helped.

"This is impossible," Bryce complained, running his hands over his face.

"I agree," said Parthenia. "We can't deal with this any longer. We simply have to Transport closer."

Carina couldn't argue. "Darius, can you Cloak us and then put us a hundred meters from the coordinates?"

The insects were gone and so was the humidity. Cool, dry air sucked the sweat from her skin. She lowered her hood. The same deep blue sky she'd glimpsed in gaps in the canopy still hung overhead, but the view had altered in every other way. Where there had once been deep brown forest floor lay an expanse of gray concrete. Towering trees had been replaced by columns of shining steel. The spacecraft that had spied on the *Bathsheba* stood on its pad in the distance, and four similar craft were positioned nearby.

The enemy didn't have just one space-traveling vessel, it had five.

The shock she felt seemed to extend to the others. For several moments, no one spoke.

Then Bryce said, "Well, we found what we were looking for. Now what?"

"I guess we get closer and see what else we can find out," she replied.

"I Cast the Cloak to a diameter of roughly five meters," said Darius. "If anyone steps outside the circle they risk being seen."

Figures moved between the columns and the shuttles. They looked more like techies and mechanics than guards, but Darius's reminder still applied. There was little chance that the sudden appearance of a bunch of insect-bitten strangers would go unnoticed.

"There's some powerful magic going on here," Bryce commented as they walked.

"It isn't magic," Carina replied irritably before asking, "What do you mean?"

"The whole place is air-conditioned and I can't see any barriers. Can you?"

As well as no ceiling visible above, forest fringed the site on every side. Something was confining the controlled atmosphere.

"Can Semblance do this?" Parthenia asked.

Carina didn't know the answer. She hadn't noticed the phenomenon the two previous time she'd encountered the Cast. In a sense, it wasn't important. Generating an illusion this vast was impressive work by itself.

An opening appeared at the base of a column and a four-wheeled vehicle sped out. It was the kind of passenger-carrying automotive she'd noticed as absent from Earth, according to Matt. The top was open and sitting in it were six men in three rows. Only one figure, seated at the front, wasn't in uniform.

"Shit," breathed Bryce.

The man in plain clothes was pointing in their direction.

"Don't worry," Carina said. "He can't possibly see us."

"Are you sure?"

She hesitated. The car was heading their way. She looked over her shoulder. Nothing stood between them and the edge of the site. "I don't *think* so."

Darius was also staring, dumbfounded, at the approaching vehicle. "I definitely Cloaked us."

The lead guard lifted a gun and aimed.

"Maybe you should..." Carina suggested as the vehicle zoomed closer.

"Uh huh." Darius took out his canister.

She put her rifle to her shoulder and stepped in front of her brother.

For some reason, Darius's Cloak didn't seem to be working, and they couldn't run from their attackers. They would never reach the forest in time before being mowed down. All they could hope was that he could Transport them before someone was hit.

The guard fired, and the round narrowly missed Parthenia.

Carina returned fire, winging the man who had shot at them. As he buckled, the vehicle veered, and the men behind him began to shoot. Bryce was firing now and so was Parthenia. Carina pressed the trigger again and a second guard went down.

A shriek.

Parthenia had been hit.

The car was only meters away. The man in front glared and grinned manically as he screamed orders at his men.

Carina's finger froze on her trigger. Her rifle spurted rounds, all going astray.

As she stared at the man, all sound seemed to disappear from the world. Everything zipped from existence until it was only her and the grinning man, alone in the universe, eyes locked.

Twenty-Two

They were back on the beach.

Parthenia was crying out in pain, but she was alive. She rolled on the sand, eyes shut tight, hands clasped to her shoulder. Darius fell to his knees and gulped elixir.

"How did this happen?" Carina wondered aloud. "How the hell could they see us?"

Poor Parthenia. It was the second time she'd been wounded. The Heal Cast would quickly take away her pain but that didn't make the wound hurt less at first. And Hsiao had been attacked too. They were lucky no one had been killed.

Darius had Transported them to a spot at the edge of the waves. A little way along the shore the shuttle stood in the shade of the trees. Bibik would notice them soon and come out to check on Parthenia, no doubt. What to do next? Return to the *Bathsheba*?

She walked to the water's edge and watched the ocean, her mind a blank. She was still coming to grips with her vision of the man riding in the front of the vehicle. The face of the woman in the mountain hideaway flashed up. Suddenly, everything slotted into place.

Bryce joined her and asked quietly, "Is it possible the Cloak Cast didn't work?"

"No way. It's always worked before, and we were standing together. No one should have been able to see us."

"Maybe there's something about that place that makes Casts ineffective. Nice shots back there, by the way."

"Thanks. Target practice helps to pass the time when spending years traveling the galaxy."

"You worked out a lot too as I recall."

He didn't know why, and she'd never told him. It was due to one of the last things Atoi had said before the Regians took her: *You're weak. You can be stronger, and you need to be to protect those brats.*

Bryce's focus had switched from her face to something behind her. "*Damn!*"

"What?"

His eyes narrowed. "Soldiers! Hostiles, in the trees!"

She swiveled. Shapes moved in the undergrowth—men and women in fatigues.

She sipped elixir. There was no time to warn Darius or Parthenia.

A pulse round flashed past and hit a wave, bursting the water into a hissing frenzy. Fighting the urge to run, she closed her eyes and Cast. A second round impacted a wave.

She'd Transported everyone hundreds of meters along the beach. This time they stood at the border of the jungle. Would the soldiers they'd left behind spot the shuttle ? She hoped not, and that Bibik had the good sense to check the area before coming out.

"What was *that* about?" asked Parthenia, putting a hand to her forehead.

"They found us somehow. I had to move us away."

"But how did they know where we were?"

"I don't know. I just had to do something fast."

"You should have Transported us into the shuttle."

"You're right. I didn't have time to think." In truth, she remained dazed with shock. "I'll Transport us there now, and we can get the hell out of here." The mission felt like another failure, despite the revelation that had occurred. If anything, it had only stacked the challenges higher.

"Do they know where the shuttle is?" Parthenia asked, concern edging her tone. "Is that the reason they found us? Has anyone tried to comm Bibik?"

"I haven't," Darius said, "but that can't be why they knew where we were. In the mountains, it was different. There were hardly any places to land a shuttle. They could guess the rough location. But this beach stretches for tens of kilometers."

"I don't believe it!" Bryce exclaimed. "They found us again."

This time, the soldiers were only meters away.

"That's not possible," Carina protested.

The enemy had appeared out of nowhere.

There was no time to Transport.

"Scatter!" she yelled. "Run into the forest! When you get a chance to Cast, rendezvous in the shuttle." She grabbed Bryce's arm. "Stick with me."

By splitting up they would stand a better chance of not being caught, and in the dense forest they might find a spot to hide long enough to Cast, but she couldn't lose Bryce. Alone, he was all but helpless.

She dashed into the trees. Instantly, the undergrowth seemed to grip her, intent on slowing her down. Tree trunks appeared and she raced around them, forcing through ferns and clinging vines, listening for Bryce as he ran behind her. The dreadful humidity descended again and sweat trickled from her face and armpits. Her lungs labored.

Where were the soldiers? Had she escaped them? Her and Bryce's passage through the vegetation would be easy to follow. She could only count on their head start and greater speed to give her the breathing space to Cast.

Casting a glance behind her, she spotted Bryce a few steps to her rear and beyond him approaching soldiers.

She ran on.

Why hadn't the Cloak Cast worked?

How had the soldiers found them twice in a row, in less than a minute? The only way they could be found so easily would be if a mage was Locating them, but that was impossible. He or she would need a personal item, something imbued with their essence, to track them down in that shadowy other-world only mages could see. Yet they'd left nothing behind on their visits to Earth.

A bamboo thicket rose up, tall and forbidding. The smooth stalks clustered thickly, yet, with a little effort...

"Let's go in here." She eased between the stems, pulling Bryce in after her.

"But we won't be able to move."

"Yes, we will. Better than someone in armor, anyway." She forced a hip into a gap and shouldered the vegetation apart, working her way deeper in. The bamboo was a trap in a sense, but it would give them the time she needed.

In half a minute, they were entirely hidden. She took out her canister.

There was a flash. A soldier had fired at the clump, despite the fact they had no visible target. Smoke billowed up. Leaves at the top of the bamboo stalks turned into flames.

"Carina," Bryce whispered urgently. "You'd better Transport us, fast."

She gulped elixir, but before she Cast, the answer to the puzzle exploded in her mind. She had left things behind in the detention center in Bridgeford. She'd been ordered to remove everything from her pockets, and she'd been carrying items she could use to Locate her brother and sister if they were split up. Someone—she was in no doubt exactly who—had recently gotten hold of her things, and now he could Cast to find her, Parthenia, and Darius at any time.

"Carina!" Bryce urged. "Why are we still here?"

The vegetation crackled as the fire moved closer. Hot air warmed her skin.

"We can't go to the shuttle," she replied. "He'll find us."

"He? Who? Who'll find us?"

She had to warn Parthenia and Darius of the danger. Rather than Transporting, she Sent.

Her sister and brother were disbelieving, but there was no time to argue. She told them her plan. As she finished, she felt Bryce grab her jacket. He thrust her into the bamboo, driving a passage through reluctantly yielding stalks.

The fire had moved closer amazingly fast. A red haze of sparks and flying embers rose behind Bryce. She could smell singed hair. His eyes were wide and desperate as he tried to protect her from the flames.

She drank elixir.

The problem was, she couldn't Transport each of them to two different places at once. Bryce had to return to the shuttle first, and she didn't have time to explain why. As the air became unbearably hot and her chest heaved, she made the Cast.

Bryce was gone.

She'd saved him, or at least delayed his capture.

Now to save herself, and deprive their enemy of his advantage.

The fire was almost upon her.

She gulped elixir, but she choked and the precious fluid erupted from her mouth. She'd dropped her canister. She picked it up and coughed. The smoke made it impossible to breathe.

She had to Cast.

She had to Cast or she would die.

The heat on her skin was unbearable. Her jacket was smoldering.

Lifting her canister to her lips once more, she saw blisters on the backs of her hands. She wouldn't need to close her eyes. They were already swelling shut. She tipped up the container, but only a few drops dribbled into her mouth. The elixir must have spilled out when she dropped it.

The bamboo at her back was impenetrable. To her front was an inferno.

There was no escape.

If only she could Send to Bryce, or any of her brothers and sisters.

Whispering a last goodbye, she waited for the fire to take her.

TWENTY-THREE

The heat was gone. No flames crackled. She could breathe again and the air was blissfully cool.

Her canister was wrenched from her hand. It hit the ground with a thump.

"Shall I restrain her, Lord?"

Lord?

Her eyes hadn't been playing tricks on her at the shuttle landing site. Only *he* would award himself such a ridiculous, highfalutin title.

"No need. Look at the state of her, and without elixir, she's useless." She felt a shadow block out the sunlight and the voice hissed in her ear, "You *are* useless, aren't you, Carina? Not so clever without your little stage prop. Bringing the Great Mage to her knees is pathetically easy."

Forcing her eyes open a slit, she beheld the man she'd seen in the vehicle giving orders. He'd Located them at the site despite Darius's Cloak. Clearly, it didn't shield from Casts. They'd never tested that capability.

Then after they'd Transported to the beach, he'd Located them again, and sent his soldiers in to capture or kill them. Transporting hundreds of meters away had made no difference at all. Another Cast and once more he'd found them. Finally, as soon as she'd stayed in one spot long enough, he'd managed to first Locate her and then Transport her to his side.

He was older than she remembered him. *Much* older. He'd aged so much he was barely recognizable, hence her shock and doubt. But it explained why the woman in the mountain caves resembled Ma, and why the entire planet seemed to be prepared for their arrival—set up to prevent her from achieving her goal of a peaceful life for her family.

"Castiel." Her voice was a mere croak.

"You do recognize me, then." He smirked. "I was wondering how long it would take until the penny dropped, or if I would have the pleasure of informing you myself."

He had to be in late middle age, if not older. His thick black hair had thinned to gray strands. The youthful visage of a mid-teens boy had creased into lines and wrinkles. Eyes that had once been round and deep brown were hooded and filmy.

How long had he traveled the galaxy? And how had he found Earth's coordinates? She'd taken the mage documents from the castle on Ostillon. He'd never even set eyes on them.

"Your little burnt face is alive with questions," he teased.

"I do have questions," she murmured, "but I'm not sure if you'll answer them."

His expression brightened with pleasure. He was enjoying himself. He must have anticipated this moment for decades, brooding over the revenge he would exact on his siblings for a childhood spent feeling inferior. His spitefulness made him weak. It was a weakness she could exploit—a weakness she had to exploit. Though her view of her surrounds was limited, Parthenia and Darius didn't seem to be here. She had to prevent him from doing the same to them as he had to her. She had to go through with her plan, albeit somewhat modified.

"Try me," he gloated. "Oh, and don't think I don't know what you're doing. You want to distract me so Parthenia and Darius have time to get away. Perhaps they might, but, one way or another, it doesn't matter. I can always Locate them again." He held up a fist. Parthenia's brooch and one of Darius's combs peeked from between his fingers. "What's more, I have you too, and they'll do anything to save you, as will Ferne and Oriana. Such are the bonds of familial love, as my dear Father knew so well. All I have to do is threaten to hurt you and they'll come running, falling over themselves in their efforts to protect you. I will enjoy destroying all of you, one by one, including Nahla and your oafish boyfriend. How odd you're still with him. But as they say, love is blind."

He leaned so close his face took up all her vision. "I can read your mind. I know what question burns at its center right now. You want to know how I arrived here ahead of you." He grinned. "For so many years I've anticipated informing you about what happened after you dumped me on Ostillon."

"When you betrayed us to Sable Dirksen, you mean?" Her voice sounded stronger. The effects of the fire were easing. She could breathe better and she didn't feel so weak, though her seared skin stung painfully.

"Betrayed is such a strong word. I prefer to see my actions as sensible and rational. Had I remained with Sable I would have eventually gained control of the Dirksen clan, vanquished the Sherrerrs once and for all, and taken my rightful place as supreme leader in the sector."

"Sable would have chewed you up and spat you out. Anyway, aren't you a bit old for all this? Clinging to the past isn't healthy."

"I believe *you* were the one who wanted to know what happened back then?"

She didn't answer, playing for time.

After a pause he seemed to conclude he'd scored a point. "You ruined my chances of success with the Dirksens, and the Sherrerrs only ever saw me as their slave. The sector was dead to me."

She had a strong feeling Castiel had ruined his own chances with the Dirksens, assuming he'd ever had any, but she remained quiet. He was on a roll.

"I decided to pay you back in kind. Why should you achieve your dream when I cannot? However, I didn't anticipate arriving before you. What kept you?" Before she could reply, he added, "It was a rhetorical question. You remember Justin? Jace's brother?"

She blinked. How had Castiel known about the mage brothers? She and the Black Dogs had taken Jace from his cell in the mountain castle, where Sable Dirksen had left him to starve, and the last time she'd seen Justin, a member of the Mage Council, had been on Pirine. She didn't know what had happened to him after the Dirksens had burned the Matching campsite. She'd assumed he'd escaped along with most of the other mages.

"You *do* remember him. I can tell."

Her heart quailed at what she imagined she was about to hear. "If you hurt him..."

"You'll do what? This may come as a surprise, but you aren't in a position to make threats. You see, I *did* hurt him. Rather a lot. But that was after he gave away his secrets to Kee. The commander is a master interrogator. I don't mind admitting it. We became reasonably good friends on our long voyage. I can see you're becoming confused, so I'll start at the beginning."

It was not confusion but compassion that was troubling her. Compassion for the kind, wise man who had suffered at her evil half-brother's hands, and regret that he'd been dragged into her business and suffered for it.

"After you abandoned me and set off on your Great Adventure..." he made air quotes with his fingers "...Kee returned to Ostillon. He knew from the Dirksens that I remained on the planet, and he sought me out to find a way he might rescue Sable. Only a mage knows what another mage can do. The poor man was deeply in love with her and prepared to stop at nothing to get her back safe and sound. But when word arrived from one of the mercenaries who resigned from your band that Sable was dead, his plan changed. He wanted nothing more than to make her executioner pay for the misdeed. He would do whatever it took to achieve his aim, and, believe me, when Kee wants something, he gets it. You and the rest of the mages might have departed Ostillon, but several had been captured on Pirine, Justin among them. I won't bore you with the details, but Kee wanted to help me follow you to Earth. Our desires dovetailed nicely. All we had to do was to wait for you to arrive, and here we are."

"The woman at the ancient mages' hideaway in the mountains—she's your daughter?"

He grimaced. "Letitia bears an unfortunate resemblance to our dear departed mother. I'm not surprised you understood who she must be."

"Letitia? What a pretty name. You must love her very much." She was being sarcastic. Castiel was incapable of loving anyone except himself.

His grimace deepened. "She's...useful. She's a mage, as you must have noticed, and not a bad one. Due to Mother's neglect of my education I couldn't teach her myself, but the mages here have done a reasonable job."

So there were more mages on Earth, and Castiel was in contact with them. Was he also controlling them? Did they know he was a Dark Mage? There was so much more she was dying to find out, but she had to act soon. He might grow bored of delighting in her downfall, and then he would seek out Parthenia and Darius. They could have already left on the shuttle but she doubted it. They were, as Castiel had said, loyal to a fault. She had to think of something to distract him, put him off his guard. What better distraction was there to a narcissist than to get him to talk about himself?

"You're an old man. Isn't devoting your entire life to getting back at me a little... excessive? You must have better things to do."

"Don't flatter yourself," he spat. "I've done plenty during my sojourn on Earth. Plenty. Dealing with you and the sad wastes-of-space who are our siblings is merely a pastime. I will take great pleasure in introducing you to my empire before deciding whether to—"

She'd fastened her hand around his throat. The simple movement sent waves of agony down her arm, but she squeezed hard, sealing off his voice and breathing. Castiel flailed, attracting the attention of his men, but before they could reach her she threw him on his back. Snatching the flask at his side, she ducked the rifle butt aimed at her head. And, as she'd hoped, no one wanted to risk a shot while she was so close to their 'Lord'.

Tearing the lid from the flask, she swigged elixir. Hands grabbed her shoulders, wrenching her to her feet, but at the same time she pulled Castiel's weapon from its holster and aimed it at him. "Release me or he's dead."

The hands left her. She quickly scooped up the items Castiel had been holding, which had fallen from his grasp. In her hand were Parthenia's brooch, Darius's comb, and a button that must have been torn from her jacket during the struggle with the guard. She then stared at her half-brother, sprawled on the ground. She had a short window of time while the elixir would retain its effect. "What's it to be, Castiel? Transport or Split?"

The arrogant confidence in his eyes wavered. "You won't do it. You wouldn't dare. Your own death would follow mine in an instant." But terror underlay his words. They'd both witnessed his father's horrible demise at Ma's hands.

"The satisfaction of knowing I'd removed you from the universe might be worth it." She closed her eyes.

"You don't have the guts to kill me, Carina Lin. Run back to our brothers and sisters if you like. I'm enjoying our game of cat and mouse, and I'll also enjoy bringing it to its inevitable conclusion."

Twenty-Four

Bryce was seriously pissed off. He hadn't spoken a word to Carina the entire shuttle ride back to the ship, and he'd maintained his silence in the hours afterward as she and her siblings came to grips with the fact that Castiel had re-entered their lives.

Bryce was the type of person to stew a while before voicing his grievance, so she left him to it. Nothing she could say would make a difference to how he felt anyway. He was right to be angry. If the roles were reversed she would have been angry too. Yet what she'd done was also right. She hadn't had a choice about it.

He waited until they were alone in their cabin before saying, "We need to talk."

She heaved a sigh. "I know." Sitting next to him on their bed, she took his hand. "I know what you're going to say, but—"

He removed his hand from her grasp. "You can't do that to me again. Ever. If you do, I don't think our relationship can stand it."

She took a breath. She knew he was upset, but not this upset. "Bryce, there was no time to explain or discuss it. I had to get you to safety, and I had to find Castiel. If I hadn't we would have forever been at risk of him Locating and Transporting Parthenia, Darius and me. The only reason he didn't do it immediately was because we kept moving. He couldn't get a lock on us. As soon as he could, when you and I were hiding in the bamboo, he captured me. And I couldn't take you with me because..." Her words petered out.

Bryce's lips had thinned to a line and he'd turned pale. The anger he was holding back dismayed her.

"Because...?"

"Because it would have complicated things. If both of us had gone to Castiel he would have used you to force me to do whatever he wanted. He would have threatened to kill you, and then what else could I do except obey? You know what it was like with his father. Castiel learned all of Stefan Sherrerr's tricks."

"So you're saying I'm a liability? That I couldn't have helped you? That I'm incapable?"

"No!" She covered her face with her hands. "You don't understand."

"I think I do. You wanted to play the hero, again."

"That isn't true! And it's not fair. Do you really think I'm so crazy I would risk burning to death just to inflate my ego? You saw how I was before Parthenia Healed me. Do you think I nearly died for fun?" She hadn't told him or anyone else that she *would* have died if Castiel hadn't Transported her. No one knew she'd spilled the remains of her elixir. It had seemed an unnecessary detail. Now she didn't think she would ever reveal the truth. Not if this was Bryce's reaction without that tidbit.

"No, not for fun." His tone was softer. "But the first thing you thought was you had to get me out of the way before tackling the problem yourself. Because you're the only one who could do it."

"That's ridiculous. I'm sorry you're hurt, but let's not pussyfoot around the facts. I was the only one who could do it. Out of the two of us, who can Cast, huh?" Perhaps her abilities did emasculate him but she couldn't help it. She couldn't deny who she was.

"Wow, that's some apology. Thanks. I feel much better."

"I'm not trying to make you feel better, I'm trying to make you see sense. There wasn't anything else I could do in the circumstances except exactly what I did. If I hadn't Transported you to the shuttle and gone after Castiel we would probably all be dead right now, Bibik included. Castiel would have Located Darius and Parthenia in the shuttle and discovered where it was. We were lucky he didn't spot us when we first landed. I guess he wasn't Casting for us then. He can't do it all the time or it would exhaust him. We would be dead or captured, and then he would have enticed Ferne and Oriana to the surface—"

"For fuck's sake, Carina. I get it!" Bryce rose to his feet and leaned over her, fists clenched. "Do you think I can live with your family for years and not understand how it works? I was there when Stefan Sherrerr kidnapped you. I was there when you escaped the *Nightfall*. I've been there, right by your side, all the time. I left my family to help yours. I gave up my future on Ithiya. I've risked my life again and again to help you. Have you forgotten all that? Or do you only see me as a pathetic hanger-on, tagging along because I don't have anything better to do? Or perhaps I'm just a lovesick nobody with no life of their own?"

She looked up at him, tears pooling in her eyes. She swallowed. "No, I don't think any of that. I love y—"

"Do you? Do you really? Is that what love is? Ignoring my wishes? Riding roughshod over my free will? Transporting me wherever you want whenever you feel like it? What else have you done? Have you Enthralled me like you did Parthenia? Did you do a little interrogation late at night while I was too sleepy to notice? Or maybe you got me to agree to something against my will. That's a funny kind of love."

"I've never Enthralled you," she whispered.

"How would I know? How can I trust you when you just Transport me out of a situation without a by-your-leave?"

"There wasn't time for anything else! How can you expect me to ignore the dangers and not do what's needed to save your life, just so you don't feel controlled?" She reached out and touched his arm. He didn't pull it away, to her great relief. "I can guess how it must feel, and, if anything, I would be even angrier. Of the two of us, I *am* the one with the bigger ego, I admit."

He didn't react, ignoring her attempt to make eye contact.

"I don't know what I'm supposed to do," she continued. "We're different. I can do things you can't, and if I and my siblings couldn't Cast we wouldn't have made it this far."

"If you and your family couldn't Cast we wouldn't even be here."

It was an undeniable truth. The blessing and curse of their abilities was what had prompted her to drag everyone halfway across the galaxy.

"The only reason we met was because I'm a mage," she said quietly. "I was on Ithiya to find Darius and try to make contact with a mage family."

Bryce sat down beside her, his shoulders high and head low as he rested his elbows on his knees. "I guess that's right," he murmured. "If you weren't who you are we wouldn't be together."

A scene from a few days ago returned to her mind, when they'd been in the Twilight Dome and she'd asked him if he had any regrets. He'd said he hadn't. Was that still true? She didn't dare ask him. Perhaps he was concluding he'd made a mistake.

"I don't know how to make things better," she said. "I don't know if I can promise to never Cast on you again without your permission in a life-and-death situation. I love you. I don't want you to die." The practical part of her mind protested. *Of course* she should save him if it came down to it. She would want him to save her. Yet she empathized with his reaction to what she'd done. For once, she managed to not speak the quiet part out loud.

He took her hand in his, but his focus remained downward. Gently, he rubbed it. "I don't know how to make things better either. Maybe we can't."

She stiffened, dreading what might follow.

"It's funny," he said. "I love that you're a mage. I love that about you, though I think I would love you just the same if you weren't. But it means we aren't equals, and nothing can change that. Maybe that's something I've been trying to ignore for too long." He released her hand and stood up, continuing to not meet her gaze. "I need time to think. I'm going to sleep elsewhere for a while."

"No, don't," she protested, a catch in her voice. "Let's talk some more. We can find a way through this."

"You're not hearing me—again."

She was silent.

Before he left, he said, "What happened today... That's why ordinary people hate mages. You make us feel useless. If you want to live safely on Earth, you'll have to figure out a way to fix that problem."

TWENTY-FIVE

After hours of tossing and turning Carina was finally falling asleep when she felt the ship move. It wasn't easy to feel the motion of a behemoth like the *Bathsheba*, but she'd spent so long aboard her she'd become sensitive to any deviation from the norm.

She comm'd the bridge, but received no answer.

She tried Hsiao instead. The pilot probably had a good reason for changing their position, but it would have been nice to be consulted.

Hsiao also ignored her comm.

As the movement continued, Carina grew alarmed. Was someone else moving the ship? In her sleepy state, she wondered if enemies boarded and everyone except her been taken prisoner. It was a wild thought, but no other explanation sprang immediately to mind. She couldn't check if Bryce knew what was happening, not after their argument and his request for her to leave him alone. She comm'd Parthenia.

To her relief, her sister answered quickly. "What's wrong? I was sound asleep."

"You're okay?"

"Of course I'm okay."

"Is Bibik with you?"

"Yes. Why?"

"Have you noticed the ship's moving?"

"No, she... Oh, you're right. She is. That's odd."

Carina cut the comm. If Bibik wasn't flying the *Bathsheba* it had to be

Hsiao, or perhaps a trainee pilot. Maybe that was the explanation. But it was risky to practice maneuvers in the current situation. One thing she knew for sure—she wasn't going to get to sleep until she knew what was going on.

She got out of bed, pulled on a robe, and walked to the bridge.

Hsiao, who sat at the pilot's station, ducked her head as she walked in.

Van Hasty was here and so was Jackson, Rees, Mads, Berkcan, Ola, and Pamuk. Even Chi-tang was present. He'd managed to give Cheepy the slip.

"Well," Carina said, "isn't this quite the delegation? Is anyone going to tell me what's going on?"

Everyone looked at Van Hasty, except Hsiao, who kept her gaze steadfastly ahead.

"We decided to take matters into our own hands," Van Hasty said, a defiant look in her eye.

We?

Carina had a strong suspicion the merc had persuaded the others to gang together and back her up.

"And that means...?"

Had the Black Dogs decided to give up the idea of settling on Earth and return across the galaxy?

Jackson cleared his throat. "We're going to take out that place your asshole little brother is running. One blast from the Obliterator should do it—and take him out at the same time. Then your problems will be over and we can go planetside."

That explained Chi-tang's presence. He was the weapon's operator.

"Are you all insane?" Carina spluttered. "Hsiao, stop the ship."

Hsiao looked at Van Hasty, who shook her head.

"Hsiao," Carina repeated, "do what I said. That's a direct order."

"You're long past the stage of giving us orders, Lin," said Van Hasty. "You might have made corporal in the Black Dogs but you were discharged a long time ago, and we're not even running your contract anymore. When was the last time you paid us?"

"But you know why we're here. You agreed to help my family. You said I still had six days."

"Five days. But it doesn't matter, not now we figured out a faster way to do it."

"Your way isn't faster or better. It's stupid. If you blow up that site it'll ruin everything, not to mention the fact that you'll be killing hundreds if not thousands of innocent people."

"Innocent?" Jackson's forehead creased into a quizzical frown. "You think those men and women working for your brother can't tell what an evil, traitorous shithole he is? But they're still working for him. Choose the wrong side and you get what's coming to you. That's what I say."

His merc companions nodded their agreement.

"Okay," Carina reasoned, "if you don't care about murdering Castiel's workers, think about the damage you'll be doing to our prospects on Earth. By all accounts it's a peaceful place, as close to a harmonious human society as you can get. How do you think unleashing the Obliterator is going to go down? What kind of introduction is that? How will the people of Earth see us?"

A puzzled look passed between the mercs.

"Why should we care?" Van Hasty asked.

"Because we want a new life, a different life, an end to all the violence and killing."

"We do?"

"First I heard about it," said Pamuk.

"Yeah," Jackson growled, "I think you're getting confused, Lin. No one here signed up to the happy-ever-after scenario you have in mind. I can't speak for everyone, but what I'm looking forward to is getting wasted and seeing some different ugly mugs for a change."

"*You're* wanted for murder," Carina said, "in case you forgot."

Jackson was another problem to be overcome. While Earth might be peaceful—on the surface—it was also technologically advanced. Jackson was known to the authorities. He wouldn't last five minutes in even a small town before being picked up.

"Are you a little old to be getting wasted?" she added. "Don't you want to settle down?"

Another look passed between the Dogs. This time it was incredulity.

Jackson gave a great bark of laughter and doubled over, clutching his sides. His companions seemed to find her comment equally funny. The atmosphere in the bridge reverberated with their whoops and giggles until finally Jackson pulled himself together sufficiently to squeeze out, "Good one, Lin."

The *Bathsheba* had to be nearly out of the Moon's cover. Soon, she would be visible to anyone on Earth who happened to have a telescope pointing in the right direction. Perhaps it wasn't important. Perhaps whoever had covered up the movements of the spy space vessel would do the same for the colony ship, but she didn't want to take the risk.

"Hsiao, please stop the ship."

The pilot shrugged helplessly. "It's seven against one. Sorry."

"Chi-tang?" Carina appealed to the pickup from Lakshmi Station. "You could refuse to fire. Then we might as well stay behind the Moon."

"Someone else could do it, and, besides, Van Hasty's promised she'll get Cheepy off my back."

"You would kill hundreds of people just to get rid of a nagging ex-girlfriend?"

"Like I said, if I don't do it someone else will. And she's *really* annoying."

The mercs nodded vigorously.

Carina opened a comm. "Darius?"

He was still awake, probably playing games on his interface. "Hi, Carina. You're up late."

"Could you Cloak the ship? I'll explain why later."

"Uhh, sure."

"A waste of time," Van Hasty commented as Carina closed the comm. "They'll know our position as soon as we fire."

"We're *not* firing," she said between her teeth.

How could she make them see sense? It wasn't only her family's happiness at stake. The hilarity the mercs had expressed at the idea of living out the rest of their lives as ordinary, law-abiding citizens wasn't shared by them all. It wasn't hard to keep track of general opinion in the closed confines of a starship, and her impression was that most of the passengers were hoping to integrate into Earth society and finally begin living normal lives. The bunch of Dogs on the bridge were the die-hards, holding onto their military mindsets.

Were their old habits also responsible for their decision to wreak havoc on Earth? Maybe it was only that, after the long, monotonous voyage, they were simply itching for a fight.

The ship had to be entirely out from the Moon's cover, and Darius's Cloak wouldn't last forever.

"You can't do this!" she exclaimed. "We came here to start a new life, a better life."

Van Hasty shook her head. "You were always a dreamer, Lin. But things don't change. People don't change. Humans have always killed each other and they always will. That's why we have to swing first. It might not seem like it but we're doing you a favor. If we wait around and play nice, your brother's gonna be here soon enough to wipe us out."

"Should I start the power up sequence?" Chi-tang asked.

"Yeah, do it."

Carina tried to think of a way to stop them, but she was out of arguments. And Hsiao was right: it was seven against one. She couldn't force them to stop. Her fingers bit into her palms as the *Bathsheba* slowly built up speed on her journey to Earth orbit. "*Please.* Don't do this."

Jackson patted her on the shoulder. "In a day or so you'll be thanking us."

The bridge door slid open. Bryce had arrived. He walked in, rubbing his eyes. "What's going on? Where are we going, and why's the bridge comm dead?" He didn't seem surprised to see her but neither did he acknowledge her presence.

Van Hasty quickly outlined the plan.

"But isn't that gonna screw everything up?"

"That's what I've been trying to tell them," Carina said.

"Don't worry," said Jackson. "We've got everything in hand."

Bryce frowned. "No, no, no. That isn't going to work. Carina's got the right idea. You have to play this carefully. Earth's different from other planets. You can't go in there guns blazing. Not if you want to live there long term."

"Yeah, about that," Jackson replied. "I can't say I've spent a lot of time down there, but from what I could tell and what I've heard, Earth seems pretty boring. It won't hurt to shake things up a little."

"But that isn't what Carina wants."

Pamuk puffed a derisive *Pfft*. "Who gives a shit?" adding, "Sorry, but you know what I mean."

Carina wasn't sure she did know, but she was grateful for Bryce's arrival.

"I do," he said, "and so does her family, and more than half this ship, I bet, including the Marchonish women. They want to follow her lead and take things slow and easy. That's why you cut the bridge comm, right? So you could act unilaterally. Then, when the deed's done, everyone has to join the battle. Better to ask forgiveness than permission, yeah?"

The less outspoken mercs began to look uncomfortable. Jackson's expression was pensive, but Van Hasty remained defiant. "Who the hell are you to lecture us? You're not even a Black Dog."

"Maybe not, but Carina was, and she deserves your loyalty. I thought that's what the Dogs were about. I thought you guys supported each other. Even if you don't think she's going about this the right way, you should give her a chance."

"She's had a chance, and we don't owe her anything."

"Yes, you do. You all owe her your lives."

"If you're talking about all the shit that's gone down after Cadwallader accepted her miserable assignment—"

"I'm not. I'm talking about before then." He turned to Carina. "You never told them, did you?"

"Umm." She actually didn't know what he was referring to but she didn't want to let on, not now he seemed to be getting through to the mercs. "No, I never did."

"It was just before the mission to rescue Darius from the Dirksens," Bryce continued to them. "You were supposed to be protecting an embassy, only your old boss had signed you up to a bum deal. The enemy had far greater numbers and you were going to be massacred."

Now she remembered, though she didn't recall telling Bryce about it. The event must have come up in one of their many conversations about their pasts. It had been the first time she'd been forced to make a Cast while on duty that couldn't be easily explained away.

Jackson's eyes widened and he stared at her. "That was *you*!"

During the embassy siege, when it had become clear all the mercs were about to die if she didn't do something drastic, she had Transported the enemy soldiers a fair distance away, giving the Dogs time to escape.

"You mean when..." Van Hasty's shoulders slumped. "... I was pinned down, no way out. Toast. Then the hostiles were gone. Vanished. I couldn't believe it. All these years, and I never put two and two together. How dumb is that? Did Cadwallader know?"

"He figured it out," Carina replied. "Later, after I'd hired the Dogs to help me on Ostillon and I had to explain to him what I can do. Captain Speidel knew, though. I had to tell him I was a mage to explain how I knew Darius's location."

"I remember Speidel," said Rees. "Good guy."

"I was there at the embassy," Pamuk said. "Got wounded. A medic told me I nearly bled out. *Damn*."

Silence filled the room.

After a few moments, Hsiao said, "Shall I, er, return the ship to her previous position?"

"Yeah," Van Hasty answered grudgingly.

The mercs began to file out. Chi-tang got up from his seat and trotted up to Van Hasty. "We still have a deal, right?"

Carina thanked Bryce. He didn't answer, only gave her a pained look as he left.

Chi-tang still at her heels, Van Hasty was the last to depart the bridge. Before the door closed behind her, she said, "Five days."

TWENTY-SIX

Officer Matt was missing. Apparently, no one had given him an ear comm and his cabin assignment didn't appear on the manifest. In a ship as vast as the *Bathsheba* it was going to be hard to track him down. Carina had tried the places she might expect to find him—the Twilight Dome, all the refectories, gyms, and various entertainment centers—but he wasn't in any of them. Asking around, she discovered that in his short time on the ship he'd become well known and well liked, though she got the impression most of the passengers thought he was a little crazy. That was probably due to his belief that everything around him was part of a gigantic hoax. But no one had seen him since the previous active shift.

She cast her mind back to the last time she'd seen the man from Earth. It had been at the debriefing Van Hasty and Jackson had crashed...along with Ava. Ava had taken Matt with her when she left, telling him she would find him a cabin.

Carina comm'd the Marchonish woman, but she didn't answer.

Why does everything have to be so hard?

She checked with the sick bay staff. Ava's shift didn't start for several hours. Cursing, she set off for the woman's abode.

The Marchonish women had taken over a small section of the living quarters. Understandably, after their experiences at the hands of their planet's menfolk, they'd been nervous around the mercs, who were mostly male, burly, and loud. The men had also avoided the women, not knowing how to treat them. They were used to female mercs, who were clear, and often physical, in their rebukes if a guy tried to take things further than they wanted. Over time some of the men had learned how to be quieter and gentler and to listen a bit better, and relationships between Black Dogs and the newcomers had formed.

The Marchonish women's section had begun to empty somewhat as couples moved into double cabins in other areas, but several of the women remained, including Ava. Carina guessed her friends helped her out with child-care while she worked.

She rang the door chime.

After waiting a minute, she rang the chime again.

Perhaps Ava was deeply asleep and her comm's alert hadn't woken her. Carina felt a bit bad waking her up, but this matter couldn't wait.

The door slid open, but only part of the way. Ava was tousle-haired, flushed, and wearing a bath robe. "Hi, Carina. I didn't expect to see you here."

"Sorry to wake you. I'm looking for Matt. Do you remember which cabin he was assigned?"

"Oh." Ava's flush deepened. "Why do you want him? Is it urgent?"

"Yes, very."

"Uhh, well..." She looked over her shoulder and then back at Carina, her face deep red.

A male voice within the room murmured something.

Shit.

Carina internally groaned. "I'm really sorry to disturb you. I'll give you a minute."

"Thanks." The door closed.

Leaning her back against the bulkhead, she rolled her eyes.

She's only known him a few days!

When those Marchonish women set their sights on someone, they moved *fast.*

Matt appeared, buttoning his shirt. He looked mildly abashed but not to Ava's level. "You want me for something?"

"I do, but..." She peeked in the cabin. Ava was tidying her bedding. She called out to her. "Could I speak to you too?"

After another minute, she came out, dressed.

"Sorry about this," Carina said awkwardly. "But I'm glad you seem to be settling in, Matt."

"Thanks. I like Ava, but nothing's changed. You're holding an officer of the law against his will, which is a serious crime. You'll pay for it when everything comes to light, though I guess you could plead insanity."

She turned to Ava. "He still believes this isn't real?"

"I've tried to explain but nothing I say seems to convince him."

He placed a hand on her arm. "I believe that *you* believe it. That's all that matters. I don't think you're deliberately lying."

Ava looked at Carina appealingly.

But she didn't know how to convince him either. When a place was so technologically advanced anything could be faked, it became impossible to tell reality from fiction.

She took them to a small, out-of-the-way room with a machine that dispensed beverages. As she'd hoped, it was empty. When everyone was settled, she began. "Matt, I need information about Earth, information we can't get through regular channels. Something strange is going on down there and I have to find out what exactly is happening. If I can't, it's going to make everything much harder for my family and maybe everyone else on this ship, Ava included. Things could be very dangerous for us if we try to settle on the planet."

He smiled indulgently. "Whatever you want to ask me, go ahead. But I warn you, I'm just an ordinary guy. I don't have access to classified information."

He was humoring her, but there was no reason he had to believe the *Bathsheba* was a real starship or that her passengers were from other planets in order to answer her questions.

"Setting your conclusion that this is all a hoax aside, *hypothetically*, if people had arrived from outer space decades ago and infiltrated Earth's governments, how would someone go about addressing it? Who would they approach?"

His eyebrows lifted. "This is worse than I thought. You seriously think all the governments are corrupt?"

"Not necessarily corrupt, but compromised. You see, mages have the ability to influence others' behavior and decisions. A mage could persuade key people to erase data, ignore information, replace files with false ones, and they wouldn't even remember doing it. An evil mage, working with others, could exert a lot of control over Earth's population."

"That's a pretty powerful spell you have there," Matt replied, chuckling.

Carina's jaw muscle twitched. "It's not a..."

Ava shrugged.

Carina took a breath and started again. "I know you don't believe me, but can you put your doubts aside just for a second and think hard? I need your help. Earth needs your help. Imagine what I'm saying might be true. As a police officer you have a duty to protect people and to bring lawbreakers to justice, don't you?"

He'd been taking a sip of his drink. He put the mug down before replying, "*If* what you're saying were true, I still couldn't help you. These 'mages' as you call them could be anywhere and everywhere, casting spells left, right, and center, tricking government officials into thinking black is white. If that was really happening, how could anyone stop them? As soon as they tried, or they were caught snooping or whatever, the mage would only have to get into their head and change what they thought. Or..." he waggled his fingers "...make them disappear in a puff of smoke."

"We can't change what others think. Not in the long term."

"Then disappearing people seems more likely. Whatever. It's moot. You're insane, and the sooner you let me go the better." He turned to Ava. "I'll make sure nothing bad happens to you. You're a victim here."

"I really do come from a distant star system, you know."

"Of course you do." He put an arm around her and kissed her cheek. Then he said to Carina, "Is there anything else you wanted to speak to me about?"

"No. You can go."

Matt and Ava left, holding hands.

Twenty-Seven

The five days Van Hasty had reminded Carina of had shrunk to four with no sign of a solution to her problems.

Parthenia came to see her. "What's wrong with Bryce?" she asked as she stepped into the cabin.

That was the great thing about siblings: they didn't bother with social niceties.

"Hi," Carina replied. "I'm doing fine. How are you?"

"There's no need to be snippy. He's been walking around with his sad puppy look for two days. Have you two been fighting?" She glanced around the room. "Is he even sleeping here?"

"He's taking some time away from me to think."

"Ugh." Parthenia sank onto the sofa. "That bad, huh? What did you fight about?"

"It isn't important. Mage and non-mage relationships are hard."

"I'm not sure that's true. Bibik and I get along okay, and so do Ferne and his endless stream of girlfriends."

"Don't exaggerate. He's only on his third."

"Which isn't bad going, considering the limited pool of candidates. Anyway, he always breaks up with them amicably. Maybe it's because he grew up so close to Oriana."

"So it's me who's the difficult one. Thanks. That makes me feel a whole lot better."

"I'm just saying..." Parthenia took another look around the cabin. "It will be nice to leave this place, don't you think? I mean, in many ways the *Bathsheba* is our home, but I would love to live in a house and be able to step outside to feel the sun on my skin."

"Me too," Carina replied glumly. "At the moment I can't see how that's going to happen. Castiel has made Earth out of bounds, and he's fixed things so the entire population is on the lookout for us. Even if we hid ourselves away somewhere remote, I'm sure he would find us in the end. And if Castiel didn't, Commander Kee would. That man's a machine. How was I to know when I executed Sable Dirksen I was killing the love of his life?"

"Hmm. You didn't tell us about Kee. I didn't know he was here too. He was the man who attempted to massacre the mages at the Matching on Pirine, right?"

"That's him, though he would have been working under Sable's orders. I must have forgotten to tell you Castiel mentioned him. Our lovely brother had a lot to say. I had a feeling he'd been rehearsing his speech for years."

"You also didn't tell us that it was Castiel, not you, who got you out of that fire."

"No, it wasn't."

Parthenia gave her a hard look.

"All right. It was Castiel who Transported me. I'd spilled my elixir."

"I knew your story didn't make any sense. How could you have found him so easily? No one's that lucky. So if Castiel hadn't accidentally saved you, you would have died. Is that what's upsetting Bryce?"

"No, he doesn't know. Don't tell him, Parthenia."

She held up her hands. "I'm certainly not going to interfere in your business. I'm only concerned about impediments to our settling on Earth. I understand now that not only Castiel stands in our way. We also have to contend with this man, Kee."

"I don't know which is worse. Our brother is evil to the core, but Kee is damned smart."

"A formidable pair. But Earth is vast. Surely we should be able to find somewhere to live. As long as we're careful—"

"As long as we skulk around, keep to the shadows, pretend we don't have our abilities. We didn't come all this way to live the same life we lived where we grew up—a half-life, always watching, always fearing discovery."

"No, we didn't. But sometimes it's better to bend than break. If we can't live openly we can still live, still take some pleasure in life. I'm tired of eating printed food, Carina. I'm sick of looking out at black, lonely space. All my adult years have been spent aboard a starship. I need something new. I need to *live*." She swallowed and added, "Even if it means never Casting again."

"You would give up who you are?"

"Being a mage isn't all I am," Parthenia whispered and looked down. Tears dropped onto her hands, lying on her lap.

Carina's sister had learned from a young age to suppress her true emotions. If she had worn her heart on her sleeve, her father would have known how much she hated him and loved her mother, drawing his wrath down on both of them. Covering up how she felt had become somewhat of a habit. For her to be in this state meant she was near the end of her tether.

Carina moved next to Parthenia and hugged her. "I'll find a way. Don't worry."

"There has to be some kind of way, a compromise of some kind."

"Maybe you're right. Maybe I've been going about this wrong, butting heads and acting before thinking." She recalled the Black Dogs on the bridge and smiled wryly. "Perhaps I'm more merc than mage."

The door chime sounded.

"My, I'm popular today."

Darius had come to see her too, with Nahla. Parthenia quickly wiped away her tears as they walked in.

"Are we having a family reunion?" Nahla quipped brightly.

"It looks like it," Carina replied. "I expect Ferne and Oriana will be along any minute. Is this purely a social call or do you want to see me about something in particular?"

Nahla sat next to Parthenia. "Isn't it obvious why we're here? We want to know when is the next trip to Earth. I would like to go this time. I'm the only one who hasn't been there yet. I've been reading all about it but I haven't had a chance to set eyes on the place."

Of all her siblings, Nahla was the one Carina was most reluctant to take to Earth. Though she was bright as a button, she didn't have mage or military skills. The revelation that Castiel was there only increased Carina's reluctance. Castiel bore a special hatred for his youngest sister, possibly even greater than the hatred he harbored toward Carina. Nahla had once been his biggest fan, but she'd switched sides—an act he would never forgive.

"I don't want to return to Earth without a plan," said Carina, "and I'm all out of ideas. As Officer Matt pointed out to me a few hours ago, Castiel seems to have everyone with any influence on Earth under his control. He's discovered and enlisted the mages there to his cause. They're all working for him. What good are our abilities now? What can we do against hundreds, potentially thousands, of mages?"

"He's enlisted them to his cause?" Nahla asked. "That doesn't sound like

Castiel. He was never the persuasive type. He would have thought it beneath him."

Carina frowned. "I'd just assumed..."

"Believe me, I know our nasty brother better than anyone. I would be very surprised if Castiel has used diplomacy to recruit a workforce. That isn't his style."

"You're right. He must be controlling them somehow."

"If we could find out what he's doing," Darius said, "maybe we could put a stop to it. Then Earth would be a friendlier place to us."

"It would be a huge task, though," said Carina, "and we wouldn't know where to start. We have no contacts. We don't know anyone down there who can help us discover how Castiel is exerting his control. If we reveal that we're from outsystem, we'll..." She frowned again.

"We'll what?" Parthenia asked. "Are you thinking about the General Alert?"

"We *do* have friends down there," Carina blurted. "There *are* people who will believe us and who might help."

"Ha!" Nahla grinned. "You mean the Exodus Testifiers."

"They would be ecstatic if planetary colonists turned up on their doorstep. It would prove they weren't cranks. They would be vindicated."

"But wouldn't it put them in danger from Castiel?" asked Darius. "He could kill anyone who associates with us."

"Yes, we would have to be careful. We would have to let them know the stakes." Yet, somehow, she felt sure the Testifiers would agree to help them.

Twenty-Eight

The journalist who had written the article about the Exodus Testifier was as unscrupulous as they came. It hadn't taken more than a little prompting and the promise of exclusive rights to a recording for him to give up the real name and the address of his interviewee. What proved a lot harder was reaching the man.

The address was many kilometers from the site where it had been safe to land the shuttle, and traveling by public transportation was out of the question. Not only was no one from the *Bathsheba* 'chipped', the surveillance systems would be primed to pick up Carina, Bryce, and Darius's faces due to their arrest on the first visit to Earth. Neither did they dare risk Transporting, so they had to walk to the Testifier's location.

He lived a great distance from Officer Matt's little town, in a city on another continent, yet the place resembled their initial experience of Earth. No motorized traffic traveled the roads, only mechanical conveyances, and many people simply walked. Delivery bots trundled the pathways, carrying their loads to their destinations, ignored by pedestrians. Metro stations were everywhere. The subsurface had to be a honeycomb of tunnels.

The ambient noise was minimal, only the chatter of voices, the clanks and clinks of bicycles and larger pedal-driven vehicles, and the faint hum of the bots. Trees and shrubs lined the streets. It seemed a plant grew in every available space, including the rooftops, which were a sea of long grasses. As they walked, Carina didn't spot anyone tending the vegetation. It appeared to have been planted—or perhaps grew naturally—to thrive in the local conditions.

Nahla had spent most of their journey vacillating between open-mouthed wonder and childlike excitement.

Bryce didn't speak to Carina as they walked, though not because he was punishing her. He wasn't like that. He was only melancholy. So was she. The end of their relationship seemed to be looming and she didn't know a way to save it. Their fundamental differences had overcome them. Perhaps it was always this way with mages and non-mages in the end.

"I like it here so much," said Oriana, trailing her hand over a flowering vine hanging from a house front. "It's so nice to be surrounded by green after living for years on a starship. And breathe the air! No faint sweatiness the filters can't scrub out."

Ferne halted. "This is it. Number 68."

Like most of the other houses they'd passed in this residential area of the Earth city, the Exodus Testifier's was two-story and had plants growing in pockets set into the front walls. The vegetation was unkempt, unlike many of the other homes. It was clear the householder wasn't interested in the upkeep of his vertical garden. In fact, the plants seemed to be weeds that had sprouted there opportunistically from blown-in seeds.

"Do you think he'll offer us a drink?" asked Oriana. "I'm so thirsty. Perhaps I could ask him for one. Do you think he'll mind?"

Carina exhaled, puffing out her lips. "Darius, are you getting anything? Anything we need to worry about?"

He was best at sensing evilness emanating from another mage, such as his horrible eldest brother and the Dark Mage, Wei, on Magog, but he also picked up on the internal life of non-mages. He closed his eyes and concentrated before replying, "I'm mostly getting Oriana, but very little from in there."

Oriana's eyes narrowed. "What do you mean, you're mostly getting me?"

Hoping Darius's impression was a good sign, Carina pressed the chime.

Grey-haired, mid-fifties and well into middle-aged spread the article had said, though the Testifier's name was not John Markham, but Alfie Binger. The door opened, revealing a man fitting the description. He was even wearing a cardigan and slacks.

"Sorry," Alfie said as his gaze quickly took in the six people on his doorstep, "I'm not interes—"

As he'd closed the door, Carina had shoved her foot in the gap. He looked down at the impediment preventing him from dismissing his unwelcome callers and then up at her face.

"We aren't selling anything," said Carina. "We want to talk to you about Exodus Testifiers."

His expression hardened. "In that case, I'm definitely not interested. Are you here because of the article? I did not give permission for that to be published. That man lied to me. Leave me alone. Move your foot or I'll call the police."

"We only want to talk to you for a few minutes. Let us in and we can explain."

"Absolutely not. Stop pestering me and go away."

"We're here because we want to be Testifiers too," Oriana said brightly. "We've seen the evidence and we believe it. Please let us in. We've walked so far, and I'm dreadfully thirsty."

"You want to join the Association?" Alfie asked suspiciously. "But you're foreigners." He pointed at their translators. "Join it in your own country."

"We live here," said Carina. "We aren't reporters. Think about it. Why would a media station send *six* people to talk to you?"

His gaze traveled from face to face and the tension seemed to go out of his body. "Okay, you can come in. But if I find out you're lying I'm calling the police and I'll press charges."

Alfie Binger's home was as cluttered as the article had implied. Boxes and stacks of printed material stood each side of his hall, the only available floor space dedicated to a path one-person wide. They followed him in single file to a lounge area, similarly filled with objects. There was more variety here. As well as more boxes and printed sheets, models of starships stood on every flat surface and hung from the ceiling. Pictures of starships and their crews in uniforms, smiling, festooned the walls. Piles of rations the article had mentioned filled the sitting areas.

"You're related, aren't you?" Alfie asked as he moved the ration packets onto the floor. "I can see the family resemblance." Straightening up, he added, looking at Bryce, "But not you. Are you the feisty one's boyfriend or something?"

Carina was tempted to reply *Something* but she kept her comment to herself. "What can you tell us about the Exodus? We don't know much, and we were hoping you could fill us in." It seemed a safer opening gambit than immediately revealing the real reason for their visit.

"Oh, before we start," said Oriana, "could I please have some water?"

Ferne tutted.

"Err." Alfie's suspicion appear to resurface. "All right. But you mustn't touch anything."

Bryce was navigating obstacles to move closer to the pictures on the walls.

"Oriana, could you stop thinking about your own comfort for once?" Ferne complained. "This is serious business."

"Carina," said Bryce, "look at this."

Oriana replied to Ferne, "How can I concentrate when my mouth is like your armpit?"

"You have no idea what my armpit's like," Ferne retorted.

"Oh shut up," said Nahla. "Both of you."

"*Carina*," Bryce repeated.

Alfie returned with a glass of water, which he handed to Oriana.

"Thank you so much." She gulped it down. "That's much better."

"Please sit," said Alfie. "Sit down, everyone."

They squeezed into the scant sitting space except for Bryce, who remained at the wall, hands in pockets as he scrutinized an image.

"What do you already know about the Exodus?" Alfie asked. "I'm just asking because there's no point in me repeating anything to you."

"Uhh, just the basics," Carina replied. "That people used to leave Earth to colonize the stars. But we've forgotten about it, right? There isn't much evidence left. Do you know why?"

Alfie lifted his hands in a gesture of bewilderment. "Beats me. But the evidence is there for anyone who looks for it. I suppose the establishment doesn't like having its views challenged."

"Carina, look at this," Bryce insisted.

Alfie said, "You like that one, do you? She's one of my favorites too. Not the most beautiful example of her kind, but special nonetheless."

"Where did you get this picture?" asked Bryce.

"It's in the national archives. A perfect example of historians ignoring what's right under their noses. They say it's an artist's creation, a work of the imagination. All I can say is, if I was an artist I would draw something that looked a bit better. If you study the picture closely, it's perfectly obvious what everything's for."

While Alfie had been talking, Carina had worked her way across the crowded room to Bryce's side. He was looking at a 2D representation of a starship.

It took less than a second for recognition to dawn.

The drawing was simple, without schematics, as if the creator had only wanted to record the external appearance of the ship. The background was plain white, not a starscape as the real backdrop would have been. A ship this vast could only have been constructed in space.

Her pulse beating in her ears, Carina turned to Alfie. "This vessel—what do you know about her?"

"The *ZSS Hangxing Zhe*? She was the last colony ship ever built. I bet you didn't know that, huh? What a ship she must have been. The pinnacle of star-ship technology. And most of it lost now, of course. So much knowledge just... gone." He heaved a sigh.

The Hangxing Zhe. *So that's her real name.*

On the wall hung a picture of the *Bathsheba*.

TWENTY-NINE

lfie Binger chuckled uneasily. His gaze flicked between each of them in turn, as if he was trying to probe the truth from their eyes. He got to his feet, stepped carefully through his hoard of Exodus paraphernalia to the window, and peered through the blinds. Then he walked to the other side of the room, where double glass doors gave a view of his overgrown yard. Craning his neck to right and left, he checked the rear of his house.

He turned to face them. "This is a joke, isn't it? A set up. Did that journalist send you here?" He scanned their bodies. "Is one of you recording this?" Though his words were aggressive his tone was semi-hopeful, as if he wanted to be proven wrong.

"No one is recording anything," Carina replied. "What I've told you is absolutely, one hundred percent true. It isn't a joke, or a lie."

They'd anticipated the Exodus Testifier might not believe they were from a starship, but no one had been able to think of a way to prove it. Any piece of technology small enough to carry could easily be from Earth. They couldn't expect him to be able to tell that it wasn't. As they'd discovered with Matt, when everything could be faked proving anything was hard. They would have to rely on Alfie taking them at their word, at least at first.

Carina hadn't told him the part about them being mages, sensing it could be a step too far and tip him over the edge into disbelief. If he kicked them out it would end any hope of having an Earth person on their side.

He took a deep breath and exhaled. "All right, let's say for now that I believe you, and that you really did arrive on the *Hangxing Zhe,* how could the ship have survived all this time? By Testifiers' reckoning she left at least two thousand years ago."

"Two thousand years in Earth time," Carina said. "You're forgetting the time dilation effect. While thousands of years passed here, the *Bathsheba*—I mean *Hangxing Zhe*—might only have been in existence for hundreds of years. We don't actually know how old she is. All we know is she's very old and she has technology that's unknown in the galactic sector I'm from."

She meant the self-repairing surfaces she'd discovered after the battle for the ship, but there was more about the *Bathsheba* that she'd never seen before. She'd never discovered what was original and what had been installed by Lomang. Now she knew the truth about the ship's origins, she suspected none of it was Lomang's doing and it was all the peak of Earth's colony ship technology.

"The galactic sector you're from?" Alfie asked. "You mean there's more than one?"

"There are four I'm aware of. There may be more. Humans have been spreading across the galaxy for a long time."

He rubbed his forehead. "It's a lot to take in. I want to believe you. I really do. But if what you're saying is true, how come you're the first to return? And why don't we receive communications from these hundreds of colony worlds? That's what people always say when arguing with Testifiers and, to be honest, I've never had an answer."

"When it comes to habitable planets Earth is in a massive desert. We had to travel a very long way to get here. We've lived ten years on our journey but we've spent even longer in Deep Sleep."

"Deep Sleep? Is that like hibernation? I've read about it."

"We also call it stasis. Basically, the body's functions slow down to a barely perceptible rate. You're alive, but only just, and there's a small but significant death rate. My guess is the colonists who survived the journey didn't want to make the trip back, and they had their work cut out simply surviving and creating a livable world for their offspring. Later generations might not have seen the point in traveling all the way to Earth when other habitable planets were much closer. Or perhaps the Earth's coordinates had been lost. We had a hell of a time finding them."

"But you did." He stared intently into her eyes. "You made the journey. Why? And why haven't I heard about it? The arrival of a starship would be all over the news."

"Would it?" Carina asked. "It seems to me, from what you've said, that people in power don't want to acknowledge there might be human life on other planets."

"There is that, but the *Hangxing Zhe* is huge. There's no hiding her. Someone would have spotted her by now. Are you saying that governments have silenced everyone who's seen her?"

"She's behind the Moon."

"Righhht," he drawled, considering, "but she had to reach the Moon. How did she travel through the Solar System unnoticed?"

Darius had Cloaked her as they neared Earth, but telling Alfie that would complicate matters.

"Look," said Carina, "if you need to be convinced, why not come and see her? We can take you to her right now."

The color drained from his face and his eyes grew round. "Travel to a starship?! Me?"

"We arrived by shuttle but we had to leave it on the edge of the city. Our pilot is waiting there. We can take you to it. Only we can't travel by public transportation. We'll have to walk."

Fortunately, he didn't question the part about avoiding the metro system. "You would take me to your starship behind the Moon? This can't be happening. Wait." He gestured excitedly. "I have to tell some people about this. No one's going to believe me! Can you take more of us? I have some friends in this city. It wouldn't take long—"

"No. Just you. It's too risky to take anyone else."

"Hmm, yeah. I get it." He tapped his nose. "We need to keep this a secret. It's safer that way."

"Exactly. Are you ready to go? Do you need to bring anything?"

"Can I bring an interface?" He rose to his feet.

"It's probably better that you don't have any evidence of what you're about to see." Carina hesitated. "Alfie, I want you to understand, if you come with us you're putting your life at risk. There's a lot I didn't tell you. You'll find out about it soon but first it's important that we convince you we are who we say we are."

"She's deadly serious," Bryce added. "Join up with us and you could die."

"Die?" Alfie sank into his seat. "It's that dangerous?"

"It is," Ferne replied gravely. "We've lost many people over the course of our journey, and not from Deep Sleep Death."

Carina said, "It's only fair that you know. But the reason we're here is because we desperately need the help of someone from Earth, and only an Exodus Testifier would believe us."

"I wouldn't say even *I* completely believe you just yet," said Alfie, "but I'm prepared to keep an open mind. And as to the risks..." His expression hardened with resolve. "All my life I've been laughed at for being a Testifier. I've struggled with jobs, girlfriends, you name it. Nearly everyone I know thinks I'm a crack-pot. They're nice enough to my face, but I know that behind my back they talk about me and snigger. Well, here's my chance to prove them wrong. I'm taking it, no matter what might happen. Besides, who would turn down an invitation to visit a freaking starship?! If it's the last thing I ever do, I won't have any regrets."

Though everyone from the *Bathsheba* was tired after their long walk, it was Alfie who was out of breath soon after they set off. He finally took seriously Carina's insistence they avoided public transportation. Naturally, they couldn't Transport to the shuttle with him in tow. He was in poor physical shape and already overly excited. She was worried a sudden introduction to mage powers could give him a heart attack. Moreover, he might be reminded of the General Alert and get spooked.

"But why walk?" he asked, two or three times, puffing and panting. "It's an awfully long way."

Rather than repeat her response that she would explain later yet again, Carina snapped, "We're wanted by the police."

This new information drew him to a halt. "What for? What have you done?" He seemed to be re-thinking his decision.

"We were picked up because we don't have chips."

"Ah, yeah. That makes sense. Okay, foot power it is, but you'll have to slow down. I haven't walked this far since I was a teenager."

He tried to get more information about the *Bathsheba* from them, but Carina shut him down. The risk of being overheard by someone who knew something about their situation was tiny, but also not worth taking.

Poor Alfie was so footsore by the time they reached the place they'd hidden the shuttle he was limping. The vessel was at the bottom of an abandoned quarry, camouflage sheeting echoing the dusty, rocky landscape.

"Where is it?" he asked as they peered over the edge. "I can't see a thing."

"You're not supposed to," said Oriana.

They followed the narrow trail down the quarry's edge. The place was as deserted as it had been when they left it, though there were signs that children came here to play. A circuit for bicycle riders had been recreated from piles of dirt and scrap wood. The sight of it made Carina's heart ache. It was an ordinary, simple construction but for her it symbolized the childhood she and her siblings had never known. Their upbringings had been far from ordinary. She hoped that, one day, their children would play happily somewhere like this, without a care in the world.

"Where is it?" Ferne asked. "I've lost my bearings. I thought Hsiao landed over there."

He pointed, and Carina also couldn't make out the lines of the shuttle. Fear gripped her guts. Was the vessel still here? Or had Castiel found it somehow and taken it?

Lifting her head, she scanned the ridges around the edge of the quarry. They seemed empty.

Alfie had been struggling to catch his breath since they reached the base of the quarry. He squeezed out: "I get it... Very funny. It isn't nice to tease an old man, you know... You really had me going for a while, though, I don't mind admitting."

Bryce had walked ahead of the group. He strode confidently forward until he reached a spot that looked no different from the surrounding area. Reaching up, he rapped with his knuckles, resulting in a hollow, metallic sound. "You're all blind."

Carina sagged with relief and removed her hand from her elixir canister. She'd been convinced they were about to come under attack.

"Thank the stars," said Oriana. "Earth is nice but I can't wait to get back to the ship and have a lovely hot bath."

There was a rustle of shifting sheeting and Hsiao emerged. "Did someone knock?"

"You shouldn't just come out like that," Carina admonished. "What if it had been Castiel?"

"If it had been Castiel I would be dead already. Help me get this sheet off and put away. Your mission was successful I see." She nodded at Alfie, whose jaw looked about to drop from his head.

Due to their repeated experience of applying and removing the camouflage the task was quickly completed. While they worked Alfie simply stood and stared. When it came time to board and return to the *Bathsheba* Nahla called out, "We're ready for you, Mr Binger. Would you step this way?"

He didn't move.

He was weeping.

THIRTY

Watching the two Earth men facing off would have been funny if the time remaining to solve the mages' problems hadn't been so tight. Matt and Alfie sat on opposite sides of the mission room, glaring at each other. Van Hasty and Jackson were here too, as well as Bryce, Nahla, and Ava. Somehow, they had to come to a decision about how the coming days would play out. But the Earthers' disagreement was getting in the way.

"You stupid young pup," Alfie said. "You're sitting inside a colony ship and you won't believe the evidence of your own eyes. How much more convincing do you need?"

"It's all fake you gullible old fool. You believe it because you want to believe it. Or maybe you're fake too. Are you part of this? If you are, I warn you you're committing a serious crime. Every single person here will do jail time when this comes out."

"Alfie," Carina said, "whether Matt believes the *Bathsheba* is real is beside the point. We've tried to get his help but he won't take us seriously because he thinks we're tricking him. That's why we've brought you here. We've explained the situation. Can you think of any way you can help us? Is there a person or an organization we can approach who will be able to root out our enemies and eliminate their influence?"

She had three days. Three days until the Black Dogs would fulfill their threat of going down to Earth. Hsiao would take them. After the crisis involving the Obliterator, Carina was in little doubt about it. And if Hsiao refused, Bibik would do it.

The mercs let loose on peaceful Earth would trigger scenarios she cringed to contemplate. Jackson had already killed someone. Wherever they went the Dogs would leave a trail of destruction in their wake. They would wind up dead or permanently incarcerated, destroying the rep of all the *Bathsheba*'s passengers in the process.

Some of them might do okay. The long voyage had tamed some of the Dogs, but the hard core bunch? Their personalities were perfect for survival on the fringes of galactic civilization, but on Earth they were anomalies, incapable of fitting in. It was a difficulty she'd never anticipated, not in all the many times she'd played out in her head their arrival at their destination. She'd become so used to the mercs' behavior and attitudes she hadn't factored it into her planning. Now, they presented as much of a problem as the mages, though an entirely different one.

"It's hard for me to say," Alfie replied after considering for a few moments. "I'm just an ordinary man. I don't have friends in high places. Heck, even my friends don't have friends in high places."

"But you know how things work, right?" asked Carina. "Where I grew up I was a nobody, a street rat, but I could have told you who was pushing the buttons on my planet. My galactic sector was controlled by rival clans, and everyone knew it. The same has to be true everywhere. There have to be people on Earth who hold the real power, people we can approach to fix things without too much bloodshed."

"I told you before," said Matt, "assuming this fantasy you're all playing out was true, approaching those people isn't going to help you. Not if your brother is manipulating them."

"I could suggest a few names," said Alfie. "Maybe that would help."

Matt snapped, "Don't encourage them. You'll only get yourself into trouble. Aiding and abetting a kidnapping is a felony."

"Some names would be a great help," Carina said. "Nahla, could you take notes?" Yet as she spoke a sinking feeling hit in the pit of her stomach. Despite Matt's skepticism he made a good point. The web of Castiel's influence had been woven over decades, with the help of mages. How could she hope to ever tear it down, let alone within three days?

Alfie wanted to see the Deep Sleep chamber again. He'd already seen them on his first, quick tour of the ship. Carina had felt obliged to show him around a little before springing the reason for his invitation upon him. She hadn't told him about mages yet and she wasn't sure he fully understood their difficulties, but at least he seemed prepared to help.

Hoping she might gain some further insights about Earth from him, Carina agreed to return with him to the chamber. While he peered into an open capsule, she stood in the center of the vast space, recalling the first time she'd set foot on the *Bathsheba*. She and Cadwallader had extracted the security codes to enter the airlocks from Lomang, and she'd used one to open the hatch that led directly to the chamber. The battle with Mezban's soldiers for control of the ship had taken place right here.

"You really spent years inside one of these eggs?" Alfie asked.

"Yep. It isn't as bad as it sounds. You're entirely unconscious. It's like going to sleep and waking up again. It's better for the body to return to consciousness regularly, so we spent years awake too."

"Do you factor the Deep Sleep years into your age? How old are you?"

She shrugged. "It's possible to figure it out but no one bothers."

"Age is just a number. That's how I think about it too." He straightened up, his rotund belly protruding, and ran a hand through his scant hair. "What wouldn't I give to travel across the galaxy? I don't suppose there's a chance you might go back one day?" He grinned cheekily.

"Are you proposing to come with us if we do?"

"Would you have me? I don't know what I could do to earn my passage, but I'd be prepared to do anything. Clean, cook, whatever."

"I'm sorry, Alfie. We won't be going back. It took us so long to get here, and people lost their lives to help us make it. I don't think I could explain it to you properly even if we had time. Your experience of life is so different from mine." *So limited.* How would she even begin to explain about the Sherrerrs, the Dirksens, Lomang and Mezban, the Regians, the mage-controlled society of Magog, or any of the other myriad people and places she'd experienced? His knowledge was limited to one planet.

"What do you mean, *if we had time*?" he asked "You seem to be in a rush to find these people who want to prevent you from settling on Earth. But you're safe enough tucked away behind the Moon. Why are you in a big hurry to fix things?"

"Did you see Jackson and Van Hasty at the meeting just now?"

"The bruisers? I wouldn't like to meet either of *them* in a dark alley."

"They're mercenaries. They helped us get here, and they're my friends. But they're impatient. They want to go to Earth now. If I don't figure something out soon they'll do it and mess everything up."

"Gotcha. You're in a pickle. I hope those names I gave you are useful."

"Thanks," she replied woodenly. "I appreciate it."

"I appreciate you bringing me here. I got the better end of the bargain, that's for sure. What else is there to see on this amazing vessel? I still feel like I'm dreaming but if I am I don't want it to stop."

She took him to the Twilight Dome. Always a show-stopper even for the *Bathsheba*'s long-term passengers, the view thrilled him so much she feared she might have to comm a medic. The sight caused him to collapse into a seat. Eventually, he said, "Why isn't it complete?"

"You mean the transparent overhead? A bomb blew a section out of it. It's the weakest part of the hull."

"A bomb?!"

"If I were to tell you everything that's happened since I first decided I wanted to come to Earth it would take a very long time. Do you want to stay here a while or see more of the ship?"

"I'll stay here," he murmured, transfixed.

"Then I'll see you later. Come and find me when you're ready." She gave him the deck and number of her cabin.

"When do I have to go back to Earth?"

"Have to go back? You don't have to go back. Or not for a while anyway. Do you want to go home?"

"Hell, no. I'm staying as long as you'll have me."

"That's good to hear. It's dangerous for us to go planetside. I'll find somewhere for you to sleep."

"Planetside," he echoed. "I love the sound of that. I could get used to that word."

"See you later, Alfie."

She went to her cabin and was disappointed but not surprised to discover it was empty. She didn't know where Bryce was spending his time these days. She checked her comms but there were no messages from him or anyone else. She didn't know what to do. It was too early to ask Nahla if she'd gotten anywhere with the names Alfie had given her. And if she did get somewhere, how would they even begin to untangle Castiel's web?

She slumped into a chair and put her head in her hands.

THIRTY-ONE

Each minute of the last two days had dragged past and yet time had also moved at an astonishing speed. Only one day remained until the Black Dog ringleaders would carry out their threat and begin a mass disembarkation of the *Bathsheba*. All Carina's plans, everything she'd done to bring her family to Earth, the sacrifices of the people who had died—it would all come to nothing. She and her siblings would be in a worse situation than they'd been in their home sector. If they'd stayed there they would have been forced to live in secret, but at least they wouldn't have faced the threat of Castiel hunting them down. She wouldn't have had Commander Kee out for her blood.

Van Hasty and Jackson had been subdued around her, as if they felt guilty for the imminent prospect of carrying out their threat. But guilt wouldn't stop them, and nor would the ties of comradeship. At the end of the day, the Dogs were hard-hearted mercenaries. They'd survived their dangerous careers this long because they put themselves first.

Fighting depression and despair, Carina went to see Nahla. She could have talked to her over comm but she yearned to see a friendly, familiar face. Bryce continued to avoid her and she'd been avoiding her other siblings because she felt she'd let them down.

"Hey," said Nahla, with a tone of surprise as Carina walked in. "I didn't expect to see you here."

She hadn't been to her youngest sister's cabin for a long time. Copies of the ancient mage documents covered the walls like strange works of art. Her bed was unmade, sofa cushions were scattered on the floor, and used dishes, mugs, and cutlery sat on the table.

Following Carina's gaze with her own, Nahla seemed to notice these things for the first time.

"It's a mess, right?" she said with some embarrassment. "I'll tidy up."

"Don't bother. I don't mind." Carina moved some clothing aside to sit down. "Are you any further ahead with the names Alfie gave us?"

Nahla had already discovered significant information on the men and women. The Testifier had been correct that they were among the greatest movers and shakers in Earth society and therefore likely to be under Castiel's influence. Yet how to reach them was unclear, or even how to approach the mages manipulating them. It was doubtful that Castiel was doing the work himself. He would have lackeys to take the fall if they were discovered, and there was no telling a mage from a non-mage by outward appearances.

"Umm..." Nahla idly swiped the screen of her interface. "Honestly? No. I've been working on it all night and I managed to access some encrypted comm channels, but it's slow work and I haven't found anything useful. I mean not immediately useful. I found out the head of a media empire is being blackmailed about serious violation of environmental protection laws, and a business mogul made some very odd deals, creating a large profit for a shady company. But—"

"These things would take weeks to get to the bottom of," Carina interrupted.

"Months, perhaps years. It's almost impossible to approach any of these people in person. They have small retinues of highly vetted staff who are the only people they interact with personally on a day-to-day basis. Castiel must have wrangled mages into these teams, but as for telling who they are, and then finding out how our brother is controlling them..." She turned her hands palm upwards in a gesture of helplessness.

"You're saying we might never do it."

"Castiel has decades on us. In a way it's remarkable that his hatred of us runs so deep he would go to all this trouble."

"He always wanted an empire. That was why he betrayed us to the Dirksens. He thought they were his ticket to dominion over a whole galactic sector. Now he has that empire here on Earth. It isn't exactly a sector, but it will do. Making my dream impossible is only a side benefit."

"*Our* dream," Nahla corrected. "It became our dream too somewhere along the way."

Carina reached out and grasped her sister's hand. "Thanks for saying that. I feel as though I dragged you all this way for nothing. I'm sorry the dream didn't come true."

Someone was comming her. She accepted it.

"Hello? Hello?" a voice shouted in her ear. "Can you hear me?"

She winced. "Alfie? Is that you?"

"Ah, good. I've just been given one of your shipboard devices. Wasn't sure if it worked."

"They work the same as they do on Earth. You don't need to raise your voice."

"Ooops, sorry."

"Can I help you?"

Alfie Binger had been enjoying himself immensely in his short time aboard the *Bathsheba*. He'd been seen all over the ship and become everyone's friend. He'd also familiarized himself with every aspect of her layout and had at least a cursory understanding of everything.

"I've been talking to that nice man about your problem. He's explained it in more detail. I'm not sure I quite believe it but my eyes have been opened so much in the last forty-eight hours I think I'm prepared to believe just about anything."

"A nice man? Who have you been talking to?" She imagined it must be Bryce, but Alfie knew his name.

"I think he's called Jackson."

Carina was entirely mystified how Jackson had gone from a 'bruiser' to a nice person in Alfie's estimation, but she couldn't be bothered to go into it. "So you know about mages? Is that what you want to talk about?"

"I'd love to when we have more time, but Jackson said your problem was urgent and you had to find the solution soon. He didn't explain why."

No kidding.

"And I think I have an idea."

She paused. What possible strategy could the man from Earth suggest? He'd only just discovered that mages existed. He couldn't have much understanding of what they could do or the depths of evilness of a Dark Mage like Castiel. Not holding out much hope she said, "Let's hear it."

"Move your ship into Earth orbit. Show the world you exist. Go public. Then go planetside. You'll be celebrities. You'll have the protection of being famous. Your brother won't dare do anything to you."

"Go public?"

Nahla was watching her, hearing only one side of the conversation.

Carina transferred the comm to her cabin's system. "Alfie, can you repeat your idea so my sister can hear it?"

As Nahla listened she met Carina's gaze. She didn't seem to immediately dismiss Alfie's suggestion.

"But will the public even find out we're there?" Carina asked. "My impression is Earth's locked up tight when it comes to the existence of colony ships. A lot of people simply wouldn't believe the evidence, like Matt. Others would be very upset about being proven wrong. So upset they might do something about it. And my brother would do his damnedest to wipe any mention of us from the media."

"That's where the Testifiers come in," said Alfie. "We're all over the place. Every country, every major city in the world. We're in all the businesses, all the professions. Of course, we aren't all out in the open. No one likes being laughed at. But at the last count our official membership stood at over 75,000. And that's only the people who've paid their subs. There are plenty who believe but don't subscribe, and plenty more who are sitting on the fence, but the minute they see images of the *Hangxing Zhe* she'll tip them right off it."

75,000? The reporter who had interviewed him hadn't done his homework. He'd guesstimated 10,000.

Nahla's features brightened with excitement. "The Testifiers would bombard the news stations with images, flood social media, that kind of thing?"

"You got it, and more besides. Send them scenes from the ship's interior. Show them Earth viewed through the Twilight Dome. We'll overload the world with information. The Return of the *Hangxing Zhe* will go viral, and then there'll be no stopping you. Everyone will want to talk to you. You'll be on every talk show, every current affairs program. No station will turn you down because you'll be who their viewers want to see."

"You'll have a platform," Nahla said, eyes shining. "You can explain all about mages and their pacifist culture. You can suggest all the good you could do in the world. And you can set boundaries so you aren't exploited or oppressed. Mages never had a voice before."

"I don't know," said Carina. "The last time mages were out in the open on Earth they were blamed for all the problems and driven offplanet."

"Earth doesn't have most of the problems it had then. What are you going to be blamed for?"

Carina was confident Castiel would think of something.

On the other hand, she didn't have a better idea and they were nearly out of time.

THIRTY-TWO

"Finally!" Van Hasty exclaimed. "You're finally seeing sense. Shove the Obliterator in their faces, then let's see what they have to say."

"That isn't what this is about," Carina replied. "Not at all." The deck shifted slightly under her feet as Hsiao pulled the *Bathsheba* away from her position on the far side of the Moon.

"Huh?" Van Hasty's lip lifted quizzically. "Then what is it about?"

"It's a publicity exercise."

"It's a what?" The merc turned to Jackson. "Do you know what she's talking about?"

"Beats me. I'm just glad something's happening and we might not be stuck inside this tin can much longer."

"We won't be stuck in here for much longer anyway," Van Hasty replied. "We've only got..." she checked a console "...nineteen hours to go, then Earth is our playground. Man, I can't wait to set foot on solid ground again."

Jackson rolled his shoulders. "I can't wait to find out what new and interesting drinks they serve in Earth bars. Who knows..." he grinned wickedly "...I might even get into a fight."

"Aren't you forgetting something?" Carina asked. "Something about being wanted for murder?"

"A tiny detail. I'm sure you guys will figure it out. You can enchant someone, or whatever it is you do."

"It's called Enthrall and... Never mind."

If mages were to live safely on Earth they couldn't ever do anything outside the law. It wouldn't take much to change public opinion about them. As Bryce had pointed out, mage powers made non-mages feel helpless and inadequate. They would have to tread carefully, and that meant no Enthralling law-enforcers. Jackson's crime was a bridge she would have to cross when she came to it.

Hsiao looked over her shoulder. "You're absolutely sure about this?"

Now you're asking me? The pilot had been more gung-ho about it when under orders from the Black Dogs. "I'm sure."

The bridge door opened and her family poured in, Bryce at their rear.

"We're starting?" Oriana asked. "This is so exciting!"

Carina had outlined Alfie's idea to them and asked for their agreement before trying it out. They'd given it, unsurprisingly. What did they have to lose? "We're going ahead."

"Where's Mr Binger?" Nahla asked.

"He's in a comm room. He wanted a private space to talk with his buddies."

Hsiao said, "Okay, we're out of the Moon's shadow. Anyone on Earth watching this part of the sky is going to see something very interesting."

"Take us there," Carina said.

"Got it. Low-Earth orbit."

The *Bathsheba* would circle the globe, visible even to the naked eye, for as long as it took for people to take notice. Which, Carina guessed, wouldn't be long.

"Better say goodbye to your favorite spots on the ship, kids," said Jackson. He hadn't gotten out of the habit of calling them that even though they were now fully grown. "Earth, here we come."

Alfie comm'd Carina. "The *Hangxing Zhe* has been spotted! It's breaking news on the media stations."

"Good. You've talked to your friends?"

"You better believe it. They're going wild down there. This is gonna be big. The biggest event of my generation. The biggest event in centuries!"

She asked Hsaio to give them a visual. A holo of Earth opened in the center of the bridge. The slowly turning blue and green globe, wreathed in clouds, steadily grew larger. Her heart seemed to beat faster at the same rate the image increased in size. Could Alfie's plan really work? It seemed impossible.

Bryce stood on the opposite side of the bridge. She wished she could go over to him and hold his hand or feel his arm around her as they waited. But the distance between them was more than ordinary space. It was a gulf of differences that she didn't think could ever be spanned.

Alfie was still chattering in her ear, but she'd missed his last few sentences, except that he'd sounded urgent. "What did you say?"

"The Head of the ETA—Exodus Testifiers Association—wants to speak to you. How do I patch her through?"

"Wait a minute. I'll come over there." It was a simpler solution than explaining the comm system. She Transported herself to Alfie's location.

And instantly regretted it.

Alfie turned white as a sheet and clutched his chest. "Where did you come from?! How did you do that?!"

"Sorry, I didn't mean to startle you. I'll talk to the person from your association."

His hand trembling, he turned the mic toward her.

"Hello?" Carina said. "This is Carina Lin of the *Bathsheba*, though you may know her as the *Hangxing Zhe*."

"Hi, Ms Lin. I'm Frankie Longbarrow, representative of the ETA. To say I'm pleased to make your acquaintance is a massive understatement. Alfie's been telling me all about you and your ship. This is going to blow all the Exodus Deniers out of the water. I can't wait to meet you in person. But I should warn you, we're already getting push back from the media. Some respected pundits are saying it's a hoax, a silly stunt, and that your vessel isn't real."

"We thought that might happen. We have someone from Earth who's actually been living here for several days and even *he* doesn't believe it." And, no doubt, Castiel and his mages were at work getting others to deny the *Bathsheba*'s existence.

"Don't worry, with the images and information Alfie's been sending us, as well as the followers we have all over the world, everyone will have to face the truth of what's in the sky. And as soon as we can get you and your crew down here we'll have living proof to back it up."

"But couldn't they say we're actors?" It was an idea that had just occurred to her.

"Not after we have your genome sequenced. You're descended from people who left Earth thousands of generations ago. Your DNA will prove it."

"Right." Giving up her DNA wasn't something she'd anticipated. It almost certainly held the secret to her magehood, and so it could be used to identify other mages within the population. Yet if they were to win public trust they had to be transparent. "I'll have to think about that."

"Fine, fine," said Frankie. "One step at a time. We mustn't get ahead of ourselves. This is amazing! I can't believe it's happened in my lifetime. I feel like this generation is the luckiest alive. So are you in a way. Several tech companies have approached the Association for confirmation that a colony ship really has returned. They'll give their eye teeth plus a lot of money for access to everything on your vessel."

"I hadn't thought of that angle."

"There will be many angles no one thought of popping up over the next few days. When will you be able to come to the surface? Alfie says you have a shuttle and he's flown in it, the lucky devil."

"We're going to sit tight for a day and see how things pan out. How does that sound?"

"Whatever you say. You're the one calling the shots. We'll keep up the pressure on the media, academia, and businesses down here. You can leave everything in the ETA's hands."

"Thanks. I should go and see what's happening on the ship."

"No, thank *you*. It's a privilege to meet you, Carina Lin."

To avoid giving Alfie another turn, Carina stepped out of the comm room before Transporting to the bridge. Everything was much as she'd left it. Her siblings had spread out around the space and Earth had grown so large it occupied the entire holo.

"Entering orbit in three minutes fifty," said Hsiao. "What's happening planetside?"

"A war of opinion from the sound of it. Castiel is trying to erase the knowledge of our existence from public consciousness and the Testifiers are forcing the *Bathsheba* down their throats."

"Who's gonna win, I wonder?" Bryce asked softly.

Van Hasty said, "You know the Obliterator's still an option, right? Wouldn't take a minute to blast Castiel's base to smoke and ashes."

"If you remember, there's the small matter of the hundreds of other people we would kill," Carina countered. When Van Hasty seemed unmoved she added, "And Castiel might not be there anymore. If he has any sense he will have left the second we flew out of the cover of the Moon."

Van Hasty shrugged. "Maybe. But it would send a message."

"Exactly the kind of message I don't want to send. I don't get why that's so hard for you to understand." Carina despaired of ever re-focusing certain mercs' minds away from violence.

She watched Earth's surface, oceans and continents moving slowly past. They were approaching with the sun at their backs. In galactic terms the planet wasn't old but intelligent life there was—the oldest human life in the galaxy, some said. It was certainly the origin planet of mages. Had those who had fled persecution ever imagined that one day their descendants would return?

She thought of the mages she'd left behind. Did the Council still exist?

Magda, the Spirit Mage had died saving Jace's life, and Justin had been murdered by Castiel. How would the young mages be Summoned to a Matching without their Spirit Mage? How would they meet, marry, and have children, when they lived secretly, often hidden even from each other?

Taking Darius from them had weighed on her conscience, but she didn't regret it. A seven-year-old couldn't bear responsibility for the destiny of all the mages in a sector. It was too much to ask, no matter the consequences.

"The *Bathsheba* is in Earth orbit," Hsiao announced.

Whoops and hollers of celebration followed.

An alarm blared out, cutting through the noise. The voices stuttered to silence until only the alarm could be heard.

"What the hell?" Van Hasty breathed in disbelief, looking up from an interface. "Hull breach. Deck Four."

"Have we been fired on?" Carina asked. "Hsiao, any sign of ships on the long range scanners?"

She consulted her screen. "Not a thing."

"I don't understand. What about an attack from the surface?"

"No way. We would have picked it up."

"Then...?" She turned hopelessly to Van Hasty, who stared intently at her console.

The alarm blared on, unremitting.

Carina comm'd the Dogs, sending a breach team to Deck Four. The *Bathsheba* would self-repair eventually, but a hull breach was too risky to leave unattended.

"Another breach!" yelled Van Hasty. "Deck Two."

But how?

Open-mouthed shock permeated the bridge.

"Should I take us out of orbit?" Hsiao asked.

"I don't know. Stand by." Carina consulted the data from the ship's sensors for herself. There was nothing to indicate they'd been fired upon. No record of a burst of energy in their vicinity or traces of an after-effect.

"Breach on Deck Seven," Van Hasty snapped. "It's the Dome."

The *Bathsheba* seemed to be splitting apart of her own volition.

Splitting apart.

"It's Split!" Carina exclaimed. "Castiel is Casting Split on the ship."

"That can't be it," said Parthenia. "The *Bathsheba* is far too large to be affected by Split. When he used it on Ostillon it only worked on shuttlecraft."

"But it isn't only Castiel," Ferne retorted gravely. "He has all the mages on Earth working with him."

THIRTY-THREE

The noise of the alarm bounced around inside Carina's skull, growing louder and louder. She realized it wasn't only the alarm she was hearing but voices yelling as the debate about what to do grew more and more heated.

"Shut up!" she screamed. "Shut up! I can't hear myself think!"

The voices quietened.

"Turn off that goddamned alarm too. We know what's happening."

Reports of more breaches had flooded in. The bridge was sealed off and everyone else on the ship was wearing EVA suits due to the threat of depressurization.

Silence fell, but it was short-lived.

Van Hasty got up in Carina's face. "We need to fire the Obliterator, now! We're not taking this attack lying down."

"Fire it on what? The thousands of mages dotted all over the planet? If you fire that thing you'll kill thousands of civilians."

"Maybe it'll make your sick shit of a brother step down."

"He won't care. He'll blame us, and rightly. We'll be the ones firing. No one on Earth understands about mages. They won't know we were trying to defend ourselves."

"Damn it, Lin!" Van Hasty spat. "What happened to you? You lost your guts somewhere along the way."

"I didn't lose anything. I gained something—the ability to think before I acted. Now back off!"

Van Hasty stepped away, glaring.

"We could try Repulse," Oriana suggested.

"Against thousands of mages?" Carina shook her head. "Even Darius couldn't fend off that many Casts all at once."

"I could try," he said.

"It would exhaust you and we need you as our last line of defense."

"The Dogs can't keep pace with the breaches," Hsiao reported. "We need to think about evacuation."

"To the surface?" asked Carina. "Where Castiel has a welcoming party?"

"I can Cloak the shuttle," said Darius.

"I hate to mention it," Hsiao said, "but it won't accommodate more than half the passengers, and at the rate the hull is disintegrating there won't be time for a second trip."

Decide who is to go and who will stay, awaiting the Bathsheba's *destruction? Who could make those choices?*

Parthenia said, "Whoever goes to Earth might be able to hide from Castiel for some time, providing he doesn't know where the shuttle lands. Perhaps we could draw lots. Little Carina and Ava must go, naturally."

Carina had almost forgotten about Ava's daughter, her namesake. Her throat constricted and she swallowed the lump that had formed there.

"And Officer Matt and Alfie Binger," Parthenia continued. "This isn't their fight."

"Alfie!" Carina exclaimed. "I'd forgotten all about him." She comm'd the Earth man. "I need you to tell me what reports are coming from Earth. Has there been any news on the state of the ship?"

"Ah, that's what all that clamor was about. Thank goodness it stopped. It was giving me a headache."

"Alfie," she repeated, "what's the news from Earth about the *Bathsheba*?"

"An awful lot of debate about her existence, but the believers seem to be winning. According to Ms Longbarrow some wonderful images of her have appeared on all the news channels."

"Nothing about her breaking up?"

"Breaking up?!"

"Sorry, try not to worry about it. Just... stay where you are, okay? Don't leave that room."

The door would seal if the adjoining passageway depressurized.

She cut the comm. "No one on Earth knows what's happening. I guess the breaches aren't immediately obvious, especially when most people have never seen a starship."

Parthenia said, "So the *Bathsheba* will fall apart and tumble from the sky, and Castiel's people will be able to play it off as if she never existed."

"Something like that," Carina muttered.

"And if any of us survive," said Ferne, "he can hunt us at his leisure."

"At least three breaches on all decks," Hsiao reported. "Decks Four through Seven fully depressurized."

"Lin!" Van Hasty barked. "Time's up. Make a decision or I will."

The deadly peril everyone aboard faced pressed in on Carina like the atmosphere of a high-grav planet. She struggled to breathe as fears hammered her mind, destroying her thought processes.

"I *wish* we had a way to Send to all those mages," Oriana pined. "If only we could talk to them and explain who we are and why we're here."

"Castiel must have fed them a bunch of lies," said Ferne, "or he's put them in fear of their lives if they don't do what he says."

Nahla said, "More likely he's put them in fear of someone else losing their life—someone they love. That's how he operates."

"But if they all stood up to him at once," said Oriana, "he would have no choice but to back down. He can't defend himself against all of them at the same time."

Ferne sighed. "There's no point in wishing. We don't know those people. We don't have any of their personal items. How could we Locate them among Earth's millions?"

Carina sucked in a great gulp of air. "We *can* Send to them. Darius can do it!"

"But how?" Oriana asked. "He doesn't have—"

"He doesn't need anything to Locate them. He's a Spirit Mage. He can Summon them."

A pause followed. Everyone was still.

Jackson frowned. "He can *what*?"

"Do it, Darius," Carina urged, adding, "Do you remember how? You do know how to Summon, right?" Anxiety gnawed at her stomach as he blinked, thinking.

He'd only spent a few weeks with the old mage, Magda. The long days he'd attended lessons in her tent had made Carina angry at the time. She'd been jealous of the woman's influence on her brother and considered the expectations she had of him too great. But now she prayed with all her heart that Magda had taught him the Cast that only Spirit Mages could perform.

"I-I think so," he quietly replied. "I'd forgotten about it until you mentioned it. I recall learning the Cast but I never had a chance to practice it. This will be my first time."

"Oh, you have to reach them, Darius," said Oriana. "Tell them mages are aboard the ship they're destroying, as well as lots of innocent people. Ask them to please stop. And tell them Castiel is a Dark Mage who will hurt them. Tell them we have another way for them to live, that they won't have to hide anymore."

"That's rather a lot," Darius nervously quipped.

Carina took her canister of elixir from her belt and set it down in front of him. "In case you need extra."

Parthenia, Oriana, and Ferne did the same.

Nahla kissed his cheek. "Good luck."

Darius looked from face to face, unscrewed the lid of his elixir bottle, and drank.

Carina caught Bryce's gaze. Making eye contact with him broke the dam and her tears flooded out. The last thing she wanted was for her youngest brother to carry the responsibility of saving everyone's lives, but they were out of options. She sank into a seat, wretched with despair.

All attention in the bridge was on Darius. Even Hsiao had ceased monitoring her screens. The young man's eyes were shut tight and his brow furrowed with concentration. Beads of sweat erupted on his forehead. His lips moved silently.

It was working. He was talking to the other mages.

A scene from a long time ago popped into Carina's mind: a little boy with a mop of dark hair mentally conversing with a starwhale, a living creature that flew between stars, asking it how it was doing, and entirely forgetting the important part of the message.

Darius would not forget this time.

Without opening his eyes, he blindly reached for another canister of elixir. Oriana snatched one up and thrust it into his hands.

He drank more elixir. The beads of sweat on his forehead coalesced and ran down his face. His skin paled and the line between his brows deepened. His shoulders lifted and fell as his chest heaved.

Hsiao swiveled to consult her screens, and then turned back to face Darius.

Carina didn't dare ask if her brother's efforts were having an effect. She didn't want to break his concentration.

Halfway through his fourth canister of elixir, his eyes opened. Instantly, he collapsed, flopping forward, propping his elbows on his knees while his head hung low. Carina stepped to his side and gently touched his shoulder.

"It's done," he whispered.

She looked to Hsiao for confirmation.

The pilot nodded, a grin wreathing her face. "No more breaches."

"Thank the stars!" Oriana exclaimed. "That was fantastic, Darius."

Nahla smiled. "You always were my hero."

But Darius was beyond hearing them. He looked utterly spent.

"Jackson," said Carina, "could you coordinate the repairs?"

"Copy. That kid's a marvel."

It went without saying.

Though she hardly dared believe it, a small flame of hope flared in Carina's chest. If Darius could speak to all Earth's mages, albeit at great expense of energy, there was a chance they could defeat Castiel. A Dark Mage could not Summon, and they would already be afraid of him. He couldn't hide his true nature for very long.

And the Testifiers were working to make sure he couldn't cover up the arrival of the *Bathsheba* with her friendly mages, here to do good and help humankind. Though things had looked dicey for a while, the publicity stunt had worked.

"Someone's hailing us from the surface," Van Hasty said. "Won't give his name. Says Carina will know who he is."

The flame of hope flickered and threatened to go out.

"It's Castiel," said Oriana.

"No," Carina said, "I don't think it is. Put him on general comm."

"Ms Lin. I felt confident we would meet again one day. I'm glad you made it here. It's quite the journey, isn't it?"

"What do you want? Spit it out."

"Castiel and I are impressed by your ability to persuade the mages to halt their Split Casts. We concede defeat. You've won. I expect we'll see you on the surface soon."

"Not if I see you first, Kee." She gestured to Van Hasty, drawing her finger across her throat.

The merc closed the comm. "Kee? That rings a bell."

"Commander Kee of the Dirksens. He's the one who helped Castiel get here."

"He must like him a lot."

"He probably despises him, but he loved Sable Dirksen."

Van Hasty grimaced. "Ugh. Awkward."

"Do you believe the bit about them conceding defeat?" Ferne asked.

"Not for a second, but, nevertheless, it's time to go planetside."

THIRTY-FOUR

As the shuttle conveyed them to the planet surface, Carina asked Oriana to switch places so she could sit next to Parthenia.

As she settled in next to her oldest sister, Parthenia side-eyed her. "You want to talk to me?"

"I've been thinking about this publicity tour the Testifiers have set up." The group had become the mages' de facto agents, arranging interviews with all the major media channels and booking their transportation and hotels. It turned out some rather rich individuals were Testifiers, and they were very happy to pay to be proved right. Everything seemed to be working as Alfie had suggested. They were already famous all over the globe. If anything happened to them hard questions would be asked in high places.

"What about it?"

"I want you to take the lead in representing the mages."

"But you're the oldest and, to be frank, this was all your idea. The journalists will want to talk to the leader of our expedition, not the foot soldiers."

"You were always more than a foot soldier, but that isn't the reason I'm asking you. You will be way better at giving interviews than me, and you'll give a better impression of mages and what we stand for."

"What?" Parthenia turned to face her. "What are you talking about?"

"You carry yourself like a queen, Parthenia. You always have. And you speak really well. Sometimes I think you have a thesaurus in your head. You know when to speak plainly and when to shut up. If an interviewer got on my nerves I might run my mouth and say something I shouldn't. Basically, you grew up in a wealthy family while I was a slum brat, and it shows."

"Hmpf. Well, I'm sure Father would be delighted that my lessons in comportment, rhetoric, and oratory paid off."

"Will you do it?"

Parthenia looked out of the window. The black of space was transforming to the crystalline blue of a cloudless sky. "What exactly do we want to tell the world about mages? This has happened so fast I haven't had time to think about it."

"I wondered about that too, but it's easy. You just need to tell them what Jace would have said, about how we don't believe in using our powers to control or hurt people, or even to gain an advantage. That we want to help people." Carina swallowed and added, "That was how my dad and Ma were trapped. Did you know? I'm not sure if I ever told you."

"No, you never did."

Though the story involved Stefan Sherrerr, Carina tried to keep him out of it as much as she could as she explained how Ba had wanted to help people trapped by an earthquake, and that was how he and Ma had been exposed.

Parthenia listened solemnly and didn't speak when Carina had finished.

She continued, "You were close to Jace and spent more time with him than anyone else. He knew mage culture inside out. If you're ever in any doubt about the answer to a question you only need to ask yourself what would Jace say? But you have to be careful about the General Alert. What you'll be saying will sound awfully like what the public has been told to watch out for. You'll need to spin it so it's clear mages aren't anything to do with that. You should question it, ask where it's from and who's behind it. When they can't answer they'll look stupid and stop asking about it. Hopefully, the Alert will fade from public consciousness."

After a pause, Parthenia murmured, "I suppose I could do it."

"Oriana and Ferne could help, and so could Nahla. Though she isn't a mage she could talk about what it's like growing up as a non-mage in a mage family. People will be interested to hear about that. You have to emphasize that mages aren't better than non-mages, only different. We can make them feel inadequate, you see. That's what Bryce told me."

"*That's* what he's upset about?"

"Yes."

"What about Darius?"

"Darius and I..." Carina glanced over her shoulder and caught his gaze. He'd been watching and listening the whole time "...we have other work to do."

"And Bryce? He knows what it's like living with mages too."

"I have no idea about Bryce's plans."

———

A sea of expectant faces awaited them on Earth. Bibik landed the shuttle at an airport in the main city of the most powerful country, according to the Testifiers. It was a place called New Tunka, capital of Ballarkland. They hadn't been here on any of their previous, clandestine visits. Carina took a moment before stepping out of the shuttle to take in the view. The city beyond the airport boundaries looked more built up than other metropolises she'd seen, such as Alfie's, and definitely way more built up than the small town Matt was from.

Officer Matt was behind her waiting to disembark. His superiors had agreed to waive kidnapping charges, accepting there had been a 'misunderstanding'. Ava was with him and so was little Carina. Alfie had elected to remain on the *Bathsheba*, unsurprisingly. It would have taken a crow bar to lever him from the ship, despite her recent brush with destruction.

New Tunka spread out to the horizon, or at least it seemed to spread out. Like everywhere else Carina had seen on Earth, the greenery of the city made it hard to distinguish what was town and what was country. No building stood higher than three stories, and no motorized vehicles ran along the roads.

"Umm..." said Oriana, standing behind her.

"Sorry." She took a step forward, but something buzzed into her field of vision. She swiped it, knocking the buzzing thing off course. "What the hell's *that*?"

"It's a camera drone, moron," Van Hasty yelled from somewhere back in the line. "Move your ass, Carina. Some of us want to get a look at Earth."

The drone returned, swooping in front of her face again. She frowned at it angrily, but then, remembering this was the first sight of a mage for most Earth citizens—that they knew about—she forced her frown away and waved at the reporters.

Despite the extreme unlikelihood of Castiel Splitting her in front of the world's media, she couldn't help tensing, fearing attack, as she descended from the shuttle.

"No camouflage sheet this time," Oriana whispered.

"Be careful," Carina warned. "I know this looks safe, but..."

"Don't worry. I know my brother well."

A barrier encircled the shuttle exit, preventing the reporters from approaching too close. Men in uniform stood inside it. One beckoned her. As she stepped forward, a barrage of questions began.

"How does it feel to arrive on Earth?"

"Where are you from? What's the name of your planet?"

"Are you one of the mages? Which of you can do magic?"

"How long did it take to get here?"

"Have you seen aliens? Is there intelligent life on other worlds?"

"What are your plans now you've arrived?"

Carina smiled but didn't answer. Apparently, the rights to the 'first interview with the returning colonists' had been signed away for a very large sum.

"Ms Lin? Ms Lin!"

She looked for the person calling her name so insistently. A florid, middle-aged woman in a thick coat was pressed up against the barrier, waving wildly. "They won't let me through," she called out as they made eye contact.

"Frankie Longbarrow?"

"That's right. We finally meet, haha."

"Please let this woman in," Carina asked one of the uniformed men. "She's, uh, part of my media team."

"I thought it was you," Frankie said breathlessly after ducking under the barrier. "Alfie described you to me very well."

Carina didn't ask what he'd said. "Thanks for all the ETA's help. We could never have done this without you."

"It's our pleasure."

The endless yelled questions continued as they crossed the open space to the nearest building.

"I need to discuss your itinerary in detail," said Frankie. "It's complicated. You're going to be very busy for the next few months until things die down."

"Actually, my sister will be the main person handling the interviews."

"Oh?" Frankie's eyebrows rose and she craned her neck, looking backward. "Which one is she?"

"You'll soon spot her. We look very alike."

"So you're handing her the reins? I understand. You have plenty else to do."

They'd arrived at the building. The doors were open and the interior looked invitingly empty and quiet. Carina wondered if she was being selfish in asking Parthenia to present mages to the world. She couldn't deny the thought of being famous and under constant scrutiny appalled her. But her reasoning was also valid. Her oldest sister was perfectly suited to the task, whereas she was more of a behind-the-scenes person.

Before entering the building, she took a look at the line of shuttle passengers, stretching back to the vessel. Oriana, Ferne, and Ferne's latest girlfriend, who came from Marchon, walked in a little group. Matt had his arm around

Ava and she was holding her daughter's hand. Parthenia and Darius followed them, looking somewhat apprehensive. Van Hasty and Rees strode behind the pair, towering a head taller. They were unarmed, at Carina's request, and didn't appear too happy about it. Nahla was with her merc partner, a man a little younger than her and far less aggressive than most of the Dogs. About halfway back walked Chi-tang and Cheepy, bizarrely lovey-dovey now they'd arrived at their destination.

The line continued on, men and women who had taken part in the long journey. In the many years of the voyage she'd come to know them all by name. They'd eaten and socialized together. There had been fallings out and reconciliations, anger, despair, and tears, laughter, joy, and delight. Soon, they were to part ways. Things would never be the same again. Everyone would create a life on Earth, get jobs, have families, put down roots. She wondered how their lives would turn out.

She had a feeling she would never know.

THIRTY-FIVE

Carina waited two weeks before going after Castiel. Though the Testifiers did an excellent job of guarding or destroying anything personal to the mages, realistically it was only a matter of time before their ranks were infiltrated and the Dark Mage would Transport his siblings to his side. As long as he lived, they would be under constant threat of disappearing, never to be seen again.

Over those two weeks a great outpouring of data had been going on from the *Bathsheba* to Earth scientists. Her logs, schematics, every bit of information about her systems and all the devices aboard. Tech companies had started a bidding war for priority access to the ship but the consensus among her passengers was they did not want to profit from her, that her tech should benefit humanity as a whole. After all, the vessel hadn't belonged to them in the first place.

"You're going to kill him?" Parthenia asked before Carina set off.

"Don't you think he deserves to die after everything he's done?"

"Yes, but…"

"I know Ma wouldn't want me to do it, but she would also want me to protect all of you. I can't do both, and it's better that I do it than one of his full siblings. I can live with myself afterward. I'm not sure you can."

"I've always hated killing. Even the Regians. You're right. I don't know if I could bring myself to kill Castiel."

"I know. It's one of the things I like about you." *One of the things I'm going to miss.*

"Darius is going too? I saw him getting ready."

"I'd rather not take him but I'm going to need him."

"And Bryce?"

"He doesn't know about it."

"You two *still* aren't talking? That's ridiculous. You're both being stubborn."

"It isn't stubbornness. I'd be happy to patch things up. He isn't interested. He's moved on. He'll find a nice non-mage partner on Earth. He has millions to choose from."

"No, he won't. Bryce has been through thick and thin with you. He won't be happy with anyone else. You two are made for each other."

"I thought so too, once. But I pushed him too far and now I don't think he can ever come back."

"He will. He just needs time."

Carina doubted it but she didn't bother arguing. She had an important job to do.

———

Near the ancient mage hideaway in the mountains, all was still. Even the ever-present wind had dropped to nothing and a hot sun baked the rocks. As Darius brought the mercs in, they quickly took stock of their surroundings.

"Where did you stash the equipment, Lin?" Pamuk asked.

Carina nodded to the dip in the slope where she'd put the armor, rifles, and other equipment she'd Transported down from the *Bathsheba*.

"I still say we should blow that place from orbit," Jackson grumbled.

"Yeah, 'cause no one's going to notice, right?" Carina asked sarcastically.

"Quit with the stupid suggestions, Jackson," said Van Hasty. "This might be our last chance for a fight and I'm gonna take it. Shit, Earth's boring. I've never known such a peaceful planet. Even Magog was more interesting."

"You didn't come with us to Magog," said Carina.

"Exactly."

The rest of the mercs were retrieving weapons and donning armor. Carina and Darius suited up too.

"Do you feel him close by?" she asked her brother over comm.

"Yes, he's already here."

Whether Castiel had set watchers who had spotted their arrival or if the mountain was his permanent abode wasn't clear, but Carina's intuition about where she would find her half-brother had been correct.

"Are we Transporting in?" asked Jackson, "or assaulting from outside?"

"There's only one entrance I know of and it's only one man wide. I want you to take a team, scout it out, and assess the level of defense. Remain outside to catch anyone trying to escape, and await orders."

"What do we do with them if they come out?"

"If they surrender take them prisoner."

"What if it's your brother or Kee?"

"Kill on sight."

Allowing either man to live was too risky.

She could only Transport mercs to the areas she'd been inside the mountain, and they were only a small portion of the whole. But it couldn't be helped. With luck they would have the element of surprise and would quickly mow down the opposition. She hoped that, on this peaceful world, their soldiers only comprised the men and women who had partaken in their galactic journey and there were few recruits from the local population.

She didn't anticipate encountering many mages. From the ones who had come forward and revealed themselves, she understood that Castiel's main method of persuasion had been convincing them that non-mages would hate and persecute them. The reception Carina and her siblings had received put the lie to his assertions and much of his support had melted away. Yet, no doubt, there were also mages he was controlling by more nefarious means. She and Darius would have to be on their guard.

"Ready?" she asked him.

"Yes."

She began to Cast. As soon as the Dogs had gone in, she Transported herself and Darius to the great chamber with the waterfall.

Already, flashes of pulse fire could be seen lighting up the exits, though their hiss couldn't be heard over the roar of the waterfall. She dragged her brother to the side of the chamber, where a protrusion gave a little cover. The cavern seemed empty, the only movement the ripples of the pond where falling water crashed into it.

"He's here!" Darius exclaimed.

She couldn't see Castiel but she didn't doubt her brother's words.

She switched her comm to external. "Castiel! Your plan has failed. We've won. You have two choices: leave Earth forever or face the consequences of your actions."

Castiel's voice floated back, thin and faint, "The consequences of *my* actions? As I recall, it wasn't I who murdered my father. It wasn't I who executed Sable Dirksen in cold blood, condemning her to a horrible fate without even the justice of a fair trial."

"They earned their deaths, the same as you'll earn yours if you don't get off this planet."

"Even if I agreed with you, I am sadly unable to comply. The starship we arrived on was destroyed long ago. So unless you plan on giving me yours..."

He was stalling. Castiel would never agree to her terms even if she put the *Bathsheba* in his hands. The immediate area was clear. She scanned upward. The walls were smooth, impossible to scale. There was the possibility that Castiel could Transport soldiers in—

Something was moving within the waterfall. The endless rush of water had scooped a hollow behind it. She fired. The soldier fell without a sound, tumbling down and disappearing into the pool.

"I see your aim has improved," said a voice.

Kee was here too.

"I had a lot of time to practice."

Castiel needed a line of sight to attempt to Split them, and they had good visibility. No one could sneak up on them. They could survive here a long time and Transport out within a few seconds, but that wasn't the point.

"Darius," she comm'd, one to one, "we have to find them."

While the exchange had been going on within the chamber, the fighting outside had intensified. An enemy soldier stumbled through one of the entrances, fell down face forward, and was still.

"I know," her brother replied.

"They must be on the far side of the pool. It's the only spot we can't see."

"I'll Transport us."

"No, I'll do it. I want you to conserve your elixir. And remember your promise, right?"

"I remember."

Before they'd embarked on the mission, she'd made him swear that if she was killed he had to leave. He would need elixir to do it and she didn't want him to run out. She comm'd Van Hasty, who was somewhere within the depths of the mountain.

"Copy," the merc replied. "I know where you are. The place with the waterfall, right? Stay put until I get there. Resistance is heavy but we're breaking through."

They waited, watching for signs of another attempt to reach them. Castiel would be growing impatient, and he was undoubtedly receiving the news that his troops were being defeated.

A comm arrived from Van Hasty. "We're in. Where are you?"

Carina Cast.

As they arrived it took her a second to get her bearings. Three figures stood under an overhang, armored up. She turned to the entrance.

It was empty.

Where was Van Hasty?

A pulse round flashed. Darius gasped. He'd been hit.

She fired back and grabbed her brother's arm, hauling him toward the gap in the wall. More pulses flashed past. Kee was firing and perhaps Castiel too, though that had never been his style. The third person had to be his daughter. Perhaps she was the other one shooting at them.

"He's Casting," breathed Darius. There was a gulp as he drank elixir.

While Darius was Casting Repulse against Castiel he was defenseless. Carina pushed him behind the entrance, but soldiers were running down the passageway. They were not Dogs. She shot at the three armored figures in the cavern, spraying them with fire, then focused on the approaching soldiers.

White-hot heat exploded at her neck. She'd been hit. She fought down a shriek and struggled to hold onto her rifle. Her suit's analgesics kicked in, forcing the painkiller through her skin, and the agony faded. But the scent of her burned flesh told her it was a serious wound. She had to Cast Heal but there was no time. She needed a reprieve. She would Cast Transport instead and get them out of the fighting for a short while.

She sucked on the tube leading to her suit's reservoir, but no elixir spurted into her mouth. The pulse round had destroyed the tube. "Darius..."

He was on his knees. He'd taken another hit, and he couldn't defend himself because he was too busy Casting against Castiel.

Where were the mercs? There had to be another cavern with a waterfall somewhere in the mountain and Van Hasty had gone there.

The enemy soldiers had nearly reached them. She shot into their midst. One fell, but the others rushed up, grabbed her, and threw her down.

They'd taken off her armor. Darius knelt beside her, also without his suit.

Castiel, Kee, and Letitia had removed their helmets.

Kee had aged significantly. His cheeks were sunken in and his eyes sat deep in their sockets, but they were as dark and intelligent as ever.

"Carina Lin," he said softly. "If I'd known you would kill Sable one day, you would never have left the interrogation cell alive."

"Strange that you would feel so strongly about such a terrible person, Kee." She winced as pain lanced her neck. "Was it really worth devoting your life to getting revenge for a monster?"

"You have no idea of the depths and richness of her personality. You did the galaxy a great disservice when you deprived it of her presence. It's long past time for a reckoning."

"*Long* past time," Castiel agreed, "for that and many other things."

"I don't know what you hope to achieve by killing us," Carina said defiantly. "You've lost the mages under your control. Parthenia will turn Earth into somewhere they can live without fear. Your time here is over, whether we live or not."

"You underestimate the great satisfaction your deaths will bring me regardless, and you overestimate Parthenia's abilities. Though she may persuade the public not to hate her, she will have *my* hatred for the rest of her life, which I aim to cut short as soon as I have the opportunity."

"Don't do it," said Darius. "We're family. You and I are brothers. We grew up together. For a long time, I looked up to you. You can still change, Castiel. You don't have to do this."

He chuckled. "Sweet little Darius. Mother's darling. How I hated you from the very minute you were born, before anyone even knew what a powerful mage you were. Ferne and Oriana were always stupid but tolerable. You, however, were something else. I knew for a long time I couldn't allow you to exist."

"I'm sorry," Carina whispered.

Darius bowed his head. "You don't have anything to be sorry for, sis."

"How sweet," said Castiel. "I would so love to make a great display of your deaths, to show the world what should be done to those evil arrivals from the stars. But, though it pains me to say it, your soldiers are closing in. We must make quick work of this and then retreat to a safer spot."

"What about you?" Carina asked, lifting her gaze to the woman at his side, who hadn't said a word during the entire exchange.

Letitia looked away.

Now Carina could get a good look at her, the likeness of the woman to Ma struck her more forcefully than ever. Tears of grief sprang to her eyes. *I did my best, Ma. I tried my best to save them.*

"Weeping won't help you," said Castiel. "You won't find any mercy here."

"Is this what you want?" Carina asked Letitia.

"How dare you address my daughter?" Castiel demanded. "Be silent. Kee, do the honors. Carina is yours and I get to kill Darius, as we agreed."

Kee lifted his rifle.

"He hates you," Carina said to Letitia. "You know that, right? You've always known it." She launched herself at Kee, head-butting him in the stomach.

Winded, the old man landed heavily.

A flash of light lit up the dim space. Someone had fired. As Carina struggled on the ground with Kee, she yelled, "Letitia, come over to our side! You can live freely as a mage." Sounds of a fight were coming from one side but she couldn't make out what was happening. "You'll never please him!" she shouted. "He'll hate you forever."

Kee was under her. She drove her knee into his chin. There was the crack of shattering teeth and blood ran from between his thin lips.

A second flash ignited in the cavern.

Kee's grip on his rifle loosened. She wrested it from his grasp and spun it around. The old commander raised his hands as if to ward her off.

She fired.

Kee was no more.

She turned.

Darius was down.

Dead?

The horrible scent of burned flesh was rank in the atmosphere.

A little way off were two figures, one kneeling, the other standing. Carina squinted at them as she crawled to her brother.

"Don't do it, darling," Castiel pleaded. "You know I love you."

"It isn't true!" Carina yelled. She touched Darius. He was warm but that didn't mean anything, and with their suits gone she had no elixir. "You *know* the truth, Letitia. You know it."

The woman's head swiveled toward Carina's.

Their gazes met.

She turned back to her father and shot him in the head.

THIRTY-SIX

She Healed Darius with Castiel's elixir. From what Darius said when he came around, Castiel had shot him but at the last millisecond Letitia had pushed her father. The round couldn't have quite hit its mark or Carina wouldn't have been able to bring Darius back.

Letitia and Castiel must have been the pair she'd heard fighting. Eventually, the daughter had got the upper hand, and with the truth of Carina's words ringing in her ears, she'd delivered the coup de grâce. Then it was only a matter of waiting for the Black Dogs to complete their mission. The hostiles Carina had shot at had been forced away to deal with the mercs under Van Hasty's command.

They left Castiel and Kee's corpses in the cavern. Neither of them deserved a decent burial, and though their presence besmirched the ancient place, the mages who had lived there had departed millennia ago. It was only a deserted cave in the mountains.

The long story of the Dark Mage's hatred for his family was finally over. They could live in peace, which in some ways made Carina's delivery of her decision even harder. After several days of gathering courage, she explained what she intended and her reasoning, adding, "It has to be this way. I'm sorry."

"No, it doesn't!" Parthenia sobbed, trembling with shock. "You can't do it. I couldn't bear it."

Oriana simply wailed, unable to verbalize her sorrow.

Darius hung his head.

"Is this what you want?" Ferne asked him quietly.

He nodded. "Carina's right."

Nahla turned away, running her fingertips under her eyes.

Parthenia asked, "Does Bryce know about this?"

"I haven't told him," Carina replied. She hadn't seen any reason to.

"Then *I* will. I bet he'll have something to say about it."

"Whatever he has to say, it won't change my decision."

Ever since asking Darius to use the Summon Cast to speak to the mages on Earth, the fate of the mages they'd left behind had weighed heavily on her conscience. They had no Spirit Mage, no way of coming together, and their lives were already hard and dangerous. If she could return to her sector with Darius and find them, she could tell them about Earth, the safe haven for mages. They could build colony ships and, one day, arrive at a true home for themselves and their descendants.

"You'll take the *Bathsheba*?" Ferne asked solemnly.

"Everything about her has been downloaded to some place or another on Earth. If someone wants to build another colony ship they can. They don't need a model to copy."

"But you can't fly her alone," Parthenia protested. "She's massive. It's impossible."

"I know I can't do it alone. Hsiao and some of the Black Dogs have agreed to come along. I got their agreement before I told you."

"No way!" Ferne exclaimed. "They only just got here."

"They don't like Earth," Carina explained.

"Don't like it?" Oriana squeaked. "What's not to like? Earth's lovely."

"They've spent most of their lives aboard starships and fighting battles. There's nothing for them here. And if Jackson stays he's going to prison."

She recalled asking Hsiao if she would be prepared to fly back across the galaxy. The small woman had grinned and replied, *You know me, Carina. I'm not interested in making decisions. I just follow orders.*

No, seriously, Carina had said, *I know it's a big ask. You'll be giving up the chance for a peaceful life planetside.*

But I'm a starship pilot. You think I'm going to have fun ferrying tourists to and from the Bathsheba? *I love that ship, and you're offering me the chance to stay with her forever. Why would I turn you down?*

Carina took Parthenia's hands. "You must continue what you've been doing, building trust between non-mages and mages. And make Letitia one of the family. She's had a hard life growing up as Castiel's daughter."

Her sister bowed her head and tears dripped onto their joined hands. "We could all be dead by the time you come back, if you ever do."

"Then I'll meet your children. They will be beautiful and wonderful, like you."

A great sob burst from Parthenia and she pulled Carina into her arms, weeping on her shoulder. Carina held onto her sister as she cried.

"We've been through so much," Parthenia mumbled.

"And we've grown to know each other so well. I'll never forget you."

For a long time, Parthenia couldn't speak. Eventually, she broke their embrace. "I understand what you must do. It's just that it hurts so much."

"It hurts me too."

Ferne and Oriana were hugging Darius. Nahla hugged Carina, and then suddenly they were all hugging.

"What's going on?"

Bryce had arrived. He was looking at them darkly.

"Carina and Darius are leaving on the *Bathsheba*," Oriana said, her voice thick. "They're going to find the mages in our sector and tell them about Earth."

He caught Carina's gaze and narrowed his eyes. Then he left.

"Well, now he knows," said Ferne.

———

The day before their departure, Carina approached Darius. Once they left there would be no turning around, and though her task would be nearly impossible without him, she felt bad about asking him to come with her. She wanted to offer him the option to back out gracefully without hard feelings.

"Darius," she said, "are you sure about this? You're young. You have your whole life ahead of you. You shouldn't have to spend it always helping others."

"Some people are born to a life of service. I was, like you."

"Like me?"

"What else do you think you've been doing all this time except helping mages?"

"I thought I was doing this for myself."

"Really? That doesn't sound like the young merc who rescued a frightened little boy from his kidnappers."

Then she knew he was right.

The Earth authorities were not aware of her plan. Telling them would have created needless complications. There would have been objections, perhaps attempts to prevent them from leaving, but in reality they had no say in the matter.

Too soon, all the tearful reminiscing and promises to stay safe and live happy lives was over. It was time to fly to the *Bathsheba* and begin the final preparations to depart the system. The core of the Black Dogs had boarded the shuttle except for Jackson who, unable to show himself in civilized regions, had already been Transported to the ship. The only new passenger was Alfie Binger. He'd begged to be allowed to join the expedition and Carina had agreed on the proviso he told no one else about it. She couldn't imagine fielding the thousands of Exodus Testifiers who wanted to come along.

Carina was saying her final goodbyes to her siblings, drinking in the sight of them, committing their faces and voices to memory. They'd spent years in close confinement on their starship voyage, too close at times. She knew and loved them inside out. It was not enough, but it would have to be.

She climbed into the shuttle and turned to take a final look at Earth and the people it was breaking her heart to leave.

Someone was riding a bicycle across the landing field. The rider was clearly new to the skill, for the bike swerved and wobbled alarmingly. When he reached the shuttle he leapt from his seat. The bicycle continued on and crashed into the vessel, bounced off it, and fell onto its side, the wheels spinning.

"Carina!" Bryce yelled. "You're really going to leave?" He ran up to her and grabbed her shoulders. "Tell me you weren't going to go without even a word."

"What is there to say? We made it to Earth. You can make a home here now."

"I don't want to make a home on Earth. I came here because I wanted to be with you."

"But I have to leave. I have to go back."

"Then so do I."

She smiled up at him, joy breaking through her sadness. "Let's make the *Bathsheba* our home."

THE END

Thanks for reading Carina's story. I hope you've enjoyed it as much as I enjoyed writing it. If you like science fantasy you might be interested in another series of mine: STAR LEGEND

Sign up to my reader group for a free copy of the *Star Mage Saga* prequel, *Daughter of Discord*, discounts on new releases, review crew invitations and other interesting stuff:

https://jjgreenauthor.com/free-books/

OF J.J. GREEN

With deepest thanks to patrons

Paul Hanrahan, John Treadwell, Joseph Lau, Peter Samuel Harness, Geeraline Marrs, Bobby Borland, John Stephenson, Chris, William Retsin, Dan Archibald, Grant Ballard-Tremeer Dale Thompson, Jean Gill, Christopher E. Marshall, Cheryl Kuchler, Shan Shwe, Steve Glasper, Donald Swan, Wayne Lampel, Janette S. Mattey, Brian Kelly, Jim, Sarah Woods, Richard L. Adams, Frank Menendez, Patti DeLang, Elizabeth Hickey, Linda Liem, Russ Kirkpatrick, Kate Wilson, Duff Kindt, Catherine Corcoran, Shaun, John Gancz, Dave, Archie Strong, Struggle Session, Susan Cook, Annie Hsiao-Wen Wang, Julian White, Dane Elliot, Iffet a Burton, Gary Johnson, Tracey Paine, Randy Berlin, Ed Cleeves, Amaranth Dawe, Neil, Alex Green, Ann Bryant, Neil Holford, Michael Claremont

---

1.

www.ingramcontent.com/pod-product-compliance
Lightning Source LLC
Chambersburg PA
CBHW070335170726
48291CB00001B/55